CHARON'S LANDING

JACK DU BRUL

TOR®

A TOM DOHERTY ASSOCIATES BOOK
NEW YORK

This is a work of fiction. All the characters and events portrayed in this book are either products of the author's imagination or are used fictitiously.

CHARON'S LANDING

Copyright © 1999 by Jack Du Brul

A Tor Book
Published by Tom Doherty Associates, LLC
175 Fifth Avenue
New York, NY 10010

www.tor.com

Tor® is a registered trademark of Tom Doherty Associates, LLC.

ISBN: 0-812-57550-4

First edition: May 1999
First mass market edition: May 2000

Printed in the United States of America

0 9 8 7 6 5 4 3 2 1

This one's for my father and
brother and our monthlong Alaska
crusade to hit every gin joint between
Ketchikan and Point Barrow.

ACKNOWLEDGMENTS

With every book, the list of those people I need to thank grows and grows. First and foremost is Debbie Saunders for putting up with my telling her, "Not tonight, honey, I have to write," way too many times. I love you. Then comes my agent, Bob Diforio, for his faith and patience. Writing has been my lifelong dream, and you have made it possible. I also want to thank everyone at Forge, especially Melissa Ann Singer, for getting this book out in a readable form. I promise someday I'll learn how to type.

I also want to thank my dad for keeping my job open while I finished this novel. Then come all those whose brains I picked, including but not exclusively: Captain Robert Foale; Michael Mccleary; Chris Flanagan, who knows more about guns than one person should; and my mom for her sharp editing pen. I give them credit for everything that's right in these pages, but I take responsibility for the mistakes. I also want to thank Clive Cussler for his fabulous quote and criticism, as well as the other Jack Du Brul, Todd Murphy, Cathey and Bill Bachman, Andy Lecount, and the Florida gang. To the guys at What Ales You, I just want to say that none of you are Harry White, but you all could be.

Lastly, to everyone who bought my first book and those who replied with so many kind letters, thank you. I can't express how much that touched me.

HOMER, ALASKA
OCTOBER, 17

Howard Small leaned over the gunwale of the charter boat and retched so violently that he nearly lost his glasses. The soured contents of his stomach hit the water loudly, alerting the crews on the other charter boats. They looked over and cheered. Howard spat several times in a vain attempt to clear the foul taste from his mouth before straightening. He wiped clotted brown smears from his lips with his parka sleeve, laid his head back against the Fiberglass hull, and moaned.

"Christ, Howard, we're still tied to the dock. Don't tell me you're already seasick," teased Jerry Small, captain of the fishing boat.

The two were cousins but couldn't have been farther apart as physical types. Howard, younger by a few years, was prematurely bald, while Jerry still retained a tangle of black and silver hair. Where Howard was slightly built and bookish, Jerry's features were broad and deeply weathered, and he carried his more than two hundred pounds on a solid frame.

"Don't blame me, Jerry. It was that sadist there that did this to me," he answered, waving an arm weakly at the other passenger on the thirty-foot craft. "We were up until about four hours ago drinking tequila shots at the Salty Dog Saloon."

In the opposite corner of the boat, the other passenger smiled like the Cheshire Cat. He leaned negligently against the transom, one leg stretched out along a bench, the other tucked against his chest, battered hands cupping his bent knee. He wore faded jeans, a plain black sweatshirt, and a leather bomber jacket. His hiking boots were of good quality but heavily worn. His clothes looked slept in, but there was still a rough elegance about the man, the way a suspension bridge or a high dam can be elegant.

Despite the few hours of sleep and the massive amount of alcohol he must have consumed, the passenger's eyes were sharp and focused. They were an unusual shade of gray, hard yet at the same time friendly and laughing. They possessed a captivating depth that caught Jerry's attention. He had to force himself to look away.

"I know just what you need." The passenger glanced at his TAG Heuer watch and took note of the still distant dawn. "Just as I suspected, it's Happy Hour in Oslo, Norway."

He fished two bottles of Alaska Pale Ale from the plastic cooler on the deck next to him and tossed one toward Howard.

"Nothing like a little hair of the dog." The man grinned, twisting the cap off what he considered the finest beer in the world.

"At four-thirty in the morning, this is the whole dog again," Howard complained, but he opened the beer and took a long swallow.

"Better?"

"Better."

"The fore lines are off, Dad. Let's get going." Jerry Small's teenage son was an even larger version of his father. The boy, man really, was at least four inches taller than six feet, with shoulders like an ox. His youthful face was incongruous on his large body.

"Get ready to cast off stern, John," Small said, as the big stern-mounted Chevy engine rumbled to life.

John cast off the final line and jumped aboard their charter boat, *Wave Dancer*, a poetic name for a stout, roughed-up craft that had fared too many Alaska winters. The two passengers joined the captain and his son in the relative protection of the open-sided cabin.

They were the first vessel of Homer's charter fleet to head out in search of halibut, huge bottom-feeding fish strongly resembling flounder. Though it was late in the season, Jerry assured his party that he could still lead them to some monsters. To starboard, the boat motored past one of the largest natural spits in the world. In the protection of the Cook Inlet, where the currents from the Gulf of Alaska met those from the Chelikof Straits, the seas had created a mile-long thrust of land, narrow enough that someone could throw a baseball from one side to the other. The spiny projection on the Kenai Peninsula's northern coast was home to some of the best salmon and halibut fishing in the world as well as the nesting site of a huge flock of bald eagles that scavenged around the sleepy town's garbage dump.

The *Wave Dancer* rounded the tip of the spit. To port, the Kenai Mountains were a murky shadow in the dim light of the false dawn. The sun was just a stroke of blush against the horizon. The temperature was a raw thirty degrees, forcing the men to hold themselves close to the cabin's heating vents. The wind was mild, and the seas were no more than three feet—a gentle ride for a boat designed to battle ten-foot swells.

"You don't strike me as one of the regular eggheads Howard usually brings fishing," Jerry Small said to his other passenger.

The man smiled. "No, I'm an independent consultant, hired to check the viability of Howard's work for commercial application."

"And?"

"And what?"

"Does my cousin's gizmo work?"

"If my recommendation holds any weight with Pacific Machine and Die, this time next year, Dr. Howard Small is going to be a very wealthy man."

Howard grinned around his hangover. This was the first he'd heard of the endorsement after the two weeks of field trials they'd just completed north of Valdez. "Thanks, Mercer."

"Don't thank me." Philip Mercer shook Howard's hand. "You did all the work. In a couple of years, the mining industry is going to be turned on its ear by what you've developed.

For the past three years, Professor Howard Small and his

staff at UCLA had been developing a minimole, a type of tunnel-boring machine that utilized the latest in laser guidance, hydraulic technology, and microminiaturization. Their creation, dubbed Minnie, had just proven itself on its first true test, under some of the harshest conditions any machine was forced to endure. The machine had bored a two-mile-long tunnel through granite bedrock with a deflection of only one ten-thousandth of an inch from her original course. Unlike other tunnel-borers, Minnie was small and economical. A crew of twenty could keep the sixteen-foot-long machine running twenty-four hours a day as she chewed out a four-foot-diameter tunnel. By comparison, the borers used to dig the Channel Tunnel between England and France were six hundred feet long and required hundreds of men to maintain.

Mercer had been hired by Pacific Machine and Die, a huge equipment manufacturer, to evaluate Minnie's utility in hard rock mining. A borer that small could potentially eliminate explosive blasting in mines and the hundreds of deaths and injuries it caused each year. With his formidable reputation in the mining industry, Mercer's recommendation ensured that Pac Mac & Die would be buying the rights to Minnie within months. Howard's years of work were about to pay off.

This fishing trip was a way for both men to unwind after the long weeks of testing. Strangers just a short time ago, they had developed a rapport that felt as if it had been forged over many years.

"Does this mean you'll finally pay for one of these charters?" Jerry Small asked his cousin.

"Don't count on it."

An hour out of Homer, Jerry slowed the *Wave Dancer* in a small protected cove, cutting her engines to a slow trawl. He and his son watched the depth finder intently, comparing the bottom reading with geographic references from shore. After a few adjustments, Small shut down the engines and allowed the silence of the Alaska coast to wash over them.

"Best fishing hole in these waters," he announced, heaving himself from his seat to prepare the heavy rods.

The Arctic Ocean pack ice, eight hundred miles north,

seemed to strip the sun of its warmth so that it gave off a cold pearly light. Backed against the low scudding clouds, the sky was like an opaque shroud, a special effect only nature could create.

Within a few minutes of getting the baited hooks in the water, Mercer heaved a ninety-pound halibut to the surface. Jerry and John used heavy gaffs to haul the fish over the gunwale. Its flat white body was smooth except for the two blisters on the top of the fish that protected its eyes. Although the halibut was one of the ugliest creatures in the world, Mercer was congratulated soundly.

"Great fish."

"Beautiful fish."

"Looks like my ex-wife. Don't tell your mother I said that, John."

Five minutes later, Mercer and Jerry helped John land a forty pounder, and then it was Howard's turn to haul in one of the monsters from two hundred feet down. For an hour it went on like this, each man catching only a few minutes after his hook reached bottom. After they had all caught one, they released the fish back into the depths. There was no real sport to this type of fishing; it was just a test of strength to bring the sluggish creatures to the surface.

Jerry compared it to pulling a queen-sized mattress from the bottom of the ocean, no fight but plenty of weight. The camaraderie was halibut fishing's true appeal. Jerry said that to experience real Alaska fishing they had to stand hip deep in an icy river while the salmon were making their spawning run. There were so many fish, they butted against your waders as if you were just another obstacle in the water. Yet, during the spawning runs the salmon almost never feed, so most fishermen just watch them swim past their lines.

"More frustrating than impotency in a whorehouse," was how Jerry described it.

Howard had recovered from his hangover enough to begin enjoying the beers Mercer kept passing to him. Jerry Small too was drinking steadily. Only John, too young to drink legally, seemed to have any interest in remaining sober. Jerry had told the boy it was all right to have a few, but John said he was training for the upcoming basketball season, so he abstained completely.

By ten in the morning, it seemed that they were catching the same fish over and over again, so they hauled in their lines, and Jerry started out for another hole farther from Homer. They motored south, the Chevy keening sharply so the *Wave Dancer* trailed a fat wake behind her. The seas were still calm and the sky had cleared enough so the sun poked through in sharp rays that flashed against the water like heliograph signals.

About twenty minutes into the run, John pointed starboard and shouted, "Dad, what's that?"

Jerry throttled back immediately and turned the boat hard over, Mercer and Howard clutching at the dash to maintain their balance. About five hundred yards away, another boat bobbed eerily in the low swells. She was larger than the *Wave Dancer* by twenty feet, a commercial fishing vessel with a small cabin hunched over her heavy bows, her afterdeck supporting a purse net derrick at the very stern.

Even at a distance, everyone could tell there'd been trouble aboard the other ship. She was unnaturally low in the water, and her upper works were darkened and scored by fire. There was a forgotten, haunted feeling to the vessel. It was the unnatural silence of the crypt that hung over her. Jerry swung *Wave Dancer* closer. No one moved on the derelict or answered his call of "Hello."

"What boat is that?" Jerry asked absently as he brought his boat alongside.

"Her name's burned off the transom," his son answered as he tied fenders to the *Wave Dancer's* gunwale. "But I think it's the *Jenny IV* out of Seward."

Mercer was in position to jump across with a line when the two came together. He secured the boats quickly. The alcohol-fueled banter had died as soon as the *Jenny IV* was spotted, and he moved with a calm professionalism, as if finding burned-out wrecks was an everyday occurrence.

Six inches of sea water washed across the *Jenny IV's* scarred decking, slopping from gunwale to gunwale as she rolled sluggishly. The waterproofing on Mercer's boots failed soon after leaping aboard the fishing vessel, and his feet quickly numbed. He looked around the deck, then turned to Jerry.

"Radio the Coast Guard and report what we've found. Tell them to take their time, no one survived." Mercer's voice possessed an edge of command that hadn't been there before.

"How can you tell?" Howard asked, leaning over between the two boats.

Mercer looked forward again before speaking. "Because the life raft is still hanging in its davit and there's a charred body at my feet."

"Oh, shit," Jerry Small said from the console of his boat. "John, make that call to the Coast Guard."

He leapt onto the *Jenny IV*, steadying himself against a scorched deck winch when he saw the facedown corpse.

"Oh, shit," he repeated.

If the condition of the boat was bad, leaking and burned as she was, the body on the deck was much, much worse. Whoever it was had obviously survived much of the fire, because the corpse's position indicated that he'd dragged himself from the cabin. He lay stretched out on the deck as if he'd been crawling from the worst of the flames before dying. The upper body was remarkably undamaged, and he still wore a safety orange coat over a checked flannel shirt, but from the pelvis downward, nothing remained except the blackened stumps of femur bones sticking obscenely from his hips. His hands were twisted claws, charred bone and tendrils of flesh that waved delicately with the water sloshing across the deck.

Mercer had no desire to turn the body and see what damage the fire had done to its face.

The odd state of the body only compounded a deepening mystery surrounding the vessel. Already Mercer's mind was worrying at a problem with the boats' condition. There had been an accident on board and a raging fire, one that had caught the victim unaware, but there was no explanation as to why the fire went out before sinking the craft. Had it been extinguished by another ship, then surely the body would not have been left on the derelict. It didn't make sense.

"Get back aboard your boat," Mercer said to Jerry. "I need a flashlight and an ax."

Jerry thankfully reboarded the *Wave Dancer* and handed the items over to Mercer. He sat anxiously against the gunwale as Mercer continued his investigation.

"Don't you think we should wait for the Coast Guard?"

Howard had a good point, Mercer thought, but something about this fire bothered him and he wasn't going to wait for the authorities to find out what.

"I won't be a minute."

Forward, a short set of stairs led up to the wheelhouse. Next to them a door led to the belowdecks area. The pilothouse, though damaged by the fire, wasn't nearly as ravaged as the deck below, so Mercer went to the door and tried to wrench it open. The wood had been so warped by the heat that it jammed almost immediately. Mercer swung the ax a few times, and the wood splintered. Half the door fell to the deck with a splash.

He flicked on the heavy flashlight and cast its beam around the cramped room below the pilothouse. A small galley was to his left next to a couple of bench seats and a dining table. Everything was burned horribly. To the right were three bunks, two of them empty save for smooth layers of ash that had been the mattresses and blankets. The third bunk contained another skeleton, this one burned so badly that no flesh remained on the bones. Empty eye sockets watched Mercer almost accusingly, sending a superstitious chill up his spine. No matter how strong the urge to escape the charnel cabin, he forced himself to remain critical and press on.

He suspected that the third crewman of the *Jenny IV* must have jumped overboard to escape the inferno. Placing his hand against a steel bulkhead, he noted the metal was ice cold. Because the night before had been so bitterly cold, it would be impossible to guess the fire's exact time until a forensic specialist went over the bodies.

The room's ceiling was scorched by the flames, but it didn't appear as if there had been enough time for the wood to burn through. Next to the door that Mercer had smashed through, another led down a short hallway to the cargo holds.

Of the door itself nothing remained, and the casing and bulk-head near it had been blown outward by an explosion farther belowdecks. That explained why the fire hadn't totally destroyed the boat. The explosion must have robbed the flames of oxygen, snuffing the inferno.

Mercer wondered what the fishing boat could have carried to cause such an explosion.

The vessel's engines were in the stern, and logically the fuel tanks would be close to them, but there would be evidence of that sort of explosion abovedecks. Certainly that would have sunk the vessel. It was something else.

Murky green water reflected Mercer's flashlight as he trained it into the holds. The smell of burned wood and plastic couldn't mask the overpowering stench of years of fishing. A thick scum choked the surface of the water, pools of fuel flashing rainbow hues in the few clear areas. Mercer took a cautious step into the flooded hold, feeling for a step as he made his way down. The water leached his body heat through the thin protection of his pants.

He knew, as he stood thigh deep, that nothing could be accomplished here without diving equipment. He was just turning to leave when the beam of the flashlight reflected something in the water one step below where he stood.

He groaned as he reached under the surface to retrieve it, soaking his arm up to the shoulder. It was a piece of bright stainless steel about ten inches long and six wide. Whatever had exploded on board had torn the steel as if it were paper; its edges were distorted like a chunk of shrapnel. Mercer turned it in the beam of his flashlight and saw the name ROGER on one side, the last letter being the point where the steel was shredded.

He slipped the fragment into a cargo pocket of his jacket and made for the upper deck. He took a few deep breaths in the veiled daylight, realizing he'd been breathing shallowly since entering the vessel.

"Find anything?" Jerry called

"No," replied Mercer, noticing the damage to the net derricks for the first time.

The top of the A-frame fishing gantry was gone, as if it

had been removed with a cutting torch. He looked closely at the two steel stumps, all that remained of the net hauling crane, and saw that the breaks were clean and sharp. There was no evidence of explosive damage. Whatever had destroyed the derrick had sheared it off. Curious, he turned and saw that the antennas for the *Jenny IV*'s radios also had been snapped off, about a foot above the wheelhouse roof.

He had no explanation.

"Did you contact the Coast Guard?"

"Yeah. They're sending a cutter from Homer. It should be here in about an hour."

"Fine." Mercer jumped back to the *Wave Dancer* after taking another look at the body on the commercial ship. "There's no sense remaining tied up. Her lower decks are flooded and she could sink at any time."

Jerry fired up the engine while his son cast off the securing lines. Once they were fifty yards from the *Jenny IV*, Jerry idled his boat and kept her at a constant distance from the derelict. There was a mystery about the burned-out vessel and its skeletal crew that went beyond an engine explosion, and all four men knew it. They were silent for many long, unsettled minutes, watching the deathly quiet *Jenny IV* as she swayed with the rolling waves. The two bodies aboard her would never give them the answers they wanted.

"Well, I guess that takes care of fishing for the day." Jerry's voice was unnaturally loud.

Mercer turned to him and smiled back his own misgivings. "Hell, fishing's just a reason to drink, and I've never really needed an excuse for that."

THE WHITE HOUSE
OCTOBER 19

The President's long-legged stride carried him easily across the informal dining room in the first family's private quarters. He smiled warmly as his sole guest got to her feet to shake his hand. She was much shorter than his six foot two inches and somewhat squat. Her clothes looked as if they'd come from the matron section of a discount department store, and her makeup seemed to have been applied with a hand trowel. Even the kind early morning light streaming through the windows overlooking the Rose Garden could not hide her creped neck or heavy jowls. In a world dominated by media sound bites and personal appearance, her looks were incongruous. Tucked away from journalistic scrutiny, she had worked her way up through the government ranks on sheer determination and the simple fact that she was always the best person for any job. Her intensity and intellect had made her one of the President's closest friends and most trusted advisers.

"Good morning, Connie, it's great to see you," the President said as he sat across the table from his secretary of energy, Constance Van Buren.

She smoothed her black polyester skirt against her nyloned legs as she retook her seat. "You know me, I never pass up a free meal."

"So what's the latest one? Don't spare me."

Connie took a sip of coffee, her eyes sparkling with humor, "Don't say I didn't warn you, because this one is cruel. Stu Hanson at the EPA said he heard it on one of the late-night talk shows." She paused. "According to the media, your latest poll was so limp that even Viagra can't help you now."

The President burst into laughter, the tension lines around his eyes easing as he and his old friend began bantering back and forth. These meetings ostensibly were for presidential briefings on energy matters, but actually they served as a respite for the President from the pressures of his office. While the two did accomplish work during these bimonthly breakfasts, they looked forward to them just for the pleasure of being in each other's company.

"I was just thinking, Connie. When Lloyd Easton from State comes over for breakfast, he brings two aides, four briefcases, and a portable fax machine in case something happens while he's here."

"Yeah, well, Lloyd had his sense of humor removed sometime between his acceptance into Mensa and receiving his Phi Beta Kappa key. What all you boys in the big offices have forgotten is that these are only jobs, important jobs, yes, but they are just jobs. I still spend weekends with my grandchildren and bake them cookies and berate my daughter for marrying a lazy husband and do all the other things normal people do."

A shadow passed across the President's eyes before he spoke. "I told you I've decided not to run again, didn't I?"

"You said you were thinking about it." She nodded. "I think it's a good idea. We both know your marriage is rocky at best. You and Patricia need some time together. And I don't know how your health is, but your hands never used to shake at eight o'clock in the morning."

The President looked down at his long tapered hands and was shocked to see a minor tremble. "Jesus, how anyone could volunteer to put himself through a second term is beyond me."

"Most of your predecessors never had to make the hard choices you've made to put this country back on track, so they never had to take the kind of political heat you've gotten."

"Like the oil thing."

"Like the oil thing," Connie Van Buren agreed.

The President had committed political suicide only nine months into his term, according to supporters and opponents alike. During his first prime-time address to the nation, he had laid out his new Energy Direction Policy. The President wanted the United States to end its dependence on foreign sources of oil within ten years. Through special discretionary funds, the administration would finance massive programs to create new sources of alternative energy throughout the country. He envisioned a nation running cleanly, cities freed from smog and the ecological disasters that had plagued the 80s and 90s. Sprawling windmill farms were to be built in the plains states and solar collector arrays set up in the Southwest. He proposed erecting a tidal power station off the coast of Maine that would provide nearly all the energy for the city of Boston.

Because of its unusual electromagnetic properties, the recently discovered element bikinium would be used to multiply the output of current generating stations. Eventually it would become a source of power itself. The automotive industry, which had been sitting on battery technology for years because it wasn't profitable, would be forced to fully develop electric cars. At the end of the President's ten-year schedule, half of all vehicles sold would have to be electrically powered. He'd said that the technology was there, America just had to have the courage to use it.

The President had given the nation a tough challenge, and they seemed eager to accept. The people were galvanized with the same sense of expectant optimism that President Kennedy generated when he promised to put a man on the moon. Environmentalists saw the glorious end to fossil fuel's rapacious destruction of the ecology. Economists agreed that the transition period would be difficult, but the ban on oil imports would help end the nation's decades-long trade imbalance. Technocrats were eager to see the emerging technology that would wean America from her dependence on oil. And the State Department was thrilled to see the Middle East's diplomatic trump card, the threat of another oil embargo, taken away from them.

Within a few short weeks of his plan, political reality reared its ugly head.

The world's seven major oil companies, known collectively

as the Seven Sisters, has a combined economic power larger than many industrialized nations. They knew their largest market was about to vanish, and they began to exert their massive influence. In what amounted to economic blackmail, the Seven Sisters began bumping up the price of gasoline in ten-cent increments until it had nearly doubled. Then, they quietly made it known within the beltway that prices would continue to rise if certain concessions weren't made. The President was realistic enough to know that the oil giants could spiral the global economy into a slide that would make the Great Depression seem like a boom time.

By pulling in every political favor he had acquired during his terms in the House and Senate and making promises that would take the rest of his term to honor, the President pressured Congress to open up the Arctic National Wildlife Refuge for oil exploration. The millions of acres of virgin tundra on Alaska's north coast just east of Prudhoe Bay were the last major source of domestic oil and one of the most delicate ecosystems on the planet. The Arctic refuge was known to hold oil deposits many times larger than those found at Prudhoe, and it was a prize that the Seven Sisters had wanted for years. That was the price the Sisters demanded for their cooperation, and that was what the President got for them. The bill had been quietly tucked in with other legislation only minutes before passage, forestalling any debate on the floor. Environmental lobbyists and activists never knew what was happening until it was too late.

Environmental concerns had always blocked earlier attempts to open the Refuge to exploitation. However, the President had no choice but to sweep those aside, knowing that he had negotiated for the lesser of two evils. He knew that no matter how many precautions the oil companies took in their scramble for this new source of crude, the land would be destroyed virtually forever. But he also felt that it was a small price to pay if his new policy led to a cleaner life for the rest of the country and eventually the world.

He never expected the severity of the uproar when the nation learned of the deal. Overnight, it seemed every citizen became a champion of the Arctic National Wildlife Refuge.

People who couldn't find Alaska on a map suddenly started spouting off statistics about the damage that oil exploration would do to the wilderness. Posters, T-shirts, and talk show guests materialized out of thin air. The arctic fox and the polar bear became immediate media sensations; hours of programming chronicling their plight choked the airwaves. Thundering herds of caribou raced across television screens night after night while serious-voiced commentators described how they would be nearly extinct within eighteen months of the first oil rig start-up. People were outraged, and dozens of environmental groups burgeoned after the President's announcement.

Boycotts of the oil companies that had been granted drilling licenses erupted across the nation. The hardest hit, Petromax, started legal proceedings against several groups, including Greenpeace, for organizing the protests. Greenpeace welcomed the media attention a pending trial would generate. They wanted to send their ship, the *Rainbow Warrior III*, into Prince William Sound as an act of defiance, but she was stationed in the South Pacific to protest the latest round of French nuclear tests.

What had started as a chance to finally cure many of America's problems turned into a pitched battle that was dividing the nation as nothing had since Vietnam. Like so many hard decisions, everyone saw the Energy Direction Policy as a good idea, but no one wanted to pay the price for its success.

The President and Secretary of Energy Van Buren had weathered the storm together, both shouldering even more criticism as now, almost a year later, men and equipment poured into the wildlife refuge to began spudding, the start-up procedure for drilling. People seemed to forget about the benefits of the President's moratorium on oil imports. All that mattered was the protection of the Arctic tundra and its inhabitants, even if that meant another generation of smog and acid rain and greenhouse gasses.

"I'm not even going to ask if we've done the right thing," the President remarked tiredly, for he'd covered the issue a million times before. "I know I'm right. We need to wean ourselves from oil. Period. At our present rate of consumption, the planet will run out by the middle of this century anyway, so why not be prepared for it? Europe and Japan will be screaming for our clean technology, and we'll hold all the cards. Doesn't anyone see that this is for the best?"

Connie Van Buren had heard all of these arguments before and said nothing. Though not well known to the general population, the Department of Energy was a favorite lobbying spot for the Seven Sisters and all the other oil concerns. She had come under even more pressure than the President. But with a forbearance found only in women, she had taken the criticism and complaints in stride, while keeping an open ear for the President to vent his frustration.

"The long-term benefits of what I've proposed far outweigh the destruction of the Arctic Wildlife Refuge, and hell, it isn't a foregone conclusion that the animals there will be wiped out like the doomsayers predict."

That last statement fell sour to the President's ears even as he spoke it. The flora and fauna of Alaska's north coast were found nowhere else on earth and were so delicate that even the most minor damage was virtually permanent. Arctic moss required a minimum of a hundred years to recover from the passage of even a light vehicle. Once the rigs and pipelines and all the other support structures were built, the land would never come back.

"But Christ," the President continued, his voice thundering, "it's a small price."

Connie threw up her hands in mock defense. "Remember, I'm on your side."

"I'm sorry." He smiled ruefully. "It's just the pressure. How in the hell do you handle it?"

Connie laughed. "I just remind everyone that America's nuclear arsenal falls under the Energy Department's jurisdiction. I tell them that I control over twenty thousand warheads and I'm prone to PMS. That seems to back them off."

The President smiled tiredly. "What's the latest from the native rights groups?"

The rights of Alaska's native people had become a hot topic as well. Connie shifted in her seat, resting her knife and fork on the china plate still heaped with congealed eggs and soggy bacon. "They're relatively quiet so far. Because they lack the international exposure of the big environmental groups, the native advocates are keeping a low profile to see how far the administration is willing to back up this initiative. Though I just heard Amnesty International is threatening to call the entire Inuit population political prisoners of the United States if we continue to infringe on their rights to the land."

"Jesus Christ!" exclaimed the President, "you call that a low profile?"

"Compared to what this group called PEAL has done, that's nothing."

"PEAL?" He cocked a bushy eyebrow. "I've never heard of them. Are they another environmental group?"

"More like eco-terrorists." Connie lifted an expandable briefcase from the floor and set it on the table. After rummaging though the detritus cluttering the case, she slid a manila file over to the President. "This is the dossier INTERPOL has compiled of crimes that PEAL has been directly or indirectly linked to in Europe. And this is just from the last year."

As the President leafed through the summary reports of bombings, protests, and assaults, Connie Van Buren gave him a brief rundown of the organization. "PEAL is the acronym for Planetary Environment Action League. It was founded four years ago by a Dutch science professor who had fallen from grace with mainstream academia. Jan Veorhoven is a classic study of the charismatic leader. He's young, not yet forty, good-looking, from a wealthy family with name recognition in his native Amsterdam, and possesses above-average intelligence."

Connie spoke as if reciting the material arrayed before the President. It was obvious that she'd been over the file many times before.

"Until this year, PEAL had remained inconsequential. They printed pamphlets and Veorhoven lectured at rallies all over Western Europe, but the group was relatively small, about one hundred active members. Many in the environmental movement saw PEAL as too radical for even their tastes.

"Veorhoven espouses a kind of pseudo-religious communing with nature, where the rights of man are second to those of the earth. He flew to Bangladesh after a monsoon that killed eleven thousand villagers and denounced those who survived for cheating nature of her just dues. Last December, after some nonradioactive cooling water escaped from a French reactor, PEAL was thrust to prominence when Veorhoven challenged the director of the plant to drink some of it. It was a media stunt of epic proportions because the director is hyperallergenic and can tolerate only distilled water, a fact Veorhoven was aware of.

"Beginning this year, PEAL became the 'in' group to join among the professional protesters. Their ranks have soared, as has their budget. In March, they bought a mothballed survey ship and renamed her *Hope*. They opened satellite offices in London, Paris, New York, Washington, and San Francisco. And they started getting violent.

"Members of the group have been arrested in Mozambique with enough explosives to destroy the Cabora Bassa dam. In Brazil, they've taken responsibility for demolishing about ten million dollars worth of heavy equipment used in forest clearing. In Washington State, a PEAL activist is facing manslaughter charges after the steel spike he put into a tree caused a chainsaw to kick back and kill the logger operating it. Your own Secretary of the Interior had a sack full of dead spotted owls left on his doorstep. The bag had the PEAL logo on it. Nothing is beyond them.

"They've destroyed gas stations in Germany, Holland, and Belgium. They are suspected of breaking into a German chemical company and destroying several million dollars worth of experiments. They've broken into laboratories to release test animals, many of them infected with diseases or experimental vaccines with unknown side effects. In short, they are highly motivated, well funded, and dangerous, and their next target will undoubtedly be Alaska."

The President was startled by Connie's summation. "How can you be sure that they will target Alaska?"

"Because their ship, *Hope*, is currently anchored in Prince William Sound, just outside the safety zone set up around the tanker shipping lanes headed into Valdez. And because Jan Veorhoven is said to be aboard."

"Have they taken any action?"

"Not yet, but I consider their very presence a threat, don't you?"

"In light of what you've just said, yes," the President agreed. "But there isn't a goddamn thing we can do about it."

"I know they have a legal right to be there, but I want to make sure they are number one on the suspect list if anything happens."

"I'll tell Dick Henna at the FBI to keep his ears open."

"I talked to him as soon as I heard the *Hope* was headed to Alaska. He promised to stay on his toes." Connie's last remark was almost flippant, but her eyes had hardened and her mouth was pursed into a tight line. She was serious. And scared.

=====

GEORGE WASHINGTON UNIVERSITY WASHINGTON, DC

Mercer stood as the large group of students began a disinterested round of applause. He was sure that they weren't applauding his presence, just the fact that they didn't have to suffer through another lecture by their regular teacher, Professor Lynn Snyder. The one hundred and twenty students in the lecture hall were mostly freshmen, and though the school year was only a few weeks old, they had already developed a special loathing for Introduction to Geology. Professor Snyder's presentation was as dry as the rocks she forced them to study.

Lynn Snyder had been a doctoral candidate at Penn State at the same time as Mercer, and despite the few years separating them, she looked fifteen years older. While he had gone to the U.S. Geological Survey after receiving his Ph.D. and later to the private sector as a consultant, Lynn had ducked immediately back into academia. It always amazed Mercer that so many Ph.D.'s spent their entire careers creating clones of themselves in a never-ending chain of teachers.

Lynn knew ninety percent of the class didn't give a damn about geology. They signed up only to fulfill the school's requirement for two semesters of science. Still, she hoped for that rare student who embraced the subject.

However, that special type of student was few and far between, so Professor Snyder hit on the idea of giving her classes a practical application of geology in the form of Dr. Philip Mercer. Mercer was a field man who'd proved that studying igneous inclusions and anticlines could mean millions of dollars in gold or oil or some other precious mineral for mining corporations and substantial finders fees for himself. Though his lecture taught nothing critical, it was usually entertaining and on the end-of-semester comment cards, his visit was always a highlight.

Mercer smiled at Lynn as he joined her on the lectern after his introduction. "Once more into the breach."

"Knock 'em dead." Lynn gave Mercer a playful pat on the arm.

Mercer adjusted the microphone and busied himself with a sheaf of notes he had no intention of using. His delay was a simple speaking tool to calm the audience and hold their attention for a few moments. The hundred students were spread throughout the lecture hall in GWU's Funger Hall, one of the urban campus's many classroom buildings. He thrust his left hand into the pocket of his light gray suit pants; his jacket was draped over a chair behind him on the dais. The room was at least eighty-five degrees despite the air conditioning. He fondly recalled the chilled air he'd felt in Alaska only four days ago.

"I know what you're all thinking, 'Great, a guest lecturer even more boring than Professor Snyder.' "

A co-ed's voice called out seductively, "That's not what I was thinking, handsome."

A chorus of female whoops and cheers followed almost

immediately. Mercer smiled sheepishly and adjusted his tie to cover his embarrassment.

As the cheering was dying down, Mercer leaned into the microphone and looked toward where the first voice had come, "You make me wish schools had never done away with spanking unruly students."

Another few moments of cheering and laughter delayed Mercer's lecture.

"How many of you are here because the university requires a year of science before they give you a poli-sci degree? And be honest." A sea of hands were raised all across the hall. "And how many of you are genuinely interested in learning geology?" A few hands shyly went up before being lowered quickly.

"To those few who planned on learning today, I apologize, because I'm not a teacher. In fact, I don't understand half of the things Professor Snyder will teach you this year. As she said in my introduction, I did get my Ph.D. at the same time as she did, but I had already graduated from the Colorado School of Mines. Her goal was to teach geology, while I wanted to apply it."

He had a relaxed, unrehearsed speaking style that caught his audience's interest as he spun tales of mining disasters and of wondrous treasures hacked from the earth. This was not the stuff of science as they'd expected but adventure stories told with a natural eye for the more fabulous elements of the tales. He talked about the fabled early days of the Kimberley diamond rush in South Africa where desperate paupers became overnight millionaires and of the Molly Maguires' strike in the Pennsylvania coal fields that led to the establishment of the forty-hour work week. He described what it was like to actually work miles below the earth in dust-choked shafts and dark tunnels where the constant strain of knowing gravity was pressing billions of tons of rocks down around you had driven many men insane.

Mercer spoke about the history of mining and quarrying, from the prehistoric days of scavenging shards of flint to make spear points to the earliest actual open pit mines where water-soaked wood wedges were used to cleave slabs of stone that became the temples and monuments along the Nile River. He talked about the ancient mines where children were forced to hand dig for ore, and their lives might last as much as a month but more often ended only days after entering a shaft. He talked about technological advances, about giant earth-moving equipment, huge machines that weighed as much as twenty thousand tons yet were still able to move under their own power. He talked about explosives, how four hundred pounds of dynamite registers seven on the Richter scale when set off on the surface and about Primacord fuses that burn at twenty-five thousand feet per second. He kept the students enthralled for an hour with stories and anecdotes from a world few of them ever knew existed.

When he finished, there was a smattering of applause centered at the back of the room, started by a single figure in the very last row. As the others stopped clapping, the lone figure, a woman, continued. Her applause was slow, almost taunting. A clap, a pause, and then another clap. And another pause.

The woman stood, strands of her hair escaping from under a red bandanna. Despite the oppressive heat in the hall, she wore a shapeless bush jacket over a dark T-shirt. Mercer couldn't really make out any details of her face as she continued her desultory applause, but there was something compelling about her posture, an undercurrent of poise and confidence that her shabby clothes couldn't hide.

"These stories are all very interesting, Dr. Mercer, quite entertaining actually, but you brag about your accomplishments with the evil candor of some Nazi scientist discussing the results of his genocidal experiments. I wonder how you sleep at night?"

Her comment surprised Mercer, but it wasn't the words that made him pause, it was the voice. He knew immediately she wasn't a student; she possessed a mature woman's voice. It had a certain music to it, a timbre and catch on certain letters that made it one of the most captivating he'd ever heard, despite the accusatory tone. It took him several heartbeats to respond, "I'm sorry, but what the hell are you talking about?"

"I'm talking about your lack of concern for what you've done to our planet. I'm talking about your defilement of something that you do not posses. I'm talking about your rape of the earth."

Here we go again, he thought.

"You've stood up there for the past hour and told us about how wonderful and beneficial mining is to mankind without once addressing the toll that has been paid by the earth. The damage that you and others like you have caused is irreparable. Our world is permanently scarred by what you've done, and you don't seem the slightest bit guilty. In fact, you're proud of your achievements. Mankind was not put on this planet to exploit its natural resources, but to live in harmony with them. The wanton destruction you freely admit to has to stop, now.

"You've talked about the benefits of technological advances that have made strip mining and other activities so simple, but you don't talk about the other advances at all. Why don't you tell us about cyanide filtration used in modern gold mining. Tell us about the $129 million needed to clean up the Summitville disaster. Tell us about the seventy billion dollars needed to clean up other the ecological disasters left by greedy mining corporations. Go ahead, tell us."

Mercer let her challenge hang in the air. He had no defense, for what she'd said was correct. Summitville was currently costing the federal government thirty thousand dollars a day, and even that money was only a temporary cure for the worst mining disaster ever on U.S. soil. Galactic Mining, a firm in southern Colorado, had been using cyanide to pick out microscopic particles of gold from ore spread on huge plastic sheets. Hasty construction of the extraction pads led to a leak that leached raw cyanide into the ground water. No deaths had resulted from the accident, but the surrounding land was effectively dead for years to come. He didn't want to mention that her estimate for cleaning the other mining sites on the Superfund list was much too low.

"You seem better informed than most undergrads," Mercer said.

"I'm not a student. I'm a member of the Planetary Environment Action League. I came here today because I knew that you would only present your side of the issue and I felt it necessary to let these students know of the destruction you've caused."

"What's your name?" Mercer asked.

"That is none of your concern," she responded sharply.

"You sit there in anonymity and hold me personally responsible for an act that I had nothing to do with." Mercer laughed, a quick bark that defused the tension that had swelled in the room. "By mentioning Summitville, you're trying to lump every mining company in with one that was grossly negligent. I'm sorry, but that kind of emotional plea doesn't wash. Nor does your call for us to live in harmony with nature. Is nature harmonious with us when she sends hurricanes into the Caribbean that wipe out whole villages or chokes thousands of people under walls of mud when the heavy rains come to Central America? The answer is no."

Normally Mercer wouldn't allow himself to be drawn into this type of confrontation, but today he couldn't stop himself. With the debate over Alaska's Wildlife Refuge raging all over the country and with so much emotionalism spent on the issue, he felt he had to present a voice of reason, if only to this audience.

"We fight nature as surely as she fights us. For every foot of ground we gain, she takes back two. Ask the survivors of the Kobe earthquake about it sometime. I'm sorry if you still don't realize that all life is a struggle. From the time of our crushing births until our last gasping breaths, we fight for what we want. Some of it may come easy and some may come hard or not at all, but we continue to fight. The nature you are so willing to defend has forced us to evolve that way.

"Your way of thinking is so self-indulgent and self-centered that it's laughable. It must be nice to be so comfortable that you can afford to be guilty about that comfort. Ask a miner in Africa if he cares that what he's doing might affect the world for his children and he'll tell you that if he didn't do it, he wouldn't have any children.

"Every animal extracts a price from nature for its existence, but it's only humans who have an inbred sense of guilt for it. To disconnect man from the nature that created him is egotistical to the point of hubris. Evolution is the most awesome force ever to exist. Right now we are at the top of its chain, but like the dinosaurs, we aren't meant to stay there forever. When nature no longer believes that the big brain of *Homo sapiens* is the key to survival on the planet, she'll do away with us. It's been tried before. Cholera, tuberculosis, and the plague nearly wiped us out, but we adapted, changed our behavior, stopped living in the filth that bred such diseases. Today, what is AIDS teaching us? In what evolutionary direction will this modern killer push us? Nature is producing viruses faster than we're able to cure them. This is a direct competition between our brains and natural selection. By denying us our right to use our minds and to use the resources we are able to exploit, you're trying to stop the natural progression of our species. And you accuse me of going against nature's wishes. I advise you to take a good look at evolution and tell me who is more in concert with nature, a person who is working with natural evolution or someone who is denying that its forces continue today. Do you think a locust swarm is concerned with the destruction it leaves behind? Why do humans, the most intelligent species ever to exist, try to deny what is natural to every other creature on the planet?"

"Are you saying we are nothing more than an insect infestation?"

"To the earth and on the geologic scale in which it exists, yes, that is exactly what I'm saying. I deal with a time line that stretches billions of years while you limit yourself to your own insignificant life span. To the planet, we are one in a long line of dominant creatures and we will be usurped." Mercer paused and shifted tack.

"I don't deny that man has the responsibility to husband nature's resources, to protect them for our future, but that does not mean that we must stop using them altogether, which I suppose is the goal of your organization. PEAL and other environmental groups see every issue as a double-sided coin, black or white, right or wrong, exploit or protect. But there's a third side of the coin, its thin edge that we call compromise. I may not like it and you may not like it, but that's the way it is.

"As we speak, the most controversial compromise in environmental history is being played out in northern Alaska. For the sake of a few thousand square acres of land, the United States may free itself from the smog that has choked our cities for generations and end our dependence on fossil fuels forever. Is the price high? Absolutely. I've seen the Arctic Wildlife Refuge. It's one of the most spectacular places on the planet. But if its use means that future generations won't have to live with acid rain or high levels of carbon monoxide or gaping holes in the ozone layer, then I believe it's justified.

"I'm sorry if you don't like it, I would just as soon see it left alone too, but that's the nature of compromise. At some point in your life, when you're not so sure that you're right all the time, you'll understand what I mean."

Mercer broke eye contact with the woman and surveyed the attentive looks of the students. They were rapt by the exchange. He smiled self-consciously, embarrassed at his long-winded soliloquy. "Ladies and gentlemen, I thank you for your time and attention. Dr. Snyder has some amendments to your syllabi before class is dismissed."

The applause was genuine and enthusiastic as Mercer gathered the notes he never needed. Just before he turned from the lectern, he caught the eye of the young woman again. She threw him a saucy smile, as if to say round one to you, but the fight will continue.

LOS ANGELES INTERNATIONAL AIRPORT

Howard Small stepped off the Boeing with an expectancy he hadn't felt since college. He'd spent four more days in Alaska with his cousin before returning home, and he was expected back up at the test site in a week. This short stay in Los Angeles was due to a prior commitment he could not avoid. While he was physically unimposing, just over five foot six with a slight frame and a prematurely hairless skull, the crowds at LAX seemed to open before his eager charge. Within the briefcase swinging carelessly from his hand were the final test data from the mini-mole. The information, while signifying a technological breakthrough, also represented a great deal of money. Once the patents were filed, Howard and his UCLA team were going to be wealthy. He smiled to himself as he walked along the crowded corridor.

His buoyant mood carried him through the hassle of collecting his suitcases from the carousel, allowing him to ignore being jostled by countless others who believed that rushing the process would somehow give them an advantage getting out of the airport.

With his valise under one arm, a case in the other, and his larger piece of luggage rolling behind him like a disobedient dog, Howard turned to the terminal's exits and the Southern California night beyond. Had the uniformed limousine driver not chosen that moment to cough, Howard would have missed the man holding a signboard with his name on it. He approached the dark-complected chauffeur warily.

"I'm Professor Small," he said.

"Ah, very good, sir," the driver responded. "Let me assist you with your baggage."

"But wait." Howard refused to give up his grip on the luggage. "I wasn't expecting a car. Are you sure you are waiting for me?"

"I was told to pick up a Dr. Howard Small arriving from Anchorage, Alaska." The driver sounded like he hadn't been in the country long.

"Any idea who hired you?"

"No, sir."

Howard laughed to himself and spoke more for his own benefit than that of the taciturn driver. His confusion had turned to delight. "Must be the guys at the lab already spending their share of our profits."

He turned over his two large cases and followed the driver

into the night. In the glare of the airport's loading ramp, a black limo glistened like a panther amid the battered taxis. The driver used a keyless entry system to unlock the doors, opening a rear one for Howard before securing the luggage in the trunk. The luxury vehicle glided smoothly from the curb before Howard could get himself comfortably settled in the plush interior. The inside of the car smelled of carpet cleaner and Armor All.

"You have my address in Glendora?" Howard asked through the intercom system. The dividing screen between the two compartments of the vehicle was up and Howard could not seem to lower it.

"Yes, sir," came the quick response, and the intercom went dead.

Since conversation with the Arab driver was out of the question, Howard contemplated helping himself to a drink from the minibar but realized he'd done more drinking in the past week with Mercer than in his entire life. He thought it wise to give his body a rest for a while. Howard chuckled again. He'd had six hangovers in seven days, and not once had Mercer shown any ill effects from the alcohol they'd consumed. The man's guts were harder than the rocks he mined.

It took more than an hour to reach the quiet development north of Los Angeles where Howard owned a modest bungalow. Between the drone of the limo's tires, the mesmerizing lights of other vehicles, and the occasional mutterings of the driver to his dispatcher, Howard was lulled to sleep, waking only as the car pulled into his development.

Howard's home was third from the end of a cul-de-sac butting against one of Los Angeles' increasingly rare patches of woodland. It was a little past ten, yet the street was quiet and dark, the only light coming from street lamps and the occasional porch fixture. The limo pulled unerringly up to Howard Small's yellow and red one-story house. The driver's familiarity with the neighborhood should have alerted Howard, but he failed to notice it.

He stepped out of the car and looked up the street, hoping a neighbor would see him with the stretch limo, but even Mrs.

Potter, who seemed to always be walking her dachshund, was tucked in for the night. The driver too scanned the street, his eyes sweeping the area with military efficiency. He recovered the bags from the trunk and followed Howard up the driveway, past the scientist's decade-old Honda. At the door, Howard fumbled with his keys while pulling a ten-dollar bill from his pants as a tip. He turned the key in the lock and was just about to relieve the driver of the bags, when the man powered a shoulder into him, shoving him bodily into the house.

Howard fell to the carpeted floor, the wind knocked out of him. He lay wheezing as the driver dumped the suitcases in the entrance and banged the door closed with his hip. A silenced automatic was already in his hand, the weapon nearly lost in the man's large fist. Before Howard could react, a living room light snapped on, revealing three other men, two more Arabs and a Caucasian with a silver crew cut and washed-out blue eyes. The two Arabs were standing, while the other man lolled in a soft overstuffed chair, a nearly empty glass in his hand. Even in this frozen tableau, Howard knew that the seated man was in charge and the most dangerous person he had ever seen.

On both counts, he was correct.

Ivan Kerikov set his drink on a coffee table, carefully placing the glass onto the ring of condensation that marred the otherwise clean surface. "No one was outside when you drove up?" His voice was low and menacing, with the thick guttural accent of his native Russia.

"No one saw us enter," the driver said, crossing the room to stand at the side of one of the Arabs. The two were of a type, large and dangerous with the flat expressionless faces of bodyguards.

The third Arab was younger by a few years, early thirties, and handsome in a cruel way with thick hair and a body that was as lean and rippled as a scorpion's. His most noticeable feature was his eyes. They were small and dark, with an inner fire that threatened to burn free at any moment.

"I told you it would be simple to capture him, Kerikov," the young Arab said, glancing at his two henchmen for confirmation.

"Shut your mouth," Kerikov snapped.

It was a risk interrogating Small in his own home but one Kerikov couldn't avoid. He had heard of Howard Small only the day before and hadn't had time to snatch him in Alaska. Nor did he have the time to establish a more private base in Los Angeles. However, there were psychological benefits to torturing a person where he felt the safest, especially in his home. Small lay on the floor, trembling like a child, his lower lip quivering so much that he had to bite down to still it. His eyes had grown huge with fear.

"Whatever it is you want," he finally managed to stammer, "please, just don't hurt me."

Kerikov's gaze didn't soften. How many people had begged for their lives before him, he wondered. A hundred, certainly. Two hundred, quite possibly. It never got easier for him, nor did it ever get harder. In the life he'd led, torture and interrogation were simply parts of his job, as necessary and familiar as a lawyer preparing a brief.

Several long seconds passed. Howard's eyes locked on the Russian as he levered himself out of the chair.

"I don't wish to make this any more unpleasant than it must be, Professor Small." There was no sympathy in Kerikov's voice. "But you must realize the seriousness of my intent."

On cue, the younger Arab, whose nom de guerre, Abu Alam, meant literally "Father of Pain," left the room for a moment, returning with a large cloth bag that writhed with anguished movement. Howard clearly heard his cat, Sneaker, screaming from inside the sack. The two bodyguards lifted Howard off the floor, carrying him to the kitchen where Abu Alam stood poised over the sink with the bag. His hand flicked out and switched on the garbage disposal.

"Oh God, no, please. I'll do anything you say. Please don't do it," Howard cried.

Alam ignored him, plunging his hand into the bag and removing a multihued calico male with four white paws. Tape bound each pair of legs so tightly that the cat could not defend itself, only squirm.

"According to the note left by your neighbor, your animal was very good while you were away, but you did not leave enough food for it so she had to go out and buy more." There was an edge of excitement in Alam's voice that bordered on the sexual. The disposal made a harsh grinding noise as he held the struggling feline over the circular drain.

Still in the living room, Ivan Kerikov listened dispassionately as the disposal's mechanical teeth stripped the flesh from the cat's forepaws and then ground the bones to splinters. Long after the pet had died from shock, Abu Alam continued to feed the carcass into the unit, its motor loading down as it chewed through heavier concentrations of bone and gristle, until the whole animal had been reduced to a pulpy mush. Howard Small struggled against his two captors and would have screamed forever had they not tied a gag over his mouth.

Listening to the grisly sounds emanating from the kitchen, Kerikov reflected that he was too old to still be doing these sorts of interrogations. He should be retired right now, living in a beautiful birch forest dacha on the Moscow River with a study full of citations and a chestful of medals. At this moment he should be half drunk on Scotch, fucking some eager blonde the State had given him in gratitude for a lifetime of service in the KGB. Had Russia not sold out, and allowed herself to be swept aside in a sea of greed, corruption, and the slick packaging of the Western lifestyle, Kerikov wouldn't be sitting in a shabby house in Los Angeles, trying to extract information from a man who was not even important enough to waste spit upon.

Kerikov had spent thirty years in the KGB, ruthlessly working his way through the hierarchy. When the Soviet Union disintegrated around him, as he had known all along it would, he headed one of its most shadowy organizations and was in possession of a great deal of information that would make him wealthy in the New World Order to follow. Unlike many others in the higher echelons of the KGB, Kerikov wasn't going to allow himself to be caught in the rubble of the collapsing Russian empire.

When the Soviet Union inevitably fractured, Kerikov was the head of Department 7, Scientific Operations, the arm of State Security involved in planning and executing Russia's most audacious operations. At the height of the Cold War,

Dept. 7 had a budget that rivaled the space program's and boasted a much higher caliber of scientists. Its operations, launched during the 1960s and '70s, were not designed to come to fruition until decades later. Yet when Kerikov took it over in the late 1980s, much of Dept. 7 had been dismantled due to financial constraints. Russia could no longer plan operations decades in advance when the government didn't know if it would exist the following month.

Knowing that the end was coming, Kerikov managed to keep active a few operations that had a certain portability. When it came time for him to escape Russia and start a new life, he smuggled out some of these plans and prepared to turn them over to an outside power. For a price.

Just after his departure from Russia, he almost succeeded in selling a Dept. 7 operation code named Vulcan's Forge to a group of Koreans for $100 million. Had it not been for the interference of an American mining engineer and a double cross by a trusted agent, Kerikov wouldn't now be struggling to bring another KGB operation out of the Cold War.

Charon's Landing. It had been conceived in the mid-1970s, when détente was at its lowest ebb and the Soviet government believed they could win a limited nuclear war with the United States. The operation was meant to be the war's opening gambit, designed to cripple America's short-term economic capabilities. Ten years would pass before Dept. 7 was ready to install the hardware necessary for its success. But the world had changed by then, and relations between the two superpowers had warmed. Yet Kerikov had gone ahead anyway and laid the foundation for Charon's Landing, contrary to Mikhail Gorbachev's direct orders. No one in the Soviet government knew of the work, so when Kerikov fled, his theft of the project went undetected.

After the failure of Vulcan's Forge, Kerikov had to wait a year for the right set of circumstances before trying to sell this other operation. The U.S. President's ill-advised Energy Direction Policy made his search for a buyer so easy that, after its announcement, he could actually choose among the bidders.

Now, hearing Abu Alam gleefully liquefying Howard

Small's cat, Kerikov wondered if he had made the right selection. He had worked with many psychotics during his life. After the war in Afghanistan, most of his squad of KGB interrogators could not function normally in a civilized society and had had to be killed rather than demobilized. Yet none of them compared to Abu Alam. The man truly lived up to his name, and Kerikov had known him only a short time. Alam was the right-hand man to Hasaan bin-Rufti, the Petroleum Minister of Ajman, and the man who had raised the money to implement Charon's Landing. Rufti was paying Kerikov $50 million for its successful completion. Part of Rufti's bargain with Kerikov was Alam's assistance during the final phases of the operation, as a way of guaranteeing the Minister's tremendous financial investment.

Kerikov had sold Charon's Landing to Rufti almost a year earlier, though Alam had not joined the Russian until just a month ago. Already the man's insanity was getting to the Russian. It was often necessary to soften a subject for an interrogation, but it had been Alam's idea to use the cat. And now, as the disposal finally wound down to silence, Kerikov knew that Alam had truly enjoyed himself. A moment later, a broken Howard Small was led back to the living room and dumped on the floor at Kerikov's feet. Abu Alam was drying his crimson-stained hands on a dish towel. Dark spots of blood smeared the black leather of his jacket.

"I have only one question for you, Professor Small, one question whose answer will save you a great deal of pain. To tell us what we want to know will cost you nothing but will spare you from unbelievable agony." Kerikov spoke slowly and clearly, knowing his subject was already in a mild state of shock. "I wish to know who was aboard the *Wave Dancer* with you and your cousins earlier this week when you discovered the derelict hull of the *Jenny IV*."

Since that first shove into the house, Howard had assumed that these men were industrial spies after the secret of the mini-mole. Never would he have imagined they wanted such an innocuous piece of information. In the few seconds it took him to get over his confusion, Abu Alam strode across the room and kicked Howard full strength in the stomach. Howard wailed into his gag as agony rippled through his body, curling him tightly on the floor.

"Answer him." Alam ripped off the gag, pushing the scientist onto his back with another derisive kick.

"Enough, Alam," Kerikov snapped. It wasn't that he felt mercy for Small, but to kick a man who was already defeated served only to prolong the interrogation. Also, Kerikov was still bothered by the botched interrogation of Howard's two cousins in Alaska.

He'd chanced upon a newspaper article in Anchorage detailing the discovery of the *Jenny IV*, which had been under his charter. The piece was only two paragraphs long, but it mentioned the name of the boat that discovered the hulk. Kerikov tracked down the owner of the *Wave Dancer*, and dispatched his two personal bodyguards, former members of East Germany's secret police. Both Jerry Small and his teenage son had died during their interrogation after revealing Howard's name but before divulging the name of the fourth member of their fishing excursion. The Germans had made the deaths appear accidental, but their mistakes forced Kerikov to California. He had to ensure that this final lead did not end up as a literal dead end as well. Too much was at stake. Knowing that someone had boarded the *Jenny IV* and possibly saw its last cargo was too great a risk to leave unaddressed. The discovery of the commercial boat could spell the end of the entire operation.

Damage control had always been one of Kerikov's best abilities because it necessitated a decisive ruthlessness and an expertise in projecting consequences far into the future. He was here now, personally tying up a loose end and making certain that there would be no further repercussions from the loss of the *Jenny IV*. Kerikov slid a silenced pistol from under his suit coat and aimed the barrel to Howard's right knee.

"The first shot will sever your leg at the knee, Professor. If you do not tell me then, I will turn you over to my more creative associates."

"Philip Mercer," Howard sobbed. "He was on the boat with us. He's a mining engineer."

The name staggered Kerikov. He thought back to Greece

where he'd been hiding since the failure of Vulcan's Forge. He saw himself sitting in a favorite café reading the morning paper over a cup of strong coffee, wiping flakes of a croissant from the pages. AMERICANS FIND NEW VOLCANIC ISLAND IN PACIFIC. The words had nearly pulled him from his seat. The volcano that they had discovered was the one Dept 7 had created with a nuclear detonation in 1954. It was his volcano, the one that was going to make him rich.

He read the article quickly, looking for the names he knew would be there. Valery Borodin, the son of the man who had initiated the project. Borodin was one of many who sold out Kerikov in those final weeks before everything fell apart. Tish Talbot, Borodin's American lover, was the sole survivor of a ship that strayed too close to the volcano before it was ready to be discovered by Kerikov's partners. The article stated that she was to work with her husband-to-be developing the mineral bikinium that the volcano brought from deep within the earth.

And then there was a name mentioned so casually that Kerikov almost missed it. The wire-service article said that the volcano had actually been discovered by an American mining engineer named Philip Mercer. Kerikov had never heard of Mercer, but he knew with certainty that this was the man who had foiled his plans. It was Mercer who had destroyed Kerikov's chances of selling the volcano and its unimaginable wealth and retiring to anonymity.

Kerikov had considered having Philip Mercer killed. He still had enough contacts to get such a simple assassination done without any difficulty. However, prudence made him stay Mercer's execution. The death of the American would certainly reopen international interest in the artificial nature of the volcano's origin and put Kerikov at risk.

Without consciously being aware of it, Kerikov fired his pistol. The bullet punched a neat hole between Howard's frightened eyes, expanded in the pan of his skull, but left no exit wound.

"Sanitize the house," he ordered. "Dispose of the body so that it's never found."

"Do you know this man he spoke of?" Alam asked as his

men bundled Howard's corpse into a body bag they had brought with them.

"Oh, yes, I know him." Philip Mercer had seen the *Jenny IV*, possibly boarded her. Maybe even now he was unraveling the mystery of her destruction. Kerikov had decided to spare Mercer's life once before, but he would not do so again. He glanced at his watch, calculated time differences, and dialed a cellular phone he always carried.

Despite Kerikov's earlier leniency, he knew exactly where Mercer lived, where he spent his time, even his favorite restaurants and bars. He had taken the precaution of having a private detective agency prepare monthly updates on Mercer's movements in preparation for the time when he would exact his revenge for Vulcan's Forge. Kerikov had been a shadow warrior his entire life, and it was time to once again strike from the shadows.

On the fourth ring, the phone was answered with a cultured "Hello."

"We have a problem."

=====

ARLINGTON, VIRGINIA

At a little past seven the next morning, Mercer threw on a pair of khaki shorts and grabbed the *Washington Post* from his doorstep. His street was quiet this early on a Saturday. Washington's famous Indian summer was in full force, and the humidity was on the rise. Sweat tickled the hair on Mercer's chest as he turned back into his brownstone.

Unlike the other row houses on the street, which held anywhere from three to six families in spacious apartments, Mercer was the sole occupant of his, and he'd done more than a little remodeling to make the house into his home. The front third of the brownstone was a three-story atrium overlooked by an oak-shelved library on the second floor and his master bedroom on the third. An antique spiral staircase corkscrewed up to the other levels. The stairs had been salvaged from a rectory just prior to its demolition and cost almost as much as a luxury automobile.

Mercer scanned the headlines as he climbed up to the second floor. He smiled to himself as he passed through the library. Though he'd lived here for more than five years, he'd just recently unpacked his large collection of books; their dust jackets looked like bunting draped across the wood shelves. The leather reading chair looked inviting for a moment, but Mercer walked on, into the room that he called The Bar.

Most houses have a family room. Mercer's had a bar, six stools lining an oak-topped counter with a brass footrail. Stemware hung from racks, and the ornately carved backbar was stocked better than most downtown establishments. The room felt like an English gentlemen's club; dark green carpet, rich leather couches, and walnut wainscoting below the plaster walls. Because the only windows faced a narrow alley between his house and the neighboring brownstone, the bar always retained a dusky, intimate feel.

Mercer slid the newspaper onto the bar and walked around it to turn up the rheostat lights. The automatic coffeemaker had brewed a scalding potion so bitterly strong that the first sip made him wince. Perfect.

He slipped an instrumental CD into the stereo next to the old lock-lever refrigerator before settling down to read the day's fare of disaster, scandal, and corruption. The Metro section made Washington's murder rate read like sports scores. Cops 5–Dealers 1.

He finished the *Post* about an hour later. After pulling out the crossword for his friend Harry, Mercer folded the paper and left it on the corner of the bar and took a back set of stairs to the first floor. He threw a couple of frozen waffles into the toaster in the little-used kitchen, then went into his office.

The room was similar in decor to the bar, wood and brass and leather. A huge desk dominated the center of the room, a computer and its peripherals occupying a third of it and half the matching credenza. Mercer's hand brushed against a flat slab of kimberlite as he strode into the room. The bluish rock resting on a side table was the lodestone of every diamond mine in the world and was a memento from one of Mercer's many trips to the mines of southern Africa and his personal good-luck piece.

The twisted piece of metal he'd recovered from Alaska was locked in the upper drawer of his desk. He grabbed it and returned to the kitchen. The toaster had burned the waffles to the texture of roofing shingles, so he tossed them into the trash and headed back to the bar. He wasn't that hungry anyway.

He retrieved a one-foot section of railroad track from the back bar and a shoe box filled with tins of metal polish, rags, and other cleaning items. As he started stroking the track with a polish-soaked piece of steel wool, he regarded the metal plate solemnly. The repetitive act of polishing had served him for years as a means to focus his thoughts on a single problem, and at the pace he was going, he'd have a few miles done before he figured out the significance of the plate.

It was ten inches long, four wide, and made of stainless steel. All its edges were ripped by the violent explosion that had destroyed the *Jenny IV*. The stencil roger, done in black ink, was its only identifying mark.

Mercer had gotten the crew list of the fishing boat from the Coast Guard before he'd left Alaska. No one even remotely connected to the ship was named Roger. He thought about the possibility that the letters weren't a proper name, but no other option came to him. And even if it wasn't a name, he still couldn't decipher the meaning.

"Come on, Rog," Mercer said to the plate. "Who in the hell were you and what were you doing on a fishing boat with personalized steel luggage?"

Mercer spent his life solving mysteries. Amassing clues as to where the earth hid her mineral wealth, interpreting data, and finally pointing to a spot and saying, "Dig here," was his stock-in-trade. He thrived on the challenge of millions of dollars and potentially hundred of lives resting on his word, but he admitted that the enigma of the scrap of steel was beyond him.

The phone rang, its shrill tone scattering his thoughts. He glanced at his watch as he reached to pluck the portable from its recharging pad on the corner of the bar. It was quarter of ten. The call had to be either Tiny telling him that he had the *Daily Racing Form* and to come over, or Harry White reminding him not to forget the crossword.

It was neither.

"Dr. Philip Mercer?"

"Yes," he replied warily. "Yes, who is this?"

"I'm sorry to bother you so early on a Saturday morning, sir. My name is Dan MacLaughlin. I'm the Chief of Police of Homer, Alaska." His voice was deep and gruff but sounded tired.

"Christ, it's not even five in the morning there."

"I'm afraid this is the tail end of a shitty night rather than an early start to a good day. Were you acquainted with Jerry Small and his son, John? They ran a charter boat here called the *Wave Dancer*."

MacLaughlin's use of the past tense was not lost to Mercer. "You know I was or you wouldn't be calling me. How'd they die?"

"I'm sorry to ask that way. I'm dog tired and pretty shook up. I've known Jerry ever since he moved here."

"I'm sorry too, Chief. I didn't mean to snap. What happened? An accident on the boat?"

"They were found earlier this morning by a neighbor who was getting back from the fish factory's graveyard shift. It seems Jerry and John had themselves a couple of drinks at home and must have wanted to go out and get a few more. Well, they both passed out in Jerry's pickup. The truck was still in the garage; the door was closed with the engine running. That was what brought his neighbor over, the running engine. Well, we figure that the fumes got 'em both."

"Jesus," Mercer breathed.

"The reason I called is, Coast Guard records show you were on that charter when Jerry found the *Jenny IV*. That makes you one of the last people to see them alive. Well, it seems the two of them had been fighting. There were bruises all over them. Jerry had two black eyes and John's mouth was pretty busted up. Like I said, I've known Jerry for a while, and he and John got along better than most parents and kids, so this fight kinda seems out of character. I was just wondering if they had any problems when you were on the charter boat with them. Arguing, fighting, anything like that?"

"No. They seemed to get along just fine. Finding that derelict shook us all a bit, but they weren't fighting." Mercer was genuinely shocked that Jerry and John had brawled. He never suspected that they would have family disputes like that. But he'd only known them for a short time. "I'm sorry, but I really can't help you. I left Homer the day we found the *Jenny IV*. You might want to call Jerry's cousin at UCLA. He stayed with Jerry for a couple of days after I left."

"I plan to wait until a little later in the day. It's still a mite early on this coast." MacLaughlin fell silent. It seemed he wanted to talk about this, get his feelings about his friend's death into the open, but he held back. "I won't keep you any longer, Dr. Mercer. Thank you for your time."

"Not at all, Chief. I'm sorry about your loss." Mercer broke the connection and let out a long breath. He made a mental note to call Howard Small later and offer his condolences. He stared into space for a moment, remembering Jerry and his son, their fishing trip, and the discovery of the eerie derelict. He had liked them both. They were honest men, hardworking and dedicated. Their deaths were a tragic waste.

Mercer stared at the metal fragment in his hands. He wondered if there was some sort of connection between the deaths and the steel shard, but he discounted it quickly. He'd learned a long time ago that happenstance could be a capricious thing. Knowing he wouldn't be able to concentrate any longer, he went upstairs to change and then left the house to meet Tiny and Harry.

Tiny, whose real name was Paul Gordon, owned a seedy bar a few blocks from Mercer's house. On Saturdays, he opened early for Mercer and Harry White, his best customers, so they could enjoy a few morning drinks and go over the *Racing Form* for the afternoon races at Belmont Park. Though once a promising jockey who had a few bad breaks, mainly his knees by some mob enforcers for not throwing a race, Paul still enjoyed horse racing as best he could. He ran book for about forty guys in and around Arlington.

Mercer had discovered the bar on his first day in Arlington. He'd expected a hulking gorilla behind the bar, but Tiny was, in fact, tiny. No more than four foot ten and one hundred and ten pounds, Paul had a special platform installed behind the bar so he could comfortably serve drinks. He was already hunched over the *Form* when Mercer pushed through the glass door.

The bar smelled of stale beer and cigarette butts, and no matter how much disinfectant Paul used, the odor never dissipated. A couple of tables were near the long bar, while the back of the establishment was taken up by vinyl booths. The peeling wallpaper was dotted with cheaply framed sports pictures. Next to the cash register were pictures of Tiny, liveried in silks, accepting handshakes from grateful horse owners, the winner he'd ridden always right beside him. Tiny was about fifty, but his small size and wrinkled face made him look like some ancient gnome.

Harry White, on the other hand, really was ancient. Pushing eighty, Harry looked as if he would die at any moment, yet he'd looked that way for all the years Mercer had known him. His face was so weathered it seemed to have collapsed in on itself. His body, though tall and erect, appeared to have withered away from something larger, giving his skin the look of a poorly fitted suit. His hands resembled bundles of sticks under sheets of liver-spotted rice paper. Despite his decrepit look, he was far from frail. He boasted of an active libido, and his eyes were bright blue windows to a sharp mind and an acid wit. His voice was a raspy snarl that crashed like a broadside of cannon fire. Maybe because of their age difference or maybe in defiance of it, he was Mercer's best friend.

" 'Bout fucking time you showed up. Where in the hell is my goddamned crossword?"

"Why don't you buy the paper yourself, you cheap bastard?" Mercer tossed the folded puzzle on the bar in front of Harry.

"Listen to him, Mr. Fucking Moneybags. He can afford to buy the newspaper every day."

In fact, Harry had a decent pension from Potomac Electric Company. He had also recently received a sizable cash gift from the government as compensation for the loss of his right leg, an injury he'd sustained fifty years ago. While Mercer knew about the money and had been instrumental in getting the settlement, Harry made him agree never to discuss it.

Harry snatched up the crossword, unfolded it neatly, and held his pen poised. "How was Alaska?"

Mercer smiled as he regarded Harry. Underneath his crocodile hide, he was a true friend. "Good time, but the damnedest thing happened."

He related the story of finding the *Jenny IV*, sparing no details. Neither Tiny nor Harry could speculate on the origin of the mysterious steel plate, and they both doubted that Jerry and John's deaths were in any way related.

Tiny poured Bloody Marys for Mercer and himself and set a Jack Daniel's and ginger ale in front of Harry. While Harry smoked a dozen Chesterfields and muttered though the crossword, Tiny and Mercer worked the *Form*, handicapping the day's fourteen races with as much attention as surgeons trying to save a patient. They broke down the indecipherable minutia of the racing paper, discarding numbers they felt were unimportant, multiplying others through secret systems and, in the end, often just went with their guts. Tiny was much more proficient at interpreting bloodlines, trainer streaks, and Beyer's Speed Figures, but he did bow to Mercer's innate ability to pick winners on instinct alone.

All through the morning, Tiny received calls from his regular customers, taking bets and laying odds as he got them from a buddy who worked at the track. By eleven-thirty, Mercer and Tiny were just about finished handicapping the last race. Harry was still working on the crossword, but he seemed to be down to just a few clues.

"Shit," he exclaimed with disgust. "I'm stumped."

"What ya got?" Tiny invited.

"Five letters, the middle one is *r*, Mendelssohn's Wedding . . ."

"Dirge," Mercer offered without looking up from his *Form*.

"Cynic," Tiny replied with a glance. "Mendelssohn's Wedding March. You know, 'Here comes the bride, da da da daa.' "

"Oh, right. I thought Mendel composed 'The Wedding March,' " Harry replied, inking in the answer.

"No. Father Gregor Mendel was the pioneer of modern genetics. He did those experiments with peas back in the 1800s."

"Really. All this time I was sure that Mandlebrot founded genetics."

"Untrue. Benoit Mandlebrot was one of the creators of fractal geometry," Tiny explained.

"Then who in the hell was the guy who developed the periodic table?"

"That would be Dmitri Mendeleev," replied Tiny.

Mercer stared at his friends. "God, it gives me the creeps when you guys do stuff like that."

As the morning wore into afternoon, Tiny's Saturday crowd began shuffling in. To a man, they were all there for the races. Uniformly, they were older, late fifties and up, paunchy, and dressed in thirty-year-old suits. They were living proof that clichés were based on fact. Mercer was the youngest man in the room by fifteen years, but he felt right at home. There was a special camaraderie among bachelors that transcended age or status. It was refreshing to be involved in conversations that didn't revolve exclusively around the other person's problems.

The racing card at Belmont was short that day; the last race went off a little after four in the afternoon. After Tiny paid off the winners, he finally allowed himself a drink, his first since the morning Bloody Mary. Harry White had been drinking bourbon as if he'd just escaped a temperance meeting, but he seemed unaffected. Mercer had switched to club soda and was sober.

"What's ya doin' tonight, Mercer?" Tiny asked, running glasses through the three small cleaning sinks under the bar. The smell of liquor was removed from the glasses, but they weren't actually clean.

"I'm throwing myself into the penguin suit tonight."

"Formal dinner?"

"I'm blowing off the dinner, but there's an open-bar reception afterward."

"Open bar?" Harry breathed enviously.

"I knew that would get you," Mercer smiled.

"What's the occasion?" Tiny asked.

"The inauguration of a new think tank called the Johnston Group, sponsored by none other than Max Johnston, the owner of Petromax Oil. The group's made up of scientists, economists, and environmentalists working on practical ways to implement the President's Energy Direction Policy."

"You going to be part of this group?" Harry asked as he unwrapped his second pack of cigarettes for the day.

"No, but I've known Max Johnston for a couple of years. The invitation to the party was in my box when I got home from Alaska."

"Hobnobbing with the rich and famous again," teased Harry. "What the hell is Johnston worth?"

"Christ." Mercer combed his fingers through his thick hair. "He owns Petromax Oil outright, plus he has control of the Johnston Trust established by his father when he started Petromax. I'd say a couple billion dollars, maybe more."

"Shit. Find out if he has an eligible daughter." Harry paused and reconsidered. "Hell, for that kind of money find out if he has a toothless grandmother who wets herself. I'm not fussy."

"For your sake," Tiny added, "I hope he does so you can pay back some of your bar tab."

Harry shot him an innocent look.

Mercer laughed. "I've got to go. The dinner's at six and the reception starts at eight-thirty. I want to be the first in line at the bar."

He walked home slowly. The day had turned out to be milder than expected, and the humidity seemed to be held in check by the angry clouds that were threatening in the east. Thoughts of Jerry and John Small had faded to their proper place. Mercer felt bad for them, but it was their own stupidity that got them killed. He felt worse for John's mother, wherever she was. No parent can deal with outliving a child.

Both of Mercer's parents had been killed in the Belgian Congo during the Katanga uprising. Being a orphan, raised by his paternal grandparents in Vermont, he had never experienced the difficult adolescent phase. Mercer's desire to follow in his father's footsteps and become a mining engineer precluded any thoughts of teenage rebellion. He couldn't imagine what would bring a father and son to physical blows. But something had made them brawl, and the consequences had turned deadly. Like MacLaughlin had said, they had both been drinking.

Just as Mercer turned the key in the door of his house, he cocked his head slightly, as if hearing a voice. In fact, he was hearing John Small again, as if he was standing next to the teenager aboard his father's boat. Mercer had just offered him a beer and the young man refused with a shake of his head. "No, thanks. I'm captain of the basketball team this year and there's a good chance I'll get a scholarship out of it."

Jesus, John doesn't drink.

Mercer raced through his house to his office, his fingers touching the piece of kimberlite like a mezuzah. He threw himself into his chair and quickly dialed information. A few moments later he was connected to the sheriff's office in Homer.

"Dan MacLaughlin speaking." He sounded better than he had earlier this morning, but exhaustion still dragged at his voice.

"Chief MacLaughlin, this is Philip Mercer. We spoke this morning about Jerry and John Small."

"Of course, Dr. Mercer." MacLaughlin sounded shocked by Mercer's call. "Can I help you?"

"You said that both of them were drunk, right?"

"Preliminary autopsy showed a blood alcohol count of over point two in both of them. They were hammered."

"Chief, John Small didn't drink," Mercer said triumphantly.

MacLaughlin was hoping for a big revelation, so his disappointment sounded especially bitter. "Dr. Mercer, just because he was a minor, don't mean he didn't drink. This is

Alaska, we do things a little different up here. Hell, I buy my kids beer on the weekends."

"That's not what I'm talking about. John mentioned his basketball team and not screwing up his chances of a scholarship. We had just found two corpses on a burned-up boat and the kid refused a beer. That sight would have made a ten-year A.A. veteran consider drinking again."

MacLaughlin was silent for a minute, the static over the line the only indication that he hadn't hung up. When he spoke, he did so softly, slowly, as the full implications of Mercer's news sunk in. "My son's best friend is on that team, and they all pledged not to drink until the season was over. It was a way to keep them focused and fired up. What the hell does this mean?"

"Either John broke his oath or something's not right and I'm willing to bet it's linked to the *Jenny IV*. Did you manage to reach Howard Small in Los Angeles?"

"No, not yet. But I left a couple of messages. He'll get back to me by tonight I'm sure. Tomorrow at the latest."

"Let me ask you, what happened to the hulk of the *Jenny IV*?"

MacLaughlin paused before answering. He didn't like the answer he was about to give. "It was scuttled by the Coast Guard the day after Jerry found it. By law, he had salvage rights to the vessel. Since the owner had died in the fire, there was no one to buy her back. There was nothing worth keeping, so Jerry had the Coasties tow it back out and sink her." He paused again and then added lamely. "Old boats make great artificial reefs for the fishermen."

"Did anyone explore inside the ship?" asked Mercer hopefully.

"No, I'm afraid not. She went out the way she was found, flooded to the freeboards."

"Shit." Mercer knew he'd just hit a dead end. "Well, I'm sorry to have bothered you, Chief."

"I appreciate the call, Dr. Mercer. And if it's any consolation, folks die every day in some mighty stupid ways. No sense making more out of this than there is."

As he hung up the phone, Mercer knew that MacLaughlin

wouldn't leave the case alone, and neither would he.

Up in his bar, the last of the coffee in the pot had burned down to half a cup of tarry residue that could have have been used as industrial solvent. Mercer sipped it cautiously while his dinner liquefied in the microwave. Something linked the *Jenny IV* to Jerry and John Small. They didn't just die; they were murdered. He was sure of it. All he needed was a culprit, a motive, and some evidence.

———

FALLS CHURCH, VIRGINIA

Mercer's jaguar was a dark shadow as it crept along the wide driveway, its throaty V-12 harnessed to a purr, its Perrelli tires hissing against the damp asphalt. A fine mist silvered the night in the twin beams of the car's headlights. His eyes strained to see the house he knew must be at the end of the lane. No one's driveway could be this long.

He glanced at the odometer and saw that he'd come nearly a mile since leaving the main road. When he looked up, he finally saw the faint glow of Max Johnston's home. The car rounded one more sweeping curve, and the house was laid out before him.

It was a massive Tudor with countless gables, oak crossbeams, and steeply pitched roofs that stretched for almost two hundred feet. While the house was enormous, its whimsical style gave it a less imposing feeling. Most of the numerous windows on the first two floors were lit, warming the damp evening with a pale radiance. Mercer counted eight chimneys before pulling his car up to the covered entrance.

A valet met him and swung open the long door of the XJS Jaguar. Mercer noticed several dozen limousines lined up at the side of the house in parade formation. He stepped from the car, allowing the young valet to slide into the leather bucket seat.

From within the home, Mercer heard the solemn vibrato of a cello accompanied by a violin and what sounded like a harpsichord. He could not name the piece, but he appreciated the beauty with which it was being played. Beneath the cuffs of his tuxedo, his beaten TAG Heuer was strapped firmly to his wrist. Nine-thirty. Perfect. The dinner, a boring affair he was sure, was over, and the real reception was just beginning.

He handed his invitation to a somewhat fuddled footman. Mercer was hours late, and the servant regarded him warily, his drooping eyes scanning the card and Mercer with equal suspicion.

"I fell into a bottle of vodka and couldn't get up," explained Mercer as he brushed past the doorman.

The entry hall was a story and a half high with wide plank floors and a plaster ceiling. A cherry wood table sat in the center of the foyer, its gleaming top nearly hidden by a beautiful arrangement of cut wildflowers. The room was scented by their subtle perfume. Above the table, a glittering crystal chandelier hung like a fragile stalactite.

In a room to Mercer's right, servants were preparing the dining table to become a dessert buffet. Tortes, cakes, mousses, and numerous other sticky sweet creations covered the table that could easily seat thirty people. The classical strains of the trio grew louder as Mercer wandered through the dining room. The nine-foot doors at the far end led to a living room larger than most suburban houses.

The furniture was all nineteenth-century revival, Duncan Phyfe and John Henry Belter mostly. Four separate conversation areas quartered the huge space, couches, love seats, and chairs arranged around identical tables like defensive fortifications. The paintings were predominantly American primitives with the exception of a portrait by Sargent of a mother and daughter and a Grant Wood Landscape. A bar had been set up along one wall, guests lined up and chatting away their wait for service.

The musicians were in the center of the room. Mercer watched them for a moment. There was something erotic about a female cellist, he thought. This one, not particularly pretty but eye-catching nevertheless, wore a deeply slit cream gown. Her stunning legs were wrapped around her instrument like a lover's embrace. He felt like a voyeur as he watched her fingers working the strings and turned away before his expression got him into trouble.

Through the series of French doors at the far end of the room, Mercer saw a huge marquee tent and clusters of tables that the two hundred guests had used for dinner. He was just noticing that the bartender had lime juice to make a vodka gimlet when a hand grasped him on the shoulder.

"What's a rogue like you doing at a place like this?"

Mercer turned, smiling as he recognized the distinctive voice. "Looking to ravage a Cabinet-ranking bureaucrat."

Connie Van Buren stretched up to give him a kiss on the cheek. "God, you're good-looking, and you smell nice too."

"Ah, but Connie, you're married."

"My husband's in New Mexico," she teased.

"And my libido's in storage."

"Forever the bachelor," she chided him mildly. "When are you ever going to get married?"

"I'll marry the first woman who leaves the seat up for me."

They had first met years before when Connie was working at the Interior Department and Mercer consulted for a German mining concern called Koenig Minerals. At the time, she was devoting a great deal of energy to blocking the company from opening a mine in Utah. They had one of the worst environmental records in the world. Mercer had stepped in at Koenig's request and to Interior's great relief, smoothly worked out a compromise that was acceptable to both parties. Connie and he had stayed in touch, keeping track of each other's rise through their chosen professions.

"I noticed you were absent from dinner. You were supposed to be on my left side. Instead, I had to suffer through some mealymouthed lawyer who spoke in press releases."

"I figured it would be bad, but I never imagined Max would invite the lawyers too."

"Max invited everyone he knows in the city. It's not every

day you endow a forty-million-dollar think tank, and he wants to make sure no one forgets it."

Mercer looked around as more guests filtered in from the tented patio. Connie was right. The room was filling with some heavy hitters. The Speaker of the House was deep in conversation with the President's Chief of Staff, and behind them, several nationally recognized television journalists were hanging on the words of a very drunk senior senator. The Johnston Group was certainly getting a big endorsement from Washington's elite.

"Where's our host?" Mercer scanned the crowd looking for Max Johnston.

"Oh, he's here, basking in the glow. He and the President played golf this afternoon, and the Old Man gave his official endorsement. Max is throwing this party just to let everyone else kiss his ring." Connie paused as she recognized a man tracking across the room toward her. "Oh, shit. Robert Baird."

"Who's he?" Mercer noted the man striding through the crowd.

"He's a lobbyist for the nuclear research division of Petromax Oil, one of Max's lackeys trying to curry favor. Excuse me while I duck into the ladies' room."

Baird actually made an 'aw shucks' arm gesture as he watched Connie's ample bottom waddle from the living room. He looked at Mercer for a moment, deciding if he was someone worth presenting his case to since he had been talking to the Secretary of Energy. Mercer flashed a dull smile, and Baird went in search of more powerful prey.

Mercer was watching him slink back through the center set of French doors when he saw her. Her back was toward him, angled away as she spoke with last year's Nobel Prize winner for chemistry. In the staid Washington social circuit, a revealing dress was seen as an affront to everything the city stood for. The women present, though formally dressed, still exuded an air of conservatism that precluded any ideas of sex.

But she looked as if she'd just come from a Hollywood awards show. Her dress, deeply black against her white skin, was cut so low in the back that with a little imagination, Mercer could almost visualize a shadow where the two halves of her buttocks split into tightly rounded hemispheres. The skin on her back was flawless. She was tall, but her height was not a distraction; rather it was a pedestal to admire her from. She turned and he saw her eyes.

The mineral beryl is a relatively common stone of little or no interest; in fact it's considered a by-product of mica and feldspar mining. Yet when aluminum is present in its makeup, beryl becomes aquamarine and is considered a semiprecious stone. And when nature adds traces of chromium rather than aluminum, beryl becomes emerald, one of man's most coveted gems. The depth of an emerald's color is determined by the amount of chromium. Too much and the stone is dark, inky, and dead. Too little and an emerald is pale and faded. This color difference is called kelly. A perfect stone, one with depth to its color while maintaining its brilliance, is considered to have good kelly, and its value soars proportionately.

Her eyes were green. A perfect kelly green that shot through Mercer like a live wire. She looked at him for a moment, scraping her nails through short hair that was dark yet blond and auburn at the same time, held to her neat skull with just a trace of gel. Mercer felt like he was drowning.

Individually, the features of her face were perfect, softly rounded lips framing a sensual mouth that seemed just on the verge of laughter. Her cheekbones swept down the sides of her face with the grace of a gull's wing, and her chin was strong with a slight cleft. Above her stunning eyes, her brows were wide and dark, shocking on such a delicate face but adding an undeniable magnetism. Her nose was small and gentle, very feminine.

From her high, broad forehead to her narrow throat, she was exquisite. There was no comparing her to the brassy trophy women that many of the men here called their wives. She had the looks of a fashion model, daunting and unobtainable, but he thought he noted a charm that those women didn't possess.

She shifted her weight from one long leg to the other. Her dress clung to hips that curved from her narrow waist with unmatchable grace. The slit up the front swept aside to reveal one smooth inner thigh and, had Mercer been able to breathe,

the sight would have taken his breath away. The front of her dress covered her body completely from her calves to her throat, but he noted that her unsupported breasts were small and high, the chill of the damp night forcing her nipples against the fabric.

"What can I get for you, sir?" The bartender distracted Mercer.

By the time he'd ordered a gimlet and turned back toward the French doors, she was gone. Damn.

He took his drink, absently muttering a thanks. It was then that he became aware he'd been physically aroused just by that quick glimpse of her. That hadn't happened to him since his eighth-grade class had a twenty-one-year-old substitute for a week.

"You can put my clothes back on."

"Excuse me?" Mercer turned and his breath jammed in his throat. She was even more beautiful up close. Her lips had an enticing pout that he unconsciously felt himself swaying toward.

"You just undressed me with your eyes, and I'd appreciate it if you put my clothing back on, Dr. Mercer." The mischievous glint in her eyes showed that she was relishing Mercer's discomfort. He guessed her age at early thirties, that perfect moment in a woman's life when she retains the beauty of youth but tempers it with the knowledge of experience.

"You know who I am?" Mercer was incredulous. He was certain that he would remember her if they'd met before.

"My, how quickly they forget." She laughed and started to walk away, her backside switching from side to side while the narrow ridge of her spine remained straight. A few paces away, she turned back. "We met yesterday morning."

She was lost in the crowd by the time Mercer realized who she was. He had been so enraptured by her looks that he had never paid attention to her voice, throaty yet soft, alluring and . . . recognizable.

Mercer nearly spilled his drink as he lunged into the crowd looking for her. She had been his vocal opponent at George Washington University. He had a hard time reconciling that shabbily dressed girl with the stunning beauty who'd just walked away. What in the hell was a militant environmentalist doing at a reception hosted by one of the largest oil companies in the world?

He moved forward quickly, apologizing to guests as he brushed by in his search. Suddenly, a man turned, and they bumped nearly face to face. Both were startled by the contact. Mercer saw that the man had gone nearly white when he saw Mercer, but his color returned quickly, and his handsome face split into a broad grin.

"Mercer, I didn't think you were going to make it." Max Johnston seemed genuinely pleased to see Mercer at his party.

Johnston was in his early sixties but looked ten years younger; his body was thin and wiry, honed from a legendary workout routine and biannual triathlons. His face was lined and weathered from the Texas sun where he was raised, but he had acquired a veneer of Ivy League polish that masked his origins. His hair was still thick and wavy, silvered just at the temples. He grasped Mercer's hand and pumped it vigorously.

The person Max had been speaking with drifted off.

"I had to mug a headwaiter to get his tuxedo." Mercer smiled back. "Quite a turnout, congratulations."

"I have a lot of hope for the Johnston Group," Max said as if reading from a prepared speech. "The President set a challenge to get America off its oil addiction, and I think we can help."

"Isn't that like cutting off your nose to spite your face?" joked Mercer.

"Hardly. Petromax is so diversified that shutting off our oil imports may actually help the company. In fact, I just closed a deal to sell off our last three supertankers. No, we're ready to help shape the future."

"Aren't you involved with the exploration of the Arctic Wildlife Refuge?" Despite his desire to find that woman again, Mercer found himself drawn into a conversation with his host.

"Yes, but that's only a small part of what we've planned. The oil we pull from the Refuge will provide Petromax with the capital to establish itself as the leader in alternative energy technology. We've already started pilot programs, and our lab people are close to developing a commercial hydrogen-cracking unit using seawater as fuel. Fusion thinking has taught us that there is more energy in matter than we had ever imagined." Johnston held up a half-full glass of champagne. "There's more power in this glass than mankind has produced since our first fire in some cave two hundred thousand years ago, and day by day we are getting closer to getting at it."

Mercer looked past Johnston's shoulder and saw the woman walking toward them, her body swaying to the chamber music while her eyes remained locked with his. He sensed he was about to be in the middle of a conflict between Johnston and the environmentalist. "Uh-oh."

Max turned, following Mercer's line of sight and muttered, "Oh, shit."

"You know her?"

Before Max could answer, she was with them, slipping a slim arm under Max's in a familiar gesture. Max regarded her indulgently for a moment, then turned back to Mercer to make the introductions. Before he could speak, she piped up.

"I apologize for lying to you, Dr. Mercer." Her smile numbed him. "We have met once before yesterday, but I doubt you'd remember. It was about ten years ago in Houston, when Petromax announced the discovery of the Edwards Plateau Oil Field. I remember that you were wearing an olive-colored suit with a black-patterned tie. You were the only man there without a cheesy cowboy hat."

"Honey, those hats are the symbol of the greatest state in the Union." Max turned from the girl and looked Mercer in the eye. It was a look of trepidation. "Well, then, I guess introductions aren't really necessary, since you two know each other."

Mercer found his voice. "I could still use a little help here."

Max gave her a fond smile. "This is my daughter, Agatha."

"My grandmother had to suffer through life with the name Agatha." She struck out her hand, which Mercer took like a pilgrim grasping a religious icon. "But I'll be damned if I will. Please call me Aggie, Dr. Mercer."

It was as if an elemental force passed between their hands.

Mercer held onto her long after a simple introduction demanded, long after mutual attraction expected. Long after . . . it was only when Max delicately coughed that he reluctantly let her go. Their eyes remained locked, clear green to cloudy gray, virgin earth to stormy sky.

"I only use my professional title when I call for dinner reservations. Please drop the "Doctor" and just call me Mercer. Everybody does."

Aggie pulled back a half step. "Are you so ashamed of your accomplishments that you're trying to hide your identity? My God, you single-handedly destroyed an entire mountain in India when you staked out the Ghudatra mines. What about your work in Australia? How many aborigines had to be relocated after the firm you worked for pegged a hundred thousand acres for an opal mine? Don't be modest, Dr. Mercer. To some, you're a hero. Right, Daddy?"

Max Johnston was looking uncomfortable. He glanced around, making sure that none of his well-heeled guests had heard his daughter's outburst. It was clear he'd listened to her views so many times that he could repeat them by rote.

"That's enough, Aggie. You promised to be my hostess tonight and not spout your drivel," Johnston hissed. "Christ, you're about as considerate as your mother was."

He turned to Mercer. "Sorry about that. Let's go get a drink."

He put a strong arm around Mercer's shoulder and led him away. Mercer turned his head and saw the look of utter hatred Aggie directed at her father.

"You don't have any kids, do you?" Max asked as the bartender fixed another gimlet and refilled the host's champagne flute.

"No. I realized young that I can barely take care of myself, so how the hell could I care for a child?"

Max smiled, relaxing slightly. "She's my greatest joy and I've been proud of every one of her accomplishments, even if they were designed to get back at me. Do you know she graduated at the top of her class at grad school? She got a degree in environmental engineering, of all things. She is quite brilliant, but she wastes it on these quixotic quests. I guess she never really had to grow up. I spoiled the hell out of her. Hell, I still do, by letting her screw around with that ecological group."

Mercer had no interest in the problems between Max and his daughter. Though he lent a patient ear, he had to make one comment. "Max, she's a grown woman. Shouldn't she be making her own choices?"

"If I let other people have choices, none of this would be here today." Max waved his glass around the room. Mercer couldn't tell if he was being flippant or serious.

"I shouldn't burden you with this." Max's public persona was back. "She and I still get along on occasion. Here, have another drink." Mercer allowed Max to put yet another gimlet in his hand. "Will you excuse me? I've got to go say hello to Connie Van Buren."

Max Johnston drifted back into the crowd, leaving Mercer thankfully free again. He finished the first drink Max had given him then took a small sip from the second. He smiled to himself as he looked around the opulent room. It didn't matter how rich a person was, common problems still reared their ugly heads.

Max Johnston wore his somewhat openly. He was a widower, his wife having succumbed to an alcohol-induced suicide wish. Mercer recalled her drinking problem when he'd first met Max in Houston. An hour into the party, Barbara Johnston was so drunk that Max had to have his chauffeur take her back to their limousine. Six years later, after countless rehab programs that the media intrusively reported, Barbara washed down a bottle of sleeping pills with a fifth of vodka. Her suicide note said, "Gone to sleep, please wake me when life is easier." And now Max was fighting with his daughter in front of some of the most powerful people in the country.

If that was the price of success, decided Mercer, Max could have it all.

He didn't see Aggie as he scanned the room, and felt a small measure of relief. Speaking to her now would be uncomfortable at best. Within a few minutes, he was talking with the co-chair of the Johnston Group's scientific arm, the ugly scene of a moment earlier all but forgotten.

Half an hour later, he became aware of her perfume. He hadn't noticed it before, it was so subtle. Mercer noted the wolflike stares from the men and the jealous glances from the women and knew Aggie Johnston was behind him. He turned around. She looked as if she'd recovered from the confrontation with her father, but he noticed a shadow behind her impossibly green eyes that hadn't been there before. Mercer knew it was best to act as if nothing had happened rather than rattle off some platitude about relationships.

"I never got a chance to rebut your attack on my profession."

Aggie gave Mercer a smile of thanks, a small lift of her lips that pleased him inordinately. Yet when she spoke, sarcasm edged her voice raw. "My father's company retains four entire law firms and a whole army of public-relations experts. They make excuses faster than the rest of the company produces environmental disasters. I'm sure you can toe the party line with the rest of them."

She paused, regarding him clinically. "Let me guess. You'll tell me how what you do creates jobs all over the world and gives hope to starving people who are still living in the nineteenth century. Does this sound about right?"

Mercer guessed she was a typical "cause and effect" protester. If there was an effect in the world, she'd join the cause. She would no doubt belong to numerous organizations, favoring new ones as they gained popularity. Harry White derisively called these people 'flavor-of-the-month liberals.' It wouldn't matter that some of her beliefs might be diametrically opposed to others as long as they were politically correct and au courant.

He used this to his advantage when he came back at her just as hard. "Do you know how many millions of young girls are denied a useful life because they have to carry water to villages often miles away? They are reduced to the level of pack animals because they don't have access to a well and a mechanical pump. Accessible water is such a commonplace item that you simply take it for granted, but to many in the world it is a luxury that they can only dream of.

"Those jobs that I help create, the ones you scoff at, can free those women. When a company I work for starts paying employees, it affects not only them but their families and villages. It gives people hope. Christ, to deny them that is to return to the colonial period of human exploitation. Is that what you want?"

It didn't matter how beautiful he thought she was, he would never allow himself to be pushed around. His reputation, both good and bad, stood as his testament and he would defend it no matter what.

Her smile was patronizing and taunting. "Nice try, Dr. Mercer. To most, that would have worked. Though I believe in women's rights and I deplore our treatment, I am an environmentalist, not a feminist. I'm not a Socialist or an anti-technologist either, so the rest of your arguments are moot. I have my beliefs and you have yours. They do not correspond."

"Did anything I said during that class yesterday make sense to you?" Mercer was hoping for a common ground, a reason to keep her near him.

"No, not at all. It might have impressed the students, but clichés and hyperbole don't impress someone who is truly informed. And as to your theory that humans are conforming to evolution by destroying our environment, well that's just bullshit and you know it."

He found her use of profanity alluring. "Mark my word, as we learn more about evolution and extinction, we're going to find that behavior contributes as much to a species' demise as changes in environment or any other factor. If our actions contribute to our destruction, then that's the deal nature dealt us. Period."

"And you see no reason to change that?" she challenged.

"I see no way to stop it. The Chinese government plans to provide refrigerators to every household in the country. The antiquated technology they use would pump out so many CFCs and other ozone-depleting gasses that any counteraction in the West would be futile. We couldn't regulate fast enough to prevent the greenhouse effect you so fear. Why isn't the Planetary Environment Action League trying to stop them?

Groups like yours are adept at stirring controversy and garnering headlines, but you don't attempt to offer workable solutions. You don't have enough facts behind your outcries, so you appeal to emotions to get your point across. You probably agree with the results of the 1992 Earth Summit in Rio, right?"

"I attended it," Aggie shot back proudly

"Do you remember Article 15 of the Rio Declaration?"

Aggie shook her head.

"I forced myself to memorize it because it made me so disgusted, I never wanted to forget it. 'Lack of scientific certainty shall not be used as a reason for postponing cost-effective measures to prevent environmental degradation.' That means there doesn't need to be proof for action to be taken. Taxpayers' money can be spent on some problem that may not even exist. Unbelievably, the United States signed this garbage, potentially handing over billions of dollars with no way of knowing how the money is being spent.

"You think you're trying to change the way mankind cares for the planet? Another document signed at Rio called Agenda 21 effectively states that the only way to stop environmental damage in the Northern Hemisphere is to pour tons of money into the third world nations of the Southern Hemisphere. Does that make any sense to you? I certainly don't get it. Like I said in class yesterday, if you're ashamed of our accomplishments, I'm sorry, but some of us are proud of them."

Mercer turned to walk away, leaving Aggie speechless and a little slack-jawed. "Just a bit of trivia before I go. The very same scientists you rely on for proof of global warming were writing articles in the 1970s stating that pollution was actually cooling the planet, forcing us into a new ice age. When you can back up your clichés and hyperbole with facts, we'll talk again."

He was gone before Aggie could react.

Because Mercer had been the last to arrive at the party and was the first to leave, the valet was able to pull his Jaguar to the porte cochere only moments after he strode through the front doors. Mercer was angry at himself for getting into the conversation in the first place and wished he'd been thinking with his big head rather than his little one. He couldn't deny an attraction, but that was as far as he'd let it go.

Mercer slid into the seat and closed the door with a slam. Just as he pulled the shifter from park, white knuckles rapped the passenger window. Startled, he pressed the power lock button and Aggie Johnston slipped into the Jag. Without a word, Mercer pulled away, the engine growling happily as he applied too much throttle. Now what?

As Mercer jinxed onto the main road, Aggie pulled a pack of cigarettes and a gold lighter from a small purse. She glared at him, defying a comment about her smoking as she lit up, the flame like a harsh flare in the intimate glow of the dash.

He waited out her silence, wondering where this would lead and secretly happy she'd followed him.

"I hate him almost as much as I love him." Mercer knew she was speaking about her father. "In so many ways he's the kindest, most thoughtful man I think I'll ever meet, but I can't help opposing him. He's a health nut, so I started sneaking cigarettes from the staff when I was fourteen, hoping to get caught, but he never noticed. He still doesn't know I smoke. Because he made all of his money in the oil business, I decided, even before I knew what it meant, that I would become an environmentalist."

The window slid down and Aggie tossed her spent cigarette into the darkness. "I sometimes wonder if he's noticed anything I've done. Lord knows he never noticed my mother's desperation until it was too late."

Mercer knew that she just wanted to talk, so he remained quiet.

"She killed herself when I was getting my master's. I found out from the chauffeur Dad sent to bring me home for the funeral. You'd think that she and I would have been close, but we really weren't. I cried at the funeral and I still cry sometimes now, but it isn't loss that causes it. It's pity. She was a pitiable person, really.

"My only strong memories of her are when she was drunk and one time, just before her suicide, when I nearly caught her in bed with another man. I wanted to blame my father so badly, but I can't. She had a self-destructiveness that forced her to stay, to give her a reason to keep abusing herself with booze and affairs. She would have killed herself even if she had left him. You talked about mankind's fate earlier. Well, the fate of Barbara Johnston was to die by her own hand, and nothing was going to stop it."

Mercer glanced at Aggie. Her hands were trembling as she lit another cigarette, but her voice had remained steady. It didn't take a trained psychologist to understand the emotional conflicts that made up her personality and motivated her actions. Her anger at her father had driven her to champion causes that opposed him. And that anger didn't stem from her mother's death but her own inability to stop it. Everything warned him to stay away from her, but he found himself drawn by her contrast of toughness and vulnerability.

"Where do you live?" he asked as they approached the nation's capital.

"Georgetown. I have a condo on the canal."

They didn't speak for the rest of the trip, but somehow the silence wasn't uncomfortable. She directed him to her street with one-syllable prompts or simple nods of her head. Her condo building had once been a warehouse along the C&O Canal. Mercer knew that the units started at a quarter of a million dollars and rose dramatically from there.

Rain had started falling, pelting the windshield with dappled splashes as he pulled up to the building's entrance. Aggie waited for the wind to die down, her purse held across her lap, her slim body enfolded by the wide bucket seat of the Jaguar. When she spoke, her voice was soft, almost timid.

"I didn't want to fight you tonight. In fact, I think I wanted to seduce you." She looked at him, waiting for a reaction that he refused to give. "When I first met you, I had this noble image of you. I thought you were different from the rest of them. I guess it was just a schoolgirl crush."

She opened the door and unlimbered herself from the car. Before she vanished into her building, she ducked her head back into the Jag. "I'm glad I learned disappointment at a young age."

The door closed softly and she was gone.

"The old Mercer charm strikes again," he muttered, hurt by her statement.

Rather than giving himself time to digest what had just occurred, he decided to thrust it out of his mind until later. But as he dialed his car phone and listened to it ring three thousand miles away, he knew that Aggie's outburst about being disappointed had been directed more at her father than at him. About her desire to seduce him, well, she wasn't the first woman he'd blown it with and most certainly wouldn't be the last.

The ringing stopped. "You have reached the home of Howard Small. I'm sorry I'm not here to take your call. Please leave a message after the tone."

"Damn it." Mercer cut the connection without leaving a message.

AT eighteen years old, Jamal Lincoln had lived a life that was all too common in Washington's poorest neighborhoods. A gang member at thirteen, he saw his first action two weeks later when he was caught in the cross fire of a deal gone bad. He'd picked up the gun his cousin Rufus dropped when a nine-millimeter blew his teeth out the back of his head, and sprayed rounds as fast as he could pull the trigger. He didn't hit anything, but the feeling it gave him was the beginning of a life that would have an inevitable outcome.

A week after that shoot-out, he'd pumped two slugs into the chest of a convenience-store clerk and used the thirty-seven dollars that that man's life had been worth to buy his first vials of crack. He slowly worked his way up through the gang, promotions coming as his body count rose. He lost his virginity at fourteen when Nyeusi Radi, the gang leader who bragged that his name meant "Black Thunder" in Swahili, gave him a prostitute for his birthday. Jamal was still in school and spent his time roaming the hallways or lurking outside school grounds selling drugs and recruiting for his gang. On both counts he was too adept. By the time he was seventeen, he had survived enough firefights to become one of Radi's chief lieutenants.

Radi was twenty-four, a millionaire with time running out.

Everyone knew that his luck would end soon. The life he led would kill him eventually, and the longer he held on, the closer his death came. And Jamal, now eighteen, was next in line to take over the gang, make the real money, have the real power. That's why he resented being sent on this mission outside his turf to nail some guy he'd never even heard of.

Earlier that night, Radi had invited Jamal into his crib, a series of large rooms carved out of a rundown apartment block in Anacostia. Radi had told him what to do and gave him a clean piece, all the while this creepy white dude watched them from a couch near Radi's desk. Everything about the white guy screamed cop, but the dude didn't even blink when Radi told Jamal to waste this other guy out in Arlington.

As Jamal was leaving the room, the white guy came up off the couch and grabbed him by his bare bicep. Jamal's arms were big, roped with muscle held taut beneath glossy skin. The guy's fingers were thin, pale, and bony, yet they sank so deeply into Jamal's arm that he was staggered by the pain.

"Make it look like a mugging. Take his watch, wallet, whatever you want, but make sure he's dead. If he's isn't, you will be."

"Who da fuck you think you are, motherfucker?" Jamal shouted, trying to pull his arm away.

The hand around his bicep tightened, forcing Jamal to his knees. "Willis, tell your dog to stop yapping, or I'll tear his arm off and beat him to death with it."

"Jamal, do the guy, all right? Don't ask no fucking questions." Nobody ever called Radi by his given name, and nobody ever put an edge of fear to his voice, but he was frightened by the white man in the dark suit.

"I'll do it, Radi." Jamal looked toward his leader, surprised to see him heave a sigh of relief.

According to the recently stolen Rolex he wore, Jamal had been pacing the street for three hours. No cops had cruised by during the wait, and Jamal had seen only a few brothers, mostly zebras, blacks trying to pass themselves off as white. He felt fairly safe, a little exposed but anonymous enough. No matter how he felt, there was no way he was going to leave the neighborhood until he'd done the guy. He didn't want to face that white dude ever again.

He'd thought about ducking into the bar up the street, especially since the rain started. His fake ID was good enough, but he didn't want anyone getting a good look at him. Once the guy was dead, all a witness would be able to say was that the attacker was a young black male in a dark leather coat. Christ, that's half the fucking city.

Jamal saw the sweep of light across the dark buildings and knew that a car had turned onto the street. He spun and saw the headlights of a vehicle about six blocks up, just past that bar. The big Glock 17 in his pocket suddenly seemed lighter. It was eleven-fifteen and all the other houses had been quiet for hours. This had to be his man coming.

A beat-up Chevy Cavalier pulled out from the parking spot directly in front of Tiny's just as Mercer turned onto his street. Not one to avoid providence, he pulled his Jag into the spot without so much as a second thought and headed into the bar. It was a quarter past eleven on a Saturday night, and there was no way he was going home without a nightcap or two.

"The anointed has returned," Harry White growled over the stereo as Mercer walked in. "What happened? They close the open bar or did they just close it to you?"

Mercer took his customary seat next to Harry and sipped the gimlet that Tiny had poured as soon as he'd entered. Tiny fingered the material of Mercer's tux, nodding his approval.

Mercer shook his head sadly, "No one appreciates the old lamp shade on the head gag anymore."

Tiny's was exactly what Mercer needed to forget about Aggie Johnston and her problems. He and Harry bantered with a biting sarcasm that would wither most people, but neither would have it any other way. An hour and a half went by, Mercer's couple of nightcaps turning into an entire milliner's shop as he and Harry as well as a few of the other regulars drank their wallets empty. Tiny closed the place at one, making sure to call cabs for those patrons too drunk to drive and assigning moderately sober drivers for the rest.

Harry left with Mercer, each of them with two bottles of beer in hand for their walk home. Harry lived five blocks away in the opposite direction from Mercer. He began swaying up the street after a few parting jibes about Mercer's tuxedo.

Mercer left his car and turned down the street, taking swallows from one bottle as he went, though each footfall made him dribble a little beer. He knew he was really drunk when his feet crossed each other and he nearly sprawled on the sidewalk. He glanced around, his blurred eyes trying to penetrate the darkness to see if anyone had noticed, but the street appeared quiet.

He continued, draining the first beer as he crossed onto the block just before his. Rather than fighting open the other, a task he knew would be impossible in his state, he simply carried it with him, each dangling by its neck in his hands. He tripped again stepping to the curb on his block and laughed at himself. He'd heard from enough people that alcohol was a depressant, but right now he had that perfect buzz that made everything funnier than hell, even the shadowy figure that stepped from behind a van parked a few paces from him.

Mercer saw the blow coming and willed his body to tense, but his alcohol-deadened nerves wouldn't respond. He was completely limp, and that saved his life. The pistol butt laid into his face, snapping his head so hard that he corkscrewed to the sidewalk. A vicious kick to the ribs turned him over twice, and he went with it, rolling away from his assailant, giving himself enough distance to get to his feet.

He staggered up, blood slicking the right side of his face and dripping into his mouth with a metallic salty taste. The Glock came down, its nine-millimeter muzzle leveled at Mercer's chest.

The suddenness and ferocity of the attack would have frozen a normal man, but Mercer's reactions were quick—if dulled by the gimlets. The alcohol coursing through his body filled him with a reckless courage. He leaped forward, ignoring the Glock, his evening shoes sliding across the rain-soaked cement. The gun never went off.

Jamal Lincoln was thrown off guard by Mercer's assault

and hadn't squeezed hard enough on the integrated trigger safety of the unfamiliar weapon. He shifted the big semiautomatic in his hand, feeling the safety disengage an instant before Mercer crashed into him. The gun was aimed at his intended victim's chest and at this range would blow him halfway down the block.

Mercer still had the beer bottles in his hands and swung them with all of the strength he could muster, each arm whipping inward so that the two bottles smashed into Jamal's head simultaneously. The full bottle exploded on impact, showering them both with frothing beer and shards of green glass while the empty bottle remained intact, knocking Jamal off balance. His right arm whirled across his body so when he fired, the shot ricocheted off a building across the street. Jamal almost blacked out from the blow but retained enough control to push against Mercer just as the return stroke of the bottle came at him, missing him by inches.

The unbroken bottle whizzed by Jamal's head, the force of the swing leading Mercer into a natural follow-through, and without thinking he plunged the remains of the shattered bottle deep into his assailant's throat. The jagged glass cut through skin and muscle and arteries with only spongy resistance. The Glock dropped as Jamal reeled away, clutching at his shredded throat. It was the last voluntary movement he would ever make.

Mercer fell to the ground at the same time as Jamal, the alcohol, shock, and fear draining his strength. Darkness crept into his mind, cutting his vision down to a haze-filled tunnel. Even the lights that had snapped on in response to the shot were just distant points, fading even as more of them lit the street. He laid his head against the cold concrete as a siren began to wail someplace in another reality.

"You're dead, aren't you, Howard? They got you already," Mercer mumbled to the cement before he passed out.

ALYESKA MARINE TERMINAL
VALDEZ, ALASKA

Under the glare of sodium arc lights, the hull of the *Petromax Arctica* was even darker than the water of Prince William Sound. The sun had not yet set in the northern latitudes though it was past nine at night. Despite the umber light, regulations demanded that the lamps high up in the oil gantries were on at all times. They bathed the VLCC (Very Large Crude Carrier), bringing out harsh shadows on her huge deck.

The ship was more than a thousand feet long, but what truly made her seem unworldly was her width. With a hundred-and-fifty-seven-foot beam, she was nearly as wide as a city block was long. Her red-painted deck was as large and flat as a parking lot, broken only by inspection hatches and a raised catwalk that ran nearly a quarter of a mile from her superstructure to her blunted bows. The tanker's superstructure was a slab-sided white box at the very stern, rising fifty feet over the deck. Cantilevered promenades wrapped around a few of its levels, and the wings of the flying bridges hung over empty space on each side of the ship. Her single funnel sat foursquare in the center of the superstructure. The emblem of Petromax Oil, a stylized oil derrick with the intertwined letters *P* and *O,* was lit by a floodlight just below the twenty-foot-tall standard.

Unlike any ship in history, supertankers, as VLCCs had been dubbed by the media soon after their debut, defy nearly every law of naval architecture. Because of their size, they cannot be built like a traditional vessel with a laid keel and massive steel supports rising up like ribs from the backbone. Tankers must be built in sections, each one floated independently and welded together in the water. According to the engineers, tankers are safe, yet they still tend to break up when nature or man's own folly stresses them too much. They are a bastard creation, spawned by an oil thirsty world with little regard for how that thirst was slaked.

The *Petromax Arctica* was a modern-generation supertanker, only three years old, double hulled and built with the latest inert gas scrubbers and other safety devices. But the most recent evolution of a dangerous idea was still dangerous. Therefore, Captain Lyle Hauser treated his ship as if she were a floating bomb with a lit fuse.

Hauser stood one hundred feet over the sound on the port wing of the flying bridge, feeling his ship settle as North Slope crude poured into her compartmentalized hull at a rate of twenty thousand barrels every hour. He'd been up there since the armored hoses of loading berth number three had started disgorging the oil hours earlier. Pulled from retirement for this trip, this was his first time on a tanker of this size and he wasn't going to allow even a minor deviation from procedure. If that meant he had to stand on the flying bridge and watch the gantries automatically pump oil into his ship for the remaining hours of loading, so be it. It was a ritual he'd acquired as a lightering tanker captain. Some superstition, deep in the back of his mind, told him that if he didn't watch the entire loading process, disaster would surely strike.

The loading system was a direct feed linked through the ship's computer, so there was no chance for a spill or the vessel losing her center of gravity, yet Hauser could still smell the heavy stink of crude oil and feel the great behemoth below his feet shift as the internal pumps transferred crude between the compartments to keep the *Arctica* level.

He pulled a walkie-talkie from the deep pocket of his pea coat. "Riggs, how're the oxygen levels in the tanks?"

"Showing five percent across the board."

While oil is one of the most combustible substances on earth, it can only burn within a narrow ratio of gases. Too much or too little oxygen and it will not ignite. Because her main engine produced emissions in the 12 percent range, the *Petromax Arctica* was outfitted with a separate Sun Rod boiler system that produced exhaust well below the threshold where oil is combustible. The Sun Rod's emissions were piped directly into the tanks to maintain an inert level.

"And what's the cargo level in starboard tanks one through three, please?"

"Twenty-seven percent. She's loading even, Captain," his First Officer responded.

Hauser knew that his ship was loading evenly; he could feel it with his wide-spaced feet. His request had merely been a test to ensure that Riggs was manning his station and attentive to his job.

Her job, Hauser reminded himself. Though she had a deep, almost coarse voice that came across the walkie-talkie as mannish, his Number One, JoAnn Riggs, was a woman, a nine-year veteran out of the Merchant Marine Academy in Maine.

Hauser hoped he'd get used to the idea of a woman under his command. Her dossier, which he'd read on his flight to Alaska, showed her to be a competent, disciplined officer. In fact, she had more time on supertankers of this size than he did. Yet there was something about her intense manner and constantly blinking eyes that he just didn't like. After forty-five years in a career that led him to work with hundreds of people, Hauser had become an excellent judge of character. His first instincts usually served him well. He just did not like JoAnn Riggs. It had nothing to do with her gender, it was just her.

Hauser plucked a cheroot from its black and gold cardboard box, slipped the packet back into his coat, and pulled the thick wool back around himself to ward off the unseasonable cold. He automatically reached into his pants pocket for his lighter, an inscribed Zippo from his wife, but it was locked in his desk in the captain's day room. He'd quit smoking the cigars over a year ago but kept the lighter with him. It was under lock and key, not as a safety precaution but as a deterrent from ever lighting one of the five cigars he chewed each day.

"Fucking Surgeon General and his ridiculous warnings," he muttered.

As he thought about it, Hauser realized that he didn't care

for the three other ship's officers he'd met this morning. Because of the tremendous fortunes tied up in tankers and their cargoes, men had to accommodate the ships rather than the other way around. It was common for new crew members, including captains, to meet their new ships in out-of-the-way places like the Persian Gulf or Cape Town or Alaska. There was no time for crews to get acquainted before the ships were back at sea. Depending on the circumstances, crewmen were sometimes choppered out to the tankers while they were under way, adding to the isolation in which these leviathans existed.

It was one of the many dehumanizing effects on ocean commerce Hauser had watched develop over the decades. The industrialized world had put itself on such a rigid schedule of supply and demand that tankers and their cousins, bulk carriers and container ships, simply became another part of the assembly line. To those who owned them and to many of the new generation that worked them, the world's merchant fleets no longer elicited the emotional responses that they'd commanded a half century before. They'd become just one more cog in the great industrialized machine.

Maybe that was why Hauser didn't like the crew he would command until the ship docked at the El Segundo refinery north of Long Beach. They were part of the new generation. They saw what they did as jobs, not callings, as he had when he went to sea at sixteen. Hauser wondered if he was just being harsh. Maybe his wife was right, that he shouldn't have allowed himself to be coaxed out of a quiet, dull retirement for one last command. Even if he could accept a woman as a bridge officer, progress might have passed him by, leaving him longing for the old traditions that were gone for good.

"Aw, hell, give 'em time. They've had a rough couple a days," Hauser said aloud. He regularly talked to himself and to his ships.

Until three days ago, the *Arctica* had been owned by Petromax Oil under the command of Captain Harris Albrecht. Then, through secret negotiations, Petromax sold their remaining tanker fleet, including the *Arctica*, to Southern Coasting and Lightering, an obscure tanker company based in

Louisiana. The same day news of the sale reached the ship, Captain Albrecht, the master of the *Petromax Arctica* for nearly six years, had suffered a serious accident.

Hauser hadn't yet learned the full story, but due to the severity of his injuries, Albrecht had been choppered from the ship while she was still two hundred miles from port and flown directly to Anchorage's Providence Hospital. Riggs' succinct report of the incident stated that Captain Albrecht had lost part of his right forearm in a machinery accident and that the severed member had not been recovered. Hauser was empathetic enough to give Riggs and the rest of the crew time to deal with the trauma before pressing for details.

Southern Coasting and Lightering had bought the crew's contracts when they purchased the vessel. However, they did not have a captain able to fill in for the injured Albrecht, so Hauser had consented to leave his retirement and take the vessel from Valdez to California. Hauser had spent most of his career on smaller vessels called product tankers, moving fuel oil, gasoline, or other oil derivatives along the East Coast. This was the first time he'd ever worked for Southern Coasting and the first time in years that he'd commanded a tanker in these northern waters.

In addition to a more complete accident report, Hauser also wanted to get the reason why the *Petromax Arctica* had been eighteen hours late arriving at Valdez. He could forgive an inadequate log entry concerning the accident, given the circumstances, but he was not about to overlook Riggs bringing the tanker into port three-quarters of a day late without an explanation. That kind of laxity was unpardonable. This had not been an auspicious beginning to Lyle Hauser's last command.

The sliding glass door leading to the bridge hissed open, pulling Hauser out of his musings. First Officer Riggs approached, her angular body buried under layers of sweaters and coats. Her face was gaunt and bony, with deeply recessed eyes of an indeterminate color. They were rather hazy and small. Her mouth was tight and lipless, and her eyelids fluttered distractingly.

"Sir, a call from the Operations Control Center." Even

without the distortion of the walkie-talkie, her voice was clipped and masculine.

"Yes, what is it?"

"The tractor trailer has arrived with the new nameplates for the ship."

Hauser blew a long breath of frustration. If his new command had not been discomforting enough, the name of the vessel was to be changed as the tanker steamed to Southern California. When Hauser was told that he was to command one of the newest VLCCs in the world, he had felt the same exhilaration as he had when he'd received his first command. Then, when he was informed that the vessel's name was to be changed during her maiden voyage as an SC&L tanker, Hauser had felt an icy tentacle of superstitious fear wend its way around his guts.

He knew that during a tanker's twenty-year life, it carried more names than the devil himself as it was bought and sold, sometimes faster than the new names could be placed on stern and bow. His last ship before retirement had been named and renamed seven times before her owners sent her to the Pakistani ship breakers. But he didn't like being on a vessel, let alone in command, while her name was being changed. Every sailor knew that it was simple bad luck.

When he heard about the name change, Hauser had asked Southern Coasting to delay it until she reached Long Beach and a scheduled maintenance cycle. But his entreaties fell on deaf ears. SC&L's Director of Marine Operations told him that Petromax had demanded the ship's name be changed en route. Out of idle curiosity, Hauser had phoned Petromax on his way to Alaska and learned that it was SC&L that had demanded the hasty renaming. They were even paying for the workers and the plates that were to be welded on to the stern, each one-hundred-pound piece of steel cut in the shape of a letter to spell out *Southern Cross*, the *Arctica*'s newest moniker.

Hauser had almost wanted to refuse to take command. Lord knew that his wife didn't want him traipsing around the world on a supertanker. The name change was bad enough, but what rankled him the most was being lied to. To him, it didn't matter who'd ordered it, but to lie about it was unreasonable and childish. However, if he didn't take the ship, there would never be another one after it. He longed, once more, to feel a great tanker under his feet and know that she was his.

"Do you want me to tell them to come aboard?"

He had been so distracted with his own thoughts that he'd forgotten he wasn't alone. "Yes. Have a couple of seamen help them with anything they need and make sure the stewards know there'll be several supernumeraries aboard for the voyage."

"Yes, sir." Riggs turned and walked the long open promenade back to the bridge.

Captain Hauser stared across the thousand sprawling acres of the Alyeska Marine Terminal. On a hill overlooking the five loading berths, huge earthen containment dikes surrounded the twenty principal oil storage tanks that had a holding capacity of more than three hundred and eighty-five million gallons of crude. Below them was the East Manifold Building, which was the terminus of the eight-hundred-mile-long Trans-Alaska Pipeline. Between the Manifold Building and Hauser's ship sat the ballast water treatment facility and the fuel bunkers for the tankers that used the port. Next to them were the Operations Control Center, the Marine Operations Office, and the Emergency Response Building. This last section of the facility had been greatly improved since the *Exxon Valdez* holed herself against Bligh Reef in 1989.

As Hauser looked toward the main gate of the terminal, a flatbed tractor trailer heaved into view, diesel smoke blowing out of her twin stacks. Dark tarpaulins covered the long trailer. A white van followed the truck closely, its headlights winking against the multiple reflectors on the big rig. A crane was also crossing the yard, its long boom thrust out like a medieval battering ram preparing to assault some ancient castle.

He watched as the three vehicles converged on the *Petromax Arctica*, as he would refer to his ship until the voyage was over. Within moments, the men from the van and the crane operator had established a smooth rapport of loading the bundles of steel plate onto the tanker. Hauser noticed that eight men appeared to be outfitted to come aboard, their duffel bags and cases piled on the asphalt quay in a heap. It looked as if only the van driver and the tractor trailer would be returning to Anchorage.

"Why in the hell would they need eight men to change the name of the ship?" Hauser's question was met by a quick gust of wind that pulled against his sparse gray hair. "And why in the hell do they have so much fucking luggage? This isn't a cruise ship, for Christ's sake."

The question Hauser didn't ask himself was one he would come to regret later. Why did the eight men coming to change the name of the ship move with the precision of a highly skilled squad of soldiers?

THE UNITED
ARAB EMIRATES

The dry desert heat beat down with the intensity of a blast furnace. Great downdrafts of molten air stirred the dust of the open rocky plain into whirling spirals that grew so large they collapsed under their own weight, vanishing as quickly as they formed. The sky was a cerulean blue dome over the barren earth, hazed only to the west where the far edge of the *Rub' al Khali*, the great Empty Quarter of the Arabian Desert, met the waters of the southern Persian Gulf. The landscape was as desolate as the surface of the moon. There was little vegetation, only a few camel thorn trees and sparse sage. Rocky outcrops were baked so fiercely by the sun that many were slit apart like overripe fruit.

The land was a thousand shades of color, from the blinding white of the sand dunes that marched in waves to the distant horizon to the deepest black of the Hajar Mountains across the border in Oman, yet much of the sand was stained pink by iron oxide. It was as if the desert were rusting. The late afternoon temperature hovered above one hundred and ten, and even with the coming evening, it wouldn't dip more than a few degrees.

The *khamsin,* the scorching summer wind that tore across the land, was still strong this late in the year. It raked the surface of the earth, gouging it, shaping it as it had for a hundred million years. It forged an uncompromising environment that supported only the most hearty species.

Prince Khalid Al-Khuddari stood proudly in the open desert, the brutal heat raising only a thin layer of sweat under the thin cotton of his bush shirt. He was a creature of the desert, as hard and uncompromising and starkly handsome as the land around him. He was naturally light-skinned, but the time he spent in the desert had darkened him, turning his face and arms a dark mahogany. His high cheekbones and strong, hooked nose made him look like an American Plains Indian, his thick black hair and dark eyes only adding to the allusion.

He was tall, just over six feet, and he held his body erect and alert. In the open V of his shirt, his chest was smooth and hairless, almost like that of a boy, but the muscles stood out sharply. His belly was greyhound thin yet rippled like a streambed. He held his left hand at chest height, his elbow crooked so he could regard the creature perched on his gauntleted wrist. If any animal captured the essence of Khalid Al-Khuddari, it was the saker falcon gripping him so strongly with its talons that he could feel their needle tips piercing the leather of the falconer's glove.

The saker, the second largest of the species *falconidae,* stood just over nineteen inches, with a reddish brown body and a neat pale head. Its beak, so sharply curved that it almost touched its breast, was as deadly as a scimitar, while its eyes were arguably the keenest in nature. The bird was known as one of the finest hunters in the world, with a determination and courage that were the basis of legend.

Used for falconry since generations before the horse was domesticated, the saker had the longest history of coexistence with man of any animal except the dog. Considered a sport of the nobled elite of Europe since they learned of it during the Crusades, falconry is as much a part of the Arab culture as the five Pillars of Islam. In decline in the West because of an emotional animal rights movement, falconry thrived in the Gulf States. It was a pastime of both the wealthy and the poor. In fact, Khalid had learned it from a desert Bedouin, an elder of one of the tribes that had wandered the Arabian Peninsula since before the Prophet heard the word of God.

This falcon, a female named Sahara, was quiescent, calmly listening to the soothing words of her master, her head covered by an ornate leather hood so that she would not take flight until Khalid was ready to hunt her. Leather jesses tied around her tarsis, the naked part of her legs above her claws, leashed her to Khalid's glove. He stroked her wings and the bird responded with a quiet *kweet kweet,* a sure sign of her contentment, much like the purr of a tabby cat.

"Are you ready, my darling?" Khalid asked the raptor, his face so close to the bird that his breath made her shift her weight. The tiny bells around her ankles chimed softly.

Though he felt alone with his falcon in the great desert, Khalid was not. Behind him, under a dazzlingly white bell tent, forty guests watched him from the tables laid specifically for the hunt. He and his guests had just finished a late lunch of lamb grilled over open fires and strong cheeses and dates, washed down with French champagne. Many of the assembled felt that they were emulating their early tribal history. Used to the air-conditioned comfort of Abu Dhabi City, they thought that the afternoon in the open country was a great adventure. That the tent had been set up for them and that a small army of servants ensured that their wine glasses never emptied was lost on them. Their roots had been yanked up by the Western influences that had poured into the country since oil was discovered in 1958.

Khalid looked behind him. Beyond the tent, the road was hidden by a small dune, but he could see the top of the two Daihatsu trucks that had brought the men and equipment for the outing. He knew that there was a fleet of Mercedes limousines near the trucks, their drivers waiting patiently while their pampered charges enjoyed themselves. He did not blame his guests for their wealth and privilege, for he was one of them, but he felt a twinge of disappointment that none of them shared his love of the land that had given them the lifestyle to which they had grown overly accustomed.

The land. Khalid turned back, ignoring the waves of greeting from a few of the women. The land. It gave no indication of the wealth it stored.

The United Arab Emirates had known three great periods of prosperity, once as one of the great pearl-producing areas of the world, once as an active piracy coast, and now as the home of one of the largest oil reserves on the planet. The fact that there were thirty-two billion barrels of oil trapped beneath the coastal plain and shallow offshore shelf of the UAE were not lost to Khalid Al-Khuddari. He knew that the open market price of Brent light sweet crude closed up a dollar and a half the day before, which translated into $750 billion buried in the desert. That wealth was spread among the Emirates' two hundred thousand citizens, giving them the second highest per capita income in the world.

Khalid tracked these numbers and knew what they meant because he was Abu Dhabi's Petroleum Minister, the UAE's official representative to OPEC. Even though all seven of the autonomous Sheikdoms that made up the United Arab Emirates now had Petroleum Ministers, only Abu Dhabi, with the lion's share of the oil, had the clout to join OPEC. After Kuwait and Saudi Arabia, the UAE possessed more oil than any other nation within the cartel and thus wielded a great deal of power determining oil policy and prices. This power and responsibility were newly laid upon Khalid's shoulders following the untimely death from lung cancer of Abu Dhabi's previous Oil Minister.

His elevation to such a position of authority was highly unusual, not only because of his youth—Khalid would turn forty in two years—but also because he was not a member of Abu Dhabi's ruling family. He wasn't even part of the same tribe as the Crown Prince Shaik. Khalid's people were the wanderers of the open desert, the Bedouin who knew no border but the ones their herds of goats and camels established. They owed no loyalty or allegiance to any but their own and the *Sharia,* the law of Islam.

Khalid's father may not have owed allegiance to any man, but the ruler of Abu Dhabi owed the Al-Khuddari family a great debt because of the support they had given during the early years of the UAE's independence from Britain. Because of this, Khalid was given a European education, Eton, Cambridge, and the London School of Economics, and when he returned to his homeland, his sharp mind and keen negotiation skills launched him on the fast track within the Emirate's Oil Ministry.

The death of the previous Minister, following so closely after the American President's announcement to suspend oil imports, had thrown the Ministry into chaos. Old guard clashed with the new generations of technocrats who had grown up with the affluence oil had brought, never knowing the poverty that had gripped the region prior to World War II. In the end, it was decided to turn the job over to someone outside of the ruling family and thus disassociated from the familial infighting.

Khalid realized that the debt to his father had been paid and that he himself was now beholden to the royal family of Abu Dhabi, a responsibility he took seriously, not only as the Oil Minister but also as an ad hoc family member. It was in this last capacity that he'd called this hunt, not to allow him an afternoon pursuing one of his great passions, but as a demonstration.

"Gentlemen," he called over one broad shoulder while stroking the breast of the hooded falcon. "Why don't you join me for a much better view."

The twenty or so men around the long table got to their feet, tossing crumpled linen napkins on their chairs and generating a polite wave of laughter from their wives and girlfriends at their parting comments. The Oil Minister of Ajman had to be levered up from the table by two brawny escorts. Hasaan bin-Rufti weighed five hundred pounds at least, his body a shapeless, bulging mass. His neck was hidden by layers of fat that hung from his chin like the dewlap of an ox. His hands resembled surgical gloves that had been inflated to the bursting point, and despite his Semitic complexion, Rufti's skin was whitened by the internal pressure of adipose tissue. The sweat and fat on his body gave him a maggoty sheen, and his white suit looked almost as large as the tent. As he labored across the loose sand, his body quivered like some gelatinous dessert.

Khalid noted that Rufti's pet psychopath, Abu Alam, wasn't present. His sources had told him that Alam had been out of the country for some time. Because Khalid's spy network was strongest in Europe and they couldn't find the French-born Algerian who tried to pass himself off as a Muslim fanatic, he suspected that Alam was somewhere in the United States.

As the men approached, Rufti taking up the rear as he wheezed across the desert, Khalid held up a hand to stop them about fifteen yards away. Any closer and they would distract his falcon.

Sahara was an eyas, a bird taken young and raised by hand, long before she had gone through her first molt and learned to fly. Khalid had several birds that he hunted, most of them haggards, falcons taken as adults and thus more difficult to train, but Sahara was his favorite, not only for her brave heart and unbounded loyalty but also because she was the first bird Khalid had trained after his return from school. Though she was getting old, almost too old for the hunt, she still possessed a special place in his heart.

One hundred yards farther out in the desert, in the thin shadow of a desiccated tree, two assistants waited by a large plastic and steel cage. Inside was a bustard, a huge game bird with a gray body and black tiger stripes across its broad back. It was a European bird, especially brought to the Middle East for the hunt. It was much larger than the indigenous birds of the Gulf, with nearly a seven-foot wingspan.

"Just so you'll know what to expect," Khalid addressed his guests in English since several Westerners were present as well as UAE citizens, "when I signal my clansmen at the cage, they will release the prey and it will fly straight for us. Don't be alarmed by its size—it will never reach us. Are you ready?"

They nodded eagerly. They might have lost some of their heritage, but the spark of their ancestors' way of life still burned within them. It could be seen in their eyes and the alert carriages of their heads and shoulders. Wealth had not quite wiped clean the slate that hundreds of generations of desert living had etched onto their spirits.

Khalid shifted his gaze and saw that Hasaan Rufti looked bored, his piggy eyes darting back to the food left on the table.

No one saw the hand signal—it was just a discreet wrist flick—but all at once the cage opened and a massive shape flew from it, lifting itself off the desert on huge outspread wings. Its flight kicked up dust until it reached a height of about fifteen feet. Despite its size, everyone knew immediately that the hunt wouldn't be a contest, for the falcon's speed was legendary and the bustard was merely lumbering through the air like an overloaded cargo plane.

The bird did not see the motionless men, or chose to ignore them in its desire to get away from the cage. It flew directly toward Khalid and the small falcon perched on his arm. Khalid had devised a system to unhood his falcon and slip the jesses in one motion so he could marvel at the swiftness with which she acquired her target and lifted to give chase. Faster than any human could react, Sahara saw the bustard and was gone, her lunge aloft pushing Khalid's arm to his side.

Khalid had timed the intercept perfectly. The bustard wheeled in the air as soon as it saw the falcon, its ungainly body seemingly turning inside out in its desperate attempt to flee as Sahara rocketed toward it. The birds were thirty yards from the men, who were tensing for the inevitable collision with morbid fascination. A couple of them actually cringed when they saw the two bodies meet in midair. But there was no strike.

Like owls and other birds that had been the prey of falcons, the bustard had a few moves left, and just as Sahara torqued her body to strike with her talons, the bustard flipped itself in the air, twisting and lifting just the few inches it needed to ensure that the raptor missed. Like a combat pilot, the bustard began driving for altitude, pounding the air fiercely.

Sahara turned the instant she realized that the bustard was still in the air and started her pursuit.

This was the type of hunt that all falconers dreamed of, the hunt that had thrilled countless ages of men who had watched their birds spiral upward, circling their slower prey so as to overtake without drifting away from their masters. As he watched Sahara dissolve into the sky, Khalid felt a special kinship not only to his ancestors but to the bird itself.

The falcon quickly caught up with the fleeing bustard and continued beyond, flying upward until she was invisible from the ground. At the apex of her spiraling parabola, Sahara winged over and stooped, tucking herself into a deadly bomb aimed at the lumbering bustard, special flaps in her nostrils protecting her lungs from the 180 mph force of her fall. She was one-fifth the size of her target, rocketing downward with the courage that was her breed.

The strike was inaudible, but those on the ground saw it happen. Sahara knifed into the bustard, breaking its back so surely that its wings folded completely in on themselves. The large bird began to fall, cartwheeling to the earth in an untidy pile of shattered bones, blood, and feathers.

Khalid didn't need the lure in the pouch around his waist to bring Sahara back to his arm; she flew to him even as the bustard was falling, alighting on his arm gently, dissimulating the power and fury she had just shown. He slipped the hood back over her head and reattached the jesses as soon as she'd finished rearranging the long feathers on her wings.

The men burst into applause, and behind them, the women added their acclamation. Sahara preened and called quietly, as if she knew the ovation was for her.

"I will be a while. Why don't you all rejoin the ladies and start off to my house at the Al-Ain oasis. I shouldn't be more than half an hour," Khalid called to his guests.

The entertainment was over, so the men were now anxious to leave. None of them offered to stay and assist Khalid while he finished his work with the falcon. This was the new way, he supposed, the way taught to them in America and Europe, instant gratification coupled with attention spans shorter than young children's.

"Minister Rufti," he said, his gaze locked on the corpulent minister from Ajman, the smallest of the Emirates. "Why don't you walk with me?"

Hasaan bin-Rufti realized that Khalid's invitation was more of an order than a request, but he tried to demure anyway. "No thank you, my friend." The pressure of fat against his vocal cords made his voice unnaturally high. "In fact, I must take my leave now and depart for Ajman. There is an important meeting tomorrow with our Crown Prince that requires my attendance. I must decline your gracious hospitality."

"Walk with me." Khalid's voice cracked like a whip.

"Of course, of course." Rufti struggled miserably.

Khalid considered the majority of the people attending this outing to be friends or at least business acquaintances, with the sole exception of Hasaan bin-Rufti. No man represented more of what Khalid hated about what had become of his country. Rufti was slovenly, greedy, and ambitious to the point of fault. It was Rufti's greed that prompted Khalid to invite him along. This little informal chat was the whole reason for the weekend hunt.

He waited for Rufti to waddle to his side and then turned and walked farther out into the desert, near where the two assistants were waiting by the cage that had held the bustard. As if sensing a tension in the hot air, Sahara constantly craned her head around. Though she was blinded by the hood, she seemed to be scanning the horizon for new prey.

"That bird of yours is amazing. I've never seen anything like that before." There was a nervous edge to Rufti's voice as he tried to dispel the heavy silence with words.

Khalid was withdrawn until they'd joined his assistants, not even turning to acknowledge the struggling figure beside him. From a smaller cage that had been hidden from view, one of the robed aides retrieved a large gray pigeon, the type found in city parks all over the world. The bird was not so big as it was fat, its breast almost sagging and its head movements sluggish.

"I thought that you would appreciate another demonstration of my falcon, one not so genteel as the earlier hunt." Khalid turned to Rufti with a knowing smile. "What you saw earlier was toned down because of the ladies, but we are both men, yes? I think you will enjoy this rather more . . . graphic hunting style."

Rufti relaxed at the words. Tension ran out of his shoulders so that an avalanche of fatty tissue seemed to roll down his arms and back. He laughed nervously but tried to act worldly when he responded, "I knew that falconry was a true blood sport and that you had held back."

Khalid laughed with him, sharing a moment between mutual men of the world. "How would you like to release the pigeon?" He saw the look of distaste on Rufti's face, so he added quickly, "It's an honor, you know."

"Yes, of course," Rufti agreed despite his reluctance. "What should I do?"

The assistant placed the pigeon in Rufti's hands, making sure that his sausage-sized fingers were wrapped securely around the fat bird. The pigeon's body was pulpy, so soft that his fingers sank deeply before meeting the resistance of bone. Khalid pulled the hood from Sahara but kept the restraining jesses in place. The raptor locked its depthless black eyes on the pigeon, its gaze hammering the bird like a physical blow.

"Pigeons are actually intelligent birds." Khalid wasn't looking at Rufti as he spoke, but his voice was as riveting as the falcon's eyes. "They eat only as much as they need to survive. Occasionally a bird will glut itself if a supply is available and there are no predators in the area. We actually had to force-feed this one. Obesity seems to be a trait found only in humans."

A pallor crept into Rufti's face. He had been nervous when he had agreed to join Khalid, and now he was terrified. He had made the connection between himself and the bird as soon as his host had started to speak, but there was nothing he could do. The last of the limousines had pulled away a moment ago, taking with it his only chance of escape. All that remained were the two large trucks that would bring Khalid and his aides to the party he was throwing at Al-Ain.

"I think that—"

"Not a word." Khalid whirled so that he faced Rufti, the

falcon nearly losing her perch on his arm. "It is time for the hunt. I believe the poor creature can still fly, but we shall see."

Rufti looked unsure, scared. He pulled the fat bird close to his chest as if its survival meant his own. "I don't think I want to see this."

"Release!"

Without thinking, Rufti did. The pigeon rose sluggishly from his hands, heaving itself into flight with sheer force of will. Khalid immediately loosed the jesses, and Sahara took to the wing.

The normal technique of a hunting falcon is to gain altitude and use its devastating dive to take down its prey, but Sahara ignored her instinct. The pigeon was so slow and lethargic that she came at it from behind, her amazing speed closing the distance in only a few beats of her wings. The pigeon didn't have the strength or the ability to alter its course as it felt the falcon closing in for the kill.

Sahara raked her legs forward, drawing her talons up so she struck with her claws. At the instant of impact, she twisted slightly, tearing the pigeon into two bloody halves that she dropped immediately, contemptuously. The chase had taken seven yards. Three and a half seconds.

The two globs that had been the pigeon landed on the desert with a dull thud, spraying bright blood that soaked into the parched sand. Sahara fell onto the dead bird, tearing at it with beak and talon, stuffing her crop with strips of flesh as quickly as she ripped them from the carcass. Khalid ignored her, letting her eat her fill. He turned to Rufti, who was visibly shaken by the slaughter.

"Even a man of your limited intelligence should see significance in this situation. There are no witnesses right now; my assistants are members of my clan and would say nothing of what occurs here. Don't think that I won't kill you where you stand.

"I may be new to my job, Rufti, but I take my responsibilities far more seriously than you can imagine. I've taken the time to learn every facet of the UAE's oil business. I've met hundreds of employees, from the managing directors down to the derrickmen in the field. I see all and I'm beginning to know all as well. I've been getting reports recently, disturbing reports of money being funneled into this country in the form of oil exploration grants, yet no work is ever done. I've seen entry and exit visas for men who do not exist, and I've heard rumors about a compound in your native Ajman, deep in the desert where no man has a reason to be."

Khalid watched Rufti carefully and he noticed a spark of defiance burning behind the fat man's eyes. His true character could be seen in that spark, for though he looked the fool there was true strength at the heart of that fleshy body. Maybe not now, not under these circumstances, but Hasaan Rufti was a very dangerous man.

"Eleven months ago, just a short time after the American President's announcement, you were seen in Istanbul meeting with a man named Ivan Kerikov, a former high-ranking member of the KGB. Not long after that, money started flowing through Ajman's Oil Ministry as if you'd just struck it rich. We both know that Ajman has no oil, but your department now has a budget of thirty million dollars in untraceable funds. Where did that money come from, Hasaan? You are too stupid to think an original thought, so I want to know who is bankrolling whatever it is you're doing."

Rufti opened his mouth to speak, but Khalid cut him off instantly. "Shut up. Don't say a word. Whatever you say right now will be a lie, so save your breath.

"Because of your position within the government and the uncertainty of the times, we both know I can't mount an official investigation, but you'd better believe that I'm not going to let this end here today. Now more than ever the UAE and OPEC have to show the world a united front. I want you to know that I will fight you, Rufti. I will fight you as the Minister of Petroleum for the UAE, I will fight you as a friend of the royal family, and I will fight you as a man who believes in justice. Consider yourself warned. Whatever it is you're scheming, will not succeed."

Khalid whirled away but turned back to the startled Rufti. "We're leaving now, my two cousins and I. When we reach Al-Ain, I'll send a truck back to take you to that important meeting in Ajman. The truck should return in about an hour. It will be the longest hour of your life. Use the time wisely. Think about what I said, because if I don't like your explanations next time we speak, there will be no truck to come to your rescue."

Khalid's parting words were spoken over his shoulder as he and his clansmen were striding across the hardpan toward the trucks. Rufti tried to follow, but his tremendous bulk slowed him to the point of capitulation. He stopped, watching the rapier figure of Khuddari gliding across the desert, the falcon on his arm, flanked by the robed Bedouin.

Rufti stood still for many long minutes after the sound of the departing trucks had been swallowed by the emptiness of the desert. When finally his rage abated to the point where he could think, a sickening smile piled up skin and fat atop his cheekbones. "You are too late, Khalid Al-Khuddari, Charon is already at his landing and ready to cross the River Styx with the soul of the United States as his passenger. You'll never know who paid the toll, because you are going to be the first to die."

ARLINGTON, VIRGINIA

Last night had ranked on the top ten list of Mercer's worst. Following the attack, he spent four hours in the pandemonium of DC General's emergency room. Ultimately, he was given an adhesive bandage for the cut on his cheek, a paper shot glass with two aspirins for his pain, and a prod in the chest to prove his ribs weren't broken. The whole time, two uniformed cops guarded him as if he were public enemy number one.

Just as dawn was tinting the eastern horizon, he was released from the hospital and taken to the Arlington police station for a further three hours of inane, repetitive questions. There was no doubt that he was innocent of any wrongdoing, but it seemed that the cops needed to fill their quota of harassment and Mercer was unlucky enough to be there at the wrong time. He was allowed to leave with a stiff warning to stay in the Washington area and to report any suspicious activities in his neighborhood.

Mercer shed his tuxedo jacket as he made his way up to the bar on the second floor of his home. Whether he picked up the jacket later that day or later that year made no difference to him. His head ached fiercely, and his mouth felt as if a furry rodent had spent the night in it. His eyes were red-rimmed and gritty. He'd had a good buzz when he'd left Tiny's, but now all he had was a raging hangover and an exhaustion that ran to his bones.

He knew that the attack last night had not been a random occurrence. He had been targeted as surely as Jerry and John Small. He was certain that Howard was also a target and more than likely dead by now. And linking them was the *Jenny IV*.

What had been aboard the derelict that was worth killing to protect? Mercer wondered. His only clue was the mangled piece of stainless steel with the name roger on it, and he wasn't even sure if there was any significance to it.

And now with two confirmed deaths, a possible third, and the attempt on his life, Mercer recognized that the stakes had been raised too high for him to play alone. He needed help. He cracked open a Heineken from the antique refrigerator, settled himself at the bar, and reached for the cordless phone. The private cell phone number he dialed was part of the directory he carried in his head.

"Hello?"

"Dick, Mercer here."

"Oh, shit. What's happened now?"

Dick Henna was the Director of the Federal Bureau of Investigation and one of Mercer's closest friends. They had met during the crisis in Hawaii and had maintained a tight relationship ever since. Mercer was always welcome for dinner at Henna's house, and his wife, Fay, was determined to get him paired up.

"That's a cheery greeting," Mercer said. "But you're right, something's up. I was attacked last night coming home from Tiny's."

"Jesus. You all right?" While technically a bureaucrat, Henna had never lost the razor edginess he'd acquired from his years as a field man.

"Yeah, I'm fine, a few cuts and bruises. The kid who attacked me is dead, and I think that it was an assassination attempt made to look like a mugging."

"Why do you say that?" There wasn't a trace of doubt in Henna's voice, but he was a cop and took nothing as fact until he had evidence.

"The kid who tried to kill me, Jamal Lincoln, was from Anacostia, which means he was ten miles from his home turf. All of the vehicles on the street around my neighborhood had the proper parking stickers or were accounted for by the police. He might have taken the Metro here, but he attacked me after midnight, which would have left him with no way to get home afterward. There had to have been an accomplice in the area last night who dropped him off, then fled after the attack went wrong."

"Yeah, and?"

"Come on, Dick, I don't need to tell you that muggings usually happen within a mile or two of the perpetrator's home, in an area well known to him. And muggers don't act in teams, with one guy waiting in a getaway car. It's usually just snatch and run and make sure your victim isn't in any shape to follow."

"You might have something, but I doubt it. He may have been in Arlington visiting friends and needed cab fare home and you were the closest ATM."

"I'd agree if two people I went fishing with in Alaska last week weren't found dead yesterday morning, and I suspect that the other guy who was with us is dead too. I've been trying to call him but I keep getting his machine."

Mentioning Alaska piqued Henna's interest. Because of the increased tension in the country concerning the opening of the Arctic Wildlife Refuge, anything that took place in Alaska was of priority importance. "I thought you were doing work with some tunnel-digging machine or something."

"I was. When we finished, I went fishing with the inventor, Howard Small, and his two cousins."

"And you're saying they're all dead?"

"I'm not positive about Howard, but I'm pretty sure. In fact, one of the reasons I'm calling is to ask you to send someone to his house in Los Angeles and see if he ever got back from the trip."

"No problem. What makes you think you're being targeted?"

Mercer told Henna the story of finding the *Jenny IV* and his suspicion that something else besides the fire had aided in her destruction. He mentioned how the heavy support arms of the net-hauling cranes had been shorn off and the radio antennas were all snapped at their roots. He held the steel fragment in his hand as he described it to Henna, giving an account as thorough as a pathologist's autopsy report.

"Any idea who Roger is?"

"No. I made a few calls to the boat's home port, and no one knew anybody connected to her named Roger. And the Harbor Master didn't remember anyone else on board the morning she left for her final voyage."

"What's your take on all this?" Mercer heard an interest in Henna's voice that surprised him. Something was definitely up.

"I don't know. Something on the *Jenny IV* exploded after she had caught fire and put out the flames. What could've detonated without tearing the ship apart is a mystery. I want to ask you to have your lab people at Quantico take a look at this piece of steel and see if they can get anything from it. I've been staring at it for a few days and it's gotten me nowhere."

"Sounds like a good idea. I'll send over a messenger this afternoon. If you were anybody else, I'd say you're being paranoid. But I know you, and I know trouble follows you like an obedient dog. What are you going to do?"

"Me? I want to find out what your lab boys can dig up,

then I'm getting the hell out of Dodge. I don't want to be around when someone makes another attempt on my life."

"Listen, Mercer, you and I both know that Alaska is the number-one topic around dinner tables in this country right now. That's why I'm taking this so seriously. It's possible your friend in California is fine, just taking a couple more days off after your trip, and your attack may be a coincidence, but until I can prove that, this has my full attention.

"I have strict orders from the President concerning Alaska," Henna continued. "Anything—and I mean *anything*—deemed even remotely threatening is run to ground, no questions asked as to how many agents it takes or how much it costs. He wants weekly reports concerning the activities of the environmental groups that have set up shop in Valdez and Anchorage and copies of the threatening letters · sent to oil companies starting to operate in the Refuge. We're averaging eighty threats a week and I've got field agents taking them all seriously. Is it possible that one of these groups is after you? As I understand, the work you were doing dealt with the building of the second Trans-Alaska pipeline, right?"

"Yes, Howard Small collaborated with the construction firm building TAP Two. His final test hole, through a mountain about ten miles north of Valdez, runs parallel to the old pipe and will be used to run the new one. The mini-mole saved about ten weeks of heavy blasting and earth moving," Mercer replied, knowing where Henna was heading. "But security was pretty tight; few people knew what we were doing up there. Besides, that wouldn't explain why Howard's cousins were killed. I admit that my evidence is circumstantial, but if it does add up, then there is definitely something going on that your agents haven't picked up."

"It's my ass in the sling if something happens to the new pipeline or the teams working in the Refuge," Henna said. Mercer knew his friend was hooked. "Circumstantial evidence is better than none at all. Listen, do you want some protection? It may take a few days to analyze that metal fragment."

Mercer thought about it for a moment and then agreed. "I'm no hero. Send a whole platoon of soldiers if you want. The more the merrier."

"I'll assign an agent until you leave town. We should be able to get to the bottom of this, provided we get something from the sample. I'll give you a call as soon as I hear from the field team in L.A. about Howard Small, and I'll make sure we have some answers from the lab by Monday morning."

Mercer gave Howard Small's phone number and address to Henna before hanging up. He drained the last of his Heineken and thought about another to counter his hangover, but what he needed was a long shower and about eight hours of sleep.

Before padding to his bedroom, he went to the locked trunk at the bottom of his office closet. Opening it, he retrieved a Beretta nine-millimeter pistol and a black shoulder holster. The gun was U.S. military issue, a gift from Dick Henna to replace the one Mercer had lost in Hawaii last year. Henna had also given him a permit to carry the weapon anywhere in the United States except on commercial aircraft. He closed the trunk, tucking the loaded gun and a spare clip under his arm. This was the first time he'd felt he'd needed it since Henna had given it to him, and its presence was a powerful reassurance.

The courier came for the steel fragment ten minutes after he'd gotten out of the shower. The bruises on his body were mottled dark rose and purple. Ignoring his bed, Mercer had been sitting at the bar, staring at the cryptic remnant when the courier arrived with the agent who was to take the first shift guarding his house. After handing over the steel plate and conferring with the guard for a few minutes, Mercer fell into a deathlike sleep.

Dick Henna called two hours later.

"I'm sorry to be the one to tell you this, but it appears Howard Small is dead. A neighbor who'd been watching Small's house said she hadn't seen Howard since he left for Alaska. There was no luggage, and the answering machine had about two dozen messages on it. A closer examination turned up a bullet hole in the floor and traces of blood on a carpet that matches Small's, and what appears to be the body of a cat lodged in the drain under the kitchen sink. The house had been professionally sanitized, no prints, no tire treads, nothing but the blood, the bullet hole, and the cat."

"Then it's no coincidence. We're being hunted." Mercer's voice was thick with unfocused anger.

"Looks that way. The piece of steel was just delivered to Quantico and Dr. Goetchell said she would have a preliminary report by late tomorrow morning. As soon as I get it, I'll let you know, and then I want you to vanish."

"Don't worry about me. I'll be the invisible man."

Mercer was woken again, just past six o'clock. This time it was a pounding at the door that dragged him from the blissful embrace of oblivion. The skylight over his bed was a darkening square, the sky above swollen with rainclouds. He threw on a pair of jeans and a shirt and spun down the stairs. His injuries had stiffened, so he moved like an old man, shuffling and slow.

He looked through the peephole and saw Special Agent Mike Peters standing next to someone he thought he'd never see again. He swung open the door with a tired smile.

"I'm sorry to bother you, sir, but this woman insisted that I tell you she was here."

If Aggie Johnston was beautiful in a designer dress, she was absolutely enchanting in jeans and a plain white T-shirt, her hair tucked under a baseball cap. Her face had the clean scrubbed look of a college coed, except for the enticing pout of her lipsticked lips that drew attention to her understated sensuality.

"You're quite a surprise," Mercer said, catching her green eyes.

"I came over with some dinner." She held up a plastic bag emblazoned with Chinese dragons and characters. "The next thing I know I'm being felt up by this guy. What's going on here?" She paused when she noticed the bandage on Mercer's cheek. Her voice softened. "Oh, my God, what happened to you?"

Mercer turned to Agent Peters, "You frisked her?"

The big FBI agent looked sheepish. "I had to make sure she wasn't armed."

"Lucky boy. I think if I'd tried that, she would've torn me limb from limb."

"Mercer, what happened to you?" Aggie cut in impatiently.

"You might as well come in. I'll tell you all about it."

He moved aside to let Aggie enter, tossing a wink at Peters as she crossed the threshold.

"I didn't expect this." Aggie eyed the tall atrium. "It's beautiful."

"Thank you. Come on upstairs. I'll fix you a drink." He followed her up the staircase, his eyes luckily at the level of her tight backside as she took the steps with long-legged grace.

She paused in the library, scanning the titles, her fingers running along the spine of one of the twenty-eight volumes of Denis Diderot's eighteenth-century *Encyclopédic Methodique*. She looked at the shelves with the rapt attention of a true bibliophile. Many of the books in Mercer's collection were early editions of some of the great works on geology and mineral sciences. She went to one shelf and withdrew *Earth in the Balance* by Al Gore. "This is one book I would never have suspected of you," she teased.

"It was a gift," Mercer defended himself quickly. "I swear to God I never read it."

In the bar, Aggie ran her hand along the massive mahogany bar top, surveying the delicate woodwork that made up much of the room. "This is more what I expected from you, masculine, overbearing, and dedicated to alcohol."

"Your father must have a higher opinion of me than I thought to give me such a glowing review. I assume he told you how to find me?"

"Actually, I sneaked your address out of his Rolodex." Aggie put the bag of food on the bar and sat on one of the stools, cocking one leg so it rested on the seat with her. Her pose unintentionally rucked her jeans into the juncture of her thighs. Mercer had to drag his eyes away from the alluring sight. "The estimate of your personality is all mine. Now, are you going to tell me why you're limping and have a bandage on your face?"

She had been teasing Mercer since the moment she entered

the house, but there was real concern in her voice that softened her jibes.

Mercer ducked behind the bar. He'd offer her a drink, but he felt it more important to put a little distance between himself and Aggie Johnston. The physical barrier of the bar, he hoped, would help him build a psychological barrier between them. In his chaotic life, the last thing he wanted was to succumb to the attraction he felt building toward her.

"White wine all right?" he asked, reaching for a bottle in the fridge.

"I'd prefer a stinger."

Mercer cocked an eyebrow in approval as he reached for the brandy and white crème de menthe. "After I dropped you off last night, I stopped at a bar just up the street to have one more for the ditch."

He set the drink in front of her and dribbled a healthy shot of brandy into a snifter for himself. There was an ashtray on the bar, used primarily by Harry White, which Aggie took as de facto permission to smoke. She left the pack and the gold Dunhill next to her drink.

"I left a couple of hours later, pretty mixed, I might add. Anyway, a guy tried to mug me as I was walking home. He did a good number on me, as you can see." Mercer touched the bandage on his cheek. "This was from a pistol whip."

"Jesus!" Aggie exclaimed. "What happened? How did you get away?"

"I didn't. I ended up killing him." Mercer waited for a squeamish reaction from Aggie, but he remembered that she was Max Johnston's daughter. It would take more than the death of a criminal to rattle her. "I'd left the bar with a couple of beer bottles. I smashed them against his head, and the next thing I knew, I'd stabbed him with the broken neck of one. I passed out, and the next thing I remember I was in the hospital with a nurse cleaning blood off my face."

Aggie was silent for a moment; this was not one of those stories that demanded some immediate soothing response full of feigned emotion. At last she asked, "Are you still in pain?"

"Only when I laugh." Mercer smiled. "Actually, the worst part about it was the high-grade hangover all morning."

"If you were the victim of a mugging, why is there an FBI agent guarding your door and pawing your guests?"

"I didn't know he'd be pawing, I swear, but he's there as a favor to me. I thought there may have been someone else involved in the attack. I'm just being a little paranoid about possible revenge."

Mercer mixed enough fact with fiction to make a credible story, but again he underestimated Aggie.

"My father has always liked you, and he knew I had a crush on you, so whenever he heard something about your career, he'd tease me about it. Your boyfriend did this or your boyfriend did that." Her tone was flippant and self-mocking as she mimicked her father. "My crush was pretty transparent when I was younger. He told me all about what you did before the Gulf War, leading a team of commandos into Iraq to evaluate their uranium-mining facility.

"He also told me that there are some people in this world who, no matter how hard they try, can't get out of the way of danger. He said you were one of them. I know you don't believe that you were the victim of a mugging, and you know that I know it too. I'll leave you your cover story and let it drop, but next time you don't want to tell me something, just say so. Deal?"

Mercer was inordinately pleased at the prospect that he would have a next time. In fact, he was mystified that she was here in the first place. He asked her why.

She lit another cigarette, more out of nervousness than nicotine addiction. When she spoke, her eyes were downcast. "I said some things last night that I shouldn't have, burdened you with a lot of skeletons from my closet. I'm a little embarrassed."

Apologies didn't come easily to Aggie, that was plain to see. Her shy, elfin smile exposed beautiful white teeth and turned the corners of her eyes into creased points. But when she looked at him, her emerald eyes were almost imploring, exposing herself as surely as if she stood naked.

She laughed, cutting the sudden tension. "Just because I'm here and I apologized doesn't mean I don't hate what you do for a living."

"I promise not to rape the planet until after you leave."

They ate the Chinese food and talked for hours. They steered well clear of talking about themselves, in an unspoken understanding that too much had been said the night before. Despite the adversarial nature of their beliefs, they were highly intelligent and well-informed people. Even when their companionable discussion turned into debate, both enjoyed it immensely. By nine-thirty, they were sitting on the leather couch, their bodies almost, but not quite, touching. And just before ten, Aggie made the first move, reaching out to take Mercer's hand. He was speaking when it happened, and his voice caught.

He paused, looking at her face. Her eyes had gone glassy smooth, and her pupils were dialated twice their normal size. Her mouth invited. Mercer read her expression expertly, cupping his hand behind her head and lifting her slightly so their lips would meet.

At that instant, Harry White's graveled voice echoed through the house. "Hey, Mercer, you home? I thought you were going to Tiny's to watch football today."

The moment was lost immediately.

He moved away from her quickly. To delay would have meant he never would have stopped. "Harry," he bellowed with frustration, "your timing sucks."

"My timing? I'm not the guy with twenty bucks on the Steelers who didn't show up to even watch the game." Harry's voice was getting louder as he made his way up the spiral stairs, his limp more pronounced with each footfall.

Suddenly the situation dawned on Mercer with a galvanizing shock. "Harry, how in the hell did you get in here?"

"With the key you gave me five years ago. What are you, stupid?"

"Take cover now!" Mercer shouted. "Aggie, get behind the bar and stay down."

For Harry to get into the house without first confronting Agent Peters meant something had happened to Mercer's FBI guard. Mercer ran from the bar, pounding up the back set of stairs to his bedroom. There was just enough light flooding over the balcony to see the ugly shape of the Beretta on the nightstand where he'd left it while he napped through the afternoon. He dove bodily across the bed. Just as he reached for the gun, the skylight above his king-sized four-poster exploded downward with the force of an automatic weapon, bullets shredding the down comforter in a storm of feathers, glass shards, and jacketed rounds.

Mercer torqued his body as he crashed to the floor, sweeping his pistol off the stand in the same motion. He landed on his back, his legs up on the destroyed bed, the gun aimed at the ceiling. It took only a fraction of a second to thumb off the safety before he started pulling the trigger, cycling through the clip as fast as the manufacturer said was possible.

He was back on his feet as the assassin fell through the shattered skylight, his lifeless corpse smashing into the bed so hard that the frame cracked, tumbling him to the floor and leaving crimson splashes on the covers. Mercer ejected the spent clip and rammed a new one home, cocking the slide with practiced confidence.

Adrenaline fizzed in his veins like agitated champagne, sharpening his senses to a fine edge. If Harry had gotten in unchallenged by Mike Peters, it was safe to assume that the agent was dead and at least one of the assailants was in the house downstairs. He could only hope that the man on the roof had been the sole backup for whoever lay downstairs.

Now that the backup was dead in spectacular fashion, Mercer had no idea what the partner would do. There was a chance he would flee, but it seemed unlikely. This was the second attempt on his life in twenty-four hours, and they would want to end it now. Since he knew the brownstone better than his adversary, his only chance was to go on the offense. He had to think about Aggie and Harry.

He stalked to the balcony, ducking his head over the railing to make sure the foyer below was empty before pumping three rounds into the marble floor, the bullets sparking off the stone like fireworks. He dashed from his perch, retracing his steps across the bedroom to the back stairs. Whoever was below him would assume that the shots were covering fire for a descent of the spiral stairs, but he planned to outflank, not charge in headlong.

The narrow back stairs were empty as he cautiously made his way down, the Beretta held at the ready, his finger no more than an inch away from squeezing off a round. The doors to the two guest bedrooms were closed. Mercer guessed that his adversary hadn't had the time to stage an ambush here, so he ignored them. The bar was a little farther along the hallway, and he was torn between forming a defensive position around Aggie or keeping on the offense. The question was answered for him.

"Come out, or your father dies." The voice was heated with anger but commanding.

The library, thought Mercer. The guy has Harry in the library and thinks he's my father. He raced down the back stairs, gliding so quickly that his bare feet barely scuffed the steps. Through the hallway that divided the kitchen and the billiards room and out into the foyer he ran, not making a sound but knowing he was going too slow. The attacker would expect an answer within a few seconds, and he'd already taken too long.

He came to the spiral stairs and started up, his gun trained before him. Just below the second floor, he heaved himself over the railing, hanging ten feet over the foyer and continued upward, his toes finding purchase on the outside of the oak steps. He raised himself to see into the library, a quick motion that would have gotten him killed if he'd stayed between the banisters of the staircase.

The gunman was positioned in the juncture of two bookcases, his back tucked into the corner, Harry held before him as a human shield. The motion of Mercer's head ducking over the railing caught the assassin's eye and he fired off a snap shot that went wide but would have drilled Mercer if he'd come up where expected. Mercer had only a split second to react; the next shot would compensate for his deception.

He launched himself off the staircase, lunging for the thick newels that lined the front balcony of the library, his body stretched far out into open space. He grasped the heavy oak in one hand, the momentum of his leap swinging him in a wrenching arc that felt as if it would tear his shoulder from its socket. The barrel of his pistol cleared the library floor.

He fired too fast. The shot caught Harry White just below his knee, the impact of the nine-millimeter slug folding his leg under him. He took the gunman down with him when he fell to the floor.

Mercer caught another banister with his right hand, clutching at it desperately while trying to maintain a grip on the Beretta. He slithered over the railing as the assassin untangled himself from a stunned Harry, ignoring the blood pooling under them both. The gunman recovered just a fraction of a second before Mercer did, raising his weapon in a steady, side-arm stance. Mercer took another snap shot, the concussive explosions coming as one thunderous sound.

A molten stream of acid ran across Mercer's shoulder as a bullet gouged a shallow trench through his flesh. The force of the shot slammed him back into the railings, splintering three of them and threatening to send him down to the hard marble below. Through the pain, Mercer saw that his shot had caught the other man in the middle of his chest, 115 grain bullet driving him off his feet as if he'd been yanked by a marionette's strings.

The body landed in the bar, sprawled on the floor in the unnatural pose of death. Aggie's shrill scream pierced the air like a siren, rising and falling in terror. Mercer ignored her; her wailing was fear, not pain. Harry lay motionless on the floor, his face deathly pale and waxen. Mercer crawled to his old friend, the drops of blood oozing from his shoulder soaking into the beige carpet. Mercer feared he'd hit Harry in the wrong leg.

"You son of a bitch." Harry turned, holding the shattered remnant of his prosthetic limb in his hands, the flesh-colored plastic shredded where the bullet had passed through. "Do you have any idea how much these fucking things cost?"

Relief made Mercer sag to the floor, his face pressed into the deep pile of the carpet, the adrenaline rush dissipating like an alcohol buzz. "Bill me," he panted.

"Mercer!" Aggie screeched, the fear in her voice jolting him like an electric shock.

The gunman was struggling to his feet, his pistol trained on Aggie where she crouched near the edge of the bar. A burgundy stain ran down from his thigh where Mercer's first shot must have caught him after passing through Harry's artificial leg. He was heaving great drafts of air, struggling to regain the breath that had been knocked from him when the second shot had been stopped by his Kevlar vest. Mercer let out a roar as he charged into the bar, his gray eyes fixed with rage.

The assassin turned toward the sound, his aim swinging from Aggie to Mercer in a quick arc. Mercer ignored the pistol wheeling toward him. He crashed into the gunman after six powerful strides, his damaged shoulder pounding into the other man's chest, throwing them both against the back wall and rattling glasses behind the bar. Mercer used his slight advantage to torque his pistol into the assassin's belly just under the protective vest that had just saved the man's life. He pushed with all of his strength, feeling the hard muscle resist for an instant. Mercer screwed the gun in deeper, almost tearing through skin, before angling the barrel up and firing four rounds into the chest cavity, tearing internal organs into wet chunks that exploded through the gunman's back and sprayed the wainscoting beyond.

Mercer staggered back, letting the corpse fall to the floor, his hand covered with the assailant's blood. He turned. Aggie had regained her feet, though somewhat shakily. She clutched the edge of the bar, her knuckles white with the tenacious grip. She stared at the body with a mixture of fear and revulsion even as she came across the room to collapse into Mercer's arms.

He gasped as her hand slid across his shoulder, forcing fresh blood to well to the surface. As he sank to the floor, Aggie went down with him, her arms still around his neck, her eyes still fastened on the body only a few feet away.

"That's, that's . . ." she stammered but could not continue.

"What is it?" Mercer panted, his heart racing three times normal speed, his hands only now beginning to tremble from the fear he'd been able to ignore.

She tore her eyes from the body and noticed Mercer's wound. "He shot you."

"I'm all right. The bullet only grazed me." Even as he

spoke, he gingerly pulled her arm off his damaged shoulder.

"Jesus Christ," Harry admonished at the entrance of the bar. "I've had my leg shot off and you end up with a woman in your arms."

Aggie gasped when she saw the source of the voice. Harry leaned against the doorjamb between the bar and the library, his body supported by only one leg. The tube of his other pants leg dangled emptily. He held the dismembered limb like a rifle at high port. Mercer couldn't help but laugh at the demented image.

"You look like an extra from a bad horror film, *Night of the Legless Drunks*."

"And fuck you too." Harry snorted. "What the hell just happened and who the hell is that?" He pointed the leg at Aggie like an accusing finger.

"What happened was the second attempt on my life in the past twenty-four hours and this is Max Johnston's daughter, Aggie. Aggie, this pathetic excuse is Harry White, my oldest chronological friend and the man we both owe our lives to. Harry, if you hadn't barged in, those guys would have caught us with our pants down." Mercer realized his gaffe and quickly added. "Figuratively speaking, of course."

Aggie waved timidly, smiling a small greeting. Harry caught the direction of her gaze and lowered his artificial leg. "Don't worry about this. I lost it so long ago I forget what it felt like to have two."

He hopped across the room, steadying each leap against a piece of furniture until he could plant himself at the bar, leaning his dismembered leg against the footrail like an umbrella. "Are you going to get me a drink while I call the police or do I have to do everything myself?"

His unflappability roused Mercer from the floor. That was the one thing Mercer could depend on Harry for, his ability to break down any situation and place it in a context that couldn't possibly disturb the pace of his life.

"Good idea." Mercer grabbed a handful of bar towels and laid them over the body before pouring a Jack Daniel's and ginger ale for Harry and a heavy slug of brandy for himself. It was a better anesthetic for his shoulder than the pills he would get at the hospital. "Aggie, another stinger? I think you could use it."

Aggie shot a glance at the body before responding, "No, I have to get out of here, now." The urgency in her voice jarred Mercer.

"It's all right," Harry growled, "he won't hurt you anymore."

"That's not it." Aggie leaped to her feet and started to the door.

Mercer followed her, catching up at the top of the spiral stairs. "Are you okay?"

It was natural for her to want to put as much distance as possible between herself and the scene of such violence and horror, but Mercer was sure there was something more behind her reaction. He'd been in enough bloody confrontations to know how people react, especially first-time witnesses to a fatal shooting, so he knew that she was fleeing for some other reason, something unrelated to what had just transpired. He put his arms around her.

"What is it?" Concern softened Mercer's voice to an intimate whisper.

"I can't be here," she replied shaking out of his embrace. "I can't be found here when the police come."

She raced from the house, the door slamming with a finality that hurt Mercer more than his shoulder.

———

ANCHORAGE, ALASKA

Kerikov slammed the phone so hard against its cradle that the slim executive handset snapped in two, the halves joined by only a few tendons of wire. His rage not yet vented, he plucked the entire unit from the end table and threw it at the far wall of his hotel suite. The phone disintegrated against the hard oak paneling. In a gesture bordering on manic, he raced across the room and crushed the remains under his heel, grinding them into the carpet until he felt shards jabbing into his foot through the sole of his shoe. His breathing and heart rate had accelerated, and sweat beaded his broad forehead.

He turned to look through the picture window high over Alaska's largest city. His suite was just one floor below the Captain Cook room of the Anchorage Holiday Inn, arguably the city's finest hotel. While he'd been in the room only a few hours since returning from the interrogation of Howard Small in California, he'd had time to notice the room's view of the snow-peaked Brooks Range and the outline of Mt. McKinley making a rare appearance from behind a layer of cloud. Between the city and the mountains were the wide black ribbons of Elmendorf Air Force Base.

When he'd first gotten into the room, Kerikov had seen AWACS radar planes flying out of the base, their distinctive flat-dish antennas clinging to their backs like some engineer's afterthought. Watching one lumber into the sky, greasy trails of smoke trailing the quadruple engines, Kerikov wondered why the Americans bothered. There was nothing left for them to spy on.

He stood staring across the late afternoon vista for several moments, concentrating on his breathing, clearing his mind, vainly attempting to corral his emotions. He knew he'd just had what he called an "episode," a period where he lost conscious thought and moved purely on raw emotion. He had lost all control of his actions, his mind blocking out anything that might have occurred. These usually violence-marred times were becoming alarmingly frequent and longer-lasting. When they had first started, during his assignment as an interrogator for the KGB in Afghanistan, they would last only a fraction of a second and occurred maybe once every two or three months.

At the time, he thought they were caused by stress, brought on by fighting on the dirtiest front of an unwinnable war. By war's end, he would black out for a day at a time, sometimes regaining consciousness in other parts of the country with no knowledge of how he'd gotten there or why. The episodes stopped when the war came to a close. After the conflict ended and the Soviet Union had withdrawn her troops with the ignominy of America's withdrawal from Saigon, Kerikov was free of blackouts for several years. Even the memories of the occurrences faded. But during the late 1980s and early '90s, they returned. When the futility of his career at the KGB became apparent, as one by one the Soviet satellite states reformed and westernized and his own beloved *Rodina* vanished under the capitalist wave, his blackouts came back, their duration and frequency increasing exponentially. By the late 1990s, men were dying during Kerikov's blind rages. He had come down from one such episode during his final months in Russia to find four subordinates dead by his own hand, each arranged around a conference table with his throat slit. He had no recollection of the acts or how he'd managed to subdue each man as he dispatched the others.

Knowing that he'd just returned from the violent edge of his own mind, Kerikov turned quickly to see if his untethered rage had caused another death. His guest, a thin, academic young man in black jeans and turtleneck stared at him through thick glasses, his misty eyes registering incomprehension of the display he'd just witnessed.

Ivan Kerikov hid his relief at seeing the young American still alive by recrossing the room and pouring three fingers of Scotch into a thick glass tumbler. Disdaining ice, he forced the drink neat, its fire ripping at his insides like claws. He carefully set the glass back on the coffee table, making sure that it stood precisely in the center of the narrow rim of spilled liquor on the glass top. The tiny ritual was a gesture of the orderliness that was wholly unobtainable in his mind.

He stood over the young man, folding his thick arms across his chest in a gesture that intimidated as strongly as if he were shaking a meaty fist. His voice was well modulated and even, the wracking emotions temporarily checked behind his personal facade. "Because of the incompetence of others, your job has just been made much more difficult."

Ted Mossey said nothing. He perched on the edge of the

overstuffed easy chair like a frightened bird about to take flight.

"That was my contact in Washington." Kerikov nodded in the direction of the destroyed telephone. "There have been two unsuccessful attempts to stop an enemy who will now be coming on the offense. I know him well, and I know that our only chance to defeat him is to step up our timetable. You must be ready within forty-eight hours. Otherwise we may be forced to abandon the project."

"No!" The anger in Mossey's voice charged his entire body, squaring his narrow shoulders and firming the soft flesh that passed as a chin.

Ted Mossey had a face shaped like a spade, his weak chin forming its point and his rounded cheeks forming the bowed top. He had no cheekbones to speak of, so his face appeared to slope in on itself; only his small nose added any definition. His glasses were hooked behind wildly recurved ears that were nearly hidden by lank blond hair. Angry red scars pocked his face, adolescent acne that followed him into early adulthood with embarrassing ferocity. But Kerikov had not hired Mossey for his appearance. He'd taken him into the fold of Charon's Landing because the twenty-eight-year-old was a computer virtuoso.

He could debug one program while simultaneously writing another, one keyboard under each of his ambidextrous hands, his eyes shifting between screens so fast that they would blend into one homogeneous image. Mossey was responsible for the parent 3-D generators used on the next-generation video games, and a program he'd designed as a geometric data cascade was so advanced that it could not be used until computer speed increased another hundredfold.

However, there was another aspect of Ted Mossey that had attracted Kerikov above all the other hotshot computer geniuses that the United States produced in alarming numbers. While many of Kerikov's earlier candidates certainly possessed the skills he needed, only Mossey had the element that made him an easy recruit. Mossey was a rabid environmentalist, an eco-terrorist who used his knowledge of computers to wreak havoc among timber companies, mining concerns, and heavy industries. While many environmental activists seemed more impressed with publicity than results, Mossey preferred to work from the shadows, destroying computer systems and causing millions of dollars in damage to those he saw as destructive to the planet. Once Kerikov approached Mossey and outlined in brief strokes the principle behind Charon's Landing, the young American almost begged to join.

"I won't let that happen," Mossey said angrily. "This is too important. I can do it in forty-eight hours, no problem."

Kerikov recognized the bravado in Mossey's voice. He didn't need assurance, he wanted the truth, so he spoke accusingly. "You're not scheduled to work at the Marine Terminal again for three days, and I'll need you at the terminal within two. How will you manage it?"

"Simple. Right after I got the programming job at Alyeska, I inserted a virus into their system that will lock out all the work stations from the mainframe. No one will be able to use their computers. I can unleash the virus from my system at home and freeze every computer on the Alaska Pipeline. In the past few months, they've come to see me as the resident expert, so they'll call me to get the system back on line." When Ted spoke about computers, he had an authority that masked his physical frailty.

"Won't they know that their system has been accessed from outside the facility?"

As much as he dared, Mossey shook his head at such an insult to his abilities. "I've already deleted the backtrack subroutine of their antivirus program. They'll have no record of an outside contact."

"If that's the case, can't you initiate my primary program in their mainframe from your own computer?" Kerikov asked reasonably, the subtleties of computer hacking lost to him yet hoping to avoid the security risk of placing Mossey within the confines of the Alyeska Marine Terminal.

"I told you before," Mossey sighed. "Your program was buried inside the computer core during the 1986 system upgrade. When your programmer hardwired it into the mainframe, he made it impossible to activate from anywhere other than the main computer room in Valdez. That way, no one could ever stumble across it at a desktop unit or find it by hacking into the system. He made it impossible to discover and at the same time very difficult to access. My antibacktracker is child's play compared to the protection your guy put into the system."

Kerikov understood that there was no other option than to get him into the computer room at Valdez in order to initiate the programs planted over a decade ago by one of Kerikov's best agents. The computer sabotage had been the only active element of Charon's Landing Kerikov had carried out prior to the collapse of the Soviet Union. Everything since then had been his own doing, with financial backing from Hasaan bin-Rufti and others. The computer codes were the only items Kerikov needed to pirate the former KGB operation.

"How soon can you lock them out and get yourself to the facility?" Kerikov asked, the ripe scent of victory already detectable. Philip Mercer might still be alive, but there wasn't anything he could do to stop Kerikov once the control program was primed.

"About four hours after I get to my apartment in Valdez. Once I freeze the system, they'll call me within minutes. After that, I can start your program in just a few hours."

"Excellent. I want you to drive back to Valdez tonight, but don't lock them out until I call you. The delay shouldn't be more than twenty-four hours, thirty-six at the most, understand?"

"Yes, sure, but why wait?"

"Initiating my computer program is only one phase of the overall operation; there are others that you are not aware of. I have to make certain that everything is in place before we take over the system entirely." Kerikov wasn't in the habit of explaining his orders.

Kerikov didn't wait for Mossey to leave before he strode from the living room to his bedroom. The phone extension there was now the only working unit in the suite. As he dialed an in-house line to reach Abu Alam two floors below, he fished in his pant's pocket for his pack of cigarettes and lighter.

"Yes," Alam answered.

"We are leaving in a few hours. There has been a slight complication. The people in Washington failed."

"Mercer is still alive?" Despite his instability, Alam retained enough professionalism to ask the right questions.

"Yes. Rather than try again, I've decided to draw him to Alaska, then send him on a wild-goose chase. We can take care of him later. To ensure he comes, we need to return to Homer. Fuel the car. I'll meet you in the lobby," Kerikov looked at his watch, "at ten o'clock."

"Should we be armed?" Even Alam had some respect for American law enforcement and traveled with his beloved SPAS-12 semiautomatic shotgun only when necessary.

"Yes. We will take my own men on this trip." Kerikov needed the steadier hands of his two German guards instead of Alam's murderous Arab gunslingers. While the former Stasi agents had bungled the interrogation of the fisherman and his son, they were well trained and disciplined, and tonight's work would need their professionalism. He cut the connection and immediately redialed the phone.

"I can't speak now, we're still loading," a voice responded brusquely, then hung up.

Kerikov looked at the mute instrument for a moment, but since he'd called to get a situation report from his agent, he was satisfied. He made another call, ignoring the time difference, not caring that he'd wake the man at the other end.

"Hello," came a sleepy voice after a few rings.

"You've failed again. Mercer is still alive." Kerikov could hear the man swing himself out of bed.

"That's not possible. I sent my best man, he's never failed me."

"One of my old contacts in Washington just called me from Mercer's block. There are about two dozen cops there right now and he said he saw Mercer talking to Dick Henna himself."

"Was anyone else involved?"

"What does that matter? Mercer is alive, and now you've failed me twice. Your ineptitude is intolerable." Kerikov left his last statement hanging in the silence.

"He'll be dead tomorrow if I have to kill him myself."

"Don't be a fool," Kerikov barked. "He's under the protective custody of the FBI now. The only way to stop him is to lure him to Alaska where I will take care of him personally. I have an old score to settle."

"What do you want me to do?"

"Nothing for the moment. Is everything set with Rufti?"

"I spoke with him this evening. He says that Khalid Al-Khuddari is suspicious, but he assures me that he's ready to strike before Khuddari has figured just how real the threat to the royal family is."

"The weapons?"

"Are stowed aboard the *Petromax Arabia*, which is berthed in Abu Dhabi for an unscheduled maintenance inspection as you planned." As the other man spoke, his voice grew more confident. "The *Arctica* should be leaving Valdez within a couple of hours, so everything is on track. Even with Mercer still alive, there's no way to stop everything we've set in motion. Don't worry, Ivan, within a couple of days America's last source of domestic oil will become inaccessible, petroleum prices will double, and the map of the Middle East will be redrawn again. And this time, no one will be able to lift a finger to change it back. All three of us get what we want— you your money, me my profits, and Rufti his own country."

"I will believe that when it occurs. Hubris has taken down greater men than you," Kerikov chided before his voice took on a thoughtful calm. "I'm concerned about Rufti. I just don't believe that fat bastard has the guts or the brains to pull off his part of the operation. If he fails, everything will come unraveled."

"Is there enough time for you to derail Khuddari?" Kerikov's partner asked.

"No. And that's what concerns me. I've pushed up our timetable by a full day, so there is nothing we can do about him. Rufti, I'm afraid, will be on his own until this is over." Kerikov kept his anger hidden. In the old days, he could have simply dispatched an assassin to kill Khuddari and tie up that loose end, but he no longer had that sort of power.

"I've known Hasaan Rufti longer than you. I too was distracted by his weakness for food and thought it connoted a deeper weakness within the man. Khuddari may prove to be difficult, but Rufti is greedy enough, and crafty enough, to get rid of him. And he won't care what it costs or who gets in the way. He has absolutely no morals. You've met his lackey, Abu Alam. Christ, Rufti is twice as sick as that lunatic and ten times as dangerous. However, I'll be speaking with Rufti again tomorrow. I'll make sure he understands your concern."

"He doesn't know that you and I are working together?" Kerikov nearly shouted, panic forcing blood to his face in an angry flush.

"Of course not," the other man soothed quickly. "He'll think that the concern is mine. Don't worry, Ivan, he doesn't know of our deal at all."

"Don't fuck this up, or so help me God, death would be a relief from what I'd do to you." He angrily hung up the phone, the cavalier attitude of his partner threatening to send him into cardiac arrest.

He'd been this close to his goals before and had them stripped away by perfidious greed and the work of Philip Mercer.

He lit another cigarette to steady his fraying nerves. He had only a few minutes to meet Alam and his two men for the trip down to Homer. Once he'd laid the false trail for Mercer, he could again concentrate fully on all the other aspects of Charon's Landing.

Before he left the suite, he had one more call to make. The connection took a few seconds longer than normal as the signal was bounced off an orbiting satellite and converted to a marine band frequency. A female answered.

"Is this Hope?" he asked.

"Yes it is," she chirped brightly.

"This is Ivan Kerikov. Tell your boss that we're pushing up the strike by twenty-four hours. Make sure that you're ready. I'll be back in touch in the morning if there are any questions."

THE J. EDGAR HOOVER BUILDING
WASHINGTON, D.C.

The headquarters of the FBI was located in downtown Washington, a massive steel and glass building that more befitted a high-tech corporation than America's premiere law-enforcement agency. Behind the walls of the building named for the most vigilant American ever born, the FBI ran countless operations all over the nation, from the mundane to the most dangerous, each conducted with a thoroughness that many felt bordered on paranoia. Yet the tireless men and women of the Bureau knew that their work secured the nation as no other on earth.

Dick Henna had a suite of offices on the top floor. When it wasn't necessary to impress guests and he needed privacy, he preferred one of the plain conference rooms several floors below. It was just one more way he tried to remain connected to his organization and not hide himself in the ivory tower of his position as had so many of his predecessors. Henna's bulldog face was heavily jowled, with a sloped nose and small eyes. His body matched his face, wide shoulders and thick gut stacked on short legs. He looked like a Teamster enforcer from the union's nefarious past. Despite his years spent steadily gaining positions in the agency and his year as the Director of the FBI, he'd never lost the look of an overworked street agent.

Across from him, Mercer slouched comfortably, none the worse after the attack and a night under FBI protective custody at the Willard Hotel, one of Washington's finest. The bullet wound wasn't deep, more of a nuisance than an injury, a weal that would mend in a few days. In deference to the meeting, he wore a suit, one that hung off of his long frame as easily as a favorite pair of jeans and rugby shirt. When the police had arrived at his brownstone the night before, with Henna and two cars of FBI special agents, they'd given him just enough time to pack an overnight bag before bundling him off to the Willard. Harry White was brought back to his own apartment for debriefing.

Until midnight, a tag team pair of investigators grilled Mercer over every element of the assault on his house, each retelling gleaning some other detail as he wracked his brain for information. He was entirely honest and cooperative about the whole affair except that he maintained that he was alone when Harry had come over. Though he felt a tremendous sense of betrayal, he thought it best not to mention Aggie Johnston. As a favor to Mercer, Harry would verify that his friend was alone when he arrived.

Mercer hadn't really had the time to analyze Aggie's reaction. The FBI had kept him up so long that exhaustion had overwhelmed him even as he was retelling the events of the previous night. But he was disturbed by her sudden departure and what it could possibly mean.

Henna was uncharacteristically subdued. He'd spoken with Agent Peters' widow the night before and was going to visit her later in the day. It was a duty he was not looking forward to but one that he wouldn't allow anyone else to handle. Though he'd never met the young agent, he took Peters' death as hard as if it were his best friend who would be buried the following day.

An aide stepped into the office with a tray of coffee. Mercer took his black and waited for Dick to dilute his with a heavy drop of milk and two spoons of sugar.

"Why is it you look worse than I do and I was the one who was attacked last night?" Mercer tried to put some levity in his question, but he couldn't cut through Henna's morose air.

"I don't know what it is about you, but since last night, the shit's really hit the fan." Henna shook his head sadly. "After you were attacked, I called the President, woke him, actually. He gave me the authority to dig around in the archives of the CIA and the National Security Agency for anything pertaining to Alaska or you." Henna pulled a tightly folded piece of paper from his pocket, easing out the creases as he spoke. "The NSA came up with this about two hours ago."

Mercer scanned the page, ignoring the bureaucratic language and extraneous words that littered any government document. The meat of the letter was that a man named John Krugger had entered the country twelve days earlier. "So?"

"The NSA's computers automatically flag passports with suspicious names. They process thousands of yellow flags per week, names and aliases that are the same or sound similar to those of terrorists or other undesirables. Naturally, most of these are meaningless coincidences. Yet the computer will red-flag certain ones depending on our interest in the person being sought. This name sent up a red flag immediately."

"Means nothing to me." Mercer was nonchalant, though the hairs on the back of his neck were beginning to bristle with premonition.

"John Krugger is an Anglicized version of Johann Kreiger," Henna said flatly.

Mercer shrugged his shoulders, but unconsciously he braced his feet as if expecting a physical blow.

"Johann Kreiger was a favorite alias of Ivan Kerikov, and according to the KGB, who still wants him dead, he has an English passport under the name of John Krugger."

"Kerikov's in the country?" Mercer rasped.

A thousand emotions swirled through him, undirected and random. Through the chaos, a pattern formed and a dominant desire cut through the tempest. Mercer wanted revenge. Ivan Kerikov, the mastermind behind Vulcan's Forge, had nearly killed Mercer a dozen times over when the Russian stole that former KGB plot. Mercer had wanted a chance to kill the Russian then, but Kerikov hadn't been close enough. He had expertly manipulated others to do his bidding while remaining safely outside the country.

But now, Kerikov was here, in America, on Mercer's home turf, and he wanted another chance to bring the Russian down. His stomach tightened with fury.

"I want him, Dick."

"We'll discuss that later. Right now, we have to figure out why he's here."

"You think it has something to do with me and Alaska?"

"Since you cost him a hundred million dollars in Hawaii, I'm sure it will involve you and, given the mood of the country and the administration, I assume everything has to do with Alaska."

There was a knock on the door, and it swung open without invitation.

Dr. Lynn Goetchell was the senior lab analyst at the FBI's Forensic Crimes Laboratory in rural Virginia and ruled her domain with the haughty demeanor of a benevolent dictator, her omnipresent lab coat taking on the importance of a robe of state. She sat next to Mercer, barely acknowledging his presence. It was not that she was a rude person, but the three doctoral degrees to her credit had called for sacrifices in her life, and social niceties had been one of the first to go. She wore a severe blue suit, and her only jewelry was a pair of paste earclips.

Mercer had no basis for reference, but he guessed that Goetchell hadn't slept since receiving the metal scrap from the *Jenny IV*. Her face was pale, and the bags under her eyes were a bruised purple. Mercer could smell traces of chemicals on her skin.

"I might as well tell you right now that I got absolutely nothing from that sample you gave me," Lynn Goetchell admitted after the perfunctory introductions. "We've had less than twenty-four hours, which isn't enough time for a definitive analysis, but I'll stake my reputation that we won't get much further with it."

"What do you have so far?" Henna queried.

"It's your basic stainless steel, unremarkable in every respect. The ink used to print the word "roger" is a standard product produced under license by twenty different companies in this country alone. It's untraceable. The presence of sodium and diatoms on the surface of the sample was explained by its immersion in seawater. Salt concentrates were consistent with the waters of the North Pacific and Prince

William Sound. We ran it under a two-hundred-thousand-power scanning electron microscope and found nothing out of the ordinary—"

"What about where the metal was torn?" Mercer interrupted.

"Shearing tears consistent with violent explosions, implosions, or rending force. Anything could have torn it apart. I can't give you anything more specific than that. There were no traces of chemicals around the damaged sections, no blast residue or explosives."

"Dead end," Mercer said miserably.

"Yes," Goetchell agreed. "We found only one thing that couldn't be detected with a visual inspection. Using computer extrapolation we discovered that the fragment was torn from a cylinder approximately thirty-seven-point-nine inches in circumference."

Mercer did the math in his head and envisioned a stainless steel tube about twelve inches wide. It still told him nothing. "So where does that leave us?"

"That leaves us with the other evidence recovered from the *Jenny IV*." Goetchell pulled a folder from her briefcase. "Autopsy reports, and very poor ones too. I should have the license of Anchorage's Medical Examiner yanked."

She opened the slimmer of the two files, the last words written about the men who had died on the *Jenny IV*. "The skeletal remains found in the boat's cabin were too far gone to get much. The level of carbonization of the bone fragments indicates a fire of over eight hundred degrees, consistent to the combustibles found on boats—wood, plastic, and fuel. There wasn't even enough to do a DNA analysis. Identification had to be made through dental records."

"And the body I found on the deck?"

"Cause of death was severe burn trauma. He'd lost forty percent of his body mass to the flames. His lungs were so scorched that even if he'd survived the fire, he'd have died within hours." She passed around a series of gruesome photographs. The corpse as horribly disfigured as Mercer remembered, burned hands with skin peeled back like shredded paper, charred stumps that had once been his legs, and a face more ruined that Mercer thought possible. There were no eye-lids, ears, or nose, and the lips had burned away to reveal crooked yellow teeth.

"What's this one?" Henna held up one of the pictures.

Goetchell peered at it. "It wasn't labeled in the ME's report, but it looks like a picture of a cell biopsy. They look like subcutaneous fat cells."

"They look like they've collapsed," Mercer remarked. He'd watched enough science programs on television to know a healthy cell structure. These looked like haphazard bricks on a crumbling wall. The cell walls, usually well defined and rigid, were smeared and distended.

Dr. Goetchell took the picture from Henna, studying it much more carefully. "I'll be damned. I missed that entirely. Another mystery on top of everything else."

"What could cause that?" Mercer asked.

"An increase in extracellular salts, sugars, and proteins will cause cells to leach out water in an effort to rebalance the concentration," Lynn Goetchell lectured patiently. "If the chemical imbalance is bad enough, the cells can't excrete enough water to dilute their protective fluid. They drain themselves and subsequently collapse, or more accurately implode. It starts out as a protective function that ends up destroying the cells themselves."

"What could make it start in the first place?" Henna asked. He was out of his element entirely and doing his best to keep up.

"Any number of chemical compounds could do it. The human body is very attuned to toxicity in its environment. Also, when a body is frozen, this kind of damage will occur."

"Jesus," Mercer exploded. "Freezing. Why the hell didn't I think of that before?"

"What's the big deal?" Henna shook his head. "The body was recovered from Alaska in unseasonably cold weather. It's no surprise that the body was freezing."

Mercer turned to him as a thin tendril of the mystery began to unravel. "Dick, pay attention to the tenses. She didn't say when a body freezes; she said when a body is frozen." He glanced to Lynn Goetchell and was rewarded with a slight nod. "What are we talking about—temperatures below two hundred degrees Fahrenheit?"

"The destruction to the cells is complete, and since the reaction wasn't timed, there's no way to calculate."

"It doesn't matter," Mercer replied. He tore a piece of paper from the legal pad at Henna's elbow and pulled a pen from the inside of his jacket. Henna and Goetchell watched silently as Mercer wrote out the name whose meaning had eluded them all: roger.

"Now, that piece of steel was ripped just at the end of the last letter r, right?" He didn't wait for a response. "But what if it wasn't an r at all." He continued the upper arm of the letter, curling it down to spell out rogen.

He looked up quickly. Lynn Goetchell instantly understood where he was leading, but Henna was still baffled, the corners of his mouth hanging down in concentration. Mercer finished the remainder of the word with a flourish, filling in the letters that had been torn away by the explosion aboard the Jenny IV: nitrogen. And then he added the word he knew proceeded it on the twelve-inch-diameter cylinder that rested within the doomed ship's hold: liquid nitrogen. He went so far as to add the triangled circle that denotes biohazard.

"I'm willing to bet that there was a hell of a lot more than one tank of liquid nitrogen on the Jenny IV," Mercer said triumphantly. "I remember that her stern-mounted crane and all of her radio antennas had snapped off. Now it makes sense. The fire must have boiled the liquid nitrogen in the holds. Since I found one body still in his bunk, the fire must have consumed the ship quickly. The other crewman was on the deck when the heat of the flames caused the tanks to explode. The ship would have been engulfed in a fog of supercooled gas that snuffed the flames. That's why he was so badly burned in some areas and unaffected in others. The fire was put out before it could finish roasting him." Mercer paused, imagining the agony of such a death. He shivered off the gruesome image. "The intense temperature change would have weakened the cranes and antennas. They snapped under their own weight."

Henna looked at Goetchell for confirmation.

"It makes sense given the preliminary findings of the autopsy. Nitrogen liquefies at three hundred thirty-eight degrees below zero, about seventy-seven degrees above absolute zero on the Kelvin scale, more than cold enough to do this type of cellular damage. And it doesn't require expensive refrigeration equipment like liquefied hydrogen or helium. A fire near the cylinders could conceivably cause them to boil and rupture, spilling their contents in an evaporative cloud. And that kind of cold will weaken metal, plastic, and wood to the point where they can collapse under even minor strain. There isn't a physics student in the country who hasn't seen a nail dipped in liquid nitrogen shatter when hit by a hammer."

"Why?" Henna directed his question at Mercer like a pistol shot.

"Hey, give me a moment. Ten seconds ago we didn't even know what she was carrying."

In the ensuing silence, the large white-faced clock on the wall clicked through five minutes, its thin red second hand ratcheting off the time mechanically, uncaringly. Mercer stretched out, his eyes staring into a middle distance that only he saw.

"Where did they get it?" Mercer asked softly. "It doesn't make sense that they got the nitrogen from the mainland and brought it out to sea with them. More than likely, they were conveying it to port when the fire occurred. Where the hell did they get tanks of liquid nitrogen in the middle of the Gulf of Alaska?"

"One more on the list of mysteries," Henna said pessimistically.

"Not so fast." Mercer turned to Lynn Goetchell. "Can you give me the date and time of death?"

"The body was discovered on the seventeenth and the Medical Examiner put the time of death at early afternoon the day before. I can't prove it, but I'll bet that he wasn't off by more than a few hours."

"Afternoon of October sixteenth." Mercer turned to Henna. "I need a phone and a couple of hours and I'll tell you where they got those cylinders. Hopefully, I'll be able to give you a why after that."

"Forget it. You've done your part."

"What are you talking about?" Mercer was shocked that his friend was taking him out of the loop.

"If it hasn't slipped your mind, there have been two attempts on your life in the past couple of days. You're out of it as of right now."

"Dick, don't turn bureaucrat on me now. You still have no idea what's happening, which means the attempts on my life aren't going to stop. If I'm at risk, then I want a say in the investigation."

"Forget it, Mercer," Dick Henna repeated sternly. "I've got nearly two hundred agents working in and around Alaska right now, looking for anything that may threaten the opening of the Arctic Refuge and the building of the second Trans-Alaska Pipeline, and so far they've turned up nothing. Christ, two gas stations in Anchorage were firebombed last night no more than five blocks from our field headquarters. Now that we've gotten a lead, my personnel are the ones who are going to track it down. Not you."

"Come on, none of those guys have my scientific background. If the FBI had had agents who knew that ammonium nitrate fertilizer and fuel oil combine to make an explosive, the Oklahoma City bombing might never have occurred. I was playing with Amfo when I was a kid."

"Dr. Goetchell, would you please excuse us." Henna's tone was tight. She got up quickly, shaking Mercer's hand and nodding to her superior before leaving the conference room.

Henna continued. "Number one, don't think our friendship means you can talk to me like that in front of my people. It undermines my authority and makes you look like a jerk. Number two, I appreciate what you've done here, but that doesn't mean I'm going to give you free rein to continue. This is an FBI investigation, not a personal crusade. I like you enough not to want to see you killed. Kerikov never got close to you last time, but now he's in the country, and if you go sniffing around, you'll end up in the same condition as your three friends. If you think I'm being a hard-ass, you're right. The country is a powder keg, Alaska is its fuse, and any moment someone's going to light it. I have enough to worry about without you making this personal."

Mercer knew that Henna was speaking from the heart. Henna was being forced against a wall by the administration, pouring a ton of man-hours into the Alaska crisis with absolutely no results. Mercer had just provided a major clue, but there was just no way Henna could let him get involved. Mercer understood this, respected Henna for it, but had no intention of backing down.

Rather than continue his entreaty, he changed tack. "What about those guys who attacked me last night? Have you found anything?"

Henna wrongly assumed Mercer's question meant he was dropping a personal investigation. "The guy you left in your bar was named Burt Manning. Before he left the CIA in 1990, he was also known as 'The Ghost.' Consider yourself lucky. As far as we can determine, you're the first man since Manning worked for the Phoenix Project who ever went up against him and walked away. The guy was the culmination of four years in Southeast Asia and twenty more as a cold warrior in the front lines against the Soviet Union. He'd run ops in Africa, South and Central America, Eastern and Western Europe, and Russia. His dossier at Langley reads like a spy thriller.

"Since retiring from the Agency, he has owned a private security consulting firm here in Washington contracting to corporations that feel their upper management is ripe for kidnapping or assassination. The other guy in your place was a former colleague of Manning's from the CIA. We figured he was hired by Manning to back him up on the hit. We raided Manning's office, but an alarm tripped when we broke through the door and crashed his computer system, erasing everything. A couple of our pet hackers are attempting to reconstruct the files, but they aren't optimistic. We'll probably never know who hired him."

"Damn," Mercer spat. "Knowing that would have saved you a shitload of time."

"Be thankful we found out who he was in the first place." Henna shot a glance at his watch. "I've got to get going. I need to coordinate with the Anchorage office and get them working on this new lead. You need anything?"

"I'm going home to pack and see about someone to repair my shattered skylight. Then I'm going on a vacation, maybe fishing in Belize."

"There's a contractor at your place right now, billed to my office. It's the least we could do. Call before you go over just to warn the agents on guard. Have a good time. We should have this cleared up in a week or two. Don't come home until then."

Back in his room at the Willard, Mercer shed his jacket as soon as he passed the threshold and had his tie undone by the time he threw his key on an oak credenza. An ornate tabletop pendulum clock stood on the large desk in the corner of the elegant room. Ten-thirty A.M.

"Screw it," Mercer said aloud and dialed room service. "I'd like two vodka gimlets and a bottle of Jack Daniel's, please, and the minibar is about to run out of ginger ale so send up a few more cans."

He cut the connection, then dialed an outside line. A moment later, Harry White answered with a rasping hello that sounded more like a curse than a greeting.

"Have fun last night?"

"Mercer, knowing you is going to kill me quicker than the cigarettes or booze."

"The women will do you in first, you lecher," Mercer teased. "How's the leg?"

"I'm going to be on the fucking peg leg for two weeks until my orthopedist can get a new prosthesis, you ungrateful bastard."

"Ungrateful, you say? How's this for ungrateful. I'll let you use my new digs for a couple of days to show my appreciation."

"Where are you?" Harry asked suspiciously.

"Willard Hotel."

"I'll be there in an hour."

"I won't be here, but I'll leave the key in an envelope with the concierge. The room number's on the key. You'll find a bottle of JD on the nightstand. Dial zero for more. There's full cable hookup, and the FBI is paying for the whole thing. You can stay until they throw you out."

"Where are you headed?"

"Back to Alaska."

"You figured out who Roger is, huh?"

"Yeah, he's trouble."

ALYESKA MARINE TERMINAL
VALDEZ, ALASKA

The light drizzle had turned into a driving slushy snow in the predawn darkness. It was merciless weather that soaked everything it touched, seeping into Lyle Hauser's pea coat as he stood on the bridge wing, a walkie-talkie clutched in his numbing fingers. In the glare of the terminal's powerful spotlights, the sky was an angry swirling mass, churned by a shrieking twenty-knot wind. The seas of Prince William Sound mirrored the ugly mood of the sky, whitecaps sliced through the slag gray water like daggers. Visibility was so poor that Hauser couldn't see the lights of Valdez nestled across the bay.

"Start of another miserable fucking day," Hauser muttered to his ship. He lifted the walkie-talkie to his lips and barked, "Status."

"Green across the board, Captain. Engines are on line, turning at sixty-nine rpms." Because of its massive size, the Hyundai engine could turn at such low revolutions and still produce over 36,000 shaft horsepower. Enough to move the oil tanker at a nominal cruising speed of sixteen knots. "All hydraulic pressures are up and stable."

"Visual inspection of the steering gear?"

"Chief says it looks fine."

While it was maritime law for the steering gear and engine

to be checked by the Chief Engineer twelve hours prior to entering harbor, Hauser wanted a second inspection to put his mind at ease about his new ship. In 1979 the 220,000 ton supertanker *Amaco Cadiz* lost hydraulic pressure to her massive rudder and slammed into the coast of France, spilling nearly her entire cargo into the English Channel. Since then, Hauser made sure that his gear was given a personal inspection by the Chief Engineer before he moved any of his charges from her berth. The visual inspection may or may not turn up an internal flaw in a weld or a slight tear in a rubber gasket, but it was better than nothing. Yet another of his many superstitions.

"First Officer?"

"Here, sir," JoAnn Riggs squawked through the walkie-talkie.

Hauser peered toward the twin towers of the manifold system located amidships, nearly six hundred fifty feet away. In the artificial daylight from the dock and at this great distance, Riggs was a tiny figure, visible only because of her bright yellow rain slicker.

"Give the order to cast off bowlines, Bridge ahead slow, please."

He watched as the massive hemp and nylon rope was slipped from the bollard and drawn into the ship by a mechanical windlass. With the last thread to land removed, the *Petromax Arctica* was free to begin her journey to southern California.

Belowdecks, the nine-cylinder diesel engine felt the strain of the water as the propeller shaft was engaged and began fighting against the ship's tremendous inertia. According to Newton's law, a body at rest tends to stay at rest unless acted upon by another force. Because this particular body weighed 255,000 dead weight tons (dwt), the force needed to move it had to be equally as large. Under her flat stern, the ferro-bronze propeller, a twisted sculpture the size of a commercial aircraft's wing, ripped at the water, torquing it so that slowly, slowly it began pulling the ship. Though located at the back of a vessel, a ship's prop works the same as that of an airplane, creating low pressure before the blades and high pressure behind them. They do not push through the water; they pull.

The pistons, each over a yard in diameter, had the power to send a shiver through a ship even the size of the *Petromax Arctica*. To Hauser, the slight rattle beneath his booted feet was a comforting feeling.

Hauser changed frequencies on his walkie-talkie before speaking again. "Alyeska control, this is the *Petro—*" He corrected himself quickly, "This is the *Southern Cross*. We are underway at 2:43 A.M., en route to el Segundo." Damn name change.

"Roger, *Southern Cross*. An ERV is standing by for escort duty."

The ERVs, or Escort Response Vessels, were one of the latest safety features incorporated at the terminal, one of the many changes following the *Exxon Valdez* disaster. Each tanker that berthed at Alyeska was shadowed by a specialized ship until it reached the Gulf of Alaska. Designed for an immediate response to oil spills, ERVs were equipped with nearly a mile of oil-absorbent material called boom that could be laid around a slick like a floating dam. They also carried drop mats for small spills and water cannons for moving oil across the surface of the Sound. The crews of the ERVs were all highly trained specialists in the field of oil spill cleanup. The 182-foot-long ship that followed the *Petromax Arctica* down the length of Valdez Bay, actually a twelve-mile-long fjord, was the newest addition to Alyeska's fleet.

The *Arctica* was on her way. Captain Hauser was the only member of the command crew with a certificate to guide a fully burdened VLCC through these dangerous waters, so he had to remain on the bridge until they cleared Prince William Sound. He moved into the bridge from the port wing and wedged himself into the master's chair, a cup of coffee at the ready. His first standing order since taking command was that fresh coffee was to be available at all times of the day or night and each pot was to be no more than thirty minutes old. He was good for at least twenty-five cups per day. He'd been able to break himself of his nicotine addiction, but his need for caffeine would never be shaken.

Already the cruise wasn't going well. The ship was running flawlessly, but Hauser was having a tough time with his crew, especially JoAnn Riggs. He had spoken to her briefly about the accident that had maimed the former Captain but still wasn't satisfied with her answers. She had been extremely evasive. The remaining officers and the Chief Engineer appeared competent, but they had not been present when Captain Albrecht had lost his arm and could add nothing to Riggs' account.

The hours dragged on without incident. The great tanker powered south, her huge bows forcing the water aside rather than cleaving through it. For a ship this big, the stormy seas of the Sound weren't even noticeable. They swirled around the hull but couldn't cause even a slight roll.

"ERV to *Southern Cross*." The radio call was the first voice on the bridge for the past two hours except for Hauser's quiet course corrections.

"This is the *Cross*. Go ahead."

"Though we can't see it, the Loran says we're at the the entrance to the Sound. You're on your own." The voice over the radio was tired.

The storm that had dumped four inches of snow aboard the tanker at Valdez had not abated. A steady white curtain was drawn against the armored windscreen of the bridge, the snow racing in one direction, then another without a moment's pause. It was impossible to discern a horizon line between the sea and sky; each was dark and angry. The tanker's bow lights looked like a dim constellation, far removed from the heated comfort of the spacious bridge.

"Roger that. This is the *Southern Cross* acknowledging that we have been escorted out of Prince William Sound," Hauser replied formally. The ship was on her own.

He waited for another ten minutes before taking his leave from the bridge, making certain that everything was functioning properly. He took a slow circuit of the huge compartment, his weathered hands clasped behind his back as he read the dozens of gauges and dials that indicated the ship's status. As he'd suspected, the ship was running in perfect order. When he'd finished his brief tour, he paused at the exit to the bridge, near the large plotting table.

"Helmsman," Hauser didn't recall the man's name from the hasty introduction just before leaving the terminal, "First Officer Riggs is eight minutes late for her watch. When she arrives, tell her this has been noted on my log. If she hasn't shown in ten minutes, call me in my cabin." Hauser had to use the bathroom so badly he couldn't wait for Riggs to replace him on watch.

Because a modern supertanker operates with just a skeleton crew of thirty, there was a great deal of space for each person aboard. Most rated a private cabin or shared with only one crewmate. The Captain, especially, was afforded every luxury. The Master's Suite was located one level below the bridge and included a large front office, called the Day Room, as well as a sleeping cabin the size of a generous apartment. The carpet was a rich blue pile, thick and soft, and the woodwork around the cabin was of the finest quality, not the cheap commercial paneling found in the other officers' quarters. There was already a stack of paperwork mounded on his desk that needed his immediate attention. He hated to admit that the job of Master had become one of administrative details rather than saltwater and hard steel. Such was the nature of the business today. Once, captains had been cut from a romantic cloth, heaped with legend and lore. Now they were nothing more than glorified managers buried under bureaucratic paper shuffling.

He kicked off his boots and shed his black worsted wool uniform jacket. He'd stuffed the tie that went with the uniform into a pocket hours before and vowed he wouldn't retrieve it until the ship was in sight of Long Beach. He'd never felt that discipline aboard ship was maintained by strict dress code. Let the crew be comfortable and they would work better had always been his style of command.

Hauser was finishing in the bathroom when the intercom chimed. "Yes, what is it?"

"Sorry to disturb you, Captain." It was the helmsman. "First Officer Riggs hasn't shown yet. I paged her cabin but got no reply."

"I'm on my way," Hauser muttered irritably. Riggs' actions had gone beyond rude. She was showing a serious dereliction of duty.

He threw on his shoes and decided against his uniform coat.

Swinging open his cabin door angrily, he plowed right into Riggs, tossing the smaller woman to the floor in the moment before she knocked. Hauser recovered from his surprise, bending to offer her a hand, a ready apology on his lips. That was when he saw the pistol on the carpeted deck where the collision had knocked it from her grip. Riggs, too, saw the weapon and struggled toward it, her arm outstretched, her fingers crabbing furiously.

He saw a look of murderous rage in her eyes and without conscious thought stepped on her wrist, pinning her hand. Riggs screamed out in startled pain, writhing to twist herself free. He was just about to demand what was happening when a burst of automatic gunfire echoed from the deck above, near or on the bridge. Hauser looked down the hall and saw an armed shadow duck from an emergency exit, dive across the hallway, and fall into the Chief Engineer's cabin.

Hauser had only moments to react, his mind churning but his instincts forcing him to flight. He couldn't risk the seconds to scoop up Riggs' pistol; he just ran. Smashing through an emergency exit, he dashed up the utilitarian stairs, his chest heaving. He paused at the top landing and pressed his ear to the door that led to a short passageway and the bridge.

Trained for and seasoned by danger his entire life, an armed conflict aboard his ship went far beyond his experience. Yet Hauser's first thoughts weren't about the situation. He thought instead of his wife, white-haired and wrinkled but still the most beautiful woman he'd ever known. Her grave expression as he boarded his flight to Alaska filled his mind and her almost disapproving gaze galvanized him into action. She'd warned him not to take this command, and suddenly he agreed with her.

Still, he was responsible for the safety of the ship and its crew. The automatic gunfire could mean only one thing. Terrorists were seizing his ship and Riggs was helping them.

Thirty seconds had elapsed since he'd first bumped into her, and already he was forming a plan. He had to get to the bridge to send a distress call.

How many more of the crew were working with them? Hauser couldn't even guess.

The door Hauser was hiding behind was halfway down the hallway that connected the bridge to the supertanker's main elevator. Once he committed himself, there would be no cover until he gained the bridge; the hall would be like a shooting gallery. Gathering the courage he never recognized he possessed, Hauser took a deep breath, threw open the door, and ran faster than he'd ever moved before.

One of the men assigned to replace the tanker's name guarded the closed doors of the elevator, the body of a crewman at his feet, shot to death as he tried to escape. He was turned away when Hauser dodged from the emergency stairwell.

The bridge was only a couple of dozen paces away. Hauser had seen the terrorist the moment he committed himself, but there was nothing he could do about it now. A dozen paces to go. The gunman finally noticed Hauser, raising his Israeli-made Uzi machine pistol at the same instant. Four paces. Hauser could hear the subdued *ping* of the radar repeater through the open bridge door. Three paces.

The hallway exploded. The Uzi opened up like a chain saw, bullets screaming, tearing into the walls, ricocheting into the bridge. The hallway filled with acidic smoke, deafening noise, and the full thirty-two rounds from the weapon's stick magazine.

The carpet caught a few of the rounds and the left side wall caught a few more but the majority raked across the control panel of the supertanker and slammed into the windscreen, creating round spiderwebs in the inch-thick glass. The helmsman was almost cut in half, two nearly separated chunks of his body crashing to the deck in a widening pool of blood. Hauser had escaped the fusillade by diving the last few paces to the bridge and rolling around the thick wooden pedestal of the chart table.

The leaden sky was still dark, night oozing onto the bridge

through the windows and portholes, gathering in the shadowed corners. A bullet had cut a wire somewhere in the tangled maze behind the controls, killing the lights with a blue arc of electricity as the system shorted. The emergency lights kicked on, and an alarm pierced the air shrilly. The murky bridge smelled of smoke, ozone, and blood.

Hauser had managed to gain a few seconds, but he hadn't escaped yet. There were two separate emergency distress systems located on the bridge console, but he didn't have time to reach either of them. His only choice was to get out onto the flying bridge where the international orange canister of the EPIRB sat in its bin. If he could reach it and toss it over the side of the vessel, the contact with the saltwater would activate the system and send a distress call over a satellite uplink. He'd worry about his options after that.

Forcing himself to ignore the helmsman's corpse, he crawled toward the insulated door to the flying bridge, his arms shaking so badly that they almost couldn't take his body weight. The rank sweat of fear slicked his body, bathing him in a clammy chill. Although he'd spent most of his adult life aboard supertankers, he'd never fully appreciated how wide they were until he was forced to crawl across the bridge of one, the fear of an assassin's bullet urging him onward.

He made it to the door, his body tensed for the inevitable shot in the back, but it didn't come. He couldn't understand what was delaying them. He stretched up from the floor, reaching for the handle to temporary freedom when an unfamiliar voice called out sharply.

"Stop where you are."

Hauser ignored the order. With a burst of adrenaline he undogged the door, throwing his weight against the icy wind that raced across the ship. He fell out onto the snow-covered flying bridge. A pistol cracked three times in rapid succession, the shots landing just inches from Hauser's slithering form, kicking up tiny geysers of snow and creating glowing hot spots on the metal deck that smelled of burned steel. He moved as fast as he could but with a tired resignation. The flying bridge was a dead end. He was trapped.

The outside visibility was only about thirty feet. Snow,

sleet, and freezing rain slanted against him, forced by nature and the movement of the ship into a forty-knot gale. He wasn't dressed for this kind of weather; the cold and wet soaked through his uniform shirt, and only fear kept him from shivering to death. Hauser knew that he wouldn't last more than fifteen minutes before hypothermia robbed him of control over his own body. The pistol roared again, the bullet fired blindly into the twisting storm but passing close enough to Hauser to make him duck. Hypothermia wouldn't have the time to kill him.

Lyle Hauser had never considered himself a brave man. True, he had done things that others wouldn't, like jumping aboard a burning barge when he was twenty to save a deckhand trapped by the flames. He had always just done whatever he felt was necessary. If others saw his acts as brave and heroic, well, that was up to them. Hauser was just doing his job.

His job right now was surviving. There was only one option, and it would take all the bravery he possessed. He raced to the end of the bridge wing and stopped to pick up the two-and-a-half-foot-tall canister of the EPIRB, but it was gone, the brackets empty. Riggs must have removed it as a precaution when she began taking the vessel. Out of time, Hauser looked over the chest-high railing of the flying bridge. All he saw below was a curtain of white, but somewhere underneath his position was the balcony of the second deck, no more than fifteen feet away. If he could land on that narrow perch, he had a chance of escaping, finding a place to hole up for a while and consider his next move. But if he missed the scant promenade that surrounded the next level down, the main deck was a drop of forty feet, and if he missed that, the North Pacific would kill him the moment he hit.

He stood just above where the flying bridge cantilevered over the side of the vessel. He had to get closer to the center of the tanker before he could jump, which meant getting closer to the men trying to kill him. They were on the bridge, weapons drawn, bright eyes peering into the storm for his shadow to come within range.

He launched himself back down the narrow walkway, his

boots finding little purchase on the slick decking. He suppressed a desire to shout as he ran, to give voice to the fear that tore at him like the wind stinging his face. Just as he discerned the red glow spilling from the emergency lights on the bridge, he gathered himself and leaped up to the six-inch-wide railing, scrambling with feet and hands and chest, breaking stride for only a second. Ignoring the oblivion that sucked at him from below, he ran on, pushing each stride when he felt his feet sliding off the ice-encrusted railing.

The armed figure looming out of the snowy night was startled by Hauser's unusual position. The man's weapon was held low, ready for a frontal charge; not this tenuous rush at the level of his shoulder. The terrorist began to twist, raising his pistol in a movement as graceful as ballet. Hauser chanced two more paces, stretching himself too far on the last step so that when he went over the railing it was more of a fall than a leap. In an instant, he'd vanished.

On the bridge, JoAnn Riggs took immediate charge of the pandemonium. There should have been no need for violence when taking the ship from the unarmed crew, but it hadn't worked as planned. Two crewmen were dead, Hauser was missing, and the bridge was virtually destroyed. Riggs' first act was to cut the alarm klaxons and return the lighting to its normal nighttime luminance. One of the terrorists who'd stormed onto the bridge following the gunfire had already extinguished an electrical fire below the helmsman's station, and two more had removed the corpse to the other flying bridge. Riggs gave orders that the Chief Engineer, the electrician, and a replacement helmsman be brought up from the crew's mess where they were being held.

She didn't try to hide her new position of authority. She ordered both crew and terrorists with equal command. At the back of the room, the terrorists watched impassively as Riggs mustered her crew into cleaning up the mess and reestablishing control of the vessel.

Everyone on the bridge paused for a moment when the door to the flying bridge opened with a blast of raw arctic air. The leader of the terrorists, a granite-faced man known only as Wolf, stepped out of the night. The crew looked at him, silently wondering what this new threat represented. Riggs and the others regarded him expectantly.

Riggs broke the tight silence. "Did you get him?"

Wolf shook the snow from his dark hair and slid the big Sig Sauer pistol back into its nylon combat harness. He spoke with a German accent, his voice brutal and clipped. "He tried to rush me by climbing onto the railing, but he never made it past. He lost his footing and went over the edge."

"How far down the bridge wing were you?" Riggs asked nervously.

"Nearly halfway. He either landed in the water or fell all the way to the main deck."

"Take some men and make sure. He can't be allowed to live." She turned back to her crew, ignoring their accusing glances. It was clear to them that Riggs was discussing their new captain.

Twenty minutes later, Wolf returned with three of his men, snow clinging to them like glittering jewels. If the weather had made them uncomfortable, they gave no outward sign. When they brushed themselves off, they did it more out of annoyance than discomfort, as if the near-freezing night wasn't even worth their attention. Riggs knew that they were former East German Special Forces and had trained for conditions much worse than those lashing the supertanker.

"Well?"

"We found no sign of him. The wind and the heat of the oil in the tanks have removed all of the snow on the main deck, so there were no footprints, but a man couldn't have fallen that far without leaving a blood trail if he crawled away. He must have missed the ship and gone overboard."

"Good, one less thing to worry about." Riggs sounded relieved.

"How bad is it?" Wolf nodded at the partially dismantled controls.

The electrician and an assistant were crawling under the consoles. Only their backsides were visible; their heads and shoulders were buried in the wires, circuit boards, and microchips that kept the tanker running.

"So far, it's not too good. The radar is out permanently, a

round shattered the cathode-ray tube and the digital image processor. It's a complete write-off. We have helm control, but the throttles can be engaged only from the engine room. We can live with that. Our biggest problem is the internal pumps. When the control panel was shot up, a power surge affected the pump control room and knocked out most of the systems. Monitors, gas pressure and ratio gauges, and the pump controls themselves were all severely damaged. We can't shift the oil within the baffles of the main tanks to maintain proper trim, nor can we tell if the fumes above the ullage line are dangerous. The pumps themselves are fine, but the tank sensors are off-line. We have no way to tell how much oil is in each tank without visual inspections."

Both Riggs and Wolf knew the importance of this particular system for maintaining control of the ship. Without the pumps, the *Arctica* could tear herself apart if they encountered rough seas. And when they reached their ultimate destination, the pumps would be critical to the success of their mission.

"Can the damage be repaired?"

"How should I know, I'm not an engineer," Riggs snapped. "Your trigger-happy soldier boy really fucked us up."

"He will be disciplined." Wolf ignored her anger.

"Lot of good that's going to do us," Riggs seethed. "I should have him locked in the mess room with the rest of the crew, but we may need him before this voyage is over." Riggs looked at Wolf pointedly. "But when his phase is done, I want him killed."

"He is under my command."

Riggs' dark expression deepened. "And you are under mine."

An ironic smirk curled Wolf's cruelly handsome face. "Yes, sir."

THE UNITED
ARAB EMIRATES

Below the whirling blades of the Aerospatiale Gazelle helicopter, the desert was stirred into a vicious sandstorm that chased the speeding machine like a relentless shadow. The military chopper was flying no more than forty feet off the desert floor, the pilot pouring all of his concentration into keeping the craft from smearing against the earth. He left the tricky navigation to the copilot seated at his right.

The sun was just lifting over the far horizon, but still the brighter stars could be seen against the deep blue sky. The land below was dark, a featureless plane of sand and rocks. Only to their right was the endless vista broken. Fifty miles distant and growing out of the night were the Hajar Mountains, jagged ramparts protecting the Arabian Gulf from the eternal pressure of the empty desert.

Colonel Wayne Bigelow lit a cigarette and regarded the other passenger with paternal fondness. He'd had a good hand in raising him from a callow youth into a fine man. Bigelow, a graduate of Sandhurst and an old Middle East hand, had lived in the Gulf for most of his life, both as a member of the British occupying forces and later as military adviser to the Emirates' Crown Prince. That post was more honorary than functional. The old man just liked having Bigelow around to tell war stories. The Crown Prince often remarked that Bigelow should have been alive when T. E. Lawrence was riding with old Faisal against the Turks. The era suited him better. Bigelow had never argued the point.

Seated next to him in the stripped-down Gazelle was Khalid Khuddari, another man suited for an earlier time but just as adept in this one. Bigelow knew how remarkable it was that Khuddari had achieved his current position, since he'd not been born into the royal family. Secretly, the Crown Prince had confided in Bigelow that he loved Khuddari more than his own sons, three of whom lived in Europe with women who seemed to need cash infusions for sustenance.

Bigelow had been present when Khalid's father had come in from the desert with his son and reminded the Crown Prince of his promise to look after the boy in exchange for the Bedouin's oath of loyalty. The Crown Prince, a man true to his word, welcomed the young Khalid into his home. Bigelow had had the good fortune of becoming one of Khalid's many tutors, a chore he relished simply because the boy was so bright and dedicated. When he looked at the man Khalid had become a quarter century later, he felt he could indulge in a little pride. A lifelong bachelor, Bigelow saw Khalid as the son he wished he'd had.

"Don't look so serious. All of the hard work is finished," Bigelow shouted over the roar of the turboshaft engine over their heads. His Arabic was flawless.

Khuddari couldn't be brought out of his dark mood. "I'm afraid that the hard work is just about to begin."

"If the Crown Prince finds out what we're doing, we'll have more to worry about than hard work," Bigelow said pointedly.

The chopper was well into Ajmani airspace without authorization. While the seven Sheikdoms that made up the United Arab Emirates were considered one country by the international community, each member maintained a great deal of sovereignty over its own portion of the desert. By flying into Ajman, Khuddari and Bigelow were in effect crossing a national boundary without prior notice. Their actions could easily be labeled an invasion.

"So tell me how you found it," Khalid invited.

Bigelow leaned toward the younger man so they could speak at a more conversational volume. Khuddari had access to an executive chopper, one outfitted with the latest silencing equipment so that the interior was as quiet as a luxury automobile, but they had agreed this machine was better suited for the trip into the desert.

"Nothing to it, really. There were no roads leading this far out from the city of Ajman so everything had to be brought to the facility by helicopter, usually at night. I had a man at the airport watching them come and go from dusk until dawn. Since we couldn't follow one of their choppers without giving ourselves away, I called in an old favor. An Air Force adviser in Saudi Arabia and I spent four months together as peace-keepers on Cyprus in '64. I saved his life during the August ninth bombings. Anyway, last night I called him just before another of Rufti's helicopter went into the desert. He had one of the AWACS planes the Saudis bought from the Yanks divert from its normal patrol of the Iraqi boarder and take a quick peek our way."

"And?"

"The coordinates he gave us were right on. Our assault team found the camp four hours ago, as easily as you find the naughty bits between a whore's thighs."

"What did you find?" Khalid asked expectantly.

The intercom squawked as the pilot interrupted their conversation. "ETA two minutes."

"Wait and you'll see for yourself." Bigelow stroked his mustache, sitting back in his seat.

The chopper thundered over a low dune, the skids nearly ripping off the top of the sand wave. The desert before them was bright enough to see the smoking ruins a few miles ahead. The ground had been scorched black by a blazing fire, a small ring of ash on the clear white sand. Tendrils of smoke still lifted into the shimmering sky.

Following the arm motions of one of Bigelow's troopers who'd scouted a solid landing spot, the helicopter landed a few hundred yards short of the camp. Khuddari and Bigelow jumped down lightly, bending low to avoid the spinning rotor. Both were dressed in desert camouflage but only Bigelow was armed, a heavy Webley Mark VI revolver buckled around his thick waist. The heat was on the rise, and beads of sweat blistered Bigelow's ruddy face by the time they were halfway to the destroyed camp, yet he continued to walk easily over the loose sand, matching Khuddari's long-legged pace.

The camp had sat in a natural bowl in the desert, a circular depression ringed by heaped sand dunes like the walls of an earthen castle. The center of the camp had been some sort of parade ground or training area; surrounding it were the remains of dozens of tents, their charred poles thrusting up like the empty ribs of some prehistoric monster. Steel scaffolds littered the parade ground, the struts blackened by fire. It was obvious that there had been a purpose to their original placement, but they now looked like girders from an Erector Set that had been tossed aside by a vengeful child. Sand was already building up against their windward edges. The two camouflaged Toyota Land Cruisers used by Bigelow's soldiers were parked at the camp's perimeter, their drivers guarding them with roof-mounted fifty-caliber machine guns.

"How did he know?" Khuddari hissed, his dark eyes gazing at the desolation around him. "How the hell did that fat bastard know?"

"Those last helicopter flights were not to resupply the base. They were already pulling out. My agent was too far from the airport to tell the difference. As near as we can tell, the place was torched early last night." It was obvious from Bigelow's tone that he hated admitting they'd been too late, but regrets would do them no good. "However, to clear out a camp of this size, they must have started pulling out a few days before you spoke to Rufti."

"For the love of Allah, he knew I was on to him already. Have your men found anything to give us an idea of what Rufti was doing out here?"

"Nothing yet." Bigelow kicked at a small pile of burned canvas on the ground at their feet. "But the scaffolds remind me of my training days with the Special Air Service. The SAS used these sorts of things to simulate buildings, draping them with cloth with squares cut out for windows. It was a cheap and simple way to train for urban antiterrorist actions. I'd bet what's left of my pension that Rufti's men did the same thing here."

Khuddari nodded and took a longer look at the frameworks. If they represented a street corner or park that he knew, he didn't recognize it. Bigelow shrugged when Khuddari shot him an inquiring glance.

"For all I know, it could be the street corner in Manchester where I grew up." Bigelow spat into the sand.

"Rufti doesn't have the imagination for something outside of the UAE. This must represent a street in Abu Dhabi City. But I don't think there's any way to tell which."

"What should we do?"

Before Khuddari could answer, one of Bigelow's troopers called to them. He was kneeling off to the right of the parade ground, far from the cluster of tents. His bright teeth were visible as he smiled under a black, drooping mustache. Bigelow and Khuddari were at his side in an instant, peering over his shoulder at what he'd found in the sand.

Bigelow picked up the item and examined it as critically as a master jeweler peering into a diamond before making the critical first cut.

"Nine-millimeter Parabellum casing," he said at once. "There's an FIO stamp on the head, which means it was manufactured by Fiocci in Italy. The primer was flattened when it was fired, so we can assume it was hot loaded. By the depth of the bullet sealant left inside the casing, I'd guess it was loaded with 124-grain bullets and Winchester AA7 powder, about nine grains or so considering the distortion."

"Can you tell what type of gun it was fired from?"

"Not without a laboratory and a couple weeks. It could have been anything from a Luger to an Uzi." Bigelow slipped the spent cartridge into the breast pocket of his fatigues. "I can tell you it was fired at least a few weeks ago; there's no trace of a cordite smell to it at all. Christ, the bloody thing could have been here since World War Two."

"I wish." Khuddari turned away and started back for the helicopter, Bigelow closing on his heels quickly. "Tell your men to head home, we've been here long enough. I don't think we'll learn anything else."

Bigelow whistled shrilly, and immediately his Sergeant Major acknowledged the order to pull out by calling to his men. The troops started for the two desert vehicles, weapons at the ready, a beautifully executed tactical withdrawal. Bigelow's men were well drilled and disciplined, like the man who'd trained them.

The Gazelle's rotor was already turning lazily as they approached, the turbine just beginning to build up to an ear-splitting whine. The two men vaulted into the cabin and buckled their seat belts. After a few moments' pause, the French-built helicopter lifted into the air. The rotor's down force threw up a cloud of dust that obliterated any sign that it had landed. Khuddari and Bigelow were quiet during the flight home, each respecting the contemplative silence of the other. Only after they were safely back in Abu Dhabi airspace did the younger man speak.

"Rufti left for London this morning to act as an observer at the OPEC meetings that start in two days. His men are obviously finished training for whatever they are planning, so I'm sure they'll strike soon. Rufti's gutless enough not to be around when the bullets start to fly."

"You're convinced that they're planning some sort of assault?"

"It's obvious. We just don't know the target. I have an audience with the Crown Prince this afternoon, and I'm going to tell him everything we've found. I'm also going to tell him that I'm not going to the meeting in England."

"Do you think that's a good idea? Your not attending won't look good to the rest of the family. This is the first Cartel meeting since you became Petroleum Minister."

"I don't give a damn about that," Khuddari snapped. "This is more important than my career. I can't afford to be in some boardroom when Rufti strikes. I should have killed the fat *Lootee* when I had the chance."

"We'll get the buggerer, mark my words."

Abu Dhabi City spread below them as the chopper flew. Only a handful of buildings were older than twenty-five years; prestressed concrete and smoked glass had replaced traditional stone architecture as the nation struggled into the twenty-first century. Not long ago men here would have fought to the death over the theft of a goat or an insult to a family member, and that ruthlessness still molded the people of the Gulf. But now, with petrodollars pushing the stakes to the highest levels, a rivalry would end not with just a single death but hundreds or possibly thousands. Rufti was working to destabilize the confederation of the UAE, one that was shaky at best. He had put a lot of money and effort into his plan, and whatever his target, Khuddari knew it could mean the end of the Emirates as a single country.

Oil had been the salvation of the nation, but perhaps the ceaseless sawing of the horse-head wells spread throughout the land were pounding out her death knell too. The money that the elite of the UAE possessed had not tempered their unyielding nature and, in fact, had fueled their ability to exercise it. Rufti's greed might very well sever the vital artery of oil that allowed him to exist.

Khuddari had to admit that if Rufti was planning a coup, he couldn't have selected a better time. The Crown Prince was at odds with most of the Supreme Federal Council, composed of the six rulers of the other Emirates, and with the Council of Ministers, the legislative arm of the nation. The schisms stemmed from the American's announcement to phase out all oil imports within ten years. That act could cripple the money-based power structure of the Emirates, weakening the Prince's position so that a coup might be seen as a beneficial act rather than one of naked aggression. The political climate was ripe for a change to face this new, uncertain future, and Rufti could be in the perfect place to exploit it. Khalid hoped that his thin evidence was enough to convince the Crown Prince that he and the nation were in danger, but no matter how credible Khuddari was in the Sovereign's eyes, a lone shell casing and a deep suspicion weren't much. He feared that his pleas would fall on deaf ears.

He craned his head as he looked out the window at the city below. This close to shore, the water of the Gulf was an iridescent aquamarine, a dazzling shade more suited for neon signs than nature. Because the water was only ten fathoms deep and nearly one hundred degrees, there was little life to cloud the sea. An empty supertanker rode high just where the Gulf turned darker and deeper, her upper deck painted a dull oxide red that matched the twenty feet of her underbelly that showed below her Plimsoll line. At this distance, Khalid couldn't read the name on her stern, but the activity of the small boats cruising around the monstrous ship indicated that she was hove to for repairs.

He turned away, absently wondering why the vessel wasn't at the huge new shipyard at Port Rashid near Dubai City. The Gazelle was coming in for her landing, and he didn't give the tanker another thought.

THE RICHARDSON HIGHWAY NORTH OF VALDEZ, ALASKA

The Richardson Highway, arguably one of the most beautiful stretches of road in the world, parallels the Teikel River as it gouges its way through a rocky canyon. The road boasts no fewer than twenty-five scenic overviews within the first forty miles north of Valdez. At points, the valley was barely wide enough to allow the river and two lanes of traffic; other times it opened dramatically into alpine meadows and side valleys with spectacular views of the Chugach Mountains and the Worthington Glacier. The highway also traversed Thompson Pass, an area fabled for holding all three national records for snowfall—seasonally, monthly, and for a twenty-four-hour period. On a single day in 1955, more than five feet of snow had covered on the top of the twenty-six-hundred-foot pass. But there would be no records tonight. A storm was dropping snow, but rain fell with it, creating a frigid slurry that squirted from under the heavy lugged tires of a fuel tanker truck as it sped north.

The beauty of the ride was lost on the driver of the eighteen-wheeled tractor trailer; the truck's powerful headlamps couldn't penetrate deep enough into the storm to reveal the towering cliffs over his head or the vistas to the left and right. Occasionally, one of the many waterfalls not yet frozen by the unusually frigid weather flashed by like a white smear against the black night, but he had eyes only for the dark ribbon spread before his truck.

Brock Holt was not a happy man despite the country music blaring from the cab's eight speakers. The conditions of the road didn't bother him too much. To a native of Prince William Sound, a storm like this was nothing but a mild nuisance. What bothered him was the full load of Petromax gasoline, nearly eight thousand gallons, in the tanker behind him. He hadn't been scheduled to make the run from the Anchorage depot for another two days, but the influx of media had supposedly emptied the service stations around Valdez. His dispatcher had assured him the early run was necessary, yet when he arrived at the Petromax stations, he found that they hadn't called for him. In fact, they probably wouldn't need the gas from his regular delivery either.

The stations' owners complained that an environmental group had targeted them for a series of protests and boycotts. While the other stations in town were doing a brisk business, collectively Petromax hadn't sold more than fifty gallons all week. The dispatcher must have assumed that since the other stations were pumping, so was Petromax. "Snafu," Holt cursed as he began the long haul back north, anxious to chew out his dispatcher, Hank Kelso.

Since he was missing a repeat of the Country Music Awards on cable, Holt soothed himself by selecting another disc on the ten-disc CD changer in the cab. His only consolation, thin as it was, was that traffic on a night like this was nearly nonexistent. He rolled the big diesel as fast as he dared in the vain hope that he could catch the show's big finale just before midnight.

ON the downhill side of Thompson Pass, in a forlorn gravel turnoff overlooking the Worthington Glacier thirty miles from Valdez, a yellow Range Rover sat as quiet as the storm, its lights off and its engine idling just enough for the heaters to work. The only indication that the luxury vehicle was occupied was the frosting of the passengers' breath that smoked the windscreen and side windows. The custom-painted Rover had been there so long that its tire tracks had been obliterated by the continuous snowfall.

Two of the three men in the vehicle had fidgeted away the past two hours, shifting constantly in the plush leather seats, sighing occasionally and staring at the cellular phone mounted under the dash in the hope that it would ring. The third man, the driver, sat calmly watching the storm, following individual drifting flakes as if they needed his permission to land. The intensity of his blue eyes was almost enough to melt snowflakes before they touched the ground.

His hands, powerful and deeply tanned, rested on the steering wheel, the occasional tap of his index finger betraying the anxiety he felt. His handsome face was as still as the glacier to their left. While the other two men sported layers of wool, nylon, and Gore-Tex, he wore only a Norwegian roll-neck fisherman's sweater and a pair of jeans. His companions shivered in the cab of the Rover and muttered complaints, but he didn't even feel the cold. He saw the low temperature as something to be embraced rather than warded off.

Nature, he thought, was not meant to be a struggle; it was to be enjoyed. To fight it only served to antagonize it and force it to oppose that much more. He'd often said that every time we attempt to show dominion over nature, she counters, even stronger than before. To him, it made more sense to accept its elemental life force and revel in its magnificence.

He'd tried to teach that to his people, but few really understood. True, some would join him when he swam in subarctic water or trekked through searing deserts, but they did it more out of sheer will than in communion. To them, it was a means of proving that they could endure the worst that nature possessed. They faced the elements not as its vassal but as an equal. He saw his actions as the highest form of worship. To stand before a natural force was to stand before God Himself.

The only other person who truly understood was Aggie. She saw nature as he did. The crashing waves of a winter storm on a forlorn coast or an intense rain that made it impossible to breathe were forces that she could appreciate. She saw these things as the highest expression of perfection. Let others stand in awe before a Picasso or the Sistine Chapel. These were man-made and thus inherently flawed. They paled before the perfect beauty of a tropical sunset or a coral reef. Aggie believed him when he said that humanity had changed so much from our original intentions that we had become a danger to the planet. She didn't balk when he said that if the end of our existence was the price to pay to save the earth, then so be it.

The ring of the phone was just a quiet chirp, but the men in the Rover started at the sound. They'd been waiting two long hours for it. There was no need to answer the call. Their lookout had already hung up and was on his way back to Valdez from his position atop Thompson Pass.

They didn't speak as they exited the vehicle, stretching for a moment to work out the kinks from so many hours of immobility. The driver opened the back door of the truck, revealing the five-gallon red plastic jerry cans that they'd loaded in Valdez. Each can weighed thirty-five pounds, and as each man heaved two from the cargo deck, only the driver didn't stagger or struggle with his burden.

The storm whipped at them without mercy, snow and wind battering all three as they crossed the parking area, heading for the shoulder of Richardson Highway. They had chosen this location for two reasons. It was the steepest part of the descent from the top of the pass, and the road curved sharply along the precipitous bank of the Teikel River, twenty-five feet below.

Their actions were well planned and carried out with a minimum of confusion. The lookout's call confirmed that the Petromax tanker truck had just reached the pinnacle of Thompson Pass and that no other traffic was headed their way. Each man emptied his cans of water onto the road in a precise area, so that a maximum amount of the highway was soon covered with a thin sheet of invisible black ice. This alone would not guarantee that the truck would skid out of control, so they had to be back in the Rover before the tractor trailer appeared.

"Hurry up," the driver urged, though he knew by earlier timed tests that they had another few minutes.

The last can was emptied, the water rushed down the inclined road for a moment before slowing to the pace of molasses as it froze. The three men hurried to the Rover, the driver shifting the idling vehicle into gear as he settled in the seat. His two companions muttered about the weather and brushed themselves off, but a childlike, expectant tension shone on their youthful faces. They'd just pulled off a bit of mischief and gotten away with it. To them, it all seemed a game.

The driver, older by fifteen years and wiser by a couple of centuries, knew what was at stake. He understood fully what they had just done and silently wished that they could do it more often.

BROCK Holt eased the truck over the top of the pass and worked the transmission up through a few gears. He'd driven this road so many times in the past six years that he knew he wouldn't need to downshift for another mile and a half, until the road really started to descend into the gorge. The storm had intensified since he'd left Valdez, but it still wasn't strong enough to concern him. He kept one hand on the wheel as he slid a stick of chewing gum from the pack he'd left on the center console. His heavily bearded jaws jumped rhythmically as he chomped on the gum and mumbled the words to the song belting from the stereo. The digital clock on the dash told him that he just might make it to Anchorage in time to see the finish of his show on the small black-and-white TV in Hank Kelso's office.

The road started to drop away, and Brock downshifted, the big diesel bellowing at the extra strain of slowing the rig. The steering wheel was a living creature under his hands, twisting and writhing as he guided the eighteen-wheeler off of Thompson Pass. As the road dipped farther, he dropped one more gear, slowing even more, cautiously easing the truck along the road. When the front wheels hit the black ice, he was traveling slowly enough to correct for the short slide, but the patch was much larger than anything he'd ever experienced before.

The cab began losing its grip on the road, Holt could feel

the wheels spinning uselessly against the slick surface, yet he had no choice but to turn the wheel to take the corner coming at him dangerously fast. He feathered the brakes and shifted down into low range, using the engine to gain just enough traction to keep the rig on the road. As the truck began to respond, he became aware that his heart had moved from his chest and was now pounding in his throat. For the barest fraction of a second, he'd almost lost the rig, but he'd gathered the truck like a wild horse bucking at the reins.

That's when he saw the yellow Range Rover pulling out of an overlook and diving straight into his path.

He mashed his foot against the brake, slamming the pedal against its stop in a purely reflexive act. Even as he cursed the idiot in the other vehicle, he could feel his rig losing control once again. The massive trailer and its forward movement was a force that the cab could not overcome. The rig began to jackknife, the trailer pushing the truck out to the side of the road in an obtuse angle. Just as quickly as the Range Rover had jumped into his path, it dove out of the way of the runaway tractor trailer. But it was too late for Brock Holt.

The cab was now perpendicular to the trailer, hurtling down the icy road in the grip of gravity, wheels slipping against the icy tarmac. The guardrail separating the highway from the deadly drop to the river was just a narrow band of steel, puny compared to the force of the truck. Brock tried to steer into the skid and once again put the cab in front, but the trailer, with its twenty-eight tons of gasoline, pushed remorselessly and could not be controlled. The front fender of the cab now touched the rounded side of the tanker as it hurtled down the road.

In a last-ditch effort, Brock Holt hit the accelerator, hoping he could whip the trailer around, setting the rig back in tandem. His gambit almost paid off. The drive wheels were out of the ice-covered lane and began to pull against the trailer, dragging it slowly under control. Had the curve been another hundred feet away, he would have made it. The back of the cab hit the guardrail first, buckling the metal so badly that when the trailer hit an instant later, the whole section let go.

With a rending scream, the eighteen-wheeler went over the edge, the tangled guardrail twisting around the truck's wheels. The rig rolled once, the top of the cab crushing against a rocky outcrop, the trailer splitting open like a wildflower bloom. The truck rolled again, spraying gasoline in a forty-foot Catherine wheel that splashed against the dark rocks and pelted the river like machine gun fire. The roll ended when the two halves of the rig locked together and the whole eighty-eight-thousand-pound mass slid down to the inky river, gouging a huge furrow into the earth.

The two passengers in the Rover sprang for their doors, but the driver halted them with a sharp command. He slid the vehicle into gear and slowly backed out of the parking lot until all four wheels were firmly on the Richardson Highway and then, just as carefully, drove forward again, guiding the Rover over its own tire tracks, making it look as though they'd just pulled into the lot.

"Flask," he said as he killed the ignition.

The passenger in the backseat twisted as he pulled a silver hip flask from his parka. He carefully poured a few ounces of its acrid contents into each of the six jerry cans before returning it to his pocket. It took only a few shakes to coat the insides of the plastic jugs.

"Remember the scenario," the driver cautioned. "We just witnessed a horrible accident and we're the first people on the scene. Make sure your footprints in the snow show our urgency to help the driver of the tanker truck. Now let's go."

They dove from the Range Rover, dragging their feet slightly as if in shock and then began running across the road to the smashed guardrail. The first nauseating waves of gasoline fumes cloyed their throats when they were still fifty yards from the precipice. At the edge, it looked as though a giant ax had struck the earth; rocks, loose dirt, and the tenacious vegetation that grew along the slope had been thrown aside by the hurtling truck.

The rig lay halfway in the swift river, like a giant overturned beetle. The trailer resembled the glossy carapace, and the mangled wheels turning on their bent axles twitched like limbs. Under the beams of the powerful flashlights all three carried, the river downstream of the destroyed truck was rainbowed by the spreading slick of gasoline pouring from the huge tank. From their vantage point, they couldn't see the fate of the truck driver, the cab was too dim even for the four-cell Maglites.

"Make sure he's dead," the driver said, meaning that if the driver had miraculously survived, he was to be killed, not rescued. "I'll go call the police."

He trudged back to the Rover, focusing his flashlight on the emblem painted on its front door. The seal depicted a very detailed globe, each continent and coastline rendered almost perfectly, yet the world was cut up into segments and laid back like the skin of an orange. It was a haunting image showing both reverence for the subject while demonstrating a concern for its future. Beneath it, in tall block letters, was written PEAL. He dialed 911. The connection to the police station in Valdez took only a moment.

"Hello, my name is Dr. Jan Voerhoven. I've just witnessed an accident on the Richardson Highway."

It took an hour for the police to arrive, two patrol cars and a single ambulance. Voerhoven had assured the authorities that there was no need for urgency since no one had survived the crash. Four satellite uplink trucks roared into the parking lot only moments after the police, each van emblazoned with the logotype of a television network. Voerhoven smiled tightly when he saw the first of the vans arrive. Perfect. The media had been listening to police scanners, as he knew they would.

The police were thorough with their questions, considering PEAL's global reputation. Two patrolmen took the time to follow their tire tracks from the highway to where the Rover had parked and studied the footprints across the snow. They seemed satisfied with Voerhoven's explanation that they had been driving to Valdez when they saw the tanker truck lose control.

The officer in charge, a heavy lump of a man with a red nose that might or might not have been caused by the cold, told one of Voerhoven's men to open all six jerry cans in the back of the Rover. He sniffed each one to confirm that the

PEAL vehicle carried its own extra fuel, an environmentally friendly blend of gasoline and ethanol that hadn't been commercially available since the 1970s gas crisis. The few ounces of gasohol poured from the flask were pungent enough to convince him that the cans had once been filled with the alternative fuel.

Cautious and considerate attention to detail had always been Voerhoven's way of ensuring that PEAL, though always under suspicion, was rarely found responsible for its actions.

As soon as the police had finished with him, Voerhoven sent his two companions back to the Rover while he went to meet the members of the press who were arrayed like a choir awaiting its conductor.

"This has all been rather difficult for me, so I don't have any sort of prepared statement, yet I'm sure you all have a number of questions." When he spoke, his slight accent and his naturally compelling voice created an instant aura of trust. His blue eyes were captivating under the harsh glare of the cameras' klieg lights.

"Given that PEAL's latest target of protest is Petromax Oil, do you think it ironic that you were the person to discover this accident?" This from a local reporter, not one of the network heavy hitters who'd been shouted down by the woman's grating voice.

"Ironic? I think it's tragic that anyone has to see what happened here tonight." He dismissed her summarily, then pointed to a CNN weekend anchor who'd been giving PEAL favorable coverage in the weeks since their ship, *Hope*, had entered Prince William Sound.

"Doctor, what is your personal reaction to what happened tonight and what is the official reaction from your organization?"

As he'd expected, the CNN reporter had just given Voerhoven the step he needed to mount his soapbox.

"How does it make me feel? To be honest, it scares the hell out of me. The driver of that truck was traveling much too fast for these conditions, indicative of the negligent attitude of the company that employed him. Petromax Oil established tonight that they can't be trusted to transport a few thousand gallons of gasoline on a well-traveled highway, yet they are about to pump millions of barrels of crude through the pristine environment of the Arctic Wildlife Refuge.

"Tonight, Petromax spoiled just a small portion of a glacial river that nature will be able to clean, but what happens when this very same company has a much more serious accident on the North Slope? The irresponsibility of one man has consequences that we can cope with, but the actions of the company he represents will be with us far into the future. When Petromax and the other oil companies turn the Refuge into a reeking plain of sludge, all the finger pointing in the world won't clean it up.

"As to the official position of PEAL, we are here to make sure that never comes to pass." Voerhoven nodded to another nationally recognized reporter.

"When the President announced that he would suspend oil imports, PEAL had no official comment, yet since the opening of the Arctic Wildlife Refuge, your organization has been extremely vocal on the subject. Would you care to comment?"

Voerhoven smiled, his eyes bright with humor. "The one announcement followed so closely after the other that we didn't have time to react." The members of the press chuckled with him. "Of course, we applaud the suspension of oil imports. Getting just one supertanker off the oceans is a major victory. And we fully support the search for alternative energy. But only a few weeks after the President's speech, we see what we have to pay for that victory. By so quickly capitulating to the power of the oil lobby, the President has shown that he really doesn't have a serious commitment to the environment. When his ten-year deadline is up and we still don't have a viable alternative energy source, you can believe that the oil companies will be there, eager to peddle their poison again."

"What about the research to be carried out by the Johnston Group, founded by the president of Petromax Oil, whose sole aim is to find a solution to the world's oil dependency?"

Voerhoven's eyes drilled into the reporter who'd asked the question. "They'll make a lot of noise, promising that they're on the verge of a great discovery, but in ten years' time they'll have nothing to show us, and the Johnston Group will quietly close their doors. Max Johnston will be right back in the oil business."

The bitterness of Voerhoven's answer prompted an even more challenging follow-up from the same journalist. "How do you respond to the accusation that PEAL is a band of so-called eco-terrorists?"

"You call my organization a band of eco-terrorists?" Voerhoven raged. "Did you get a close look at the truck that went over the guardrail, pouring thousands of gallons of gasoline into that river? It doesn't say PEAL on the side of the trailer; it says Petromax Oil. Don't call me a terrorist when they are the ones working to destroy the planet."

"Dr. Voerhoven, you know what I mean. Many feel that the tactics used by PEAL to promote global environmental awareness are so extreme they border on terrorist acts."

"Why is it when someone fights for a belief that you disagree with, he is called a terrorist, yet when you are sympathetic to his cause, he's referred to as a freedom fighter?" Voerhoven challenged. "In today's world, context no longer determines meaning. Today it's all a matter of perception. Are the goals and methods of PEAL extreme? To some, I'm sure that they are, but to call us terrorists is to place yourself in opposition to the environment. If you believe the health of our planet isn't worth fighting for, then yes, we are eco-terrorists. But to those who see our cause as just and our methods as necessary, we are freedom fighters, engaged in a war to save the very place that gave us life.

"To win this war, we must win each and every battle. Alaska is about to face a massive assault by oil companies fixed on making a quick profit, and PEAL is here to lend a hand in her defense. But as we saw here tonight, nature is not entirely defenseless. She has made a clear statement. The oil companies and their eagerness to destroy will not be tolerated." Voerhoven turned away from the cameras without another word, striding purposefully toward the Range Rover.

A man had died that night in a horrible crash, leaving a widow and two young daughters, and as the press packed up their gear, they felt almost good about it. Such was the power of Jan Voerhoven's oratory.

GEORGETOWN

Forty-eight hours earlier, everything had been simple; her life had fit neatly and flowed. One event led naturally to another with hardly a thought. Private school to college, college to grad school. From there into a field she had such a passion for that it didn't seem like work at all. Jan Voerhoven had come into her life ten months ago, and while he hadn't formally proposed, it was a forgone conclusion that they would marry. She'd been able to make decisions easily, with little regard to the consequences. Just one month shy of her thirty-second birthday, she was on her way in the life that she'd envisioned for herself: a career, a cause, and a soul mate.

But now everything was different. The choices more difficult, and their aftermath would change her life forever. True responsibility scared Aggie Johnston more than she wanted to admit.

It had all come crashing down when Philip Mercer had walked into her father's party, his tuxedo accenting his lean, powerful body, his hair so thick it seemed to crackle, and his eyes as seductive as the devil's own. Mercer's smile was a challenge no woman could resist.

Aggie got up from the couch and crossed the living room to the glass balcony doors. Her condo looked over the C&O Canal, and the balcony, which cantilevered over the murky water, was one of her favorite spots. Joggers passed on the other side of the waterway in an almost constant parade. She stood there until the afternoon humidity made her uncomfortable in her own skin, her cropped T-shirt clinging to her body. She turned back into the air conditioning, sliding the door closed with a finality she didn't feel.

The condo was decorated with some of her father's castoff furniture, precious woods and oils that she neither liked nor appreciated but kept to make him happy. The only item she really loved was an old easy chair she'd bought from a thrift shop when she was at prep school. She carted it around like a faithful pet. Over the years, the chair had been repaired so many times that little of the original remained. Yet to her it was still the same chair she'd had since those easy days at Westminster. She fell into it gratefully, slouching into its embrace so she almost felt like it was hugging her. Something she needed desperately right now.

She'd known that Mercer was on the guest list of the party; her father had teased her about it from the time he'd sent the invitations. She'd hoped that he wouldn't show while praying that he would. When his RSVP was not returned, she felt a strange mixture of relief and loss. And then he walked in from the dining room, and her girlhood crush came back with such force that she again felt like the callow coed she'd been when she'd first met him. Her simple life suddenly grew more complex than she could have possibly imagined. New thoughts, new ideas, and new options tumbled in her mind until all she could do was act rudely to him when they finally met.

She didn't know why she'd gone to his house yesterday; however, either consciously or not, she'd worn her skimpiest lingerie. From the moment she'd walked into Mercer's brownstone, she hadn't given Jan the slightest consideration. Her feelings for Mercer could not be denied, and that frustrated her. Such a rush of emotions had never happened to her before, not even when she'd met Jan for the first time.

"Damn it!" she said, launching herself angrily from her chair.

She hunted for her cigarettes, locating them on a cluttered kitchen counter. She lit one quickly, calming herself.

She shouldn't have gone to him last night, but like an addict she couldn't refuse herself. She was in love with Jan, was going to be his wife. That was what she wanted. He represented everything that she respected in the world. Why would she throw that away for a man she found reprehensible?

She considered this until there were three fresh cigarette butts in the overflowing ashtray, but she couldn't find an answer. She didn't know what this meant to her life. Would she always be unfaithful, giving in to casual affairs every time someone caught her eye? Or was Mercer a special case, a once-in-a-lifetime infatuation? Aggie had never doubted herself until this day. And there was another question plaguing her, one that was undoubtedly more important. Every time she came close to thinking about it, the fear of the answer forced her away. It felt like those times when she missed her period and was more afraid of taking a pregnancy test than of actually being pregnant.

In her confusion, the question finally slipped into her mind. Why had her father sent Burt Manning to kill Mercer last night?

Manning had worked for her father for years. Aggie had known him since her senior year of college. The attack on Mercer's house had been the most frightening experience of her life, but when she saw Burt dead on the floor, it was too much for her to handle. She fled as fast as she could, immediately understanding why her father had told her not to see Mercer. He knew Burt was going to Mercer's house to assassinate him.

Tears filled her eyes, spilling onto her chest. She thought she'd cried herself out the night before, but as she reached for a tissue from the box half buried in the junk on the counter, she knew she might never get this out of her system. Her silent tears turned to racking sobs that shook her whole body. She slumped to the tiled floor, pressing herself against the cabinets.

Consequences were catching up to her faster than she could handle. In the past forty-eight hours, everything she'd worked for and dreamed about had been turned upside down. Her fiancé, a man she loved and respected more than anyone else, paled in every comparison to Philip Mercer. And her father, whom she'd never liked but always loved, had turned out to be a monster who employed hit men. She wanted to close her eyes and sleep it all away, to wake up again and find it was all a horrible dream.

When the doorbell chimed, it was just subconscious ringing, far in the distance. But then she heard a key turning the front door lock and struggled up from the floor, steadying herself. She combed her fingers through her hair, thumbing salty tears from under her eyes.

Her father came into the kitchen, his face showing a deep concern. He wore his typical uniform, a perfectly fitted dark suit, a white shirt, and a subtly patterned tie. Even in her pain, Aggie saw that his shoes were like they always were, not exactly scuffed but well worn. He didn't believe in highly glossed shoes, feeling they were an affectation sported by those more concerned with image than substance.

"I've been trying to call you all day, but your line's been off the hook. I was worried about you," he said before he noticed the tear tracks on Aggie's cheeks. "Sweetheart, what's the matter?"

It didn't matter now that her father knew she smoked. Aggie lit a cigarette. "I was there last night, Daddy. I know what you tried to do."

"Aggie," Max Johnston said tenderly, "what are you talking about?"

"I was at Mercer's house last night. I was there when Burt Manning tried to kill him."

"Burt Manning?"

"He broke into Mercer's house. Him and another man. They were there to kill him. And I know you sent him there. I know you wanted to have Mercer killed." Despite her anger, Aggie began crying again.

His eyes went wide with shock. "Burt Manning tried to kill Mercer last night? Are you sure?"

"I was there, Daddy. Burt and another man broke into the house. They killed an FBI agent. Burt almost killed me before Mercer shot him. Mercer was shot in the shoulder and a friend of his in the leg, though it was an artificial leg so he was okay." Aggie knew she was babbling. She'd wanted to be strong when she confronted her father, but it came pouring out of her in a torrent. "I know you sent them. That's why you didn't want me to see Mercer again."

Max took Aggie in his arms, holding her trembling body close to his, stroking her hair, all the while muttering softly in her ear. "It's okay now, you're all right."

A few minutes passed as Aggie recovered, her sobs easing into silence. When she calmed, Max held her at arm's length so that he could look her in the eye. "You weren't hurt?" Aggie shook her head, and he hugged her again, relief making him clutch her tightly.

"Aggie, listen to me," he said at length. "Burt Manning doesn't work for me anymore. He hasn't for months. He has his own business as a security specialist. I knew even when he worked for Petromax that he was unbalanced. He was good at his job, but he was too unstable to control. I fired him last spring. I don't know anything about him trying to kill Mercer, but I can tell you it has nothing to do with me."

Max smiled, his own eyes glistening with concern and love. "Ever since you were little, you've accused me of a lot of things, and some of them were even true. But I draw the line well short of murder. Besides, why would I want to kill Mercer? He's a good friend of mine."

"But you told me not to go near him again," she accused quietly.

"Sweetheart, I did that to protect you. I know you've had a crush on him and I just didn't want you to get hurt. He has quite a reputation with women. A schoolgirl infatuation is one thing, and even though it's been years since you've seen him, he'd surely break your heart. I like Mercer, but I wouldn't trust him with you. That's why I warned you away. Oh, my poor little girl." They hugged again as she wished they'd done more when she was a child, but even now it wasn't too late.

"Aggie, I know you're involved with the leader of that organization you work for. I don't approve of him, but I know he treats you well and makes you happy." He didn't know that they were discussing marriage. She'd never had the courage to tell him. "Get Philip Mercer out of your mind. It's for the best. Okay?"

Aggie nodded slowly, her tears finally drying up.

"How's this, kiddo? I'll make you a deal. I won't say anything about you smoking or ask why you were at Mercer's house at quarter past ten last night, if you promise to forget about him."

Aggie smiled up at her father, a frail, hurt smile full of trust. She threw her arms around him again, losing herself in him like she did with her favorite chair. "I love you, Dad."

"And you are my life, sweetheart. Don't you ever forget that. Are you going to be all right?"

"I'll be fine. I think I'll leave town for a while. I just need to get away."

"Sure, you do that. Listen, nobody's using the company house on Hilton Head. A Petromax jet could have you there in an hour. Do you want me to arrange it for you?" Aggie nodded. "Excellent. How's this? I have to go to London for a couple of days. After I get back, what do you say I join you?"

"That would be great." She smiled as best she could.

As soon as her father had gone, Aggie dialed US Airways. The ticketing agent came on the line after a few frustrating minutes of voice mail.

"What's your next available flight out of Reagan Airport?" Aggie demanded sharply.

"What is your destination, miss?"

"Alaska eventually but right now it doesn't matter, I just need to get out of Washington." Aggie hadn't told her father what time she was at Mercer's house last night, yet he had known.

Oh, God.

ARLINGTON, VIRGINIA

While Aggie Johnston was making frantic preparations to flee the nation's capital, Mercer was only ten miles away doing the exact same thing, though without the urgency of fear. When it came to packing, he considered himself something of an expert. Rarely would he carry an item that he wouldn't use or forget anything essential. Not only was he economical in his selections, he was quick. Eleven minutes passed from the time he tossed his leather garment bag and hand grip onto his destroyed bed until he zipped them both closed.

Since leaving the Willard Hotel late that morning, this was the first eleven minutes he'd spent away from the telephone. If he was going to leave the protective custody of the FBI, he was going to give himself the best possible odds. Getting information he might need in Alaska, Mercer called in almost as many favors as he'd promised. Even with Kerikov trying to kill him, and knowing the Russian would redouble his efforts, there was still no way Mercer was going to let this drop. He was enraged that his home had been violated and his friends put in danger. The threats to his life were something he could handle, but not when they involved those he cared about, especially Harry and, now, Aggie. He'd gotten her unlisted number from a friend at the phone company but had been frustrated by a continuous busy signal.

His phone rang as he was ready to carry his bags downstairs. The portable was on the nightstand. "Hello."

"Dr. Mercer? This is Chief MacLaughlin in Homer. I have a message here that you've been trying to reach me."

"Thanks for returning the call. I have a suspicion that I'd

like you to check for me. It's connected to the deaths of Jerry and John Small."

"I'm afraid that'll have to wait, Dr. Mercer. We had a murder here last night that's got the whole town real jumpy."

"A murder? What happened?"

"A fishing boat was found beached about a mile south of town. The owner was discovered in a forward cabin, his throat slit. Pretty gruesome stuff, if you know what I mean."

"Was it a local boat?" Mercer felt hair raising on the back of his neck.

"Yeah, she was kept at the marina. The owner was born and raised right here in Homer."

"What kind of boat was it?"

"I'm sorry, Dr. Mercer, but I really don't have time for this right now." There was a weariness to MacLaughlin's voice, like he'd seen and done too much in the past couple of days.

Mercer sympathized, but he persisted. "I wouldn't ask if it wasn't important."

"She wasn't a commercial vessel but a good-sized charter boat. In fact, she's the largest in town. Can handle a twenty-person charter, she can."

"Chief, would the victim have known the Loran coordinates where the Coast Guard sank the hull of the *Jenny IV*?"

"Sure. The Coasties make them available so the chartermen can use them when they turn into reefs after a few years."

"You've got to send someone out to drag the bottom and make sure that the hulk is still there." Mercer already guessed it wasn't, but he had to make sure.

MacLaughlin bristled at Mercer's demanding tone. "Now just a damn minute. I appreciate your cooperation concerning the Smalls, but I've got an important investigation and don't have time for this."

Mercer relaxed his tone. "I'm sorry, but if my suspicions are correct, you'll find the boat's owner was killed last night after being forced to use his boat to haul the *Jenny IV* away from where the Coast Guard deep-sixed her. There was something on the wreck that no one noticed, some piece of evidence that wasn't supposed to be found, ever. The same men who killed Jerry and John Small as well their cousin, Howard, undoubtedly committed this latest murder too."

"And who are these men?" MacLaughlin asked suspiciously but nonetheless intrigued.

"I don't know yet," Mercer lied, "but you can believe that I'm going to find out."

MacLaughlin responded after a long silence. "I suppose I can ask my brother-in-law to go out in his boat to snag the hull with a grapple hook on the end of a rope. I guarantee he'll find her on the first pass."

"Don't bet on it, Chief. The *Jenny IV* won't be there. You won't be able to reach me at home by the time he gets back. I'm flying up to Alaska this evening, so I'll call you later."

"Yeah, sure. In case I'm not here, let me give you my home phone number."

"I can't tell you what this means to me," Mercer said. He took MacLaughlin's number and snapped off the phone.

He exhaled a long breath, relieved that the Alaskan had agreed to help. Mercer didn't like lying to MacLaughlin, but he felt he had no choice. He doubted that MacLaughlin's investigation would lead him beyond the Homer town line, so the less he knew, the better his odds of avoiding Ivan Kerikov's interest. There was no amount of warning he could give that would prepare the Chief for an international terrorist like Kerikov, and Mercer couldn't take another death on his conscience if MacLaughlin got too close. But having him look into the whereabouts of the *Jenny IV* did free Mercer to pursue other avenues.

He hefted the bags off the bed and noticed that the powerful sunlight beaming through the new skylight was drying the first coat of joint compound. In just a day or two, all the physical evidence of the attack would be gone. As promised, Dick Henna had hired a crew to restore his house. There was already new carpeting in the bar where Burt Manning's blood had been spilled, and a master carpenter was repairing the bullet holes in the library and on the balcony and the antique staircase.

Mercer knew from experience that the psychological effects of the assault would take much, much longer to mend.

The phone rang again when he was halfway down the

stairs. He left his luggage in the library and rushed to pick up the extension in his office.

"Enrico Caruso said it," a voice said triumphantly before he could say hello.

"Took you long enough," Mercer chastised with a smile.

David Saulman, a longtime friend, and Mercer had been engaged in a grueling trivia contest for as long as they'd known each other. Each enjoyed the tests immensely, Saulman because it allowed him to use his inexhaustible research skills, and Mercer because it taxed his phenomenal memory.

The latest question had been posed by Mercer three months earlier and it had taken all that time for Saulman to find the answer. "Who was quoted as saying, 'The chandelier tried to touch the ceiling and the chairs chased each other across the floor,' in reference to the great San Francisco earthquake of April 18, 1906?" It was one of Mercer's most esoteric questions, but he felt vindicated by posing it because he hadn't remembered that Benjamin Briggs was the Captain of the *Mary Celeste*, the answer to Saulman's last query.

Invariably, Mercer's questions dealt with earth sciences or engineering while Saulman limited his to maritime lore and history. Both were experts in their chosen fields and could draw from an unfathomable well of knowledge.

David Saulman had been an underage deckhand aboard merchantmen during the Second World War, slowly working his way through the ranks, "up the hawse pipe" in the vernacular. But an engine explosion in the early 1960s had cost him an arm and cut short his career. Forced from the working ranks, he turned his experience to the legal side of maritime commerce, putting himself through law school. Since then, he'd become one of the best marine lawyers a tremendous amount of money could buy. His offices in Miami boasted nearly one hundred fifty associates, and his new satellite office, recently opened in the shadow of Lloyd's in London, was doing better than expected. With contacts ranging from stevedores to tycoons, he knew more about the industry than anyone in the world.

"I got your message from my secretary this morning," Saulman said, his Brooklyn accent still crowding his speech after so many years. "I just now got the information you wanted."

"I'm surprised you got it so fast."

"I can't remember how the hell we did business before computers," Saulman said with the respect of those who really did remember the world before silicon chips took over. "So who do I bill the time to?"

Mercer laughed. Although Saulman would have done the research *pro bono*, he knew that when Mercer asked for a favor, there was always someone else equally interested in the information. "Charge it to the FBI. A bill from your office won't seem too bad when Dick Henna finds out that I lied to him about my travel plans. What have you got for me?"

"All right." David Saulman paused and Mercer could hear him arranging papers on his desk. "There were one hundred and three ships in the Gulf of Alaska at the time you asked about. Ninety-four private or commercial fishing vessels, including the *Jenny IV*. There were also four large ferryboats operated by Alaska Marine Highway. Three container ships owned by the Lykes Line, either running equipment north for the new pipeline or deadheading south. Finally, a vessel named *Hope* owned by an environmental group called PEAL and a tanker headed to the Alyeska terminal at Valdez."

The mention of PEAL sent a charge through Mercer. "What do you know about the *Hope*?"

"An old English survey ship bought about a year ago and converted into a pseudo-research vessel. She's more about public relations than hard science. You'll find her wherever there's some ecological controversy. She's been anchored in Prince William Sound for nearly three weeks."

"Has she left the area recently?" Mercer asked quickly, a glint of victory in his murky gray eyes.

"Sorry, no." Saulman dashed his hopes.

The PEAL vessel would have been his logical choice for smuggling large quantities of liquid nitrogen, but if she hadn't left Valdez, she couldn't be the one. "Okay, what about the tanker?"

"Ah, let me see." Saulman searched for the specifics of the tanker. "Here we go. It was the *Petromax Arctica*, a 255,000 ton VLCC making her regular run between Valdez and Long Beach—"

"Petromax?" Mercer interrupted. "I just talked to Max Johnston a couple of days ago. He said they sold their tankers."

"If you'd let me finish, I was about to say that she sailed into Valdez as the *Arctica* but left the day before yesterday as the *Southern Cross*. Her new owners are Southern Coasting and Lightering out of New Orleans. It's a big step for SC&L."

"What do you mean?"

"They're a midsized outfit. Their biggest vessel before they bought Petromax's fleet was a fourteen-year-old hundred-thousand toner. They shelled out 150 million dollars for the *Arctica* and her sisters. For them, its like going from a Yugo to a collection of Bentleys in one move."

"Did your firm draw up the papers for the sale?"

"No, it was handled in Louisiana. But when I heard about it, I was a little suspicious and did some checking. It was weird right from the start. Petromax almost tripped over themselves unloading those ships. The first day anyone heard that Max wanted to dump the tanker arm of Petromax oil, Southern Coasting comes along and, pretty as you please, cuts him a check for the $150 million, no negotiations, no financing, nothing."

"Sounds like he was anxious for the money," Mercer said.

"The Greeks or the Japanese would have bought those tankers in a heartbeat for a hell of a lot more. Christ, the *Petromax Pacifica* is only eight months old. She must be worth $75 million all by herself," Saulman pointed out.

"No shit."

"Yeah, no shit," Saulman agreed. "And here's another weird one. Southern Coasting demanded that the all ships' names be changed immediately upon signing of the deal, not just in the books but physically changed on the ships as well. They're even paying for a crew to fly to Valdez to rename the *Arctica* while she's en route between Alaska and California."

"What about the other two tankers?"

"The *Petromax Arabia* is in the Persian Gulf. Her new

name is the *Southern Accent*, and the *Petromax Pacifica* is unloading in Tokyo where she becomes the *Southern Hospitality*."

"Strange, but it doesn't really help me any." Mercer kept the disappointment from his voice. "Do you have anything else?"

"Well, the *Arctica* was eighteen hours late arriving at Valdez, and her captain had to be choppered from the ship to Anchorage after he was involved in some sort of accident."

"Jesus, why didn't you tell me that in the first place?"

"Hey, you wanted a list of ships in the Gulf of Alaska. You never told me why."

"Sorry," Mercer replied sheepishly. "Is a tanker running late a common occurrence?"

"Like hell. One of those monsters costs roughly a thousand dollars an hour to operate, so we're talking eighteen thousand dollars just for fuel, wages, and insurance. That doesn't factor in lost haulage time and lateness penalties paid to the chartering companies. Tankers are never late."

"Any idea what happened to the captain?"

"No. All that's listed in the accident report sent to Lloyd's was that he lost his forearm. Petromax is paying to have him sent to a specialist in Seattle."

Mercer was silent for a few moments. He wanted to believe that the *Arctica* was the ship that smuggled the cylinders of liquid nitrogen to a rendezvous with the *Jenny IV*, but that didn't make sense. Petromax was a world leader in oil exploration; they wouldn't be involved in a smuggling operation, especially something as innocuous as liquid nitrogen. Their position in Alaska was already difficult because of opposition to opening the Arctic Wildlife Refuge, and they wouldn't do anything to jeopardize it further.

"I think we're barking up the wrong tree," Mercer finally said.

"Tell me what you're looking for and maybe I can find it," Saulman offered.

"I can't, Dave, I'm sorry. Listen, you've helped me by telling me where not to look. That's more than I had before."

To lift Mercer from the black mood Saulman heard in his

voice, the lawyer offered another trivia question. "Well, before I go, who designed the original *Monitor* for the Union navy?"

"Too easy," Mercer replied without hesitation, "John Ericsson." He hung up the phone while Saulman cursed him out good-naturedly.

A few minutes later, Mercer slid his Jaguar into a spot next to Tiny's well-used Pontiac in the parking lot behind the former jockey's bar. He tossed his bags into the backseat of his friend's sedan before locking his own car.

The bar was empty except, to Mercer's surprise, for Harry seated on his normal stool, a nearly empty drink gripped in his bony hand, a cigarette hanging limply from his pale lips. Next to him was a large cardboard box, the unmistakable labels of Jack Daniel's bottles peeking over the lid.

"What the hell are you doing here?" Mercer asked as he entered the bar through the little-used kitchen.

"You won't believe it." Harry was excited as a child at Christmas. "I've ordered four cases of JD and the idiots at the hotel keep bringing them to me. They even called a cab for me to lug 'em over here. A couple more hours of this and I won't have to pay for a drink for the next year."

"What are they charging per case?" Mercer asked, fearful of the answer. Henna was going to kill him when he got the bill.

"I don't know, like a hundred dollars a bottle." Harry dismissed, finishing his drink just as Tiny set another before him. "God bless Uncle Sam and his bottomless pockets."

Mercer paused. He could be angry for Harry's abuse of his offer to use the suite or he could join in the spirit of larceny. "Next time you go back, grab me a couple of bottles of Absolut vodka, but make sure that this is your last run. I'm sure that the Willard's going to alert Henna's office before too long. And grab a bottle of Remy Martin for Tiny; I know he's out."

"Mighty generous of you," Tiny said sourly. "Do you have any idea what'll happen to my business if Harry has his own source of bourbon?"

"Charge him double for the ginger ale, he'll still come," Mercer joked. "Paul, I need a favor."

Tiny caught the seriousness of Mercer's last words and replied instantly. "Name it."

"I just need a ride to the airport. And for you to hide my car for a few days."

"What's going on?" Despite his inebriation, Harry heard Mercer's tone.

"I've got a lead on those bastards who shot up my house last night."

"I thought that the FBI was handling that."

Mercer shot Harry a scathing look. "They're out of their league on this one. Kerikov's back."

Harry was quiet while he absorbed this piece of information. He felt a phantom spasm in the missing leg. It was the Soviet plan, Vulcan's Forge, that had cost Harry his leg, and it was Kerikov who had controlled it at its bitter end. Tiny didn't understand what had just passed between Mercer and Harry; he didn't know what a malevolent force Kerikov represented. But Harry and Mercer knew all too well. They had often discussed the probability of Kerikov resurfacing, and now it was happening. Harry's missing limb twitched again; he could feel it as if it were really there. "You think he's after revenge?"

Mercer shook his head. "There are too many other things involved, but if I get taken out in the cross fire, I'm sure the son of a bitch won't shed any tears."

"Well, it can't be a coincidence," Harry said pointedly.

"No, but it could be fate." The last time he'd squared off against Kerikov, the United States had almost erupted in civil war. He was truly frightened of what would happen this time.

"Tiny, take him to the airport. I'll watch the bar." A line like that from Harry would have usually demanded a number of quips, but Tiny untied his apron and tossed it on the bar without comment.

Mercer was almost out the back door following Paul Gordon's diminutive figure when he turned back to Harry. "If I don't come back, stay low, will you? He knows who you are too."

"If you don't come back, I might as well commit suicide and save Kerikov the hassle of killing me." Harry looked down at his drink for a moment and when he glanced up again, his eyes were heavy with emotion. "Take care of yourself, Philip."

It was the first time since they'd met that Harry had used Mercer's first name, and it sounded so much like a final good-bye that Mercer paused, locked eyes with his old friend, and then nodded almost imperceptibly.

PRINCE WILLIAM SOUND

Built by Yarrow and Company in 1964 as a Hecla class survey ship for the Royal Navy, the *Hope* retained her sparse military lines even under coats of garish yellow paint that made her look like an oversized bathtub toy. Her flat bows rode almost perpendicular to the choppy swells, and her stern was equally blunted. She was two hundred thirty-five feet long; two thirds of her main deck supported a three-level superstructure, her squared funnel thrust through the center. There was a helicopter pad on the aft deck, and a garage below the bridge that housed her two yellow Range Rovers. A ten-ton crane angled forward, ready to swing the vehicles to or from shore.

With accommodations for one hundred twenty-three crewmen, she had more than enough space for the twenty-two members of PEAL who crewed her and the up to sixty others who accompanied her on her voyages. Her twenty-thousand-mile range allowed the *Hope* to cruise anywhere in the world, calling attention to environmental damage. She wasn't quick, possessing a top speed of only thirteen knots, but the bow thruster running athwartships made her maneuverable. Her three Paxman Ventura V-12 turbo diesels and her strengthened hull made her safe in heavy ice.

When PEAL had bought her, they had done little to change her interior specifications, leaving in place the two laboratories, the photographic studio, and her large cargo holds. Seablue carpet had been laid in all passages and companionways, and her utilitarian gray walls had been repainted in soft pastels of mauve and cream. Many of the interior spaces were covered with posters. The prints ran to a similar theme: entreaties to save rain forests and oceans and endangered species. Pandas and whales were the two most common animals pictured, along with disturbing scenes of industrial pollution spoiling air and water alike.

The most evocative picture hung in the place of honor in the mess hall and was used by PEAL in their ad campaigns. It showed a six-year-old South American Indian boy wearing nothing but a ragged pair of shorts. Behind him, a wall of smoky flames shot high into the air as fire consumed the edge of the Brazilian rain forest. The boy gravely regarded a huge earthmover treading toward him, its driver's face hidden behind a bullbous gas mask. No caption was necessary.

Because she drew fifteen and a half feet of water, the *Hope* couldn't tie up to one of the piers around the town of Valdez. She lay at anchor a few hundred yards offshore and was the largest vessel in Prince William Sound except for the steady procession of tankers running to and from the oil terminal across the bay. She'd approached the coastline only once since arriving in the Sound, so that one of her Range Rovers could be lifted ashore at the ferry terminal.

The ship's offshore position gave Jan Voerhoven a few minutes to watch his guest being motored to the *Hope* aboard one of their custom yellow Zodiacs. Despite the bright sun, the air was bitterly cold. An arctic front held all of Alaska in its grip, dropping temperatures fifteen to twenty degrees below normal. The locals were saying that this could be the worst winter in the past quarter century and it was only mid-October. The two men manning the Zodiac were hunched against the frigid gusts blasting across the Sound, their slickers pulled high around their heads, but their passenger seemed oblivious to the weather. He sat stoically in the middle of the inflatable boat, his shoulders squared, his cannonball head held erect. He didn't even take the precaution of wearing a hat to help preserve his body heat. Voerhoven could easily see the silvered bristles of his crew cut.

Jan Voerhoven had faced nature that way many times in his life, always seeking to feel closer to her, but this man came not to taste nature's power but to dominate. Even at this distance, Voerhoven could see his arrogance. He looked as though he felt nothing for nature, not her gentle caresses or her harsh torments and seemed almost contemptuous of the cold. Voerhoven felt the bile of hatred building in his stomach, churning and roiling bitterly.

From the time of his very first memories, Jan had always loved the world around him, not the cities and roads and manmade canals of his native Holland, but the natural world, the world of wind and oceans and land. As a boy, he spent hours enraptured by the interplay of the clouds as they ranged above his backyard. He thought nothing could be more perfect than the soil on which he lived. He was ten when he found out it was all a lie.

He learned that his whole country, everything that he'd ever seen in his young life, had been built on land stolen from the North Sea. His teachers had proudly explained that it had been "reclaimed." Earthen dikes and dams had been built along the coast so that the once fertile sea floor could be drained, cultivated, and developed. The teacher said it was a marvel of human ingenuity and perseverance.

Young Jan saw the creation of Holland as deliberate theft. How could something be reclaimed if they had no claim on it in the first place? At ten, he realized that one of the greatest engineering feats was nothing more than the plundering of an untamed region just for man's greedy desires. He believed that the Dutch had no right to do what they'd done. He realized that nature had no way of stopping them, no way of protecting her balance as mankind began wrenching her apart.

That day, that very instant, he dedicated his life to pushing the balance back into nature's favor, to stopping humanity's unending thirst for the destruction of the planet. He'd been too young to join the beginning of the Green movement that swept Europe, but he kept active during his college years in the early 80s, organizing often violent boycotts and demonstrations while majoring in environmental studies. The halcyon days of his youth were filled with police clashes and tear gas raids, late-night debates and underground newspapers.

He pursued his doctorate more out of an interest in staying around the restless students than any other factor. There was never a doubt that he would teach after receiving his Ph.D., expounding his particular blend of environmental activism and violence. He'd been run from academia four years ago, chased away because his fervent pleas were becoming too radical for even Europe's liberal academic circles. He was no longer bitter about being censured because that had led directly to the formation of PEAL. Had he still been teaching, he never would have had the time to create the organization that now stood at the brink of eclipsing Greenpeace as the most active environmental group in the world.

The Zodiac was nearing the *Hope*. Her slick rubber hull knifed through the water with the agility of one of the many otters that lived in the sound. Voerhoven's thoughts again returned to the man coming to see him.

Voerhoven had dealt with many dangerous people before— neo-Nazi skinheads he'd hired to disrupt his own rallies for greater media coverage, professional arsonists contracted to burn gas stations in Holland and Belgium, and burglary gangs hired to teach PEAL activists how to break into research facilities where animal testing occurred. As fanatical and ominous as these others had been, none could compare to the man approaching the *Hope*.

Their first meeting had taken place over a year ago. The man had entered PEAL's cramped office near Amsterdam's train station, and after the barest introduction, the visitor had laid a bank draft on Voerhoven's desk. At the time, PEAL had fewer than twenty members, mostly volunteers, and a budget of fifty thousand dollars, much of it coming from Voerhoven's trust fund. The check had been made out to PEAL in the amount of ten million dollars.

"There is a condition attached to this money," Jan's bene-factor had stated simply.

Voerhoven remembered looking into the man's icy eyes and seeing death, but it did not stop him from agreeing read-ily, giving away his soul as surely as if Lucifer himself had made the offer. Ivan Kerikov was a malignancy as deadly as cancer. Through his contacts in Europe, Voerhoven later learned that Kerikov was a former KGB officer turned rene-gade and was being hunted by the United States, his former Russian masters, and a number of other groups. His reputation for violence seemed the stuff of nightmares.

Within weeks, Kerikov had turned PEAL into a tightly or-ganized outfit, building on Voerhoven's natural charisma and his unflagging dedication to the cause. Kerikov made possible the purchase of the old survey ship that became the *Hope* and hired a well-respected advertising agency to manage PEAL's publicity campaigns. Gone were the photocopied flyers sta-pled to telephone poles around the Low Countries and PEAL's word-of-mouth recruiting style. PEAL moved to a luxury suite of offices in a downtown bank building, complete with secretarial staff, massive computer system, and enough space for two hundred employees. Within a few months, PEAL's membership had jumped 1000 percent and continued to grow at a phenomenal pace. PEAL had been a small cadre of dedicated volunteers; now it bloomed into a major force that people paid to be a part of. It took a short time to trans-form PEAL from an obscure organization on the fringe of the environmental movement to one of the world leaders in ec-ological preservation.

Kerikov managed all of this with Machiavellian aplomb, never revealing himself to anyone other than Voerhoven but getting results like no one the Dutchman had ever seen before. Kerikov had the ability to make problems simply disappear, and people as well. When a gas station owner was acciden-tally killed in a fire set by a PEAL crusader, his outraged and outspoken widow vanished a short while later. Kerikov was single-minded and ruthless in his dedication to building PEAL, though he never once gave his reasons. Voerhoven took Kerikov's money and aid, not daring to question what price he would eventually have to pay for the Russian's patronage.

Only three months ago had Kerikov finally revealed the condition he had first mentioned when he came to PEAL. Voerhoven was enthralled by the bare sketch of Kerikov's proposal and was astounded to learn how far the plan had progressed without his knowledge. Kerikov was providing PEAL the outlet for the ultimate act of environmental protest, an opportunity to prevent an inevitable environmental disaster and save an entire ecosystem. Kerikov's plan would ensure that there would never be another *Exxon Valdez*–type spill and that the Arctic Wildlife Refuge would be beyond man's ability to ever exploit.

The Zodiac slid up to the *Hope* near the steep boarding stairs. While a crewman on the rubber boat held the craft steady against the platform, Kerikov heaved himself up the swaying steps to the deck of the PEAL ship, moving easily for a man in his mid-fifties.

Voerhoven stood at the top of the landing to greet the Russian. Kerikov made no move to shake hands and Voerhoven did his best to hide his discomfort. This was an unscheduled meeting that Kerikov had called for only this morning. Voerhoven had come to understand that Kerikov did nothing without a specific reason, but he did not know the purpose behind this conference.

"Let's go to your quarters." Kerikov knew the ship well and led the way to the spacious cabin that had once been the Officers' Wardroom.

Voerhoven had taken over the largest cabin aboard the *Hope* when he joined her here in Alaska. The rooms didn't feel like they were on a ship. The steel bulkheads had been Sheetrocked and painted, and the carpet had been double padded to cushion the metal decking. The two small, rounded portholes were the only indication of the suite's nautical origins. There were three rooms: a full bath tucked behind the bedroom and an office complete with an oak desk and a conference table big enough to seat ten.

As soon as Voerhoven closed the watertight door, Kerikov grabbed him by the shoulder, spun him around, and slapped him so hard across the face that he staggered against the wall, knocking a framed picture to the floor.

"What the fu—"

Kerikov slapped him again, this time over his temple. Voerhoven toppled to the deck, cutting his hands on the glass shards lying on the carpet. "Shut up," the Russian said conversationally. "I'll tell you when you can speak again."

He moved across the wide room, taking the chair at the head of the conference table, leaving Voerhoven to pull himself from the floor. Kerikov watched Voerhoven with reptilian eyes as the Dutchman slid into a chair across from him. A thin trickle of blood oozed from the corner of Voerhoven's mouth, but he made no move to brush it away.

"I won't ask you what you were thinking when you pulled that stunt last night because I know you weren't thinking at all." Kerikov's voice was even and well modulated, but there was an undercurrent of anger clipping each syllable. "I've pumped ten million dollars into this operation, built up your pathetic little protest group and worked for more than a year to bring us to this point, and you draw attention to us by killing a truck driver just so you can throw a few sound bites on the evening news."

"I didn't kill him—Petromax did," Voerhoven replied quickly.

"Shut your fucking mouth," Kerikov snapped. "You may convince the world about your noble cause and the greed of the corporate world, but I don't care. You killed the driver, Petromax killed the driver, fucking aliens killed the driver, it doesn't matter. You were there when it happened and were ready to capitalize on it for network television. I authorized your boycott of Petromax gas stations here in Valdez because it lends authority to your cover here. But I didn't give you permission to carry your crusade beyond Prince William Sound. I've got enough problems right now with some copycat group burning gas stations in Anchorage. And if I find out you were behind that too, I'll tear out your intestines and hang you with them."

Voerhoven said nothing but he kept his eyes downcast. He would never dare openly defy Kerikov.

"Now that we've settled this unfortunate incident, we'll turn to other matters." Although the topic had shifted, Kerikov's menacing tone was still in place. "You were able to secure enough liquid nitrogen to replace the cylinders we lost on the *Jenny IV*?"

"I think we depleted the entire supply in Vancouver and Seattle, but yes, it's here, in Fairbanks, actually. We managed to get four tons."

"Six tons were lost when the *Jenny IV* burned."

"Two tons of her cargo were extra insurance for the mission. That's a luxury we can't afford. There just aren't enough medical supply stores and chemical companies in the Pacific Northwest to give us that margin again. To avoid suspicion, my people from the San Francisco office had to be pretty creative with their cover stories."

"What did they tell the suppliers?"

"They posed as special effects coordinators for a big-budget action film."

"Excellent." Kerikov lit a cigarette.

"Please don't do that," Voerhoven said, pointing at the smoldering Marlboro in Kerikov's hand.

Kerikov looked at him sharply, dropped the cigarette to the floor, and ground it into the carpet with his foot, leaving a tarry black mark. He lit another derisively, blue-gray whorls filling the room. Voerhoven kept his silence. "We'll have to transport the liquid nitrogen cylinders to the target site in helicopters, and it'll take several runs. That leaves us more exposed than I like."

"Enough money will ensure that the pilots keep quiet," Voerhoven replied.

"It's not the pilots I'm concerned with; it's the ground personnel and others at the airport." Kerikov was quiet for a few seconds. When he finally spoke, his voice was firm and decisive. "Have your people rent a truck and move the tanks northward, to the town of Fox or some other village that has an airport. We'll have the choppers pick up the nitrogen there, again using the cover of a film company." We'll kill the pilots after they've transported all of the cylinders. Kerikov kept this last thought to himself.

120 MILES WEST
OF BRITISH COLUMBIA

The waves started far out in the ocean, churned up by currents and tides into great sloping mounds of water that rushed across the Pacific at nearly thirty miles per hour, building momentum and force with each passing moment. They were not the surface swells whipped up by stormy winds that were the delight of surfers along America's Pacific coast. These were pulsating mountains that shifted millions of tons of water as if driven by the very engine of the earth. The *Petromax Arctica*, now called *Southern Cross*, took these massive rollers along her beam, her quarter million tons lifting easily, her deadly cargo shifting so the steel baffles within her tanks groaned. When she took an errant wave head-on, an explosion of white foam and dark green sea would blow over her bow. In the pale afternoon, the collisions looked like torpedo strikes, great plumes of water lashing the deck, each hit sending a shudder through the tanker.

She'd been built for these seas, and despite the seeming violence of the confrontation between ship and sea, she rode them well. Only the larger commercial fishing boats and tankers braved these waters. The endless procession of ferries and cruise ships that sailed to Alaska never strayed from the protection of the Inside Passage, a marine route protected from the ravages of the open ocean by a string of islands that stretched from Vancouver to the Gulf of Alaska.

The tension on the bridge, which was an almost tangible presence, had nothing to do with the deteriorating weather. Since the takeover, every member of the crew regarded the situation with equal doses of fear and expectation, fear for their lives and hope that there would be an opportunity to retake the tanker. When not on duty, the crew was kept in the main mess hall under the watchful eye of at least two guards. Conversations at the long tables were kept to ship's business and nothing more.

Despite their incredible size, VLCCs are operated with only a tiny crew, twenty ratings and ten officers. And since there were only three key areas that needed monitoring—the engine room, the tank control station, and the bridge—the eight terrorists under JoAnn Riggs' command could maintain control for as long as necessary.

Riggs sat in the port side Master's chair, one of the two comfortable seats located on each side of the spacious bridge. Since the takeover, she had sat there braying orders, watching the bridge crew with predatory eyes, and smoking cigarette after cigarette in an unending chain. To her right, a helmsman kept a firm grip on the two levers that acted as the ship's wheel. When his eyes were not scanning the open horizon, he either studied the digital engine displays or glanced at his new captain. Behind the helmsman, Wolf, the terrorists' leader, stood against the aft bulkhead, a machine pistol dangling below his crossed arms. Despite his presence, Riggs felt exposed and vulnerable. To hide it, she lashed out at the crew, screaming orders that would normally be spoken in a whisper, forcing them to work extended shifts to repair the damage from the terrorists' attempt to subdue Lyle Hauser.

JoAnn Riggs was not supposed to be in charge of the supertanker or the terrorists, but due to the misfortune of the ship's original captain, Harris Albrecht, she found herself in this position. Albrecht should have commanded the ship back to Long Beach and led the terrorist takeover, with JoAnn acting as First Officer. But then he lost a good share of his lower arm and had to be evacuated, forcing Southern Coasting and Lightering to ask Petromax for a replacement because Riggs didn't have experience in these waters. Riggs had to rework her plan and had intended to use Hauser until the ship was safely away from Alaska, then lock him with the rest of the crew. She would then captain the vessel to their final destination. With Albrecht gone, Riggs' payment for her involvement had doubled, but she was left as the only officer working with Wolf and his men. The responsibilities were daunting, especially with a crew who were virtual prisoners and many critical systems either off-line or destroyed.

Another wave crashed into the bow a quarter mile away, thick spume rising up nearly to the height of the bridge before slamming back to the deck and racing to the scuppers like a river at full flood. Just as the deck cleared of water, a series of yellow and red warning lights went off all along the control console. An alarm sounded.

Riggs reacted instantly, coming off the chair like a panther. She was at the helmsman's shoulder before the crewman realized she'd moved.

"What happened?" she snapped, fearing that the wave had stove in the bow.

"Automatic engine override. The computer shut the main down."

"Why?"

"I don't know yet. The diagnostic is still cycling," the helmsman answered.

Riggs picked up the hand mike for the intercom and dialed the mess hall. "This is Riggs. I want the Chief Engineer and three of his men in the engine room immediately." She snapped off the button but held the mike in case she needed to issue more orders. "Do we have a fire?"

"Negative. Engine room heat is nominal, and the suppression system hasn't tripped."

She looked out the bridge window and was relieved to see that the horizon was clear. Even if they couldn't get the engine restarted right away, there was little cause for concern. There wasn't any other shipping in the area, and they had plenty of sea room before the tanker drifted close to shore. Because of the inertia built up by the two hundred thousand tons of oil in her tanks, it would take seventeen miles and about six hours before they came to a stop. After that, they would be at the mercy of the North Pacific.

"Bridge, this is the engine room." George Patroni, the ship's Engineer, sounded tinny through the onboard intercom. "There's no emergency. I can have us under way in about an hour, but we've got another problem."

"What is it?" Riggs said, then quickly countered herself. "Belay that. I'm coming down."

The engine room of the *Southern Cross* was a towering cavern of steel, aluminum, and copper. The ceiling lofted four stories over the bottom decking and was obscured by the tangled junctures of the countless miles of piping conduits, duct work, and electric cables that meandered throughout the ship. Though spotlessly clean, the room was permeated with the heavy stench of marine-grade diesel fuel and machine oil. The smell coated everything and clung to the clothing and skin of anyone who entered.

The engine itself was the size of two overland buses laid end to end with two others stacked on top of them. The huge diesel wasn't running, but there was a palpable feeling of power emanating from it. In a vessel that taxed superlatives to their very limits, the engine suited the ship perfectly. When it was operational, no one could tolerate the deafening roar of the nine-cylinder power plant, but even now, the noise produced by the auxiliary generators and steering gear pumps was just below the pain threshold.

When she stepped off the tranquil elevator at the main engineering level three floors above the bottom deck, JoAnn Riggs was pushed back by the noise as if physically struck. Patroni stood on a catwalk suspended over the molded block head of the engine in a huddled meeting with his assistants. He was built like a fireplug. Wolf had somehow beat Riggs here and watched the engineers from a few paces away, one of his men at his side. Because of the noise, no one was aware of her presence until she tapped Patroni on his hard sloping shoulder.

"Well?" She had to scream into his ear to be heard over the machinery.

Patroni held up a scarred finger, then bade Riggs to follow him.

The walk to the engineering control room was hot and uncomfortable; the smell made her nauseous. Patroni slid open the glass door to the control room and waited until they had all entered before sealing the room again. Through the thick glass enclosure, they had a commanding view of the engine room, but the noise was reduced to a dull rumble by the sound insulation, and the air was fresh thanks to air conditioning.

"Well?" repeated Riggs.

Patroni ignored her for a moment as he studied the countless banks of control consoles that hugged three walls of the room. With each display he checked, he grunted a bit louder and the scowl on his pug face deepened.

"I told you we needed to keep engineering manned at all times. This accident is your fault entirely," he accused, ignoring the two machine pistols trained on him.

"Just tell me what happened," Riggs ordered angrily.

"According to the computer logs, there was a buildup of scale on the fuel filter for number-five cylinder. Had someone been in here, it would have been easy to switch over to the backup injector, clean the filter, and reactivate the primary, but me and my staff weren't here. The filter failed, and the fuel pumped into number five was contaminated. It started running lean. The computer picked it up, but again," he glared at Riggs, "no one was here. Had the seas been calm we would have felt the engine vibrating as cylinder five started to predetonate. As near as I can tell, she was running so lean, she blew the head right off the piston. The computers sensed the presence of that much metal grinding through the machinery and initiated an emergency shutdown."

"You said you could get her running again."

"Sure. I just release the compression on number five and let her cycle without power, but we've got a couple hundred pounds of scrap metal in the crankcase right now and it's going to tear the rest of the engine apart when we restart."

"Drain the oil and refill it with lubricant from ship's stores," Riggs replied.

"That'll get out most of it, but not all," Patroni pointed out. "She'll foul up again. At reduced power we just might make Seattle before the whole engine seizes solid."

"I don't care what you do, Chief, but this ship will make it to San Francisco or, so help me God, you'll watch as every member of the crew is castrated before I kill you myself. Am I clear?" Riggs turned to Wolf, whose eyes showed respect at Riggs' handling of the situation. "Any chance this could be caused by sabotage?"

"No one has been down here since we took the vessel except for the inspection, which my men watch. This is a natural accident."

"Accidents are never natural," Riggs snapped before leaving the control room, heading back to her sanctuary on the bridge.

"All right, boys," Patroni turned to his three assistants. "Ken, Paul, I want you to go to the stores and grab three barrels of oil. Pete, start pulling the drains on all the cylinders. I want you to set some filters under the drains so I have an idea how much shit is in the crankcase. I want to flush the whole system once, turn her over a couple of times with the primary starter, and wash her out again. Then we'll fill her up. Oh, and check the fuel preheater, will ya, make sure it's ready. The fuel's going to be cold again by the time we're ready for a restart. I need to go put on my working rig." Patroni's men were already wearing their heavy overalls, but he was still in his uniform and had to change before tackling the messy job of changing eighty gallons of engine oil. He glanced at Wolf and asked ironically, "Is that all right with you?"

Wolf waved him away with a flick of his wrist. He was more concerned about Patroni's men somehow sabotaging the engine repairs. He felt certain that the Chief Engineer knew what was at risk and would soon return to the engine room.

George Patroni angrily stabbed at the elevator call button and quietly cursed everyone involved with fouling his beloved engine. First, of course, was the bitch Riggs, followed closely by Wolf and the rest of his band of cutthroats, then came the idiots who had installed the faulty fuel injector and the morons who'd built it in the first place. He was still adding people to his list when the elevator arrived and he stepped into the empty car.

He wasn't even aware that the emergency hatch on the top of the elevator was open until a voice called down to him, "Did I stop the ship?"

Patroni nearly jumped out of his skin, slamming himself

against the back of the car and staring up at the dark opening over his head. He watched, slack-jawed, as Captain Lyle Hauser peered through the hatchway.

"Jesus, Mary, and Joseph," Patroni muttered.

Hauser snapped him out of his near panic. "Disengage the alarm and stop the car."

Patroni peeled himself off the wall and opened the small panel cover beneath the elevator's controls. It took him a second to cross-wire the elevator alarm so when he hit the stop button, the bell remained silent. Hauser almost fell from his perch at the sudden deceleration.

"I thought you were dead," Patroni said after finally finding his voice.

Hauser eased through the hatch and dropped to the floor next to Patroni, the car shuddering with the impact. "So did I."

Hauser's life had been spared by a fraction of an inch. When he leaped from the bridge wing the night before, he had lost his footing at the critical instant and had slammed into the stout railing that surrounded the lower promenade. Through the agony of the crushing blow, he had enough presence of mind to clutch at the railing before falling another forty feet to the main deck. He clung precariously for many long moments as his breath returned in aching gasps.

He knew that Riggs would send someone to make certain he was dead. He had to find refuge. Cold, numb, and racked with pain, Hauser had broken into one of the ship's three enclosed lifeboats, the one that hung directly at her stern. The other two boats, both port and starboard, were visible from the bridge and therefore not options. Hauser had thought about launching the craft and escaping, but he was the captain of the *Petromax Arctica* and there was no way he would abandon his ship and crew.

Despite his fear, Hauser had managed to eat a little of the emergency stores cached in the craft. He had donned one of the yellow survival suits to retain his body heat and had even managed to sleep for a few hours. By the time dawn finally arrived, he was rested enough to implement the plan that had come to him during the night.

Hauser had spent only a few hours aboard the *Petromax Arctica* before she was seized, but he'd been around ships, especially tankers, his entire life. It was easy to work his way into the multiple layers of crawl spaces and access tunnels that were sandwiched between the decks. This gave him full run of the supertanker while avoiding any chance of detection. He'd been able to watch guards and crewmen alike as he lay in the cramped confines of the heating ducts.

When he reached the engine room this morning, he'd found Patroni and an assistant oiler doing a scheduled inspection under the malevolent glare of one of the terrorists. His hopes of sabotaging the tanker were dashed. There was nothing he could do as long as the engine room was occupied. But even as he prepared to make his way back to the sanctuary of the lifeboat, the guard herded Patroni and his aide back to the elevator.

Because of the complexity of the forest of pipes running to and from the power plant, inspection hatches were placed in readily accessible areas. One of them gave him access to the primary fuel bunker for the odd-numbered cylinders. The metal shavings he found on the floor of the machine shop adjacent to the engine room were perfect for what he had in mind. He simply dumped a few handfuls into the viscous diesel fuel and waited for them to grind the engine to a halt. The tanker wouldn't be delayed long—he hadn't done enough damage—and he hadn't wanted to disable the ship permanently, fearing the dangers of her drifting out of control. Still, he'd hoped that he could grab a few minutes alone with a member of the crew during the confusion. Finding the Chief Engineer in the elevator was a godsend.

"We don't have much time," Hauser said to the still-startled Patroni. "They'll wonder about your delay, so give me a quick rundown of the situation."

"Well, terrorists have seized the ship and Riggs is working with them."

Hauser cut him off. "I know all that. What's the status of the ship and crew?"

"Whatever you put into the fuel system only affected cylinder five before the computer shut the engine down. We'll have her running in an hour or two. But we'll only be able to goose fifty percent power without destroying the rest of the engine. Riggs told me that the ship has to make it to San Francisco."

"Frisco? Why Frisco?"

"She didn't say, but she made it damn clear that that's where we're headed."

"How's the crew?"

"We're doing okay. They keep us in the main mess hall when not on duty. We're fed only once a day and have to sleep on the floor or in chairs, but it could be a hell of a lot worse. They've made a few threats, and so far two are dead, one of them was Larry Walker, the helmsman who took the bullets meant for you."

"What about the rest of the ship? I know the bridge was shot up pretty badly."

"Yeah, it was. The radar system is a complete write-off; I'll never be able to fix it. And the tank pressure sensors were taken out too. She wants those sensors back on-line ASAP. In fact, she's got the ship's electrician scavenging parts from other systems to get them running again. The helm controls still work fine, but changing engine speeds must be done manually in the engine room."

"They don't have throttle control, yet they leave the engine room on UMS status?" Hauser was shocked by the negligence. UMS, or Unmanned Ship, is the automatic system that controls the power plant during the engineering staff's off-duty time. In normal conditions, a tanker is run under UMS only at night and in calm seas.

"I'm not issuing the orders. I'm just following them."

"I wonder why tank control is so important to them. It shouldn't be prioritized above regaining remote throttle control." Hauser spoke almost rhetorically. Neither he nor Patroni could second-guess the motivations of the force that had taken their ship.

"Do you know anything about the terrorists?"

"Only that the leader is named Wolf, and even he takes orders from JoAnn Riggs."

"What's your take on all of this? You've sailed with Riggs."

"I don't know, Captain. I've sailed with her, yes, but only twice before. I'm almost as new to this tub as you are. All I know is that she was pretty chummy with the former captain, Harris Albrecht."

"Do you think Albrecht was involved with this?" Hauser asked, putting two and two together but still coming up with three.

"I'm sure of it."

"Do you know what happened to him and why the ship was late getting into Valdez?"

"Albrecht confined most of the crew to their quarters while we wallowed in the Gulf of Alaska. Nobody was allowed topside except him and Riggs. And it wasn't the first time we stopped out there, but it was the longest. I don't know what happened to Albrecht's arm. But I do know that they never recovered the limb, if you know what I mean."

"What are you saying?"

Patroni looked at Hauser for a second as if he couldn't believe that the captain didn't catch his meaning. "Hey, this ship is big and dangerous too, but if you lost an arm, you would damn well find it real fast and hopefully have a doctor sew it back on. Captain Albrecht never got his arm back, and the medevac helicopter was here only twenty minutes after the accident. What happened to the severed limb?"

"Overboard?"

"What was he doing at the rail that could take his hand off?"

Hauser had no reply.

"I've been talking to the guys who'd been sailing with Riggs and Albrecht for a while. They've been doing this for a few months, stopping in the middle of nowhere and confining the crew belowdecks. They were paid a small bonus for the inconvenience, so no one complained."

"Petromax never said anything about these delays?"

Patroni shook his head. "Not as far as I know."

Hauser looked at his watch, "You'd better get going before they wonder where you are. I'm holed up in the aft life raft.

I need you to pass me any information you can get."

"Yes, sir. I want these bastards off my boat as bad as you do."

"Listen . . ." Hauser hadn't been in command long enough to know the names of his officers.

"George," Patroni offered.

"Listen, George, it may be necessary for me to leave the ship, the emergency radio in the life raft doesn't have much range and we have to tell the outside world what's happened. I want you to think of a way of launching the life raft without arousing suspicion. I don't want my escape causing problems for the crew."

"I understand," Patroni replied. "I can arrange a short on the master control panel that will kill the indicator lights when the raft goes up on her davits. Don't forget, the aft boat can be self-launched, but the timing has to be perfect."

"It won't happen for a while," Hauser said as he prepared to heave himself back onto the roof of the elevator. "But be prepared. I'll be in touch as soon as I can."

Once on the top of the elevator, he turned and looked back through the open hatch. "George, take care of the crew. No matter what happens, they come first."

"I will, sir, you can count on it." A moment later the elevator lurched upward as Patroni disengaged the manual arrest button.

ABU DHABI CITY
UNITED ARAB EMIRATES

Khalid Al-Khuddari didn't mean to slam the antechamber door of his office suite when he entered, but his pent-up frustration got the best of him and the nine-foot door crashed against its jamb with the concussion of a rifle shot.

Siri Patal, Khuddari's personal assistant, looked up with startled doe eyes, her fine features showing concern as Khalid stood by the door trying to calm himself.

"Sorry," Khalid said with a guilty smile. "It's already a rotten day and it's not yet noon."

Siri regarded him with barely hidden adoration. Since she'd started working for him, she thought of little else than being with him, but circumstance and tradition ensured that that would never come to pass. She was Indian, the second daughter of a successful merchant who'd moved his family to the Gulf during the boom years of the 1960s, and Khuddari was an Arab. He was a Muslim while she was Hindu. The divides were uncrossable.

She thrust her own confused emotions aside and smiled brightly. "That bad?"

"Yes, that bad." His handsome face couldn't hide his disappointment.

Khalid had just returned from a meeting with the Crown Prince. The meeting had originally been scheduled for the day before, but the ruler of the UAE had canceled at the last minute. Instead, they had met for a late breakfast, which in itself was not a good sign. Because the Prince was in his late seventies, most important meetings occurred in the mid-afternoon, after his postluncheon nap. The Prince's age did not affect his ability to rule, but as the years wound onward, he was forced to make concessions to his body. Khalid had arrived dutifully at ten and reported his findings to the droopy-eyed ruler, dispassionately laying out his suspicions of Hasaan bin-Rufti. He also told the Prince about his cross-border excursion with Bigelow.

The Prince had listened quietly, his expression hidden behind a wispy gray beard that was so withered it resembled the loose feathers of an old chicken. His dark eyes, still sharp and quick, gave away nothing as Khalid spoke. It was impossible to tell if the Prince had been fascinated or bored.

When Khalid had finished with his briefing, he'd eased back against the Regency dining room chair, cocking one arm over the walnut back in a relaxed gesture that he hoped would hide his agitation. The Prince poured another cup of coffee for each of them, his hands shaking slightly as the Turkish coffee dribbled into the demitasse cups. His voice was almost as frail as the rest of his body, but age didn't diminish the strength of his words.

"Not since Allah's prophet Muhammad has a world leader not faced a direct confrontation of his authority. You might say it is an occupational hazard." He spoke in a style better suited to an earlier century, proper and formal.

"Now you come to me with the love of a son in your heart and my best interests in your mind and tell me of another attempt to wrest power from me. I thank you for your dutiful application to your work, Khalid. However, you have overstepped your province. You are not a policeman. You are Petroleum Minister, in charge of the safekeeping of our greatest natural resource. You should not have done what you did. Overflying Ajman airspace without authorization is a very serious act. I don't believe you realize the position I would have been in had you and your band been caught. You are as much aware as I that my authority on the Supreme Federal Council is at the weakest it's ever been. Your incursion could have dealt me a severe blow."

Khalid had tried to interrupt the Prince but was waved down with a sweep of the ruler's bony hand.

"I know you felt justified. The evidence you've gathered against Rufti points to some sort of attempt on my life. But we can't lower ourselves to his standard and break the sovereignty laws of our neighbors. Colonel Bigelow's complicity in this act is something I will deal with at a later time. He is old and wise enough to know better than to follow a young man on such a quest."

Khalid had to speak on his mentor's behalf. "Colonel Bigelow isn't responsible for his actions. Although I have no authority to give him a direct order, he agreed to come with me after a great deal of personal coercion."

The Crown Prince smiled for the first time that morning. "If I know Bigelow, he volunteered as soon as he heard what you had planned, but your loyalty to him is laudable. Listen to me, Khalid, I realize that what you've done, you did for me. But you have to understand that there is more at stake than you realize.

"Hasaan bin-Rufti is only the latest incarnation of an old threat that goes back to the time when man first decided he needed leaders. There is always someone ready to question and to eventually try to seize what is not rightfully his. While Rufti may be more potentially dangerous given his timing, he is no more or less of a threat than I have faced before. I have known of his intentions for several months, almost a year really, ever since he went to Istanbul last winter.

"However, I cannot make a move until he does. I am bound by my office to remain on the defensive. I can't authorize any offensive action without incurring the wrath of the other members of the Supreme Council."

"You will do nothing?"

"If I have him arrested, the Sheik of Ajman will denounce me immediately, and I fear that he will garner the sympathy of Dubai and several other Emirates. Such a coalition would be powerful enough to oust me as head of the Council.

"We are facing a crisis right now, not only within the UAE but throughout the Gulf, and most people don't even realize it. For fifty years we have had the power to grind the West to a halt by shutting off the flow of oil. The embargo in the 1970s was just a reminder that we here in the Gulf cannot be ignored. The President of the United States has taken away the one trump card they feared we would play again. When America stops importing oil and turns to alternative fuels, Europe and Asia won't be far behind. And where will that leave us? We will be like saddlemakers after the invention of the automobile. Oil will be a quaint curiosity used by only a few diehards.

"The sole reason the UAE exists as a nation is our possession of one of the world's largest oil reserves. When that no longer has meaning, when oil has been replaced, our country will crumble, as will much of the region. Do you think if Kuwait didn't have oil, President Bush would have sent a half million men to defend her?"

Khalid was quiet as he absorbed this. He realized that despite his age, the Crown Prince could still see the world through very keen eyes. However, Khuddari was dubious of the Americans. "Do you really believe that they can live without oil?"

"I learned to never underestimate the United States. They swagger through the world like an overeager child, touching everything they come into contact with. But like a child, they possess a resolve that goes beyond reasonable understanding. They are a clever people, and if they say that they will find an alternate source of energy, you'd best believe it."

Khalid was doubtful of the Prince's estimation of America. Returning to the original subject, he asked, "So what do you want me to do about Rufti?"

"You are expected at the OPEC meeting in London. I want you there. You are the Petroleum Minister, not my bodyguard. You must be in England, looking after the best interests of the country, not here wet-nursing an old man."

"But the training facility we saw?"

"There are still ten years before the Americans stop buying our oil. In that time we will face a great many challenges, but the deadline is too far off to think that Rufti is a threat quite yet. The presence of that training ground *is* disturbing. However, I don't believe Rufti will make an attempt on my life in the near future. In the the decade before the American moratorium, he will continue to grow fat on the profits our oil brings into his coffers both as a citizen of the Emirates and as Ajman's Petroleum Minister."

"The British thought they had time when they signed a ninety-nine-year lease for Hong Kong. They have now lost the lease and you can ask anyone involved, the last ten years were the quickest," Khalid said sharply and immediately realized that he'd overstepped his bounds. He stood quickly to cover his embarrassment. "If I am to go to the OPEC meeting, I must take your leave."

The Crown Prince was ready to dismiss Khalid, but he stopped the younger man with a question. "Do you read much detective fiction?"

"No, sir. I rarely find time for pleasure reading."

"Too bad," the Prince said. "There seems to be an axiom among investigators that I always found interesting. When you don't know someone's motivation, look to the money."

"I don't understand," Khalid replied.

"Just because I told you to forget Rufti doesn't mean I expect that you'll obey. When you continue your research, remember those words." The old man's eyes glinted with fondness as he spoke.

Now, back at his office, Khalid shed his suit coat. Though many businessmen in the Arab world wore the traditional flowing wraps of white cotton, he preferred Western-style suits. His were not the overpriced boxy Italian suits favored by the Saudis and Kuwaitis, but a conservative English cut of superior cloth. Siri came from behind her expansive desk to hang the jacket properly on an ornate stand. Khalid stalked into his office beyond the antechamber, closing the door behind him as if that simple act would shut out the problems he was facing.

Siri entered a moment later, her body moving with a rhythm all its own. Khalid paid no attention to her as she took a seat before his desk.

His office was large, much too large for his austere tastes. The walls were richly carved panels of cherry, oiled daily so that they glowed with the light beaming through the tall windows behind the neatly kept desk. The floor was also wood, most of it covered by an intricate rug of either Afghani or Uzbeki origin. There were only a few pictures on the walls, one an official reproduction portrait of the Crown Prince and the others original paintings of the native landscape, each scene seeming to capture the essence of the open desert lurking just beyond the glass and steel confines of the city.

"Has Trevor James-Price phoned yet?" Khalid asked, absently shuffling through the papers Siri had set on the blotter during his meeting with the Crown Prince.

"No, the phone's been quiet all morning." It was odd for his phone to be silent for five seconds let alone an entire morning. But most people probably thought he was already in London. "Are you going to the OPEC meeting?"

Khalid looked up tiredly. "I have no choice. You might as well book me on the next available flight. And keep it quiet, no official reception at the airport and no bodyguards either."

"You could take one of the corporate jets."

As Petroleum Minister, Khalid ranked a board seat on AD-NOC, the Abu Dhabi National Oil Company, and thus was allowed many of the perks that went with the position. Yet for some reason that Siri couldn't figure, but which endeared him even more to her, Khalid refused many of the benefits, preferring to use commercial flights and dispensing with the usual retinue that went with his position.

Siri went back to her office to make the arrangements, leaving Khalid alone with his thoughts, which frustrated him to the point of distraction. Rather than deal with the summary reports Siri had left for him as preparation for the OPEC meeting, he swiveled around in his chair and looked out across the Persian Gulf. Immediately, he noticed the tanker he had seen when returning from his reconnoiter with Bigelow. The vessel was still hove to, although today he couldn't see any movement around the behemoth. She looked like a ghost ship.

Khalid spun back to his desk, putting the ship out of his mind. He spent a few minutes working on the papers before curiosity got the best of him. Jim Gibson, a consulting petroleum geologist, occupied an office a couple of floors below his. The American had a beautiful brass telescope next to his desk that he used to ogle sunbathers at the Sheraton Hotel. Khalid grabbed the telephone and dialed the in-house number. Gibson answered on the first ring.

"Jim, Khalid Khuddari. Anything worth looking at up the beach?"

"No, last time I checked there was just a couple skinny broads and some woman who must weight four hundred pounds, Minister." The north Texas twang made the phone lines resonate.

Khalid laughed with the libidinous American. "In that case, can you do me a favor and tell me the name of that tanker sitting out in the bay?"

"Sure, give me a second." Gibson set down the phone and was off the line for about a minute. "My angle is pretty poor, but it looks like *Southern Arabia*."

"Thanks, Jim. I noticed her yesterday and just wondered who she was."

"Yesterday, shit. That tub's been here for two weeks."

"Know anything about her?" Khalid's interest was piqued.

"Sorry, I just find the stuff, I don't haul it around." Gibson was referring to crude.

"Well, thanks anyway. Let's get together after I come back from London."

"Surprised you're not there now."

"A bureaucrat's job is never done, no matter how highly placed." Khalid hung up before Gibson could ask any questions about Khalid's delay at attending his first OPEC meeting as the UAE's official representative.

Khalid's personal computer was already working, the screen saver bouncing geometric shapes against the VDU's edges like Ping-Pong balls. It took him a few minutes of scrolling through countless menus to find the information he wanted, an alphabetical list of tankers that regularly plied the waters of the Gulf. Using the mouse he jumped down through the list but found no reference to the *Southern Arabia*. Curious, he was just about to call the port authorities when Siri's melodious voice came over the intercom.

"Minister, Trevor James-Price is on line one."

"Thanks, Siri," he said, reaching for the phone. Smiling to himself, he recalled the times he and Trevor had spent together at Cambridge.

During their university days, Trevor had been the only one of Khalid's friends who didn't see life as a series of obstacles to be overcome. He viewed each day as a precious commodity to be maximized until every second of every hour was used to its fullest potential. Whether it was cramming for final exams or relaxing at a pub with a pint and a pretty girl on his arm, Trevor had the knack of making the most of each moment. He'd once explained the mathematical improbability of any person's life, the innumerable random events that had occurred since the creation of the universe to allow one person to exist while denying another. He'd summed up by saying the chance that we were alive was somewhere in the realm of infinity-to-one. Why not make the best of living through the greatest long shot in history? Trevor had taken a double first in philosophy and classical literature, graduating with one of the best academic records in Cambridge's long history.

Trevor had published his first work of philosophy when he was only twenty-four, and by thirty he was the darling of the European intellectual elite. By thirty-five, he was a burned-out alcoholic with an ex-wife and three kids he hadn't seen in years. He now eked out a living as a freelance journalist and was currently working on an exposé of the OPEC cartel. Khalid had asked James-Price to keep an eye on Hasaan bin-Rufti during his time in London.

"Trev, how're things in soggy old England?"

"I don't know what's more damp, the weather or the lasses' knickers."

"Come to think of it, I'd heard it hadn't rained in Blighty in quite some time."

"Allow me a little fantasy life, won't you, old boy? God, how I hate a harsh taskmaster." Trevor moaned theatrically.

"How's the meeting going?"

"The preliminaries are over with, and all of the little functionaries have scurried around enough to ensure they'll stay off the dole for another year. As you know, the heads of OPEC meet tomorrow. The static over the wire leads me to believe that this isn't a local call, am I right?"

"I'm still in Abu Dhabi. Is anyone else missing?"

"Just you and Juan De la Bruille from Venezuela. All of the other petro-nabobs are present and accounted for, including your corpulent friend."

"Rufti's no friend of mine," Khalid reminded James-Price mildly. "So what's he been up to?"

"Do you want the full room-and-board itinerary or just the highlights?"

"Keep it short. I've got a ton to do before I leave the Gulf."

"So the anointed one is going to join us, then?" Trevor teased.

"As that American you had as a roommate for your second year would say, anoint this."

"Touchy, touchy."

"Actually, Trev, I am. Things aren't so hot here. In fact

you could say that our house of cards is facing a stiff breeze."

"Trapped between Scylla and Charybdis, eh?"

"You could say that, but I've no idea what it means."

"Classical Greek mythology. Loosely translated it means caught between a rock and a hard place."

"That sounds about right," Khalid breathed.

"We'll talk about that later, then." Trevor had caught the undertones in his friend's voice and wisely backed off the subject. "Well, Rufti has been very chummy with the hand-maidens and even with a couple of the scullery wenches."

Trevor referred to the representatives of the Seven Sisters, the seven great oil companies, as the handmaidens. The scullery wenches were officials from any one of the smaller petroleum companies.

"Anyone in particular?"

"Actually, yes. None other than Max Johnston himself. He and Rufti have been as thick as thieves since Johnston's arrival this morning."

"Any rumors flying about them?"

"The latest I heard is Rufti wants some of Petromax's money to sink exploratory wells in Ajman. It sounds like they're talking about a smash-and-grab operation. Bleed whatever oil they can and move on to the next site. Given the Yank's time line for oil importation, it seems to be the only thing they can do."

"It makes sense," Khalid conceded. "Ajman does have some oil reserves that they'll want out of the ground before the American moratorium."

"Qatar and Kuwait are negotiating similar deals with the Big Seven," the journalist agreed. "They're taking a massive price cut just to get the oil to market."

"Do you get the impression OPEC is planning an across-the-board price reduction?"

"No way," James-Price said. "These deals are sub rosa, the mercantile exchange boards won't know a thing about it. In public, the ministers are talking about a four-cent-per-barrel increase in response to the rise in Brent Light Sweet prices."

"So you don't see anything suspicious about Rufti's behavior?"

"I didn't say that. Rufti as well as the Oil Minister from Iran and the newly reinstated representative from Iraq have been holding very quiet meetings, usually in out-of-the-way places."

"Iran and Iraq? What in the hell is he doing with them?"

"Haven't a clue, old boy. Security around those meetings is tighter than a vicar's robes though not as easily bought. During the day, all three men keep their distance from one another, but for the past two nights, their limos have all been seen parked in front of the same hotel or restaurant. Whatever they are discussing is high level and extremely hush-hush."

"Trev, I need you to find out what they're talking about."

"I would, but I do have a piece to write. Playing detective for you has been a nice diversion, but I've got child support payments higher than most countries' gross national products. I need to get back to my story. I'm sorry."

"I'm writing a check right now for one hundred thousand dollars. Get me that information and it's yours."

"Khalid, I don't need your beneficence," Trevor said angrily.

"But I need yours." Khalid set down the phone without saying good-bye.

―――――

ALYESKA MARINE TERMINAL
VALDEZ, ALASKA

As a frequent traveler, Mercer had developed an immunity to jet lag. He could force himself to stay awake or fall asleep upon arrival, depending on how much time he'd shifted. He could be fully acclimated in only a single day, whether he got thirteen hours of sleep or three. However, his flight to Alaska, by way of Chicago and Sea-Tac in Seattle, had been interrupted by both weather and a mechanical delay at Midway, forcing him to spend a night at an airport hotel. He finally landed in Anchorage at a little past ten in the morning, clear-eyed and sharp.

Mercer rented a four-wheel-drive Blazer and drove the three hundred miles south to Valdez, stopping only for fuel, coffee, and the occasional al fresco bathroom break. He arrived in town shortly before four and decided to head straight for the marine terminal rather than checking into his hotel.

He rolled the Blazer to the small guard booth at the entrance to the sprawling facility and was relieved to find his name still on the guest list from when he and Howard Small had used the terminal as a base for their mini-mole tests. Mercer drove into the terminal, around the East Manifold building that monitored oil pouring down the pipeline at 88,000 barrels per hour, and past the huge holding tanks that processed the contaminated seawater that ballasted tankers on their runs to the site.

He slid into an "Authorized Vehicle Only" spot in front of the Operations Center, just inland of berth number four, where a midsized tanker was having her belly filled with North Slope crude. Once he was out of the protective cocoon of the truck, the biting cold struck him head-on, the wind coming off the Sound like needles. Snow had blanketed much of the terminal, but it had all been plowed into huge mounds in parking lots and just beyond the sharp curves of the roads that crisscrossed the installation. To say the weather was unseasonably cold was to say that Cain and Abel only argued on occasion.

Quickly, Mercer dashed from the Blazer into the Operations Center, unzipping his coat as soon as he felt the blast of warm air from the building's heaters. The receptionist was reading a thriller novel and regarded Mercer so angrily that he was sure he'd interrupted a climactic scene. "Can I help you, sir?"

"Yes, I phoned earlier. I'm Philip Mercer."

"Oh, yes, you're here to see Andy Lindstrom." She got up from her chair, the metal legs scraping as she shifted her considerable bulk. "Right this way. He's not expecting you for a while, but I'm sure he won't mind."

Lindstrom, the terminal's Chief of Operations, stood behind his desk as Mercer entered his office. He wore jeans and a heavy flannel shirt, his head covered by a Seahawks baseball cap. Of average height and build and still in his forties, he looked much older, his skin heavily weathered by twenty years in Alaska and a two-packs-a-day cigarette habit. His jaw was stubbled with a couple days' worth of reddish beard, and his blue eyes were wearier than Mercer remembered from the last time he'd seen him.

The office was small and institutional, the light provided by a single window and a bank of fluorescent fixtures suspended from the drop ceiling. Lindstrom's desk was piled with papers placed haphazardly in spiraled stacks that seemed in imminent danger of toppling. A credenza and file cabinet were also buried under papers, thick technical manuals, and parts catalogs. The only furniture not covered was a pair of old wooden chairs in front of the desk. On one wall was a large topographical map of Alaska crudely bisected by a jagged red line representing the pipeline. On the opposite wall was a garish travel poster of a well-bikinied beach.

Lindstrom acknowledged Mercer with a raised finger, then pointed at the telephone receiver clutched in his other fist. His complexion was reddened by whatever was being said on the other end of the conversation.

"Now wait just a goddamn minute. I sent the armature up to the depot in Fairbanks two days ago. If you haven't gotten it yet, bend their ear, not mine." He paused and rolled his eyes at Mercer. "Hey, listen to me, I'm not your fucking whipping boy. This sounds like an internal problem to me. I just tried to do you a favor, don't think it means I want you calling me every time you have a glitch with one of your machines. Maybe next time you'll buy American."

He set the phone down and blew out a long breath.

"Let me guess," Mercer said as Lindstrom lit a cigarette. "One of the oil companies up in the Refuge."

"You got it. Alyeska promised to help them out, and the next thing you know they're calling me when they run out of toilet paper. Christ, it wasn't like this when we opened up this state. Those roughnecks knew how to work.

"I was a little surprised to get your call yesterday," Andy said as they shook hands. "I thought you'd left the state after completing those tests with Howard Small. And I'm downright curious why you wanted my Chief of Security present for this meeting. Mike Collins will be here in a few minutes. Mind telling me what you're doing back in Alaska?"

"I'd prefer to wait until Collins gets here. It's a pretty complicated story, and I only want to tell it once."

"Am I right in guessing this has something to do with your project up on the hill?"

"Indirectly. Have you heard about Howard Small?"

"No, what about him?"

"He's dead, I'm afraid. Murdered. And whoever killed him has made two attempts on me."

"Jesus. All for that tunnel-boring machine of his?"

Before Mercer could reply, there was a knock at the door, and without pause, Mike Collins entered the office. He was big, a solid two hundred twenty pounds, and old enough that Mercer assumed the scar jagging its way across the right side of his face was a constant reminder of the Vietnam War. Like Lindstrom, he was dressed casually, jeans and a flannel shirt, a pair of Tony Lamas on his size-thirteen feet.

Because he and Mercer hadn't met during Mercer's earlier stay in Valdez, Lindstrom made introductions. Collins' grip was sure and firm, his hands almost as callused as Mercer's. The Operations Chief told Collins about the death of Howard Small and the two attempts on Mercer's life.

"So this is about Minnie?" Lindstrom asked again.

"No, not at all. After we finished up our tests, Howard and I went fishing with his cousin in Homer. While we were out, we found a burned-out derelict fishing boat floating maybe forty miles offshore. What we found aboard her got him killed."

"Yeah, and what was that?" Collins asked with the sharpness of a cop who couldn't take retirement.

"It took the full efforts of the FBI lab in Washington to figure out that a piece of steel I'd salvaged from the wreck was a fragment of a liquid nitrogen containment tank. Our best guess is the boat was smuggling cylinders of the stuff into Alaska."

"Why would someone do that when it's commercially available, and why would someone then try to kill to cover it up?"

"The Feds are working on that right now," Mercer answered. "What concerns me is what they're going to do with it."

"You think this may have something to do with us?" Collins asked.

Before Mercer could answer, Lindstrom spoke. "How much liquid nitrogen are we talking about?"

"Before I left Washington, I called the Harbor Master in Seward, the boat's home port. He told me that the *Jenny IV* had gone out eighteen times in the past year, yet none of the canneries or fish-processing plants that I called have any record of buying fish from her. The Harbor Master also told me her captain had just paid cash for a new pickup, so he was making money somehow. Figure she went on at least eighteen runs and had a capacity of about thirteen tons, you do the math. That's a shitload of liquid nitrogen."

"I still don't get it. It's not a drug or explosives or anything illegal. I mean it's just cold. What's the big deal?"

"The only thing that makes sense to me, and I believe that Dick Henna of the FBI agrees, is sabotage," Mercer continued over the startled looks of the two men. "Liquid nitrogen can alter the molecular strength of any material exposed to it. It weakens steel so badly that it can fracture under its own weight. And there would be no trace of tampering. Say someone sprays a piece of equipment with the stuff. Later, when it's used, the equipment would fail with no logical explanation and no detectable cause. What if they use the nitrogen to weaken a section of the pipeline? When it collapses you've got a major spill on your hands for no reason. You've been under the media microscope since work started on the new pipeline from the North Slope, so I figured you guys would be tailor-made for this kind of terrorist action."

Mercer could see he'd caught Andy Lindstrom's attention. But by no means was the third-generation oilman convinced.

Instinctively, Mercer stayed quiet, letting Lindstrom think through the logic. But still he had to struggle not to show his agitation. He'd just dropped a bombshell on the Operations Chief's desk, and Lindstrom didn't know that Mercer wasn't given to paranoid fantasies and conspiracy theories. Come on, damn it, come on. You know this could be a possible threat.

"The pipeline would make a choice target, but it wouldn't work," Lindstrom said at last, pulling a fifth of bourbon from a desk drawer and splashing some into three small styrofoam cups. "The pipe walls are high-tensile steel, about a half-inch thick, with a maximum rated internal pressure load of nearly one thousand two hundred psi. Even if someone froze a section, they'd still need a bulldozer to crack it open, and our response team would be there long before they made their getaway."

"What about the VSMs?" Mercer fired back, knowing he had to work fast or his warnings weren't going to amount to anything.

The aboveground sections of the pipeline were supported above the frozen tundra by 78,000 VSMs or Vertical Support Members. The towers were spaced approximately sixty feet apart and were designed to allow the pipeline to shift within its bed up to twelve feet horizontally and two feet vertically to compensate for expansion and contraction of the pipe casing. The VSMs also served as a buffer in the event of an earthquake like the one that devastated Alaska on Good Friday of 1964. The bases of the stanchions were buried anywhere between fifteen and sixty feet deep depending on the depth of the permafrost. They utilized passive ammonia cooling to ensure that conductive heat from the flowing oil didn't melt the frozen soil that kept the pipeline stable.

"Same again. Even if you weakened the supports with liquid nitrogen, you'd still need heavy equipment to make them fail. Remember, it took 1347 state and federal permits to get the line constructed, and you can bet dollars to doughnuts that they covered their asses and made sure the whole system was so overbuilt that God himself couldn't take it apart."

"They said the same thing about the *Titanic*." Mercer let his last statement hang in the air for a minute before continuing. "How about some of the bridges? Isn't there one over a thousand feet long?"

"Where the pipeline crosses the Tanana River, there's a suspension bridge of twelve hundred feet, but again, even after weakening the anchors and caisson supports, you'd need dynamite to bring it down. Why bother freezing the steel if you have to use explosives?"

"I know you guys have to put chemicals in the oil to augment its natural heat and make flow easier on the way from Prudhoe. What about just freezing the oil in the line, plugging it up solid? Would something like that cause severe damage?"

"If the oil froze, thermal expansion wouldn't be enough to crack the pipe casings, and we could have the pipe cleaned out in just a few months," Lindstrom retorted. Mercer could see that Lindstrom was ready to tear his idea apart. "And you're also forgetting some other prime targets in Alaska like Elmendorf Air Force Base, or the string of radar-tracking stations along the north coast. And what about the new production facilities in the Refuge? A couple of them are already up and running, piping crude to Prudhoe Bay for transshipment here on the TAPline." Lindstrom lit another cigarette while a new idea struck him. "The only place Alyeska could be targeted is up at our equipment depot in Fairbanks where we've got about half a billion dollars worth of drill string, cutter heads, and other equipment."

"They spray a bundle of drill string, the sections of pipe used to bore into the ground, then smack them with a hammer." Collins hadn't detected the sarcasm in Lindstrom's voice and was seriously considering the possibility. "The pipe wouldn't crack, it's too strong, but there would be microscopic fissures. When those turbines on the pads spool up, the string would shatter, fouling the bore hole for eternity."

"What's security like up there?" If Mercer could convince just one of the men about his fears, it was better than nothing.

"The expensive stuff, like the diamond cutter heads, are under lock and key, patrolled twenty-four hours a day," Collins replied. "But the lengths of string are just lying around in big stacks ready to be transported to the North Slope." Collins rubbed a hand across his balding head, a gold Marine

Corps ring catching the final rays of the setting sun through the window.

"I suggest you beef up your force," Mercer said mildly.

"I don't see it," Lindstrom remarked, still unconcerned. "If they shipped over two hundred and thirty tons of liquid nitrogen, they're after something a hell of a lot more important than spare parts sitting in a warehouse."

"What's your estimation?" Mercer tried to draw Lindstrom in again, hoping that the Operations Director would take his warning more seriously.

"We're secure here at the terminal, and Prudhoe Bay is so isolated it doesn't make a logical choice."

"Which leaves?"

"Not much. The pipeline is just too tough for something like you suggest. Alyeska may be a prime target for terrorism, and I'm not ruling us out before this crisis over the Refuge ends, but using liquid nitrogen just doesn't make any sense."

Mercer turned to Collins, hoping he still had the other man intrigued. "Why did you say that the terminal itself is secure? I didn't have any problems getting in."

"You're still on the guest list; all others are being turned away. We've even suspended the regular visitors' tour bus from town. Besides the access road, there's no other way into the terminal. Fences, active and passive detectors, and patrols keep everyone from getting within a mile of any vital area."

"Mercer, you've been focusing on why someone is smuggling liquid nitrogen into Alaska. Have you stopped to ask yourself who?" Though Lindstrom obviously didn't believe in a threat to his private domain, he acknowledged the possibility of terrorism.

"Oh, I already know who," Mercer said sharply.

"PEAL?" asked Collins.

"No. This may be their type of operation, but it's way out of their league."

"PEAL?" Lindstrom didn't immediately recognize the name. "Oh, wait, aren't they the environmental group with the big research ship anchored in the bay?"

"Yeah," Collins said. "They've been here for a couple of weeks, boycotting Petromax gas stations, giving interviews to the army of reporters that follow them around, and generally making everyone around here as edgy as hell."

"They don't have anything to do with this," Mercer repeated. "They want to stop the drilling in the Arctic Refuge, but this is just too big for them. Boycotting gas stations is one thing, but coordinating an attack against Alyeska is entirely different. Listen, guys, I'm not up here in any official capacity; the Feds are handling the investigation. In fact, I'm in Alaska against the FBI Director's direct order. But while they're off looking for clues, I think they're forgetting to watch over targets. I'm surprised no one from the Bureau has been here to talk to you. That's what you get for having too many law school graduates and not enough people with brains."

"You sound like you know who's smuggling the liquid nitrogen. Who is it?" Collins asked.

"A former KGB Colonel named Ivan Kerikov. I've dealt with him before. He's utterly ruthless. He would kill without a moment's hesitation. Oh, shit, that reminds me. Can I use your phone?"

Lindstrom nodded, and Mercer dialed quickly, the phone number being one of the hundred or so he was able to keep straight in his head.

"Homer Police, Chief MacLaughlin speaking."

"Chief, this is Philip Mercer—"

MacLaughlin cut Mercer off before he could continue. "How the hell did you know the *Jenny IV* wouldn't be there?"

"Just a hunch."

"Bullshit," MacLaughlin exploded. "No one gets hunches like that. I've just changed the deaths of Jerry and John Small from misadventure to murder. Add them to the death of Dave Heller, the guy we found in his beached boat, and it means I've got three unsolved killings in a town that hasn't seen a murder since I became Sheriff. I want some fucking answers."

"You'll have them as soon as I do, Chief. I'm sorry, but that's all I can say right now. I can tell you that you won't find the murderers in town; they're long gone."

"No kidding," MacLaughlin said sarcastically. "Just because I'm a small-town cop doesn't mean I'm a simpleton."

"I'm not saying that, but I think your investigation will be better served if you concentrate on finding where the *Jenny IV* was sunk the second time."

"Fat fucking chance. After my brother-in-law failed to find her by dragging the bottom, I sent out nearly every boat in the harbor. Forty boats, all equipped with fish-finding sonar, failed to find anything. They must have searched a hundred square miles."

Mercer could imagine their search. Captains and crews half drunk, thrilled at playing cop for a day, running randomly across the water without any logical search pattern. Mercer guessed that MacLaughlin's one hundred miles was more like ten. There was no sense in pointing this out. MacLaughlin was so angry right now that any criticism would probably set him off like a volcano. Mercer couldn't blame MacLaughlin; he was caught up in something so big that he didn't know which way was up.

"Really?" Mercer said, trying to sound impressed while thinking that he might call Dick Henna and have him get an antisubmarine vessel into the area. With its side-scanning sonar, it would be able to find the hulk on its first pass. "I appreciate that, Chief, I really do. I'll let you know if I get anything more on my end."

Mercer cut the connection before Maclaughlin could protest.

"What was that all about?" Collins asked suspiciously.

"Maybe something, maybe a red herring. But a couple of nights ago, the *Jenny IV* was moved from where the Coast Guard had sunk her. Whoever did it killed the owner of the boat they used."

"You think it was this Kerikov guy?"

"Either him or someone working for him," Mercer said, keeping a tight rein on his building anger. "Like I said before, I really don't have any right being here and talking to you two. But my ass is on the line here. I'm the only living witness to the discovery of the *Jenny IV*, and I don't think Kerikov's going to stop until I'm dead. My only choice is to stop him first. I don't want to end-run the authorities, but if anything, and I mean *anything*, out of the ordinary happens here I'd like to know about it."

"Nothing will, but sure, we'll keep you in the loop," Lindstrom answered indulgently.

Mercer gave him the name of the hotel he'd be staying at. He felt he'd done the best he could with what little information he had and could only hope that his warnings wouldn't go unheeded.

Twenty minutes later, he parked the Blazer in front of his hotel, a large clapboard structure that had seen better days. It wasn't the best place in town, which suited him fine. After settling into his room and taking a quick shower, he enjoyed a salmon dinner in the nearly deserted dining room. The adjacent lounge was almost as empty, so he decided to head out for a while and maybe talk to some of the PEAL activists who might be in town.

Although he didn't think PEAL was involved with the smuggling of the liquid nitrogen, he wanted a better handle on the group, partially for his own investigation and partially because he wanted to know more about Aggie Johnston, and PEAL seemed to be a major portion of her life.

Ever since she had stormed out of his house, thoughts of her weren't too far away. At first, he'd tried to simply will her from his mind, but he gave that up. Aggie was not the type of woman Mercer could forget. In just a short time, she had worked her way into his head so deeply that he found he could recall the specific scent of her hair and the way her eyes softened when she first saw the bandage on his face from the pistol whip. Mercer had never believed the old adage about opposites attracting, but then he'd never really faced it before. He was both hurt and confused that Aggie hadn't tried to contact him. But he had too much going on to allow himself to be distracted by thoughts of her, yet he still wanted to find out more about her, a lot more. Everything.

He walked along North Harbor Drive, paralleling the small boat marina. The sun had set, and the sound of waves slapping against the hundred pleasure craft came out of the darkness like an eerie recording. The few streetlights cast hazy puddles on the sidewalk, their glow barely glinting off the chrome trim of the nearest boats. The air was heavy with the tangy perfume of the ocean. Although the sidewalks were fairly crowded for a town of only three thousand, there was a loneliness here that was found in all of Alaska except for its larger cities. Out in the harbor he could see the running lights of a large vessel he knew must be the *Hope*.

Mercer finally came across a bar that looked promising, its advertising neon signs casting garish splashes of color into the night. Country music blared from within as a young couple entered, Mercer following close behind. He nodded his thanks to them and surveyed the room.

The bar was one step below a hole in the wall but better than a dive. The floor was chewing gum–smeared carpet with a pile so worn it looked like cement. The walls were yellowed by the cigarette smoke that hung in the air like smog. The U-shaped bar could seat about twenty people, and as he approached, he saw that its heavily varnished top was covered with carved initials. Like so many bars, this place relied on a gimmick to attract patrons, in this case, the immortality of etching your name into the bar top. There were about a dozen tables in the room, a tiny dance floor, and an even smaller stage, although the music was now coming from the battered jukebox next to the front door. The establishment was maybe half full.

Mercer wanted a vodka gimlet, but this was the type of place where you drank either beer or straight whiskey. He ordered a beer from the busty bartender and took a corner stool next to a guy he figured was a fisherman, given his size and the rubber boots he sported. The woman behind the bar bent deeply as she slid a Coors to Mercer, giving him an excellent view of what she kept barely hidden under her plunge-necked blouse. He smiled at her for both the beer and the view. If bars had gimmicks, well, so did bartenders.

"Are you an Us or a Them?" the man sitting at Mercer's left asked without preamble.

"I guess that depends on who we are and who they are." He couldn't tell if the man was drunk or crazy.

"*They* are that ecology group and the mess of reporters here with them." He nodded at a group of tables pushed together against one wall, the ten or so people forming an exclusive enclave. "*We* are just about everyone else."

"Trust me, I'm one of us." Mercer caught the man's humor. "I'm a mining engineer. You?"

"I work aboard one of the ERVs, the ships that guide the tankers out of Prince William Sound," he responded before taking a swallow of his beer. "I tell you, I just don't understand how these protesters can survive. Do they get paid for fucking around with other people's lives?"

"You'd be surprised how well funded most environmental groups are. And at least one member of this group has got more money than God."

"Figures, the idle rich feel guilty, so they try to make sure no one else can make any money."

"Modern noblesse oblige," Mercer muttered.

He took a moment to study the group at their tables. Deciding who was a journalist and who was a member of PEAL was simple. The reporters had a hard-edged cynicism, whether gained through experience or affected, that they all wore like a badge of honor. The environmentalists were usually younger, fresh-faced and eager, with open smiles and easy laughs that made them look like a victorious college football team and their girlfriends. There was a scrubbed innocence to them and a strong sense of camaraderie that bound them much more strongly than simple friendship. They were crusaders, brothers in arms fighting a holy mission.

"So what do you know about them?" Mercer asked his neighbor, who, like so many Alaskans, was more than willing to talk to a stranger.

"Not much, other than I want 'em out of my town," he spat. "They been here a few weeks, them and the reporters. One group getting in everyone's faces, preaching at us about this and that, treating us like morons." Then he quipped, "And the protesters are even worse."

The ERV crewman had just started telling Mercer about the overturned fuel truck when the door to the bar opened, letting in a blast of cold air. Mercer turned to see a large group of people enter, laughing as they stepped across the threshold. There were nine men and five women, though it was hard to distinguish between the two if one judged by hair length alone.

When he saw her, he wasn't surprised. It was logical that she'd be in Alaska. Her organization's largest protest was happening right here in Valdez, and their flagship was anchored in the bay. There was no reason why she wouldn't want to be part of it. And this bar was the closest to where Mercer had seen several PEAL Zodiacs tied against the public docks. He wondered, as he looked at her, if his being here was as random as he liked to believe. Or had he come to this particular bar hoping that she would be here too? Even if some part of him had wished for her entrance, he was unprepared for her arrival.

Aggie Johnston didn't see him as she was swept into the bar with her friends, her face radiant. They immediately headed for the tables already staked by PEAL and the sycophantic reporters. Like the day he'd first seen her at George Washington University, she wore a shapeless green anorak.

His eyes tracked her across the room, listening to the joyous cries of her fellows as she joined them. It was obvious that they had not seen her in some time, and her presence was the reason for their celebratory mood. He watched for a few moments longer, then turned away abruptly, angry at himself for acting like a lovelorn teenager suffering through the end of a summertime romance.

"Jesus," Mercer's neighbor breathed, "I'd rather feel that than feel sick."

Mercer looked and saw that Aggie had taken off her coat, revealing a tight black turtleneck. He expected that his friend's taste in women ran toward the bosomy centerfold type, yet he too had felt Aggie Johnston's allure.

"I don't think you can't have one without the other," Mercer said darkly.

Two beers later, Mercer was getting ready to leave. The bar was filled to capacity and the band was just going on its first break, the house lights coming back up. A few of the locals had tried to approach the PEAL table to ask the women to dance, and had all been rebuffed with casually cruel snickers. Aggie had had the most potential suitors, and while her refusals seemed a little kinder, they were no less absolute.

One of the men at the table, a black-bearded giant who appeared to be some sort of leader given the deferential quiet he received when he stood, hoisted his glass to make a toast in the silence following the band's last song. "To Brock Holt, a polluter who paid for his actions."

Although the toastmaster spoke to his group, his eyes scanned the crowd, clearly hoping for a response. His eyes were glazed with fervent conviction and several pitchers of beer. No one knew he had been on that lonely stretch of road with Jan Voerhoven. Even the jaded reporters were stunned by his inappropriate words.

He didn't have to wait long for a response. A voice from the far side of the bar, ten or so stools from Mercer, bellowed drunkenly, "What the fuck did you say, asshole?"

"I don't believe I was talking to you," the environmentalist menaced.

The air in the room had gotten tight. The bartender was already reaching for the phone to call the police. The club's three bouncers would be sorely outmatched if things turned ugly.

"Brock was a friend of mine." The local stood on drunken legs, his lips rubbery but his emotions as clear as crystal. He wore a blue parka with a Petromax logo over his left breast.

"Then you should be as relieved as we are that he's no longer hauling poison across the state," came the reply with a mocking sneer. Aggie tried to pull her friend back to his seat, but he shook her off, too hyped to think about what he was saying or where he was.

The antagonists started walking toward each other, and chairs began scraping back from tables as the room galvanized into two camps. This fight between activists and locals had been brewing since PEAL had arrived in Valdez, and after a few more heated insults, the room exploded, each side believing that it was right; the ecologists knowing their struggle was to save a planet, the locals fighting to preserve their livelihoods and families. The reporters ducked behind their tables and watched the melee with ghoulish glee.

It was apparent that only about thirty of the locals wanted

to get involved; the rest made for the door as quickly as possible. Nearly all twenty-five members of PEAL were eager to brawl, including several women. At first, Mercer wanted to join the hurried exodus, but as he was moved toward the exit, he realized that he couldn't leave Aggie until he knew she was safe. He turned and struggled back into the bar, shoving and pushing through the panicked throng.

Forcing himself into the clear, he heard her scream over the shouts and yells, over the grunts and cries, over the breaking of glass and the crash of furniture. She was pinned near the far wall of the bar, bent backward over one of the band's large speakers, red stage lights flashing against her pale, pained face. A swarthy man in a black leather jacket held her hands over her head, a sheen of eager sweat gleaming on his skin. To get there, Mercer fought his way in, out, and around a half dozen fights, punching and kicking with little regard for his target.

A blow landed solidly in his stomach and another caught him on his jaw. He rolled with the shots, giving himself a few moments to recover. A PEAL advocate came after him, hands held low and at the ready. Mercer let him come, gauging the man with an expert eye. As soon as his attacker had committed himself to a powerful roundhouse punch, Mercer eased back just enough so that the fist slid past his chin. He grabbed the man's outstretched arm, steadied his target, and fired off a series of punches at the man's exposed flank, fists sinking into the hard pad of muscle below the activist's arm. A couple of ribs snapped with sickening pops.

Mercer sidestepped the falling environmentalist and targeted the man holding Aggie. Her attacker had freed one of his hands so he could grope between her legs. His shoulders were hunched to protect himself from her futile ripostes. Mercer shoved aside two struggling men who staggered into his path and reached Aggie only sixty seconds after the fight had broken out.

Had her assault not turned sexual, Mercer might have been willing to let her feel the consequences of her action. She was playing with other people's lives as a pet project, disregarding what was at stake for the men and women who lived in Valdez. Protests like this were strictly geared for the media. PEAL wasn't in Alaska to raise environmental awareness, just the world's awareness of the group's existence. Their interest in Valdez would last only as long as they could hold the media's attention, then they would move on. But the man holding Aggie had made the mistake of trying to satisfy some perverse desire by fondling her.

Even as Mercer swept a half-filled beer bottle off one of the few unoverturned tables, he hoped that a less amorous man had pinned Aggie. She wanted to be part of the Green Revolution, and this was its reality. Tear down what exists and worry about the aftermath later. With a strong downward jerk, the bottle shattered over the man's head and he hit the floor before the last of the disintegrated glass found its way to the carpet.

Aggie was pulled off balance by his fall, sliding off the speaker and onto her feet. Her eyes widened to almost impossible proportions when she recognized Mercer standing before her.

"Now, what's a nice girl like you . . . Oh, never mind, let's get the hell out of here." Mercer grabbed her wrist and led her out a back door just as the police stormed into the bar. As they fled, Mercer took an instant to notice that nearly all the PEAL activists were still fighting while the floor was littered with the dazed forms of Valdez's toughest citizenry.

The alley behind the bar was dimly lit and the Dumpster next to the back exit was filled to near overflowing. Aggie tried to stop, but Mercer wanted to be as far away from the bar as possible. He didn't want to spend the night in the town's drunk tank with a group of hungover antagonists whose fight was far from over. He dragged her to a lit street, one block inland from the bar.

Once under the protective pool of a streetlight, she stopped and jerked her arm out of Mercer's grip. "What the hell are you doing here?"

"You're welcome."

"Answer me, goddamn it."

"Hey, I was in the right place at the right time. If you want to go back, be my guest. I'm sure that guy would love to have another go at you." Mercer said with more anger than he felt.

"Fuck you."

"Good-bye, Aggie." He started to walk away and was relieved when she ran up and grabbed his sleeve.

"I'm sorry. I don't care why you were there tonight, but I'm certainly grateful." She looked up at him, her eyes like gems.

He wanted, more than anything else, to kiss her, to capture that mouth with his. But he turned away instead and continued walking. He hated being this confused, and his natural reaction was to leave, as if getting away from her presence would ease the hurt in his mind.

"Mercer, wait!" She caught up to him again, and they began walking in stride, her long legs matching his angry pace. Without a word, he shed his leather jacket and draped it over her shoulders. She snuggled into it like a favorite blanket. After a moment she said, "We need to talk."

"I really don't think we do."

"The man who broke into your house, I knew him."

"Yes, I know," Mercer replied evenly, thankful she hadn't dodged the other issue that had been plaguing him since that night. "I've never seen anyone face death the way you did. Your expression wasn't fear or disgust, it was recognition."

He might have expected her first revelation, but he wasn't prepared for her second. "He worked for my father."

"What?" Mercer stopped, whirling her around so that she faced him.

"Well, he used to. I confronted my father about it yesterday. He told me Burt Manning hadn't worked for him for a couple of months."

"And you believed him?"

"Yes. No. Well, maybe. I don't know."

"Aggie, we're talking about lives here, mine in particular."

"When I talked to my father, he knew what time I was at your house and the only way he could have known that is if Manning had told him before breaking in to kill you. Manning must have been working for him." Aggie went quiet for a second, on the verge of tears. "I just can't believe it. My father is a monster, but he would never have someone killed, especially you. You two are friends. After I talked to him, I was so scared, I didn't know what to think, so I came here a couple of days before planned."

"Aggie, do yourself a favor and get the hell out of Alaska. You're not safe here."

"I'm safer here than I was in Washington." They started walking again.

"Manning wasn't after you. He was after me, and his reasons have nothing to do with your father. Go home."

"What does being in Alaska have to do with anything?"

"More than you think, but I don't have time to explain." Mercer had shut down the emotional side of his brain so when he spoke again it was without the trace of bitterness he expected. "You and your PEAL friends should just pack up and go somewhere else."

"None of us are leaving until our work is done." Her tone was absolute.

"Hey, you guys want to go chain yourselves to trees and stage marches, that's fine, but people are dying here and I'm afraid it's not over yet. Don't you understand? You are about to get caught up in something more dangerous than that barroom brawl. Is your life worth more than making a little noise about the environment? Listen, Aggie, your father didn't have anything to do with that attack on my house. It was coordinated by a former KGB operative named Ivan Kerikov, and he's in Alaska now and has already killed four people including three of my friends."

"But my dad knew when I was at your house," Aggie persisted.

They'd walked back to the docks, where a crowd of PEAL activists were clustered around the two large Zodiacs. By their laughter, it seemed that only a few had been arrested and none seemed the worse for the fight. Mercer guessed that the lenience was due to the media's presence. His impression that they were like a bunch of collegiates out for a good time was reaffirmed. He paused, while he and Aggie were still in the shadows of a storefront, and watched the environmentalists a little more critically. They appeared too relaxed, and something about that niggled at the back of Mercer's mind.

"Well, there are your friends. I know you're not going to listen to my advice because you're too stubborn, but I want you to be careful, all right?"

"Mercer, I—"

"Just be careful." He turned and vanished into the night so quickly that his absence surprised her.

A moment later she'd rejoined her friends, laughing with them as they recounted their prowess in the fight before boarding the Zodiacs for the brief run out to the *Hope*. She kept peering into the darkness, hoping to see Mercer watching her, but he was gone.

As the group clambered aboard the rubber boats, another figure was watching them, tucked deeply in the shadows. He languidly massaged his crotch as he watched Aggie ease herself into a Zodiac, her taunt body straining against the denim of her jeans as she stood for one instant stretched between the wharf and the boat.

She's got the backside of a young boy, Abu Alam thought. He touched the lump on his head where the bottle had collided. He couldn't have his revenge against the man tonight; Kerikov was expecting a report about PEAL's activities in town, but he now knew the man's face very well. And once he was out of the way, there was nothing to stop him from discovering if her ass felt as tight as it looked.

MV *HOPE*

The wooden steps slung from the side of the research ship could be lowered from the main deck to water level like a medieval drawbridge. The men and women waited in the Zodiacs with the anticipation of marauding Saxons eager to storm a Norman castle, ready for their party to continue aboard their ship. Aggie went up with them, mindful that the graphite strips on each tread were slicked by a chilly fog. She did not share the high spirits of the other activists.

She was carried up the last few steps by a big Norwegian student nearly ten years her junior who laughed as he set her on the deck with a gallant flourish. His hair was almost as white as his toothy grin. She tried to smile back, but everything suddenly began to feel unreal, as if she shouldn't be here, as if this was no longer her world.

The feeling of disquiet clung to her as she entered the main salon, grateful for the heat blasting from the ventilators. It was only then that she realized she was still wearing Mercer's bomber jacket. She brought the collar to her nose and inhaled the rich aroma of worn leather, a trace of his musky after-shave, and the unmistakable scent of the man himself. The smell was pleasing, comforting. She shed the jacket, tossing it over her chair in a quick guilty gesture as if those around her somehow knew what she'd just been feeling.

She felt disconnected from the party that was continuing around her, barely acknowledging the bottle of beer that was put in front of her or the animated chatter of the people. She wondered if she'd been away too long and just needed a little time to reacclimate herself to their boisterous lifestyle. Or had she changed in the month since she'd last been aboard the *Hope*, when she'd been part of this extended family?

Certainly things in her life had affected her—Burt Manning's death, her father's possible connection. And Mercer. She absently fingered the rough texture of his coat, finding the leather scarred and worn like its owner.

She'd felt absolutely powerless when the man in the bar had grabbed her and began to grope. He could have raped her right there and she doubted anyone would have noticed in the confusion. And then, suddenly, Mercer was there, like the hero of the trashy romance novels she'd read as a girl. How he had come to be there she still didn't know, but she was grateful. Not that she'd shown it. The conflicting emotions he generated were almost too much to take. He attracted her with an irresistible magnetism, yet whenever they were together, he managed to infuriate her with just a few words or even a look.

She wondered if she lashed out at him because of her own insecurities, wanting to build a wall between them. Aggie knew she shouldn't even be thinking about Mercer in this way. She loved Jan and hoped one day to be his wife. She had no answers, just a vague sense of falling into something much bigger than she could handle.

Aggie lit a cigarette and got up mechanically, ignoring the party and the beer that sat in a clear pool of condensation on the table's Formica top. Jan hadn't been aboard the *Hope* when she'd arrived in Valdez. She knew she should have waited for him to return instead of joining the party. She hadn't seen him in a month, and should be looking forward to their rendezvous. But she felt hollow, like a fragile shell that would crack with only a slight touch.

She walked blankly down the corridor in the direction of Jan's large stateroom, cursing herself for her lack of resolve. She'd always known what she'd wanted and always gotten it. But now? God, I hate this, she thought. She knocked timidly on his cabin door and entered without waiting.

Jan sat behind his desk, wearing a heavy sweater despite the warmth of the cabin. It was obvious that he hadn't been aboard very long, otherwise he would have changed, for he had an aversion to heat. There were papers strewn across his desk, and his head was bowed in concentration over them, a pen poised to strike if needed. He scribbled a furious notation before finally looking up, smiling when he saw Aggie standing at the door, her body partly shielded behind it as if awaiting punishment. He was so beautiful to her.

"Aggie! Oh, my God, I'm so glad to see you." He came from around the desk, his long arms opening wide, crushing her to him tightly. He tilted her face up to his, pressing his lips to hers. When she didn't respond, he backed off slightly. "What's wrong, my darling?"

"Oh, Jan." Aggie paused, not sure herself what was wrong. "I was so scared tonight. You heard about the fight at the bar."

"Yes, I was already told. Heinz and Pierre are both in jail

until morning on a drunk and disorderly charge. Someone said you were almost molested but some local managed to sneak you out the back door. It must have been terrible."

"Yes," Aggie replied simply, relieved that Jan didn't suspect that there was something else on her mind.

"I wish I'd known you were coming to Alaska early. I would have met you in Anchorage. Why didn't you call me?" Voerhoven held her at arm's length, looking deeply into her impossibly green eyes.

"I didn't know myself. I kind of came here on the spur of the moment." She didn't mention the panic that had precipitated her flight from Washington.

"Well, it doesn't matter. I'm just glad you're here." Jan smiled at her, his intentions evident in the huskiness of his voice.

"Please, Jan, not tonight. I know I haven't seen you for so long, but I just don't feel right. Clean, I mean. That man . . ." Her voice trailed off.

"Oh, darling, that's not what I meant. Well, partially that's what I meant. But listen, great things are about to happen here. Things that I want you to witness, to be a part of."

Suddenly Mercer's warning flashed in her head. "What things, Jan?"

"Aggie, we're about to strike a real blow against the fascist corporations whose greed is destroying the planet."

"My father's included?" She didn't mean to sound like she was defending her father, but her tone was harsh and accusatory.

"We've talked about that," Voerhoven said, holding up his hands as if warding off a physical assault. "I thought you understood that he has always been one of our fiercest adversaries. Petromax is one of the most ruthless exploiters in the world. I thought you were okay with what we are doing. You've said countless times how you want to get back at him. Now is your chance! We're on the verge of something great here, something that will save Alaska and maybe the rest of the world as well. In the next couple of days we are going to force the world to live without oil, Aggie. Don't you know what that means?"

"No, Jan, what does it mean?" she replied sharply. The spell he could so easily weave around her seemed no longer to hold her enraptured. For the first time she was seeing him for what he was, not what she wanted to see. What has Mercer done to me? she thought.

"You'll understand when we're finished. You will see. We are about to save the planet from its greatest scourge, its thirst for oil."

Again Aggie found herself thinking about Mercer's words. "What will you replace it with?"

"What?" Jan asked tenderly.

"If you shut off the world's oil, how will you supply energy for schools and hospitals, provide jobs for the millions of people who depend on oil for their livelihoods?" Aggie shook herself free from his embrace.

"Aggs, I'm not going to shut off the world's supply of oil. I'm going to make it such a repugnant source of energy that no one will want to use it."

"What are you talking about?"

He took her into his arms again, pressing his engorged groin against her body, his hands traveling the length of her back in fervent strokes. "Later, Aggie." He kissed the hollow of her throat, his tongue deftly stroking one of her most sensitive areas.

"Jan, please. I told you."

He ignored her pleas. "Aggie, I haven't seen you in so long. *God*, I want you."

She felt herself being maneuvered out of the office portion of his cabin and into his stateroom. Allowed herself to be maneuvered, she thought, for she could have resisted. If he felt the stiffness of her body, he ignored it.

At his bedside, he laid her gently on the eiderdown duvet. "You are so beautiful," he breathed, his face flushed with desire.

"Jan, please don't," Aggie whispered. Why was this happening? Why was she allowing this to take place? As much as she wanted to stop him, part of her mind told her she owed him. And even as she thought it, she knew it was wrong. She owed him nothing.

He unsnapped the top button of her jeans and slowly pulled down the zipper. She made no move to help him, nor did she try to stop him either. His hands were so familiar on her body, caressing her narrow hips, tracking across her breasts. Didn't she owe him? They'd been lovers for nearly a year. Surely this was right.

He undressed himself and a moment later entered her painfully, for her body had not responded to his advances. He seemed not to notice. He covered her completely, his nude form supported by his hands as he pistoned up and down, head arched back, eyes closed. He came, burying his head into her shoulder in a silent explosion.

Aggie felt like a whore.

MERCER made it back to his hotel room about midnight, his mind cleared, his raging emotions of an hour earlier kept firmly reined in. He was frozen to the core. Having surrendered his jacket to Aggie, he'd had to walk to his hotel in nothing more than a shirt, and this was not the weather for it. He thought of taking a shower, but a quick check of the time told him that he should make his call before turning to his body's needs.

He dialed and was surprised that four rings went by before the other end of the line was picked up by a gruff, "What?"

"Evening, Dick, Mercer here."

"Jesus Christ, Mercer, where in the hell are you?" Henna exploded. "I've got an entire task force searching for you right now."

"Come on, Dick, I'm at the Willard Hotel, where you left me," Mercer replied innocently.

"Laugh it up, funny guy," Henna snorted. "You're going to get the bill for all the booze Harry smuggled from the hotel. Now, where are you?"

"Valdez, Alaska."

"I fucking told you to stay away from Alaska. Are you deaf or something?"

"Come on, Dick. The coelacanths are on their spawning runs. The fishing's supposed to be great."

"For your information, coelacanths are found only in the Indian Ocean."

"That's why I haven't caught one yet," Mercer laughed. "I thought I was using the wrong bait."

"Okay, so you're in Alaska," Henna said with resignation. "What have you found?"

"Nothing concrete, yet, but I've got my suspicions," Mercer replied. "By the way, Dick, where are you?"

"I'm at the White House with the President and the Secretary of Energy. Care to talk to either of them?"

"Tell Connie that she should ditch those sensible shoes she's wearing."

Mercer heard Connie Van Buren's distinct laughter and knew Henna had put his cellular on speaker mode.

"How are you doing with Max Johnston's daughter?" Van Buren called. "I saw you two leaving the reception together."

"You know me and women, Connie," Mercer chuckled. "She hates my guts. Listen, Dick, I need a favor."

"What else is new?"

"You know that group PEAL? The environmentalists? Well, I think they may be up to something here."

"That's not the way we're reading it on this end, Mercer. We're tracking the Kerikov angle to what's happening. PEAL doesn't fit in."

"I just watched a few of them tear apart a barroom full of rednecks. These guys moved like a trained army. Not your typical style for a bunch of earth-loving druid wanna-bes."

"If you'd listen, I was about to say we've found Ivan Kerikov," Henna exclaimed. "And he appears to be working with some Middle Eastern types, not a group of trust-fund radicals."

"What do you have?" The last traces of humor vanished from Mercer's voice.

"We tracked his false passport to the Holiday Inn Tower Hotel in Anchorage. He took three different rooms. A suite for himself and two other rooms for what sound like bodyguards. The staff remembered that three of the guards, Arabs, and a man matching Kerikov's description did leave the hotel for a couple of days. The time frame corresponds with when

Howard Small vanished. Unfortunately, when we raided the hotel this morning, we missed them by a couple of hours. The whole party had already checked out."

"Shit," Mercer said bitterly. "Wait, did he make any calls?"

"Dead end there too, I'm afraid. He did make a couple, but they turned out to be a private manual exchange in New York."

"A what?"

"It's like a dead letter drop only for telephone calls. You phone the place and they patch you through to another line using an old manual PBX, that way any traces end with the exchange, not with the person you're trying to reach. KGB used them for years in this country."

"Shit," Mercer breathed. "It still doesn't add up. More than two hundred tons of liquid nitrogen have been smuggled into Alaska over the past couple of months. Kerikov is going to need more than a few Arabs and a couple of bodyguards to do anything with it."

"And you think PEAL is somehow involved?" It was the unmistakable voice of the President, who'd been listening to the conversation.

"Yes, sir, I do. I don't have any proof, but they make me suspicious as hell."

"What do you want done?" Henna asked.

"Search their ship, find out if the liquid nitrogen is aboard or if they have any special type of refrigeration units, something they could have used to store the stuff. Arrest them all if you find even a goddamn ice cream machine. I know they're involved."

"Mercer, I can't just go around seizing ships flying foreign flags."

"Come on, Dick, you control the goddamn FBI. Surely you can think of something to get men aboard the *Hope*. Use the cover of health inspectors checking for Brazilian crotch lice, I don't know. Anything."

"If you're wrong about this, your ass is going to be in a sling," Henna threatened.

"I thought it already was for coming to Alaska in the first place," Mercer quipped.

"All right, what else do you have?"

"Nothing. Or maybe everything. I found out that Burt Manning used to work for Max Johnston. And Johnston knew exactly what time the attack on my house took place."

"What are you saying?" The President sensed a scandal immediately. He'd just played a round of golf with Johnston.

"I don't know, sir, but I just spoke with his daughter and he's got her pretty spooked."

"Mercer," Connie Van Buren chimed over the speaker phone, "you don't think Johnston's involved? He's got more at stake in Alaska than almost anyone."

"I agree with you, Connie. That's why I'm not sure yet if he's in any way connected. It's just a piece of information I picked up and wanted to pass along."

"We'll check out the *Hope* for you, but I want you back in Washington ASAP," Henna interrupted.

"I will, Dick," Mercer said seriously. "But I want to be part of the team that boards the *Hope*."

"This is a federal matter. You're just a civilian."

"Come on, give this civilian some credit. I may have given you a lead, while the couple hundred agents you've got bumbling around the state haven't turned up anything."

"Dr. Mercer, I'll make sure you are part of the assault, but only as an observer." The President's tone was cool and neutral. "However, I want your personal guarantee that you will be on the next plane back to Washington afterward."

"Trust me," Mercer said.

Richard Henna shut off his cellular when he realized that Mercer was gone and leaned back heavily into his chair. He and Connie Van Buren were seated before the President in the Oval Office. While they were dressed casually, there was a stiff formality in the air.

They had been here for almost two hours, discussing the implementation of the President's energy policy and Henna's involvement to ensure that it went through smoothly. None of the more powerful Washington insiders were naive enough to believe that there wouldn't be serious recriminations, both nationally and internationally, for what the President had proposed. Oil companies and environmental groups weren't the only players who saw themselves threatened by the proposed isolationist move.

A large number of the oil-producing nations saw this as one more step in the American plan to destroy their way of life, and they were currently meeting in London. Militant factions within OPEC could threaten and browbeat the United States because they still held a powerful economic weapon. The three people seated around the large desk had to make sure that possible reprisals never touched America's shores.

"That son of a bitch," Henna said fondly as he strode to a sideboard near one wall that acted as a small bar. He poured a heavy dose of Scotch into a glass and downed it in one easy swallow.

"Why do you say that?" Connie asked.

"Because he knows more than we do. Again. I swear to God, he creates these crises just to make me look bad," Henna said tiredly. "But I don't think you handled that very well, Mr. President."

"Why not?" The chief executive bristled.

"Because he might actually follow your order and come home, and we'd lose the best man we have in Alaska."

"What about the rest of your agents, two or three hundred of them, I believe?" Connie asked.

"I've got two hundred agents who've turned up nothing. I've had men following FedEx delivery people if a package looks suspicious. That's how desperate I am. In just a couple of days, Mercer has given us more leads than my entire staff combined. None of my men have his scientific qualifications or the savvy to make the connections he does. Mercer knows what liquid nitrogen can do and what it could be used for while I've got a lot of eager men with short haircuts and linebacker attitudes waiting to kick down doors and crack skulls. None of them are piecing this thing together the way Mercer is. He's our best asset in Alaska, and if he decides to head home, we may all pay the price for it."

"Dick, I've known Mercer even longer than you," Connie Van Buren said. "Don't you think you're giving him just a little bit too much credit?"

"Connie, you weren't part of the Hawaii crisis," the President replied sagely. "Nothing Mercer does could surprise me anymore." He turned to Henna. "Do you think there is anything to his suspicions of PEAL and Max Johnston?"

"PEAL, maybe. Their leader is one pathological bastard." Henna fell back into his chair. "But Johnston, no way. The guy is true blue all the way."

"Dick," the President's voice was heavy with the gravity of the situation. "We both know Philip Mercer. He bailed my ass out of that Hawaiian incident. If he's suspicious, well, so am I. Do a little digging on Johnston. Quietly."

VALDEZ, ALASKA

Dawn was hours away and the night sky was as black as pitch. Even the stars seemed especially remote and cold in the silence of space. The town, too, was quiet. Only the gentle lapping of waves and the occasional whistle of wind through loosely strung power lines disturbed the night. It was almost four in the morning, the time when humans and all other nonnocturnal creatures were at their lowest ebb. Even with electric lighting and sophisticated technology, man still feared this time of night and hid from it as surely as his primordial ancestors had eons ago. It was the time of witches and devils. It was the time of Ivan Kerikov.

The still of the night was stirred by a persistent buzzing noise approaching the town from the north. The buzz built into a whine and then to the throaty roar of two fuel-injected six-cylinder engines of a Cessna 310 prop aircraft, its landing lights brilliant in the darkness. The pilot keyed on his mike and the automated runway lights of Valdez's airport sparkled on, outlining the single 6,500-foot asphalt strip. He crabbed the aircraft, mindful of the crosswind coming from the Sound.

With just the right touch of throttle and flap, the executive plane scuffed the runway, then settled on its tricycle landing gear, the pilot giving himself more than enough room for his rollout. A flashlight beckoned him to the hard stands where a small group of people waited at the otherwise deserted airport. Their breaths were like cigarette smoke in the predawn chill.

The pilot cut the engines, and silence once again enveloped the field. A few moments later, the rear passenger door hissed open and Kerikov stepped down to the tarmac, unlimbering his bulky frame from the six-passenger aircraft. His face was drawn and deeply shadowed in the Cessna's dim cabin lights, but his pale eyes retained their deadly stare.

"Voerhoven?" he called evenly.

Jan Voerhoven stepped away from his men and strode to the aircraft, keeping the beam of his flashlight on the silvery wet asphalt. He'd arrived at the airport just moments before Kerikov's plane, leaving Aggie curled up and asleep aboard the *Hope*.

"You are ready." It was a statement, not a question.

"Yes, everything's set," Voerhoven replied. "And I have good news. We found that our intelligence about the road to Pump Station number 5 was incorrect. Permits to travel on the Dalton Highway aren't necessary unless one wishes to travel beyond Atigun Pass. After that, the road is secured for Alyeska vehicles only. Because we used a helicopter to transport the freezing packs to sites north of Pump Station number 5 last month, I assumed we would need them again. I was mistaken. We can move the last of the liquid nitrogen by trucks, which I have waiting for us in Fairbanks."

"What's the distance to the pumping station?"

"Just over two hundred miles from where we've stored the nitrogen. However, much of the road is unpaved. We'll need at least four hours to get there."

Kerikov snapped back his cuff to look at his watch, a crisp, almost military gesture. "That will put us at the pumping station at around twenty-one-hundred hours. Traffic on the road will be negligible and patrols by Alyeska workmen shouldn't be a factor. Excellent, Jan. I congratulate you on your thinking."

"Listen," Jan hardened his voice, "I need to know what kind of exposure my people can expect."

"What do you mean, exposure?"

"All of the other freezing packs we've attached to the pipeline were done at remote locations, with almost no risk of discovery. This time, we're going to march right up to a pumping station staffed with workers."

"Don't tell me you're having doubts," Kerikov mocked, his lazy half smile challenging Jan as surely as an insult.

"No, but I want to know if my people are going to be in any danger."

"Our diversion in Fairbanks is all set. At most, we'll be facing only half of Pump Station 5's crew." Kerikov then laughed, an unnaturally loud sound in the deserted airfield. "Besides, Alyeska's crew are all unarmed. It'll be as simple as killing an unarmed truck driver, Jan. If your people are as eager as you say about freezing the pipeline, I'm sure they're looking forward to a little action. But if you wish, they can remain by the trucks while my men quell any resistance."

Voerhoven opened his mouth to protest. Then he remembered the humiliation he'd felt two days earlier when Kerikov had slapped him around, and he remained quiet. Kerikov saw Jan's reaction and nodded, knowing full well he had the Dutchman under his control.

"Get on the plane. We'll take off in just a moment."

Kerikov moved farther away from the Cessna, deeper into the night. He slipped a thin cellular phone from his jacket pocket, punching in one of the many numbers the device kept stored. He had to call twice because an answering machine picked up the extension before waking the person he wanted to reach.

"Hello," a voice muttered thickly.

"Mossey, this is Kerikov. It's time."

"Christ," Ted Mossey complained. "It's four o'clock in the morning."

"Yes, I know it is," Kerikov agreed with the young computer expert. "Voerhoven and I are about to head north to place the final shipment. I need you at the terminal facility. I'm about twenty-four hours away from initializing the original computer override virus. You have to begin installing it immediately."

Mossey came a little more awake at this revelation, his weak voice firming slightly as he realized what was happening. When he spoke, there was a breathless anticipation behind his words. "So soon? Oh, my God, this is fantastic! I'll have their systems down in just a couple of hours. They'll call me right away. Oh, man, this is great!"

"Calm down," Kerikov snapped. "Once you freeze their computer and they call you back to the terminal, you said it would take about ten hours to get our old program up and running, correct?"

"Yes, ten, maybe twelve. Looking over the documentation of your program, I saw that your guy buried it pretty deep in the main frame. It's not something I can get to very easily."

Kerikov cut him off quickly before he started another of his intolerable lectures about computers and their abilities. "And once it's in, I can activate the program remotely, correct?"

"All you need is a telephone, even that cell phone you carry can do it. Oh, man, this is going to be fucking great. The ultimate hack. And I'm getting paid for it too. No one is ever going to believe this one."

With those last words, Kerikov knew that the computer expert had to die. Voerhoven and his people willingly took risks because they believed they were right, that their cause came before all other considerations, but Mossey was different. Kerikov knew it wasn't only his environmental activism that drove him to assist in Charon's Landing; it was also his ego and the desire to pull off the impossible. The PEAL activists would never reveal their involvement because it would cause just too much damage to their organization. Especially when Kerikov tied the two disparate sides of this operation together. But after a while, Mossey's ego would force him to talk to someone, some other computer freak, and all too soon, the whole world would know. A swift bullet would ensure his perpetual silence.

"Calm down," Kerikov admonished the younger man. "We're not there yet. Remember, no one at the terminal can suspect that anything of consequence is wrong."

"Don't worry, it'll be a snap. To them I'm just another digit head. Good old Ted, you know. By the time you make the call to trigger the program, I'll be halfway to Japan and a much better life. You have any idea what they pay good programmers there?"

Kerikov paused for a second. He could delay Mossey from leaving Valdez long enough to get Abu Alam in position to kill him, maybe when Mossey was driving up to the airport in Anchorage. That was the beauty of Valdez—there was only one road in and out, a dangerous road that had claimed a life only a few days before. Mossey's death wouldn't be that suspicious, thanks to Voerhoven's unauthorized activities.

"Ted, after you initiate the control program, go back to your apartment and wait for a call from me," Kerikov improvised.

"What in the hell for?"

"Because I order it," Kerikov bellowed, then lowered his voice when he saw Jan look over. Kerikov had never revealed the hacker's presence to Voerhoven or the effects of the computer virus he was going to unleash. "I'll make sure you have enough time to get out of Alaska before I set off the virus."

"Hey, that wasn't part of our bargain," Ted Mossey whined.

"It is now." Kerikov shut down the phone and fished a cigarette from an inside pocket. The flare of his lighter was blinding for the instant it took to light the Marlboro.

He placed another call, this time using his own memory rather than that of the cellular. Abu Alam answered after only one ring despite the time. He sounded as if he hadn't slept yet, if he slept at all.

"I didn't take her tonight," he said by way of greeting, for he knew only Kerikov had his cell phone number.

"What happened?"

"There was someone with her. We had a good opportunity, I almost had her, but some bastard hit me over the head and escorted her back to the PEAL ship. We couldn't grab her without taking him out first, and you said you wanted her kidnapped with the least amount of resistance."

"Jesus Christ! It was only one man and you didn't move in?" he said disgustedly. "One man isn't an obstacle. You should have beaten him and snatched her when you had the chance. Listen to me and listen good. I want her taken no later than tomorrow night. After that, I want you to stay with her on the platform. Guard her well, Alam, but do not touch her. Is that clear?"

"Why guard her? There's no place Aggie Johnston can go."

"No names, goddamn it! I need you on the *Omega* to go over the final preparations, including taking out our computer expert after I fire off the nitrogen canisters."

"What's going on here, Kerikov? You assured Minister Rufti that you had everything under control, that you trusted your people, that you didn't need any help. This will be the second time you've asked me and my men to bail you out. Are you certain that you know what you're doing? I believe it is time to inform the Minister that things here are not going as planned, yes?"

"No, they are going as planned, it's just that you don't know the full plan," Kerikov said angrily. "Just grab the woman, get her to the *Omega*, and await my instructions. You knew when Rufti bought into this operation that you would be much more than an observer."

"Rufti will hear of this," Abu Alam threatened. "You can be sure of this. You are not the person you think you are."

"Oh, yes, I am." Kerikov folded his phone back on itself and put it in his pocket.

After a lifetime in the intelligence game, Kerikov never ceased to marvel how quickly an asset could turn into a liability. Ally and enemy weren't antonyms; they were they same thing. Only circumstance and timing made them different. It was as true of superpower relations as it was of personal relationships. And in the spy trade, it was the truest of all.

He pitched the cigarette butt onto the tarmac, grinding it

to a shredded pulp under his heel before turning back to the aircraft. The pilot saw him approach and kicked the engines back to life, their knife-edge blades cutting into the cool air so quickly they disappeared into silvered discs.

———

VALDEZ, ALASKA

The pounding on the door had the sharp rhythm of machine gun fire, crisp and piercing. Mercer covered his ears for a moment before rolling out of bed. Forgetting where he was, he took the covers with him as he plunged to the carpet, nearly concussing himself against the nightstand. He pulled himself together quickly, moaning as his aching brain reminded him that he was in Alaska—and that he'd had more to drink the previous night than he'd thought.

He threw on a pair of jeans and answered the door. Three men stood in the hallway outside his room, all of them wearing dark blue nylon windbreakers. Mercer knew that the backs of their jackets would read FBI in large gold letters. It was time for the raid on the *Hope*.

"Dr. Mercer, my name is Dave Fielding," the agent in the middle said. "I was instructed to pick you up this morning before we moved on the PEAL ship." Fielding was a solid statue of muscle, sinew, and testosterone, his heavy forehead sloping into strong hazel eyes. Had his chin been any sharper, it would have cut the air.

"Just give me a minute," Mercer said as he turned away, leaving Fielding and the two other agents at the door.

Mercer grabbed a heavy shirt from his garment bag, buttoning it on the way to the bathroom. As he peed, he licked a dollop of toothpaste from the tube he'd left on the vanity top. Swishing it around his mouth, he zipped up his jeans, washed his hands, then rinsed with a palmful of water. In the mirror, his eyes were equal shades of red and gray.

Fielding and his men waited as Mercer slipped on a pair of socks and laced up his heavy boots. They were out of the room only two minutes after the knock. It was just before 6:00 A.M.

The harbor was only a couple of blocks from the hotel. As they walked to the water's edge, Mercer wished fervently for a cup of coffee, but it was obvious by the tension in Fielding's stride that he was eager for the raid. The morning held the unmistakable expectancy of trouble. The holstered pistol under Fielding's windbreaker wrinkled the material of his jacket.

At the harbor, a forty-foot Coast Guard vessel burbled softly at idle, its gleaming white hull and superstructure slashed by the distinctive orange stripe of the service. Twin fifty-caliber machine guns were mounted in a cupola midway along her foredeck while a half dozen armed sailors cluttered the aft cockpit, their M-16s held tightly, fingers never far from the triggers. There wasn't another soul at the docks; the big fishing trawlers sat quietly at anchor. The charter and pleasure boats were equally forlorn and abandoned. Mercer had no doubt that fishermen heading for their vessels had been told to take the morning off and bill the lost time to the FBI.

He hoped he was right about PEAL.

Fielding ushered Mercer onto the Coast Guard boat and escorted him to the bench seat running along the transom. The FBI men and the Coasties moved with a rigid efficiency. They had been up for hours, planning for this morning's raid. For the Feebies, this assault was the payoff for months of dead-end investigation work. They'd been in Alaska for too long, waiting for some action, and this morning it had finally come. Mercer alone knew that the morning raid was meant to be a warning more than anything else.

He was certain that they wouldn't find anything aboard the *Hope*. Even if his suspicions were correct about PEAL's involvement with Ivan Kerikov, they wouldn't be foolish enough to leave evidence lying around. This morning's assault was designed, in Mercer's mind, to be a type of harassment, letting Kerikov know that he was now being hunted.

Mercer guessed that Dick Henna realized his intentions last night on the phone, otherwise he wouldn't be here now, but it appeared that Henna hadn't fully briefed his men. They seemed ready for a full-scale naval battle. The M-16s had a smooth greasy smell to them.

A sailor in a Kevlar vest and combat helmet cast off the bowline, his actions mimicked by another in the stern, and suddenly they were free of the dock. The helmsman edged the throttles forward and the vessel jumped from the quay. As the boat pulled out into the quiet bay, Agent Fielding sat down next to Mercer, an assault rifle propped between his knees.

Using a windproof lighter, Fielding sparked a cigarette after offering one to Mercer, who declined. The mountains surrounding the bay looked like sleeping animals under their thick canopies of pine and oak, each ridgeline bristling like a badger-hair brush. The air was sharp and clean as it blew across the Scarab-built patrol boat. It caused tears to stream from Mercer's eyes and brought a little function back to his brain.

The *Hope* lay dead ahead, gentle swells running sedately along her lemon yellow hull. The empty arms of her portside davit hung over the main deck railing like skeletal arms eager for an embrace. Only a few portholes emitted any light; the rest were just dark spots on her paintwork. She appeared quiet. No one was on the decks this early in the morning, and only a trace of smoke escaped her blunted funnel. A couple of seabirds, puffins or terns, floated just off her stern, scavenging the food scraps the chef had thrown over the side during the night.

"This is kind of unprecedented," Fielding said over the din of the engines. "As I understand it, you called in this tip, right?"

Mercer nodded. He still wasn't awake enough to speak. The excitement that held the men enthralled hadn't affected him.

"I want you to wait aboard this boat until we've secured the *Hope*. We're not expecting any trouble, but it would be safer if you stayed out of the way. You are more or less an observer, right?"

"Mr. Fielding, this isn't an invasion," Mercer said, finding his voice finally. "There's no real evidence behind this raid, just gut feelings. I suggest that both you and your men calm down a bit. These people aren't going to offer any resistance other than a few mumbled complaints."

"Well, just in case." Fielding unzipped his jacket and unsnapped the safety strap of his shoulder holster. The big Colt .45 was ready for a quick combat draw.

"May I make a suggestion?" Mercer pointed back toward the docks, now two hundred yards distant. "There're three thousand people in that town, most of them early risers. Unless you want to make yourself into a public spectacle, I think it would be smarter if we boarded the *Hope* from the starboard side, away from prying eyes. Last night, I noticed that PEAL has two Zodiacs. I didn't see either of them at the town dock, nor are they on this side of the ship. I'm guessing that they're tied to a boarding ladder on the far side."

Agent Fielding looked at Mercer angrily. It was obvious from his expression that he hadn't thought about this and may have actually been looking forward to storming the PEAL vessel using grappling hooks and ropes. He broke eye contact with a shake of his head, then went forward to tell the helmsman to swing around the *Hope* and come up on her starboard side.

The patrol boat cut a wide arc through the water, its wake widening into a boiling white fan. Its hull canted over so sharply that the freeboards were only a few inches above the waves. Rounding the stubby vertical bows of the *Hope*, the agents saw a set of stairs that had been lowered to the water level. The Zodiacs were secured to the bottom landing. On the main deck above the steps, a man watched the Coast Guard boat through binoculars, a rifle held in his other hand.

Seeing the weapon, Fielding and the other agents reacted instantly. Those not clutching their weapons did so, lifting assault rifles from the deck or slipping pistols from holsters. Their actions were so fast that Mercer was startled. Someone tossed a megaphone to Fielding; the agent caught it with his off hand and swung it to his lips fluidly.

"This is the FBI. Lay down your weapon and place your hands on top of your head. Do not move from your position, or we will open fire." His amplified voice echoed over the water in the silence created by the now idled engines of the patrol boat.

As inertia edged the Scarab closer to the *Hope*, the agents' weapons tracked the man on the deck with the precision of antiaircraft guns. The environmentalist on the research vessel made no move to lower his weapon, though he did let the binoculars dangle from a leather strap slung around his neck.

"Drop the fucking gun. Now!" Fielding shouted.

"You cannot board this vessel," the man called, his voice small compared to Fielding's electrically enhanced hails. His accent was French, maybe Dutch. "We are registered in Holland, you have no jurisdiction. We fly the flag of a friendly nation."

"Asshole, you are in United States territorial waters," Fielding shouted angrily. "If I want, I've got the jurisdiction to blow your boat out of the fucking water."

His words were punctuated by the mechanical crash of the twin fifties' bolts being slammed home, their belts of ammunition rattling like chains.

More figures appeared on the deck, most fully dressed, which told Mercer that they had been watching the Coast Guard boat ever since it left the docks. Fortunately, no one else was armed that he could see. The Scarab was nearing the boarding platform. The crew on the *Hope* leaned over the railing, watching the sleek vessel and the agents.

"François, put that gun down now," a female voice called out. Mercer recognized her instantly. The combination of natural authority and throaty allure was unmistakable.

"Aggie, we can't allow them to board us," the man named François protested. "You remember what the French did to the *Rainbow Warrior*."

"Do it."

While François was talking with Aggie Johnston, Fielding and his men leaped the few feet separating the two ships, their boots pounding against the heavy marine-grade wood as they swarmed up the stairs. In just a few seconds all eight government men were aboard the *Hope*, screaming orders for everyone to lie flat with their fingers laced behind their heads. Masculine shouts mingled with feminine screams as the FBI men pushed the PEAL activists to the deck. Mercer heard Aggie shout, and he was in action, ignoring Fielding's order to remain behind. He was on the *Hope* in a flash, searching for Aggie among the supine figures.

An agent plucked a small automatic pistol from the waistband of one man's jeans while another trained an M-16 on the man's head. Along the promenade, a series of plate-glass windows looked into the mess hall. Faces appeared there, then rushed off when they saw their ship being assaulted. Screams of fear and panic could be heard from the interior of the vessel.

"Goddamn it, Fielding, you're making this worse than it has to be," Mercer shouted.

Fielding turned to him, eyes glazed with battle lust. "I told you to wait behind. Get the fuck out of here."

"Like hell I will," Mercer shot back, striding to where Aggie lay on the deck. He knelt at her side and laid a gentle hand on her back. She lifted her head and turned it until she could see who was behind her.

Seeing Mercer, her green eyes blazed with anger. "You son of a bitch."

"I just wanted my jacket back," Mercer smiled and helped her to her feet. Aggie wiped her hands and backed away, as if contact with Mercer had somehow dirtied her.

One agent stayed behind to cover the ten or so activists while the rest entered the superstructure through a bulkhead just forward of the boarding platform.

"Listen, Aggie, this can go a hell of a lot easier if you get Voerhoven on the intercom and tell your people to cooperate." Even as he spoke, they both heard a high-pitched scream from inside the ship followed by an almost eerie silence.

Suddenly a gunshot rang out, and the prisoners flinched. Several got to their knees.

"Stay the fuck down," the agent covering the deck party

shouted, the barrel of his assault rifle sweeping across the environmentalists.

"Aggie, do it for Christ's sake."

"He's not here," she said flatly, the enormity of the situation finally reaching her.

"Come on," Mercer said, grabbing her hand.

He led her into the ship, almost having to drag her along the deserted passageways, guessing his way toward the bridge. He found it up two flights of narrow steps and though a watertight door. Two armed PEAL men were there, training their pistols with unerring accuracy at his head, their fists steady as they gripped the big automatics. Without a gun of his own, Mercer had no choice. He released Aggie and held his hands over his head. Beyond the windscreen, the bay was as smooth as a puddle.

"No," Aggie Johnston said to her two comrades, "it's all right. He's with me."

They lowered the weapons but regarded Mercer with a mixture of mistrust and anger. Aggie crossed to the communications set and lifted the hand mike from its steel clip.

"Attention." Her voice sounded throughout the ship. "This is Aggie. Everyone please cooperate. Don't put up a fight. That's what they want. Believe me, this is going to cost them a lot more than it will cost us. Just do what they say for now and we'll have them by the balls." She snapped off the microphone and turned to Mercer. "You have no idea what you've done here. My God, this couldn't be any better if we'd staged it ourselves."

"Sorry to beat you to the punch. I hear staging events is a normal PEAL practice," he mocked, then turned deadly serious. "Where is Jan Voerhoven?"

"I told you, he's gone."

Mercer detected a shadow behind her eyes and he realized that she and Voerhoven were lovers. The revelation jolted him. Suddenly, he was very jealous of Voerhoven and that made him angry at himself. He should feel nothing for her, but he did and it hurt. He felt a tremendous sense of loss, though Aggie had never really been his. "Aggie, your trust fund isn't going to bail you out of this one. Tell me where he is."

"I don't know. He left in the middle of the night."

"I left you about midnight, and he took off a couple of hours ago. Must have been a great reunion."

"It was better than anything you're capable of," Aggie spat.

Standing before him in an oversized T-shirt and an old pair of sweat pants, her hair floating around her head in a wild tangle, her face flushed from sleep and by the action of the past few minutes, she was still the most beautiful woman Mercer had ever seen. Why did it have to be like this, he asked himself, the ache in his stomach growing. Why did they have to face each other as enemies for a cause that was so much bigger than either of them?

He angrily pushed these questions aside, once again burying his emotions under a protective veneer that seemed so much thinner around Aggie than it had been for any other woman he'd known. He didn't want to think about the consequences if it ever cracked.

Fielding and another agent burst onto the bridge as Aggie and Mercer glared at each other, tension crackling between them like a static discharge. One agent had his M-16 rucked hard against his shoulder, viewing the scene through iron sights. The two PEAL crewmen laid their weapons on the main navigation console, their hands going up.

Mercer ignored the commotion and spoke so softly that it seemed unnatural. "Where did he go, Aggie?"

"Like I would ever tell you." She raked a hand across her scalp, taming her hair so it settled back against her head. But again that shadow was there, some deep part of her was hurting.

"I'll tell you right now, Voerhoven doesn't know who he's dealing with. Kerikov will crush him and the rest of PEAL when he's finished here. Your boyfriend is in too deep to realize it. Help me, Aggie. Help him. If need be, I can have everyone on this ship arrested. Those not holding U.S. passports will be deported, and all the American citizens will be charged with whatever I decide. I told you that you're involved with something far more dangerous than you thought.

Last night was your first warning, and I'm not going to give you a second one."

Dave Fielding had lowered his weapon, his head twisting from Aggie to Mercer and back again. He saw, even before Aggie knew, that she was going to give in.

"He didn't tell me, all right?" she said angrily. "We went to bed last night and when I was awoken this morning by you and your fascist friends, he was gone. I don't know where he went. He was acting strangely when we talked. He said something was about to happen, but he didn't tell me what it was." Her voice lowered to a menacing hiss, "I hate you."

"I want to be able to say the same, Aggie, but I can't."

Mercer left the room, brushing by Fielding's agent as if the man wasn't there, Fielding following a moment later. He caught up to Mercer one deck below the bridge. Grabbing Mercer by the elbow and spinning him around, Fielding pinned him to a wall. Mercer let himself be manhandled. Fielding's face was reddened, knotted muscles bunching at the hinge points of his jaw as he fought to keep his anger in check.

"What the fuck was that all about?" Spittle bubbled at his lips as he spoke.

"You did your job. Charge the guys who carried guns with weapons' possession and then get out of my face." Mercer said tightly. He tried to twist away, but Fielding held him, his meaty hands pressing Mercer's shoulders against the wall.

Mercer jacked up his knee, slamming it against the juncture of Fielding's thighs. The FBI agent doubled over, his breath exploding. The pain radiating from his groin dropped him to the deck, his lungs nearly in convulsions. Mercer stood impassively as Fielding tried to ease the agony by massaging his crotch.

"This mission was intended to be a warning," Mercer said evenly, looking down at the FBI agent. "However, the person I wanted wasn't here. I can only hope that maybe I got through to someone even more important."

Mercer looked in the direction of the bridge, a saddened

smile on his face. He turned and went below to the main deck, eager to get off the research vessel.

Only time would tell if he'd done more damage than good.

The squawks and calls of the gulls above the *Hope* sounded like laughter.

———

VLCC *SOUTHERN CROSS*

The seas had calmed. The huge ship no longer rolled or yawed but ran as smoothly as skiff on a mountain lake. Her main engine, though damaged, still moved her tremendous dead weight through the water at a healthy ten knots. Fat wedges of deep green water peeled back from her bows and raked along her sides in an unending rhythm. The wind was backing the tanker at the same ten knots of her speed so the massive decks felt becalmed.

Belowdecks, the mess hall smelled of unwashed bodies cramped too long in one space, stale cigarettes, and the heady stench from the overflowing bins of garbage next to the scullery. Because the doors leading to the nearby head were left open and nervous men had poor aim, the stink of the lavatory reached deep within the large mess. All together, it was nauseating.

The crew, who'd been prisoners for four days now, were quiet, subdued by both a pervasive sense of torpor and the omnipresent machine pistols of the terrorist watchers. Faces were ashen under grizzled beards, eyes dull and lifeless. As they mechanically slurped from coffee cups that they continuously recharged, their gestures were slow and deliberate. Such was their depth of despondency that the crewmen rarely made eye contact with their shipmates.

When the ordeal had begun, there had been fervent glances and subtle gestures of reassurance, keeping alive some hope of escape or rescue. But as time dragged, one day leading to the next and the vigilance of the terrorists waxing rather than waning, hope quickly dimmed. Now they sat docilely, heads hanging, cigarettes dangling from slack lips even among those who'd never smoked before. Rather than experience the much-hyped Stockholm Syndrome, where captives commiserate with their keepers, the officers and crew of the supertanker had fallen into a stupor.

All except Chief Engineer George Patroni and his three assistants.

Patroni had managed to inform his two men about Hauser soon after he'd been confronted by the Captain in the elevator. He'd told them just as the engine went back on line, its deafening roar ensuring that their conversation wasn't overheard by their two guards. They were professional enough not to let the news distract them or make them act any differently from the rest of the listless crew. Apart from their regular inspections and heavy workload, they sat in the mess hall with the others, sleeping on the floor when they could, or slurping coffee with slow regularity, not once betraying their special knowledge.

Short and stocky but incredibly strong, Patroni was the son of a New York longshoreman and had grown up knowing that he would spend his life at sea. While his father had wanted him to finish high school and then follow in his footsteps, unloading the giant vessels that kept New York City filled with goods from around the globe, the older Patroni understood when seventeen-year-old George had signed on with a container ship as an oiler.

When he'd gotten his first look at the massive power plant that moved the cargo vessel, George Patroni knew that someday he would master one of these huge machines. It took twenty years before he would make chief engineer and another five before he could tame the tremendous engines of supertankers, but he never once regretted his youthful decision. Today, his wife and three teenage kids were secure in a modest slice of Jersey City. They packed more family bonding and love into his infrequent leaves than most people who worked the nine-to-five treadmill.

Patroni had been in a few scary situations in his life. For much of his tanker career, he'd worked the Persian Gulf–to–Europe run, rounding the Cape of Good Hope during its infamous winter storms and braving the Straits of Hormuz when Iranian and Iraqi gunboats were launching missiles at anything that moved. Patroni had watched the *Seawise Giant*, the largest tanker in the world, take a missile no more than a mile from his own ship.

Yet nothing had prepared him for this—the palpable fear of his mates, the angry expressions of their captors, and the ugly presence of their weapons.

Patroni sat at his own table in the mess, his arms making stout pillars on the Formica table to support his bowed head. An empty coffee cup sat in a dried ring of spilled liquid only inches away. A press-formed tin astray lay before him, the half dozen crushed butts looking like fallen stumps in the ash. His eyes were downcast, his mind a near blank, when suddenly a tiny folded scrap of paper appeared as if it had risen from the table itself.

Patroni made no move for it but lifted his eyes and peered around the room. No one was paying him any attention, and there wasn't anyone close enough who could have thrown it to him. He leaned back in his chair, yawning widely so that his spine arched against the molded plastic chair and his face pointed toward the ceiling. Above him was a ventilator grid, mounted flush with the ceiling tiles. As he watched, the grid moved slightly as it was set back in its proper location.

He swept up bits of ash and tobacco from the tabletop and with the same gesture pressed the tiny piece of paper to his palm. When he smeared the debris against his coveralls, the scrap vanished into a pocket. His gesture was so smooth that no one even glanced in his direction.

In keeping with the terrorists' instructions, Patroni raised his hand until the guards estimated that it was worth their time to escort a batch of their prisoners to the bathroom.

Shepherding them with machine guns, two terrorists maneuvered the six other crewmen who'd raised their hands from the room, their hard eyes anticipating any threat. While the door to the head was always kept open to make communication easier for the terrorists, the crew were allowed the privacy of the toilet stalls. Patroni patiently waited his turn, his hands held casually at his side. Only a slight tic in his right cheek revealed any sign of his agitation. Finally he gained access to a stall. He unzipped his coveralls, dropping them to his ankles, and sat on the still-warm seat. Killing two birds with one stone, he voided noisily and retrieved the note from his pocket, smoothing it out with his thick fingers so that he could read the neat script.

I am well. No one has come close to detecting me. I've overheard Riggs talking about moving up their plan and doing it in Seattle. By my calculations, we are 3 days out from this new target. We must act before we reach the city. I know now that there is no way for you to contact me but I must get off the ship and get close to shore to use the emer. radio. If you can, short the system tonight at midnight and I'll launch. If not possible, tomm. night same time. Hauser

He dropped the note into the bowl, finished what his body demanded, and left the stall. As he washed his hands, one of the guards watched him from under heavy brows, a German-made H&K MP-5 cradled nonchalantly in his arms. Patroni could feel the terrorist's eyes burning the back of his neck. Yet he showed nothing of the thoughts swimming in his head.

They were required to wait in the restroom until the last man had finished, and only then were they led back to the mess hall. The terrorist who'd been watching Patroni gave him a sharp jab to the kidneys that propelled the engineer across the hallway and into the mess. He just managed to remain on his feet by clutching a seat back.

Patroni whirled around, his fists coming up as he settled into a defensive crouch. Then a hand reached out and pressed against his hip. It was the ship's electrician, whose chair he'd stumbled into. "It's what he wants," the electrician whispered so softly that his lips didn't move.

Patroni relaxed, straightening his body and lowering his beefy fists. He ambled back to his customary seat, a secret smile on his face. Somehow he would find a way to help Hauser.

HAUSER was too old for this and knew it. His heart pounded against his ribs like some wild animal trying to escape its cage, and sweat poured into his eyes, reducing them to painful slits. The air in the crawl space above the mess hall was so fouled with cigarette smoke that it felt as if he was drawing battery acid into his lungs. To think he used to smoke voluntarily. He clung to a thick steel conduit line running through the crawl space, his legs slung over the piping, his hands gripping so tightly his fingers ached. His shoulders were afire with the strain of holding himself in position. If he lost his grip, he'd fall through the acoustical tile ceiling below him. His labored movements kicked up dust that threatened to bring about a sneezing fit at any moment.

Captain Hauser began to haul himself back out of the space, inching along like a caterpillar. The air whooshing through a twelve-inch ventilator trunk line nearby was loud enough to cover the sounds of his ragged breathing. Once he was above the kitchen, he lowered himself to a more comfortable position—the ceiling was hardened to make it flameproof and could support his weight. His chest pumped like a bellows, and long minutes passed before his hands stopped quivering.

"Too damned old by half," he muttered quietly.

It took another hour of crawling, worming, and squeezing through the tanker's numerous mechanicals spaces for him to reach a ventilator shaft and outside hatch. The cool sea breeze drawn in by the air conditioners blew across his face. It was a welcome relief to the smoke, dust, and heat he'd just endured, but the trip had been well worth it. He knew that Patroni would find a way to disable the bridge indicators when he launched the raft and make sure that no one was blamed. That was the key. Make sure the terrorists didn't suspect that anyone had escaped.

Although his contribution to the Vietnam War had been

running oil and cargo to Southeast Asia, Hauser had met enough soldiers to know that anyone with a gun in his hand suspected everything and everyone. Anything out of the ordinary meant trouble, and the only logical reaction was to open up with automatic fire. If the terrorists became suspicious, Hauser knew that some of his crew were going to die.

Easing the ventilator grid from its clamps, Hauser slid from the shaft and dropped lightly to the deck. He was near the tanker's fantail, no more than fifteen feet from the life raft on its launching rail. As he'd hoped, he was alone. There were too few terrorists and too much ship for them to patrol effectively.

He allowed himself the luxury of watching the sea hiss past the vessel for a moment before undogging the waterproof hatch of the fiberglass lifeboat and jumping inside the claustrophobic craft. While the tanker carried a crew of thirty, as a safety precaution, each of her three life rafts could hold twenty men. Each boat carried emergency locator beacons and a two-way marine transceiver. A stay in one was never meant to last more than a day or two, especially in the busy shipping lanes that tankers ply, but they carried enough food and water to last a week.

Sitting on one of the plastic bench seats, Hauser checked that the few Plexiglas portholes were covered with blankets taken from the boat's stores before allowing himself to relax. In a few hours, Patroni would cover for him while he launched the boat. He would motor away until some other vessel or shore-based radio picked up his broadcast. Until then, he had to wait, painfully watching the hours tick away. He turned to the question that had plagued him since he'd overheard two terrorists talking while he hung in a crawl space above a cabin.

Seattle. What was Riggs planning to do in Seattle?

Thoughts and ideas rumbled through his head, but nothing solidified enough to give him an answer. Even as he drew together every scrap of information he'd learned about the ship and the terrorists, nothing made Washington State's port city seem important. He tried to remember which system Patroni had said was so crucial to Riggs. Tank control, that was it. She wanted to be able to shift the tanker's cargo from hold to hold. The system was normally used to keep the vessel trimmed in rough seas or if she unloaded part of her cargo and then moved to another port to discharge the remainder. Maintaining equilibrium was significant for normal ship's operation, but it should not be such a high priority.

It didn't make any sense.

The continental United States northernmost port and the ability to shift oil within the monstrous hull . . . what was the connection? Suddenly Hauser knew. And fear and horror almost made him gag.

"Oh, dear God, they wouldn't do it. No one would."

LONDON, ENGLAND

There are two options for London's weather in the midfall: warm and rainy with a heavy overcast, or cold and rainy with an even darker overcast. In the few moments it took him to duck from a limousine to the lobby of a discreet Belgravia hotel, Khalid Khuddari was chilled almost to the bone, the heavy rain forming camouflage splashes on his Burberry overcoat. He shivered in the marble and gilt lobby for a second, wringing water from his thick hair with one flattened hand. The doorman watched him gravely, taking Khalid's rush into the lobby as a personal affront, for the umbrella in his hand could shield a family of four.

A concierge led Khalid to the registration counter, actually an eighteenth-century ormolu and teak desk inlaid with mother-of-pearl along its delicate recurved legs and bordering its broad, glossy top. An exact replica of the table shimmered up from the white Cararra marble floor. The receptionist's smile was almost warm enough to make Khalid forget the miserable weather. "Good afternoon, Minister Khuddari. I apologize about the weather. The telly said it should have cleared by now."

Khalid wasn't surprised that she knew his name; hotels such as this knew everything about a guest. "I'll be sure to take it up with the management," he grinned boyishly. "I specifically requested no rain for my entire stay."

"I'll pass on your request to the BBC weather bureau and see what can be done about it." She mirrored his smile.

Like the older and more discriminating banks of Switzerland, which looked nothing like a place of business from the outside, the St. James Belgravia didn't look like a hotel at all. It more resembled a large well-kept private home. Georgian in style with leaded casement windows and stone walls thick enough to turn away cannon fire, it even lacked a sign at the front advertising its presence. The lobby felt more like a grand entrance hall, with the desk and three oxblood wing chairs around a low cherry table. A sideboard hugging one wall under a giltwood mirror held crystal decanters, matching glassware, and the distinctive green neck of a Dom Perignon bottle in a sterling ice bucket.

One had to have money to even know that such hotels existed and even more to actually stay.

Khalid smiled tightly, knowing that Siri had not only booked the first-class flight from the UAE but also arranged for the hotel and the limo from the airport. It was her way of teasing him and demonstrating her affection, of which he was not unaware.

"Minister, I normally wouldn't ask this of you," the receptionist said almost apologetically, "however, you have never stayed with us before. I must see your passport for just a moment."

He slid the document from his breast pocket, laying it open for her. She copied what she needed onto a guest card and handed back the diplomatic passport with another smile. "Thank you very much, Minister. The bellman will have brought your luggage to your room by now and will see to it that it's unpacked if that is what you wish. You're in room number seven. Alfred will take you."

In his suite, Khalid dismissed the two bellmen without letting them unpack his bags. He noted that they didn't wait for a tip, and he smiled again. Hotels like this never bothered their guests with such plebeian tasks as paying gratuities, but he was certain that having the men lead him to his room probably cost more than his grandfather made during his entire life. After a quick shower and shave to rid himself of the flight from the Gulf, he was back out of his room. The limo was waiting for him, as he had instructed earlier.

"The Savoy," he told the West Indian driver as he eased into the plush leather of the black stretch Daimler.

Remarkably for such a big car, they managed to bull through the snarled city traffic in record time and were soon edging down the alley that led to perhaps the most famous hotel in the world.

Given his natural good looks and the fact that he could recite ten thousand lines of romantic poetry, it was little surprise that Trevor James-Price was talking to the most attractive woman in the Savoy's American Bar. James-Price and the woman sat at the long bar angled toward each other with the intimate and exclusionary attitude of illicit lovers. Even as he approached, Khalid heard the woman's laughter, sweet and clear with a hint of sexual throatiness.

"Ah, there you are, Trevor. The other warders have been looking for you all over town when we discovered you'd left the asylum without your medication." With Trevor, Khalid could let his long-suppressed schoolboy humor flow.

James-Price looked up quickly, the sandy cowlick hanging over his forehead lifting and falling like a bird's wing. His eyes sparkled with pleasure. They shook hands warmly.

"Khalid, please meet Millicent Gray. Millie, this is the Thief of Baghdad, Khalid Khuddari." Trevor paused for a beat while Khalid shook the woman's hand. "Now, if you will excuse us, I've got to talk him out of blowing up Parliament. I'll meet you at Les Ambassadeurs at nine."

She brushed her hand along Trevor's as she stood, then smiled at Khuddari and sauntered through the room. At least half a dozen heads turned to watch her go. •

"Les A, huh? I thought you were broke," Khalid teased.

"What can I say, she invited me." Trevor knocked off the last of a club soda and nodded for the barman to bring two more. "Glad you could make it to your first OPEC meeting as a Petroleum Minister."

"I almost didn't come," Khalid said darkly.

"So I gather. You want to talk about it?"

"Not really. I think I may be jumping at shadows or I could be facing real darkness." Khalid shook his head.

Trevor was quiet for a moment. "Well, you might be facing the Abyss after all. I found out about Rufti's commiserations with the Iraqis and Iranians. If they pull it off, that hundred-thousand-dollar check you said you wrote won't be worth the paper it's printed on."

Before Khalid could react, Trevor continued, "I finally got someone to open up to me, a Saudi prince who says he's being blackmailed by Rufti and wants to see the fat bastard taken down. Seems the royal personage is tired of being extorted because of his exotic tastes in pleasure.

"Last year, Rufti met with a former KGB agent named Ivan Kerikov in Istanbul aboard this prince's yacht. I've found that this Kerikov has also met with the Iraqis and Iranians on separate occasions since then. I guessed that all of them are involved with something unsavory, so I bribed the living shit out of a waiter at the restaurant where Rufti and his cohorts met last night. He secreted a tape recorder under their table."

"And?" Khalid prompted when Trevor paused for dramatic effect.

"Because of the economic pressure of the American decree, the Iraqis and Iranians have agreed to put aside their religious differences for the greater good, namely their Swiss bank accounts. With the help of the UAE, they're trying nothing less than to take over the entire Gulf. As you know, Iran, with a little help from the Emirates, can choke off the Straits of Hormuz to all seaborne traffic, tankers and warships alike. Then, with a combined army of ten million men and chemical and biological weapons that the UN inspectors never even suspected, Iraq and Iran will swallow Kuwait and a good chunk of Saudi Arabia long before anyone knows what's happened."

"That's ridiculous. The Americans would respond immediately, with NATO backing them. It would be a replay of the Gulf War."

"Would it?" Trevor arched a pale eyebrow. "When Saddam invaded Kuwait in 1990, he made only one miscalculation. He never imagined that U.S. soldiers would be allowed to use Saudi Arabia as a base for retaliatory attacks. And if you recall, it was by only a narrow margin that the Saudis agreed to let foreign troops on the Arabian Peninsula. You wogs are real touchy about who gets to walk on sacred sand and all that rot.

"Saddam never would have paused at the Saudi border had he realized America would be given those bases. This time, you can bet the tanks won't stop rolling until they're parked in downtown Riyadh.

"Furthermore, despite President Bush's assurances to the contrary, the Gulf War was fought over oil and nothing else. The Americans didn't care about the plight of the Kuwaiti people. Until the war, most Americans probably thought Kuwait was a type of fruit. No higher principles, no moral calling, just good, sound economic policy. Well, in ten years, nine now, America won't give a goddamn about oil. They're going to turn off the valve and let the Middle East collapse. If a combined front of Iraqis and Iranians try again, Congress is going to say the hell with it." Trevor slipped into a mocking American accent. " 'Let the fig-eating sand niggers kill each other all they want. It no longer concerns us,' some southern senator will say. They won't commit combat troops to a cause that doesn't affect American wallets. Period.

"With Saudi Arabia cut in half by Iraqi troops and Hormuz closed by Iranian and UAE gunboats, the Americans couldn't do anything anyway. They would have no tactical presence in the region. They'd have to use airfields in Turkey and Cyprus, at the extreme range of Coalition jets, and a land-based invasion force assembled in western Anatolia would face rugged mountains that have staggered armies for millennia. They wouldn't stand a chance, no matter how many smart bombs and stealth fighters they used. No, my friend, it would most certainly not be a replay of the Gulf War. And think of this—with Iran and Iraq ruling the Gulf with the help of a UAE puppet regime, you can bet the dominoes would start falling. Jordan, Syria, even Israel could be swallowed as soon as the dust settled."

Khalid sat back as if physically struck. What Trevor said was entirely feasible. The defining principle behind the United States' Middle Eastern policy was the assurance of an uninterrupted flow of Gulf crude. Take away that need and the region became as unimportant as Togo or Bhutan. America poured billions of dollars into the Levant in the form of military loans in an attempt to maintain a balance of power between the nations. Usually these attempts were one-sided and heavy-handed, creating the very dictators the United States feared. Still, oil had flowed for fifty years with only a few minor hiccups.

Without the thirst for crude, America had really no interest in Middle Eastern politics. They would rattle their swords and pass a few condemning resolutions in the United Nations, but they wouldn't act. History was full of wars. Most textbooks highlight their causes and effects, as if warfare was the watershed in civilization's development. Without exception they had all been fought for economic gain.

"I see one major flaw in your thinking," Khuddari finally replied. "The UAE would never join Iran and Iraq if they invaded Kuwait or Saudi Arabia."

Trevor had the uncanny knack of a school headmaster, the ability to shrivel another person with just a glance. "With the exception of the great democracies, the average life span of a ruling government for most nations is something like eight years. The UAE has existed for nearly thirty, and I think your time may be up."

"You mean Rufti?"

"Precisely."

"I spoke to the Crown Prince about the same thing, and I have to agree with his assessment. You may be right about Rufti, but the threat is still several years away, more than enough time to deal with him."

"Are you dense, old fruit? He may not try for the whole government right away, but I'm damned certain he wouldn't mind occupying your office for a while. Christ, the way he's been swaggering around London, you'd swear he was already Petro Minister for the entire UAE, not just his own dusty corner of the country."

Khalid hadn't considered this.

While his job was to a large degree administrative, Khalid knew that an OPEC Oil Minister still possessed a great deal of respect in the international economic community. It would be a great starting point for someone wanting to gain power without calling attention to himself. Given the tense climate within the UAE's seven-member Supreme Federal Council, it would be possible for the smaller Emirates to pressure the Crown Prince to appoint Rufti if Khalid was somehow not able to carry out his duties. If he was, for example, dead.

"Steady, old son, you look as if you'd just seen a ghost," Trevor said, snapping Khalid from his thoughts.

"Yes, I did. Mine." The training facility that he'd inspected with Bigelow took on an even more ominous dimension. "Listen, are you sure about Rufti and the Iraqis?"

"Well, I put a lot of it together myself," Trevor admitted. "The information from the tape was sketchy, but it certainly fits. Especially in light of the way you've been acting recently."

"Shit." Khalid looked at his watch. "I've got to go to a reception at the British Museum. The Saudis are lending a bunch of early Islamic texts to the museum, and tonight is the opening. It's supposed to be a big gala and it's part of the OPEC agenda, an informal get-together before tomorrow's meetings. Listen, I wouldn't ask this normally, but we need to get together later at my hotel. It would mean breaking your date with Miss Gray."

"If it means that much, and I know it does, I'll be there." Trevor stood with Khalid and they shook hands. "And by the way, it's Mrs. Gray, not Miss. Well, Lady Gray, actually."

Khalid waited for a moment under the Savoy's dark portico for his limo to be brought around. A doorman escorted him to the Daimler, and seconds later they were back in traffic, heading toward the Bloomsbury section of London and the British Museum. Uncomfortable in limousines, Khalid wanted to talk with the driver to help pass the short commute, but the dark glass partition between them was closed and would not respond when he tried to lower it.

He considered rapping on the glass but instead sat back to watch the parade of interesting people as they drove through Soho. At Cambridge Circus, they turned right onto Blooms-bury Street, where the darkness of the night was held at bay by theater marquees and advertising signs. Rain streaked past the windows of the limo like Christmas tinsel.

Past New Oxford Street, the whole character of the city-scape changed. Low Tudor buildings, wooden signs swinging over cramped storefronts, and the occasional gas streetlamp gave an impression reminiscent of Dickens. The great stone edifice of the British Museum was just ahead on the right, an unnatural glow pouring down Great Russell Street from the television lights set up to capture famous faces headed into the opening. Even from this distance, Khalid could see the reflection of flashbulbs popping like lightning. Such enthusi-astic photo taking could only mean a film or recording star had just arrived.

The limo turned on to Great Russell, the museum looming before them on the left, a small side street to their right shoot-ing down between heavily windowed eighteenth-century buildings. Just past the gates of the museum entrance, the road was blocked by police cars, a security van, and a couple of motorcycles. Uniformed bobbies manned a temporary bar-ricade to keep back junior members of the press and the hundred or so curious onlookers. Senior reporters and pho-tographers were on the museum grounds, solidly flanking the steps up to the building.

The scene was familiar. Although he'd been to the museum many times during his schooling, Khalid had the feeling that he'd somehow seen this night before. The barricade, the streets, and even the buildings were like the vague outline of a dream.

The desert, a training camp just recently abandoned but thoroughly destroyed, streets, buildings, this place.

Even as the realization struck him, the partition between

the passenger and driver compartments began sliding down. The limo had stopped in a line of other luxury automobiles waiting to enter the museum grounds. The West Indian who'd driven him from his hotel to the Savoy had been replaced by a Turk, or maybe an Afghani. Khalid had just enough time to notice this when the man raised an automatic pistol into view.

Khalid lurched to the side, a silenced shot punching a neat hole in the leather upholstery, the compartment filling with the sharp smell of gunpowder. He grabbed for the door handle and threw himself out of the car. The second round tore the seam at his suit coat's shoulder, missing his body.

He hit the wet pavement hard, rolling once against the curb, then scrambling to his feet and lurching behind a heavy flower planter. Already he felt the eyes of cameras turning toward him. He had never felt more naked in his life, but he could not move. The driver's window was open and he could see the man looking for him. The planter offered minimal protection.

Khalid thought about running behind the car and ducking down the side street, hoping that he wouldn't be detected. Then he remembered the nine-millimeter shell casing that Bigelow had found at the abandoned training camp. Khalid knew enough about guns to recognize that the driver had used a .22-caliber automatic. There were others hunting him.

A bloom of light appeared in a window across the street, two floors up in what appeared to be a residential apartment. It turned into a streak that raced across the space between building and car in a fraction of a second. Khalid was in motion again, running as the shoulder-fired missile struck the Daimler squarely in the hood and exploded.

Burning fuel, molten metal, and deadly shrapnel filled the air as the limo disintegrated. Khalid was lifted from his feet and tossed through the air. He smashed against the wrought-iron gate that fronted the museum, the breath sucked from his lungs by the concussion. The driver/assassin behind the wheel of the Daimler had been vaporized.

Even as he fought to recover his breath, even as his ears

rang, Khalid heard automatic gunfire, like the ratcheting of some great machine. He looked behind him and saw a whole army rushing toward him, their guns spitting tongues of flame.

OVER THE
ATLANTIC OCEAN

Like a blunt-nosed arrow, the shining Boeing 737 sped through twenty-seven thousand feet, its turbofans purring sedately under half their intended strain. The aircraft had been designed as a medium-sized commercial long-haul air carrier, built to ferry several hundred people. But this aircraft carried only one passenger in the kind of decadent comfort that hadn't been seen since the time of the British Raj.

Max Johnston lay sprawled in one of the leather chairs in the cabin's main salon. Behind him was a galley capable of five-star meals, a conference room with an African stinkwood table, and a private bedroom with an antique Shaker four-poster bolted to the cabin floor. The dresser in the bedroom was Regency in style and predated the aircraft by more than a century, and the silver backing of the mirror above it was so flecked with age that its reflection was like an old photograph. The carpeting throughout the aircraft was a rich maroon pile accenting the tasteful wallpapers and oriental throws that somewhat hid the airliner's functional outline.

Ostensibly, the aircraft was owned by Petromax Oil and was available to every upper-level executive of the company. However, it was understood that the Boeing was Max Johnston's private plane, and in the two years since the corporation had purchased it, only Johnston himself had ever used it.

The Scotch in his slack hand was so diluted with melted ice that it looked like urine, and when he took a quick gulping swallow, it tasted as vile. His suit coat lay balled up in the seat next to him, so wrinkled that it would probably be replaced by his valet when he returned to Washington. His shirt was soiled with spilled liquor, and his uncoordinated struggle to pull off his tie had left it knotted tightly inches below his throat. His skin was pale and waxen, dark smudges under his eyes highlighting the pouches that had developed in just the past few sleepless nights. He looked like a hanging victim after being lowered from the gallows.

Johnston heaved himself from the chair and poured his drink into the dip sink of the concealed wet bar. Ignoring the ice bucket, he recharged his glass with a twenty-four-year-old single malt and knocked it back like iced tea. It was his fourth drink in just the two hours since the plane took off from London's Gatwick Airport. Although he was feeling drunk, his legs unsteady so that he had to brace himself against a television console, his feelings of self-loathing and disgust had not gone away. In fact, they were stronger, clutching deeper into his flesh, taking hold of his very soul.

He collapsed back into his chair, his chin sinking against his chest in a pose of utter defeat and despair. Tonight was the eve of his greatest coup. In several bold moves he was about to launch Petromax Oil into the lofty realm of a supercorporation, in league with the likes of General Motors, Exxon, or IBM, a company whose name and power would be known throughout the world. Taking risks far and above those of normal business practices, Johnston had quite literally traded his soul to scrabble those last steps to the very pinnacle of success. When he'd left London, he'd felt like one of the merchant princes of the Renaissance, making deals that not only affected his own purse strings but the fate of entire nations as well.

But now, just a few hours after sealing his pacts, he was drunk and despondent. The depression had come as soon as the aircraft labored out of England, but he knew he'd heard the voice nagging him even as a limousine was whisking him to the airport. The voice.

His father's voice.

The ghostly hand of his father touched his shoulder, and

Max Johnston jumped, spilling his drink on the Egyptian silk-on-silk rug that lay under his seat. The imagined gesture, as so often before, brought back a crush of emotions. But like all the other times he'd felt his father's spectral presence, thoughts and feelings were quickly burned away, distilled into one crystal bitter memory. No matter what Johnston did, no matter how much he accomplished, he realized that his success would never erase what happened to him when he was sixteen years old and the scathing remarks that followed.

The teenage Johnston had helped a friend cheat on an exam by giving away his answers. Of course, they were caught, and both boys were suspended from school. That night, waiting in the study of the mansion that had become their home after Keith Johnston, a hardscrabble wildcatter, had struck it rich, young Max had been afraid. Keith Johnston had made his fortune by hard work, determination, and a large dose of luck, pulling in two fields within six months and launching Petro-max Oil, a company named for his only child. Max imagined disappointment from the man he saw as a god, and the shame he felt was unbearable. His dad was an hour late coming home that night, and Max waited as if he were a soldier facing death, ready to accept whatever fate had in store.

Keith Johnston entered his study that night wearing a dusty suit, for success had not kept him out of the field. He still loved to visit the pumps, machinery, and men that made the oil flow from the south Texas plains. His wife had told him of Max's suspension, and his mood was foul. Max, a large boy for his age, physically cowered.

"Cheating!" the elder Johnston had screamed. "There is nothing worse than someone who cheats, except someone who cheats for another's gain, except someone so weak that he grants permission for somebody to rob him. Listen to me, boy, because this is the only time you are ever going to hear this.

"I built this company for you. I lied and cheated and stole to create all of this for you, so you could go on in my footsteps. And now I find my sole reason for working is nothing but a weak, impotent lackey, who gives away what he's earned. Had you been cheating so you could get a better grade, I would have understood, but you knew the material for the test and gave it away so someone else could get as good a grade as you. You are a disgrace, a ready victim for anyone who comes along. I can't believe that you are my son.

"We came from nothing, and you goddamned better not drag us back down to nothing or so help me Christ, I'll kill you myself." The hatred in the old man's voice was the worst thing Max had ever heard in his entire life. "You disgust me."

That was the last day they spoke to each other. Keith Johnston did not attend his son's graduation from high school or from Texas A&M where Max gave the valedictorian speech. He didn't go to Max's wedding, nor after his retirement did he offer congratulations when Max became CEO of the company named for him. The old man was still alive when, under Max's guidance, Petromax topped one billion dollars in assets; however, he never said a word. The last lines of Keith Johnston's will, read by an embarrassed family lawyer, cut Max so deeply that he actually fired the man who had been a friend for years.

"Just because I'm gone doesn't mean I can ever forgive you or forget what you really are. No accomplishment will ever erase the fact that you are weak. Someday it will destroy you and the company you never deserved."

The bitterness still burned the back of Max Johnston's throat. He tried to wash it away with Scotch, but the respite was only temporary, for even as the liquor exploded in his belly, his jaw tensed and acrid saliva flooded his mouth.

"You'll respect me," Johnston said softly, a defiant plea for the acceptance of a man who could never give it.

Academics hadn't impressed his father, himself a high school dropout who'd worked since he was twelve. Being at the top of his class in high school and college had not gained Max the praise he so desperately wanted; he should have known that such honors would mean nothing to his father. Max realized his father had been driven by the desire for wealth, not knowledge.

Certainly turning Petromax into a global holding company with far-flung interests and billions of dollars would get to the old man, reclaim the love he needed. Surely a balance sheet of half a billion dollars would get his father's attention. When the respect did not come, Max turned the company into a one-billion-dollar behemoth. Then two.

When that failed, Max thought about what all that money represented. What was wealth's purpose? It took him years to finally see what his old man had seen, to understand that the accumulation of wealth was nothing. It was the power that went along with it that was the reason for money's existence. That was what the old man coveted, that was what the old man respected.

Keith Johnston was a drooling invalid who couldn't use a bathroom by himself when Max gained his first White House invitation, and the old man had been dead for six years when Max financed his first successful campaign, buying himself a junior congressman for a mere eight million dollars. Even with his father dead, Max single-mindedly pursued those things that he hoped would impress the elder Johnston, gain the credibility and character that his father believed he did not possess. Now the President of the United States regularly consulted with Max about the Middle East and on energy matters, yet still he knew the old man was not impressed.

Power. The ability to control the lives of others with impunity.

Max Johnston was about to gain more power than any human being had possessed since the days of Josef Stalin and Adolf Hitler. It wasn't the scholastic honors gained through late-night studies. It wasn't the mountains of money made through shrewd financial dealings. Nor was it being courted by politicians more concerned with reelection than actually accepting the responsibility given to them. This is what Keith Johnston had always wanted, the accumulation of so much power that the entire world would take notice. Now is when Max would finally regain the old man's respect. Everything in his life had been a prelude to this moment. All the learning and all the money boiled down to this ultimate prize, the one thing that would make his father love him again.

It didn't matter what was left in the wake of what he was about to do. The deaths were meaningless, no matter how many or who. Wars were about to start because of him, nations destroyed, possibly even his own, but when that moment came, when his father finally respected him and the voice late in the night finally fell silent, it would all be worth it.

Johnston hated what he'd become, hated everything about himself, from the urbane sophisticate he presented to the world to the shame-faced sixteen-year-old boy who still lived within him. He'd become the same cold, hate-filled, intractable man who'd dominated his entire life. He'd broken ethical codes, skirted moral ideals, and ignored international laws on this quest, and there was nothing he wouldn't do now. No boundary was too far for him to cross. Nothing else mattered.

Somehow the glass he'd been gulping from had emptied and he got up to pour himself another, shying away from his mirrored reflection behind the minibar. When he finally did look at himself, staring deeply into his frantic eyes, he saw only shadowless clarity and single-minded purpose.

Max Johnston's chance to finally lay to rest his personal demons was about to change the face of the earth, lay waste to thousands of square miles of land, and cause the deaths of countless thousands of people. Staring at his reflection, he knew that the price was cheap. He would do anything, achieve any goal or destroy any obstacle, to finally gain the love of a long-dead monster.

Knowing that his daughter was in Alaska, unintentionally in the middle of his personal crusade, Johnston knew even her death would be meaningless if his father finally left him alone.

LONDON

After everything had returned to normal at the British Museum, the question would still linger as to who reacted first to the sound of gunfire echoing though the marble halls—the women who started to scream as soon as the shots erupted outside the building or the countless bodyguards, secret policemen, and other security professionals who'd been hired for the event. By the time the terrorist missile had destroyed Khalid's Daimler limousine, the guards were herding their panicked charges toward one of the "Authorized Personnel Only" areas at the back of the building that afforded the easiest defensible exit.

Most of the well-heeled guests, Arab and English alike, had lived under terrorist threats before, whether Islamic extremists or IRA separatists, and many found themselves behaving much more calmly than they had expected. With an orderliness born from acceptance, they allowed the guards to take them to safety. They talked little as they moved in a large group down long marble corridors, passed glass-faced display cases groaning under the weight of precious artifacts and archaeological treasures. Surprisingly, the Arab couples displayed more affection for each other than their English counterparts, taking their spouse's hands or muttering reassurances as they were hurried by the urgency of armed guards.

Throughout the ordeal, not a single bullet was directed at the museum.

IN the few thriller novels Khalid had ever finished, he'd read that bullets made a whining sound as they passed close by and that sometimes one could feel their passage disturb the air. However, no author had ever mentioned the intense heat as rounds sped by close enough to burn the skin of his face and neck.

Chunks of concrete were gouged from the sidewalk around him as full-metal jackets tore into the cement, stinging his hands and face and eyes. He rolled as fast as he could, trying to minimize his body as a half dozen gunmen advanced on him, their rifles chattering.

Automatic gunfire was now being returned by the police stationed at the barricade farther up Great Russell Street. A deadly crossfire arrowed just above Khalid's prone form. There was no cover to be found; the burning wreck of the Daimler was too hot to approach, but the oily smoke rising from the twisted mass offered a thin veil in which to hide. A bullet raked across his back, a fiery furrow running from shoulder to hip, as he scrabbled into the smoke roiling from the limousine. Lunging, he managed to roll back into the street, the six-inch curb feeling like the armor of a battle tank compared to the openness of his earlier position.

His suit began to smolder from the heat of the burning wreck and his left hand, the one closest to the car, started to blister. Khalid dared not move.

Two of the gunmen were down, blown back by the scathing fire from an FN FAL rifle carried by a police sniper, and two others were wounded. The terrorists were about one hundred feet from Khalid, but the smoke and fire hid him enough for their bursts to be off by several yards. The gawkers assembled to watch the gala opening of the special exhibit had fled in panic, stumbling and tripping over one another, heedless of those few unfortunates who fell under the mob's frantic escape.

None of the journalists flinched when the attack began. Ever since Herb Morrison's eyewitness account of the *Hindenburg* disaster made him a household name and forever changed journalism's impact on the world, every reporter's dream was a moment like this. All of them were making the most of it. As calmly as spectators watching a tennis volley, they collectively turned from a member of Parliament as he alighted from his car toward the carnage just a hundred yards down the road. And as one, their bovine expressions of boredom changed to sanguineous delight as the bullets started to fly. One journalist actually laughed when the Daimler exploded.

Khalid saw none of this as bullets streaked around him, every moment expecting to feel nothing ever again. His eyes were so tightly closed that squiggles of phantom light danced against the darkness of his eyelids. Yet he remained completely still in the gutter of Great Russell Street. Nothing in his experience could have prepared him for this kind of terror, and even as death sought him out, he was amazed at his composure.

Then, as suddenly as it started, it was over. The blistering fire from the police barricade took down the last two charging terrorists only forty feet from Khalid, one felled by a single bullet through his left eye and the other torn nearly in half by a ten-round burst fired by a young Special Branch agent. The whole scene was captured by motor-driven Nikons and Leicas.

Enough rain had fallen so that a tiny stream poured along the gutter, eddying around leaves and bits of loose cement and the twist-off cap of a cola bottle, washing the grit and dirt from the side of Khalid's face. Its coolness made him moan, not in fear or pain, which would come later, but in the blessed relief that he was still alive.

Police sirens punctuated the silence after the attack. Ambulances too were on their way, and more soldiers and more reporters and more of everybody. Khalid stayed in the gutter, letting the rain drum against his back and snake along his neck before trickling onto the roadway. It was only when he heard someone approach and say, "Jesus Christ," that he finally tried to get up.

He managed to lever himself only a few inches before choking waves of pain washed over him. He'd been wounded far worse than he realized.

"He's alive," the voice shouted. "Get a bloody doctor here, now."

A steadying hand touched Khalid's shoulder, and he gasped.

"You'll be all right, mate," the voice said with as much reassurance as the sight of so much blood on one man would allow. "You may have more holes in you than the links at St. Andrews, but you'll be fine."

"Any idea who he is?" a paramedic asked the soldier as he began his minstrations.

"Yeah, the luckiest son of a bitch I've ever seen."

HASAAN bin-Rufti slapped the man before him as hard as he could. While the blow contained as much strength as he possessed, the fat hanging like slabs of suet under his arm prevented his hand from swinging naturally, and much of the force was absorbed by his own considerable bulk. The backhanded follow-through was much more effective, especially when a four-carat diamond pinkie ring flayed a strip of flesh from the other man's cheek. Delighted with the bloody weal, Rufti slapped him again in much the same fashion. This time, the fat on his finger closed over the stone's sharp table edge, and it was his own flesh that bled. Cursing, he greedily sucked the finger into his mouth as if afraid he'd lose sustenance with the drops of blood oozing from the cut.

"I have always been surrounded by fools," Rufti cried plaintively to the two men standing behind the man cowering before him. He pulled his finger from his mouth long enough to ingest a piece of caviar-smeared toast. Rufti replaced the bleeding finger with a loud slurp and continued to speak around it.

"How hard is it to fire a missile at a stationary target? You were told to fire as soon as they stopped, but you decided to wait long enough to let Khuddari escape."

"But please, the driver, he was like my brother, surely you must know this?" the supine Kurdish freedom fighter wailed.

"I've given your organization a million dollars in return for the death of one man, and you tell me you're not willing to make some sort of sacrifice for your cause? The driver was supposed to die, you both knew that. He was supposed to shoot Khuddari and then die in the missile explosion. His martyrdom was the key to the entire operation. How in the name of Allah and his Prophet do you expect to further your cause if no one even knows who the fuck you are? For that you need martyrs." Rage and frustration caused Rufti's rubbery lips to flap obscenely. "Did you know in English, with only a slight change in spelling, Kurd is a formation of cheese? With a name like that your people are already a laughingstock. Kurdish homeland. It sounds like a home for dairy cows and cheese makers."

Rufti looked at his watch, one with a special band to encompass his twelve-inch wrist. "In ten minutes the BBC is going to get a letter stating that tonight's attack was the work of your organization, Kurdistan United, and that the assaults will continue if your demands for an independent nation are not met. After this fiasco, the world will say, 'Go ahead, keep attacking. Seven Kurds dead and only a little concrete shot up. In enough time you'll have no fighters left to carry on, so please keep them coming.'

"Our deal," Rufti continued to rant, his multiple chins quivering, "was money in exchange for the assassination of Khalid Khuddari. I know that you are too stupid to understand how important his death is for me, but don't grovel at my feet and whine to me about how you had second thoughts at the last moment."

In these precious moments, Rufti felt exactly as he saw himself. He had power right now, real power. His two aides would kill the Kurd if he said so, which he would, but the thrill of having the freedom fighter at his feet was too intoxicating to let it end quickly. He would stretch this out, savor it, feel the power he felt he deserved, the power of right and wrong, of life and death. Caligula must have felt like this, he thought.

From the huge Daulton serving platter that Rufti used as an appetizer plate, he selected a water cracker covered with goose liver pâté, cramming it into his mouth so quickly that the second one he brought to his lips disappeared in the same couple of chews. He considered keeping the third cracker in his hand as he pointed at the Kurd still on his knees, but temptation got the best of him, and it too disappeared. He drained a fluted glass of de-alcoholed Brut, so eagerly re-charging the delicate crystal that much of the pale faux champagne splashed onto the low settee next the armchair that cradled his bulk.

When not in conferences with the Iranians and Iraqis, Rufti had spent much of the past several days preparing his speech for tomorrow's opening ceremonies of the OPEC meeting. He'd carefully blended the right amounts of grief and admiration for Khalid Khuddari, outrage at the senseless attack that took his life, and weary acceptance at becoming the United Arab Emirates' official representative at the meeting. While the plan for Khuddari's assassination had been set for weeks, months really, he'd left the writing of his speech for the very end to give it just enough of an impromptu feel to lend credibility.

He felt his bowels give an oily slide when he thought how he'd explain to the Iranians and Iraqis why Khuddari was still alive. The assassination was supposed to trigger so many events that Rufti had a hard time keeping track, and now none of them would transpire. The Iraqis especially would seek retribution. They had put up the lion's share of the money for training the Kurdish freedom fighters, much of which had ended up in Hasaan Rufti's personal account, and they were going to want an explanation.

What was it the Iraqi representative had said? Twenty thousand men and eight thousand tanks would be transferred to their southern border upon the announcement of Khuddari's death. Rufti gulped at his glass again while his smooth, porcine features hardened at the Kurd in front of him. I want to kill this goat fucker with my own hands, he thought.

Far off in the ten-room condominium suite, a telephone rang softly. A moment later, an aide knocked at the door. He held a black portable phone handset on a silver platter, offering it like a piece of dark confectionery.

"What?" Rufti snorted.

"It's Tariq, Minister. He's at the hospital where they took Khuddari." Tariq was one of Rufti's own people.

"Allah be praised." Rufti snatched up the phone, shooting

a meaningful look at his other men. "At least someone shows a little initiative."

Into the handset his voice was sharp and authoritative, not petulant as it had been a moment before. "Tariq, tell me you have great news and the jackal has died from his wounds."

"No, Minister. Khuddari's still alive, but his condition is listed as critical. When I arrived, an orderly was still mopping his blood from the emergency room lobby."

Rufti knew that Tariq was speaking to him over an unsecure cellular phone and admonished him for the use of names, then continued as if his own misgivings didn't pertain to himself. "Listen to me. Stay there at the hospital, but do not approach Khuddari. I can't have your presence linked to me. What's security like there?"

"Lax, so far. I don't believe they know who Khuddari is." Tariq put as much nerve into his voice as possible. "I can get to his room easily. What will one more bullet matter?"

"No. Just stay close. I need some time to think. I may send this Kurdish idiot to finish Khuddari once and for all." Rufti snapped off the phone and pointed at the Kurd still kneeling. "Lock him up for now. I'm not finished with him yet."

Rufti wished Abu Alam was with him. He would have stormed Khuddari's room with his shotgun blazing and escaped long before the authorities realized what had happened. Rufti didn't have the same confidence in his second lieutenant. Tariq was good but cautious. He lacked Alam's psychotic fever. Yet Alam was needed in Alaska to guard against treachery from Kerikov and to oversee the kidnapping of Aggie Johnston, to make sure her father didn't get any ideas about backing out of his part of their bargain.

AGONY tore at Khalid Khuddari, etching his features so deeply that the pain lines would never fade, dulling his eyes so much that they would never be bright again. The pain. It started at his buttocks and traveled up his back, radiating from his spine along the thousands of nerves that branched away like tangled roots off a plant stem. The pain wrapped around his shoulders like a cloak, crushing him flat to the bed. But it especially centered on his head. His head ached with an unholy agony, as if his brain had swollen and pressed against his skull. His face felt as if it had been stung by an entire nest of desert wasps.

Khalid moaned and a voice said, "Aha!"

He heaved one eye open, fearing that his eyeball would roll out of his head. The owner of the voice was an Indian man, about fifty, with salt and pepper hair and an almost white mustache. His skin was the color of strong tea, and his eyes appeared unfocused behind a pair of wire frame glasses. He wore hospital greens. A stethoscope coiled around his throat like a dead snake.

"I am thinking," the Indian doctor said in that peculiar blend of snobbish English arrogance and generations of in-bred servitude, "that you are in a great deal of pain right now, but I am not knowing if you wish the use of morphine to ease it, most certainly. I am thinking that you are Muslim and your religious beliefs may not allow the use of such drugs, no?"

"Give me the fucking shot," Khalid managed to croak through gummed lips.

"Oh, most assuredly, I will give you the medication, sir." The doctor got busy injecting morphine into the plasma bag dangling over Khalid's bed.

Oh, God, Khalid thought. My life is in the hands of a cliché.

"You are a lucky man, most assuredly. But first, my name is Dr. Ragaswami. I was your emergency room physician. You came to me bleeding most heartedly, I assure you. But not once were you shot through. No, most certainly not shot through. Three bullets grazed your person, some leaving very long scars requiring many stitches, but none of them caused more than superficial harm. I also took nearly forty grams of concrete from you as well, fragments kicked up by the shots fired at you, I am guessing." Ragaswami watched the heart monitor next to Khalid, satisfied that it was reporting a man on the mend.

"How long?" Khalid gasped.

"It is now ten in the evening," Ragaswami said in his high-pitched voice, studying the face of a cheap digital watch.

"You have been here for more than five hours. It is most amazing that you are even awake right now. You are a very strong man, most assuredly. A lesser man would be unconscious until tomorrow at the earliest."

Ragaswami would have continued, most assuredly, had Khalid not cut him off. "I need to make a call."

"Oh, yes, I was just going to come to that. Your identification was lost before you were brought here. We have no way of contacting your family."

The morphine was starting to kick in. Khalid felt the flames licking at his back subside, the fires slowly extinguishing.

"I have no family here," Khalid muttered thickly, "but I have a friend, Trevor James-Price. He's having dinner tonight at Les Ambassadeurs."

It took a few minutes for Ragaswami to tell a duty nurse to track down James-Price, during which time he examined the superficial wounds that peppered Khalid's back, mumbling to himself and once exclaiming proudly about the tightness of the stitches he'd laid.

"I'm sorry, but the restaurant didn't have a reservation for a James-Price," a haggard nurse said, poking her head into the doorway of Khalid's room.

"Wait, it's not his table." Khalid played back his meeting with Trevor, remembering the woman with him. It didn't seem as if they'd known each other long, and the dinner was her idea, not his. There was no way someone like Trevor could get a short-order reservation at Les A.

"The table is under Millicent—" He paused for nearly a minute, the morphine taking a stronger hold of his mind, blanking out not only the pain, but his entire consciousness as well. His world was turning . . . gray. "Millicent Gray, she got the reservation. Tell Trevor I need him."

Five minutes later, Khalid was on the edge of blackness, a deep void that beckoned him in, one that he desperately wanted to enter but fought off like Saladin against the Crusaders at Ghalali. The nurse finally returned with a portable phone, holding it to the bed so Khalid could speak without moving and possibly tearing the stitches that ran in every direction across his back.

"I say, old fruit, this goes beyond the pale," Trevor said somewhat sharply. "I thought we were meeting later tonight. It's not often I get taken out by a bink like Millie."

"Shut up, Trev," Khalid moaned. "I'm in deep shit."

"What else is new? You bloody wogs are always in deep shit. It's the Koran, you know, all that jihad rot. It's too violent by half and you're all reared on it like it was a children's story."

"Trevor, will you shut up." The drugs were making speech easier, but he was losing track of what he was saying. "I'm in a fucking hospital with an Indian quack, most assuredly. I need you here. And I need your girlfriend too."

"What are you talking about?" Concern cut through Trevor's normal cavalier airs.

"I've been bloody shot, you ass. I need you to get me out of here. It hasn't ended. It won't ever end."

"I don't know what you're talking about, Khalid. Let me speak to the doctor."

"No," Khalid said. Ragaswami had left the room with the promise of returning in just a few moments. "Not tonight. I won't be able to make it. Tomorrow morning you've got to come here and bring Millicent Gray. She's tall enough."

"What are you talking about, Khalid? Jesus, you've got me spooked. Are you all right?"

"They have me on drugs. I can't talk for much longer." Khalid's speech slurred as he drifted back into oblivion. "Tomorrow morning, I need you here with Mrs. Gray. Dress her in a chador, full veils. She must be covered from head to toe like a devout Muslim woman. Tell them she's my wife. You understand?"

Trevor heard the desperation in Khalid's voice. "Trust me, my friend, we'll be there as soon as they let us. Christ, for you, I'll wear the fucking veil."

Khalid had slipped into a drug- and pain-induced unconsciousness. Had he been awake he would have heard those last few words and saved his friend's life. As it was, he was out, the phone dropping to the floor so hard that the battery pack snapped out from its concealed cradle, cutting the connection as if Khalid had hung up the phone.

Back at Les Ambassadeurs, Trevor handed the phone back to the hovering waiter and turned to his libidinous hostess. "Do you remember my friend at the Savoy? Well, it seems he needs our help."

"Don't tell me he knows my husband is a member of Parliament?"

"My dear," Trevor took one of her slim hands in his, pushing aside a plate of fine Scotch beef to get to what he really wanted. "Nothing so pedestrian. Tomorrow morning, you are going to be a harem master. And I shall be your harem."

"I thought all members of a harem were virgins?"

"True, but after tonight I fear that you'll have corrupted me."

MV *HOPE*

The heat coming from the central system had a dry, ozone tang that made the cabin smell like an electrical appliance that had just shorted. The antique system rattled every time it cycled water through the creaking pipes, popping so loudly that Aggie, already edgy, jumped when a pipe sounded off like a pistol shot. Outside the porthole, the late afternoon sun was hidden by layers of clouds and a wispy fog. Icy rain pelted the glass, driven by a stiff wind blasting down from the barren reaches of the Arctic Circle. According to the digital thermometer hanging near the cabin door, the outside temperature was twenty-eight degrees, but with the windchill it hovered in the midteens.

It was only the middle of October, and winter had already begun to grip the Land of the Midnight Sun.

The interior of the cabin was a comfortable seventy, but to Aggie it seemed much, much hotter. She'd just finished fifty sit-ups and was now lying on her back, her long legs held at a thirty-degree angle above the floor so that the rippled muscles of her stomach quivered. She'd been working out for two hours doing isometrics, aerobics, and step exercises, using a metal footlocker. She'd done two hundred advance lunges from her fencing lessons, each attack so focused she could almost feel an imaginary blade striking an opponent. Perspiration glossed her body and held her hair plastered to her head. Her sweat shorts and T-shirt clung like a second skin.

Getting up to begin her warm down, Aggie caught her reflection in a wall-mounted mirror. Used to seeing herself after exercising, she wasn't much concerned with her hair or her clothes or the sweat that dripped from her chin. But her eyes . . . they still burned with a cold emerald fury. The hours of exercise hadn't dimmed any of the anger that burned within her.

"Fucking men," she spat at her reflection.

She'd spent her entire life proving her independence, taking on challenges, facing them and more often than not vanquishing them with relative ease. Her master's degree was her own, her sleek body, once gawky and angular, was the result of her own effort, her personality validated years of fighting the influences of her parents and their warped lives. She had earned the respect that was her due, paid for it with time and dedicated work. But in the past twenty-four hours she'd been treated as if she were just a piece of furniture, or maybe a pet.

"Screw them both!"

Jan, with his mysterious errand and his ravings about making oil so repugnant no one would want to use it ever again. Mercer, with his patronizing order to leave Alaska for her own safety. This wasn't the nineteenth century, and she wasn't some simpering damsel needing to be rescued. They both acted as if they knew what was best, as if her wishes and her opinion meant nothing. Jesus Christ!

For all practical purposes, Jan had raped her last night. The man who wanted her hand in marriage had forced himself on her with little regard for her feelings at all. She could have been an inflatable doll for all he cared, a masturbatory toy.

She'd thought she loved him—his mind and feelings were so similar to hers—but now she saw, for the first time, how different he was. She'd known all along about his ego and self-absorption, but now she saw how driven he was by them. Even thinking about him made her uncomfortable, as if some multilegged insect was crawling across her flesh.

And what of Mercer, with his testosterone-charged assault this morning, guns drawn and orders shouted, as if they were storming some highjacked airliner? And his threatening to arrest everyone on his authority? He should have done it; everyone on the *Hope* was willing to go to jail for their beliefs. This was just another way for him to patronize her. A little slap on the wrist for the trust-fund environmentalist. Be careful, Aggie, she could almost hear his voice, you're playing with grown-ups now, and we don't want you to get hurt.

Hey, I'm an adult too, she thought bitterly, I know what I'm doing. A month shy of her thirty-second birthday and he was treating her like a six-year-old. So many men in her life had taken that attitude with her, treated her like some precious object that must be protected at all cost. Her father, especially, had hidden his problems with her mother until it was too late, fearing that a divorce or even a separation would hurt Aggie too much. That was a laugh. Like her mother's suicide wouldn't bother her?

And what in the hell did Mercer mean by, 'I want to be able to say I hate you too, but I can't'?

To her amazement, Aggie saw her eyes soften in the mirror, the tension in her face easing, and the scowl almost but not quite becoming a smile.

She knew what he meant.

"All right, Dr. Mercer, you're going to get what you want." Aggie spoke aloud, steel in her voice. "I'm going to leave. I'm going to leave Jan and Alaska and, most especially, I'm going to leave you. But not before I have my say and put a stop to this silly crush that should have ended years ago."

When Jan and she had talked about marriage, he had not given her a diamond ring. He'd said that he could not condone the devastation caused by mining and thus would not help the industry by buying into their popularist notion that

a diamond signifies a lasting love. The ring he had given her
as an engaged-to-be-engaged present was fashioned from ant-
ler. It seemed quaint and appropriate for what they both believed. She dug it out of her luggage, its tiny velvet box too
elaborate for the simple beige bauble.

"You're a cheap bastard," Aggie scoffed and left it on Jan's
desk, the lid open as if the little box was laughing.

She took a shower and dressed, hiding her wet hair under
a baseball cap. She packed a few things into a knapsack,
ignoring most of the clothing and "essentials" she'd brought
with her to Alaska. She'd buy what she needed when she got
to San Diego, the home of an old college friend. Aggie just
wanted to leave everything behind: Jan, Mercer, PEAL, this
whole wasted year of her life. She'd played close to the edge,
and it was time to return to normalcy.

Aggie knew the name of Mercer's hotel from the dinner
receipt she'd found in his jacket pocket. She thought about
calling him but decided surprise would be much more effective.

MERCER lay against the headboard of his hotel bed, the television bringing him a great college football game between
Florida State and Georgia. It was the third quarter, the score
only ten to fourteen, both defenses able to thwart numerous
well-executed drives just short of field goal range. A beer
rested within reach on the nightstand, a thick ring of condensation surrounding the smoky bottle of ale like a medieval
moat.

Taking a sip, he flashed a look at his watch and hoped that
the rest of the waning afternoon would pass quietly. Since
the raid, Mercer hadn't strayed more than a few feet from his
phone, fervently wishing it wouldn't ring but knowing it
would.

He was having *that* feeling again. Something was very
wrong. Jan Voerhoven not being aboard the *Hope* was just
the most obvious sign, but there were others, things he
couldn't explain, even to himself. Mercer ran through the connections again, the little things that made him so certain. This
kind of second-guessing was unnecessary and dangerous, but

it was also his nature to keep working at a problem, no matter how easy the solution seemed to be.

It started with tons of liquid nitrogen being smuggled into the state. Why? Who would do it and for what purpose? Second, the most radical environmental group in the world is already in Alaska, its leader missing on some mysterious mission that his girlfriend didn't know about. Then there was Ivan Kerikov, an international terrorist or, more accurately, a terror broker. A man with no loyalty except to himself but with seemingly unlimited resourcefulness. He was in Alaska too, with a couple of Arabs. What was their role in all of this?

Now what would a former KGB agent, a couple of Arab henchmen, and an environmental group do with liquid nitrogen on the eve of the opening of the Arctic Wildlife Refuge? The presence of even one of these elements was enough to give pause. But there was more.

Aggie's disclosure about her father, for one thing. She asserted that Max Johnston knew what time she'd been at his house, the exact moment of a devastating attack that only Harry White's timely interruption had prevented from turning into a massacre. Was Max connected somehow? Wasn't it one of his tankers that had been late arriving at the Alyeska Terminal to take on her cargo of Prudhoe Bay crude? Was that even significant?

Mercer shifted on the bed to reach for the phone. He wanted to call Dave Saulman in Miami. He wanted the marine lawyer to give him an update on that tanker. It was a long shot, a potential wild-goose chase, but sometimes wild geese lay golden eggs. His hand was only an inch from the phone when there was an loud knock on his door. He got up, and when he opened the door, he took a quick pace backward. Aggie Johnston wore jeans, a sweater, and her olive anorak. A baseball cap covered her head, tendrils of hair as delicate as silk threads falling down past her ears. She carried his leather jacket under one arm. Behind her angry expression, he saw a deeper emotion, a secret place that she didn't know existed, for surely she'd have tried to hide it from him. She was hurting, he knew, and scared. Mercer's heart slammed in his chest.

Her voice was brittle. "I need to say a few things to you."

"Do you really?" He had to force his voice to remain neutral.

. Aggie pushed her way into the room, closing the door behind her. "I just want you to know that I'm leaving Alaska and I'm leaving Jan."

"Why?" There was an intrigued smile on Mercer's face.

"Why what? Why am I leaving?"

"No, why are you telling me?" Mercer's smile deepened as he saw the uncomfortable play of emotions on Aggie's face. It was clear she hadn't expected that question.

"I just want to," Aggie replied, flustered. "I've had enough. Enough of Jan with his ego and his condescension and you with your overblown hero act."

"It's not an act," Mercer teased.

"Goddamn it, Philip, is everything a joke to you?" Aggie's use of his first name surprised him as much as it did her. Suddenly the room was an intimate place charged with something palpable.

"No, Aggie." His voice took on a tenderness he'd never shown her before. "I don't think Kerikov is a joke, or your ex-boyfriend. I don't think the attacks on my house were a joke, or the deaths of Howard Small and his cousins. None of this is a joke. That's what I've been trying to tell you."

"And what about us?" Aggie asked so quietly he hardly heard her.

It was his turn to be startled by a question he'd not expected. Before he could respond she turned back to the door, dragging her eyes away from his.

"Never mind," she said. "It doesn't matter. It's all over for me—PEAL, Jan, and even my crush on you."

She was reaching for the door when Mercer called out her name. He couldn't let her go and his desire thickened his voice. It was the first time that neither of them was on the defensive. They faced each other not as adversaries but as a man and a woman who were ready to admit a strong attraction, two minds coming together as surely as their two bodies wanted.

Aggie came across the room, stripping off her jacket. She crashed into him with enough force to push him back against the bed, her hands clutching at the sides of his head, pulling his mouth to hers, crushing his lips savagely.

Mercer's arms circled her body, one hand pulling her T-shirt out from her jeans, the other tracing up the smooth skin of her back to rest against her slim neck. She pulled him tighter to her body as if trying to burrow into his embrace like a frightened animal, yet there was nothing timid about her tongue, which roamed his mouth with slick, velvety strokes.

Their movements were feverish, hands never resting, urged onward by the desire to explore, caress, possess. Without conscious thought, they fell onto the bed, the comforter adding to the sliding movement of their bodies as they pressed against each other, their lips parting only enough to emit low moans and gasps.

"Why?" asked Mercer with reverent curiosity.

"Shut up, this is what we both want." She grasped his buttocks, pulling him to her.

Aggie's shirt was tangled up around her throat. She wriggled free for the instant it took to shed the cotton garment. She wore no bra, and Mercer's glimpse of her breasts brought him to the height of sexual tension. As if willed on their own, his hands could not be denied. One palm found her left breast, cupping it fully, the tips of his fingers extending along the cage of her ribs. Her breasts were small, almost girlish, peaked with tiny flushed nipples no larger than nickels.

He had always been self-conscious about his hands when it came to touching a woman's body. They were callused and scarred by a lifetime of physical labor, his palms like the horned skin of some desert reptile. His fingers were so hardened that the joints resembled chinks in medieval armor. When his skin raked against Aggie's breast, she broke the kiss and cried out. Mercer pulled his hand back immediately, fearing that he'd hurt her, but just as quickly Aggie pressed it back with her own, scraping the rough palm against her most sensitive flesh, increasing the tempo in time with her labored breathing.

"Oh, my God," she managed to squeak into Mercer's mouth.

Aggie pulled his hand from her chest and guided it to the juncture of her thighs. Even through the layer of denim, Mercer could feel the wet. He tore at the button fly of her jeans with mindless abandon, all thoughts blocked except for his desire. As his fingers worked the fastening, his mouth came in contact with her breast, his tongue washing over it, stiffening its tip until it looked like an over-ripe raspberry, sweet and alluring. The final button came undone. Her panties were just a soaked wisp of silk, deeply clefted by her arousal.

The phone rang, its chime as intrusive as a church bell.

Never in his life did Mercer want to ignore a call so much, but he knew he couldn't. He pulled himself off Aggie angrily, looking down at her as the phoned purred again. The confusion on her face was the most painful thing Mercer had ever seen. Forcing himself to ignore it, he picked up the receiver. "Hello."

"Mercer, Mike Collins at the terminal." Mercer pictured Alyeska's Chief of Security, the calm watchful eyes of a former cop, the long jagged scar of a former soldier.

"I've been expecting your call," he said bitterly, watching Aggie dressing again, her back to him.

"Andy Lindstrom thought you might. All hell has broken loose. We got some sort of riot at our principal depot in Fairbanks, and all the computers at the terminal are locked out. Andy asked me to give you a call. Since you knew something was going to happen, you got any ideas?"

"I'm on my way over. Have you called the authorities yet?" Mercer watched Aggie struggle into her jacket. She looked at him for a moment and then she was gone, closing the door quietly behind her. Mercer couldn't stop her, and he realized that she hadn't wanted him to. Aggie had made her choice while Mercer had none. He sadly turned his full concentration back to Collins.

"Not yet, at least not about our computer thing. It was the cops who called us about the trouble up in Fairbanks. Seems

some sort of protest at the depot's main gates has gotten out
of hand. According to the Fairbanks police, it's not PEAL
but some natives' rights group, jawing about us swiping sacred land."

"Don't worry about the riot, it's not important." Mercer
had the phone clamped between his shoulder and his head,
freeing his hands to lace up his boots. He gave Dick Henna's
personal cellular phone number to Collins. "Call him, tell him
who you are, and tell him I want Elmendorf Air Force Base
put on alert."

"Why? You just said the riot in Fairbanks is nothing. Just
a bunch of 'skimo lovers getting a little rowdy, is all. I've
already got some of my security people from farther up the
TAPline en route. It'll be dispersed within a couple of hours."

"Yeah, but when your men are chasing at shadows, Kerikov is going to make his real attack somewhere else and your
security people won't be near enough to deal with it," Mercer
said sharply. "I'll be there in twenty minutes."

There was no sign of Aggie in the parking lot as he fired
up his Blazer. And unless he went looking for her later on,
he knew he would never see her again. An emptiness formed
in the pit of his stomach, though he felt this was probably for
the best.

Aggie had waited in the vending machine alcove a few
doors down from Mercer's room. She watched him leave
through tear-blurred eyes. Giving back Jan's ring had been a
definitive act of closure, ending their relationship and her af-
filiation with PEAL. She'd wanted the same from Mercer, a
final moment together to satisfy all the questions she had
about him and about them. But it hadn't happened. Once
again, they hung in some sort of limbo, neither enemies nor
lovers. She knew now that she'd come here to sleep with him
and purge herself of her feelings. Because that hadn't happened, her feelings were even stronger than before. Somehow,
by not making love, she'd managed to prolong the possibility
of a relationship. But watching him walk down the hall, his
purposeful strides carrying him farther and farther away, she
felt her chest ache. Tears finally spilled from her eyes.

Aggie waited for a few more minutes before leaving the

hotel, making certain that Mercer had gone. The parking lot was nearly deserted; a dark van was parked near the exit doors and a dilapidated pickup occupied the closest space to the hotel's lounge. Aggie's rented car was next to the van, nosed in close to the building.

She fished her keys from her pocket, the large key ring snagging until she dug it out with considerable effort. Her concentration was centered on the silver circle of the key latch on the door of her car, and she didn't notice that the van's engine was running. When the side door of the van crashed back against its roller stops, Aggie snapped around, shifting the key in her fist so that it stuck from between her fingers like a metal claw. It was a purely reflexive action, practiced many nights walking to her car in Washington.

Two figures leaped from the side door of the van. They moved in concert, trapping Aggie between them, penning her between the two vehicles. She whirled, facing both men in a fraction of a second, growing frantic as she realized how well set up this had been. One of the men held a white rag in his hand, carefully keeping it away from his body as if the scrap of cloth contained something unspeakable. Aggie recognized him as the man who'd tried to molest her at the bar the night before. She turned her back on the unfamiliar assailant to concentrate on the threat she recognized. When she did this, the other man rushed up from behind, grasping her arms and locking them behind her back, holding her immobile.

She snapped a foot against the instep of the man holding her. As his grip relaxed for a fraction of a second, Aggie twisted from him, whipping around and raising her arm to smash her elbow into the man's jaw. The attacker staggered against the van, not quite knocked unconscious, but dazed. There was a small gap between him and her car and Aggie shot for it, jinxing herself to break free.

The attacker holding the rag jumped for her. A strong hand grasped her shoulder, steel fingers digging into the flesh below her neck. Aggie was nearly paralyzed by the pain. She tried to shake herself free, but the remorseless pressure increased until she cried out, falling to her knees.

A hotel window in front of the two vehicles opened and a

bare-chested man thrust his head out of the opening normally reserved for a screen. His face, ruddy but kind, was stubbled with gray beard. The thick hair on his chest and belly was as black and tight as the pelt of a mink.

"What the hell you doin' there?" His voice had a thick backwater drawl.

Abu Alam released Aggie Johnston and dropped the chloroform-soaked rag, twisting his body so that his coat twirled up, clearing the pistol grip of his SPAS-12 shotgun. His hand found it instantly and brought it to bear, the Velcro of the special shoulder rig parting with just the slightest tug. The first blast destroyed the window glass, the birdshot not spreading quite enough to hit the fatally curious hotel guest. The next shot, the two coming so close together that the sound blended as it rolled across the parking lot, hit the man full in the face, stretching his head backward like a rubber Halloween mask until it reached a breaking point and the contents of his skull sprayed the hotel room walls.

One second he was leaning out of the window, mildly concerned, the next second he was a headless corpse leaching purple-black blood from a ragged stump that had once been his neck. Alam tucked the Fianchi shotgun back under his leather coat and faced Aggie once again. Her face had gone completely white, her lips juddering as she lay at his feet.

"Get in the van," Alam ordered as he picked up the drugged rag.

Aggie couldn't move. She stared over Alam's shoulder at the space that had been a human being. But as Alam came forward, his tight mouth locked in a sickening leer, Aggie began to recover, scrambling to her feet. The man she had hit before had recovered and grabbed once again, this time keeping a vise grip on her arms, bracing his legs out of her range. Aggie could feel the man's erection being ground into her buttocks. Abu Alam clamped the rag over her mouth, her green eyes going wide.

Despite her best efforts, she couldn't fight the cloying, hospital-sweet chloroform, and her mind began to dim, her body to lose feeling. One man's hard fingers rubbing against her crotch no longer felt real to her. She had become a mannequin, a plastic effigy of herself that was being carefully folded into the back of the van, her legs positioned apart so that Abu Alam, Father of Pain, could stare at her denim-covered groin while his assistant drove.

MERCER expected bedlam, pandemonium, or at least a small-scale riot when he arrived at the Alyeska Terminal's Operations Control Center. However, the parking lot in front of the blocky building was devoid of the usual fleet of red Alyeska trucks, and the loud hailers mounted under the eaves of the roof were quiet. Atop the building, the skeletal radio tower was completely hidden by fog, and up behind the OCC, the power plant and the three hundred-and-ten-foot-tall stacks of the vapor recovery plant could be seen only because of their flashing safety strobes. Within the building, the hallways were empty, eerily quiet. His boots were heavy and strident as he headed toward the control room.

Andy Lindstrom, Alyeska's Chief of Operations, was standing over one of the blue-faced command consoles, a coffee cup resting on the fake wood-grain desk nearby. Seated in front of him was a young man in a black turtleneck that showed a heavy dusting of dandruff on his sloping shoulders. The young man's blotchy red face was rapt as he watched computer code scrolling across one of the multiple screens. Mercer could see that his glasses were filthy, and where they curved over his lumpy ears, the tips had been gnawed.

Mike Collins was on the phone, a booted foot on one of the black and chrome chairs, a large cigar clamped between his teeth. The underarms of his western-style shirt were dark with perspiration stains, and the scar on his cheek was a vivid purple. Lindstrom and the computer operator ignored Collins' verbal assault on whoever was on the other end of the line.

"Fuck you, Ken. You've never had a problem borrowing our equipment and even my men when you've got some crisis, so don't tell me that the riot at the depot is an internal matter and shouldn't concern your State Police, all right? I've got men en route from Pump Stations 5 and 6, but it's going to take them a few hours to get there. According to my people on the scene, the Fairbanks police have units at the riot, but they're overmatched by the sheer number of protesters." Collins paused as he listened to the State Police representative. His scar turned from purple to red and his eyes hardened. "I know they haven't called you for backup. For Christ's sake, why the hell do you think I'm talking to you now? *I'm* requesting aid. Jesus, Mary, and the Unlucky Bastard who Never Fucked his Wife, aren't you listening to me? We need help at the equipment depot, Ken, and we need it now!"

Collins dropped the receiver back in its cradle with a satisfying crash and turned to Mercer, anger and frustration written all over his face. "To think I used to be a cop like that and just as stuck on the fucking rules and regulations. Christ, what a mess."

"What's going on?" Mercer asked, slipping out of his jacket and tossing it on a table at the back of the room.

"Everything," Andy Lindstrom answered for his Security Chief. "Mercer, this is Ted Mossey, our resident computer expert, though right now the infernal machines seem to be a few runs up on him."

Mossey made no move to stand or shake Mercer's hand, but he did glance over his shoulder. Mercer recognized him from the night before. Mossey had been in the bar during the fight between the oil workers and the PEAL activists, although he had not gotten involved. He knew Mossey recognized him too, for the womanly young man turned away too quickly, reabsorbing himself with his computers. For just an instant, Mercer was sure that Mossey was frightened of him.

What the hell was that about?

Lindstrom lit a cigarette from the spent stub of the last one. He knuckled fatigue from his red-rimmed, watery eyes. "The shit seems to be hitting the fan around here. Early this morning, some of our security force at the Fairbanks depot found four people inside the perimeter fences, near the next shipment of material heading for the North Slope. They arrested the trespassers and called the cops immediately. Then, about ten this morning, PEAL held a big press conference in Fairbanks claiming we're holding several of their people illegally. Accused us of snatching them off the streets like a bunch of Gestapo storm troopers, for Christ's sake. The fucking reporters never thought to call us and hear what really happened, they just ran with PEAL's press kit. Within a couple of hours, about two hundred people were protesting outside the depot's main gates. It was peaceful at first, but it's turning into a damn riot now, bottles being thrown over the fences, protesters lying down on the access roads, that sort of shit. Get this—the protesters there now aren't even PEAL. It's a mishmash of groups, mostly native rights advocates and antinuclear demonstrators, which doesn't make a whole hell of a lot of sense, but hell, once someone starts griping, every nutcase in the state is ready to join in. These mobs multiply and mutate faster than a fucking virus."

"Any connection to your computer problem here?" Mercer asked.

"No," Lindstrom said tiredly. "The computer problem is cluster fuck number two for the day. A couple hours ago, the whole system crapped out. It froze up solid, keyboards wouldn't work, disc drives, nothing. Ted's been trying to find out what happened."

"What do you think?" Mercer directed his question at Mossey's vulturine shoulders and back.

"Lock down like this? I'd guess a glitch in the config or maybe a power spike fried the operating bats."

"Any chance a hacker did this?"

"No, the problem's too deep. The security protocols would have detected an unauthorized entry, stopped it automatically, and backtracked so fast the hacker would have been busted still at his terminal. This system's tighter than the FBI mainframe."

"Shit, that reminds me." Mercer turned to Collins.

Anticipating, Collins spoke first. "Yeah, I called. I can't believe you have the FBI director's personal cell phone number. Jesus, that was really something, talking to Dick Henna, I mean."

"Deep down, Mike, he's a cop, just like you. He has a bigger office and a longer title, that's all. Did he say that he would contact Elmendorf?"

"Yes, he said Admiral Morrison contacted General Kelly,

the Air Force's man on the Joint Chiefs. We've got full co-operation."

"Mercer, the Air Force? What are you expecting, World War Three?" Lindstrom remarked jokingly.

"Boy Scout training, Andy. Be prepared."

"Guys," Mossey spun himself from the computer, his face pinched. "I'm having a hard enough time with this without you talking, okay? I could use a little quiet while I work. And I certainly don't need that cigarette smoke."

"Yeah, sure, Ted," Lindstrom said, taken aback by Mossey's harsh tone. The computer operator had been nothing but docile since starting work at Alyeska. Lindstrom assumed that Mossey was more confused by the system's problem than he was letting on. "We'll head back to my office. Call if you find anything."

"Fine," Mossey breathed and turned back to the scrolling screen, his bony fingers poised over the keyboard like a musician waiting for his cue.

Back in Lindstrom's office, the wait began.

"Jesus H. Christ, relax," Lindstrom said, seeing how anxious Mercer appeared. "We talked about this yesterday. We all agreed that if someone wanted to use liquid nitrogen to disrupt the oil flow, the only logical place would be the equipment depot in Fairbanks, and we caught the bastards at it last night."

"Did they have any nitrogen tanks with them? Any stainless steel cylinders?" Mercer shot back moodily.

"Well, no. They were probably there to scout around for the best places to use their stuff. Shit, that depot is something like forty acres, with buildings and piles of equipment scattered all over the grounds. It takes a couple of hours just to find the bathrooms."

Mercer's silent glance quieted Lindstrom immediately. Mike Collins nodded his approval at Mercer, the assuring compliment of one professional to another.

A few quiet minutes went by.

"The computer system," Mercer asked, "how much of your operation does it control?"

"Well, hell, everything. You know the way the world

works nowadays. Nothing happens unless the computer gives you permission first."

"Could it shut down the entire pipeline?"

"Sure. We can remotely operate the whole system from here, but we don't. All of the pump stations are autonomous, monitored twenty-four hours a day, and they have ultimate say as to what happens at any location. If they have a problem, they can shut down the line too."

"Is there any sort of automatic override? Any way the system can take over from the pump stations, cut them out of the loop and run independently?"

"I don't follow you."

Mercer spoke slowly and clearly so there could be no question as to his meaning. "Can your computer take over the pipeline?"

It took Lindstrom a few seconds to respond and when he did, he didn't like his answer. "I don't know."

The phone rang, and Collins and Lindstrom both gave a startled jump. Lindstrom answered, listened for a few seconds, then handed the phone to his Security Chief. He turned to Mercer, nervous fingers fumbling to light a cigarette. His eyes had gone wide and his face was dewed with sweat despite the chill seeping into the building. Collins spoke little, just grunting a few times and once muttering a quiet obscenity. When he hung up, he had visibly whitened and his hands were trembling.

"That was Ken Bassett with the State Police. There's been an accident. Both vans carrying men from Pump Stations 5 and 6 to augment security at the depot went off the Dalton Highway. There are two cruisers there now, but it appears no one survived."

"When?" Mercer's voice was like a whip crack.

"The police just got there, but the vans may have gone off the road awhile ago. Guessing from where they crashed and what time they left the pump stations, I'd say at least six hours."

Mercer looked through the open miniblinds covering the window behind Lindstrom's desk. Twilight was just a few minutes away. It would be totally dark soon after. Rain fell in silvery channels down the glass. "We need to get up there."

"That's five hundred miles north of us."

"Then let's not sit here and discuss mileage," Mercer snapped. "You must have a chopper with that kind of range?"

"Yeah, but . . ." Lindstrom was obviously out of his element. He had a crisis on his hands and didn't realize it. Mercer moved easily into the vacuum created by his hesitancy.

"Mike, call up those Pump Stations. Make sure everything is okay."

"They can be accessed through the computer," Collins pointed out.

"The computer's down, or had you forgotten? And the majority of the men working those stations have been called away to Fairbanks and are now dead. I need you to make sure that the men they left behind are still alive."

Collins immediately recognized the possibility that the three apparently separate situations were linked. He raced from the room to make those calls from his own office.

"Andy, contact your pilot and have him file an emergency flight plan to get us to the Dalton Highway. I'm going out to your receptionist's desk to call Elmendorf. We're going to need them." Mercer was already headed for the door.

"What's happening?" Lindstrom was visibly shaken now.

"World War Three."

ALYESKA MARINE TERMINAL

Twenty agonizing minutes dragged by, the ticking of a wall clock sounding like the heartbeat of a dying man. Mercer's call to Elmendorf had secured two Hueys with eight fully equipped Air Force commandos in each of the helicopters. True to his word, Dick Henna had galvanized the powers that be in Washington. Andy Lindstrom had phoned one of Alyeska's on-call chopper pilots, a cowboy he thought would jump at the chance of the flight to the northern pump stations. The pilot would meet them at the Valdez Municipal Airport in thirty minutes. Mercer and Lindstrom were waiting for Mike Collins to get off the phone. Then they'd get a final word from Ted Mossey on his progress reactivating the pipeline's computer operating system.

With ten minutes to go before they were to rendezvous with the helicopter pilot, Collins finally emerged from his office, his weathered face wearing a dark expression. His eyes had gone glassy and lifeless. The plug of tobacco jammed in his left cheek looked to be the size of a softball.

"I can't reach Pump Stations 5 or 6, I've tried the phone, the two-way radio, and the shortwave. Even the fax machine. There's no response."

"What do you mean, no response? You didn't send everyone down to Fairbanks, did you?" Lindstrom asked, panicked.

"Of course not. Do you think I'm that stupid?"

"Knock it off." Mercer recognized the beginning of an ass-covering session and stopped it as quickly as he could. He had neither the patience nor the time for such bureaucratic idiocy. "We've got a major situation on our hands and don't have the time to sit here and point fingers."

Once again, Mercer found himself making decisions for Lindstrom and Collins, and again the two men obeyed without question. "Andy, I want you to stay here and coordinate our communications. Also, work on your computer guy. It's imperative that you regain control of the system. Mike, you and I are heading up to Pump Station 5. On-site intel is crucial. Does your helicopter have the right gear for me to contact Elmendorf?"

"I don't know," Collins admitted. He switched his chew from one distended cheek to the other, a small jet of yellow juice shooting from his pursed lips. "You'd have to talk to Ed, the chopper pilot, about that."

"Well, let's go talk to Ed, then." If Mercer felt any hesitancy, it didn't show. He was moving on a deeply intuitive level that he'd learned to never question.

By the time they got to the airport, night had settled with deceptive ease, darkening the sky completely. The rain, which had been constant all through the afternoon, had finally stopped, leaving the trees heavy with water. Even the slightest breeze brought another shower falling to the earth. But slight breezes were not in order for this night. A stiff wind scoured the open field, with gusts strong enough to alter Mercer's stride.

The lone Bell Jet Ranger among the Cessna 182s, Twin Otters, and a single private jet looked like an overgrown insect bathed in artificial light as it sat forty yards from the terminal. A dark figure leaned nonchalantly against the sharply angled Plexiglas windscreen, hands crossed over his broad chest.

Lit as they were, the pilot could see his passengers before they could get a clear image of him. He peered into the light beaming from the terminal and laughed roughly when he recognized one of his passengers.

"Don't even think of coming one step closer, Mercer," the pilot warned in a deep baritone. He was African American. "The Judge Advocate General said I've got the legal right to kick your ass if you come within fifty feet of me."

"Eddie?" Mercer called. "Eddie Rice?"

"None other, white boy, and I ain't kidding, you stay away from me, man. You carry some seriously bad juju and I don't want you around me again. My flying record was perfect before your sorry ass entered my life, and I plan to keep it to just that one crash until the man give me my gold watch."

"They give you a gold watch, Eddie, you'll hawk it for a couple of forty-ounce malt liquors. You still drink when you fly?" Mercer called back, pacing a little ahead of Collins.

He and Eddie Rice came together, hugging as friends who thought they'd never see each other again. Even in a padded flight suit, Eddie was a solid person, his body dense and roped with muscle. He was not as tall as Mercer, but his shoulders were wider and his neck was as thick as a tree stump. Rice was handsome, the way a sports figure or music idol was handsome. His skin was glossy smooth and his deep-set eyes were wide and bright, only a single dark vein in his right eye marring their bluish whiteness. His only unattractive feature were small, misshapen teeth, two jagged rows of yellowed tablets that were either too crowded or too gappy.

A year ago, Eddie Rice had been a lieutenant in the navy, a chopper pilot commanding a Sikorsky Sea King off the amphibious assault ship *Inchon*. He'd had the bad luck of ferrying Mercer from the aircraft carrier *Kitty Hawk* to the *Inchon* during the crisis in Hawaii. Mercer had hijacked Rice's helicopter, ordering him to fly to Hawaii so he could prevent a catastrophic invasion that would have forever crippled the United States. While making their escape after preventing a nuclear missile launch, Mercer, Eddie, and a Russian scientist named Valery Borodin had been forced to ditch their helicopter in the North Pacific. Eddie had been the most severely injured in the crash, spending three months in the naval hospital at Pearl Harbor. The last Mercer knew, the navy had given Rice an honorable discharge and set him up on a disability plan that would make him comfortable for the rest of his life. Mercer more expected to see Nanook of the North in Alaska than Eddie Rice, USN (Ret.).

"I'll have you know, I have maintained twelve hours bottle-to-throttle since about twenty minutes ago," Rice teased back.

On their desperate flight from Hawaii trying to track down a rogue Soviet sub, Mercer had offered Eddie a beer, which the pilot had gratefully accepted considering his chances of surviving to face a review board were about zero. It was one of the many things the two men had laughed about during their time in the hospital. The previous Christmas, Eddie had sent Mercer a single Sapporo beer, the brand that the two had shared on that fateful flight.

"What are you doing here?" Mercer questioned.

"Shit, I should ask you the same question. I get a call on my day off for some emergency flight, and who shows up but the most dangerous man I've ever met. What's your story?"

"You remember the Russian behind the Hawaii affair? He's back, and right now may be just a few hours north of us."

"Who, that Ivan Kerisomething? You shitting me?"

"I wish I was."

"Shit, that guy is the Tonton Macoutes and Baron D'Mort

all rolled into one," Rice said, blending his Haitian grand-mother's two greatest fears, the former Haitian Secret Police and one of the dark figures of traditional voodoo.

"Throw in Jack the Ripper and you've got it half right."

Moments later, the stress on the Jet Ranger's landing skids eased, the struts flexing so they seemed to help launch the chopper into the air. The Teikel River Valley was soon a narrow ax stroke in the ground beneath the rapidly climbing craft. Mercer sat in the copilot seat while Collins occupied the back cabin, his feet stretched almost into the cockpit. All three wore radio earphones, which gave their conversation a muted, distracted sound. The light from the cockpit gauges was an eerie green.

The Jet Ranger's nose-mounted strobe flashed a lonely signal into the night.

"So what's this all about?" Eddie asked after he got the helicopter settled into their designated flight path.

"A couple of hours ago I sent some men down to Fairbanks from Pump Stations 5 and 6," Mike Collins answered, the throat microphone too close to his mouth so that his voice was garbled. "They were all killed in an accident, two vans full of guys that I've known for years. Then, just about forty minutes ago, we lost communication with the rest of the men I left at Numbers 5 and 6."

"This have anything to do with the trouble at the equipment depot I heard about on the news?"

"Yes," Mercer answered. "But that's just a distraction. I think the real trouble is at one of the pump stations."

"All right, Mercer." Collins sat forward, thrusting his head between the two cockpit seats. "You seem to have some special knowledge about what's going on here, and I think it's time you told me. I've lost some men tonight, and something tells me the killing isn't done. You know something you're not telling me and goddamn it, I have a right to know."

"What happened to the captain of the *Petromax Arctica*?" Mercer replied.

"What?"

"The original captain of the *Petromax Arctica* was taken off the ship, choppered to Anchorage, and then taken to Seattle aboard a private medical flight paid for by Max Johnston himself. Do you have any idea why the ship was several hours late berthing at the terminal? If they went through the expense of pulling Harris Albrecht from the tanker, don't you think it was to make sure the *Arctica* docked on time? So why was the tanker late? What the hell was an empty VLCC doing running around the Gulf of Alaska without a captain while a berthing space was being held for her?"

"What are you talking about? That doesn't have anything to do with this situation. The *Petromax Arctica* docked long before—"

Mercer cut him off before Collins could finish. "Answer the question and I think you'll know."

"Harris Albrecht was taken to a trauma specialist in Seattle, a doctor specializing in limb reattachment and stump repair for prosthesis."

"Did you check him out, this doctor?" Mercer torqued himself around so that his eyes bored into Collins.

"I made a couple of calls when it happened."

"And?" He cocked one dark eyebrow.

"Tissue repair following frostbite was his true speciality. He's one of the foremost . . ." Collins went silent.

The rotors were thumping over their heads so loudly they drowned out the sound of the Jet Ranger's turbine. Eddie kept the craft straight and level, ignoring his desire to dip into the valleys and fly nape of the earth as the military had trained him to do. In the Gulf War, he'd flown Recon Marines into the hottest landing zones, and that wild flying style had never left him.

Mercer spoke. "How many times has the *Arctica* docked at Alyeska without incident in the past year? How many times has Harris Albrecht snugged his tanker into your docks without so much as a bump? Tell me how he could lose an arm and need the attention of a frostbite specialist on a normal run from Long Beach, California, to Valdez, Alaska. He's been smuggling frozen nitrogen into Alaska right under your nose. But on his last trip, something went wrong."

"You don't think this is all related?"

Mercer shot him a scathing look. "For Christ's sake, of

course its all related. Why do you think I'm in this fucking helicopter with a madman at the controls while I could be back home having drinks at my neighborhood bar? Mike, Howard Small is dead, his cousin is dead, and so is his cousin's son. People have taken potshots at me all because we stumbled onto the boat ferrying the canisters of liquid nitrogen from the *Petromax Arctica* to shore. Kerikov and PEAL are trying to cover themselves by eliminating anyone who stumbled onto their operation. Your computer problem? It isn't a coincidence, despite what your computer guy says. The riot at the depot, the accident with your vans? Whatever Kerikov has planned is happening right now!"

He hadn't intended to go off like that; it wasn't his style, but tension was starting to eat at him. There was a nagging feeling telling him he was already too late. He wasn't angry at Mike Collins for not recognizing the dangers; he was mad at himself for not recognizing them fast enough. When Aggie Johnston had told him her boyfriend was gone on some mysterious mission, he should have acted then, called in the cavalry so to speak, and ordered a statewide search for PEAL's leader. He was certain that Kerikov would have turned up in the same dragnet and this desperate flight wouldn't have been necessary.

"Eddie, what's our ETA to Elmendorf AFB?"

"I don't know, I filed a flight plan to Fairbanks. What's at Elly?"

"A couple of helicopter gunships and some gung-ho soldiers." Mercer grinned at Rice. "There's no way I'm going to get shot at again."

"Amen to that, brother." Rice smiled back, his teeth looking iridescent in the glow of the cockpit. "I'd say about another hour and ten minutes in these conditions."

"As soon as you can, get me in radio contact with them. They're expecting my call." Mercer then switched to a more relaxed tone. "So how does your wife like living up here?"

"She doesn't," Rice said ruefully. "She and I split up while I was still in the hospital. It seems I wasn't the only one receiving injections from my doctor at Pearl."

"Man, I'm sorry."

"Ah, shit. Life goes on, don't it? Besides, a black man up here? I get more ass than I can handle." Eddie's grin was back, though there was a hint of sad bitterness in his voice.

An hour later, Anchorage was a bright blur on the ground beneath the Jet Ranger. The waters of Cook Inlet were an inky black stain. The storm that had pounded Valdez during the afternoon had moved northward and now pummeled Alaska's Queen City. Rain lashed the helicopter, striking the windshield so hard that it sounded like stones thrown against the Plexiglas. The wipers turned the torrent into arcing streaks across their field of vision. Wind rocked the craft, sluing it dangerously despite Eddie's best efforts. He made no apology for his flying. His face was tight with concentration, his hands and feet dancing over the controls. A pilot of lesser skill wouldn't have dared flying tonight.

"Alyeska Flight One-eleven, we have you on radar twelve miles out, flying three-oh-five degrees."

"Roger that, Elmendorf," Eddie confirmed. "ETA in five minutes. Approach three-ten, squawk zero-two-two-zero. Confirmed."

"Confirmed One-eleven."

"You know what you're doing?" Mercer teased Rice.

"No fucking clue."

Four minutes and forty seconds later, Eddie settled the Bell chopper onto the tarmac near a huge corrugated steel hangar. Two Huey UH-1 troop transport helicopters were next to the spot where ATC had sent the Alyeska helicopter, and even in the murky light spilling from the hangars, they looked deadly. The side doors were open, revealing gimbal mounted M-60 heavy machine guns. Even before the Jet Ranger's blades stopped turning, technicians were swarming around the craft, oblivious to the icy rain buffeting the airfield. A fuel truck drew alongside and two men prepared to attach the thick hose to the chopper.

Mercer ducked from the Jet Ranger, dashing for the protective cover of the hangar, his boots kicking up violent waves in the puddles on the asphalt. A cold chill lapped under the raised collar of his leather coat, and his hands felt frozen by the time he entered the glowing hangar.

The huge building's heating eased the chill on Mercer's exposed skin, but his insides were still cold with fear and apprehension. Two delta-shaped F-15 Strike Eagles dominated the space, their twin tails rising up almost twenty feet from the polished concrete floor. Behind them, at the back of the hangar, a cluster of men waited quietly, their faces blackened with camouflage grease, their M-16A1 assault rifles held competently in demigloved hands. They paid little attention to Mercer as he approached, satisfying themselves with a dismissive glance before turning back to the perpetual task of checking and rechecking equipment. Mercer kept walking toward them, and finally a single man detached himself from the collective.

He was short and heavily built, with bristle-cut hair and a face that needed a razor. His brows were heavy tangles of wiry hair that met above his hooked nose. His eyes were dark and wrinkled at their corners, but Mercer saw that they were level and quick. His mouth, incongruously, was full-lipped and sensitive.

"Colonel Knoff?"

"You must be Mercer." Knoff's handshake was like having a hand caught in some sort of farm machine, a relentless grinding pressure. Mercer briefly considered matching Knoff's handshake but realized this wasn't some sort of macho test, just Knoff's natural grip. "I gotta say, you've caught us a little off guard here. An hour ago, I was watching porno movies with a few of the guys, and next thing I know, I'm on the phone with General Samuel Kelly, the Air Force's Chief of Staff. I can't even guess who you are to pull that kind of string."

Mercer immediately liked Knoff's attitude. He didn't have a career soldier's disdain for anyone not in uniform. It was clear that he hadn't forgotten that it was civilians he was trained to serve. "Ask any politician and he'll tell you I'm the most powerful person in the country," Mercer smiled. "An American taxpayer."

"You mind telling me what this is all about?"

Mercer could understand Colonel Knoff's question and the concern he felt for his men that made him ask it, but none of them had the time to stand around and discuss it. He had to get them moving.

"Colonel, if I've managed to convince your superiors about this mission's importance, put your trust in their judgment and just go along with it. This may be a waste of your time, but if it's not, if I'm right, we're going to face a seriously hot LZ. I can't give you any of the overall picture, but I need to know if you have any tactical questions about tonight's op. If you don't ask now, some of your boys may not be coming back."

"Mr. Mercer, I wouldn't worry about us." The ramrod in Knoff's back got about two degrees straighter, if such a thing was possible. "General Kelly briefed us on what to expect. What bothers me is the presence of you and your slick in our convoy. My pilots don't know your man, and the last thing we need is a civilian helicopter flying in the same area where we're making a hot drop."

Mercer had expected such a concern, and his reply was the reassurance that Knoff wanted. "I flew with this pilot during last year's flap in Hawaii. Plus he's ex-navy and a Gulf War veteran. I plan to keep us a couple miles back from your landings and monitor from the radio. You guys are the ones who make the big bucks for getting shot at, not us. Have your lead pilot give instructions to my man, and he'll follow them to the letter."

"What about you, what's your experience?" Knoff asked.

"Were you in Iraq?" Knoff nodded. "I'd already been in and out before the Abrams tanks broke through the berms. I was a specialist for Delta Force's Operation Prospector, to make sure none of you boys faced nukes on the battlefield. I've probably seen more firefights than all of your troops combined, and we can sit here all night and compare scars, but I don't have the time. Anything else?"

Knoff was slightly taken aback by Mercer's response. The Special Forces community, though rife with interservice rivalries, was close-knit, and stories of black operations circled freely in watered-down versions to avoid compromising ongoing missions. It was obvious in his reaction that Knoff had heard of Operation Prospector and knew that a civilian had turned a debacle into a success while saving most of the team sent to protect him. "No, sir. That should do it. I've got the coordinates for the pump stations and the quick sketch map faxed to us by a guy named Lindstrom. I figured we'd hit both simultaneously."

"Negative," Mercer replied evenly. "If we split your forces, we'll be outgunned and probably outmanned. By the time we get up there, I'll have the intel on which station was taken."

"All right." Knoff didn't have any more questions.

"Then let's go," Mercer said with more bravado than he felt.

IVAN Kerikov settled into a chair behind the pump control console, a Heckler and Koch MP-5 resting across his knees. The corpses of the few Alyseka employees who'd remained at the station had already been dumped outside. He removed his heavy overcoat and was thinking about taking off the bulky black sweater he wore beneath it. In the late 1970s, he'd been attached to a KGB commando team as an intelligence officer. As a training mission, they'd once had to retake a 'terrorist-occupied' natural gas pumping station deep in the heart of Siberia. He'd never forgotten the loneliness of the station far out in the tundra or how drab and utilitarian and unbearably cold the facility had been. Expecting much the same in Alaska, he'd dressed several layers too thick for the assault on Pump Station Number 5.

So far, overdressing had been his only miscalculation.

Ever since he'd arrived in Alaska, he'd been plagued by setbacks, delays, and a thousand other problems. He'd handled them all in his typical manner. If the problem is mechanical, replace it; if it's timing, stall it; and if it's human, kill it. But now, all his groundwork was paying off. Thanks to the former Captain of the *Petromax Arctica* and the PEAL workers, there were eighteen hundred tons of liquid nitrogen encasing strategic parts of the Alaska Pipeline. The specially built packs needed to keep the supercooled fluid from prematurely freezing the pipeline were disguised as the metal sleeving that encased the forty-eight-inch-high carbon steel pipe. The nitrogen packs had been so well built that even close inspection by Alyeska workers couldn't differentiate them from the normal sleeves. Kerikov had gone so far as to have them weathered to duplicate the quarter century of wear the pipeline had withstood. To the inspectors, the slightly larger size of the packs never raised any suspicion, and some of them had been in place for months.

Using PEAL had been Kerikov's greatest masterstroke. But as he sat in the control room, he allowed himself one more degree of conceit and admitted that creating PEAL had been the masterstroke. Hasaan bin-Rufti had been leery of Kerikov's plan. He had wanted to use some of his own people to carry out the delicate operation of placing the nitrogen packs, but Kerikov had pointed out that fifty Arabs running all over Alaska would arouse too much suspicion. However, Kerikov said, a group of environmental activists, common all over the United States and especially in Alaska since the President's announcement about the Arctic Refuge, wouldn't raise even an eyebrow, let alone an alarm. Like the purloined letter, they could hide in plain sight, protesting at various sites and cities along the pipeline's route while their companions booby-trapped the pipe.

The beauty of PEAL, too, was that they didn't know that their actions had a darker motive. Jan Voerhoven and his sad band of codependent flotsam didn't realize that their sabotage went so far beyond an environmental statement. They naively believed that when the nitrogen was released it would freeze the oil in the line and forever prevent the Trans-Alaska Pipeline from transporting crude. They believed this because it was what Kerikov had told them and was what they wanted to believe. Not one of them had ever considered that just freezing the line would present only a temporary setback to Alyeska and the opening of the Arctic Wildlife Refuge.

Voerhoven was the worst of them. He was intelligent, probably possessed a genius IQ for all Kerikov knew, but he was warped by his inflated ego. Ivan Kerikov had transformed him from a member of the lunatic fringe into a driving force in the war on industrialism, and Voerhoven thought that he'd done it all on his own. Twenty years with the KGB in various functions had taught Kerikov how to manipulate others.

Sometimes it took money and sometimes fear; with Jan Voerhoven, all it took was a little ego stroking and the Dutchman
was off and running. By the time PEAL began setting the
packs around the pipeline, Voerhoven had convinced himself
that the idea for the strike had been his all along.

"Sir." One of Kerikov's people entered the control room,
a dusting of snow covering his wide shoulders. "It'll take
another two hours to secure the nitrogen packs." He spoke in
German-accented Russian and his voice was apologetic. "Our
intelligence didn't specify that the pipeline would be so high
off the ground when it reaches this station. We only have two
trucks equipped with cranes, so the work is slowed considerably."

Kerikov's feeling of self-satisfaction evaporated.

The final packs, the linchpin for the entire operation, had
been lost when one of them had split during transfer from the
Arctica to the fishing boat *Jenny IV*. Captain Albrecht had
had one of his arms frozen off when it was doused in two-
hundred-degrees-below-zero nitrogen. During the confusion
following the accident, a fire had broken out on the *Jenny IV*.
The crew of the boat had been unable to put it out before it
boiled the cryogenic tanks already stowed aboard. The re-
sulting explosion had all but destroyed the fishing boat.
JoAnn Riggs had assured Kerikov that the hulk wouldn't float
for more than an hour after they cut her away from the tanker.
Of course, the *Jenny IV* hadn't sunk and was discovered the
next day. Though Kerikov had been forced to act against the
men who found the derelict, his more pressing demand was
to find additional liquid nitrogen and get it in position. The
original KGB blueprint for Charon's Landing had called for
eighty tons of liquid nitrogen to be placed in a remote area
on the downward leg of the pipeline as it descended the
Brooks Range, fifty miles north of his present location. Without that quantity of nitrogen to work with, Kerikov had had
to modify the plan and place a much smaller amount directly
at Pump Station 5.

He'd timed the attack so there would be only about twelve
hours between the assault on the pump station and the release

of the nitrogen, but every second they spent here increased their chances of either being caught or being forced to release the nitrogen prematurely, reducing its effect. In a small way, he blamed himself for not telling Voerhoven to sabotage this critical section during the beginning of the operation and not waiting for it to be the last set of packs coupled to the pipeline. Coming here was a calculated risk, but like any calculating man, Kerikov planned to stack the odds in his favor.

"Tell your men to stop helping the PEAL members placing the packs. I know it'll slow us further, but I need you and your troops ready for the American response. By now, they must know we're here. I expect a counterassault shortly." Kerikov spoke with confidence. He was back in his element. "Deploy the Grails and the RPG-7s and send a vehicle down the road as a rear guard. The authorities haven't had enough time to organize their attack, which gives us the tactical advantage. And remember to make sure the missile strikes count. If you miss even one of their helicopters, they'll be able to radio for reinforcements. I'm sure by now, those vans of Alyeska employees that were run off the road by the trucks have attracted police interest. The cops could show up quickly if they knew something was happening here."

While the brunt of the PEAL activists had arrived at Pump Station 5 in the lumbering trucks transporting the heavy nitrogen packs, Ivan Kerikov, Jan Voerhoven, and Kerikov's two bodyguards had flown to the station in a helicopter. He thought that if the Americans managed to land a large number of shock troops, they could use the chopper again to escape, leaving the environmentalists to fend for themselves.

If Voerhoven had any misgivings about allowing his people to be used as cannon fodder, it didn't show. He was outside, braving the arctic storm, cheering on his workers like this was some great adventure that they would all reminisce about in the years to come.

There was no way Kerikov would allow any of them to live even if they somehow survived the imminent American attack. He smiled tightly and lit a cigarette.

VLCC *SOUTHERN CROSS*

According to the tiny constellation of luminous dots on Lyle Hauser's watch, it was twenty minutes before midnight, twenty minutes until his deadline for Chief Engineer Patroni to shield Hauser's launching of the lifeboat from the vessel. But that would not happen now. Those twenty minutes would tick by. Midnight would come. Then go.

An hour earlier, he'd heard a rippling stitch of automatic gunfire through the lifeboat's fiberglass hull. The shots sounded as if they'd come from the bridge, but to Hauser, the sound was as deadly as if he'd been shot himself as he lay cocooned under layers of blankets, the crumbs of iron ration crackers sprinkled around him. The gunfire could only mean that Patroni had been prevented from deactivating the bridge indicators for the three lifeboats. JoAnn Riggs and her terrorist comrades must have discovered Patroni's actions and killed him, sawing his body in half with lead slugs from their Uzi machine pistols. Hauser couldn't get the gruesome image out of his mind.

All was lost. Riggs would surely investigate why Patroni wanted to disable the indicator panel, and trapped as he was, there was nothing Hauser could do. There were no weapons in the craft, only an orange flare pistol, its great muzzle over twice the size of a ten-gauge shotgun. But to fire it within the life raft was tantamount to suicide. The phosphorus flare would ignite the boat, its toxic fumes overcoming anyone trapped within, leaving them incapacitated as liquefied plastic and Fiberglas poured onto their inert bodies as the craft melted around them.

Ten minutes till midnight.

Patroni was dead, but maybe Riggs didn't know what he had been attempting, Hauser hoped. Maybe he could hide in the hyperbaric lifeboat for a few more hours and then decide what was best, not only for himself but for the rest of the crew. If he launched now, the panel on the bridge would light up, sounding a number of alarms. Riggs would have plenty of time to send a soldier to investigate long before Hauser could motor away from the tanker. A machine gun from the stern rail would make his the shortest escape in history.

He began working on a new plan. It was obvious that he couldn't get off the *Southern Cross* undetected. Riggs and her followers had the ship locked up too tight. His only hope lay in sabotaging the vessel again and making sure that she didn't reach a continental port. Hauser remembered hearing how important it was to Riggs that the tanker reach Seattle. According to his dead reckoning, they were still a day away from Washington's port city.

Suddenly a nearby voice called into the night. "Checking aft lifeboat now."

Hauser reacted instantly, thrusting aside the blankets, bringing the flare gun to bear on the boat's hatch. Outside, hands fumbled with the double closure of the craft.

This was it. Of all the fear Hauser had faced, nothing could compare to this. His throat was dry, his hands trembling as they gripped the flare pistol. Sweat slicked his face, burning his eyes as he watched the inner door of the life raft rotate to the unlocked position. A few more ounces of pressure and the terrorist would swing the hatch inward and discover Hauser's secret hiding place.

No matter what, he would fire. Riggs knew about him through Patroni's actions, and it had been only a matter of time before he was ferreted out and summarily shot. It was better that he discharged the flare at the terrorist as he peered into the life raft. Hauser would die, but he would take one of the bastards with him.

The inner hatch finally released, a slight hiss escaping as the circular door was pushed against its internal stops. Lyle Hauser had tucked himself back under the blankets so only the open mouth of the flare gun gave away his presence. It wasn't until the outer door was opened that he became aware of how stale the air in the lifeboat had become. The cold, tangy breeze that enveloped the terrorist as he leaned into the lifeboat was like a moist caress, intimate and loving and just as fleeting.

The guard was dressed in black, an Uzi draped around his broad shoulders and a Colt .45 automatic pistol gripped in one fist. He pushed himself half way through the boat's tight entrance. His flashlight, a mini Maglite, was clamped between his teeth like a cigar. In its erratic glow, Hauser was nothing more than a dark lump. The terrorist held a walkie-talkie in his left hand, his thumb resting lightly on the transmit button. Hauser didn't know that the guard hadn't recognized him as a person until he unintentionally shifted on the tough rubber floor mats, the blankets on his body moving like a wave.

"I think I've found somebody," the guard shouted into his radio.

In that instant, Hauser was more alive, more perceptive than he'd ever been. The guard's eyes went wide and white at the sight of the flare pistol, and he barely managed to open his mouth to scream before Hauser pulled the trigger.

The ignition of the flare gun was a concussive thump that sucked all the oxygen from the lifeboat. The molten ball of red phosphorous shot from the gun and hit the guard square in the chest. His heavy parka burst instantly into flames. Hauser saw that the burning body blocked his only escape from the lifeboat and knew his death was not far away.

JOANN Riggs was feeling the strain of her new command; it etched her face and darkened the circles under her eyes. She was exhausted, her mind dulled. The brief respite she'd had an hour ago, when Wolf had shown her how to fire one of the Uzis, was all but forgotten. Firing rounds off the flying bridge had delighted her; holding the weapon as it spat fire and shook in her arms was intoxicating. But now she was back on the bridge, ever vigilant, watching her captive crew.

Wolf, the commando leader hired by Ivan Kerikov, whose real name was Wolfgang Schmidt, stood behind her as she sat in the Master's chair. The flap of his holster was undone and tucked back so that he could reach his automatic in just a fraction of a second. A helmsman held onto the dual controls of the ship's wheel while a navigation officer stooped over the plotting table, trying hard to ignore the terrorists. George Patroni knelt into an open access panel under the bridge's main console, his buttocks half exposed like a suburban plumber as he traced a wiring fault. The ship's electrician was bent down next to him. Another of Wolf's men watched them closely, his eyes squinting in the vermilion gloom of the vessel's night lights. His Uzi dangled at his hip.

The *Southern Cross'* throttle controls were still out. However, Patroni and his men had been able to jury-rig a tank monitoring system, scavenging components from equipment that Riggs had deemed unimportant. Their work had been nothing short of miraculous considering the time constraints put upon them and the constant threat of death if they failed. Getting the throttles back in order was their last task, and it was one that Patroni was going to take his time completing. With the help of the electrician, he'd already delayed the system's restoration by several hours, intentionally shorting it out so that a wave of white smoke billowed from under the console. He'd warned a wary Riggs that it might not be repairable, so she was not too concerned by the delays.

Patroni was on the bridge for another, more important reason; to launch Captain Hauser's lifeboat. But the indicator lights and alarms for the boats were on the other side of the bridge from where he worked. He could fake it for only so long before Riggs became suspicious. She knew just how long Patroni would need to either fix the throttles or determine that the system was a write-off.

"Well, Patroni?" she rasped around a cigarette between her pursed lips.

"I'm sorry, but it may be a total loss. The main power bus is shot to hell, voltmeter's showing zip through the whole system. This isn't like the tank control unit that I could patch together; the throttles require specific replacement parts we don't have." Patroni stood, massaging his back and resettling his heavy testicles under his overalls in a deliberate taunt to Riggs.

"You will fix it," Wolf said from the back of the bridge, menace sharpening every word.

George Patroni was reaching his limit with Wolf and Riggs and the rest of the terrorists. "You want this thing fixed?"

As he spoke, Patroni moved along the main console, opening up the cabinet doors to reveal the tangled mass of electronics within. To anyone other than him and the electrician, the wires, circuit boards, and other equipment were just an impenetrable forest without any indication of their function. "Well, come on over here and give it a try yourself. Have at it, you son of a bitch. No? Don't think you can? Then get off my fucking back."

Wolf gave no reaction, but the other commando rushed forward, gouging Patroni's ribs with the barrel of his machine pistol. He looked to be only an instant away from pulling the trigger and tearing Patroni in two.

"Nein!" Wolf shouted.

Patroni hadn't moved, seemingly oblivious to the gun held against him, a lazy smile still on his face. He stood before the open access door of the launch detection board. His hand was inches from the breaker that fed power to the panel.

The guard pulled back, tucking his Uzi against his side, arcing the weapon to cover the other crewmen. His eyes didn't rest on one spot for more than a moment before flicking on. Everything he saw was a potential target.

JoAnn Riggs exploded off her chair, rushing across the bridge in just three quick strides, her right hand raised to strike Patroni. Although she hadn't known the Chief Engineer long, she knew that this outburst wasn't consistent with his personality. There was something odd going on. Wolf stepped forward just as the black radio clipped to his waist crackled.

"I think I've found somebody," said a disembodied voice.

The electrician was the first to move; he spun up from his position on the floor, a heavy torque wrench in his fist. He let the tool fly. The shining chrome flashed as it sailed across the space between him and the trigger-happy guard. Wolf yanked his pistol from its holster and fired even before he was sure of his aim, but the nine-millimeter slug caught the electrician under his right arm, tearing through the pad of muscle, puncturing both lungs, and tearing his wildly beating heart into shreds.

Patroni's reaction had been a fraction of a second quicker.

HAUSER'S own life meant nothing. It was forfeit the moment his ship was seized, and in his final seconds he realized that and accepted it. The flare burned brightly as it bored its way into the man's chest, blistering and bubbling his flesh as it ate him.

He was sickened by the sight of the dying terrorist, and nothing could have prepared him for the man's unholy scream. The gunman couldn't clutch at the burning wound in his chest. Even in his agony, his nervous system knew enough to keep his hands away from such intense heat. The temperature in the lifeboat skyrocketed from thirty degrees to one hundred and twenty degrees in a just a few seconds, hissing smoke filling the enclosed space with a noxious combination of charcoaled flesh and burned phosphorus.

From outside, the craft looked like a Japanese lantern, its toughened support struts standing out starkly against the crimson fire burning within. Smoke coiled from it only to be swept away by the stiff breeze created by the tanker's forward momentum.

The terrorist had dropped his Colt .45 when the flare had tunneled into his chest, but unbelievably he began reaching for the Uzi slung around his neck, the molded plastic grip of the Israeli weapon fitting neatly to his hand. Even as he burned, even as his life boiled away, he raised the machine pistol, leaning forward so he was half in and half out of the life raft. His last act on earth would be to send a fusillade into his killer. The Uzi's stubby barrel came up, his finger squeezing slowly, ready to send Lyle Hauser to oblivion.

THE torque wrench hit the guard in the throat and his gun dipped before he could pull the trigger. Bullets raked across the bridge, shattering glass, chewing through the control panel, and destroying more of the delicate electronics within.

Four holes appeared in the electrician's chest and his already lifeless body was launched through the bullet-weakened main windscreen.

George Patroni was already in motion, oblivious to the destruction around him. He barreled into JoAnn Riggs, shouldering her aside even as she swung at him. Her hand connected with the back of his head and would have stunned a normal man, but Patroni was a man possessed. Even as nine-millimeter rounds sprayed the bridge, Patroni was tearing at the guts below the launch detection panel, pulling at wires and circuit boards, overriding the manual system and launching all three boats simultaneously. Frigid air blasted into the bridge, whipping away the smell of the discharged shots. Patroni's shoulder block had dropped Riggs to the deck in an untidy tangle, where she frantically clutched his legs.

Wolf's H&K spat once, then again, the second round no more than an afterthought as Patroni pitched forward, arms outstretched as he fell against the helmsman's station, ragged holes blooming on his drab overalls like summer flowers. The helmsman was already dead, a chunk of his skull having vanished during the first seconds of the melee.

Patroni had planned to launch Hauser without anyone noticing. He could have done it so surreptitiously that it would have gone undetected until the next day or possibly never at all. He'd discussed it with the electrician, convincing the frightened man that the risk was worth it. JoAnn Riggs and her followers, he'd said, would never have suspected anything.

How many more of his crew would die tonight in reprisal, Patroni thought as he died.

AT the last possible second, even as the barrel of the Uzi was facing Hauser, George Patroni succeeded. Heedless of the terrorist standing at the entrance of the lifeboat, the mechanical davits swung outward, yanking him off his feet and fouling his aim. Machine gun fire ripped through the roof of the lifeboat as the dying terrorist hung in the hatchway, his feet dangling high above the tanker's frothing wake.

Lyle Hauser was too stunned to react. The flare's noxious

smoke had created such a dense cloud that he couldn't clearly see what was happening. The automatic launch sequence continued, dropping the lifeboat so quickly it felt as if gravity had found new strength.

At the full extension, there was only a two-foot gap between the lifeboat and the flat stern of the *Southern Cross*. When the winches released the boat, the terrorist was caught in this narrow chasm. His legs fouled against the ship's railing while his upper body was still in the lifeboat. The drop sheared him neatly in two, his still-burning torso spilling into the lifeboat and his disembodied legs pinwheeling into the turgid North Pacific.

Hauser screamed maniacally as the larger section of the body fell into the boat with him, sizzling like a steak on a summer barbecue. The lifeboat hit the ocean with a bone-jarring crash, a cascade of water spilling in through the open hatch. An instant later an arc of electricity flashed through the lines securing the lifeboat to the *Southern Cross*, cutting the cables as easily as threads, and suddenly the boat was free, tossing on the tanker's wake.

The two lifeboats stowed port and starboard hit the water at the same time as Hauser's, but the supertanker's forward momentum caused both to capsize and sink only moments after being released. Because it was located in the stern of the tanker, Hauser's craft remained upright, though the ride was rough until it slipped from the ship's wake.

Nearly overcome by the chemical smoke of the phosphorus flare, Hauser kicked at what was left of the terrorist, forcing the charred member out of the hatch and into the water. Despite his revulsion at the burned and blistered hunks of flesh that coated the bottom of the hatch, Hauser forced himself to close the aperture.

It was two minutes past midnight.

Not knowing what had transpired on the bridge to allow him to escape, Hauser wanted to make certain he made the best use of what providence had given him. With the radar still out, he knew that Riggs would never be able to find the lifeboat in the empty expanse of the North Pacific. But it was possible that she could triangulate his position if he made his distress call too early. The lifeboat's radio was small, with only a limited range in the best of conditions. To make it work properly, and to protect himself, Hauser had to get far away from the ship and much closer to shore and hope that someone was listening this dark night. He was two hundred and thirty miles from the coast and, unknown to him, the nearest receiving post was an eleven-year-old boy charged with monitoring the radio aboard his father's fishing trawler.

The boy was fast asleep.

———

MIAMI, FLORIDA

Widowed for so many years that getting to work at ungodly hours was the norm, David Saulman moved through the mazelike warrens of his office like a lord, turning on lights and grabbing express mail envelopes from the desks of his associates as he made his way to his personal suite. A coffeemaker slaved to the light switch in the reception area had started making a potent brew as soon as he'd entered the offices that took up an entire floor of a Miami bank building.

By the time Saulman got to his desk, there was a full pot of coffee waiting. Filling a mug the size of an oil can, he ignored the first salmon hint of daylight peeking over the watery horizon. Twenty-seven floors below, the city slumbered, eking out its last moments of quiet before the day seized it in another scorching session of existence.

The first thing associates learned when they joined Berkowitz, Saulman & Little was that there was no Berkowitz or Little, never had been. The names were figments of Dave Saulman's imagination, weighty names to give his firm a solid feel when he'd first started out three decades ago. The second thing they learned was that no matter how early they arrived at the law firm, their boss would be there before them—and he'd be going through their mail.

Dave Saulman was a benevolent dictator who was once quoted as saying, "If it's delivered to my office, its mine." During the mideighties, when bicycle messengers routinely delivered drugs to some of the younger lawyers, he came to possess almost as much cocaine as Metro Dade Police. He never chastised those lawyers who used, knowing that normal people couldn't put in the hundred-hour workweeks lawyering demanded. Saulman figured there were some very happy fish in Biscayne Harbor because of him.

Only a dozen red, white, and blue priority envelopes had been delivered last night, distributed through the offices by the firm's utility service. He opened and read them all in just a few minutes, categorizing most as hyped-up client anxiety. It was amazing how a few million dollars, when it was hanging out in the open, could panic a client.

Saulman wore a dark suit, faint chalk lines accenting his spreading figure. His silk tie had not been fully knotted, its juncture hanging an inch below the unbuttoned top of his starched shirt. Because he had a meeting at eight-thirty, he wore a prosthetic limb to compensate for his missing arm. Given his choice, he kept his empty sleeve hanging limply, but the sight seemed to bother many of the clients. The straps holding the plastic arm in place were already chafing.

Only a half dozen inches above five feet and starting to paunch, Saulman appeared taller because of the tremendous amount of nervous energy his body demanded he expend. He was never still. His right leg bounced constantly, whether he was seated or standing, his one good arm and his stump always in motion. Even his eyebrows, dark intimidating slashes, leaped and danced as he spoke. There was no deliberation to his movements, only an innate sense to move, and it served him well. He could intimidate almost everyone he met despite his stature.

Seated behind the broad expanse of his ash desk, his leg juddering like a palsy victim, he finished with the letters sent to his associates and turned his mind to the new London office he'd opened. It was midmorning there and they should be doing a brisk business. Most of the London people were involved with a leveraged buyout of a Dutch tug firm by a group of Germans, but there were enough lawyers left over to pursue more mundane if less lucrative ventures.

He was just reaching for the phone to put the fear of God into them when an apparition staggered into his office. Saulman recognized him immediately, but the man's tattered appearance shocked him more than he cared to admit. Bud Finley slumped into one of the highbacked oxblood chairs facing Saulman's desk. He was a private investigator.

Finley looked like a waste of space, his suit cheaply put together, his haircut not much better, a few greasy strands combed over a red, weeping scalp. He was heavily built, his shoulders like the crossarms of a gallows, his arms as menacing as an executioner's rope. His gut, though ponderous and straining against his discount store shirt, was solid. Finley's face was florid, widened by the years and pummeled by the experience, but his eyes were quick and intelligent. He had the look of a sewer rat and twice the cunning.

Although he'd expected Finley, the lack of self-respect the man showed himself still dumbfounded Saulman. Finley, never a neat man, looked like he'd just come from an industrial accident. "You're early," Saulman said to cover himself. He distinctly remembered relocking the outer office doors, a fact that seemed not to have slowed Finley.

Finley flared a match off his thumbnail, and as it burned toward his his fingers, he calmly pulled a pack of generic cigarettes from a suit-coat pocket and torched one before speaking. His voice was pure Deep South, garbled by a family tree without enough branches. "Ah donnit think you'd a wanted ta wait ta hear what Ah got to say."

Ever since Mercer had called him requesting information about tankers in the Gulf of Alaska and most specifically Petromax Oil vessels, Dave Saulman had been hooked, sensing one of those challenges that Mercer was famous for stumbling into. At his own expense, Saulman sent his best investigator, Bud Finley, to Petromax's main offices in Delaware and then to Louisiana, where Southern Coasting and Lightering had established their headquarters.

While they'd known each other for years, Mercer never failed to fascinate Dave Saulman. He could produce the easy solution to a complex problem, or find the obscure pattern buried in a simple issue. Mercer's instincts were uncanny. Saulman was well aware that when Mercer called for a favor, it was just the beginning of something a lot more intricate.

So when he'd called a few days ago asking about vessels in the Gulf of Alaska, Saulman knew that there would be much more buried under such an easily answered question. If there was something dangerous behind the *Petromax Arctica*'s delayed arrival at the port of Valdez, an investigator of Finley's expertise would find it. And while Saulman himself had casually asked around about the strange provisions of the sale of the Petromax fleet to Southern Coasting and Lightering with little result, he was confident that Finley would uncover the real truth behind the deal.

Saulman hadn't expected Finley until late that evening at the earliest; the man had had only about forty-eight hours to gather information. He couldn't imagine Finley getting anything out of a slick corporation like Petromax, let alone the shadowy SC&L, so quickly. None of Saulman's contacts, even when pressed, could tell him anything more than SC&L had themselves been bought recently by an unknown party. Saulman was appalled that anyone could move within the labyrinthine but somewhat closed world of maritime commerce without his knowledge.

"Ever heard of a Arab named Hasaan bin-Rufti?" Finley invited.

Twenty minutes later, after having heard the full story from Finley, Dave Saulman was on the phone with Mercer's answering machine. "You know who this is. Give me a call ASAP or sooner. Finding that the *Petromax Arctica* was late for her latest run is only the tip of the iceberg. Call me at home. After what I've heard this morning, I'm taking the rest of the day off."

LONDON

The hospital lobby was a strange combination of institutional coldness and the grief of those forced to wait within it. Families clustered in tight enclaves of nervous expectancy and wailing. Amid the sanitized tiled walls and threadbare carpet paced by innumerable feet, Lady Millicent Gray cut a striking figure. Her long legs, mostly hidden beneath a loose-fitting linen dress, slid with an easy grace, the magnificent cinnamon mass of her hair flamed like a beacon. Her face, beautiful even at this early hour, with only subtle traces of makeup to mask the more obvious signs of the previous night's sexual excesses, radiated the right trace of God-given confidence and royally appointed favor. Heads that until a moment before were bowed with grief came up and regarded her openly, their pain forgotten if only for the instant of her passage.

If asked later, none of the forty or so people who saw her stride through the lobby's double glass doors would have remembered the figure who walked with her, an Arab woman fully covered and veiled as was proper for the more conservative sects of Islam.

At the hospital's security desk, Millicent spoke to the figure at her elbow out of the corner of her mouth. "I hope you know, Trevor, that I want to wear that outfit when we're finished here and I want you to ravage me like some Barbary pirate."

"Are you kidding," Trevor James-Price quipped quietly, "I may never give it up. I know why women wear skirts now. My God, the breeze blowing up to my bollocks feels wonderful. The old clappers have never known such freedom."

"God, you're incorrigible," Millie Gray smiled.

The security guard at the duty nurses' station didn't question Millicent about her connection to Khalid Khuddari or why she was here. He could barely tear his eyes away from her breasts long enough to notice she wasn't even alone. He tripped over his tongue telling her that Khalid had a private room on the fourth floor. Millicent Gray and the disguised Trevor James-Price veered toward the elevators, both of them suppressing the desire to hold hands. Lord Harold Gray would be back from his African hunt in fifteen days, and any second of their affair they squandered would never be recovered.

Five minutes after Trevor and Millie stepped onto the elevator, an intense young Kurd walked into the lobby. The lump bulging out the left breast pocket of his khaki overcoat was a folding cellular phone. The lump at the right was a silenced Sig Sauer P220.

Tariq had met him in the parking garage in front of the massive hospital and told him Khalid's room number, having learned it last night after a lengthy reconnoiter. The Kurd had exactly twenty minutes to reach Khuddari, kill him, and make his way back to the parking garage where Tariq waited to drive them away. The young man paused in the lobby, squandering five of his minutes trying to steel his courage. Security was lax, but there were two burly guards at their station, talking easily with reporters who were waiting to get a statement from the unknown victim four floors above.

The gunman decided that now was his time to strike. If he was somehow caught, he knew he would take his own life, redeeming himself for the failure yesterday. His martyrdom would be secured. The silencer attached to the big automatic had never been used; it would work at optimum efficiency. The shot would be undetectable from more than a couple of yards from Khuddari's room. The guards didn't even glance in his direction as the gunman headed for the multiple banks of elevators.

Khalid Khuddari had been awake for nearly two hours, pain insidiously bringing him out of his drug-induced sleep. The scabs on his back felt hot even through the layers of gauze protecting them, and they itched fiercely. Every time he blinked, the delicate muscles around his eyes pulled against the raw wounds on his face, bringing fresh tears streaming down his cheeks. And when the tears stung the cuts, it was quite literally adding salt to a wound.

The thought made him chuckle painfully.

"You can't be that hurt if you can manage to laugh at this ungodly hour."

Khalid looked across the room. He barely remembered Millicent Gray, but he knew the voice from under the veils. He hadn't heard them enter. Trevor James-Price pulled the black veil of the chador from around his head, his fine hair dancing with the motion before falling naturally over his boyish face. Despite his cocksure smile, there was true concern behind his bluer-than-blue eyes. "God, Khalid, you look terrible, even for a wog."

"You have no idea."

"I won't be pedestrian and ask you how you feel. And since I talked to that obtuse doctor last night and read the papers this morning, I don't need to ask what happened either. All I need to know is why you wanted me here and why this outrageous getup? By the way, do you know that security here is an absolute joke?"

"Not surprising. No one knows who I am, and I want to keep it that way until after I'm gone." Slowly, like an old man near death, Khalid struggled into a sitting position, each movement deepening the grimace on his face. By the time he got his feet dangling over the edge of the high hospital bed, he was out of breath and sweating freely.

"Easy, old fruit." Trevor crossed the room and laid a hand on Khalid's shoulder. Khalid winced at the slight touch.

"I have to get out of here, Trev," he panted, his face deathly pale, his lips appearing blue. "I need to get back to the UAE,"

"I don't think you should be going anywhere," Millicent offered, moving next to Trevor. Although she didn't know Khalid, it was hard not to look at him and feel anything less than total sympathy.

"I am going, Lady Gray. Trevor can explain why, but right now I need your help, not your pity," Khalid said with a dedication that chilled the room.

Trevor was already pulling the black robes over his head. Contrary to his earlier tease to Millicent, beneath them he wore the suit pants and white shirt he'd had on the night before. There was a lipstick smear on the right collar of the Turnbull and Asser shirt. "What do you need her to do?"

"She should have worn the chador. I told you that last night." Khalid was bothered that they hadn't listened to him.

"Doesn't really matter, old boy," Trevor said flippantly, trying to soothe his friend. "Besides, I've always wanted to try cross-dressing."

Khalid didn't say anything further as Trevor produced a bundled package of clothing pilfered from Lord Gray's dressing room. Millicent Gray's husband was a large man, with a waist size that could accommodate two of Khalid with a little room to spare. After helping Khalid to dress, Trevor slipped the robe over his head, pulling it down so that only his shoes were visible below the black cotton. "I hope you know what you're doing, Khalid. You're in no condition to leave this room, let alone fly back to the UAE."

"I don't have a choice." Khalid rode another wave of pain, each crest being just a little easier than the last. It was hard to believe, but his body was becoming accustomed to his injuries.

Millicent stepped forward quickly and grasped the arm of the swaying Khalid. "Trevor, you shouldn't be helping him, he's half dead."

"There are more lives at stake than just his, Millie," James-Price said with quiet understanding. "I'm sorry to get you involved like this. I've no right, but I ask you to please help us. The men who came after him yesterday at the British Museum will most certainly have another go. He's a target sitting in this room."

"Why not inform your Embassy?" she asked.

"Because I don't know whom there I can trust right now. This is the best way," Khalid replied.

"But he won't be able to get a flight without reservations." Millie continued to talk to Trevor as if Khalid wasn't there.

"Diplomatic passport. He'll get a flight." Trevor held up the slim volume he'd taken from Khalid's hotel room. "That's where I went earlier this morning. Since the hospital didn't know who he was last night, I figured he'd left his ID in his hotel."

Khalid nodded gratefully to his friend, taking the passport. "The only perk better than the diplomatic license plates on the embassy cars I get to use. Lady Gray, I'm sorry, but there's no other way. And like Trev said, there are a lot of lives at stake."

"All right, I'll help. But Trevor, you make bloody sure that there are security people waiting for us at Heathrow. And a doctor too." While she thought the two men were being over-dramatic, she would go along with it, if for no other reason than that she was the trophy wife of a millionaire member of Parliament and bored out of her beautiful skull.

"It's best that she stays, Trevor," Khalid said. "We could be followed once we leave the hospital."

"Nonsense," Trevor said, pulling the veil over Khalid's head. "No one is going to pay you the slightest heed."

He fished out the keys to the old Bentley he'd been driving since his divorce and placed them in Millicent's waiting hand, caressing the tight junctures between her fingers. She smiled at the intimate gesture and he winked wolfishly. "Can you manage to get him out of the hospital? I could give you a hand down to the car."

"No!" Khalid said. His voice was muffled by the veil but still carried the weight and fear of his words. "Two people came into this place together and two are going to leave. We don't want to attract attention. I'll make it."

At the door, Khalid paused and turned back to thank his friend. The pale sunlight streaming through the window gilded James-Price's hair. "I'll see you soon, you bloody Pom bastard."

"Take care of yourself, you stinking wog."

Falling into the role of a bereaved family member leaving a dying relative and trying to remain as erect as possible, Khalid allowed Millicent Gray to lead him from the room. Neither of them paid the slightest attention to the trench-coated man headed down the hall toward them. Millicent had no idea how to spot any sort of trouble, and Khalid was struggling not to faint. Had they turned, they would have seen the man reach into his coat as he approached the door to Khalid's room. They might have saved Trevor.

When the heavy door of the room swung inward against the articulating arm of the automatic closer, Trevor was just entering the bathroom. He half expected that Millie had returned for a good-bye kiss.

He was actually smiling as he turned. A fusillade of hastily fired nine-millimeter rounds tore into the bathroom door, one catching him squarely between the eyes. The wound didn't bleed, for his heart had already stopped pumping, and only a few drops scattered as he pitched to the hard linoleum floor.

The assassin glanced back into the deserted corridor. Seeing that no one had heard the shots, he entered the room, letting the door silently close behind. Before examining the body, he lowered the cocked hammer of the automatic and slid the weapon back into his coat. Only then did he realize he'd made a critical mistake. The man on the floor was not Khalid Al-Khuddari.

The phone in his pocket shrilled.

He reached for it and activated the unit but did not speak. Suddenly his voice had gone, abandoning him as he realized the seriousness of his failure.

"Well?" It was Hasaan bin-Rufti. The Kurd hoped it would have been Tariq, for the man seemed a little easier to deal with than his corpulent superior.

Without thinking, the gunman told the truth. "He has escaped, *effendi.*"

"What?" Rufti roared into the phone.

"He had already left the hospital by the time I arrived. I don't know when or where he's gone." Lying was the only way the man could think to save his life. Rufti would kill him for his failure.

FIND him, or by the blood of the Prophet, I'll flay you alive and use your skin as a car-seat cover." Hasaan Rufti slammed down the phone and turned to the steward hovering over him, the man's jacket so snowy white it almost gave off a light of its own. "Tell the pilot that if he doesn't take off within the next sixty seconds . . ." Rufti paused, and when he couldn't come up with a really good threat, he repeated himself. "Tell him I'll flay him alive and use his skin as a car-seat cover."

"Yes, Minister," the steward said, bowing like the toady he was. He slunk forward through the cabin of the Hawker Siddeley private jet, ducking his head to pass into the cockpit.

While the appointments of the aircraft were the finest that the Hawker company offered, Brazilian woods and Turkish leather, there was no escaping the fact that the plane was small, headroom sacrificed for the sake of economy. Most people would have been thrilled to have such a plane at their disposal, but Rufti was chafed by the Hawker. Khuddari rated a Boeing for his personal use, if the fool ever chose to use it, a wide body with almost enough room to install a trampoline if the mood struck him.

That plane should belong to someone who would appreciate it, Rufti thought. Someone like himself.

They were still on the apron at Gatwick Airport, delayed now for two hours because an El Al flight had declared an emergency on its inward leg to Heathrow and had opted to land at Gatwick instead, stacking up dozens of aircraft and delaying the takeoff of dozens more, including Rufti's HS 125 600. He was supposed to be in Abu Dhabi by ten, and the way it was looking, he would be at least four hours late.

"Fucking Jews," he muttered darkly, as if that one oath covered all his problems.

Kerikov was set to detonate the icepacks attached to the pipeline in Alaska, the Iranians and Iraqis were poised to start their troop movements at a moment's notice, and he was stuck on the ground waiting for a bunch of rich Jews to get off their plane and buy up more of the world. He had two hundred of his own troops waiting for him in the the Gulf, ready for him to lead them on the glorious taking of the United Arab Emirates from the puppet the British had set up in 1970s.

The Crown Prince, though wary, was not suspecting a revolt. Rufti knew that the early timing of his revolution was the key to taking the Persian Gulf. To delay, while Saudi Arabia, Kuwait, and the UAE geared up for the changes brought about by the suspension of U.S. oil imports, would only hamper his cause. He must strike now, while the governments were unsure of what the future would bring.

Rufti didn't remember where he'd first heard the adage, but it was one that served him now: A hungry man is easy to lead and a confused one is easy to defeat.

The Gulf was confused right now, governments in turmoil, ripe for his plucking. The timing couldn't be more perfect. Over the past year, ever since buying into Ivan Kerikov's scheme to cripple the Americans' domestic oil resources, Rufti had worked tirelessly, sub rosa, to make his grand scheme a reality. Without Iran and Iraq, he could never really hope to usurp the throne of the UAE and keep it for himself. Yet if he failed to produce the agreed upon trigger, Khuddari's death, he could forget about ever ruling in the Middle East, in fact, he could forget about seeing too many more sunrises either. The Iraqis especially had warned that if he failed, Rufti would die.

Iraqi tanks were ready to roll into Kuwait once Rufti neutralized the American threat. By taking out the pipeline, he would create a domestic crisis within the United States that would leave them unable to counter the invasion. Kuwait would fall within a few days, Saudi Arabia just a week or so later. A few anthrax-laden Scuds targeting Tel Aviv and Jerusalem, and the war would be over. America would have no bases from which to launch a counteroffensive, and they would never resort to nuclear weapons to dislodge the Iraqis and their newly allied Iranian comrades.

Without oil from Alaska, and having a strategic reserve that would last for only a month or two, the United States would be forced to deal with the new Middle Eastern triumvirate of Iran, Iraq, and the UAE. Rufti envisioned a tenfold increase in oil prices. And that was just the beginning. He saw himself becoming one of the richest men in the world. And with billions of barrels of oil in reserve under the scorching sands of the Emirates, he could do it.

If only he could get the fucking plane into the air and on its way to Abu Dhabi City.

The phone recessed into the armrest of his seat bleated like a lamb, a discreet chirp that he almost ignored in his agitation. On the fourth ring he finally picked it up.

"What?"

"Sir, it's Tariq." After Abu Alam, Tariq was Rufti's most trusted lieutenant. An orphan from Lebanon's brutal civil war, raised in the refugee camps on a diet of hatred and death, Tariq was fiercely loyal and utterly without morals. When it came to killing, Abu Alam did it with the burning need of an addict, but Tariq carried out his duties with the coldness of a professional. Rufti had sent him to the hospital as a backup to the idiot Kurdish national.

"What is it?"

"I'm on the motorway, headed toward Heathrow Airport following a blue Bentley." His voice was distorted by the cellular phone connection. "Shortly after the Kurd went up to Khuddari's room, two people left the hospital garage, two women, one western, one Arab. The Arab woman was dressed in a chador, her face veiled. I'd seen them enter the hospital garage earlier. It appeared that the vehicle belonged to the Arab woman, for she drove here, but when they left, it was the Western woman who was behind the wheel and she didn't seem familiar with the car's controls."

"Get to the point, Tariq," Rufti snapped.

"I believe that the robes are a disguise and that I'm following Khuddari as he attempts to flee the country."

"Are you certain?" The glimmer of hope Tariq offered reminded Rufti that he hadn't eaten for nearly thirty minutes. As he continued the conversation, he rang for the steward. "Is it really Khuddari?"

"My instincts tell me yes."

"How far are you from Heathrow?"

"Only about ten minutes from the main gates. I suspect that they're headed to the international terminal, Terminal 4."

"Yes yes yes, let me think." There wasn't time before Khuddari entered the secure perimeter of the airport to launch an attack. What Rufti needed now was a way to delay Khuddari in London for a few hours, enough time for him to get to the UAE and put into motion his side of the coup. "Do you have any explosives with you?"

"I have just a couple of grenades," Tariq admitted, his voice breaking up as the radio waves of his cell phone encountered the pulsing radar beams given off by Heathrow Airport.

"Perfect," Rufti glowed. The steward put an entire salmon before him, the flesh of the fish so pinkish and light that the slit along its flank resembled the intimate lips of a woman. "After I hang up, call that Kurdish fool and relay my orders. Now here's what I want you to do . . ."

WHILE the Bentley had seen its finer days nearly a decade earlier, such a luxury vehicle still commanded respect as it hissed along the M-4, just east of Heathrow. Millicent was now familiar enough with the automobile to intimidate other drivers into giving her the slight advantage she needed to edge the old Bent forward another spot or two on the clogged expressway. A tandem trailer truck honked at her aggressive driving, which she riposted with an unladylike curse and the extension of her middle finger. She apologized to Khalid for the gesture but explained that no one ever complained when she drove her Rolls Silver Cloud so martially.

Khalid had been silent for most of the drive, consciously fighting the pain that flashed like sheet lightning across his back and lower legs. One moment, he could keep it at bay, forcing it back with sheer will, and then suddenly it would peak. There was so much he was supposed to be thinking about, so many plans he had to make, but his mind was too addled to concentrate. He could feel Millicent Gray glance at him every once in a while, but he could not bring himself to turn and look back at her.

They swerved through the sweeping curves of the access road, patches of lawn and shrubbery giving way to great expanses of asphalt and corrugated steel warehouses. Millicent followed the overhead signs toward International Departures, jinxing around the buses that dominated the narrow roads, their backsides belching clouds of smoke on their endless loops around Heathrow's thousands of acres.

"Which airline?" Millicent asked as they neared Terminal 4.

"It doesn't matter," Khalid replied listlessly, slipping out of the chador. "Once inside, I can call a reservation number to get me the next flight to Abu Dhabi."

"Are you sure about this?" She eased the Bentley up to the curb before one of the numerous British Airways doors, tucking neatly behind a motor coach disgorging dozens of poorly dressed people finishing their whirlwind European package tour. "I can take you to a different hospital or maybe to the trauma station here at the airport. I'm sure they have a doctor on duty."

From his pant's pocket he pulled a twist of tissue, which he opened to reveal a few capsules. "I'm sure," he said, swallowing them in a quick movement. "I've been saving these, Percodans, I believe. They should see me through."

"Wait, shouldn't there be some security people waiting for us here?" she asked.

"That was a bluff on Trevor's part to get you to cooperate. He wouldn't have had the time to set up something like that. I have to go now." Khalid opened the passenger door. "Thank you, Lady Gray. I think very soon you will see the results of your act this morning."

He stepped from the car, gingerly testing his strength before taking the first tentative steps to the terminal building, oblivious of the throngs jostling around him. Once within the building, he was swallowed by the crowds, invisible, just another face to the thousands of passengers and well-wishers milling and queuing up. His legs trembled and the clothing touching his back and shoulders scalded the multiple wounds even through their thick bandages. If the pills didn't kick in soon, he would collapse.

It took him a few minutes to secure a seat on the next flight to Abu Dhabi by way of a British Airways flight to Riyadh. He need only produce his passport at the VIP lounge to get his ticket. It was the first time he'd ever used such a diplomatic privilege, and he vowed that he wouldn't ever make a habit of it—but it was reassuring to know he could.

Trevor had thoughtfully placed a handful of twenty-pound notes in the pants pocket, one of which he used to buy a stout umbrella and a pair of sunglasses. He used the umbrella like a cane so he could keep his weight off the worse of his two legs. While the large glasses didn't hide all the wounds on his face, they camouflaged a couple of them, and with his hair raked forward, he could almost pass as the victim of a recent auto collision.

At the top of an escalator, just before the security X-ray machines, a young woman in a blue uniform approached him.

"Minister Khuddari, my name is Vivica Smith," the British Airways hostess smiled brightly. She was young, barely in her twenties, with bobbed blond hair and soft eyes. She checked his passport against the information given to her by the airline's executive ticketing service. Seeing how he hobbled, Vivica Smith called over one of the airport's electric carts to carry them to where a Boeing 767 was waiting for its final passenger.

"Thank you for your prompt attention, this is really quite welcome," Khalid said. The painkillers were finally beginning to take effect, blunting the edges of his sharper wounds. While they trundled down the carpeted hallways, he borrowed Vivica's cellular phone to call Colonel Wayne Bigelow in Abu Dhabi. The old desert rat wasn't in his cluttered bachelor's apartment, but Khalid left word on his answering machine that he would be arriving in a few hours, giving the particulars of the flight and asking Bigelow to pick him up at the airport.

Heavily burdened passengers parted before the cart as they glided past the duty-free shops, countless magazine stands, and elegant boutiques that were the pride of Terminal 4. It took just a few minutes for them to reach Khalid's gate. Vivica Smith jumped from the cart and swung around a wheelchair that had been left by the gate's entrance. With a minimum of fuss, he was wheeled to the aircraft and led to his First-Class seat. To get such a seat on this short notice and to have the plane delayed until he was aboard cost nearly ten times the regular ticket price. Privilege wasn't cheap.

No longer able to remain awake, Khalid fell into the blissful sleep he'd been fighting as the big jet lumbered away from its hard stand.

* * *

THE delaying fuse of a Czech-manufactured RGD-5 grenade had been altered from its normal four seconds to a full sixty, making it an ingenious terror weapon for crowded areas where more sophisticated devices could be detected if left for too long. Waiting until the second hand of his watch made the final tick of their schedule, Tariq slurped down the remainder of a container of soft drink, pulled the grenade from his coat pocket, and dropped both items into the trash bin he'd been waiting near for fifteen minutes. Calmly, he meandered back out of the airport and headed toward his car stowed in short-term parking. Even if someone recognized him as the man who'd planted the device, this was his first action outside the Middle East and it was improbable his description would lead the authorities to him.

Fifty-nine-point-eight seconds after the grenade's handle released, the 120 grams of TNT within its rounded body exploded, embedding the lid of the trash container in the terminal's ceiling. The concussive force also blew outward, the weapon's fragmentation liner dicing the weapon's outer casing into hundreds of tiny shrapnel shards. A nineteen-year-old Norwegian au pair returning home caught the brunt of the blast, larger portions of her dismembered body landing yards from the explosion. Eight other people were wounded by the blast. One of them, a Nigerian priest, would later die in the airport's medical facility.

Even before panic could ripple through the large building, the phone in the airport administrator's office rang. Already in a foul mood because of the traffic reroutings caused by the El Al emergency landing at Gatwick, Geoff Wilberforce didn't want to answer his extension.

"What?" he barked, expecting some spineless air traffic controller at Gatwick.

"At the precise moment your phone rang, an explosive was set off in Terminal Four's main concourse. The blast was small in comparison to what we have planted throughout the airport, including several of the aircraft waiting clearance to take off.

"If any planes attempt to leave Heathrow after two minutes of the termination of this call, I will detonate the rest of the bombs. The blood of the innocents will be on your hands. I will allow aircraft to land for the next hour, but if any planes attempt to do so after that, I will detonate the remaining explosives. Heathrow Airport is shut down on order of Kurdistan United."

The caller cut the connection, leaving Wilberforce listening to the steady drone of a dial tone, much like the flat-line sound on a heart monitor. He was just getting to his feet when his secretary burst into his office. She was near tears.

"Geoff, there's been an explosion."

THE big engines of the British Airways Boeing 767 were still idled to a low whine as the huge craft moved across the taxiways behind a New York–bound jumbo. They were fourth in line for takeoff when suddenly the engines were cut to dramatic silence. The cabin lights dimmed and the air-conditioning units switched to their much weaker internal power.

"Ladies and gentlemen, this is your captain speaking. I'm afraid there is a mechanical problem here at Heathrow. The main radar unit just died and took the computers with it. We may be stuck here for a little while until they can sort everything out. On behalf of British Airways, I and the rest of the crew apologize for this slight delay, and I will certainly pass on any information as I receive it. In the meantime, I've authorized the fight attendants to start a complimentary beverage service. Thank you."

Khalid Khuddari slept through the entire announcement.

FIFTEEN MILES SOUTH OF
FAIRBANKS, ALASKA

At five thousand feet above the low bowl of ground on the banks of the Chena River that is Fairbanks, Alaska's largest interior city, the swelling fires raging to the southwest of the urban center were easily discernible. They seethed and roiled upward and outward into the night, unaffected by the rain that fell in a wind-driven downpour. The fire was centered near the International Airport at Alyeska's new equipment depot. Eddie, Mercer, and Mike Collins could see the frantic movement of men and equipment trying to battle the fierce blaze. Revolving lights atop the emergency vehicles winked furiously. From their high vantage, it appeared that the number of fire engines was woefully inadequate for the size of the conflagration. At least a couple of acres were obscured by undulating sheets of flame and black chemical smoke.

"Jesus Christ, what's going on down there?" asked the fourth man in the helicopter, a young sergeant assigned by Colonel Knoff to handle communications between Eddie Rice and the two Huey gunships about half a mile in front of them.

"One hell of a diversion," Mercer replied from his place in the back of the JetRanger. "Looks like we're not going to get any ground support from Fort Wainwright."

Before leaving Elmendorf, Colonel Knoff had suggested sending a convoy of Military Police from the Fort Wainwright Military Airfield in Fairbanks up the Dalton Highway toward Pump Stations 5 and 6. Mercer had agreed, knowing that the three choppers would reach the pump stations long before the MPs, but if Kerikov had already left, he would run right into the army vehicles.

An emergency as large as the fire burning below would surely take precedence over Mercer's mission in the eyes of the local government. Any able-bodied soldier from Wainwright would certainly be assisting in crowd control, search and rescue, and medical treatment. The three helicopters thundering north were on their own.

Mike Collins sat next to Mercer and stared out the window, his face pressed tightly to the Plexiglas as he studied the devastation. His lips were compressed and bloodless and his hands flexed nervously in his lap. "Do those fucking lunatics realize that there're about a thousand tons of seismic charges and other explosives warehoused at that facility?"

"Probably," Mercer observed mildly.

"This isn't some fucking joke." Collins turned and glared at Mercer.

"Mike, I know it's not, but I guarantee that this is just a sideshow; the main event is still to come. Kerikov knows there would be a response once we lost communications from the pump stations, and he's trying to sidetrack us."

"How do you know that? How do you know the fire isn't what he wanted all along?"

"Because I know how the bastard thinks, and this just isn't big enough for him." Mercer was going to continue, but the sergeant interrupted. Colonel Knoff wanted to speak with him. Mercer put on his headset. "Yes, Colonel, what's up?"

"I just got a priority message from Wainwright. They need our choppers for medical evacs to Anchorage. Facilities in Fairbanks are swamped; they need every available aircraft to get patients south and doctors and supplies north."

"Negative, we go on."

"You said yourself this might be a wild-goose chase, and there are people dying down there. They need us."

"There wouldn't be a fire down there if one of those pump stations hadn't been attacked. It's a distraction, Colonel, nothing more."

"That distraction has already claimed twenty-three lives, Dr. Mercer," Knoff said acidly.

"My mission takes precedence, I'm sorry. Mercer out."

"You cold son of a bitch," Mike Collins said, then turned

back to the window as Fairbanks vanished behind the helicopter's flat bottom.

Mercer sat quietly, arms folded across his chest, eyes flat and unpenetrable. Behind the facade, his mind was working furiously. Am I right? he asked himself. Or am I consigning innocent people to death by refusing them these helicopters?

"Mercer, call from Andy Lindstrom," Eddie Rice said through the headset. "He says no answer from Pump Station 5, but 6 is on line, a skeleton crew standing by. He's asking if he should send some men down to 5."

"No! Under no circumstances are those men to leave Pump Station 6. They'd be cut to ribbons long before they reached the control building. Number 5 is under the control of terrorists. Sergeant, call Colonel Knoff. Tell him the target is Pump Station 5. Eddie, what's our ETA?"

"At least another hour and twenty minutes. This weather is really killing us, and those Hueys are even slower than we are, especially fully loaded."

"Shit! Pump Station 5 went off line hours ago. It's possible Kerikov's already gone."

Time slowed. Whenever Mercer twisted his wrist to look at his watch, a shorter and shorter arc of the minute hand had swept by. The rhythmic throbbing of the rotor blades over his head had a lulling effect, sending him into a kind of daze, his mind emptied of everything, so he was just barely aware of the JetRanger's turbine engine and the occasional mutterings between Eddie Rice and the pilots of the two Hueys. And then the thoughts came, fear and doubt the strongest, but also a deep exhaustion, a gritty feeling behind his eyes that made blinking painful. He had been awake for twenty-two hours. But that wasn't what was really nagging him.

Suddenly the quest for the unknown, the search for knowledge that had dominated his life, that made him who he was, was no longer so important. He felt like telling Eddie to turn the chopper around and head back to Anchorage. This wasn't his problem, it wasn't their fight. He had done this too many times now, put his life on the line for an ideal, a belief that he couldn't really define or name.

This was always the worst, the waiting. He'd been here

before, with Eddie in fact, but with other men too, hurtling into harm's way, fear like a weight in his stomach, doubt like a nagging headache behind his temples. He'd long ago stopped wondering why he found himself constantly surrounded by danger, but he still questioned how much longer his strange obsession would allow him to live. How many more times could he descend into the earth in some mine shaft in need of immediate repairs? How many times could he climb aboard a helicopter to face someone like Ivan Kerikov and actually return? Pessimism burned hotly behind his ribs.

God, I'm tired.

"Ten minutes to the Pump Station," Eddie called.

Mercer straightened up, noting the queer look Mike Collins shot him, as if Alyeska's Chief of Security had been reading his mind. He ignored Collins, leaning forward to peer out the cockpit canopy. In the darkness, the running lights of the two Air Force Hueys looked like flashing jewels, a cold, comforting light signifying the presence of other humans amid the great expanse of forested nothingness below. Thousands of square miles of birch and white spruce separated the Alaskan Range mountains from the Brooks Range, whose foothills they were approaching. The area was crisscrossed by dozens of rivers, streams, and tiny lakes.

"Any traffic on the Dalton Highway?"

"I haven't seen anything, and we've been over it for nearly half an hour. I didn't even see any police cars where the Alyeska vans reportedly went off," Eddie replied. "It's like the road isn't even there."

"Call Knoff. Tell him we're almost there."

"Already done. His boys are chomping at the bit."

"Good. I want you to hang back at least a mile until they've landed and Knoff gives us the all-clear sign. If Kerikov and his men are still here, Knoff's troops should be able to handle them. He won't be expecting this strong a reprisal because of his pyrotechnic display in Fairbanks."

"Does this mean you've lost your death wish?" Eddie teased. "Last time we flew together you had me land at ground zero of a nuclear explosion with about two minutes to go."

Mercer laughed. "Government cutbacks have slashed my danger pay to below minimum wage again. I only raid liquor cabinets unless given a direct presidential order. Which reminds me, I could really go for a . . . What the fuck?"

A flash of light, like a laser beam, streaked up from the dark ground so quickly it appeared as a solid line rather than a moving object. It intercepted the lead Huey, the two coming together in a violent blast, the helicopter outlined briefly in the fire of its destruction. In an instant, the chopper was falling to the earth in a flaming ruin. The pilot of the second Huey had just started evasive action when a second SA-7 Grail missile rocketed skyward on a brilliant cone of expended solid fuel.

Known by NATO forces to be wholly inaccurate and underarmed with just six pounds of high explosive in its warhead, the Grail was still deadly against low-flying helicopters, especially those with exposed exhaust ports like the UH-1. The Grail fired at the Huey didn't have the upgraded cryocooling unit to aid its infrared sensors at finding hot signatures, yet it still had no trouble locking onto its target against the cold background of the Alaskan night. The second Huey disintegrated.

Mercer was just recognizing the attack for what it was when Eddie Rice banked the JetRanger, applying max power to the turbines and the rotors, eking out every bit of speed as he tried to get them out of range of the shoulder-fired missiles. Debris from the first two choppers fell to the earth like meteor showers, the hulls hitting in explosive wrecks, fuel and metal and bits of their crews thrown up in fountains of flame and shrapnel. Patches of forest around the crash sites were ignited by the burning choppers, pine trees flaring like matchsticks. It would take hours for the rain to douse such a fuel-rich fire.

"Watch for those missiles!" Eddie shouted, jerking the controls first one way then the next in an attempt to foul the aim of the terrorists below them. The JetRanger, designed more for comfort than agility, groaned at Eddie's flying, the bulkheads and structural members straining well beyond their design specifications.

"I've got a launch, starboard side," Mercer called out,

watching with morbid fascination as another missile lifted
from the black forest.

"Got it." Eddie hauled the JetRanger onto its side, tightening his turn so quickly that the helicopter lost nearly a thousand feet in just a few seconds.

The Grail passed behind them, its infrared sight unable to
lock onto the exhaust ports of their chopper. Its rocket motor
ran out of fuel and toppled the missile back to earth. During
the violent maneuver, no one saw another Grail hurtle into
the air.

It was almost directly ahead of them, its guidance system
seeking them out with single-minded resolution. At last finding the heat signature it had been hunting for, the fifty-three-
inch-long missile slightly altered its attack vector, shallowing
its approach so as to come up under the Bell helicopter.

"Oh, fuck!" Mike Collins shouted, while the young soldier
in the copilot's seat screamed and screamed.

Mercer let himself go limp. The fear that had squeezed his
chest when the first two helicopters were hit released him at
this last moment so he could face his death calmly, watching
it happen with almost clinical dispassion.

Of them all, only Eddie Rice hadn't given up. The moment
before the warhead struck the underside of the JetRanger, he
again jerked the craft hard over, presenting the now tilted
bottom of the chopper to the missile. It struck a glancing blow
where the secondary rotor boom attached to the fuselage, and
exploded.

Most of the blast was directed away from the helicopter
because of Eddie's quick thinking and exceptional reflexes,
yet the JetRanger was mortally wounded. Smoke filled the
cabin even as the chopper was thrown violently through the
air, turned almost completely upside down by the explosion.
The electrical system failed and a second later the turbine
skipped, caught briefly, then began faltering as it starved for
the fuel gushing from the severed lines. The raw stench of
avgas gagged the four men as they struggled to regain proper
seating in the bucking aircraft. Mercifully, it hadn't ignited.
Yet.

Relying on instinct alone, Eddie managed to get the Jet-

Ranger onto an even keel; the smoke was so thick that he couldn't see the instrument panel only feet from him. They had started to auto rotate as they fell to the ground, the chopper spinning on its own axis in a tightening circle, pressing the men outward against the fuselage. Eddie used this to his advantage, slowing the descent by using what little lift remained in the still-spinning main rotor.

"I can't fucking see," he shouted above the jarring noise of the fragmenting helicopter.

Mercer leaned forward, groping blindly through the smoke until his hands felt the cold metal of the Heckler and Koch MP-5 submachine gun the sergeant had lost when the chopper was hit. Straightening, he cocked the weapon. "Cover your face!"

Aiming over Eddie's shoulder, he loosened a hail of bullets against the windscreen.

The Plexiglas starred, then lost all integrity, flying into space in nearly one whole chunk. A few fragments whipped into the cockpit, one dagger-size shard burying itself in the shoulder of an unconscious Mike Collins. The swirling torrent of wind sucked the smoke out of the cabin, taking with it the paralyzing smell of avgas. Once again Eddie could see, his hands taking tighter control of the spiraling aircraft.

"We ain't gonna make it," Eddie yelled over the din.

A thousand feet below, the ground was a featureless, dark abyss, the starless night revealing nothing. They couldn't tell if there were rocky mountains or a soft field or water below them. Eddie would have to try to make the landing blind, not even able to rely on the altimeter to get a fix on their position. It had frozen when they were hit.

"There!" Mercer shouted, pointing to their left.

Out of the gloom came a stand of tall, straight spruce trees, their high pyramidal tops like medieval church spires. The grove appeared tightly packed and would soften the controlled crash of the falling helicopter. Eddie banked toward the site, the engine coughing as the remaining fuel was burned up at a prodigious rate.

"It ain't happening, man. It looks close, but it's at least half a mile away," Eddie shouted. Rain soaked them all. The soldier used a sleeve of his BDUs to wipe the water from Eddie's dark face because the pilot couldn't afford to take his hands from the controls for even a second. Suddenly Eddie was struck with an idea. "Both of you, your doors have emergency release pins on the hinges. Pull them and let the doors drop away."

Mercer and the sergeant did what Eddie asked, tugging at the large red handles and kicking the doors outward. More rain surged through the cabin, wild eddies swirling in all directions at once. The wind reached a banshee pitch.

"I can hold it for only a second, and the drop is still gonna be about twenty feet to the tops of the trees, but it's the best I can do."

"No way, Eddie," Mercer shouted. "I'm not leaving you and Collins."

"Mercer, either we all die in the crash or just maybe I can save the two of you. Don't take that chance from me, goddamn it."

Mercer didn't argue with Eddie's dying wish. Bracing himself near the open doorway, his clothes rippling and snapping around him, he watched as Eddie brought them to the edge of the forest, just above treetop level. Echoes of the beating rotors kicked back from the hard earth below. On closer inspection, the evergreens were not nearly as dense as he'd first thought. There were huge gaps between many of the trees, and a straight fall from this height would split a man like a dropped sack of cement. He held the MP-5, waiting for Eddie's signal, one hand clutching the empty door frame as the wind tried to suck him into the void.

"Jump!" Eddie screamed, reining in the chopper to an unsteady hover for an instant. He then turned the JetRanger away so when the rotors hit the trees and flew apart, the fragments wouldn't slice into Mercer and the sergeant.

The soldier hesitated for a second, not launching himself until the helicopter was already heeled over. The delay threw off his timing and he missed his intended tree, his body falling through space, picking up speed exponentially so that he barreled into the loamy ground at eighty miles an hour. The impact broke his skull, spine, ribs, shoulders, hips, arms, and legs. He was dead before his nervous system could perceive the injuries.

Mercer had been watching Eddie and jumped the moment the African American opened his yellow-toothed mouth, not waiting to even hear the order. He tumbled only eleven feet before crashing into the topmost branches of a particularly tall tree, the thin boughs grabbing at him as he fell, each impact jarring him mercilessly but nonetheless slowing his descent. He hit the first thick branch with his shoulder, the rough, scaly bark rasping against the layers of his leather jacket.

Downward he plunged, branches whipping him like switches, flaying his hands and face, one catching him in the stomach, knocking the air from his chest, another on the thigh, deadening his entire right leg from groin to toes. The ground rushed at him too fast. Each new contact was a torment, the tree tearing at him like a wild animal even as it saved his life. Finally, after almost forty feet of torture, he fell onto a larger branch. Scrabbling to hook his hands around it, he missed but managed to clutch the next one down, arresting his descent with only six feet to go before he dropped from the tree's canopy and plummeted to the ground. He hung there, exhausted, one arm and a leg hooked over the bough, dangling like a gibbon, blood dripping from his face and hands.

Then he felt the JetRanger crash, the rotor blades chopping through the tops of nearby trees and then coming apart, spiraling outward like scythes, sending bits of wood and whole branches swirling in their destructive path. A bit of the rotor passed only a foot above Mercer's position, and rather than chance another close call, he let go, falling the last few feet and landing in a tangled heap.

The helicopter struck the high canopy so violently that the weakened tail boom separated and fell independently, cutting a six-foot gouge in the earth. The rest of the aircraft became enmeshed in the thick branches of several closely packed trees, the fuselage never actually hitting the ground but hanging up nearly twenty feet in the air, swinging precariously as the trees resettled themselves.

Mercer lay on his back. The rainwater that struck him in the face was slightly acidic because of its contact with the spruce tree. It burned his eyes and forced him to turn over. It took a minute for him to gather enough strength to actually stand, moaning as his back and shoulders cracked and popped from the strain they'd just endured. When he heard a clear call for help, he moved quickly, gathering up the machine pistol that had landed next to him and taking off at a fast trot. Torn bits of metal and whole sections of newly cut trees littered the ground.

After only a couple dozen yards he came upon the crushed body of the sergeant. Mercer needed only a quick, gruesome glance to tell that the young soldier had not been the source of the distress call. Continuing on, he came upon the crash site, or more accurately, he stumbled underneath it. Looking up, he could see the main cabin of the JetRanger tangled over his head, the chopper secured by tightly entwined branches. Eddie shouted again and then coughed wetly.

"Eddie, what the hell are you doing up there?" Mercer forced levity into his voice. "Don't you know when you crash you're supposed to hit the ground?"

"Oh, man, did anyone get the license of that truck that just hit me?"

"How you doing?"

"Not bad, considering. A branch came into the cockpit and snapped off about ten of my teeth. I think my jaw's broken too. Shit, I'm probably as ugly as you now." Eddie paused, fighting off waves of blackness. "Collins didn't make it. I can see his neck is broken."

"The kid didn't make it either. But two out of four is better than none. You did real good. Can you hold on up there until the cavalry arrives? I've got no way of getting you down."

"Don't worry about me, but if you're in any shape to go on, kill those motherfuckers for me, will you?"

"Doesn't matter what shape I'm in, they're gonna pay." There was a flinty edge to Mercer's voice. The hidden spring of his endurance had just been tapped, and the doubts he'd felt before were gone. "Eddie, the sergeant had a combat harness in the cockpit with him. It was on the floor by his feet. Do you see it?"

"Hold on." A second later Eddie called back down to the ground, "Yeah, I got it."

"Throw it down; I'm gonna need it. But keep the pistol for yourself." The heavy harness came crashing through the branches, almost hanging up a couple of times before landing a few feet from Mercer. He picked it up, looping the nylon suspenders over his shoulders and cinching the belt around his waist. Along with a knife, med kit, flashlight, and most important, a compass, he had four additional clips for the machine pistol.

"Eddie, it may take a while for the Air Force to send out a search and rescue team. I doubt we were on radar when the missiles hit. But when they do arrive, use the Beretta to signal to them. You know the distress call, three rapid shots. Just in case I fail at the pump station and Kerikov sends out a party to make certain none of us survive, be sure it's the good guys before you call to them."

"You gonna be okay?"

"I'll tell you tomorrow over drinks at the Great Alaskan Bush Company," quipped Mercer, mentioning Anchorage's most famous strip joint.

"You're buying," Eddie laughed back, but Mercer had already taken bearings from the compass and moved off.

The heavy rain masked the sound of him moving through the trees, allowing him to break into an easy loping run. His eyes were very sensitive to even minimal light, so he could find a clear path, avoiding stumps and thick brambles and anything else that might slow him. He figured that Eddie had flown at least two miles from the area where the missiles had been fired, so he didn't worry about stumbling into a recce patrol.

Ignoring the aches that cramped his body, he made it to the Dalton Highway in just thirty minutes, the last quarter mile being a ragged struggle up a steep defile. Calling it a highway was presumptuous—it was nothing more than a tightly packed gravel strip originally built as the haul road for the construction of the Alaska Pipeline. Mercer was badly winded, and sweat mingled freely with the rain that soaked through his clothing. The temperature was hovering just over thirty-five degrees, and as wet as he was, he ran a real chance of becoming hypothermic, his skin leaching away his core body heat until he collapsed and died.

The pipeline was on the other side of the road, held off the ground by spindly supports, the VSMs. In the rainy darkness, the forty-eight-inch pipe had a silver, maggoty sheen as it stretched north and south into both murky horizons. The gravel of the highway had been heavily compacted by years of fully loaded semitrailers tracking to and from the oil-rich Prudhoe Bay fields. Along its verges, fireweed grew, the countless purple blossoms all but wasted by the summer so that the topmost parts of the stalks were barren, sticking in the air like arthritic fingers.

Somewhere to Mercer's right was Pump Station Number 5, an unknown number of terrorists holding it, armed with rockets and God alone knew what else, while to his left was an open stretch of road leading back to civilization. He would find help only a few miles away, a warm ranger's cabin, a cup of scalding coffee, a bed. He snicked off the safety of the H&K and turned to the right, continuing northward into the unknown, relying on his superior eyesight and instincts to keep him from falling into an ambush.

The second mile on the Dalton Highway merged with the third and into the fourth, Mercer's mind all but shutting down, conserving his energy to keep his feet running. He couldn't remember a time when he had been so utterly exhausted, both mentally and physically. His stamina was waning and, with it, his coordination. He found himself stumbling more, lurching forward and one time pitching to the ground, the gravel digging deeply into the already torn meat of his palms.

Lying on the slick road, his face pressed against the dirt, his eyes closed in pain and weariness, he heard the unmistakable sound of a truck engine starting, revving up and then settling as the transmission was engaged. He looked up and through the drizzle saw headlights retreating back into the night. Had he been five minutes quicker, he would have jogged right into Kerikov's rear guard. The vehicle retreated northward toward Pump Station 5.

Mercer wasn't certain if this meant Kerikov was about to pull out of his position, or that he no longer feared a land-based assault up the Dalton Highway and wanted his men in a tighter defensive position. A new sense of urgency gripped him. If Kerikov was about to leave the pump station, Mercer would never have his chance. There was nothing he could do with a single machine pistol against a convoy of trucks. A single vehicle, yes, but he was sure that Kerikov would have used at least four trucks to transport enough men and equipment to seize the station and be able to deploy troops armed with missile launchers. He had to get to the station before they evacuated if he was to get his chance to eliminate Kerikov before the Russian was whisked to safety once again.

His strides felt lighter, more sure as he began running again, his focus sharper. The rain intensified, turning the hardened gravel road into a thick morass, clay lodging into the heavy tread of his boots. Mercer edged closer to the verge where the road had a rougher aggregate and he could gain a stronger purchase. Clearing a blind corner around a jagged tor of rock that cut off his view northward, Mercer dove off the road, rolling down the low shoulder and landing in a small stream of rain runoff. Ahead of him was the pump station, lit by powerful truck-mounted halogen lamps, the squat building and its immediate surroundings bathed in a pool of white light. And suddenly Mercer understood why Kerikov had taken the risk of attacking the pipeline directly.

Six flatbed trucks were pulled up against the pipe, cranes mounted on two of them swinging long cylindrical collars into place over the oil conduit. Men and women scurried around the site, and even at this extreme range, Mercer could hear their cries and oaths and shouts. This was what Kerikov was doing with the liquid nitrogen. He was placing it around the pipeline, encapsulating strategic parts of its eight-hundred-mile length in supercooled gas in an attempt to stop the flow of oil. This must be the last of it, he surmised, the replacement for the cylinders that he'd discovered aboard the *Jenny IV*.

Watching closely as the protective sleeve surrounding the

pipeline was cut loose with a torch and its virtual twin was set in place, Mercer realized how cleverly they had carried out the operation. Had he not seen it actually happen, he never would have believed that there was anything out of the ordinary to the doctored section of pipe. Who knew how much of the line they had laced with liquid nitrogen?

He moved forward, wriggling through the water and mud in the drainage ditch, shutting his mind off from the the rain and the cold and his own pain. Even with their yellow rain jackets and water-darkened hats, Mercer was able to recognize a couple of the PEAL activists he had seen at the bar in Valdez. They moved with the competence of an experienced construction crew, hoisting the original sections of pipe sleeve onto a truck. When they released the nitrogen within their fake lining, it would take weeks or even months to discover the sabotage, and even then, who would believe such a bold and cunning plan?

Remembering what Andy Lindstrom said about freezing the oil in the Trans-Alaska Pipeline, he could believe that PEAL would be satisfied with shutting down the pipeline for the months it would take to clear the solidified oil from it and replace any damaged sections, but Mercer had a hard time accepting that Ivan Kerikov would work on such a symbolic but otherwise worthless act of eco-terrorism. There was something else to this, something that Mercer couldn't quite grasp. The steady whine of the pump station's main turbine sounded like a muffled dentist's drill, droning on and on despite everything happening around it.

The hard prod at the back of his neck was a concentric circle, its inner ring exactly nine millimeters in diameter. The barrel of an Uzi pressed into his flesh was held by one of Kerikov's former East German assassins. Mercer hadn't heard him approach—he'd been too rapt by the sight before him—and as he slowly locked his fingers behind his back, he cursed himself for his lack of caution.

"Up," he was ordered, and as he stood, he was warned to do so slowly, the gun pulling back so that he couldn't twist around and grab its barrel. The man who captured him knew precisely how to handle a prisoner.

Mercer dragged himself to his feet, turned, letting the H&K machine pistol dangle from its strap against his chest. Seeing the weapon for the first time, the German took an involuntary step back, tightening the grip on his own weapon. His left foot slid a fraction of an inch in the mud at the edge of the drainage ditch, his concentration switching from his prisoner to his own balance for just an instant. Mercer used it to his full advantage, predicting it so accurately he was already in motion when the man slipped.

He dove forward, pounding into the man, throwing up his arm so that the Uzi rose harmlessly, its stubby barrel pointed into the trees. The bullet wound from Burt Manning's attack on his house screamed with newfound pain as the lips of the long gash split open again, fresh blood welling through the opening. Mercer's momentum took both men down into the ditch, the German pinned in the wet mud by Mercer's body. Mercer cocked his right arm, punching as hard as he could, one, two, three powerful shots to the jaw. The German was still conscious, but just barely. Without a second thought, Mercer held the assassin's head under the babbling stream flowing at the bottom of the ditch until his body went completely still.

Only after the man was dead did Mercer become aware that his heart was racing with fear, his chest pumping as though he couldn't get enough oxygen. His fingers twitched with adrenaline. Lying in the ditch, his back pressed into the greasy mud, he tilted his neck and opened his mouth, letting cold, sweet water seep to the back of his throat, easing the raging thirst the sudden adrenaline rush had given him. He rested a moment longer, then crawled out of the mire to see if the fight had caught the attention of the workers at the pump station.

Peeking over the rise, he saw that no one had noticed; they were still working at securing the final nitro pack to the pipeline. The sound of the big turbine within the building and the rumbling diesel engines of their trucks must have masked the noise Mercer made killing the picket.

Without warning, a fountain of dirt exploded in Mercer's face, throwing wet grit into his eyes, clogging his nostrils, and filling his mouth. He ducked again, burrowing into the ground as the sound of machine gun fire reached him an instant later. Just to his left, another burst kicked mud from the embankment, so close he could feel the heat of the bullets as they hit the dirt. He was pinned down and very vulnerable. The next move belonged to whoever held the gun.

"The man you just killed had been a member of the East German Secret Police and had received the finest training possible under Soviet sponsorship. I must congratulate the competence of America's Special Forces. You did very well indeed." The voice that called out into the darkness was thick, gutterally accented, the words clipped so tightly that all emotion had been trimmed from them. "However, I don't believe that you are bulletproof. You will throw your weapon away from your position, hold your hands over your head, and step out of the ditch."

Twice caught in under two minutes, Mercer tossed the Heckler and Koch and stood. A flashlight snapped on from about forty feet up the road, just outside the perimeter of the pump station, rain slashing through the beam. The man who'd seen him had been able to watch the entire fight from his position though he had not interfered, even when he had a clear shot while Mercer was drowning the guard. Mercer had no explanation why his life was spared, but he knew that he wouldn't like the reason.

"So tell me," the flashlight bobbed and weaved as the man approached Mercer, "are you an Army ranger or Marine force recon? I know that your government hasn't had the time to activate a SEAL or Delta unit and get them to Alaska this quickly."

"Sorry to disappoint you, but no one thought your threat was worth sending in real troops. I'm a Boy Scout leader, Dan Gerous is the name. Heck, I'm not even a soldier, I'm a geologist."

Rounds of nine-millimeter ammunition chewed up the ground at Mercer's feet, bullets zinging off stones and ricocheting back into the forest. He could do nothing but stand there as the earth around him was clawed with deadly ferocity.

"I came out here to investigate when my picket radioed he had spotted an intruder. I never imagined it would be you, Dr. Mercer. I can't tell you how pleased I am to hold your life in my hands. You are going to die a very horrible death, geologist. That I can assure you." Mercer realized that he'd been captured by Ivan Kerikov himself.

Seconds later, two men flanked him, yanking his hands from over his head and clapping on a pair of handcuffs, the steel links so tight the blood drained from his hands and wrists. He was shoved toward the backlit figure of Kerikov with a well-placed rifle butt to his kidney. From this distance, it appeared that the Russian's shoulders spanned the entire width of the Dalton Highway.

"I have been anticipating this day for a year now," Kerikov said as the henchmen held Mercer before the former spymaster. "After I heard it was you who destroyed operation Vulcan's Forge, I considered hiring an assassin to kill you in your Arlington town house, but I decided that I really wanted the opportunity personally."

There was a cruel twist to Kerikov's mouth as he spoke, and his eyes, washed-out and pale blue, glittered like flat chips of glass. Even in his moment of triumph, he showed little emotion. The juxtaposition of his words and his expression was unnatural, far more frightening than had he raved and gloated.

No matter how revolted Mercer was by Kerikov, by the malignant taint he possessed, he wasn't about to show it. He would not give in to his own fear, not now, not in front of the Russian. "If you dedicated your life to getting revenge on a nobody like me, Kerikov, I really think you should reevaluate your career goals. You're pathetic."

Kerikov dropped his assault rifle to the road and rushed forward, his right hand swinging. He caught Mercer on the point of the chin with so much force that Mercer's eyes turned back into his skull before he hit the ground. He would be out for hours.

"Take this sack of shit back to the helicopter," Kerikov ordered his men. "And tell the pilot to get ready. We're leaving."

Kerikov turned away, heading back toward the pump station compound, secretly massaging his right fist. He winced once as he popped a dislocated knuckle back into place, but the pain didn't break his stride.

The work on the pipeline was almost complete. The last sleeve of liquid nitrogen was slung under the line, its two halves hinged open so they could clamp it around the pipe. The leader of the work crew signaled the crane operator. He hoisted the cradle holding the false section of pipe sleeve, deftly following the quick hand signals of the PEAL activist standing on the pipe itself. Once the bottom of the nitrogen pack hit the underside of the pipeline, the crane operator heaved it up another couple of feet, and the two halves closed together naturally, encasing another twenty-foot section of the Trans-Alaska Pipeline with two more tons of supercooled nitrogen, held in stasis by a thin vacuum seal. Cleverly hidden bolts were shot home, tightening the sleeve to the pipe. Another section of the line was vulnerable to Kerikov's attack.

A female technician climbed up to the pipe as workers unhooked the crane. With a portable computer, she activated the electronic triggering device built into the nitrogen pack, setting it to the frequency Kerikov had chosen to detonate the device. She also checked to ensure that it was reading the tiny transmitters in the other packs PEAL had set in place, guaranteeing they would go off in predetermined series, a cascade that would cause the most damage. With fingers made stiff by the cold, she checked the primary and backup circuits, making certain there were no faults or shorts. She unplugged the computer from the jack built into the sleeve, then snapped off the jack so that only a microscopically thin filament remained as evidence. The released nitrogen and a small explosive charge would take care of the other electronics, leaving behind nothing but a few pieces of shattered plastic and wires when the device was set off. The pack was virtually undetectable. She gave a thumbs-up to the foreman.

"That's the last one, Jan," the foreman yelled to Voerhoven, who stood a little way off.

Kerikov came up to Voerhoven, wondering silently why the Dutchman wasn't frozen to death wearing just a thin windbreaker over his T-shirt. "Tell your people to pack up. The trucks must be destroyed and everyone must get to the *Hope* as quickly as possible. When we release the nitrogen tomorrow, I want all of your people back in Valdez, looking as innocent as schoolchildren."

Having them aboard the *Hope* by morning would also make it that much easier for Abu Alam to kill them quickly. The Arab butcher wanted to do it singly or in small groups, but Kerikov decided that blowing up the research vessel made more sense.

"They performed better than you expected, didn't they?" Voerhoven said with obvious pride.

"You've all done well," Kerikov replied, knowing that Voerhoven needed another dose of ego building. "You have excellent people, and their loyalty to you is remarkable. In fact, as a reward, I want to give you this." Kerikov handed over a black cellular phone. "This is the trigger for the devices. All you have to do is dial 555-2020, then hit SEND. The signal will reach the nitrogen detonators within a tenth of a second. You hold in your hands the future of this entire state, Jan, that is how much I trust and admire you. You will go down as the earth's greatest protector."

"Sometimes I've wondered about you, Ivan, about your motivations, your convictions. But this," Voerhoven held up the phone, "this shows me more than your words can ever tell. When the time comes, I won't hesitate."

Kerikov wanted to laugh at the environmentalist, but he managed to keep his voice level and authoritative. "It's time to go. I want you to come back with me on the helicopter. When he regains consciousness, there's someone I want you to meet."

"Are we going back to the *Hope*?"

"No, we're taking a short detour to drop off my prisoner first, and then we'll go to Valdez."

Walking back up the road to the waiting helicopter, Kerikov called Ted Mossey at the Alyeska Marine Terminal on another cell phone. The computer genius assured him that the original KGB program was now installed and just needed the activation code to cycle through the system. As soon as Kerikov sent the code into the computer, they would have complete control of the entire eight hundred miles of pipe and the ten pump stations. Once in their control, there would be no way to stop the preprogrammed series of events.

————————

HEATHROW AIRPORT
LONDON

There was no earthly reason for Khalid Al-Khuddari to come awake. His body was so battered and racked with pain that a normal person would have been in a coma for at least twenty-four hours. Yet something had brought him to consciousness, something that cut through the layers of pain and fatigue and drugs and dragged his mind back from the coveted bliss.

He kept his eyes closed, but slowly, too slowly, his other senses began to feed him information. A minute passed before he realized he couldn't hear the comforting whine of the jet's engines, nor could he feel any sensation of movement, none of the tiny dips and corrections autopilots must make to keep their charges on an even keel.

Startled, he looked out the window of the aircraft. Expecting to see open skies and the scrolling sand waves of the Sahara Desert, he saw instead terminals and huge maintenance hangars. Across the open vista of the taxi ramp, he saw a long line of gaily colored aircraft parked nose to tail, like elephants performing a circus trick. Dishwater gray clouds clung to the ground, allowing only a few rays of sunlight to strike the earth.

Khalid turned to the passenger next to him, a heavily built woman working furiously at a laptop computer, her hundred-dollar manicured nails tapping a fast-paced tattoo. He could tell that she was trying desperately not to notice that he was awake. Considering the state he must look, he didn't blame her.

"I'm sorry, but I fell asleep just after boarding. Why are we still on the ground?" he asked solicitously, forcing out his best upper-class British accent.

She turned to him with distaste and sighed heavily. When she spoke, she did so as if each word cost her personally, as if she'd been given only a finite amount of them and didn't want to waste a single one on him. "As I understand it, we are being held hostage."

She affected the studied nonchalance of a woman who thought that to make it in a man's world she must suppress herself to the point of becoming an automaton.

"What?" Khalid's heart flopped in his chest.

The woman saved the file she was working on and turned to him, speaking slowly, as if to an idiot. "Terrorists have seized Heathrow and ordered that aircraft not be allowed to take off or land. Otherwise they will set off the bombs they have planted, supposedly on some of the aircraft as well as within the terminal." She spoke with an eerie, unnatural calm. Khalid found it hard to believe what he was hearing.

"At first, the pilots tried to tell us that it was some mechanical problem with the radar," she continued. "But after I noticed that planes were still landing for the next hour, I knew it wasn't true. I pointed this out to the stewardess, and after a couple of exchanges between me and the pilot—a dreadful man, I must add—he told the passengers what had actually happened. A bomb had gone off in Terminal 4, killing two people. So far, security has yet to turn up any more explosives.

"I believe that this is a hoax." Once the woman decided to talk, there was no stopping her. "It's surely some lunatic, a foreigner no doubt, trying to ride the coattails of the attack at the British Museum last night. As Melville said in *Moby Dick*, 'Madmen beget madmen.' One terrorist attacks and suddenly everyone wants to jump on the bandwagon. I suppose after Lockerbie, officials must take every precaution, no matter how inconvenient."

Khalid was appalled by the woman's callousness. Two people were dead, and she was bothered by the inconvenience of the situation. He would never understand Westerners, and for that he was grateful. Looking at his watch and trying to remember what time his plane was supposed to take off, he realized that he didn't know how long they had been stuck on the ground. He asked the woman.

"Four hours now," she complained after looking at the slim diamond-encrusted watch she wore.

Khalid's mind began to come around, letting him think clearly, at least for a little while. The pain in his back and shoulders was no more than a dull ache that he could almost ignore. He caught the attention of a nearby flight attendant. "Is there a reason why we haven't been allowed to deplane?"

"I'm sorry, sir, this is part of the terrorists' demands. None of the planes on the taxiways are allowed to move. A second communiqué from them came shortly after the first one. They said that if any aircraft attempted to move or let off the passengers, they would detonate all the bombs simultaneously. They claimed to have the airport under observation. I'm very sorry for this, Minister Khuddari. I've heard what you've been through. Is there anything I can do for you? I'm afraid that I don't have anything stronger than Midol, but maybe you'd like a drink?"

"Nothing right now, thank you," Khalid demurred quickly.

For the first time in his life, he was tempted to break the dictates of the Koran and have liquor. It wasn't to dull his pain but to deaden the realization that Rufti was going to win.

Khalid realized that fat bastard must have known that he was trying to get back to the United Arab Emirates, probably had him tailed from the hospital. He didn't even want to consider the consequences if Rufti knew that Trevor and Millicent Gray had helped him. Both were in grave danger. Considering the four hours he'd been asleep, it was probably too late to help them.

Khalid thrust aside his concern for the lovers and considered what was really at stake. Rufti was surely well on his way back to the UAE. Once there, he would immediately start his plan to overthrow the government,. The Crown Prince was

vulnerable right now, trapped between appeasement of the
United States and the militancy of more reactionary forces
within the Gulf, old enemies made newly volatile by the shifting world oil situation.

Rufti could take the Emirates so easily that the coup would
certainly be called "bloodless" by the international media.
And then, Iran and Iraq would advance, and the Gulf would
fall under a tight dictatorship. Using oil as an economic
weapon, the conspirators would bring Europe, Asia, and
America to their knees in a matter of weeks.

"I need a phone." Khalid didn't realize he'd spoken aloud
until the woman next to him looked at him strangely.

He called the stewardess again and explained that he
needed to make an important call. She said emphatically that
no phones could be used while the aircraft was on the ground.
The authorities feared that any outside electronic interference,
such as a radio or a cellular phone, might detonate the explosives.

"There are no more explosives, I assure you. I must have
a phone, now."

Again she shook her head and turned away.

"Then let me talk to the Captain," he demanded harshly.
With more stability than he thought he possessed, he pushed
himself from his seat and faced the young attendant.

"I'm sorry, Minister, but that isn't possible either," she replied as strongly as she could in the face of Khalid's insistence.

"Now, goddamn it!" he shouted. She backed away silently
as Khalid moved into the aisle, his feet thudding against the
deck like Frankenstein's monster. The stiffness of his wounds
had robbed him of nearly all coordination.

Deferring to his ministerial status, she lead him to the flight
deck. The crew sat in their starched white shirts, black ties,
and trousers and looked suitably impressive even in their impotent positions. The Captain, a silver-haired man with deeply
tanned skin and calm eyes, twisted to see who had intruded
on his sanctum sanctorum. When he saw Khalid in the ill-
fitting clothes with barely healed scars on his face and hands,
he tightened his hold of the aircraft's control yoke.

"Captain Darson," the stewardess said formally, "this is Minister Khuddari, that passenger that was brought aboard at the last moment."

Darson continued to scrutinize Khalid from behind a veil of suspicion. "Yes, Minister, what can I do for you?"

"The attack at the airport was meant to delay me reaching home, Captain. There are no other explosives and no terrorist plot. A rival of mine is trying to overthrow my government, and I'm the only person aware of his intentions. By closing the airport and stalling this flight, he may succeed in wresting control from our legitimate leader." It was a struggle for Khalid to speak clearly. His mind was beginning to swim again, his vision to blur.

"Am I to assume that you wish to leave the aircraft?"

"Yes, sir, and it that's not possible, then at least allow me to make a call and send a warning."

"I understand your situation, sir, but you must understand mine. I am under strict orders not to use my radios until the authorities determine that there are no more bombs in the airport or on any of the planes. Despite what you say, the government is taking this threat seriously, considering what happened last night at the British Museum."

"Captain, I was the target of that attack. It was me they were trying to kill, don't you understand? This," he waved his arm toward the view through the cockpit windshield, "this whole elaborate plot is intended to delay only one person, myself."

"I'm sorry, but my hands are tied. The antiterrorist police should have everything checked out in another few hours. They're being careful in case the terrorists really do have the airport grounds under surveillance. I'll make sure you are taken off the plane as soon as we're vetted. I'm sorry, but that is the best I can do."

"That's not good enough," Khalid yelled. The copilot stood quickly and began moving toward him, a grim expression on his face. His intentions were clear, and Khalid allowed himself to be shepherded from the cockpit, realizing that he had nothing more to gain.

The stewardess led him back to his seat. Khalid sat, his

mind working furiously, not only against this dilemma but also the pain that threatened to overwhelm him again. He had to get off the Boeing, contact Colonel Bigelow and have him warn the Crown Prince. Nothing else mattered.

Slumped over, with his head cradled between his hands, he felt the first waves of defeat washing over him. Despite his own Herculean endurance, his sacrifices and stamina, Rufti was going to win. He had little option other than sit here in the First-Class section and wait until his country was destroyed by a power-crazed maniac.

Like hell. Khalid was in motion before he was fully aware of what he was doing.

The main cabin door of the aircraft was only a couple yards away. Lurching drunkenly, Khalid made his way toward it, tripping over his startled neighbor but ignoring her protests. From the corner of his eye, he saw a stewardess a quarter way down the aircraft's length turn to look at him, but she didn't register alarm until she saw his hand reach for the pressure door handle. She shouted a warning, dropped a bundle of blankets onto the lap of a coach-class passenger, and started running forward.

Another attendant, the only steward on the aircraft, ducked his model-handsome face around a bulkhead, his eyes going wide when he saw the ragged passenger heaving at the handle.

With what little strength he had remaining, Khalid pulled on the door handle until finally the seal broke. The door, as perfectly balanced as Boeing engineers could make it, pivoted easily, folding back on itself and leaving a wide aperture beckoning to freedom. Frightened passengers began screaming, several of them leaping from their seats and running toward the tail of the aircraft, fearing that Khalid was part of the terrorist threat. Some people watched in horrified awe as Khalid braced himself for the drop to the tarmac.

The steward lunged to grab onto Khalid's clothing in a vain attempt to stop him, but he fell short by a few inches, his outstretched hand grasping empty air. He had to clutch at the door frame to keep from tumbling after Khalid.

For a brief instant, as Khalid dropped the ten and a half

feet to the taxiway, his mind and body felt as one again, both of them seemingly weightless, adrift in a sensationless void. And then he hit the ground, his legs folding completely, his head smacking against the asphalt like a heavy melon. He kept his body loose, never once thinking to tense for the impact.

Lying on the taxiway, he could hear the shouted protests from the crew of the aircraft. It meant nothing. He was free. He could call Bigelow, end this charade, and hopefully restabilize the Middle East. As he tried to stand, he realized he couldn't move. His legs lay quietly as his mind screamed orders for them to get moving, to lift him up and carry him away. In a sickening rush, he remembered hearing a dry cracking sound when he hit the ground, almost like a piece of timber snapping in a high wind. He was certain he'd broken his back on impact. The belly of the Boeing 767 curled above him like the abdomen of a pregnant whale, a solid swell reaching almost to the ground. He struggled to roll under the hull's curvature, but he simply couldn't move.

A tanker truck, its drumlike sides emblazoned with the logo of a septic company, pulled up to the 767, stopping under the sewer outlet of the big Boeing. With practiced competence, three men leaped from the truck and hooked a heavy rubber hose to the plane's underbelly, while secretly four other men dodged from under the diesel truck and raced to Khalid. After one look, it was clear to these members of the SAS, Special Air Squadron, Britain's most elite fighting force, that moving Khalid could kill him. However, they were under specific orders to check every aircraft on the apron for anything suspicious and report back to the terminal.

Every second the airport was shut down cost tens of thousands of pounds, and the quicker they could secure the area, the quicker that debt meter would stop spinning. Two men grasped Khalid under the shoulders and dragged him back to the septic truck they were using as cover. They had orders to vet four other aircraft before returning to the terminal, but with Khalid as a possible suspect, the non-com in charge decided to return to base immediately.

Fourteen minutes later, a near-dead Khalid Khuddari was

dumped into a spartan office within the terminal, two commandos taking up position just inside the office door. Another ten minutes passed before Geoff Wilberforce strode into the room, his heavy eyelids hanging so low they almost obscured his eyes. His face, florid in the best of situations, was livid, red blotches raised on his throat, cheeks, and forehead. In twenty-eight years of airport management, he was facing the worst day of his life, and he was looking for someone to blame. Rightly or wrongly, it didn't matter. He was not taking the fall for this situation.

"Hey?" Wilberforce said, slapping Khalid on the cheek as he lay on a steel desk in the abandoned office. "Wake up now or forever hold your peace."

His body pummeled far beyond human endurance, his mind stretched so tautly it resonated with internal tension, Khalid ratcheted open his eyes and craned his head to regard Wilberforce. His expression was dulled and lifeless, arranged like a mask by the pain, yet he still managed to capture Wilberforce with the power of his eyes, obsidian-sharp and focused.

"I need a phone," Khalid croaked.

"You may get one," Wilberforce gloated, "in about fifty years when you're let out of the gaol. International terrorism is about the only crime this country takes seriously anymore and you're going to get the full brunt of the law on this one, mate. Your friend shouldn't have killed a teenager and a priest. Bad mistake."

"I'm the target," Khalid said lamely. He struggled to reach his passport and establish his credentials, but his stamina had finally deserted him. "They were after me."

"Tell it to the bloody judge, you wog bastard."

A police ambulance carried Khalid Khuddari away from Heathrow, its siren honking like a foghorn as it tore along the route back to London. He was sedated by the paramedics, two veterans of some of the most gruesome scenes in all of England. Neither of them could believe the struggle their newest patient had put up. To the last possible moment before the new round of drugs knocked him out, Khalid was demanding a telephone and trying vainly to explain who he was.

ONE HUNDRED EIGHTY MILES NORTH
OF PUGET SOUND

The sea was as dark as a slag heap belched out of a blast furnace, hard and relentless. The waves were undulating furrows arching westward, pushing aside everything that got in their way, including the fishing boat *Suzy's Pride*, a bow-heavy purse seiner. The thirty-year-old boat was out well beyond her limit, chasing fish so far into the Pacific that her antiquated radar system could no longer see the jumbled coastline of the mainland.

It was the black hour, the lowest ebb of the night between one and five when everything except the desperate slept. For nearly seventy hours, Steve Hanscom had guided his boat behind a school of feeding sea bass in hopes of coming across a large shoal of Pacific sardines. Such was his luck, he'd had two possible catches scattered by a pod of orcas that had decided to shadow his tired boat.

While at first delighted to point out the killer whales to his young son, Hanscom now cursed the capricious mammals for their dogged loyalty to *Suzy's Pride*. A fourth-generation fisherman who realized that there would not be a fifth, Hanscom still tried to make a living from the sea that had provided for his family since the middle part of the last century. With a mortgage on his boat and one on his house and a car that used more oil than gasoline, he knew all too well what a big catch meant to him and his family. Two, possibly three, more runs out into the open waters beyond Puget Sound and he would be bankrupt if he didn't come up with a big haul.

That was why Steve had pulled his eleven-year-old son, Joshua, out of school for the month and put him to work on the boat. In the few weeks they would have together, Steve hoped to teach the boy what it meant to work for yourself and to instill the pride that his own father had taught him. In a few months, surely by spring, Steve would be just another guy putting in his time for someone else, but right now, he was his own man, and by God his son would know what that felt like.

Though others would suffer by Steve losing his boat, particularly old George Boudette, the grizzled sea dog who'd forgotten more about fishing than most men would ever know, Steve Hanscom worried most about his own son. Josh had been raised by the lore and lure of the sea. It was simple economics—and the harsh reality that the Pacific Northwest was being overfished—that was driving him out of business, yet Steve still blamed himself for not being able to pass on the legacy that had been passed to him. He saw it as his own personal failure.

The ship's wheel moved effortlessly under Steve Hanscom's gentle touch, the varnished oak made smooth by generations of constant contact. Standing alone in the wheelhouse as he had since *Suzy's Pride* had left Seattle, Hanscom watched the depth finder, hoping to see the shoal of sardines pass under the boat again, signaling him to throw the big purse net back over the flat transom.

"I'll spell ya." The voice penetrated his personal world, startling Hanscom so that his fists tightened on the wheel.

He turned. "No thanks, Georgie. Get some sleep."

"I'm eighty years old. I don't need any more sleep. I've had my share until the big one comes." George Boudette's eyes were alight with the last spark of life, like a lightbulb burning brightest before it faded forever. George had crewed with Steve, Steve's father, and, as a boy, Steve's grandfather.

"How's Josh?" Steve asked. His son was below.

"Asleep at the radio like Marconi's assistant." George said fondly. "You shouldn't have sent him to bed and told him to listen to the set at the same time. He took your second order a lot more seriously than the first."

"We aren't going to catch any fish, so he might as well feel like he's doing something on this trip. Listening to the chatter of the big container ships heading to Seattle is better than sitting on the deck and twiddling his thumbs."

"We'll hit fish before dawn," George said with undeniable confidence.

One deck below, Josh Hanscom was coming awake again, gripped by the same excitement that had held him enthralled since his father had told him that he didn't have to go to school this month. It was like Christmas morning in the quiet hours before his parents woke. Yet behind it was a stronger emotion. He had been given a job to do. His father had told him to keep listening to the radio and that was exactly what Josh intended. He didn't realize that his task was more to keep him occupied than for any legitimate purpose.

Ashamed that he'd fallen asleep on duty, Josh rubbed at his eyes and yawned before concentrating on the transceiver. This was the third straight night that he'd been in the same clothes, and like his dad, he'd gotten into the habit of spraying frigid deodorant under his arms as soon as he woke. Josh even mimicked his father's shocked expression when the aerosol hit his tender skin. After hosing himself with Right Guard, Josh scaled up through the frequencies listening for anything that might help his dad find fish. He worked the twin dials with delicate fingers, easing from one frequency to another so subtly that the transition was unnoticeable unless one really listened to the pitch of the static coming through the speaker.

He nearly missed it. In the lower band of the VHF there was a quick squawk of white noise, different from the background static but so much the same that Josh almost ignored it. Yet he dialed back, and suddenly there it was again. Someone was definitely transmitting, but the signal was too far away to get in clear. It was just garbled noise, a harsh squelch much like what the older kids at school called music. Not knowing the consequences of capturing a signal at 2182 MHz, Josh listened intently until a voice emerged from the static. "Mayday, Mayday, Mayday. This is the VLCC *Southern Cross* posting an All Ships Signify."

Startled by the hail, Josh rushed from the cabin, scrambling up to the bridge. "Dad, hey Dad," he shouted.

"Hold on there, Jakey," Steve Hanscom said, using his

son's nickname. He stood hunched over the sonar scope, George Boudette at his shoulder, one scarred hand holding the wheel steady without having to actually look at the sea.

"Look at the size of that bastard," George breathed in awe, despite his decades at sea. "I've never seen a shoal like it."

"Goddamn it, Georgie, we struck gold." Steve straightened and turned to his son. "Jake, go rouse the men. We've got some fishing to do."

George Boudette idled the engines down to trolling speed, twisting the wheel so that the *Suzy's Pride* started a wide arc around the huge mass of fish roiling just below the surface, driven mad by the predatory sea bass darting through their midst. Steve turned from the sonar, confident that Georgie would handle the bridge duties while he and the two deck-hands prepared to cast the seine net around the school of sardines.

"But Dad," Josh persisted, "I just heard a Mayday on the radio. It was on 2182."

It took a few seconds for Steve Hanscom to understand what his son had said. "You heard a call on 2182? Are you sure?" Suddenly the excitement about the shoal beneath them wavered.

"Yeah, a man said Mayday and everything," Josh replied excitedly, not knowing the consequences of what he was saying.

"Get ready to cast off the purse," George cried, concentrating fully on the task of bunching the fish onto the surface until the sea was bowed with their tremendous numbers.

Steve hesitated, looking at his son's eager face, wanting to believe that the boy hadn't heard a call on 2182 MHz, one of the international distress frequencies. He had to make a decision in the next few seconds or the shoal would disperse, driven off by its swollen size.

"Cast!" he shouted down to the deck where his mates were already prepared, alerted by George Boudette's foot pounding the deck above the cabin where they slept.

The net was shoved over the back of the boat with sheer muscle power, yards and yards of material and dozens of floats and weights tossed into the water until their own drag helped haul them over the transom. The release was timed precisely with the steady throb of the motor and with the easy circle the boat drew in the water. The net was paid out at the very perimeter of the shoal in order to capture the greatest number of fish.

Normally, Steve would have been on deck assisting in the release, making sure his expensive net didn't become fouled as it oozed into the Pacific, but he had grabbed his son by the hand and dragged the confused boy back into the cabin, to where the radio transceiver sat on its built-in shelf.

"Show me," he said tight-lipped, his body almost quivering.

Scared, Josh powered up the venerable Motorola, avoiding his father's eyes as the set warmed, its dials glowing whitely in the dim cabin. He scanned the frequencies, zeroing in on 2182 MHz. Nothing came through the speaker except snow— dead white noise. Steve began to breathe again, thankful that his son had been wrong. There was nothing out there tonight; no one was calling for help.

Had there really been a distress, maritime law dictated that the preservation of human life came above any other consideration. Steve would have been forced to cut away the heavy nets paying out behind the vessel and make the best possible speed to render assistance. If that had happened, he could forget ever coming up with the money to replace them. But Josh had been mistaken. There was nothing out there, and Steve had some fish to catch.

He was just reaching to turn off the radio when a loud, clear voice burst from the speakers, so close it sounded as if the person was in the cabin with them.

"Mayday, Mayday. This is the Captain of the VLCC *Southern Cross* requesting an All Ships Signify. Mayday. Mayday."

Hanscom's blood went cold. Yet it was not the loss of his own future that frightened him; it was the message itself. He knew enough about ships to know that a VLCC was not some small coastal vessel but one of the supertankers cruising between Alaska and California. He recalled the hours of television he'd watched following the *Exxon Valdez* disaster. If one of those monsters burst her belly and spilled its poison near Puget Sound, Hanscom would be one of thousands of fisherman who would never work again.

Steve took only a moment to weigh his decision, for he really had no choice. Not only was he obliged to help the tanker if she'd sent a Mayday, he also wanted to go to her aide. If, in some small way, he could prevent a catastrophe, and maybe save the waters leading to the Sound, he had no reservations about cutting away his nets and racing to give any assistance he could.

"Josh, tell Paul to cut the nets and have Georgie power up the engines," Steve said forcefully. If he was going to lose his boat because of this, he was damned sure it would not be in vain. He checked the numbers of the radio's direction finder and quickly calculated the course. "And tell Georgie to steer 342 degrees true and burst the engines if he has to."

Josh ran from the cabin, his high, clear voice shouting excitedly but with the authority of a man on a mission. Steve picked up the hand mike. "This is the master of the trawler *Suzy's Pride*, reading you strength four, please amplify your signal. I am running at top speed to your location. Verify your position and state your emergency."

Relief washed over Lyle Hauser with the fever of sexual release. "Thank God you're out there, Captain. I didn't think I would be close enough to shore for my signal to be picked up for another ten hours. My ship has been taken over by terrorists who were working with some of my crew. I'm adrift in a life raft approximately two hundred and fifty miles north-northwest of Bellingham. I can't give a more accurate position fix."

Steve thought he was hearing something out of *Mutiny on the Bounty*. A ship seized and its captain set adrift in a lifeboat? This was the dawn of the twenty-first century. That sort of thing didn't happen anymore. It defied belief. Was this some sick hoax?

But the *Suzy's Pride* was well beyond the range of nearly all shore-based radio sets, and the direction finder said that the signal was coming from somewhere out to sea. It could be true. *Jesus*, he thought, terrorists in control of a super-tanker?

"You must relay a message to the authorities," continued the voice from the speakers, "but under no circumstance are the owners of my ship to be informed. I fear that they may be involved with the terrorists."

"I don't understand. Please clarify last transmission. Captain, I cannot radio shore this far out; my set isn't powerful enough. I will reach your position in a few hours." Steve felt his boat gaining speed.

"Negative. Make your quickest landfall and report what's happened to the Coast Guard. They must stop the *Southern Cross*. The tanker should be close to Seattle by now, and I believe they intend to destroy her in Puget Sound."

Steve snapped on the overhead lights and pulled a chart from the cabinet under the radio, anchoring its corners with two empty coffee cups and a navigation reference book he'd been using to teach Josh. He scanned it quickly, making a few rough estimates before responding.

"Captain, I am equidistant between Port Hardy and Bamfield, British Columbia. I can rescue you and still make quickest landfall. Say again, I will be at your position in about," Steve calculated an approximate distance using the signal strength and power of his radio, factoring in atmospheric conditions as well, "five hours, and we'll be within radio contact with Port Hardy another three hours after that. It's the best I can do."

"Understood, Captain," Hauser replied, realizing he'd drifted much farther out into the open Pacific than he'd thought and understanding just how lucky he'd been that someone was monitoring a radio this late in these usually quiet waters. They were almost two hundred miles from the nearest sea lanes.

"We'll monitor this frequency until we have you visually. *Suzy's Pride* out." Steve set the mike back onto its cradle.

He climbed back up to the wheelhouse. George Boudette stood behind the wheel, riding the waves that were starting to buck against the boat's blunt prow. Josh stood next to him. Steve noticed that George had the engines throttled back an inch or so away from their maximum stops. He reached over and slammed the twin handles all the way forward. The diesels under the deck bellowed harshly in reply, and the ship started to vibrate. To run at this speed for more than a few hours would cause permanent damage to the engines and prop shafts.

"If the bank ends up with my boat after this, I'm going to make damned sure she isn't in working order when they get her."

COOK INLET,
ALASKA

From the dawn of civilization, man has demonstrated an uncanny aptitude for making use of the common natural elements found near his earliest settlements. But since the time of Sumer and Mesopotamia and ancient Egypt, humans have had few uses for the black sticky resins that bubbled up from deep within the earth. While some civilizations used the tarry substance for road construction and caulking boats, and Egyptian embalmers wrapped bitumen-soaked linen around mummies, the true potential of oil would remain unknown for millennia.

It wasn't until the middle of the nineteenth century, when the wheels of the Industrial Revolution began grinding together, that man returned to the stinking, slick pits of oil dotting the globe. This naturally skimmed oil was refined to make ideal industrial lubricants. At the same time, commercial whaling fleets were decimating the world's cetacean population, driving up the prices for whale oil until it was no longer a viable option for illuminating homes and factories. Again an oil derivative, kerosene, stepped in to fill this niche, ringing the death knell for New England's whalers. For approximately sixty years, as the oil companies refined kerosene, they burned off the waste products, most notably a highly flammable but useless product called gasoline. Untold millions, possibly billions of gallons were put to the torch.

Except for Edwin Drake's use of an old brine-well drill in Titusville, Pennsylvania, there were very few innovations in oil exploration and recovery during this time. His simple drilling rig and the collection of surface oil easily kept pace with the growing demand for kerosene. Necessity had no need to nurture invention, until two German engineers, Nikolaus Otto and Gottlieb Daimler, combined their respective inventions: one, a four-stroke internal-combustion engine fueled by gasoline, and the other, a carburetor device that injected a fine spray of fuel into engine cylinders. Daimler's idea had actually come from his wife's perfume atomizer.

In conjunction with Edison's development of the electric light in 1879, the automobile shifted refinery production from kerosene to gasoline. The race was on to supply the unparalleled demand for fuel that kept the new automobiles on the roads.

The oil industry, as we know it today, was born.

By 1901, the modern rotary drilling rig was in use at Spindletop in Texas, and within a year there were nearly four hundred wells in the area. Very quickly, the hunt for oil began reaching out into the oceans. H. L. Williams' early experiment in drilling for oil from specially built wharves in Summerland, California, led to freestanding drill platforms built on log pilings driven into the silty waters of the Gulf of Mexico. The demand for oil forced companies to push deep into the realm of discovery and invention as well as search geographically. By 1930, a worker could almost walk across Venezuela's Lake Maracaibo on the huge number of drilling rigs.

The search pushed farther into areas where man was an outsider, an unwanted interloper who, without modern technology, wouldn't stand a chance of surviving, let alone recovering the huge amounts of oil society was now demanding. The drilling rigs went deeper, one hundred feet, two hundred, a thousand, three thousand. The search would end only when the oil ran out. Yet depth wasn't the only obstacle needed to be overcome by these offshore platforms.

Such is the capriciousness of nature that she placed some

of her greatest oil reserves in her most inhospitable spots: the Persian Gulf, where searing temperatures turn lubricants to water; the Gulf of Mexico, where African's great sandstorms eventually became two-hundred-mile-per-hour hurricanes; the North Sea, where the full fury of the North Atlantic batters the European coastline. And now, oil companies were making their first tentative forays into the ice-choked waters of Prudhoe Bay in the Arctic Ocean, defiantly building structures designed to withstand the crushing pressure of the polar ice sheet.

While every innovation in offshore technology is hailed as the latest, state-of-the-art development and is sure to prove to be the last word in design, it is always eclipsed by something newer and better, usually within just a few months. However, sitting in the mouth of Cook Inlet, anchored in the shallow waters and rising like a city above the dark waters, the *Petromax Prudhoe Omega* would deservedly carry the banner as the latest and best design in oil drilling and production rigs well into the twenty-first century.

Built as a Tethered Buoyant Platform (TBP), the *Omega*, as her name implied, was the last word in drilling technology. Her rectangular base, called a template jacket, encompassed nearly three acres and was supported by four floating caissons nearly ninety feet in circumference. Each leg was anchored to the seafloor with five pretensioned catenary mooring lines. She loomed two hundred and seventy feet above sea level to the top of her tallest utility crane and weighed roughly 425,000 tons.

In a line that stretches unbroken from the building of the Great Pyramids up to the modern age, the *Petromax Prudhoe Omega* represented the latest expression of man the builder and his desire to show both his will and ingenuity.

The helicopter carrying Mercer, Ivan Kerikov, and Jan Voerhoven had made good time rocketing southward from Pump Station Number 5. As the sleek craft headed out over the water, the pilot eased the chopper lower, the whirling disk of its rotors now only fifty feet from the flat surface of Cook Inlet.

"Tides," he said to an uninterested Kerikov, who sat next

to him in the cockpit of the executive helicopter, "that's the real danger of the Inlet. Oh, sure, you get a few big waves coming up from the Gulf of Alaska and occasionally a tall iceberg in winter, but the big danger is the tides. They'll rise thirty or more feet in ten hours and produce currents that'll stop a freighter under full steam. That's why most cargo is dropped at Whittier and trained into Anchorage, rather than struggle up the inlet."

The pilot hadn't shut his mouth since leaving the TAPline pump station, and his inane observations were driving Kerikov mad. Despite the capture of Philip Mercer and the few hours remaining before Charon's Landing's imminent success, Kerikov was in a black, foul mood. His stomach was knotted tightly, acids eating away at his insides so fiercely that he could feel the rumble even with the helicopter rattling around him. He feared he was slipping into another rage, one of those mindless blank periods where violence and death lurked.

He fought it grimly, the way a passenger on a rough boat fights seasickness, jaw clenched, mind tuned to anything other than the present surroundings. He felt as if there was another person within him fighting to be free, forcing him to struggle to maintain his own identity. The tension of the past year, of his entire life, was finally tearing him apart. He held on doggedly, refusing to give in, refusing to lose himself to his own madness. If only the simpleton flying the helicopter would shut his mouth.

He jerked his head sideways when the chopper pitched violently, amazed to see blood drooling from the corner of the pilot's mouth. Kerikov glanced down and saw a matching stain on the back of his hand. He had no recollection of striking the man. The pilot regarded him with shocked fear, and Kerikov smiled in response. He turned to see how his passenger was doing.

Mercer sat between Kerikov's bodyguard and Jan Voerhoven. He was bound and gagged with silver duct tape, yet there was a defiance to him and a fathomless look in his eyes. As Kerikov watched, Mercer winked, and behind the thick gag, he was sure the geologist was smiling at him. Trussed and under armed guard, totally helpless, Mercer was mocking him.

Unbelievable.

"There it is," the pilot said timidly after a few minutes.

In the darkness, the true size of the *Petromax Prudhoe Omega* could not be fully appreciated, especially when she was not in production, her two-hundred-foot-long flare stack dim, her deck lights all but extinguished. Only a few of her eight hundred portholes were lit, and these were so spread apart that they looked like they were on different structures. The red warning strobes atop the cranes were separated by five hundred feet and towered two hundred feet above the helicopter. Yet even the barest outline of the rig demanded awe and respect.

Nearing the *Omega,* the chopper gained enough altitude to reach one of the two helidecks cantilevered off the side of the living module. The crew's living quarters was a boxy structure the size of a city block, able to accommodate six hundred men, and yet was the smallest of the four modules that made up the rig's superstructure. The others, the utilities, the production, and the drilling modules, independently built and attached to the rig before it was towed to Alaska, were many times larger. In the glow cast by the chopper's landing lights, the upper works of the rig gleamed whitely, contrasting with the red decking and the spindly yellow stalks of her cranes and flare boom. The Petromax Oil logotype was stenciled on the landing pad, a grate that allowed the down blast of the rotor to pass through and ease landing operations.

The chopper flared for its landing, the retractable gear just kissing the steel deck. Two workers rushed forward to secure blocks around the tires. The turbine spooled down, and the rotor slowed until it turned with little more effort than a tired ceiling fan. Kerikov was the first to jump from the craft. He opened the passenger door and grabbed Mercer by the shoulder, dragging him out of the chopper and across the windswept deck. His dark mood had been eclipsed by a brittle cheer that was just as dangerous.

Duck-walking his bound prisoner, Kerikov led Mercer to the edge of the landing pad. Without pause for the dramatic effect of standing one hundred feet over the frigid water, he shoved at the small of Mercer's back, and Mercer flew out into space.

With his hands tied and his mouth gagged, Mercer couldn't even scream as he began to fall. His gray eyes went wide with fear and dismay. A second later, he hit the safety netting slung around the landing pad, one leg falling through the thick ropes, his headlong plummet arrested after a drop of only six feet. He was high enough above the waves crashing against the caisson legs to hear Kerikov's deep laughter over his head.

"Did you shit your pants, brave man?" the Russian called down joyfully. "I bet when my men get down there to pull you off the net, they'll have to hold their noses."

He hadn't soiled himself, but it had been a near thing. Lying on the net, Mercer's breath came in painful draws through his nose, his heart hammering against his ribs. The suddenness of the push had panicked him more than the drop itself. It had been so quick, so unpredictably violent. As two men came to roll him off the netting and onto a narrow catwalk, Mercer knew that before the night was over, he would be going over the edge again, and the next time there would be no safety net.

He was right.

ALTHOUGH the title Tool Pusher connotes a hardened, hands-on type job, one involving the very heart of drilling operations, right at the rotary table and elbow deep in gushing crude and drill mud, it is in fact bestowed on the foreman of the drilling crew. On a rig as large as the *Omega,* the job was largely bureaucratic in nature. Therefore, the cabin reserved for the Tool Pusher was large and quite comfortable, much like an executive suite in a luxury hotel.

Ivan Kerikov was sitting on a deep green couch with a glass in his hand and a fresh cigar glowing amber in his right fist, when Mercer was brought into the room. The lights in the cabin were harsh compared to the gloom of the helicopter, but it took his eyes only a second to adjust. There was no sign of Jan Voerhoven. Kerikov's face still registered the pleasure he'd felt pushing Mercer off the platform.

"It's ironic." Kerikov waved for one of the guards to un-wrap the tape binding Mercer's mouth. "Had you not iden-tified yourself as a geologist, I would have killed you on the spot, never guessing that the man I wanted most in the world was before me. Granted, I would have lost the pleasure of watching you die slowly, but it would have spared you hours, maybe days of torture. Your humor is going to cost you more pain than you thought possible."

The tape came away like searing water poured across his lips, and Mercer gasped. While he had wanted to come across Ivan Kerikov again at some point in his life, Mercer would have preferred the circumstances to be reversed. But he wasn't about to show that his current predicament bothered him much. "Tell me, that rock you crawled out from under, are you sure it didn't move away from you on its own?"

"Always the wit, eh? Is this to be the great verbal duel between the villain and the hero, the forces of good and evil speaking before the final confrontation?"

"If that's what you want, I'm game. Me, I'm just stalling until the army arrives with a couple dozen gunships and re-duces this oil rig to scrap."

"Like those choppers I destroyed tonight? I don't think so. Not this time." Kerikov sipped his drink, his face and voice calm, conversational. "You haven't had enough time to mount even a rudimentary counterattack. Tonight's minor annoyance was the best you could come up with. Considering your rep-utation, I expected a little more from you."

"Give me some credit," Mercer smiled with mock modesty. "I did dodge two assassination attempts in the past week."

"Amateurs hired in haste, nothing more," Kerikov dis-missed. "My mother could have handled them in her sleep."

"Remind me never to piss off your mother," Mercer mut-tered quietly. "Does PEAL know that Alyeska will have the line back in service within a few months?"

"Trust me, they won't. While our little ecologists believe that their acts are designed to clog the pipeline, I assure you it is going to burst in about eighty places and spill around five hundred thousand barrels of oil." Kerikov paused. "That's about twenty-one million gallons of crude, roughly double what the *Exxon Valdez* lost in 1989."

"Freezing the oil in the line won't crack the pipe. The steel liner is over a half inch thick, and there's not enough internal pressure to split it," Mercer pointed out.

"You're right, but when I say so, there's going to be more than enough pressure to see oil scattered a couple of miles from the line." Kerikov gave him a greasy smile.

Suddenly, Mercer was afraid for much more than his own life. There was little doubt that Kerikov was telling the truth. He had a way of bursting the Trans-Alaska Pipeline like an eight-hundred-mile-long balloon. As someone who'd worked in some of the more pristine places on the planet, struggling to balance the needs of mankind with the delicacy of nature, Mercer didn't want to think about the devastation such a catastrophe would create. The state of Alaska would be bisected by a black line of crude, an ugly stain that would take years to clean, assuming it was possible to fully erase so much damage. He couldn't believe, no matter how radical and dangerous PEAL was, that they would condone such a heinous act in order to further their cause. This situation made as much sense as a Palestinian terror group using a nuclear bomb on Jerusalem. Groups like PEAL wanted to garner attention to their cause, not destroy the very thing they strove to protect.

They would readily agree to freezing the oil, shutting down the TAPline for a couple of months or forever if that's what they'd been lead to believe. That would be a great victory for their cause. But to actually destroy it? Spill the hundreds of thousands of barrels of oil it contained? They would never agree to it.

He tried to imagine Aggie Johnston being part of something so repugnant, something that went against every law of nature and man, and he felt that she never would. There was no way she would sit idle while her group destroyed Alaska, leading Mercer to believe that she knew nothing about Kerikov's ultimate goals. And if she, Jan Voerhoven's girlfriend, knew nothing, then it was certain that the rank and file of the organization had been equally duped. Anger welled within him, anger at Kerikov and anger at himself for not realizing the danger sooner, for not sounding the alarm when he first found the *Jenny IV*.

Kerikov watched as the change swept through Mercer. He was a good enough judge of moods and character to almost read the thoughts of those around him. It was a gift that had served him well throughout his career in the Soviet Union. "You are just beginning to see the enormity of what I've done," he sneered. "Consider this: What happens here, the destruction of the line and the devastation to the precious ecosystems, is nothing more than a sideshow for my true aims. It's only one tine in a three-pronged operation. Had Russia ever had the balls to use it, Charon's Landing would have ended here in Alaska, but I've expanded it, adapted it to the world today and made it astronomically profitable. You would be amazed at the number of people who want to see the United States still dependent on imported oil," he chuckled harshly. "And you'd be surprised to learn that many of them are Americans themselves."

"Charon's Landing? That's the name of this little adventure?"

"Originally it was a Cold War scheme to slow American oil production while our forces launched a lightning attack into Western Europe. The plan called for a combined commando assault against the pipeline and the terminal facility. The planners envisioned the region around Valdez turning into a conflagration of mythic proportions, so they named it after the site where the mythological ferryman, Charon, docked his boat after leading the souls of the dead across the River Styx."

"Hell."

"Precisely."

"Why don't you tell me your other fronts," Mercer invited as casually as possible. "What do you have to lose?"

As soon as he'd spoken, Mercer knew he'd made a mistake. Kerikov's entire carriage changed. No longer did he slouch in his seat. He set his cigar in the glass tray on the table to his left and put down his drink, taking a few seconds to arrange it on a previous water stain. Kerikov's face, brutal at its best, was absolutely deadly when he turned back to his prisoner, his thick eyebrows pulled tightly together as if to keep his eyes from bursting from their sockets.

"Just because I've found you wanting as an adversary doesn't mean I'm going to get stupid with you." Kerikov's voice was chilling, dredged up from some deep well of hatred. "Alam, get in here!" The paneled door swung open and Abu Alam, "Father of Pain," entered, the Fianchi SPAS-12 semi-auto shotgun hanging from its special rig against his lean flank. There was a dangerous edge to him that Mercer could feel from across the room.

"Can I have him now?" Alam asked.

"No. I want him locked up with the other, and I don't want either of them touched until later. We have a great deal to finish tonight."

"You promised me, and by the blood of the holymen, I'll make you pay if I don't get them."

Mercer knew that the jittery maniac was afraid that the opportunity to kill him and some other prisoner would be taken away from him. And it was clear he would enjoy the task.

He also saw there was a rivalry between these two. Anyone could tell that the Arab resented taking orders from Kerikov. Without knowing who, Mercer sensed that Alam worked for someone else and that his being with Kerikov was on behalf of this other person. The alliance was one of convenience, nothing more. Not that it really mattered, he thought, considering his circumstances, but Mercer would have loved to know who that other person was.

"We have more important tasks than to worry about our guests." Kerikov glanced at Mercer, no longer considering him a threat, then looked again at Abu Alam. "Get a few satchel charges from the stores I brought aboard. After we're finished tomorrow, I guarantee you'll be able to enjoy yourself with our esteemed doctor here. The other prisoner, well, we have to wait about that for now."

"It's time to do away with the activists?" Alam asked brightly.

"It's time to make the preparations, yes." Kerikov's patience with Alam was wearing thin. It appeared to Mercer that he was having trouble reining in the Arab's desire for death and his love of pain and suffering. "Now take him below, get the explosives, and meet me back here. I want to be off the rig within the hour."

To Mercer, it sounded as if part of Kerikov was patronizing Abu Alam while some deeper element was in total accordance with the young assassin. Despite Kerikov's more sophisticated polish, and his more urbane attitude, he was just as sick as the Arab killer. It was like comparing the madness of Hitler to that of his henchman, Joseph Goebbels—darker and lighter shades of the same evil.

Alam yanked Mercer from his chair and shoved him across the room. Mercer calculated the odds of escape and rejected the idea as suicidal. His hands were still bound, and Alam and his two agents had seven visible guns between them. He knew they would love a chance to draw one or all of them and cut him in two, so he allowed himself to be pushed around. The sinking feeling of defeat was overcoming him. He was facing an optionless situation, a trap with no escape, a puzzle with no solution. But he would not let it end here. At the doorway, Mercer turned to look at Kerikov once more. The Russian quietly sipped his drink as if he hadn't a care in the world.

"It's too bad that the computers in Valdez detected a drop in the temperature of the oil moving through the pipeline two weeks ago. One of your nitrogen packs leaked, Kerikov. Alyeska has been following behind your PEAL work crew, removing the packs just as quickly as they were attached."

Kerikov swiveled around, searching Mercer's face with an expression bordering on pity. When he spoke he almost sounded sad, as if Mercer's bluff was too pathetic to warrant a response. "Of course, you're lying," he smirked. "I've had control of those computers for nearly a month. There hasn't been a single anomalous reading since I tapped in. I really did expect more from you."

Gotcha, Mercer said to himself.

Abu Alam jammed the barrel of his shotgun into Mercer's back, forcing him out into the hallway. For now, his only choice was to allow Alam to lead him into the mechanical decks of the rig, where the brightly lit corridors gave way to a warren of twisting crawl spaces and work shafts whose function Mercer couldn't even guess.

They walked for nearly fifteen minutes, and even with his strong sense of direction, developed over years of working in labyrinthine mines, Mercer was lost. He knew he was deep within the superstructure of the oil rig, but he couldn't pinpoint exactly where. The dark serpentine walkways merged from one to another so easily that every new junction resembled the previous. If he had any hope of escape, only Ariadne's string could save him from this maze.

They stopped in front of a six-foot hatch, its dogging wheel all the way open. It was as unremarkable as the two dozen similar hatches they had passed during their silent march through the *Omega*. Mercer spun, but his captor had already stepped back, the black SPAS-12 held levelly.

"Open it," Alam barked, and one of his men heaved at the doorway, revealing a tiny room beyond. Alam had his shotgun ready, as if he expected to see someone standing in the phonebooth–sized cabin. Mercer realized that he was looking into an elevator car. The drilling rig was so new that the lubricant used to grease the hatch was still a clear yellow, not yet darkened by dirt and grime.

"Inside." Alam prodded Mercer again.

He stepped into the small elevator, expecting Alam to disobey Kerikov and shoot him in the back, but the blast did not come. Although he knew it was futile, Mercer tried to reason with Alam. "You know you're not going to get away with this. You're going to be caught and killed."

"I pray for nothing more than a martyr's death fighting the Great Satan," Alam said, and his two men nodded in agreement.

"Be careful what you wish for, it may come true." The door was slammed in his face, and the car began to drop.

There was no real elevator car, just a cagelike platform guided by a rail on its back side. It fell sedately into one of the rig's massive hollow support columns, the walls opening up around Mercer, widening and curving like the insides of a huge grain silo. Looking out over the open edge of the car, he guessed the fall to be about one hundred feet. The bottom of the shaft was just a dark circle from his perspective, no larger than a manhole cover.

Down the platform dropped, the guide wheels passing slickly along its rail, the great open void sucking at him. Mercer had never suffered from vertigo before, but it didn't seem a good time to push his luck. He kept his eyes fixed on the opposite wall of the featureless shaft. The air was chilled and humid, condensation droplets clinging to the pale blue walls like clear, fat leeches. At one point, Mercer could feel that the elevator had passed below the water line, the temperature plummeting a further twenty degrees. He pulled his leather jacket tighter around his body.

When he finally reached the bottom, it took only a few minutes to cut the tape binding his wrists by rubbing it against the accordion gate affixed to the floor. He located the controls that would send the elevator back to the top of the support leg to his right, but they had been sabotaged. The call buttons dangled from their housing on a few blackened wires. Mercer mashed the green button anyway, pressing it with all of his strength as if sheer force would convince the disabled elevator to begin rising.

Nothing happened. It had been shorted so only the upper controls still functioned. He was trapped in a modern-day version of the medieval pit. Without waiting for the full effect of his predicament to sink in, Mercer began to explore for another way out, starting first with the elevator itself. The cable that lowered the car was his best hope, and he scrambled on top of the open-sided car to examine it more closely.

As he expected, the finely braided steel cable was slick with grease. It was so slippery that he was barely able to grasp it and knew it would be impossible to climb. Yet he had to try, and just as he gathered himself to begin pulling himself upward, a voice from the gloom warned him.

"When I tried that, I fell and almost broke my leg."

"Aggie?" Mercer couldn't believe he'd heard correctly, but it was her voice echoing inside the huge cylinder. "What the hell are you doing here?"

He looked around the dimly lit space at the bottom of the support leg. The circular room was enormous but spartan. Half of it was occupied by machinery that looked as if it had come from the nightmares of a demented plumber. It was impossible to completely trace the twisting path of even one of the hundreds of pipes with their countless valves, gauges, and spurs. A low counter with storage doors and a near-empty tool rack stood a little way off from the tangled steel forest. The deck was mostly solid plating, but there were several large grates that would give access to even lower levels.

"Rereading *War and Peace,* what do you think I'm doing? I'm a prisoner just like you." Aggie stepped from around a large watertight cabinet and into a dim pool of light given by a low-watt bulb.

Mercer jumped back to the floor, crossing the distance between them in a few quick strides. He gathered her in his arms and pressed his lips to hers, feverishly kissing her as if nothing else mattered or ever would.

A moment later she stepped back, breathless. "Where did that come from?"

"I don't know," Mercer replied with a sheepish smile. "But you can't deny it felt good."

"You won't hear me complaining, but you haven't picked a very romantic spot to demonstrate your affection." Her eyes were a bright, rich green, although the rest of her was ragged, worn by whatever ordeal she had undergone.

"Are you okay?"

She nodded. Mercer asked how long she'd been on the rig.

"I was grabbed in the parking lot of your hotel just after I left you. Two men attacked me. They killed some poor hotel guest and then drove me away in a van. They drugged me, and when I came to, I was here." Her voice was strong and filled with determination, but she looked delicate and frail, like a child. At the same time, she was such a woman that Mercer was distracted from his current predicament and stole a minute to just look at her, to drink her in. Aggie became self-conscious almost immediately, raking her hand through her short hair in a nervous gesture.

"What?" she said. "Don't look at me. I'm a mess."

"No, you're not. You're beautiful," he breathed, embarrassed by his emotional response to her presence. He broke eye contact, looking around the space quickly. "We've got to find a way out of here and stop them. Do you have any idea what your group is about to do?"

"I didn't until I talked with that sick Russian bastard. He told me about how he and PEAL are going to freeze the oil in the pipeline."

"That's only half of it. He plans to split it wide open and spill five hundred thousand barrels of crude all across Alaska."

Aggie turned pale, her deep sense of love for the environment shaking her to the core. "God, no, he can't do that."

"I'm afraid he can and will, unless we can stop him. And another thing. Your boyfriend has been in the thick of this thing since the very beginning."

"No way," Aggie defended Jan Voerhoven automatically. "I believed Kerikov when he told me Jan helped attach the liquid gas canisters, but there is no way he would allow the pipe to be cut and its contents spilled. He would die first."

"It's possible he doesn't know all of Kerikov's plans," Mercer admitted. "But that doesn't mean he's not a willing accomplice to the largest act of sabotage in history. Now, I want to see if I can get that elevator working."

"I already tried. The power's been cut to the controls down here, and there's nothing we can use to jumper the circuits." She spoke with authority. "It's my bet that the breaker was shut off at the topside box."

Mercer felt a twinge of chauvinism, thinking that she probably didn't know anything about electronics and that he could somehow sort out the jumbled wires hanging from the control. He looked at them briefly, then turned back to Aggie. She watched him with an almost patronizing smirk. "I thought you had a degree in environmental sciences or something?"

"That was my master's. My father demanded that I do my undergrad studies in mechanical and electrical engineering."

"Really?"

"It was all part of his grand plan to get me ready to take over Petromax. He knew I never would, of course, but he still had hopes that I'd give up environmental activism."

"Okay," Mercer conceded. "What about option two?"

"Which is?"

"I don't know. Hell, I don't know where we are, except to say we're not in Kansas anymore."

Aggie took on the persona of a bubbly tour guide. "Before you, we have the auxiliary buoyancy pump controls for support column three of the *Petromax Prudhoe Omega,* a TBP built for Petromax Oil by Sosen Heavy Industries in Pusan, Korea, at a cost of $1.4 billion. Commissioned in 1998 and completed eighteen months later by a crew of two thousand men working around the clock. The *Omega* uses every safety device yet developed for offshore structures, from Baldt Moor-Free acoustic detonators on all twenty of the compliant tension cables to no fewer than fifteen lifeboat spaces for every member of the crew. Since she was designed to work in arctic conditions, the *Omega* utilizes an Integral Riser system for all subsurface flow and control lines, pre-tensioned to prevent shearing due to surface conditions or ice buildup. Her multiple blowout preventers are rated at sixty thousand pounds per square inch to keep down hole gas and oil from bursting up to the surface.

"She has accommodations for six hundred men, carries 250,000 gallons of fresh water, 500,000 gallons of diesel for her pumps, drills, and other machinery, and when in full production can provide the total energy needs of a city the size of Rochester, New York." Aggie smiled saucily. "Anything else you want to know? Don't forget this is my daddy's rig. He managed to get me to launch her for him last June before she was towed here for pre-staging and testing. She's going to be brought to Prudhoe Bay next spring."

Mercer was impressed. "I've always loved a smartass, especially when she's right. If you know so much, then how do we get out of here?"

Aggie turned quiet again, chastened. "The elevator is the only way, so we're stuck until Kerikov or that disgusting Arab comes for us. By the way, he was the guy you clobbered in the bar, the one groping me. He was also part of the duo who kidnapped me at your hotel."

"Reasons two and three for me wanting him dead." Mercer tried to make that sound light, but his voice was frigid. "Let's look around, inventory everything that's down here and come up with a plan."

Twenty minutes later they had scoured the huge auxiliary control room, pulling tools and other supplies from water-proof cabinets and stowage lockers. When they finished, the pile of equipment was pathetically small, most of it worthless; two boxes of hand tools, wrenches, screwdrivers, pliers, and the like; four rolls of duct tape; four sections of one-inch pipe, the longest one only six feet in length; and a torn Sterns flotation suit, its safety orange cover blackened by grease and several of its Ensolite foam flotation cells punctured and empty. They found a large blue polypropylene tarp and two empty oxygen cylinders like the type worn by firefighters, but no masks or regulators. The room also gave up a first aid kit, a diver's flipper, and a container of decayed food forgotten by a worker during the construction of the rig.

"It's hopeless." Aggie put a voice to what both were feeling.

A minute passed. Mercer looked at the clutter, then glanced up to the top of the huge cylindrical caisson. It was like looking up from the bottom of a well. Another minute went by until finally he looked at Aggie, his eyes brightening. "You said auxiliary pump controls?" She nodded. "Can you run them?"

"Yes, but what does it matter?"

"I'll have us out of here in a couple of hours," Mercer predicted with a devilish smile.

"Are you nuts?"

"No. I float."

ABOARD THE *PETROMAX*
PRUDHOE OMEGA

Kerikov stepped from the shower cabinet, his usually gray skin now pink and glowing, the hair on his chest and back matted down like a pelt. He wrapped one towel around his waist and used another to dry himself. He'd already shaved, using the comforting routine of morning ablutions to revive himself. It was now three o'clock in the morning, and he hadn't slept for nearly thirty hours. The shower had done wonders, almost as much as the second Scotch he'd poured himself before entering the bathroom.

He was just beginning to dress when there was a knock on the cabin door. Abu Alam entered without being invited, swaggering to the couch and eyeing Kerikov's nudity with a mixture of hatred and sexual interest. The Arab disgusted Kerikov like no one he'd ever met before.

"He's down in the hole with the woman now," Alam reported. "I don't understand why we just don't kill them both."

"Because I won't be rushed in dealing with Mercer. It's a personal matter. As for the woman, she's the daughter of one of our principals, and her presence here is to ensure he fulfills his end of our bargain. If Max Johnston decides to expose us after he learns of our double cross, the woman will be yours for as long as you wish, provided we send videotapes of your time together to her father." Kerikov imagined the young heiress being raped and sodomized to death by Alam and his two assistants. "However, if he fulfills our agreement, she is to be released immediately, and if I hear that she has been touched, I'll kill you myself."

Alam was skeptical. "No one frightens me with idle threats."

Kerikov ignored his posturing. "Go find our friend Voerhoven and let's get back to Valdez. When PEAL pulls out from Pump Station 5, they're going to make the road northward impassable by blowing up several bridges. That leaves us only a few hours before the authorities are finished with the fires in Fairbanks, freeing up helicopters to investigate what happened at the station. How much time do you need to plant the explosives aboard the *Hope*?"

"Do you want it totally destroyed, or just sunk?"

"I don't want a piece of debris larger than a postage stamp," Kerikov intoned.

"Maybe an hour, two at most. I've got to be able to get the charges around all the fuel bunkers and, using Primacord, time the detonations so the concussion blows out both sides of the hull simultaneously." Alam spoke with the competence ingrained in him by years of terrorist training, first in Algeria and later in the streets of Lebanon and the desert bases of Libya, Iran, and Iraq.

Kerikov watched the slight nervous twitch that had developed in Alam's cheek. It was so subtle and infrequent that had he not been looking for it he never would have noticed. Alam, Kerikov suspected, had orders to kill him as soon as he'd destroyed the Alaskan Pipeline and orchestrated the sinking of a supertanker off the continental coast of the United States. Rufti was going to betray him.

Kerikov had known this would be coming even before he approached Rufti. The Arab was so transparent it was almost sad. Did he really think that Kerikov didn't have ways of protecting himself from a double cross?

Lord protect us from the ambitions of imbeciles.

MERCER managed only a few words of explanation about his escape plan when Aggie's face went bright red with fury. "You're out of your mind. Do you have any idea what that would do? The balance of one of these monsters has to be monitored twenty-four hours a day. When winter hits, even though she won't be in production, a crew will be aboard to make sure that ice buildup doesn't affect the rig's stability. On a platform this size, a two-inch coating of ice weighs something like four hundred and fifty tons and could turtle her if left unchecked.

"And you're talking about knocking out the balance by a magnitude of a hundred. If the *Omega* is deck loaded, her pipe racks filled with drill string, her bunkers and drill mud storage ponds full, she'll flip long before we reach the top of the leg. Remember the 500,000 gallons of diesel I mentioned earlier? That'll become a slick covering the entire inlet if the rig nose-dives."

"Aggie, if you'll just let me—"

She cut him off as if he hadn't opened his mouth. "Environmental considerations aside, you can't possibly think we'd survive long enough in the water even if we did manage to make it all the way up. Jesus, it's just above freezing in here. We'd be hypothermic in twenty minutes and dead five minutes after that."

She was working herself into a frenzy, and although she had very valid points, Mercer knew it was fear that was making her protest so much. He couldn't blame her. What he proposed scared the hell out of him too.

"Aggie, for Christ's sake shut up for a minute and let me finish." She quieted, pulling at the collar of her anorak protectively. "You know as well as I do it's the only way. If we stay here, we're both dead, so why not at least try to escape? And do you think anyone's going to give a shit if this rig flips and spills its fuel into Cook Inlet when the rest of Alaska is covered by ten inches of crude? If there's a chance to get out of here, if we don't die of exposure, if the rig doesn't flip, and if we can warn Andy Lindstrom at the Marine Terminal, we can stop this whole nightmare before it starts. I know how Kerikov is going to split the pipeline after PEAL freezes the oil. All I need to stop him is a phone or a radio to make a ten-second call."

She wavered, her fear slowly dissipating as she too saw the larger issues at stake. Either way it went, their lives were over, so why not die trying? He could see it in her eyes when she decided to agree to his plan. "I still think you're nuts."

"It'll work. Trust me."

"Last time I heard that was from a forty-nine-year-old professor I agreed to go to bed with," she joked. "It didn't."

Mercer's plan was born of desperation but was, in theory, incredibly simple. He intended to flood the hollow support column of the *Petromax Omega*. Using the manual override on the auxiliary pump controls, they could fill the entire two-million-cubic-foot cylinder with seawater. He and Aggie would float on the surface of the rising water until they reached the elevator doors one hundred feet above. As Aggie pointed out, the greatest danger was unbalancing the entire rig as thousands of tons of ballast filled one support while the others remained empty. For that, Mercer could only hope for the best. As to her other concern, hypothermia, Mercer had a plan to keep them dry. While he got busy building an improvised raft, one in which his own body formed the bottom, Aggie worked on the bewildering forest of pipes, valves, and controls that made up the pump units. The pumps, six in total, were located a farther fifty feet below them, but all their controls were here. At Mercer's prompting, she explained the system as she worked.

· "Each jacket—that's what these legs are called in the oil industry—is computer linked from the primary pump control in the Operations Center, so each one can be individually ballasted depending on the conditions. In heavy seas, the entire rig can be lowered until the main deck is almost awash, or she can sit one hundred feet above the waves. The catenary mooring lines run through hydraulic lifts so that their tension is never reduced and the anchors remain firmly bedded, no matter what the attitude of the rig.

"My father," she admitted with a trace of pride, "was instrumental in the development of the entire system. His initial sketches were the basis of the entire forty thousand pages of the rig's blueprints.

"The weakest link, apart from your little raft capsizing, is the anchors themselves. I suspect they're Flipper Deltas built by the Dutch company Ankar Advies Bureau. They must be at least twenty tonners, which gives each anchor about four hundred tons of reactive force against the drag of the rig. That type is perfect for the soils around Prudhoe, but I'm not too sure about here in Cook Inlet. This is only a temporary anchorage for the *Omega*, and dead-on stability is not as critical as when she's in production. When the rig begins to dip with the added weight, and the kinematics angle of the anchor lines changes by as little as ten degrees, those anchors are going to lose about thirty-five percent of their efficiency. Push them too far, and they'll pull free completely."

Mercer understood maybe half of what Aggie said. He didn't have the slightest idea what a kinematics angle was nor did he really care. He just wanted to keep Aggie talking, let her calm herself, and him too, just by the simple act of using her voice. She continued on about tripping angles and flukes and palms and about the pump mechanisms themselves. Her knowledge was encyclopedic, her voice brisk yet incredibly alluring.

"Ready," she announced after nearly a half an hour. "I've taken the safeties off the flow regulators and depth gauges; the pumps will keep running even past the Never Exceed point. The system will shut down only when the topside electrical panels are shorted by flooding water."

"What about any warning indicators in the master control room?"

"There's nothing I can do about that," Aggie admitted. "Their board will light up like a Christmas tree when the cycloids kick on. We just have to hope that Kerikov hasn't left enough men on board to monitor those warning panels. If they do, your scheme can be shut down with a flip of a switch upstairs."

"Then let's hope they're in the bathroom right now, because I'm ready to go."

Mercer had repaired the torn Sterns survival suit, using an entire roll of duct tape to seal the countless rips and punctures in the nylon outer fabric. There was so much of the silver tape he looked like he wore a suit of armor. Almost as important as the suit, he tended himself with the supplies found in the first aid kit, spending almost ten minutes dressing his wounds, stanching the blood that still seeped from some of his deeper cuts and swallowing a couple of the codeine tablets he'd found. He'd need the drugs if he hoped to survive the upcoming ordeal.

His raft rested on several toolboxes and was a creation only Rube Goldberg would love. The four lengths of pipe they had found were taped together in a diamond shape, the tarp spread below it and secured to the framework with more tape. The craft was sized so that when Mercer lay his head at the apex of one corner, his hands could grab two others with his feet hanging over the bottom juncture. The indentation of his body against the loosely strung tarp would create the draft the raft needed to stay afloat and hopefully keep Aggie out of the water. Mercer wore the suit in case some water did slosh over the raft's low freeboard. With Aggie riding on his chest, she should remain dry. If they were swamped, the few extra minutes of protection Mercer got from the Sterns suit wouldn't really matter.

He had managed to scrape several large handfuls of grease from the elevator cable. Aggie watched in amazement as he smeared a large amount of it on the back of his head, working it through his thick hair, right to his scalp. "Don't worry, you're next."

"What for?"

"Channel swimmers have been doing this for years. The grease prevents the icy water from touching your skin, thus avoiding the greatest threat of the heat loss," he explained as he stooped before her and raised up her pant leg, smearing the thick grease against her smooth skin, trying hard not to think how erotic it felt.

He did the same to her wrists and neck. As his hands ran slickly over her throat, Aggie mewed almost like a contented kitten. "I wish you were doing this someplace else and the oil smelled like passion fruit, not heavy machinery."

He kissed her on the forehead and then began using the last roll of duct tape to cover her in long overlapping strips, masking her from head to toe. "Once we reach the top, we'll have to abandon the raft and tread water until we can open the elevator doors." He handed her the largest of the screwdrivers, and eighteen-inch piece of high carbon steel and plastic, a perfect pry bar to force the hatch at the head of the support column.

Aggie was trembling, and it wasn't only the cold air causing it. Both of them could be dead within the hour. For Mercer, it was a feeling he'd experienced before but had not grown used to. But it was something that went far beyond Aggie's realm of experience. Her beautiful face was pale, and her pouting lower lip quivered. Her eyes were glassy with unshed tears.

"We're going to make it, Aggie," Mercer said. "We have to."

She nodded up at him and could not resist kissing him, pressing herself against his body, wrapping her arms around him. It could be the last embrace either one would ever experience, and they made it special, something beyond fear and beyond a physical touch. A current passed between them in the frigid pump room, something tangible that neither could, or wanted to, deny. If they survived the next hour, it was something they both wanted to explore together.

"Are you ready?"

"Let's do it," Aggie replied, steeling herself.

Mercer settled himself on the raft, his head and feet in perfect position, his grease-slicked hands slipping through the loops of tape he'd made as handholds. The toolboxes under the framework would allow water to creep up underneath the raft and float them free. Otherwise, the raft would have simply filled with water as the cavernous chamber flooded.

Aggie went to the controls, pressing several rubberized buttons in succession, each motion bringing another pump online. The noise of the huge turbine pumps built quickly, echoing off the steel walls in a shrieking cry as four thousand gallons per minute were forced through each one.

"The noise will die after the pumps are submerged," Aggie screamed, closing the watertight pressure doors that housed the electronic controls. "We've got about ten minutes before the water reaches this level."

"Get into position now," Mercer said from the floor. "We can't afford to be surprised."

Aggie lay down on top of him, her back pressed to his chest, her bottom cupped around his waist almost sexually. He shook under her to dislodge her.

"Not like that. Stay on your back but turn around so your

head is on my thighs, your legs around my head. That'll distribute the weight better."

She did as he ordered, shifting nimbly. Their position afforded Mercer a view of the mysterious place between her spread thighs. He quickly purged his mind of those thoughts and concentrated on the task at hand.

The wait was interminable. They lay quietly, not speaking to each other even when the pumps were finally submerged and their piercing whine was dulled to a low whoosh. The water was rising so fast they could feel the air being pushed ahead of it in an icy gale, a tease of the true cold to come. Minutes dragged by. Mercer kept glancing to the side, expecting to see the water rushing through the floor grates in a frothing roil. Yet it would not come.

Every second felt slower than the previous, expectation and fear bringing them both to the point where neither could lie still. They nervously scratched at imaginary itches or twisted to get more comfortable. Mercer was breathing so deeply that the motion of his lungs forced Aggie to bend even farther in an already uncomfortable position.

The sound of the rushing water was getting louder, the wind blowing more fierce. It would happen at any moment. Mercer turned once again to look to their left. Just then the water came like a geyser.

"Here we go!" he shouted over the din. They were lifted up off the toolbox cradle even before he had finished speaking.

Like a kite caught in a brutal updraft, the makeshift raft was plucked from the deck in a gut-wrenching swoop. Water splashed over the side at an alarming rate, drops hitting their exposed faces like needle jabs. Within seconds, six inches of icy saltwater were pooled around Mercer's bent waist, inches from soaking into Aggie's buttocks. If any more came aboard and drenched her, she would be dead before they reached to the top of the caisson.

But Mercer couldn't dwell on that now; he had something more immediate to worry about. His weight, plus hers pressing down on him, was almost too much for him to bear. The straps he'd fashioned for his hands dug into his flesh, wrenching his arms painfully. It would take them thirty minutes to reach the top and he was already afraid he couldn't hold on for another thirty seconds.

The eddying water twisted the craft around, spiraling it on a tight axis. The raft was surprisingly stable considering the turgid water, but as they spun, more water slopped over the side. Mercer could feel it against the survival suit in the few areas where the insulation had been lost. The cold was biting. It numbed him so that his thigh felt as though it had been burned. And that was through the waterproofing of the Sterns suit and his jeans. If water got against his skin, he knew he wouldn't be able to stand it for more than a few minutes.

"How you doing?" he managed to ask, his teeth clenched from the stress of holding his body rigid.

"I don't think this is going to work," Aggie cried.

"That's what the Wright brothers said to each other." Mercer tried to put a little cheer in his voice.

"They failed the first time."

"We don't have that option."

While at first the ascent up the support leg seemed quick, the little raft rising alarmingly, their perception changed as the true nature of the challenge unfolded. Aggie was within a couple inches of being submerged by the water flooding onto the tarp, and there was nothing they could do about it. Mercer needed to keep a vise grip on the scaffold to maintain the raft's stability so he couldn't try to bail, and Aggie was having a hard time just holding her precarious balance. The first ten minutes were an absolute agony, and there was no reprieve as they continued.

Mercer's arms began to tremble as his strength waned, his body unconsciously sinking farther against the tarp, Aggie coming that much closer to hitting the water. She noticed the dip and cried out. He tightened up once again, his stomach and back knotting in great bunched cords. The strain was only slightly less than the gymnastics maneuver called the iron cross. It was forty-two degrees in the column, and he was sweating, salty sheets running down his face.

Aggie could sense his struggle. "Is there anything I can do to make this easier?"

It took him a few seconds to gather the strength to reply—
he was tapping out and they still had another sixty feet to the
top of the shaft. "Go on the fastest crash diet in history."

Slowly, too slowly, the water level rose, and the surface
calmed considerably from those first frightening moments
when they were caught in the initial upwell. The weld seams
on the walls marked their passage, each weld another ten feet
of progress, another ten feet less until the torture was over.
The top of the caisson still looked impossibly out of reach, a
shadow high over their heads, a dim goal that got darker as
another of the lights strung along the circular walls submerged.

At first, Mercer thought the pain that suddenly shot through
his upper thigh was a sharper stab of muscle cramp. A second
later, he realized that his suit was leaking. The near-freezing
water had found a way in through a tear he had missed, or
more likely the tape was beginning to fail. The water felt like
acid.

He cried out, his pain echoing over the sound of the pumps
and the bubbling water.

"What is it?"

"Hole in my suit, the water's getting in."

"Is it bad?"

"It ain't good," he moaned as more of his skin was doused
in icy water. So strong was the urge to try and rub some
warmth back to the spot, he had to shut his eyes and concentrate to maintain his grip on the scaffold. They had thirty feet
to go. "Aggie, you've got to arch your back, take your weight
off of me. I can't take this much longer."

She did as he asked, digging her boots into his shoulders,
her shoulders pressed against his shins so that when she
shifted, arcing in a parody of orgasm, the strain was taken up
by his bones rather than muscles. He gasped as her weight
came off of him, his back and stomach relaxing for the first
time in twenty minutes. The position was now as painful for
her as it had been for him. She bore it as long as possible,
her body made supple and strong through years of fencing
and exercise, but after only a few minutes, she had to lower
herself against him again.

"I'm sorry," she panted, "that's the best I can do."

"I'm all right now," he lied. "Besides, we're almost there."

Deep below the rig, in the black waters of the Sound, buried under eighteen feet of silty mud, the five huge anchors restraining number three support jacket were losing their mooring integrity as the leg began sinking, pulling at the fifteen other anchors holding the rig in position. To maintain their strength, the mooring lines must be rigid at all times. Aggie had been forced to take the automated tensioning hydraulics off-line in order for her to flood only the one leg. As more water filled the support, the catenary lines began to sag beyond their fracture points, and one by one they parted. The seven-inch-thick steel wires sheared cleanly, the anchored ends dropping silently into the gloom, the remainder hanging from the underside of the rig like the tentacles of some enormous jellyfish.

The other plow-shaped Delta Flipper anchors were so well placed that they hadn't dragged, and their tension was so strong that the rig began to pendulum back. Rather than listing toward the filled support leg, the *Omega* swung one hundred and eighty degrees in the opposite direction. Though the dynamics of the entire anchoring system was measured in the thousands of tons, the rig was now so unbalanced that every gallon of water cycling through the pumps and into the support column shifted the structure just a little more.

The twenty-knot incoming tide rushing past the platform was the only thing keeping the rig upright, pressing just enough against the legs to keep them stable. But the delicate balance of force, counterforce, weight, buoyancy, and drag wouldn't last as the pumps continued to fill the *Omega*'s buttress.

"Only a couple more feet," Aggie announced in amazement.

"How far are we from the elevator opening?" Mercer asked grimly. The proximity of their goal couldn't overcome his pain and the numbness that had spread through his lower body.

"We're coming up right below it. Your feet are only a couple of inches from the cable."

"As soon as we get close enough to the door, you have to jam the screwdriver between it and the casing. There should be a mechanical release to open it in case the automatic system doesn't work and someone is trapped in the car."

"Like in the movies?"

"Exactly."

Aggie tried to extend her arm, simulating the motions she would need to pry open the door. As soon as she moved her hand, she fell off Mercer's chest with a scream.

She hit the water pooled on the tarp and began to thrash, ripping through the plastic, and destroying the raft. Mercer let go of the struts, falling into the water with Aggie. The survival suit kept him buoyant, and he grabbed Aggie as she flailed. He pulled her close, trying to calm her before she drowned from her own panic.

"Oh, my God, it hurts. Oh, sweet Christ, I can't, I can't . . ." Her lips were blue as the freezing water seeped around the tape Mercer had used to cover her. "Mercer, please, oh, God, I'm going to die."

"Aggie! Aggie!" Mercer shouted, looking into her eyes but seeing he'd already lost her to fear. She stared back vacantly and he feared she'd gone into shock. He barely noticed or cared that the Sterns suit had failed and that he too was soaked to the skin. He had to get them out of the water in the next few seconds.

Just then, four of the twenty-ton anchors securing the off-shore platform were wrenched from the seabed in clouds of drifting silt, tearing huge furrows through the mud, relinquishing their combined thousand tons of counterforce. There was no stopping the *Omega* now. She was going to flip. There was too much weight on one corner of the rig, and without the anchors, the buoyancy of the other three legs would capsize her in minutes. Of the eleven anchors still holding fast, only three more had to fail before the platform upended and vanished beneath the waves.

The effects within column number three were instantaneous. One moment, Aggie and Mercer were struggling just below the elevator door, and the next second, the rig had dipped and rushing water forced them into the empty elevator vestibule. They were pressed to the very ceiling by Mercer's survival suit, totally submerged and held helpless by water pressure.

The icy water beat against Mercer's temples, sharp stabbing pulses that made him nauseous. His mind was nothing but a swirling gray cloud of pain. His reserves were gone. He'd failed. They were going to die.

Aggie's movement was so slight that he almost didn't feel it, yet unbelievably she pressed on his hand, opening his fingers and placing something against his palm. He didn't want to look, didn't want to open his eyes to the saltwater, but something forced him on. He glanced down and saw in the watery light that somehow, through her thrashing and her fear and her proximity to death, Aggie had maintained her grip on the screwdriver and had the presence of mind to place it in his hand.

He plunged the tool at the door, missing the seam by a good six inches with his drunken lunge, but the angle of his attack forced the flat point of the screwdriver to gouge along the door and lodge firmly in the crack. The tip found the release on the pressure bar. He hauled back on the handle and the door swung free, pushed outward by tons of water.

Aggie and Mercer burst through the narrow door in a rush, like the life-giving spill of birth, borne along the hallway by thousands of gallons of water, careening off the bulkheads and tumbling forty feet before smashing against a twist in the corridor, water surging around them in a diminishing torrent.

Both of them retched until their lungs ached, shivering in the steel hallway as water continued to gush past. They needed to stop, to take time to recover and strip out of their soaked clothing, but they couldn't. The *Petromax Omega* was bobbing like a pleasure boat caught in a rough storm, the tensioned mooring lines stretching beyond their maximum tolerances yet amazingly still holding. But each swing against them was stronger and stronger, as the top structure of the platform arced fifteen degrees against the gracefully swooping catenaries.

"We have to move," Mercer gasped, his jaw chattering like a jackhammer. "Can you walk?"

Aggie didn't respond—she had slipped into unconsciousness.

Ignoring his own needs, Mercer took the time to strip Aggie out of her clothing, yanking off her sodden jacket, sweater, and T-shirt and peeling her wet jeans from her legs, gaining a few more minutes before she froze to death. He looked down the corridor, closing his eyes for a moment, thinking back to the winding journey he'd taken to this spot while under guard by Abu Alam. He closed his mind to everything—his pain, the cold, the imminent destruction of the rig—and reconstructed the route corner by corner.

After defeating the Minotaur in Greek mythology, Theseus used a string to guide him back out of the labyrinth. Mercer had only his own clouded mind. Carrying Aggie, he ran through the empty passages, his feet pounding the steel battle deck as he backtracked the tortured path. Yet unerringly he negotiated intersections and stairs and doorways, making the correct decisions every step of the way, instinct driving him on. Had he stopped to think, he would have been lost in moments. The stark corridors of the rig's underworks were indistinguishable from one another. There were no remarkable objects to remind him of the proper route, yet still he ran, covering the distance back to the living module in half the time it had taken Alam to bring him to the support leg. Utilitarian steel walls gave way to faux wood paneling and thin carpet as he burst through an open hatchway and into the crew's quarters.

The deck was canted at least twenty degrees now, pushing him headlong down a wide hallway. The paneled doors of individual cabins blurred by as he ran, Aggie lying limply in his arms. He didn't dare pause to feel for a pulse. Alarms shrieked all along the corridor, red strobe lights pulsing like frantic heartbeats. Over the din, a computer-generated voice was telling all personnel to abandon the rig immediately.

Mercer kicked open an exit door, twisting himself so that Aggie passed through without hitting her head or dragging her legs against the steel frame. The stairs looked like something out of a funhouse, tipped so steeply that they were almost vertical. Mercer started up carefully, cautious to keep his balance as he climbed. It was like trying to scale a cliff face, and every second the rig pitched to a steeper angle. He slogged up two more flights before reaching the main deck and then dashed out into the windswept night.

When sensors had detected that the rig was listing, the computer had activated the emergency lights, bathing the deck in a pink sodium-vapor glow, the flare tower and cranes backlit against the darkness like monuments. Mercer strained through the glare as he searched for one of the yellow escape pods he'd noticed on the chopper ride in. They were slung along the edge of the module like lifeboats on a luxury liner.

Out in the open, the tilt of the huge platform was much more apparent. Mercer had thought they had a few minutes, but now saw that in seconds the *Petromax Omega* would flip onto her side and sink. He could only hope that Kerikov and Alam were still trapped belowdecks, but he knew it wasn't so. The helicopter that had carried them here was gone.

Aggie was dead weight against him as he lurched toward the edge of the towering platform, slipping on the deck as the rig angled further. The alarm bells were maddening in their insistence. Mercer crashed against the railing, managing to shield Aggie from the blow, his shoulder hitting only inches from an escape pod's razor-sharp propeller. The upper deck of the pod was a perfect cylinder, while its hull was deeply veed to give it stability in the roughest seas.

Not knowing how to work the sophisticated davits that would launch the raft, Mercer could only pray that the mechanism could be activated from within the pod. He wedged Aggie against the railing, freeing his hands to work the hatch, when suddenly the lifeboat lifted, swung out over the water, and vanished from sight so quickly he felt himself swaying toward the void it had created.

Some of Kerikov's men must have already been in the pod and used it to make their own escape.

Mercer had wasted time he couldn't afford. The next pod was twenty feet away. He gathered up Aggie and ran toward it, his hip scraping against the railing as he went; without its support he wouldn't have been able to keep on his feet. Halfway to the lifeboat, it too lifted up and away, disappearing as swiftly as the first.

"Shit!"

Pushing himself harder than he thought possible, he sprinted, his feet slipping with each step, the abyss to his right sucking at him constantly. His breath was a ragged explosion every time it burst from his mouth, while his right leg screamed each time he put his weight on it. He ignored the next two pods in a dangerous calculated risk, focusing all of his attention on the last pod on this side of the living module.

Reaching it, he didn't take the time to set Aggie onto the deck. Instead, he slung her over his shoulder and pulled at the handle securing the hatch. It lifted easily, and the hatch swung inward. Lights in the pod automatically snapped on and heaters began warming even as he unceremoniously tossed Aggie onto the padded bench that lined the sides of the raft. He dove in after her, twisting as he landed so he could resecure the hatch. Next to it was a small control panel with two buttons. He pressed the one marked Launch.

It seemed to take forever but actually happened in less than ten seconds. Hydraulic pistons lifted the pod off the deck, but the rig was angled too steeply. The underside of the escape pod hung up on the railing, balancing almost perfectly. The davits started to unspool the lowering lines. The pod teetered for a second, then started to fall back toward the deck. Mercer and Aggie would be trapped aboard the *Omega* when she went over. Mercer had felt what was happening and reacted instantly, diving across the pod and slamming himself against the outside wall, his weight tipping the forty-foot craft the other way.

The pod slipped from the railing, and as he'd predicted earlier, Mercer was free-falling off the rig once more. Enough cable had unwound from the davits for the pod to fall twenty feet before being yanked short, almost wrenching itself from the lines. It danced against the restraint, tossing Mercer and Aggie around the enclosed cabin ruthlessly.

Without warning, the escape pod smashed into the waters of Cook Inlet, inertia and weight driving it below the surface before it pluckily burst back up, throwing off water like a hunting dog after a retrieve. Mercer lay stunned on the floor of the raft, Aggie on top of him, her head resting against his chest as if she'd merely fallen asleep. He had to get up, unhook the pod from its shackles, and motor them away from the doomed rig, but he couldn't move. He just wanted to stay where he was, cradling Aggie until all the pain went away.

The last anchors finally gave way, stressed far beyond what their manufacturers ever dreamed possible, and the *Petromax Omega* lurched violently. The crane towers and flare stack snapped off cleanly, falling into the water only a couple dozen yards in front of the escape pod. Four hundred lengths of drill string in bins atop the production module came pouring off the rig like a log slide, followed closely by countless drums of chemical drilling mud.

As the platform toppled, it began breaking apart. The living module sheared off, the entire thirty-thousand-ton structure falling into the sea in a catastrophic explosion of water and debris that flung Mercer and Aggie's escape pod to the very limit of the lowering line, but they still remained attached to the swiftly sinking module. The upper decks hit the water next, and as they did, the number two support leg lifted completely out of the water before breaking away to fall independently from the rest of the platform.

Diesel fuel poured from ruptured storage tanks, making contact with one of the many electrical fires already raging, and ignited in a wide sheet of flame, black smoke lifting high into the air. As the rig settled into the water, it pitched and bucked as more pieces fell clear. It sank slowly, fighting almost as if it were a living creature that realized it was drowning. Explosions rumbled from deep under the flaming water.

Throughout the final moments, Mercer lay still, his breathing settling as he soaked up the warmth that blasted from the pod's multiple heaters. He knew that there was something he had to do, something that compelled him to get off the floor, but he could no longer remember what it was. Yet he forced himself from the floor and moved to the stern where the motor and steering controls were housed in an economical dashboard. He was working on getting the engine started when he remembered that he hadn't unshackled the pod from the living module!

Cook Inlet was two hundred and seventy feet deep where the *Omega* had been temporarily moored, and the lines securing the living module to the escape pod were only one hundred and fifty feet long. He raced back to the davit controls, just reaching a hand outward when the module sank beyond that one-hundred-and-fifty-foot tether. The lines came taut, then the little craft was capsized in a fraction of a second, hauled down toward the murky bottom, condemned to a watery grave.

Once again Mercer and Aggie were thrown violently, falling to the ceiling as the raft tipped upside down and was yanked below the surface in a headlong plunge. While it had been designed to be watertight in the most adverse surface conditions, the pod's fiberglass hull was not designed to survive a prolonged submergence. In seconds, the seams where the upperworks and hull joined were creaking and popping, a tiny jet of water shooting from around one of the gasketed mounting bolts.

Seconds before the hull imploded, Mercer scrambled back to the controls and pressed the second of the two buttons. Spring clips securing the tethers to the hull snapped open. Free of the plummeting living module, the escape pod rocketed back to the surface of the Sound, surrounded by a champagne fountain of air bubbles. It was launched completely out of the water, like a humpback whale breaching during its annual migrations. Its design was such that it quickly settled on an even keel, even if its two occupants were no longer in any condition to care. It took all of Mercer's remaining energy to strip himself out of the survival suit and wet clothing and curl up under several of the blankets that had been dislodged from a storage locker, Aggie Johnston held tightly to his chest.

"We made it, darling," he mumbled and then remembered that escaping the rig was only half the battle. The real fight was still to come.

THE UNITED
ARAB EMIRATES

The television image was grainy and broke up every few seconds due to atmospheric disturbances as it bounced back to earth from a communications satellite. On the screen, a woman stood in front of the massive facade of Heathrow's Terminal 4, her beautiful face composed of equal parts of pity and eagerness. As a professional broadcast journalist, this was the type of incident she lived for. The doors behind her were cluttered with swarming rescue workers in heavy flame-retardant gear, uniformed police, and suited members of Special Branch. The incident that had brought them all here had occurred on the other side of the building, out on the huge apron where aircraft had been waiting for clearance from the bomb detection teams. The sound from the BBC Special Report was much sharper than the pictures beamed into the Hasaan bin-Rufti's Hawker Siddeley now only fifteen minutes from touchdown at Dubai, the closest international airport to the Emirate of Ajman.

Rufti was seated in the main cabin, his bulk sagging over and around the confining arms of the luxury seat. His fingers and lips were greased with the molten butter dripping from the lobsters he was consuming. He had just finished sucking the pale red meat out of the tiny underclaws of two huge imported Maine lobsters when the report had broken into the financial news he had been watching. The napkin hanging down his chest was the size of a tablecloth and was streaked yellow with butter, like a urine-soaked diaper.

Although he didn't pause from his afternoon snack as he listened, his piggy eyes did brighten somewhat.

"This is Michaela Cooper reporting live from Heathrow, where the terrorist threat has intensified in the most horrifying way. Twenty minutes ago, while the airport was still under a high security alert following a bomb explosion in the main concourse, a refueling lorry was driven, apparently by suicide bombers, into a grounded British Airways Boeing 767.

"Unconfirmed reports so far indicate that the entire aircraft was destroyed by the collision between the plane and the lorry. A source here has told me that the bodies of the tanker's real crew were found in a maintenance hangar shortly before the explosion, their throats slit, but again this is unconfirmed." She glanced down to the notes in her hand, her shimmering blond hair falling around her shoulders. When she looked up, the hair remained draped over the silicone swell of her breasts. "The aircraft was scheduled to depart for Riyadh, Saudi Arabia, several hours ago. However, it was halted on the tarmac by the ongoing terrorist threat, now said to be the work of a group called Kurdistan United. They are the same terrorists claiming responsibility for the attack at the British Museum yesterday evening."

"So the monkeys did it after all," Rufti said aloud as he watched the broadcast, bits of lobster dribbling from his liver-shaped lips.

Having Tariq detonate the grenade in Heathrow's international concourse and the making of a couple of well-timed phone calls to the airport manager's office had bought enough time for the suicidal Kurds to set up a proper assault on Khalid Khuddari's plane. Even as he made preparations to return to the UAE and confront the Crown Prince, Rufti had managed to put together a spur-of-the-moment plan that had worked brilliantly, with no exposure to himself. While he had personally made the two calls to Heathrow, his pilot had assured him that the communications gear aboard the Hawker would prohibit the signal from being traced.

Rufti had spent millions of dollars recruiting, training, and arming the Kurdish nationals to attack Khuddari at the British Museum. The operation had been planned down to the finest detail so that nothing could possibly go wrong. But of course it had. It had been left up to him to improvise a new plan to eliminate his greatest rival. With no prior planning and only the barest minimum of time, the Kurds had managed to use the window created by Tariq's grenade to infiltrate Heathrow's grounds, overcome the fuel company workers, and slam their truck into the parked Boeing.

"Unbelievable," he muttered, shaking his fat-swaddled skull back and forth slowly.

The attack at the museum had been simplicity itself, while launching an assault at an airport already on high-security alert had to be the most difficult operation a terrorist cadre could accomplish. How the Kurds failed at the first but managed the second was a mystery. "Truly unbelievable."

The camera view shifted to a long-range shot, a thousand-millimeter lens focusing on the pandemonium on the runways. After the explosion, the authorities had evacuated the rest of the planes immediately. They stood alone on the tarmac, yellow inflatable slides hanging from their exits. The passengers had been bused to a cargo warehouse for temporary shelter, three Fox combat reconnaissance vehicles standing sentinel outside the sealed doors, their 30mm Rarden cannons at the ready. The remains of the British Airways 767 were nothing more than a smoking heap on the asphalt, a charred ruin that was the funeral prye to 165 passengers and crew. The camera sharpened even further, showing fire trucks pumping white foam onto the twisted remains, crews in silver fireproof suits edging as close as possible to the hot aircraft.

Michaela Cooper's tone was doleful as she continued her report, but Rufti no longer paid her any attention. Khalid Khuddari had been on that plane, and now he was dead. Rufti had lived up to his part of the bargain with the Iranians and the Iraqis. It was now up to Kerikov to destroy the Alaska Pipeline and sink the tanker off the western coast of America, and within days the maps of the Middle East would have to be redrawn once again. The Saud family would be dead, their huge nation becoming a territory held jointly by Iran and Iraq, Kuwait would be absorbed by her northern neighbor, and he, Hasaan bin-Rufti, would be the new absolute ruler of all the Emirates.

Rufti was almost giddy. From the jaws of defeat, he had

scored a stunning victory, proving himself to his partners. His negotiations with the ministers from Iran and Iraq, stretching over many months but culminating only days before in London, had hinged on both him and Kerikov first accomplishing their parts. Rufti could now settle back and wait comfortably for Kerikov to execute his side of the operation. Once done, the combined armies of the Middle East's most belligerent neighbors would sweep southward while the United States and Europe sat impotently as their precious oil was taken from them.

He had to admit that Kerikov was a genius to come up with such an audacious operation, but then remembered that Charon's Landing had once been a Soviet plan and the credit really went to their Cold War paranoia. It was Rufti's own doing to include other nations in the coup. Kerikov had been interested only in crippling America's domestic oil production, increasing her dependence on the Gulf states, thus Rufti's interest in financing some of the plan. But Rufti had seen this as an opportunity to do much more. With America starved for oil, this was the time to finally rid the Muslim world of Western influence, drive the United States out of Arabia and expose Israel to attack. To make great again the Arab empire that once ruled so resolutely in centuries past.

"Minister Rufti," the pilot's voice broke into his reverie, "we're on final approach now."

He looked at the clock set in the forward bulkhead of the cabin. A few more hours and it would all be over.

COOK INLET,
ALASKA

When flying to the *Petromax Omega,* the sea had appeared placid to Mercer, only a gentle swell marking the movement of the surging tides. However, in the small escape pod, caught up in the full motion of the twenty-knot tides, the surface of the Inlet was a steeply rolling plane, rising and dropping with gut-wrenching ferocity. Mountains of water broke over it like avalanches, plunging the craft into the hollows between the waves, giving only an instant's reprieve before hauling her up to the next crest. White spume crashed against the windscreens as thick as foam. The life raft was a bright yellow dot on an otherwise black, empty sea.

Mercer woke to the sound of vomiting, a harsh barking that seemed as if its source was tearing its very intestines from its body. As he became more conscious, he realized that he was that source. Bitter bile scored his mouth and throat, pooling under his chin as he lay on the pitching floor. The stifling hot cabin smelled like the bottom of some zoo animal's cage.

"Oh, Christ," he moaned. "Talk about adding insult to injury."

Having experienced seasickness only once in his life, he'd forgotten just how miserable it could be. His stomach felt like a nest of writhing snakes eager to escape. Knowing it was useless to resist his heaving stomach, he let himself throw up until he felt he would split open. Once purged, he felt a little better, but he knew dry heaves would shortly follow.

He checked on Aggie as she lay next to him at the stern of the pod, curled into a tight fetal ball. He felt her skin and sagged with relief. She was warm to the touch, her complexion back to its natural color. He tapped at her fingers and she mewed in her sleep. She hadn't lost any sensitivity in her extremities, so frostbite was no longer a concern. She was in the deep sleep of exhaustion, not a coma as he'd feared.

He took a second to watch her, thinking about what a remarkable woman she was. They would both be dead now without her. Her levelheadedness on the offshore rig, knowing how to operate the pumps, and being able to do so under pressure had saved them both. Mercer's life had been saved many times by many people, but never by a woman he felt so . . . He shut himself off from those emotions. He couldn't afford to have a bachelor's catharsis now and turned to more important tasks, first tucking more blankets around her.

The pod's engine was purring on idle, the gauges all reading normal, and the compass bolted to the dash indicated that the boat was headed north, toward land. Mercer eased the throttles, and the life raft reacted instantly, meeting the waves more aggressively, shouldering aside the swells as best it could, a slim wake wedging out from her stern. The raft had an autopilot, which he engaged to continue them toward the northern side of the Inlet. According to his watch, they'd been in the raft for fifty minutes, giving them just a few hours to contact Andy Lindstrom at Alyeska and stop Kerikov from destroying the pipeline. While there were more towns on the Kenai Peninsula to the south, Mercer decided to head to the mainland. Landfall was significantly closer, and he hoped to find a radio or telephone at one of the many fishing camps on the Inlet.

With the raft motoring in the proper direction and feeling moderately human again after his sleep, he investigated the storage lockers, searching through the provisions to see what, if anything, would be useful. From a medical kit he took several Triptone tablets. The anti-motion-sickness pills were most effective before the onset of symptoms, but he figured swallowing a few, if he could keep them down, wouldn't hurt. He discovered several woolen jumpsuits and donned one quickly, taking an extra minute to dress Aggie as she slept. She barely stirred. Behind the medkit, tucked between two flashlights, was perhaps his greatest find, an unopened bottle of bourbon. Though he didn't recognize the label, he thanked the gods it was there. He took a heavy swallow, the spirits hitting his stomach like liquid steel poured from a crucible.

Expecting to be sick again, he was pleasantly surprised to feel his stomach calmed by the liquor. He considered the amount of bourbon Harry White absorbed daily and realized that his friend might be on to something.

He mopped up the water and vomit sloshing on the floor with a blanket and covered Aggie with several more, tucking them carefully around her body, running the back of his hand along her smooth cheek. God, she's beautiful. Again he was assailed with emotions he couldn't deal with and he turned them aside, concentrating on the reality of their current situation rather than the fantasy of any future they might have together.

He took his position at the controls and pushed the little craft as hard as possible. As they pounded northward, he activated the automatic distress beacon, the single-ping transponder sending out a repetitive signal on an emergency frequency of 121.5 MHz. He gave a few seconds' thought about using the radio to call for help but knew there were at least two other life rafts from the *Omega* making their way toward land. The last thing he wanted was to broadcast that he and Aggie had survived the capsizing of the platform. For now, they were alone, arrayed against an army and totally cut off from help.

For the next two hours, Mercer fought the sea and his own sickness, the Saab engine under the rear cowling running flawlessly. Aggie remained unconscious during the trip, her exhaustion so complete that even the wild pitching of the escape pod could not wake her. Mercer was not so lucky. The farther they traveled, the worse his stomach reacted. For a while he tried to steer the raft with the outer hatch open to allow fresh air into the stuffy cabin, but too much water poured through the low opening.

The only thing keeping him going, the only spark that gave such a miserable experience any meaning, was the hope of stopping Ivan Kerikov. Without that drive, he would have given up long ago. But as his stomach convulsed for the twentieth time, dry hacks that left him sweaty and weak, he knew that he could endure anything to stop the Russian.

Dawn arrived slowly, silvering the sky in a pearly half light that only hinted at the coming of the new day. Through the wave-slashed windows, the northern coast of the Inlet was a gray-green strip cutting between the dark waters and the sky, the horizon undulating with pine-covered mountains. Rocky hills and nameless streams carved their way to the water's edge to be ground down by the lunar pounding of Cook Inlet's harsh tides. It was an uncompromising land, a rugged place inhabited by only the strongest.

With the coming day, the sea eased some, the great waves giving way to a more gentle swell that rocked the pod but no longer threatened her. Mercer was finally able to leave the hatch open, reveling in the foggy air that cooled his skin and cleared his gummy red eyes. He needed sleep so badly he'd forgotten what it actually felt like. His back was as stiff as a steel rod, his shoulders as tight as staying hawsers.

He began paralleling the coast, powering toward Anchorage but praying to find some sort of shelter long before that far-off city. There had been no sign of the other lifeboats from the *Petromax Omega*, but he kept a sharp eye out. To run into one of them now, with only a knife taken from the emergency stores to defend themselves, would mean his and Aggie's recapture or, more likely, their death.

To his left, the coast scrolled by in a featureless panorama of rocky beach and towering forests beyond. After twenty minutes, Mercer began to think he'd made a serious mistake. Perhaps he should have gone south to the fishing communities on the Kenai Peninsula. The precious time he'd saved heading north was rapidly being whittled away as he searched for a fishing cabin. The coast gave way to a deep bay, the shoreline curving inward, carving deeply into the land. At the center of the wide-mouthed bay, a river disgorged the last of its summer runoff, white water cascading over rocks before reaching the ocean.

And on the bank of the river stood a cabin, the rough logs of its exterior weathered by decades of exposure. The cabin was one story with a native stone chimney rising from one side like a parapet and a low tumbling veranda leaning toward the river. It looked like an Appalachian homestead without the amenities, but to Mercer it was the most inviting building he had ever seen.

He guided the lifeboat shoreward, bucking through the swells that built against the coast, and as he neared the shack, he saw something that made his heart lift. Hidden behind a screen of dwarf spruce trees, a red seaplane was moored where the river met the Inlet, held fast against the swirling waters that licked at its torpedo-shaped pontoons by heavy manila lines.

If the cabin didn't have a radio, which he suspected it didn't, the plane surely would.

Beaching the lifeboat twenty feet south of the river, he drove it hard against the pebbly shore until it was firmly grounded, then cut the motor. His legs wanted to sway as if he were still on the water, but as he waited, the feeling left slowly, steadying him once again.

He jumped from the pod, his boots digging into the rocky beach. The morning air was sharp, scented with pine and the low fog that hung just above the treetops. He envied whoever owned the cabin for having such a remote and beautiful getaway.

Mercer paused to look through the cabin's filthy windows and saw through the gloom that the cabin hadn't been occupied for a while. Dust sheets covered the few pieces of furniture and cobwebs hung elegantly from the framed photographs on the stone mantel. From what he could see, the cabin was very primitive. The kitchen consisted of a small sink fed by an iron pump handle and a camping stove. He guessed that its communications would be equally crude. His best hope lay with the plane.

The airplane, an old Cessna, was in immaculate condition, its paintwork glossy, and when he opened the rear hatch, the interior cargo space was spotless. Mercer guessed that the single-engine plane was left here as a play toy while the cabin's owner used a newer aircraft or perhaps a motor yacht to reach the camp from Anchorage. Mercer couldn't believe that anyone would leave such a plane unprotected for the winter, but he was in no position to question the practices of others.

He ducked into the cockpit, checking for the radios as he settled himself into the pilot's seat. He scanned the simple instrument package once quickly and then again with more concentration. The space where the radios should have been was an empty hole in the molded plastic dash. She carried no communications equipment.

In frustration, Mercer beat on the control wheel. He and Aggie were stuck until rescue workers, searching for survivors from the *Omega,* stumbled upon the cabin. That could take days, long after the Alaska Pipeline had been destroyed by Kerikov and his PEAL allies. Mercer had spent hundreds of hours being ferried to remote mining locations in small aircraft and he watched pilots intently, getting pointers, but he'd never had any formal flying lessons. It was one of those thing's he'd promised himself he'd do but never found the time for. He cursed himself now for procrastinating.

The controls before him seemed so familiar, and starting the plane would be a snap, but he wasn't sure of the proper combination of rudder, yoke, throttle, trim, and fuel mixture that would make the plane fly. But he'd been through too much to give in now. If escaping the oil rig hadn't killed him, then surely stealing a plane, flying it a hundred miles, and landing it again wouldn't either, he thought insanely. And as soon as he realized he was going to do it, his stomach was cramped by fear, a paralyzing stab that almost coaxed him out of his decision.

He concentrated, relying on his near-photographic memory to replay exactly the motions he'd observed so many times before. Upwind, fuel mixture rich, throttle to full, ease back, and you were airborne. It was easy. But landing? The pilots just seem to do it, settle the plane, glide down, and the next thing you know, you're on the ground.

Sitting there, he felt as lost as a teenager on the first day of driver's education. Everything was so familiar, yet bewilderingly complex and frightening. Oh, Jesus.

And then a new thought struck him, and he smiled. He didn't have to take off. He could use the floatplane like a boat, letting the Lycoming engine zip them across the waves rather than haul them through the sky. That was something he could handle.

His newfound self-satisfaction evaporated when he heard the hum of a marine diesel engine far out in the bay. Its distance was hard to judge because of the fog rising from the water, but it sounded like it was heading toward shore. He'd hoped to leave Aggie in front of a fire in the cabin before starting out on his suicidal mission, but that was no longer an option. The engine noises could only mean that Kerikov's men who'd escaped the *Omega* were approaching.

"Mercer Airways flight 666 to Hell now boarding," he joked as he leaped from the cockpit, running back down the beach to where he'd left Aggie in the escape pod.

Aggie was still sleeping as he scooped her up, keeping the blankets around her. Shimmying out of the pod, one item caught his eye and he grabbed it.

"Complimentary beverage service and everything." He raced back to the Cessna, the bottle of bourbon clutched tightly.

Mercer laid Aggie in the open cargo section of the plane, securing her to the deck with tie-down straps, then stripped away the vinyl coverings over the pitot tubes. Rather than taking the time to untie the aircraft, he simply cut the ropes with the pilfered knife. He jumped back onto the Cessna as the swift flow of the river grabbed it, pushing it out into the bay. The sound of approaching motor was much closer, seemingly right on top of them, but still lost in the fog.

Once seated and strapped in, the daunting task he'd set himself became all too apparent, especially after he turned the ignition key and got no response from the plane's engine. "Come on, baby, don't do this to me."

He tried again and got nothing for the second time before remembering to throw the toggle marked Master Switch. Not knowing the exact purpose of the magnetos, he left them set at BOTH and tried the ignition again. The engine kicked over once, died, kicked again, then boomed loudly, a gray spout of exhaust jetting from the motor.

"All right," he said aloud.

He looked at the quivering engine gauges and decided their order of importance quickly.

"Oil temperature, who cares?

"Manifold pressure, who cares?

"Carburetor heat, who cares?

"Airspeed indicator, too fucking slow." He opened up the throttles, wincing when one of the cylinders prefired and then settled again.

In a moment, the plane was heading into the bay, rapidly picking up speed. The twin pontoons carved deep slices in the water. Mercer made sure the fuel was set at Full Rich to give himself the maximum amount of power from the engine. He experimented with the rudder pedals, and the floatplane responded to his commands, turning gently. He tried to estimate where he'd last heard the lifeboat and steer a course around it—for in the fog he was virtually blind.

Feeling a bit more confident, he dialed the flaps down one notch, increasing the wings' lift. The plane felt lighter in his hands, the ride smoothing and his speed increasing. He glanced at the indicator and was startled to see they were doing more than seventy knots. The floats skimmed the surface like arrows, and the Cessna felt like it wanted to fly. The plane was steady, but he felt the excessive speed was too much for him to handle, and he reached forward to reduce the throttle.

Like Leviathan rising from the sea, one of the *Petromax Omega's* escape pods appeared out of the fog directly in front of the hurtling aircraft. With just an instant to react, Mercer unthinkingly pulled back on the control yoke, and the Cessna came unglued from the water, flashing only a scant foot above the rounded top of the lifeboat. His first thought was to get the plane back on the water again, but she continued to climb steadily, the safety of the water receding with every passing second. Panic gripped him, and his hands felt like lead weights on the yoke. *Oh, shit.*

He purposely lightened his deathlike grip and let the plane settle into its natural environment as it rose through the silvery mist. Fighting his mounting fear, Mercer tried to remember the width of Cook Inlet and the height of the mountains on the other side. But as the plane climbed above three thousand feet, breaking out into clear sunshine, he saw that the mountains of the Kenai National Refuge were too distant to be a threat to the soaring aircraft. He took several calming breaths, wiping a new coat of sweat from his brow, but his heart continued to hammer at his chest. He'd just gotten himself and Aggie into a mess he had no idea how to fix.

Not giving in to his panic, he started to experiment with the plane. If he was to land them safely, he had to teach himself how to fly before the fuel gauges dropped to empty. Fortunately, the air was calm, and it took him only a few minutes to get used to the quick control response of the Cessna. After ten minutes, he set a course to Valdez and had the plane flying straight and level, throttled to 70 percent power and cruising as if he'd been flying all of his life.

Like hell.

In a vain attempt to distract himself from their predicament, he thought about Kerikov and how the Russian would destroy the pipeline. As Andy Lindstrom had said earlier, freezing the oil in the line wouldn't do it; the steel making up the pipe segments was too thick. But if Kerikov had gained control of the computers that ran the pumps, which Mercer suspected he had through Ted Mossey, he need only wait until the line was mostly solidified and then crank the turbine pumps to maximum. The free oil in the unfrozen sections would create tremendous back pressure when it met the frozen oil plugs, and even with a rated pressure strength of eleven hundred eighty psi, the line could not hold against the combined power of its ten active pump stations. It would split in a hundred different places depending where Kerikov had placed the nitrogen-freezing packs.

Mercer looked at his watch. If he didn't get to Valdez and warn Andy Lindstrom about Mossey, Kerikov would succeed. Ignoring the steadily plunging fuel gauge and the near redlines of the engine indicators, Mercer opened the throttles a notch farther, eking out a few more miles per hour. Another twenty minutes dragged by before the Cessna cleared the eastern coast of the Kenai Peninsula and broke out over the waters of Prince William Sound.

Gently, he banked the plane northward, hugging the coastline. The town of Seward was only four minutes south of their present location, but in his concentration, Mercer had failed to see it nestled between the mountains. He could have landed there and saved himself the ordeal yet to come.

THE Planetary Environment Action League research vessel *Hope* had the carnival air of a cruise ship that had just reached some tropical paradise. The crew, all young and idealistic, were toasting their success from bottles of cheap champagne. They were only an hour or two from completing the greatest attack on the industrial polluters in the history of the environmental movement. All of their previous actions—the arson attacks on gas stations, the rallies and fights, the shouted chants, and spray painting of slogans—had led to this moment. And this one had been pulled off so easily that many of them realized that large acts of eco-terrorism were much simpler than the small protests they had been part of before. A few were already talking about their next reprisal against the industrial world.

Jan Voerhoven stood surrounded by his followers in the *Hope*'s wardroom, a glass of champagne in his hand, a smile lighting his handsome face. He basked in the mood around him like Caligula before his hand-picked Senate, drawing strength from their adoration. The only shadow in his deep blue eyes was the fact that Aggie wasn't there to share it with him. He knew the significance of her leaving the ring he'd bought for her. She had meant a lot to him; however, the buoyant celebration helped dispel the loss he was already feeling less strongly. Several unattached women eyed him predatorily, for the rumor of Aggie's departure had spread quickly.

One woman, a girl really, no more than nineteen, caught his eye, and when he smiled, she matched his gaze with a frank desiring expression. No, he thought as another champagne was placed in his hand, he would probably have a new bedmate this very night.

"How much longer, Jan?" someone shouted from the back of the crowded room.

"Not much more," he called back, grinning. He had the
detonator in his shirt pocket, the slim cellular phone tucked
against his chest.

One deck below the raucous party, Abu Alam was making
his report to Kerikov. He'd spent the past three hours in the
engine room of the *Hope*, securing charges of plastique to
fuel lines, oil bunkers, and other strategic locations. When
they were detonated, there would be nothing left of the research ship but the twisted backbone of her keel. His clothing
was filthy, his dark complexion sooty and streaked with oil
and grime, and his hands were so black with dirt that they
looked gloved. They were alone in Jan Voerhoven's spacious
cabin, Alam's footprints staining the carpet's rich pile.

He gave his report without emotion, dictating the locations
of the charges and the fact that he had had to kill three engineers who had come too close to his work. His eyes were
flat and hard. Alam contained his excitement with difficulty,
trying to remain impassive under Kerikov's critical stare.

Is he aware? Alam wondered.

It would be natural for Kerikov to suspect treachery from
Alam—their entire world was created from deception—but
he couldn't tell if the Russian knew it was coming so quickly.
Hours now, not days.

Alam had not thought through his timing yet, for the del-
icacies of it were somewhat beyond him. He was a soldier,
not an officer, and certainly not a strategist. Hasaan Rufti had
made it clear that the pipeline must be destroyed and that
there could be no possible link between the act and the Minister himself. Eliminating PEAL was a desire of both Rufti
and Kerikov; neither of them wanted a group of young ide-
alists bragging of their achievements afterward. But killing
the Russian was going to prove far more difficult. Alam had
to make certain Kerikov detonated the nitrogen packs and
activated the hidden computer program that would rouse the
multiple pump stations before killing him with a quick knife
thrust or blast from his SPAS-12 shotgun. Ideally, Kerikov
would die when Alam set off the explosives secreted throughout the ship, but he didn't know how to properly time such
an occurrence.

Trust in Allah, Alam reminded himself, and his Prophet will guide you.

"Very well," Kerikov cut into Alam's transparent musings, for the Arab's duplicity was obvious. "It's nearly time. The crew should be drunk by now, and once we detonate the nitrogen packs, they won't notice when we leave the ship. That will give us the window to destroy the *Hope*. Bring Voerhoven to the bridge. I want to see his face when he realizes what he's done to his precious environment."

THE Cessna was a bright speck high over the gray water of Prince William Sound, the plane so high its droning engine couldn't be heard by a ferry heading eastward from Seward to Valdez. At least that is where Mercer hoped the vessel was heading as he used it as a reference to make his turn slightly north and head up into Valdez Bay.

Everything was going perfectly—so far. He almost felt comfortable in the pilot's seat, his hands and feet light but firm on the controls. The terrifying prospect of landing was still a few minutes away. What bothered him most now was the relentless movement of his watch's second hand as it ground down toward the end. There was nothing he could do to stop it or even slow it. The plane was already at maximum power. The margin to reach the *Hope* was so thin it was practically nonexistent.

The great expanse of the Alaska mainland lay before the aircraft, the early morning light giving the vaguest hints of the beauty of the state, its towering mountains and icy streams and huge forests. If he failed, it would become a cesspool of unmanageable devastation. He knew the resilience of nature, what her forces could do to clean the scars left by man's existence, and while the process was slow by human standards, nature always seemed to recover. But something like what Kerikov was attempting would take generations to heal. Alaska would be ruined well into the twenty-second century.

Amazingly, when he pushed a little harder on the maxed-out throttle, the engine beat picked up just that tiny bit more. He looked back to see Aggie still asleep in the cargo hold. If only he could be certain they were headed in the right direction. While there were some charts in the plane, Mercer wasn't familiar enough with the region or with navigation techniques to use them. They lay folded in a vinyl pouch on the floor below the copilot's seat.

"God is my copilot and hope is my navigator," he breathed between tight lips.

Up ahead, he spotted a long, narrow island sitting a couple miles off the north coast of the Sound. He watched it for a moment and then reached over to dig out the maps. Maybe he could use them after all; the island was so symmetrical that recognizing it on the charts would be relatively easy. When he straightened back, he saw the long trail of white water backing against the island and realized it was no landmass at all but a supertanker heading south from Valdez. Even from three thousand feet the vessel's size was staggering. Looking around at the insectlike Cessna, it was hard to imagine that both craft came from the mind of the same species, for surely the tanker was proportioned for the gods.

While he admired the ship, he also realized that it had just saved him from making a disastrous error. Mercer was on a too easterly course; they would have flown beyond the entrance to Valdez without ever realizing it. Quickly adjusting their route to follow the wake of the ponderous tanker, Mercer took a second to check his watch again. Not enough time, but still he had to try.

One of the first things an instructor teaches a student pilot is that the use of the elevators must correspond with the throttle in order to avoid stalling or power diving. Usually after the verbal lesson, the instructor will demonstrate this fundamental by heeling the plane over at full throttle and scaring the student half to death in a dive-bomber stoop that quite often spills the student's lunch.

Mercer had never been a student pilot, and the throttle was at the gate when he pushed the yoke away from his chest. The Cessna responded like a horse given free rein, dropping out of control, Prince William Sound filling the view from the windshield, and every second brought the sight into sharper focus. The engine screamed, and the plane began to buffet as its wings reached, then passed, their structural tolerance point. They were traveling straight down at one hundred forty-five miles per hour.

His stomach, already turbulent from the ride in the escape pod, went into full revolt, liquid acids rearing into his mouth, gagging him with their foul taste. Knowing he'd just committed a critical error, Mercer pulled back on the yoke, but the pressure of the wind against the control surfaces was too strong for him to fight. His greatest effort only managed to stretch the control cables running from the stick to the elevators, suddenly making the yoke feel mushy in his hands. The plane was going down, and no matter how hard he strained, he couldn't stop it. The altimeter spun backward in a solid blur, unwinding their altitude faster than the barometrically controlled needle could accurately follow.

He never considered the throttle until an elegant hand reached for it and gently backed it off, the engine calming immediately. Without saying a word, Aggie Johnston wedged herself into the copilot's seat, fighting against the force of the plane's severe pitch. She added her strength to Mercer's, and with the aid of a slowing engine, they managed to pull the plane's nose upward, slowly at first and then as the wings felt lift, quicker and more smoothly, the airframe stopping its mad shudder as the craft came level only eighty feet above the choppy waters.

"The last thing I remember, we were about to drown, and now we're about to crash," she said so calmly that Mercer could not believe her quietude. "What is it, can't decide how you want to die?"

"Of course I can." He matched her nonchalance, relieved at her obvious flying skills. "I see myself killed by a ricochet while passing a kidney stone. How about you?"

"Let's put it this way, I don't want to be killed by another of your idiotic ideas." Aggie had the plane in trim now, gaining altitude steadily as she followed the course Mercer had set. "It's clear you don't know how to fly a plane, so do you mind telling me what's going on?"

"We escaped the *Petromax Omega* about ten seconds before it capsized." She looked at him sharply. "I know what you're thinking—any fuel that she spilled was burned up in a fire that would have inspired Dante. We made it to shore a couple hours later, where I found this plane and decided that stealing it was a much better option than being recaptured by Kerikov's goons. I never intended to take off, but, well, you know how these things sort of happen. While I thought out the beginning of our escape, I don't mind the fact that you're stepping in to finish it. You do know how to land this thing, don't you?'

"Two hundred and fifty-seven hours in my log. Where's the closest runway?"

"Ah," Mercer tried a charming smile to cover his trepidation. "This is a seaplane, and we're only about five miles from the *Hope*. But you can land a seaplane, right?"

"Oh, shit." The color that had returned to Aggie's face drained once again. Her hands tightened on the spongy yoke of the unfamiliar Cessna. "I've never been in a floatplane before."

"Sure you have," Mercer quipped. "We've been airborne for a while."

He ignored the sour look she shot at him and continued seriously. "Besides, we don't have the time to discuss the differences between a seaplane and a regular plane. For now just consider it semantics, because there's the *Hope*."

Looking much like a yellow toy, the MV *Hope* sat at anchor in the middle of Valdez Bay, equidistant between the town and the sprawl of the Alyeska Marine Terminal. The mountains looming at the head of the Sound were a bleak snowcapped backdrop. Valdez was a tumbled gray blur to their left, enmeshed by a spiderweb of docks and jetties. The tired fishing and pleasure boats looked like detailed models.

"Aggie, you have to land this plane. Kerikov is on that ship, and you and I are the only ones who can stop him," Mercer said harshly. "I've never given up on anything in my life, and I know you haven't either. If you care, I mean if you *really* care about the environment, then don't think about putting this plane down, just do it."

Mercer considered having Aggie land them at the Alyeska breakwater, but he didn't think they had the time. It would take several minutes to cross the Sound and even more time they didn't have to reach Andy Lindstrom at the Operations Center. And even then, there was no guarantee they would be able to stop Kerikov from cycling the pumps and destroying the pipeline. His only choice was to stop the Russian from detonating the nitrogen in the first place.

Aggie didn't speak, didn't even take the time to look at him. Even though she was piloting a strange aircraft and forced to fly from the right-hand seat, she was quick and sure with the controls. She eased the throttles back farther, added ten degrees of flap to the wing, and edged the nose higher, the Cessna happily following her lead as if it knew that its previous pilot was a total incompetent and that it now enjoyed the ministrations of a professional.

Coming in low over the water, actually having to rock the plane around a fishing boat headed out to sea, Aggie brought the Cessna in for its landing. Without knowing the weather conditions, pressure, wind direction, or any of the myriad other pieces of information pilots used to land successfully, she relied on her own training. The altimeter read that they were still forty feet above the seas, but she knew they were no more than twenty. She recognized that Mercer had not set the altimeter when he took off. The plane was much bigger than the aircraft she had flown before, and the two pontoons under the hull acted as drag as she crabbed the plane in, her hands and feet dancing on the controls like a pianist during a concert solo.

Adding more flaps and pitching the nose even higher, Aggie realized that they were too close to the *Hope* to land and still have enough room for a rollout or, more accurately, floatout. The vessel was just a hundred yards away, and the floats under the Cessna were still ten feet above the Sound. She should pull up and come around again, but she continued grimly, her anger at Jan making her reckless.

Now only four feet from the water and held aloft by the ground effects of the wide wings, the Cessna was open to the variability of the winds that slued the plane hard to port. Aggie stomped on the right rudder to compensate and eased the plane down as best she could, the pontoons smashing into a wave, breaking clear through a trough, then barreling into another of the two-foot swells.

The Cessna almost flipped as if it had been plucked from the sky, the prop coming dangerously close to digging into the water. The plane fought its way through the next swell as it slowed, droplets spattering the windshield. They had landed. Aggie had done it. She heaved a sigh as the aircraft wallowed like a spindly dragonfly.

"Flying pigs be damned, I'm a pilot," Aggie breathed.

Mercer guessed the non sequitur was some ritual.

"Yes, you are now, go!" he said, on the edge of an adrenaline overdose. He jammed the throttle back in just before the last of the spark in the motor died away. It bellowed at full power, and the plane began racing across the water. The *Hope* was twenty yards away, shimmering in the late dawn light.

"Get me alongside," he ordered, "near her stern if you can. I've got an idea."

Aggie wasn't yet over the shock of their escape from the *Omega,* not to mention Mercer's suicidal nosedive or her near fatal landing. She was too tired to argue with him, didn't have the energy to do anything but follow his orders. She guided the plane toward the *Hope*, her feet playing alternately against the rudders as swells slammed into the deeply settled pontoons.

The hull of the *Hope* loomed quickly, too quickly, her yellow sides towering up and over the Cessna's cockpit before Aggie realized they were that close. She desperately tried to avoid contact, but just then a heavy wave smashed the plane into the research vessel, the thin aluminum skin and support members of the port wing crumpling against the hardened steel of the ship's hull.

"Damn it," she cursed her own misjudgment, but no one was there to hear her epithet.

Mercer was at the rear cargo door, wrenching it open, letting in a harsh blast of frigid air to cleanse the stench of fear from the Cessna. The main deck of the *Hope* was twelve feet over his head, and there appeared to be no way up. He jumped down onto the pontoon and shimmied forward so he could grasp the angular strut supporting the starboard wing. The pontoon was slippery, forcing him to struggle onto the wing using his arms and shoulders, new pains tearing into the old ones.

Grunting and straining, he managed to haul himself onto the undamaged wing, then stood on the unsteady platform. Prop wash whipped at his hair and clothing like a hurricane gale. The dynamics of the tides and waves kept the Cessna hard against the side of the *Hope*, the plane scraping against the vessel with every surge. Even with the wing's added height advantage, it was too far of a jump to reach the steel railing circling the vessel's deck.

Mercer dodged to the far tip of the wing, his weight dipping that side of the plane farther into the water, and then ran to the other side, stopping just short of the damage caused by Aggie's mistimed approach. He repeated the process, slowly building a steady rocking motion, every dash raising the damaged wing closer to the deck. At the instant he thought the plane would pitch no higher, he raced onto the wrinkled section of the wing, springing upward even as the weakened section sagged under his weight.

His leap was fouled by the wing giving way, and he had to scrabble to maintain his grip on the scaly opening of a deck scupper, the molded steel giving almost no purchase as his feet pumped against the glassy smooth hull. Hanging in space, Mercer prayed that Kerikov hadn't posted any deck guards. The approach and subsequent crash of the Cessna had the subtlety of a slap in the face, and it would only stand to reason that someone would come out to investigate. If Mercer was discovered hanging from the side of the ship like an unwanted barnacle, he could be cleaned off with an easy shot through the top of his skull.

Mercer pulled himself upward, his feet scrabbling. The rough steel edges of the scupper tore into his hands, releasing a fresh torrent of blood from his raw palms and fingers. He ignored it and heaved himself onto the empty deck, scissoring his legs under the railing in a last desperate effort.

"Aggie," he shouted down to the plane, his voice almost stripped away by the engine noise and still-spinning propeller.

A second later, the prop juddered to a stop, and the engine went dead. The only sound to be heard was the lap of water against the hull of the ship. Then, through the silence, Mercer heard laughter coming from within the superstructure.

"Aggie," he called again, and her pale face appeared in the opened cargo door of the Cessna, her short hair swept across half her face. In the tricky light of the morning, her green eyes appeared luminous. "I need you up here, otherwise this will never work."

Mercer wanted to send her to shore so she could alert Lindstrom, but he needed her with him. Because he'd led the Coast Guard raid against the *Hope*, he was certain that the crew would try to stop him. But with Aggie at his side, he hoped that her presence would arouse less suspicion, freeing him to go after Kerikov.

"I can't jump up there." Aggie stood on the floatplane's pontoon.

"Wait." Mercer ducked from her view, rushing to the the stern of the research vessel where a fluorescent orange life-preserving ring hung from the railing, attached to the ship by two hundred feet of heavy nylon line. He ran back to the side of the ship, casting quick glances forward, thankful that no one had investigated the Cessna.

"Grab onto this. I'll pull you up." He threw the a ring over the side, and it landed in the narrow strip of dark water between the ship and the floatplane, the line dangling in front of Aggie's face.

Without question, for she was well beyond that point, Aggie wound the rope around her fists several times. She walked up the side of the PEAL ship in time with Mercer's tugs. At the top, with one hand bracing the rope, Mercer leaned over the side, grasped Aggie by the loose waist of her coveralls, and hauled her over the rail. She fell in a heap at his feet, cursing at him for scraping her chest against the railing.

"Okay, now what?" she breathed, looking at him critically.

"We find Kerikov and kill him," Mercer replied, his eyes fixed in a deadly stare. "After the crew sees we're together, I want you to get to the radio room, contact the Marine Terminal, and tell the manager there, a man named Lindstrom, to stop their computer technician. Mossey is his name. Tell Lindstrom that Mossey was responsible for locking out the computers and he's planted a new operating system that is keyed into the nitrogen detonators."

He saw that Aggie didn't have the slightest idea what he was talking about. There wasn't enough time to explain further, so he changed plans. "The hell with it. Stick with me and just make sure none of your PEAL buddies think I'm the enemy."

They ran to the superstructure, tossing open one of the heavy doors, and dashed down a deserted hallway, the ship's heaters feeling like a steam room compared to the cold air on the open deck. Most of the cabin doors they passed were open, the rooms empty. The sounds of the party grew steadily as they tracked its source.

"That better not mean we're too late," Mercer said tightly, his fists bunched at his sides as he dodged through several hatchways, Aggie at his side.

Bursting into the main dining room, Mercer and Aggie were stopped short by the sight of the ebullient crowd. The celebration was in full swing, and the transition from the horrors of the past hours to this took them both aback. A roar went up as the environmentalists recognized Aggie, some with delight, others with surprise.

They took scant notice of Mercer, obviously not equating him with the man who'd arrested several of their comrades during the FBI raid. In an instant, he and Aggie were enveloped, people jostling to get close, plying them with glasses of champagne. Mercer felt so out of place, it was as if he'd just broken in on his own funeral.

"Has it happened yet?" he shouted over the festive din, and from somewhere a voice responded that it would in a couple more minutes. They were ready for the final countdown.

Aggie looked at Mercer fearfully. Her eyes were huge. It was obvious that no one knew the full effects of what was about to take place. "Where's Jan?" she asked a PEAL activist standing next to her in the mass of drunken revelers.

"On the bridge, I think," came the response, and Mercer

was carving a swath through the crowd, pushing aside those who got in his way as he lunged for the door.

IVAN Kerikov was posed before the bridge windows when Jan Voerhoven found him. His hands were behind his back, his thick chest puffed up, his chin thrusting boldly at the wild land beyond the thick armored glass. His flint-hard hair was silvered in the dawn, like the fur of a winter fox. There were fewer than fifteen years between their ages, but Jan felt like a callow youth in the Russian's presence. He stood silently for several seconds, fearing to disturb Kerikov's repose.

"The time has come for you to take your place as the spark that begins the third great revolution of modern times." Kerikov turned the full brunt of his mesmerizing eyes on Voerhoven.

Jan thought that those must have been the eyes that Rasputin had, not in color but in intensity. "The third?"

"Of course, the Russian Revolution of 1917, the Fascist Revolution that swept in Hitler, Tito, and Mussolini, and now the Green Revolution," Kerikov replied, giving an answer that would soothe the agitated environmentalist. Kerikov kept to himself that the third revolution would actually be the unifying of the Middle East under joint Iraqi and Iranian control. "You have the detonator?"

"Right here." Jan pulled the phone from his shirt pocket, snapping open the mouthpiece. Everything around him seemed unreal. He suddenly felt that he was being dragged into something he no longer wanted to be a part of. Yet he could not stop himself. Kerikov nodded to him to proceed and, as if the Russian actually had control of his fingers, he began to dial.

Mercer heard only that Voerhoven had the detonator as he crouched at the entrance to the bridge. The Russian was out of sight, and he had no time to determine Kerikov's position, but Jan was standing right before him, near the central control console. Mercer rushed from his hidden position, closing the gap between himself and Voerhoven. He crashed into the Dutchman with the force of a cannon shot.

Both men flew over the console, the phone flying from Voerhoven's hand as he smashed to the deck, ribs cracking as Mercer's full weight landed on his chest. It took only two powerful punches to knock the activist into unconsciousness, but the delay gave Kerikov enough time to reach for a holstered pistol. Mercer came to his feet, whirled, and saw the weapon leveled at his head.

Echoing across the open expanse of Valdez Bay, sirens wailed like a rape victim in a deserted parking lot, a haunting cry that came too late to prevent the inevitable.

There was an emergency at the Alyeska Marine Terminal.

Both men glanced out the windscreen toward the sprawling facility, as if they could see evidence of the awful destruction taking place along the eight-hundred-mile length of the pipeline. Mercer looked back at Kerikov, his gray eyes darkened by reckless hatred.

"Too late, Dr. Mercer." Kerikov revealed yellow teeth in what passed as a smile. "Last time you beat me by a few hours. This time I beat you by only seconds."

"I'm going to kill you, you sick fucking bastard." Mercer shifted his eyes to Kerikov's right as he spoke.

"Afraid not." Kerikov twisted to follow Mercer's gaze and when he did, Aggie Johnston came out from an open flying bridge door to his left. Kerikov never saw the fire extinguisher she used as a bludgeon. He crumpled, blood pouring out of the wide gash in his skull.

"Glad you were here to back up my threat," Mercer said as he recovered Kerikov's gun, training it on the Russian. He knew the man was still dangerous as he lay moaning on the deck. Aggie's attack hadn't been strong enough to knock him out, and already he was moving, struggling to clear his head.

"What's that sound?" Aggie asked over the klaxons shrieking from across the harbor.

"We're too late. Voerhoven set off the nitrogen packs."

Screaming like a madwoman, Aggie ran across the bridge to where her ex-lover sprawled on the floor. She kicked at him, yelling his name and swearing as if she would never stop. Her face was bright red and tears raged in her eyes. No one could have done her a more grievous injury than what Voerhoven had just done to Alaska. She felt the land's pain as if it was her own body covered in toxic poison.

"Aggie, stop it!" Mercer shouted, grabbing for her shoulders as her feet continued to pummel Voerhoven. "I have to contact the Terminal. There may be a way to reduce the damage. Aggie! Listen to me!"

She stopped, finally, looking at him as an eerie calm settled over her.

"Where are the radios?" Mercer was still shouting, his nerves frayed like a rope about to part. Voerhoven's cell phone was at his feet, damaged beyond repair.

"They're destroyed. I saw that Arab smashing them on my way here. He stole a Zodiac and is headed away from the ship right now. I thought coming to the bridge was more important than trying to stop him."

Like a sprung trap, Kerikov came off the floor where he'd been momentarily forgotten. Mercer saw the movement out of the corner of his eye and shouted for the Russian to stop, but Kerikov was in full flight out the bridge wing door. Mercer triggered off one round, the bullet puncturing Kerikov high on the left shoulder, staggering and slowing him but not stopping his dash to freedom. He was already on the narrow flying bridge, the tails of his coat streaming around him in the wind, an arm crossed over his shoulder to clutch at the oozing wound.

Mercer didn't have time for a second shot before Kerikov reached the end of the deck and tossed himself over the side of the ship, dropping thirty feet into the frigid water. He was just starting to race after Kerikov to get another shot when he resurfaced, but he stopped himself, spun around, and grabbed Aggie by the hand.

"Don't talk. Run."

They raced back through the ship, fear hounding Mercer like never before. For Kerikov to flee as he had, he must have believed that taking a bullet in the back and jumping into the freezing water was a more survivable option than staying aboard the *Hope*. He had run the instant he heard Aggie say Abu Alam was no longer on the research vessel. Mercer recalled that the two of them had rigged the ship with explosives, and he guessed the psychotic Arab must have a detonator of his own.

They burst into the dining hall to find the party even more wild than before, European rock music blaring from a stereo set up at the head of the room and most of the people dancing with abandon. Mercer took only a second to aim through the crowd, fired once and then again.

The music suddenly stopped as the speakers disintegrated in showers of black plastic and wires.

"Get off the ship. It's going to explode." Having given a warning he didn't feel they deserved, Mercer grabbed Aggie again and rushed to the aft deck where the Cessna seaplane was still held fast against the side of the *Hope* by the tide.

He jumped down to the plane, the wing dipping under his weight even though he cushioned the fall by flexing his knees. He turned and looked up at Aggie at the railing. "Jump!"

He expected her to hesitate for a moment, but she didn't. She threw herself over the side before he had properly braced himself. She landed in his arms with so much force that they both almost rolled into the water. Struggling, Mercer held on to Aggie as her feet dangled off the trailing edge of the wing.

"Can you reach the pontoon?" he asked, gently lowering her.

"Almost . . . Wait . . . I'm on it."

He let go, and even as he got into position to follow her, Aggie ducked into the plane, readying it to get them away from the *Hope*. As he jumped down to the pontoon, the engine kicked over, and the prop wash nearly blew him off the eight-inch-wide float. Struggling against the wash, he edged forward until he hopped into the cabin.

"Go. Go. Go, Goddamn it, go." He screamed.

Aggie hadn't bothered with her safety straps since the damaged wing prevented the Cessna from ever flying again. She sat on the edge of her seat, like a child driving a car for the first time, her eyes wide with fear. She had enough sense to keep the yoke pressed forward, spilling off any lift the wings might produce as the plane moved away from the doomed research ship. In a moment, Mercer was in the copilot's seat at her side.

"Those people . . ." she said, referring to the PEAL members still on the *Hope*.

"Signed their death warrants when they allied themselves with Kerikov," Mercer finished. "We gave them a chance they never would've had."

"Where are we headed?" Aggie resumed that calmness that so fascinated Mercer.

"To the Marine Terminal. I don't know, maybe there is something we can still do." Mercer knew it was too late; the damage had been done. All that remained was to help clean it up. Even over the vibration of the plane and the whining drone of the engine, he could hear the sirens calling from across the water.

———

VALDEZ HARBOR

Abu Alam had barely left himself enough time after planting the explosives to disable the *Hope*'s radio equipment and dash down to the boat deck. He had cut the margin much too thin. He was a good mile from the rocky beach at the head of Valdez Bay when he heard the alarms from the Marine Terminal. Kerikov had triggered the nitrogen packs. Alam was too exposed on the open water to detonate the explosives aboard the *Hope*. To do so now would attract attention, and he still needed time to steal a vehicle that would take him to Anchorage's airport.

Every second now increased Ivan Kerikov's chance to escape the doomed ship, and one of Rufti's most explicit orders was that the Russian must not survive. Alam balanced caution with his desire to kill Kerikov. He knew that until he reached land, caution by necessity must prevail. He'd considered motoring the Zodiac toward Valdez, but it was very possible that he had been spotted kidnapping Aggie Johnston. It would be smarter for him to head for the Alyeska Terminal where he

could beach the rubber raft a short distance from the facility
and steal a vehicle during the confusion created by the detonation of the liquid nitrogen.

Looking over his shoulder, he saw the decks of the *Hope*
were quiet, the young people obviously still enjoying their
morning celebration. Alam hated using explosives. It was too
distant, too impersonal. He much preferred seeing his victims
die, smelling their fear as their life drained from a slit throat
or a bullet in the chest. He had used bombs before, but he
felt a little cheated inside, as if the explosives did the killing,
not him.

A big wave grabbed at the Zodiac, forcing Alam to concentrate on his course. Just beyond the outside perimeter of
the tanker loading facility, a small stream emptied into the
bay. It was screened on both sides by thick copses of trees
and would make an ideal landing spot. Even this far out, Abu
Alam could see a low bridge crossing the water-washed ra-
vine. The Alyeska access road was only a couple dozen yards
away. Perfect.

Because he was unfamiliar with the workings of small
boats, Alam focused all of his attention on bringing in the
Zodiac and didn't turn back again until the bow was bucking
against the stream's flow, the motor churning brown silt from
the bottom. When he finally twisted around, he immediately
reached for the detonator in his jacket pocket. A steady stream
of tiny figures were leaping over the yellow side of the *Hope*.
At this distance, they looked much like the proverbial rats
leaving a sinking ship. The PEAL members were escaping,
Kerikov probably among them. Alam didn't waste time thinking of this, didn't even notice the red speck that was a damaged aircraft racing from the ship. He though only about the
pounds of artfully placed explosives aboard the *Hope* and the
deaths they were going to cause. Clearing the detonator from
his pocket, he keyed an activation code, noted the green indicator light, and pressed ENTER.

LIKE a crippled fledgling that doesn't know it can't fly, the
aerodynamics of the Cessna kept trying to loft Mercer and
Aggie Johnston skyward as they skimmed along the surface

of Valdez Bay. Aggie struggled to keep the Cessna level, forcing nearly all of her weight against the starboard rudder pedal to compensate for the destroyed port wing. As it was, she could only manage to crab the plane sideways across the bay, the nose pointed almost thirty degrees away from their direction of travel.

Mercer now knew enough about planes to know he didn't know enough about planes to help her. He kept his hands and feet clear of the controls. He focused instead on the tiny mirror placed high on the dash and watched the *Hope* shrink in their wake. No matter how fast they traveled, it seemed they were still too close to the research ship. If it had been rigged with enough explosives to panic Kerikov into his suicidal jump, he and Aggie were in for a rough ride. With nothing better to do, Mercer grabbed the bottle of bourbon still in the cockpit and dosed himself with a little liquid courage.

The MV *Hope*, formally a Hecla class research vessel in the British navy, vanished just as the bottle came away from his lips.

One second the ship was centered in the mirror and the next it was gone in a blooming explosion of red, yellow, and black, huge slabs of the hull splitting apart, chunks of metal, wood, and flesh arcing through the air. The devastation was total. Even before the shock wave hit the fleeing Cessna, the main part of the ship had sunk beneath the rippling bay, nothing to mark its existence except a greasy fire raging on the surface and the human misery wallowing near its grave.

The overpressure wave blew out every storefront window in Valdez, killing four people, and overturned all but the largest boats laying at anchor in the public harbor, claiming a further eight victims. Had the explosion been delayed by a few more minutes, the civilian death toll would have been much higher, as onlookers were just converging at the shore to see what had caused the alarm at the tanker facility that shared their waters and gave many of them their livelihoods. Of the PEAL environmentalists, Mercer's shouted warning had saved all but twelve. Eight died immediately and four later in the hospital.

Two potential victims the blast did not claim were Aggie

Johnston and Philip Mercer, but it was a close call all the way.

"Brace yourself," Mercer shouted as soon as he recognized what had happened, dropping the bourbon to the floor.

The concussion of the explosion grabbed the Cessna, tipping it so high that the prop ripped at the water, slicing it into a plume that obliterated their view. Aggie pulled back on the yoke immediately, releasing the rudder at the same time. The plane tried to lift, and for a precious moment it was back on an even keel, the pontoons barely keeping purchase, the forces of the wings and that of the concussion wave holding the aircraft steady.

Then the concentric swells radiating from the explosion caught up to the plane, lifting it higher and, like a body surfer caught on a perfect crest, bore it even faster along the Bay of Valdez. The water raced from the explosion's epicenter at nearly one hundred fifty miles per hour, piling up a mountain of water thirty feet high, and at its very crest, Aggie maintained an unsteady control of the Cessna, not sure if her adjustments to yoke and rudder were effective in keeping them in place or if the aircraft was at the whimsy of the raging onslaught.

As her ears stopped ringing and she became aware of the sounds of the torrent around her, she also heard Mercer laughing. "What's so goddamned funny?" she shrieked.

"Half hour ago, you were complaining about my flying. I don't see this as an improvement."

Before Aggie could come back with an obscenity-laden rejoinder, the wave smashed into the breakwater protecting the Alyeska facility, the top of it battering the seawall built specifically for just such a tsunami, although the designers expected waves generated from earth tremors, not catastrophic explosions. The pontoons were ripped from the Cessna by the concrete wall, and much of the force of the wave was beaten down by the massive cement structure, leaving the plane to sail clear for an instant before it plowed into the rocky ground, its belly scraping off their speed brutally, the prop blades folding back around the engine cowling like the tentacles of some sea creature.

The threat of fire was real, and both Aggie and Mercer launched themselves from their seats as the plane finally ground to a stop.

"Remember, this flight counts double for your frequent flier miles. We want to thank you for flying Mercer Airlines. Have a nice day." He was out the cargo door of the Cessna as the last words rolled from his lips, with Aggie right behind.

The sprint to the Operations Building took forever, both of them hampered by their injuries and by the countless vehicles they had to dodge as technicians and employees raced to evaluate the situation. Mercer pounded through the door, tossing a hapless employee back about ten feet as the edge of the door caught her square in the chest. He raced for the control room, ignoring the dazed woman completely. The room was packed. Voices clashed angrily over the wail of countless alarms, the normally calm professionals driven to the point of panic by the scope of the catastrophe facing them. Andy Lindstrom was in the center of it, his face red and his shouts muted to angry growls from hoarseness. He scanned the multiple panels and video display units, assessing the damage to his precious pipeline. Twenty or so engineers were gathered around him, ranked by seniority so the most experienced was at his shoulder and the juniormost stood in the back of the room. The windowless room was filled with cigarette smoke and the smell of fear's sweat.

"Andy!" Mercer shouted over the arguing voices, but the noise drowned him out.

To gain attention, he pulled out Kerikov's pistol and fired into the floor, silence echoing after the shot.

"Andy, how bad?" Mercer asked calmly. If he was bothered by the stunned crowd around him, it didn't show on his stony face.

"Jesus Christ, Mercer, what the fuck are you doing?" The shock on Lindstrom's face was a combination of seeing Mercer with a pistol, seeing Mercer even alive, and the stress of the nitrogen packs freezing his pipeline as solid as a popcicle. "Great to see you again, but I don't have time for this—your friend the Russian has destroyed my pipe."

"I know." Mercer couldn't afford the delay caused by emotional answers. "I need to know if the pumps are running right now."

Before Andy could answer, an engineer seated at the console spoke up. "No, the computer logs show they shut down about a minute before the nitrogen packs went off. Right now they're off-line. And it looks like they'll never run again. Preliminary reports indicate at least forty spots where oil flow has stopped completely and a couple more with minimal flow. It looks as if there are at least two ruptures, one at the center of the Tanana River suspension bridge."

"The bridge collapsed?" Mercer asked fearfully.

"Yeah. Oil is flowing toward it through open check valves like a spigot."

"Where is that computer guy, Mossey?"

"He was in the computer room a moment ago," replied a technician standing near Mercer.

Mercer turned so fast he bumped into Aggie, whom he'd all but forgotten. She was sickened by the fact that the pipeline had been cut by the nitrogen freezing. As a member of PEAL, she was, by default, responsible. "This isn't over yet," Mercer said and ran down the hall.

The computer room, in comparison to the Op-center, was sterile and clean and empty save for one frantic figure stuffing papers and computer discs into a soft-sided leatherette bag. Mercer didn't give Ted Mossey a chance to even turn around. He used his left hand to smash Mossey's head down to the desk while his other pressed the automatic pistol into his face so hard that Mossey's teeth ripped the delicate inner skin of his cheek. When Mercer spoke, his voice was a white fury, his eyes glazed with hatred.

"Shut the fucking program down! Now!"

"I can't," Mossey stammered, saliva and blood dripping from his mouth onto the computer station. "I was locked out as soon as Kerikov triggered the nitrogen."

Mercer snicked back the hammer of the pistol, the small click sounding very final in the quiet confines of the room. "That's too bad. You've had the program for a couple of months. I'd thought you'd have broken into it and set up a back door. Last mistake you ever made, pal."

He was willing to let the bluff go for a few seconds before knocking Mossey unconscious, but it wasn't necessary. Mossey folded instantly. "Wait, please God, don't kill me. There is a back door. I put it in soon after Kerikov hired me to reinstate his old program."

"Use it now, you little ferret, and stop the pumps from coming on-line or, so help me Christ, I'll pull the trigger and use your brains as finger paint." Mercer let Mossey back up but kept the pistol screwed into his ear. The younger man started working on the terminal, his fingers blurring across the keys.

Aggie stood in awe at the back of the room, fascinated by the absolute control Mercer showed of both the situation and Ted Mossey. It wasn't the gun that gave Mercer power, it was the man himself. His conviction and his unwavering belief in himself held her rapt. As unpredictable and wild as his actions had seemed to her, once the resolution became clear, his was the only logical course. Standing as he was, grim-faced and tensed, Mercer was the most desirable man Aggie had ever seen. The sight of him gave her a delicious thrill.

"I'm in," Mossey said at last. "Just a minute more."

"I blow your skull apart in thirty seconds." No one, not even Mercer, knew if he was still bluffing or not.

Andy Lindstrom had followed Mercer and Aggie to the computer room and, after watching the drama unfold for a moment, crossed to a terminal next to Mossey, the computer screen before him indicating pump and pipeline status. Though the program had been installed by a mole at the height of the Cold War, only now was it active. All ten pumps had spooled up to full power, building a tremendous back pressure against the solidified oil plugs. Mercer had been too late to stop that from happening, but pipe integrity was still holding. If they could shut down the pumps in time, the line wouldn't blow apart as Kerikov had planned.

"Internal pressure?" Mercer demanded without taking his eyes off Mossey.

"Twelve hundred pounds per square inch within the pipe casing at nearly every sensor," Lindstrom cried. "We're over the maximum rating. The whole thing's going to let go at any second. Pumps are still in operation. This isn't going to work."

"Someone already told me that today." Mercer stole a glance at Aggie, who smiled at him in response.

Mossey pushed himself from his keyboard computer, his slight frame spent. "That's the most I can do."

"Status?" Mercer barked.

"Twelve hundred twenty-five psi. The fucking thing is going to burst. Fuck!" Lindstrom screamed. "Massive pressure drop at one of the sensors, pipe blowout. Pumps are still . . . Wait, pumps are off-line, they've stopped." Lindstrom's voice trailed off as he watched fearfully. The internal pressure sensors placed within the line continued to climb higher and higher, now 15 percent beyond their rated maximum tolerance. Finally he spoke again, filling the thick silence, excitement crowding his words together. "Pressure going down across the board, steady drop. My baby held together. Oh, thank you, God, and thank the union welders for making this bitch stronger than we ever thought."

Mercer looked over at him in relief, his face and body showing the extent of the battering he'd been through since last night. "What about the steel mills that rolled the pipe sections?"

"Fuck 'em, it was a Japanese firm." Lindstrom laughed, emotion bubbling over. While still facing a major disaster— there were three huge leaks belching out thousands of barrels of oil—the extent had just been reduced to manageable levels. With Mossey as a witness, Alyeska would be found blameless for the entire affair.

"Human error," Mercer said, as if reading Andy's mind. "Not the negligent kind, but the type found when people do the wrong thing for the wrong reason."

"How'd you know about Mossey?"

"I'll tell you everything tomorrow. Right now I need a drink, a hot shower, and a bed—in whatever order they come."

"Drink first," Andy grinned. "That I have in my office. But no matter what you did here today, I'm not sharing my bed with you."

Mercer glanced at Aggie and smiled at the shy look on her face. Andy followed his gaze, forcing Mercer to make introductions. "Andy Lindstrom, this is Aggie Johnston, Max Johnston's daughter."

"I know your father." Lindstrom shook her hand as he led Aggie and Mercer back to his office. "Listen, I don't have time for that drink. I've got to get crews to the damaged sections of the line and start on the repairs. I can tell from the sensor panel where PEAL placed their nitrogen. There are miles of open pipe between the plugs, so we're going to lose a shitload of oil. The leak on the Tanana Bridge is spilling something like five thousand gallons an hour. Every minute we wait is going to make this more of a mess than it already is."

Lindstrom paused, then asked, "Listen, Mercer, can you stick around for a while? I need to get details of what happened at Pump Station 5, we still haven't managed to get a team up there. The fire at the depot in Fairbanks is still raging out of control, tying up a lot of my people."

"Eddie didn't make it?" Mercer was stunned. He thought rescue crews would have found the fearless chopper pilot before his injuries claimed him.

"Eddie's fine. He's in a hospital in Fairbanks right now, but he's been sedated since his arrival. An army chopper picked him up last night, but they didn't return to the pump station. They're still ferrying the injured out of Fairbanks."

Somehow, knowing Eddie Rice had survived meant more to Mercer than preventing Kerikov from destroying the pipeline. But that was how he thought; human life always took precedent over all other concerns. In mine rescue work, he had spent millions to save one lowly worker, and to him it was a bargain. And whether it was money he was gambling or the environmental fate of an entire region, his decision was always the same. Life, anyone's life, came first. Perhaps it was a superior attitude to take considering the new-world thinking, but it was the way he was.

"Andy, seriously, there's nothing I can give you about your pump station. I never got within a hundred yards of the pump house before I was captured." Mercer was almost asleep on his feet. "I'll tell you everything I can tomorrow, but for now, I'm worthless."

Lindstrom wasn't even listening. He was already engaged in a discussion with an engineer, the two of them arguing about materials allocation for repairs. Mercer turned away, guiding Aggie into Lindstrom's office and closing the door quietly behind them. The soft click of the door closing became a punctuation mark to what they had been through, an end to what had happened before and a beginning to what would now come between them. They both felt it, glancing at each other with both longing and trepidation, as if the adventures they'd shared had been a necessary distraction from what they now faced.

The air sizzled.

"Drink?" Mercer twisted himself away from her eyes, reaching into Lindstrom's desk for the bottle he knew would be there.

"Yes, please," Aggie said, acquiescing to Mercer's desire to sidestep their emotions.

He poured Scotch into two paper cups, slopping each one nearly half full. Of all the morning drinks he'd had in his life, and there had been quite a few, Mercer believed that he and Aggie had actually done enough to warrant this one. He finished his in a heavy swallow, pouring another by the time Aggie had taken a first tentative sip. She found a pack of cigarettes on Andy's desk and smoked one of them almost as fast as Mercer drank.

"Is it over?" she asked.

"You know, I think it really is." They were standing close together, the top of her head well above his shoulder, her face tilted to his, her lips full and inviting. There was an unmistakable gleam behind her emerald eyes.

As he stooped to kiss her, the door to Andy's office flew open, the matronly receptionist from the front office almost falling to the floor in her rush. She was about to speak, but when she saw that Andy wasn't there, her face collapsed. Mercer realized she was really in distress, far more than the others dealing with the emergency.

Not recalling her name, he asked her if anything was

wrong, and in a rush it came pouring from her so fast there was hardly a pause between words.

"There was a shooting at the main gate, Ralph, the nice older guard is dead, another person, I don't know who, is lying in the street, blood all around his body. A man attacked them, shot up the booth with some sort of machine gun and stole one of the company trucks. Oh, God, poor old Ralph, he was just a nice man."

She fell into a chair, overcome by everything that had happened, her doughy body pooling around the wooden chair, her rounded cheeks stained with fresh tears. Mercer shot a look at Aggie, who immediately understood that he wanted her to look after the receptionist, and then he was gone again, running out of the building, shouldering aside those already in a scurry over the crisis.

The air was bitter cold under a pewter sky as he raced toward his rented Blazer still sitting in the Op-center parking lot. Despite everything he had been through since the previous afternoon, he'd managed to keep his keys, transferring them to the deep pocket of the coveralls when he'd donned the garment in the escape pod. The engine roared with the first crank, and a second later the truck slashed through the terminal's gates, threading nimbly around the people clustered near their fallen coworkers. As he sped from the facility, he hoped one of them had had enough sense to alert the authorities in Valdez.

The pistol he'd taken from Kerikov was lodged behind his back. He pulled it out and set it on the plastic console between the two front seats. He drove furiously, the heavy-duty tires screaming as he took corners fifteen or twenty miles faster than posted. He estimated that ten minutes had elapsed since the attack, factoring in the distance between the main entrance and the Op-center and the time it took witnesses to get themselves in motion after the initial assault.

If he had had his Jaguar, he could have made up that time effortlessly, but the Blazer was built for rugged off-road use, not high-speed pursuit.

He didn't waste more than a second realizing who it was he was pursuing. With Kerikov dead in the harbor, only Abu

Alam remained unaccounted for. It made sense that after triggering the explosives aboard the *Hope*, Alam would leave Prince William Sound as fast as possible. Because of the heavy traffic around the town caused by emergency vehicles headed toward the harbor, there would be no way for him to get to the airport. His only other option was the Richardson Highway and Anchorage a couple hundred miles north. Once there, he would be lost forever.

The road uncoiled before the Blazer, the powerful Chevy engine roaring under the broad hood, the wheels reacting eagerly to Mercer's guidance. As he drove, he shoved aside his exhaustion, knowing that he couldn't push himself much farther or his body would simply fail to respond. This whole affair had all started here for him, at a test with Howard Small and his tunneling device, and he was going to see that it ended here too, probably no more than a few miles from Howard's mini-mole site.

His mind cast back to that time only a few weeks before, recalling that the turnoff to the site was around a couple more bends in the road. Mercer didn't realize his concentration had wavered until he rounded a sharp corner, and there, stretched across the two-lane road, was an overturned tour bus, glittering fragments of glass spread around the motor coach like handfuls of diamonds tossed onto the macadam. Dazed people milled around the scene, many of them stained by their own blood, others still struggling out of the destroyed vehicle.

Using both feet, Mercer ratcheted the brakes to the floor mat. Greasy black slicks burned off the tires, a sharp stench filling the confines of the Blazer. One elderly woman, her eyes owl-wide, stood transfixed as the truck careened toward her. Mercer yanked the wheel over, fishtailing the Blazer to a stop only feet from where she stood. Even as the body of the truck settled back onto its suspension, Mercer jammed the accelerator.

When he whipped his truck around to miss the woman, the Blazer lined up with a dirt track that forked off the Richardson Highway and climbed up to its right, heading straight to where the pipeline crossed over Thompson Pass. Mercer knew the track well. This was where he and Howard had been conducting their tests.

As the Blazer left the asphalt and the tires dug into the muddy road, he guessed at what had happened just moments before. Alam must have rounded the corner wide, directly into the path of the oncoming bus. Like Mercer just now, he would have hauled his truck to the right to get back into his lane and noticed the road leading up into the hills. Ignoring the swerving bus, he would have made a quick escape toward the testing site, while below him, the driver of the bus lost control of his heavy charge.

Mercer could not allow himself to consider that Alam had managed to squeak past the bus and continue toward Anchorage.

The access road twisted sharply in hairpin switchbacks, and almost immediately Mercer noticed fresh tire tracks in the hardened dirt, darker sprays of soil churned up from the wheels of a speeding vehicle. With Howard dead and the site shut down until people from UCLA came to get the mini-mole and all the other equipment, there would be no reason for anyone to be here. Alam was just ahead and this was a dead-end road. Mercer grabbed the automatic pistol and set it on his lap.

The road was narrow, trees and greenery scratching the side of the Blazer as it powered upward. When he finally burst into the site itself, the thick forest gave way to a huge field at the base of a solid wall of rock towering two hundred feet above the tallest trees. A steel cyclone fence had been erected around the area and where it crossed the access road, the gate was smashed back, hanging limply from one hinge.

The scene looked exactly as it had when Mercer and Howard had left for their celebratory fishing trip. Two enclosed trailers sat side by side, cement blocks placed under their integrated jacks keeping them level. A flatbed eighteen-wheeler was parked a little way off. Minnie herself sat at the base of the cliff under a tarp, heavy cables running from her to spools that were attached to large portable generators. She was still lined up to the main test-boring hole in the mountain, a perfectly round aperture that was so black it seemed to absorb light. A red Alyeska pickup truck sat next to one of the travel trailers Howard and his team had used as an office.

Pocketing the keys to his truck, Mercer dashed to the cover provided by the huge flatbed semi, ducking under the low trailer and training the pistol over the wide expanse of the site. He quickly ran through Alam's options in his mind. Alam hadn't had enough time to pick the lock on one of the trailers and hide inside, nor did it seem he was using the rig to hide behind because he could have easily gunned down Mercer as he ran toward it. The surrounding field was mostly alpine grass and offered no protection, so Alam wasn't running on foot, nor did he appear to be climbing the cliff, a difficult task for even an experienced climber. That left Minnie, the generators, or the couple of pallets of gear clustered near the entrance to the test hole. The four other holes nearby were no more than a couple of feet deep, dug as calibrating bores before Minnie's main hole, and he could clearly see that Alam wasn't lurking in any of them.

Instinctively, Mercer knew Abu Alam was trying to make his escape through the mountain in the four-foot-wide tunnel. But just in case he was wrong, he crawled the fifty yards to where the generators sat, his body tensed for a shot that never came.

Mercer worked the controls with one hand while the other held his pistol leveled at the tunnel entrance, and the generators, big Ingersol-Rands powered by eight-cylinder diesels, fired after only a second. Once they were running, he stripped off Minnie's cover, revealing the ugliest machine he had probably ever seen.

The miniature boring machine operated much the same as its larger cousins but refined to near perfection. The cutting blade, a four-foot-diameter disk, was composed of carbon fiber polymer and diamond chips held together with the recently discovered carbon molecule called buckminsterfullerine. It could turn the hardest bedrock into microscopic dust in an instant. The body of Minnie was a rounded box that housed the sophisticated pumps and valves for the hydraulics and a third-generation global positioning system that gave her more accuracy than the American navy's nuclear submarines.

For propulsion, two hydraulic legs, rams designed much like the legs of a grasshopper, were mounted on either side of the machine's body. They provided enough holding power and forward pressure for the cutting blade to core through granite at the unheard-of pace of two feet per minute. An enormous fan mounted on the very back of the machine blew the dust and debris created by the disk back down the tunnel it had created.

"Alam, I know you can hear me," Mercer shouted at the tunnel, his voice booming down the length of the shaft. "That noise you hear is the boring machine that dug the hole you are running through."

Abu Alam ran doubled over along the pitch-black passage, but he paused at the voice. It was distorted as it ricocheted off the walls, but he caught just enough to force him to stop. He recognized the voice as the person Kerikov had captured during his attack at the pump station. He had no desire to turn back and finish off the man. Philip Mercer was Kerikov's enemy, not his. All that mattered to him was getting out of this hole and escaping. Behind him, the tunnel opening was only a pinhole, while ahead, there was only blackness.

"It was built by the man you killed in California," Mercer continued as he readied Minnie, checking connections and making sure the cutting wheel was freely turning on its shaft. "He was testing it here just before you murdered him. Unfortunately for you, Alam, we never finished this hole before deciding the test was a success. It ends about five feet from the other side of the mountain."

Alam went white.

Mercer engaged the ram/legs and stepped aside. Like a tired beetle, Minnie started forward, the cutting head spinning at fifteen thousand rpm. Without having to cut through rock, Minnie could travel about twelve feet per minute with its peculiar lurching gait. It would take an hour for it to reach Alam. Mercer couldn't afford to wait until the end, so he programmed the machine to automatically shut itself down after boring through two additional feet of rock at the shaft's terminus. He turned away and started back to his Blazer. "Die hard, motherfucker."

Abu Alam, Father of Pain, would cower until the last possible second at the end of the shaft, curling himself into a ball against the rough stone before Minnie reached him. His body was liquefied by the cutter head. Days later, when the mini-mole was pulled from the hole, the largest piece of him found could have been squeezed though a toothpaste tube.

Back at the base of the access road, Mercer took on three of the most seriously injured of the bus passengers, none of whom were in any real danger. He deposited them at the Valdez hospital but left before anyone could detain him with questions about anything other than the crash's location. It was only after the Blazer was rolling into the terminal facility that he remembered something Ivan Kerikov had said the night before on the *Petromax Omega*.

"Shutting down the pipeline is only one tine in a three-pronged attack."

Mercer was about to find out that the second prong of Kerikov's plan was as sharp as, and even deadlier than, the first.

ALYESKA MARINE TERMINAL

When Mercer got back to the Operations Building, Andy Lindstrom was in his office, one phone clamped to his head and another one lying off its cradle on a pile of papers, a tinny but strident voice calling from it like an irate Lilliputian. Two workers stood in front of the desk, their heavy utility clothes streaked with crude. Andy saw Mercer standing at the threshold and waved him in. He barked an order into the phone, cut the connection, and scooped up the other launching into a new set of commands before dropping that one too into its receiver. Instantly both started ringing again.

"Christ, this is fucking nuts," Andy said, lifting one of the phones. He shouted into the mouthpiece, "Give me a second, will ya?"

Without waiting for a response from the caller, he set the phone on the desk. Ignoring the other ringing telephone, he took a moment to light a cigarette. His ashtray was overflowing with half-smoked butts. He used the glowing cherry of the cigarette like a finger to point at the two workers. "Introduce an instrument pig from Pump Station 10. I need to know the condition of the line between us and the Tanana River. The on-site guys say there's no external damage, no sign of tampering, but I need to be sure. If you run into a frozen section, cut the pump immediately and call me. I'll try to scare up another jet heater from the Air Force."

The two men nodded quickly and left.

"Mercer, I've got a problem even bigger than this mess. Go down to the communications room. They'll fill you in."

"Andy, I'm going to bed," Mercer said flatly.

"I need you, man. Without Mike Collins, I've got no security chief. I heard that someone was shot at the main gates an hour or two ago, the local police are screaming about that PEAL ship exploding in the harbor, and already oil companies are demanding revised delivery schedules. Alyeska's board is telling me that *I will* have the line back up in three weeks, and I don't even know how bad it is yet. Shit, worldwide crude prices are up three dollars since this morning, and it doesn't look like they're coming down any time soon. Help me out, will ya?"

"All right," Mercer breathed resignedly. He didn't acknowledge Lindstrom as he strode from the room, his dulled mind thinking that Andy's new emergency might be another of Kerikov's fronts.

The communications center was a small office dominated by a built-in counter with several multiline phones, fax, and teletype machines, plus two powerful marine transceivers. Three people were monitoring the fax, the teletype, and the huge radio sets, while a fourth was deep in conversation at a desk phone. Aggie Johnston was standing over by the desk, a cigarette smoldering between her fingers. She ran to Mercer when she saw him enter, pressing herself tightly to him.

"What happened?" she said against his chest.

"Abu Alam is dead. You don't want to know the details. What's going on here?"

"A tanker has been seized by terrorists, but its captain escaped. He's on the phone right now. He thinks the ship is going to be scuttled somewhere near Seattle."

"Is this another PEAL operation?"

"Mercer, almost the entire active core of PEAL was on the *Hope* when it exploded," Aggie said sadly. "All that's left of the organization are the office workers and the fringe members who used us to be in with the smart European set.

"I'm sorry, you're right," Mercer replied, shamefaced. Until yesterday she had believed in them and their cause, and this morning she had lost a great number of friends and her ex-lover. Under the circumstances, her response was much milder than it could have been. "This is something Kerikov must have planned with another group. What's the captain's name?" He directed the question at the woman on the phone.

"Hauser, Captain Lyle Hauser."

"Has this call been verified? It could be some crackpot."

"Authentication protocol has been used. Hauser is the captain of the VLCC." She didn't protest when Mercer took the handset from her.

"Captain Hauser, my name is Mercer. I'm the acting head of security here at Alyeska. I'm sorry, but I need you to run through what happened again."

"We don't have time for this," Hauser shouted. "Those lunatics are going to sink the ship and cause a slick the size of Lake Superior."

"Where are you now?"

"Victoria Island, British Columbia, a little town called Port Alice. I was dropped here by the commercial fishing boat that rescued me."

"Was Seattle the destination of your vessel?"

"No, for Christ's sake, how many times do I have to go through this with you people? We were headed to Long Beach when my First Officer and a group of terrorists masquerading as workers took over my ship. I managed to sabotage the engines and maybe delay them by a couple of days. The damage I caused forced them to change their plans, so rather than scuttle the *Arctica* in San Francisco harbor, they chose Seattle instead."

"*Arctica*? Is this the Petromax vessel?" Mercer asked, and Aggie looked at him sharply when she heard the name of her father's company.

"Yes. No. Well, it was. The ship was just sold, but that's not important right now," Hauser persisted. "We've got to stop them."

"You're goddamned right we've got to stop them." Pieces were falling into place, frightful conclusions that Mercer really didn't want to explore. "Captain, I need to make some calls and then get back to you, but I want you in Seattle as fast as you can make it. Chartering a plane is your best option. But for now, give me your telephone number and stay close by. I'll be in touch within ten minutes." Mercer was about to hang up when he remembered something critical. "Captain, the name of the company that bought your ship is SC&L right?"

"Yes."

"I'll call right back." Mercer cut the connection and dialed Dick Henna's cellular phone.

As he waited for the connection to be made, Aggie approached, her face lined with concern. "What's that about Petromax?"

"It's one of your father's tankers that was hijacked."

"But he sold them."

"Maybe," Mercer said, then turned away brusquely as the director of the FBI came on the line. "Dick, it's Mercer, no time for bullshitting. Get a pen and write this down. I need to know if a company called Southern Coasting and Lightering has filed a flight plan for one of their corporate jets from either Sea-Tac Airport or the one in Vancouver, British Columbia, destination someplace in Louisiana. There's a tanker in Puget Sound that's been taken by some of Kerikov's people, and whoever seized it will be needing a quick getaway after they scuttle her. I also need you to arrange some special forces troops, SEALs preferably, to stand by in Seattle. We've got just a few hours at the outside."

Henna tried to interrupt, but Mercer cut him off before he managed more than a syllable. "Dick, no questions, just do it. I'm sure you've already heard what's happened up here. Kerikov warned me that the action against the pipeline was just a distraction. Seattle is about to become a toxic waste dump if we don't get moving. Call me here when you find out about that plane." Mercer gave the number taped to the phone and hung up.

"Mercer, what was that all about?" Aggie sank into a chair next to him. He noticed that she had showered and changed into loose-fitting coveralls, the heavy denim cuffed at wrist and ankle and belted tightly around her narrow waist. She looked lost in the baggy outfit.

"Kerikov is dead, but his plan is still in effect. He hold me that destroying the pipeline was only a feint. I have a feeling that sinking a tanker is also another piece of his sleight of hand, misdirection to cover something even worse."

"Like what? And what does this have to do with my father?"

"I don't know Kerikov's true aim, nor do I know what your father's involvement may be, but prepare yourself, because I'm sure he's part of this in some way."

"How can that be? He's in the oil business. Destroying the pipeline or sinking a tanker is the last thing he would want, especially one of his own."

"You may not believe this, but the very ship now in the control of terrorists is the same one that transported the liquid nitrogen used to freeze the Alaska Pipeline. I suspect your father's involvement may go even deeper than that. Remember that was your father's oil rig we were held on last night, and I didn't see any evidence that Kerikov had taken it by force."

She sat silently, her gaze drawing inward as though she did not want to see what Mercer presented. Her body, already appearing fragile in the big coveralls, looked even more delicate, like porcelain.

He turned away from her again, giving her room to think, to believe what could be true. Mercer dialed Dave Saulman's office in Miami and was told that the lawyer had gone home for the day. He was about to try Saulman's home number when the phone shrilled.

"Yes, Dick, what have you got?"

"Southern Coasting and Lightering has a charter plane under contract and it filed a flight plan yesterday from Vancouver to Baton Rouge, a Gulfstream IV. The plane is already there, arriving last night from—"

"San Francisco," Mercer finished for Henna.

"How the hell did you know that?"

"Because that was where Kerikov had intended sinking the tanker, but the captain, who managed to escape, sabotaged the ship. His action forced them to change their plans and target Puget Sound instead of San Francisco Bay. The plane had been on stand-by in California and was then moved north to Vancouver when the tanker couldn't make it that far south."

"What do you know about the ship itself?"

"Not much. You'll have to get her particulars from the Coast Guard, but Dick, this is the ship that originally transported the liquid nitrogen that I discovered aboard the *Jenny IV*. According to a friend of mine, she was just sold to a small tanker company called SC&L but she had been part of Max Johnston's fleet. She's filled to the gunwales with North Slope crude, and if they burst her in Puget Sound, it's going to make what's happened to the Alaska Pipeline look like spilled milk. How are you coming with those SEALs?"

"I haven't even started yet. I can't just order them up like eggs, for Christ's sake."

"Don't get bureaucratic on me. Get hold of Admiral Morrison and tell him you need those men. Lean on the President if you have to—he owes you enough favors."

"I'll do what I can," Henna replied, suddenly catching on to the urgency of the situation.

"We're probably going to have to launch our assault on the tanker from Victoria. You'll have to clear this with the Canadian government. I know that they're our neighbors and all, but they get real touchy about sovereignty issues like this."

"I've already thought about that. You and I need to stay in touch. You're closest to what's going on. Are you going to be near this phone for the duration?"

"No, I'm going down to Puget Sound. It's about a five-hour flight from here, but if I'm to coordinate this, I need to be right on top of it. As soon as I've got communications set up, I'll get back to you."

"All right," Henna agreed. "Is this the last we're going to hear from Kerikov?"

"I wish to God I could say yes, but I doubt it." Mercer cut Henna off then dialed Captain Hauser. "Captain, this is Philip Mercer. Have you made arrangements to get to Seattle yet?"

"Yes, I've hired a floatplane. The pilot says he can get me there in about two hours."

"Good. But you've got to change your destination to the city of Victoria. That's where the terrorists will have a boat ready to take them off the ship."

"Are you sure?"

"SC&L has a jet on stand-by in Vancouver to take their people back to Louisiana. Once they scuttle the tanker, they'll want to clear out of the region as fast as possible. I'm looking at the map on the wall in front of me, and the quickest way is a boat from the *Arctica* to Victoria, then a short helicopter hop from Victoria to Vancouver, and they're home free."

Hauser couldn't fault Mercer's logic. "Okay, then what?"

"I'm leaving Valdez in a minute, but you'll get to Victoria about three hours before I do. Wait in the airport's main terminal. I'll have you paged when I've got more for you." Even as Mercer was talking with Hauser, he mouthed to one of the office workers to go and get Andy Lindstrom. "I've already alerted the director of the FBI about what's happened so far. Wheels are in motion, Captain. Don't worry, they won't hurt your ship if I can do anything about it."

"Mr. Mercer, it's not the ship I care about. It's Puget Sound."

Aggie grabbed Mercer's wrist as he was about to dial again. "What are you doing? You can't go to Vancouver."

"Aggie, I've got to," he said, knowing that she wouldn't understand.

"You're dead on your feet. You've done enough already. Let someone else handle this."

"Don't you think I want to? But this is who and what I am; this is what I've always done. When people say, 'Let someone else do it,' Aggie, I'm that someone else."

"The world isn't your responsibility," she snorted.

"You're right, but that little part I can do something about is." More than anything in his life, Mercer wanted to walk away from this mess, go someplace far away with Aggie and forget everything. For an instant, he wished he was one of those people who blindly hoped that there were others to fix all those things wrong with our world. He spoke with a tired resignation. "Aggie, I have to go and take care of this, see it through to whatever end there may be."

She loved him for his dedication but realized that no matter how much that love might one day be reciprocated, he could never be there for her. There would always be something else in his life, some challenge or crisis that would lure him away the way other men were lured away by affairs. Though she wasn't the type of woman who wanted to possess the man in her life, she knew she wanted more than Philip Mercer could give. And if he became what she wanted, the change would mean he would no longer be the man she had fallen in love with. It was a Catch-22 whose only resolution was to end it now before she became more hurt than she was at this moment. The very thought of stopping their relationship before it even began created a void in her chest, a physical ache that felt as though it could never be filled.

"I understand," she lied.

"When this is over, I want to . . . I mean if you and I . . ." He stammered to silence. "I think you know what I mean. I'll get in touch with you."

"Of course," she said, her emotions in such a turmoil that she couldn't look him in the eye. But she steeled herself, and when she looked up to tell Mercer that she did not want to see him again, he was gone.

Mercer met Andy Lindstrom just outside of the Operations Director's office. Without preamble he said, "I need a jet to get me to Victoria, British Columbia, as fast as possible."

"What's happened?"

"As I figure it, Kerikov planned to destroy the pipeline and then have some more of his people scuttle a supertanker off the coast of San Francisco. The tanker's captain sabotaged the vessel so she couldn't make it that far south. The terrorists are now poised to sink her in Puget Sound. This is Kerikov's second front. All along, his intentions have been to stop the flow of oil from Prudhoe Bay and then make it impossible to transport it along the West Coast. Following the *Exxon Valdez* accident, the sinking of a tanker in Puget Sound will end crude movement to California forever. The EPA and the environmental groups would never allow it again. Even if you managed to get the pipeline back in operation, your oil would have no place to go. The destruction of the pipe and scuttling a tanker go hand in hand to block America's newest and potentially largest domestic source of crude oil."

Andy nodded. "But what's the final result? I mean, what is he after?"

"Was after. Kerikov's dead, but I have no clue what he wanted to accomplish," Mercer admitted. "For now, all we can do is head off his tactical attacks and hope the final strategy becomes clear when we're successful. Do you have a plane?"

"Yeah, sure. And you're in luck, it's here in Valdez. Alyeska usually keeps it in Anchorage."

"Call the airport and tell them to get ready for a flight to Victoria International Airport at the best possible speed. Tell them to pick up some food for me too. I haven't eaten in God knows how long." He turned to go.

"What's your plan?"

At the doorway, Mercer glanced at Lindstrom. "As soon as I make one up, you'll be the first to know."

Thirty minutes later, Alyeska's corporate jet, a recently purchased Citation, hurled itself off the runway and turned south for the journey to the greater Seattle/Vancouver area. While heading for the airport, Mercer had managed to grab a change of clothes from his hotel and pack a small bag for himself, including Ivan Kerikov's pistol. Not knowing how long he would be gone, he'd told the hotel to store the rest of his belongings and check him out of the room. Someone at Alyeska could take care of his rented Blazer.

Pressed back in the supple leather seat of the aircraft, Mercer worked at something Andy Lindstrom had asked him, something about Kerikov's final outcome. What could be so big that the Russian would consider destroying the Trans-Alaska Pipeline and sinking a tanker as nothing more than mild diversions. There was something he was after, something related to oil obviously, but something that would require America to stop using her own resources.

The answer was so evident he cursed himself for not realizing it sooner. He put it off to his own exhaustion and reached for the phone, checking his watch to see what number he should call. It was eleven in the morning Alaska time, which made it just four in the afternoon in Washington, D.C. Taking a quick gamble he dialed his home number and was about to give up after three rings.

"Hello." Harry White sounded as though his vocal cords had been filed raw with sandpaper.

"What the hell are you doing at my place, drinking my booze, when you just stole a couple of cases from the Willard Hotel?"

"Tiny was charging me four bucks for a glass of ginger ale. Besides, your pretzels are fresher."

"I hope you've got a huge life insurance policy and I'm the beneficiary, you old bastard."

"Funny, I think the same about you," Harry replied.

"Are you on the portable phone?"

"Yeah, why?"

"Go down to my office. I need you to do something for me." Mercer remembered Dave Saulman saying Petromax had sold two other tankers to Southern Coasting and Lightering, one of them near Japan and the other off the coast of the United Arab Emirates.

"I'm in your office," Harry finally said after creaking down the stairs from Mercer's home bar.

"Okay, turn on my computer and scroll through the menus until you come to the electronic Rolodex."

Mercer waited a few minutes, listening to Harry curse as

he fumbled with the powerful computer. The jet engines of the Alyeska plane were a droning whine.

"Son of a bitch. How do you do it?" Harry finally asked disgustedly.

"Use the mouse," Mercer said.

"No. Not that. How do you turn on the computer?"

"All right, Harry, today is your first lesson in modern technology. There's a small button on the back of the machine, to the right of all the wires. Can you feel it?" Oil. Petromax. The Middle East. "Come on, Harry."

"Ah, fuck this. I'll dig out the old typewriter you used to keep in the closet. That's something I can understand."

"Not the same thing, Harry. I need the computer." Mercer had heard on the radio driving back to the terminal from the mini-mole test site that a UAE diplomat had been attacked in London. Connection? Probably.

"All right, all right, hold on here. There, it's on. The TV on top of the square box is flashing like the neon sign outside a strip joint."

"Great. Do you see the gray pack of cigarettes on the desk? It's called a mouse. You move that and it moves the little arrow on the TV."

"I'll be goddamned, it does." Harry was delighted with his accomplishment. "Oh, hey, this is a nice little feature."

"What?" Mercer asked with trepidation.

"The automatic drink coaster that slides out below the TV. Your highball glasses fit in it perfectly."

It took a second for Mercer to understand. "No, Harry that's the tray for the CD-ROM drive. It's not a coaster."

The United Arab Emirates. Few Americans had ever even heard of it. Would they notice if it were suddenly taken over in a coup? As long as oil prices remained stable, Mercer knew the answer was no.

It took a further ten minutes of instruction for Mercer to guide Harry White into the electronic Rolodex, Harry responding like a child every time the computer reacted to his commands. "This thing is great. I've got to get one," he kept saying.

"Now Harry, I've got the Rolodex cross-referenced to geographical locations. Double click the little map of the world, and when the map expands on the screen, double click again near the Middle East."

"I've got it," Harry said. "Man, just call me a hacker now."

"You only hack in the morning when sixty years of cigarettes come coughing out of your lungs."

"Great talking with you, Mercer," Harry teased. "I've got to go now, Tiny's is open."

"Very funny. There's a name there, I can't remember what it is, but he's a petroleum geologist working in the United Arab Emirates. Scroll through the list, reading off any name that has UAE written after it."

Harry read through names. Many of them Mercer didn't recognize and many more he knew no longer worked in the Gulf. He hadn't updated his Rolodex in over two years, and the oversight was costing him time.

"Wait, what was that last name again?"

"Jim Gibson."

"That's him," Mercer said triumphantly, remembering the big florid Texan and the brass telescope that traveled with him wherever he went. Mercer had met Gibson in Nigeria years before when both men were working to expand the West African nation's natural resource exports. Gibson was an oil man, while Mercer had been working on a promising diamond field in the center of the country. Being two of only a handful of Americans in Nigeria at the time, they made it a point to have a couple of drinks whenever they were both in Lagos. Gibson used his telescope to spy on young village girls bathing in a stream near where they were drilling test holes. He bragged that he could spot a pretty girl on the moon if he had to. "Give me the number and thanks a lot, I owe you one."

"Don't mention it. I lied to you anyway. Even though I have that Jack Daniel's at home, I've been drinking your Jim Beam."

"You're a true friend, Harry." Mercer dripped sarcasm.

It was midnight in the United Arab Emirates so Mercer had to content himself with a message on Gibson's voice mail at the Petroleum Ministry, leaving his number on the aircraft in case Jim got to his office early but telling the oil man that he would be back in touch in the morning.

The flight took just under five hours; Mercer allowed himself to sleep only three. He used the rest of the time to organize the counterstrike against the *Southern Cross* née *Petromax Arctica*. The nap had gone a long way to revive him, but he wasn't even close to working at his peak. In the remaining hours before landing, he placed calls to Washington, D.C.; Victoria, British Columbia, where Captain Hauser was standing by; and to Andy Lindstrom in Valdez, who had wisely turned over the responsibilities of assessing the damaged pipeline to a subordinate. One of his calls, to Dave Saulman in Miami, had taken nearly half an hour, but had been worth every minute. Saulman's research had cast a shadow over Mercer's plan, but he had no option but to continue.

By the time the Alyeska jet touched down in Victoria, everything was in place. Hauser had a rental car ready to take him and Mercer down to the port, where a SEAL team from the naval base at Bremerton, Washington, was standing by. Henna had said that he'd had to pull in every favor ever owed him to get the President to authorize the use of the team.

"Have the Canadian authorities been notified?" Mercer was still on the phone as the jet taxied to the general aviation hangar.

"Be thankful I've gotten as far as I have with our people. Politicians have the memories of five-year-olds and half the attention span. It's going to take more time to get the Mounties on line too. The Canadians are in agreement in principle, but they want to get their own special forces in place. So far they've agreed that the SEALs can have the actual assault, but their men must be on scene as backup."

"Dick, Captain Hauser suspects that the terrorists are waiting until the tide turns. Then they'll spill the oil into the Juan de Fuca Strait with the rising water. According to a guy Hauser talked to here in Victoria, the tide turns in about thirty minutes. We're going as soon as I get to the waterfront, with or without the Canadians. It's one of those situations when you ask for forgiveness, not permission."

"Mercer, I can't allow you to do that. There are international considerations here."

"You don't understand, I'm not asking for your blessing—I'm telling you I'm going." Mercer hung up on his friend just as the pilot spooled down the engines and a ground worker opened the outer hatch. A customs agent was standing with him.

"Welcome to Canada, *Bienvenu au Canada*. Do you have anything to declare?"

"Yes, an emergency," Mercer breathed as he dragged himself out of the plane.

LYLE Hauser was waiting next to a Ford Taurus in the parking lot outside the general aviation building. He wore a pair of fisherman's overalls and borrowed gumboots. His clothes were clean, but his face was unshaven and drawn. "If I had a mirror, I bet I look as bad as you do."

"I'm that bad, huh?" Mercer replied, warming to the captain immediately. "Are we set?"

"Just waiting for you. I've been contacted by the naval personnel. They're standing by in the harbor with one of their assault boats."

"Have you briefed them about the people who seized your ship—numbers, types of weapons, that sort of thing?"

"I did the best I could. Most of what I know I got second-hand from the Chief Engineer before I escaped," Hauser said, slipping behind the wheel of the rental and gunning the motor. "The SEALs' commanding officer told me that they've practiced this kind of attack before. He said they have it all figured out."

"We'll see about that." Mercer agreed with Hauser's less than enthusiastic assessment.

It was only a ten-mile drive from the airport to Victoria harbor along Blanshard Street, Mercer and Hauser maintaining a companionable silence. Neither felt the need to discuss the outcome if they failed. The consequences were too horrifying to consider.

The sky was a clear robin's-egg blue with only a few smeared clouds high overhead to stain its perfect dome. While there was a bite to the air, the sun was strong enough to warm everything and give the autumn day a springlike feel. If the crude was spilled, the very air would turn to poison, the hydrocarbons so polluting the atmosphere that even a short-term exposure would mean burned lungs and the very real threat of cancer.

At the docks, the five-man SEAL team was as inconspicuous as a bottle of Scotch at an Alcoholics Anonymous meeting. They stood on their assault boat in body armor, their black outfits blending in with the boat perfectly but looking ridiculous compared to the L. L. Bean shirts and gaily colored jackets of the crowd that gawked at them like zoo patrons. The boat, an evil-looking deep-hulled craft skirted with a rubber pontoon ring and powered by twin outboard motors, looked like an ugly duckling compared with the sleek pleasure craft around it.

"Jesus Christ," Mercer exclaimed. "The fucking circus is in town."

He and Hauser moved across the docks as quickly as possible, praying they got to the boat before the Harbor Master spotted the assault craft and decided to investigate. "I can't believe they haven't been carted off by the local gendarmerie."

"Lieutenant Krutchfield?" Hauser called. "I'm Captain Hauser and this is Dr. Mercer." They jumped down to the boat, their combined weight having no impact on the stable craft. Mercer took a second to shake the young lieutenant's hand before ordering him to cast off.

Krutchfield's face was baby smooth, with cornflower blue eyes and a nose so sharply upturned his nostrils resembled the muzzles of a double-barreled shotgun. He didn't have that hard-edged look of the other soldiers in his team. He looked too eager, more like a puppy looking to be petted.

"Dr. Mercer," Krutchfield shouted over the throb of the engines. The boat was already rocketing at nearly fifty miles per hour, coming on to plane faster than any high-performance boat Mercer had ever seen. "I heard about what you did last year in Hawaii with another of the Teams, sir. I must say it's a pleasure to meet you."

When Mercer didn't acknowledge the compliment, Krutchfield continued. "It was just our luck that we were in Washington when the call came through."

"Lieutenant, only one SEAL survived that attack in Hawaii. I'd hold off on your enthusiasm until this is over," Mercer said darkly. "How far is the *Southern Cross*?"

"Satellite intel shows her holding a position about forty miles up the Strait. We'll be there in fifty minutes."

"Not in this death trap we won't. They'll blast us out of the water as soon as they see us coming. Do you guys have any civilian clothing, a disguise of some sort?"

"No, sir. We were briefed that this was a straightforward assault, no need for that sort of thing." Krutchfield didn't like having his tactics questioned.

"So much for subtlety," Hauser said.

Mercer's entire plan revolved around intercepting the boat meant to pick up JoAnn Riggs and her cadre of terrorists and using it to make their approach to the supertanker. However, even getting close to the pickup boat without tipping their hand would be tricky, considering the conspicuous nature of the SEALs' assault craft and the fact that they still didn't know which of the hundreds of vessels in the Strait was the one sent to fetch the terrorists. Without that piece of critical information, they might as well go home and watch the worst environmental disaster in American history on television. "What kind of communications gear do you have aboard?"

"Just this." The young commando held up a small portable radio, its antenna no more than a blister at the top of the armored casing.

"What the hell is that?"

"Devil Fish, Devil Fish, this is Mud Skipper. Come in, over." Krutchfield handed the radio to Mercer. "You're now in contact with the fast attack submarine USS *Tallahassee*. She's about forty feet below us and keeping pace all the way to the tanker. You aren't going to find a better comm center than a hunter–killer nuclear sub, Doctor. Since the alert was put out a few hours ago, they've been monitoring marine channels in the area, feeding all contacts into the computer and creating a chart of every ship in Puget Sound. My CO said Admiral Morrison of the Joint Chiefs thought you might appreciate the help. Seems he's a fan of yours."

"Devil Fish standing by," a voice called from the radio in Mercer's hand.

While Mercer was stunned by the presence of the submarine and just how much faith the Chairman of Joint Chiefs placed in him, he didn't allow it to affect him as he spoke. He was totally focused on what lay ahead. "Devil Fish, we're looking for a boat that left Victoria within the hour and is en route to the *Southern Cross*. She would have made at least one contact with the tanker, a brief message. The key word I'm looking for is *Arctica*. Do you have anything matching that description?"

"Stand by, Mud Skipper." A moment later the submariner came back. "Affirmative. A twin screw boat making revolutions for twenty knots left Victoria forty-seven minutes ago, one transmission to the tanker, traffic as follows. '*Arctica*, this is Rescue, en route, ETA 1420 hrs. Confirm?' The tanker replied, 'Confirmed.' That's all. Active sonar lash shows the target to be thirty-six feet long, eleven wide. Our best guess is she's a fishing boat or a seagoing cabin cruiser. Over."

"Roger, Devil Fish. Mud Skipper out." Mercer handed the radio back to Krutchfield. "It's going to be tight. We have to take that boat before she's in visual range of the tanker. Otherwise we don't stand a snowball's chance."

"How'd you know she'd be called the *Arctica* again? Her name was *Southern Cross* when I left her." Hauser was standing next to Mercer in the tiny cabin of the boat.

"I have a good lawyer," Mercer said without elaborating, then turned to Krutchfield. "Is this as fast as this pig can go?"

"Hell no," Krutchfield grinned, and the man at the helm dropped the throttles to their stops, the wind on the exposed deck screaming around them now at sixty miles per hour.

Mercer turned back to Hauser and filled him in on what had happened to the Trans-Alaska Pipeline earlier in the day and about Ivan Kerikov. "This is the second part of his plan, sinking a tanker in American waters, polluting the coastline for a couple of hundred miles. Max Johnston was part of this from the beginning, using one of his ships to transport the liquid nitrogen. He knew the ship was going to be scuttled, and to avoid the few billion dollars for the cleanup, he quietly sold his fleet, including the *Arctica*. He made certain his key people, like this JoAnn Riggs you told me about, remained on board."

"That's right. The *Petromax Pacifica* was to be renamed *Southern Hospitality*, and the *Arabia*'s new name is *Southern Accent*," Hauser stated.

"You were the wild card, since the *Arctica*'s former Captain, another conspirator I'm sure, was injured and had to be replaced. No offense, but they hired a captain who was at the mandatory retirement age and hadn't been at sea for a couple years. It would be easy to pin an 'accident' on you once you were dead."

"It doesn't add up. If Max Johnston sold his tankers, why is the ship still the *Petromax Arctica* and not *Southern Cross*?"

"Because early this morning, according to Dave Saulman, my lawyer friend, the sale of Petromax's fleet to SC&L was canceled. Their ownership reverted back to Johnston, including the responsibility for the two-hundred-thousand-ton oil spill that's about to occur."

"I don't get it." Hauser looked at Mercer with a blank expression.

"Somehow Kerikov was the money behind Southern Coasting and Lightering, and he planned to double-cross Max Johnston all along. He needed Max's equipment, the tanker and an offshore oil rig, but didn't want him as a full partner. There's still something else at stake that Kerikov didn't want Johnston a part of. Kerikov kidnapped Johnston's daughter to ensure that he never revealed his part in this plot. Max would be stuck with the cleanup and couldn't utter a word about his own complicity," Mercer replied, then fell silent.

With a hand braced against one of the cabin's tubular support stanchions, Mercer needed to take time to prepare himself for the attack. If things went according to plan, the SEALs would have little trouble seizing the escape boat and then using it as cover to take the supertanker. Hauser had said there was only a handful of terrorists holding the ship, and

SEALs were known to be the best special forces troops in the world. Like their name implied, they were equally comfortable on land as in the water. Taking over a ship, according to Krutchfield, was their stock-in-trade.

On the other hand, Mercer was in no condition to be part of their assault. In fact, he shouldn't even be breathing right now considering what he'd been through. He was spent. His body was one large aching bruise, and his shoulders, legs, and chest were beaten to the point where he felt light-headed. He had no illusions of himself in a firefight. His reactions were slow, his reflexes dulled by exhaustion. It took him a few moments to notice Krutchfield tapping on his arm.

"Message from Devil Fish," Krutchfield shouted into Mercer's ear. "Their sonar says we're about five miles behind our target and about seven from the tanker. Like you said, this is going to be tight."

"What's your plan?"

"Basically, come up next to them, and when we're abeam, open fire at the same time two of my men jump from this boat to theirs."

"And if you miss everyone with the first barrage and they manage to radio a warning to the *Arctica*?"

Krutchfield grinned his boyish smile. He was really loving this. "On my command, the *Tallahassee* is going to jam every radio transmission within a fifty-mile radius. There're going to be some pissed off disc jockeys in a few minutes."

The Juan de Fuca Strait here was wide, more like a broad lake than a strait, forests and cliffs towering on both sides but so far away they appeared to be held at bay by the surging water of the channel. In a different time, under different circumstances, Mercer would have enjoyed the ride. He grimly held on and watched the narrows before them, hoping to spot the telltale wake of the terrorists' boat. Mercer used the last few moments before contact to borrow some 9mm ammunition from one of the SEALs and transfer it into the clip of Kerikov's pistol.

"There!" Hauser shouted, his trained eyes finding the distant rescue boat much quicker than those of the younger men. He had a much stronger vested interest in saving the *Petromax*

Arctica/Southern Cross. To the SEALs, this was another hot op, but to him it was personal. She was his ship, his command.

From this distance, the boat was just a white dot on the gray water, its wake like a ghost image behind it. The tanker was still beyond visual range. It was impossible for those on the fleeing craft to see them. The black hull of the SEAL boat was all but lost amid the swells, its unusual silhouette making it all but invisible from beyond five hundred yards. But Krutchfield wasn't taking any chances. He lifted the radio to his lips as soon as he spotted the boat.

"Devil Fish, this is Mud Skipper. It's lights-out time. Repeat, it's lights-out time. Give us seven minutes, monitor, and if there is no contact, jam again until you hear that fucking tanker breaking up. At that point, go to condition Bravo."

"What's condition Bravo?" Mercer asked.

"The *Tallahassee* surfaces, targets the tanker with a MK48 torpedo and finds out if these assholes are willing to die for their cause."

Mercer didn't feel like pointing out that torpedoing the tanker would accomplish the terrorists' goals for them. But he could not remain silent. "Don't tell me if you have a condition Charley. I don't want to know." He fingered the pistol in his hands, absently clicking the safety.

"Lieutenant, I have an idea," Hauser said just before they were spotted by the pickup boat. It took only an instant for him to explain and everyone to agree.

They came up to the hurtling craft. She was a fat-hulled pleasure boat, her white freeboards badly discolored by years in the murky waters of the North Pacific, her upper works weathered by the region's notorious summer rains. She looked tired, and it was no surprise that at twenty knots, her engines were grinding out as much speed as she could muster. Because the terrorist team hadn't had enough time to make proper arrangements since being shifted from San Francisco, the owner of the vessel was stuffed into a fore storage locker, the contents of his skull adhering his corpse to the fiberglass walls. The men who'd stolen the boat, the crew spirited to Vancouver on Southern Coasting and Lightering's executive jet to assist JoAnn Riggs, were taking no chances that they would ever be connected to the destruction of the supertanker.

The SEALs' boat closed the gap between itself and the cabin cruiser so quickly that the navy commandos had to scramble to get themselves into position. Crouching behind the gunwale didn't offer them any protection if they encountered return fire, but they were invisible as the boat cut into the wake of the cruiser, sluing around until the two vessels were running parallel. Captain Lyle Hauser stood at the helm of the assault boat with Mercer, each looking relaxed in their civilian clothes. Hauser lazily throttled back the twin outboards until both boats were traveling at the same speed, only a few feet separating them, as if to say to the men on the white cruiser, "Hey, look at my new toy."

On the cruiser, the three men huddled in the flying bridge looked startled when they saw the sleek craft pull up next to them. To allay their fears, Mercer and Hauser waved enthusiastically, smiling as if this were nothing more than a pleasurable afternoon jaunt. Krutchfield and his SEALs were still out of sight.

"What's the layout?" Krutchfield was crouched behind Mercer, a machine pistol in his hands.

Mercer kept his smile in place as he spoke out of the corner of his mouth. "I see three men on the bridge, Arabs I'd guess. No visible weapons, but all of them are wearing windbreakers that could conceal just about anything. It looks like there is at least one more in the cabin below. I see movement in one of the small windows. I can't tell if he has a gun."

"SEALs, we go in thirty seconds," Krutchfield called quietly to his team. "Captain Hauser, ease us forward by about twenty feet, and when I yell out, bring us back abeam and put us right against her side."

Hauser acknowledged the order by grabbing the throttles. Instantly, the attack boat pulled ahead of the cruiser, cutting through the wedge of water that peeled off her bow. Mercer waved again but got no response.

The timing of the SEAL commandos was uncanny. Krutchfield hadn't even shouted when the boat's regular helmsman bumped Hauser from the conn and burped the engines, bringing them back alongside the weathered cabin cruiser. The three men on the pleasure boat's deck turned in unison as they started to overtake the odd-looking craft that had just passed them. But by the time they suspected anything was amiss, three of the SEALs had appeared over the gunwale and opened fire while Krutchfield and another commando leaped the narrow gap between the two speeding craft.

The H&K MP-5s the SEALs carried whined like buzz saws, pouring a hundred rounds into the cruiser in just a few seconds, blowing off pieces of fiberglass and worn wood-work, dicing the three men at the controls. There was a steady pulse of return fire from the boat's lower cabin, the distinctive chattering crash of an AK-47. Krutchfield's partner was caught halfway through his leap to the cruiser, the Russian-manufactured weapon stitching across his Kevlar body armor. None of the bullets pierced the vest's ballistic material, but the hydrostatic shock tossed him into the empty space be-tween the boats, his body vanishing in the clouds of cordite smoke that fouled the air. He hit the water with a bone-breaking splash, but his scream went unheard as the running battle continued.

Another burst from the SEALs tore a jagged hole in the hull around the porthole where the shots had originated. There was a brief scream piercing the sounds of automatic fire, and suddenly it was over. Krutchfield was at the controls of the cruiser, standing proud in an ankle-deep mire of blood and shattered bodies. He cut the engines at the same time as his helmsman slowed the assault boat, both craft hissing to a slow crawl, the echoing sounds of the battle dying away.

Mercer was the first from the SEAL boat onto the cabin cruiser, whose name he saw was *Happyhour*, with Hauser only a breath behind him. Krutchfield's other two SEALs swarmed over next, like extras in a pirate movie, their eyes bright with battle lust, their gun barrels hot from the fray. The helmsman arced the assault boat away from the *Happyhour*, carving a tight crescent in the Strait to pick up their fallen comrade, the powerful motors bellowing like caged animals as he gave them their head. While Krutchfield heaved bodies over the side of the captured boat, his two teammates ducked down the narrow steps to the belowdeck cabin. By the time Krutchfield had finished, they were back on the bridge. One of them, a compact Hispanic with a gap where one of his teeth had been, was wiping his knife against a napkin he'd taken from the galley. Red smears bloomed from the blade's passage.

"There were two of them, *jefe*," he remarked casually, slipping the blade back into its inverted scabbard on his combat harness.

"Shit," Krutchfield exclaimed. He turned to look over his shoulder at the distant wake of his boat.

There had been five terrorists on the boat. With one SEAL down in the water and the other out to get him, there were only three commandos on the *Happyhour*.

Mercer knew what the navy lieutenant was thinking and spoke before Krutchfield did something rash. "We don't have time to wait for them," he said. "JoAnn Riggs is expecting this boat in a couple of minutes. We don't need to make her any more suspicious by being late. There were five men sent to pick her up. There are five of us, including Hauser and me."

"Dr. Mercer, we've been trained for this type of sortie; it's what we get paid for. I understand why you and Captain Hauser are here, but I can't authorize you to board the *Arctica* until we have her secured."

"We don't have time to argue about this, Lieutenant. Let's get going. We'll discuss it on the way, but no matter what, we can't wait here for your other men." Mercer knew that Krutchfield would have no choice but to allow him to come along. They were going to need the extra firepower.

"Mercer, JoAnn Riggs would recognize me right away, I'd be more of a liability than an asset," Hauser pointed out.

"I know. I just thought about that. How about if you follow us about five minutes after we board? We should have the area around the boarding ladder secured by then. Believe me, we're going to need you if Riggs has already started to scuttle the ship. I don't know anything about tankers."

"I thought you said you worked for Alyeska?"

"No, I don't. I'm here as a favor to Andy Lindstrom, the

Chief of Operations. Kind of filling in, so to speak."

"Oh, shit, we're in trouble," Hauser breathed.

"Tell me about it." Mercer was staring over the bow of the racing cabin cruiser. A half mile ahead, the VLCC *Petromax Arctica* appeared, her one-hundred-sixty-foot-wide beam making her head-on profile look like a solid wall of preformed steel tucked against the north bank of the ten-mile-wide Juan de Fuca Strait.

While the sight of her unimaginable size was awe inspiring, Mercer couldn't help but think she looked like a ghost ship.

ABOARD THE *PETROMAX ARCTICA*
JUAN DE FUCA STRAIT,
BRITISH COLUMBIA

As the cities of Seattle and Vancouver expanded during the '80s and '90s, fueled by immigration from Asia and the technology companies that seemingly grew out of every garage and basement, great pains were taken to ensure that the pristine Pacific Northwest was left as virgin as possible. Unlike the megalopolis that stretches from Boston to Washington, D.C., that's been spoiled forever by two hundred years of sprawl, the environs of Puget Sound were still beautiful rugged forests and mountains and clear cold waters that supported both commercial fisherman and the needs of the avid sportsmen. Wildlife flourished, especially in the Sound itself, where marine creatures from majestic whales to playful otters abounded. The crab beds around Seattle were legendary, teeming with the delicious crustaceans even after years of harvesting, and the national forests were perfect habitats for deer, beaver, and dozens of other woodland species.

To all but the most vehement environmentalists, the area was the model of ecology and industry working together in productive harmony.

Where the sea rushes between Victoria Island and the mainland, a few miles from the city of Port Angeles, the VLCC *Petromax Arctica* hulked low in the water, her belly swollen by 200,000 tons of oil so her rails seemed only a few feet above the waves sliding against her. While tankers were not an uncommon sight in the Strait, one of the *Arctica*'s dimensions was. But more disturbing than her presence was the feathery tail of smoke leaking from her square funnel. Her engines were turning only enough for station's keeping against the tide flowing into the Sound.

While the past quarter century is full of stories of supertanker accidents, the *Exxon Valdez*, the *Amaco Cadiz,* and the *Torrey Canyon* being the most famous, many of the giant vessels have been lost through storm or accident or mechanical fault. During a single month in 1969, three tankers of over two hundred thousand tons were lost or severely damaged, and few outside of the oil industry ever knew of these incidents. While the causes of disasters vary, it's rare that a single fault can sink one of these behemoths. Many factors, from weather to a simple human mistake to a complete design flaw, are necessary to pull a supertanker under the waves. Not until the space shuttle has a single device possessed so many backup systems and fail-safes—all designed to prevent the type of disaster about to unfold in the waters leading to Puget Sound.

In Ivan Kerikov's plan, the destruction of the tanker was to occur shortly after the cancellation of her sale to Southern Coasting and Lightering. Since the crippled ship could not make it as far south as San Francisco Bay, the plug had been pulled on the deal a few days early, a minor detail that only slightly altered the the intended outcome of the operation. Captain Hauser's valiant actions merely shifted the target city to Seattle. While not as sentimental as San Francisco, it was an equally fragile ecosystem that would suffer just as cruelly when the crude washed up on its coastlines.

JoAnn Riggs' job now was to ensure that as much oil as

possible was dumped into the sea, while making her actions appear accidental rather than intentional. With the ship's crew shortly to be killed and the extraction boat on the way, there would be no witnesses and no physical evidence that the largest oil spill in history was an act of sabotage. The most conservative estimate predicted oil spreading from Bellingham to Everett, and the best-case scenario saw a slick covering a one-hundred-seventy-four mile stretch of coast from Vancouver to Tacoma, an area that included thousands of miles of irregular shoreline and numerous inlets, islands, and bays.

Giving the order to kill the remaining crewmen was a decision that gave JoAnn Riggs pause. It was an order that should have fallen to Captain Albrecht but now was her responsibility. While the million dollars that was to be her share for this operation would go a long way to assuaging her guilt, she was still reluctant to give Wolf the nod to do it.

Sensing her unease as they stood on the port side bridge wing, Wolf knew he would have to kill them without getting the direct order. There were so many murders in his past that a few more didn't cause him undue concern. However, he did lose some respect for the woman who had executed the takeover of the tanker as if born to terrorism. As he turned to go, he took Riggs' silence as a tacit approval. While Wolf would be doing the actual killing, the responsibility was still hers. Riggs gathered herself to finish what she had been paid to accomplish.

Max Johnston had made certain when the *Petromax Arctica* was built that she incorporated every automatic and systematic safety device to prevent her from ever spilling even a drop of her cargo. Therefore, to intentionally sink the vessel and make sure that crude poured from the hull in such volume that nothing could prevent it took the concerted effort of the entire terrorist cadre except for Wolf and one man he kept to assist him, each of them assigned a specific task and timed with military precision.

The great hull of the *Arctica* was segmented into eighteen separate tanks, a system used not only to prevent the entire cargo from being lost if she were ever holed but also to make the vessel much more stable in rough water. A complex system of valves and pumps connected the tanks, used mostly to keep an even keel when part of the cargo had been pumped off the ship. The computer that monitored the level of oil in each of the cavernous tanks prevented the ship from ever becoming unbalanced in even the roughest storms, compensating automatically to the conditions of the vessel and of the sea.

Riggs and her team had to take the computer off-line and manually operate the pumps, valves, and float cocks that controlled oil movement. The computer could not produce the conditions necessary for dumping her cargo—there were mechanical checks as well as those programmed into the system. Human hands, driven by greed or madness, would have to run many of the controls, opening them wide even as the computer was demanding they close. The machine's binary morality put that of humans to shame.

The first part of their plan to dump the *Arctica*'s cargo was the sea suction inlet located at the stern of the vessel. This thirty-inch-diameter pipe, in conjunction with the *Arctica*'s three cargo pumps, was used to draw seawater into the tanks during cleaning and ballasting operations. To allow the cargo to drain from the hull out through the inlet, eight different valves of the double-segregated system had to be opened. Then, gravity would force the two hundred thousand tons of crude into the open sea. Perversely, the ship would rise in the water as its cargo discharged, increasing the pressure through the outlet and spraying oil in a two-hundred-foot jet when it cleared the waterline. Unless a salvage diver explored the tank control room after the ship had been scuttled and checked each of the valves, there would be no evidence of sabotage.

The second part of the plan involved temporarily removing the deck covers over several tanks and using the manifold system to flood the deck with oil. Once Riggs was ready to open the sea suction inlet, the covers would be replaced, again—to remove evidence of tampering. The crude would then be ignited as the remainder drained away. Spill response teams would waste precious time battling the flames, never realizing that much more significant damage had already been

done in the pump room. Third, shaped explosive charges were
to be detonated in the crawl spaces between the vessel's double hulls, timed so that much of her oil would already be
oozing toward shore when her bottom was blown out. If
things went according to design, the reasons behind the sinking of the *Petromax Arctica* would remain a mystery.

Riggs waited in the pump control room while part of her
team were in the labyrinthine tangle of the inner hull spaces
planting explosives and others removed the covers to six of
the tanks. So far, the computer monitors showed that the system was nominal. The tanks were in perfect trim, the ratio of
gases in the inert mixture that prevented the oil from ever
catching fire was within the proper range.

Riggs had wanted to coordinate efforts with hand-held
walkie-talkies, but they appeared to all have failed at the same
time. She couldn't get even a faint whisper from any of the
units. Thinking it was a bad batch of batteries, JoAnn never
suspected that the signals were being jammed. Relying on a
quickly drawn up schedule, she waited for the appointed time
to deactivate the computer and spool up the huge pumps that
controlled the oil flow within the ship.

As soon as a hatch cover was removed from one of the
brimming tanks, an alarm sounded in the control room that
indicated the gas ratio had changed and was becoming dangerously explosive. At each alarm, Riggs flipped several
switches, and the valves controlling oil flow forced crude into
the open-hatched tank. It came bubbling through the openings
in thick clots like some primordial tar pit, spreading in ever
widening pools. At fifteen thousand tons an hour, it took only
a few seconds for the pumps to coat the main deck in an
inches-deep slick, heavy ropes of oil draining through the
scuppers to pour into the Strait. The alarm for the Saab ullage
radar, which measured the height between the top of the cargo
and the tops of the tanks, wailed an even more strident note
than the other sensors. Riggs ignored it, making certain that
the entire four-and-a-quarter acres of the deck were awash
with North Slope crude. The mixture of oil vapor and air
became a destructive cloud over the hull. Satisfied, she shut

down the pump and waited for the crews to wrestle the hatches back into place through the stinking black slime.

She had emptied oil from only six of the eighteen tanks in a zigzag pattern that caused the hull to creak mournfully from the added strain of her now uneven load. Once the explosives in the ship's belly detonated, this additional stress against her keel would speed up her destruction. A shining pool that scintillated like a rainbow had already formed around the *Arctica*'s dark hull, and a few inches of her oxide red Plimsoll line showed above the waves.

Riggs looked at her watch. It was ten minutes past two. The boat sent to fetch her and the others would be here in minutes. As if echoing her thoughts, Wolf appeared at her shoulder and said, "The boat is approaching. It is time to go." His accent masked any emotion he might have had, though Riggs doubted he was capable of feelings.

"Is it done?" Riggs asked, referring to the murder of the crew.

"Yes, they're dead."

As a precaution if any bodies were recovered or washed ashore, Wolf and one of his men had forcibly drowned each member of the *Arctica*'s crew in the saltwater swimming pool on the funnel deck. Each man had to be led up to the pool individually, rendered unconscious by a blow to the head, and held under water until his struggles had ended. It had taken them much longer than anticipated to kill all twenty-four.

Riggs and Wolf waited in silence for a few minutes, giving the deck crews enough time to resecure the hatches. Once Riggs' watch swept past 2:20 P.M., she manually opened the eight screw valves that led from the sea suction inlet to the main lines feeding from the ship's cargo tanks. As the final valves opened, the pressure of oil venting through the ten-inch pipes could be felt as a palpable presence in the room. The flow sounded like a locomotive hissing through a long tunnel. Where the three lines combined into the main thirty-inch artery, the torrent made a noise like a continuous explosion. Crude began pouring from the vessel, life blood from a mortal wound.

Riggs smiled. "Let's get off this coffin ship. I just need to stop and use the radio to complete our cover as hapless victims about to die, and then we're gone."

ANY conversation Mercer and Krutchfield planned to have about the two civilians helping to retake the *Petromax Arctica* became moot when they saw the cauldron of oil blooming around the supertanker's fantail. Even from a distance of half a mile, the sharp smell carried to them on the salty breeze.

"*Madre de Dios*," the Hispanic SEAL mumbled. He crossed himself quickly.

"They didn't wait for the rescue boat." Krutchfield stated the obvious. "We're too late."

"Maybe not," Mercer said tightly. He looked at Hauser, who regarded the crippled ship with horror. "Captain?"

"I don't know," Hauser finally said. "I can't tell how bad it is until I'm aboard. It looks as if they reversed the sea suction and used it as a discharge outlet. Or they may have holed her. I can't be sure."

The *Arctica*'s stern pointed toward the open ocean and her bow speared eastward inside Puget Sound. The cabin cruiser raced along the entire quarter mile of her length to where a rope ladder dangled from her aft port rail. Like an iceberg that hides four-fifths of its bulk under water, the true dimensions of the supertanker could not be fully comprehended even as they passed down her hull. The ship's side, as black as sin and as smooth as glass, scrolled by endlessly as Krutchfield guided the *Happyhour* to the boarding ladder. It defied belief that something so vast could have been wrought by human hands, yet Mercer and the rest could see only part of the ship. Below them, the hull sank into the depths for sixty feet, the equivalent of a six-story building.

At the stern, Mercer looked behind them to see the full scope of the tanker and was reminded of the photographs he'd seen of China's Great Wall, a continuous slab stretching to infinity. It was a chilling sight.

The entire hull was surrounded by a thick poisonous moat of oil.

"Hold fast," a voice called from high above, a tiny blob

that was a face peering over the rail of the *Arctica*. "We are coming down."

Krutchfield and his two remaining SEALs had put on yellow rain jackets to camouflage their black uniforms, and so far it seemed to have fooled the man on the tanker. The next few minutes would be telling as the SEALs started up the ladder, their weapons hidden under the rubberized slickers.

"No, go back down. We're finished," the terrorist aboard the tanker shouted, his words torn away by the breeze tunneling down the Juan de Fuca Strait.

Krutchfield ignored the order as he scrambled up the swaying rope ladder, his feet kicking effortlessly on the rungs, his remaining team members following closely. They looked like a single organism as they climbed, undulating upward in a fluid motion. Mercer waited for half a beat before he committed himself to the task, knowing that Hauser would follow. The Captain no longer cared if he was recognized by Riggs or one of the terrorists. The *Petromax Arctica* was his ship, nominally under his command, and he would do whatever was necessary to prevent her destruction.

Mercer was three quarters of the way up the ladder when Krutchfield heaved himself over the railing and onto the deck. He thought about the ladders he used to climb as a boy in the granite quarries of Barre, Vermont, where he was raised. He used to be able to scamper up them like a monkey, unburdened by the fear that now clamped onto his stomach and knotted every aching muscle in his body. Above him, the last of the SEALs reached the top and disappeared from view. Without knowing what waited, he followed.

Suddenly the rope ladder jerked, bucking so hard that Mercer paused to see if Hauser was in trouble below him. Looking down, he saw the older man shaking the ladder to catch his attention. Reflexively, Mercer glanced upward in time to see one of the SEALs pitch over the side of the ship. A heartbeat later, the sound of gunfire reached him.

The lifeless corpse of the Hispanic commando flew by, pinwheeling through space until he landed flat on the water, white spume like a policeman's chalk outline erupting around his body. Mercer jerked the pistol from his belt as he listened to the gunfire over his head. He couldn't stay where he was, exposed and vulnerable, and rather than backing down, he surged upward, bobbing his head quickly over the railing to assess the situation.

The deck was empty except for a handful of shining brass shell casings that rolled on the white steel deck. Wisps of acrid smoke still filtered from the necks of the spent shells, singeing his nose even sharper than the leaking crude. There were thick strings of blood splashed across the deck leading toward a closed hatchway.

A mechanical-sounding voice almost made Mercer lose his precarious perch. "Devil Fish calling Mud Skipper. Standing by."

He'd forgotten that he had Krutchfield's comm link to the *Tallahassee*. Tucking his pistol under his arm to free his hand, Mercer reached for the radio. "This is Mud Skipper. The condition is . . . Oh, shit, I don't know. Just wait. I'll be back in touch."

He jammed the radio back in his coat pocket and rolled onto the deck, finding cover under the port side lifeboat davit, the empty mechanism offering protection from every side.

The pain he had endured before, the agony of being beaten and shot and crashed and drowned and nearly incinerated, meant nothing at this instant. Adrenaline, the natural drug he had become addicted to so long ago, coursed through his body, giving clarity to everything he saw or felt or sensed. Mercer was on automatic and nothing else mattered.

"Hauser, move it, we don't have time," he called, rushing past the rope ladder.

Mercer slammed his shoulder against the superstructure door as Hauser came onto the deck. The heavy steel crashed back against a bulkhead, and beyond lay a dim carpeted hallway. Eight feet down the corridor, a dark lump on the deck revealed itself to be the body of one of the terrorists, his chest ripped open by a SEAL's machine pistol. As Mercer stooped to pick up the pistol left lying near the corpse, Hauser came up behind him. The smell of oil lay heavy in the air, coating their throats like a thick mucus and burning their eyes so that they were red and raw.

"We have to get to the pump room." Fear and tension made

Hauser speak unnaturally loudly, his voice booming in the corridor.

Gunfire rippled in the distance. A fierce battle raged a deck below them.

"We're not going to make it this way," Mercer said, guessing they were cut off from the pump room.

"We can get there from the other side of the ship, but we need to go back outside and cross the hull on the funnel deck. I'll lead you."

"No, stay behind me. I can't risk you if we get ambushed. Just call out directions." Mercer was already running the way they'd come, the two automatic pistols held in his fists like a western gunslinger.

Hauser guided Mercer up several flights of stairs, their feet slipping on the steel treads. On the lower bridge deck, the area that housed the crew's mess, theater, library, and dispensary, Hauser paused to look into the mess. Seeing that it was empty, a dark look crossed his face. He feared the worst for his boys. They crossed the width of the ship on the funnel deck at the very top of the superstructure. From this vantage, nearly eighty feet above the water, Mercer could see the widening stain of oil like a cancer around the supertanker. He had no way of judging the amount of crude already lost, but even a single drop was too much. A high wave passing down Juan de Fuca Strait met the resistance of the slick and was crushed under the oil's weight into a ripple that could barely undulate the sea's glossy surface. The two men dashed across the funnel deck, the *Arctica*'s Captain on Mercer's heels as he dodged between vent stacks, mechanical housings, and the elevator's machinery shack. Hauser almost ran into the mining engineer when Mercer stopped just short of the swimming pool. The limp bodies of Hauser's crew floated on the surface of the water like so many neglected toys. The gruesome tableau held both men immobile for long seconds as they stared mutely at the horror before them.

"I want them, Mercer. I want them all to pay for this. . . ." Words failed Hauser as he looked at what had become of his crew. Tears of rage and frustration pricked his eyes as he struggled to keep his emotions in check.

"We both do," Mercer said quietly. No matter how many times he'd seen death in its thousand guises, he could not, would not, harden himself to it. He was as shaken as Captain Hauser.

A door opened beside them. Mercer instantly noticed the man's clothes as he peered onto the deck. It wasn't one of the SEALs, and Mercer's two guns spit in rapid succession, eight rounds fired as fast as he could pull the triggers. Six of the shots caught the terrorist, stitching him from thigh to throat. He was dead before he hit the deck.

Deep below the waterline, at the very keel of the *Petromax Arctica*, microscopic welding flaws in the hull plating began to expand into long jagged rents as the strain of the uneven cargo load grew. Like a tree caught in a high wind, the ship moaned, metal rending against metal in a deep resonance that echoed across the Strait. The *Arctica* was beginning to break up.

"Let's go. We've got to stop this ship from splitting apart."

Hauser led Mercer to the forward edge of the superstructure just above the bridge. Both men were struck dumb. Expecting to see the red-painted main deck stretching the length of three football fields, they were greeted by a wide expanse of crude oil. Only the elevated catwalk that ran the length of the ship and the twin towers of the manifold located amidships were visible above the stinking black morass.

"What does it mean?" Mercer found his voice.

"They probably plan to ignite the ship too. It's not enough just to pour her cargo from her—they want to set her ablaze as well."

Far beyond the bow of the tanker, miles away it seemed, Mercer could just make out the white knife-edge prow of an approaching Coast Guard cutter, but it was already too late for the cavalry's arrival. Poison was dumping from the tanker so fast that by the time the authorities arrived, tens of thousands of tons would be polluting the virgin waters of Puget Sound.

"We've got to close the sea suction inlet," Hauser shouted.

"Lead on," Mercer cried and followed Hauser at a fast run toward the interior of the VLCC.

They ran through the crew's portion of the superstructure, both men ignoring the possibility of an ambush. If they did come across one of Riggs' terrorists, it would be a chance to vent some of their hatred and anger. At a T-junction at the end of a long hall, Hauser directed Mercer left, then down two more flights of stairs. So far the coast was clear. The ship had begun to list, and it felt more noticeable as they entered her bowels, forcing both men to run with one shoulder braced against the wall. The chemical stench was getting stronger with each passing breath.

"How much farther?" Mercer's lungs burned from the combination of exertion and the petrochemical mist he inhaled with every step.

"One more deck down," Hauser panted. "We're almost there."

Mercer set off again, his jaw locked in determination. Twelve hours ago he had been struggling to escape a doomed oil rig and now he was racing into the heart of a doomed oil tanker. The irony was not lost on him, and he chuckled grimly.

All at once, he heard voices at the foot of a staircase and flattened himself against a wall to listen. Over the shriek of several alarms, he couldn't distinguish the words. The voices, one male, the other female, seemed to be retreating down the hallway he and Hauser had almost entered.

Taking a chance, he ducked around the stair landing and saw two figures walking away, neither of them apparently concerned with the vessel's predicament or the alarms crying around them. Hauser looked too and almost started after JoAnn Riggs and the terrorist named Wolf, but Mercer restrained him, forcing the Captain against a bulkhead so that he could look the older man in the eye.

"They're not important. I know how you feel, but we've got to save the ship first. You've got to stop the oil."

Reluctantly, Hauser nodded, and the two men dashed down the dim corridor and into the pump room. The Captain immediately set about righting his ship, spooling up the three pumps in an effort to suck the oil-contaminated seawater back into the vessel. It was a desperate act that did not succeed.

The weight of crude remaining in the tanks exerted too much pressure for the pumps to overcome. Oil continued to belch from her. Hauser was forced to close the double valves on the thirty-inch main and each of the three smaller pipes, managing to stem the leach of petroleum. While Hauser was doing this, Mercer worked on deactivating the alarms. The sound was rising and falling so shrilly that his teeth felt on edge.

"How's it going?" Mercer shouted over the klaxons. Hauser was working frantically, moving from one workstation to another, flipping switches and checking dials before returning to the Damatic computer system, running through menus and sliding the mouse around like a child with a toy race car.

"I think we're going to make it. I'm trying to redistribute oil within the holds. I need to rebalance the ship." Hauser looked up at Mercer seriously. "If we were a minute later, there wouldn't have been anything I could do. The ship would have broken up."

Without warning, the air in the pump room came alive as if an electric charge had arced through the space. A wild burst of nine-millimeter ammunition smashed into the steel walls and ceiling, fragmented into hundreds of supersonic pieces, filling the air like a maddened swarm. Over the shriek created by the fusillade came two concussive booms of a larger-caliber gun. Mercer was spared from the assault by a metal cabinet used to store crude samples taken from the tanks during loading. Hauser was not.

The Captain caught a brutal spread across his broad back, red blooms erupting on his coat where the hot metal punctured cloth and skin. He pitched forward, screaming. He hit a desk, balanced for a second, and then fell to the floor, writhing as though caught in a seizure.

Mercer ducked around the cabinet in time to see a dark figure lurch from the doorway, getting off a snap shot he knew had been too slow. He edged to the door to take a quick look down the hall and almost had his throat slit for his effort. Lieutenant Krutchfield was leaning there, his face blackened and bloody. There were three bleeding holes in his uniform, and his Kevlar body armor looked as though it had been stampeded by a herd of buffalo. The knife he held at Mercer's

throat had drawn a thin line of blood before the SEAL realized he was about to kill one of the good guys and checked
the motion.

"I almost had the son of a bitch, but I'm out of ammo."
Krutchfield's pistol was locked back empty and still smoked
in his other hand. "I thought you were his backup."

"Christ, he just opened fire in this room." Fear stripped
Mercer of his usual calm. "Do you think he would have done
that to his own man?"

"Sorry." Krutchfield was fading fast. "I'm a bit fucked up
right now. I can't seem to think too well."

"No shit. You've lost a lot of blood." Mercer guided the
commando into the pump room and laid him on the floor next
to Hauser. The Captain had quieted to an occasional whimper.
Mercer couldn't tell if he had gone into shock. "Krutchfield?
Is your other man still around?"

"I don't think so. We got jumped pretty hard coming up.
There were at least six terrs waiting for us. After securing the
top of the ladder, we separated and went into pursuit. That
wasn't one of my best ideas," the SEAL admitted.

"Just make sure you live to regret it." Mercer checked the
clips on his two pistols, combining the half-empty magazines
into one fully charged weapon. "Stay with Hauser. Do whatever you can for him. I saw a Coast Guard ship headed our
way, probably called in by Devil Fish. Help will be here in
just a few minutes."

Mercer was almost out of the room when Krutchfield called
to him. "Be careful of this guy. I had him in my sights when
I pulled the trigger, but he'd moved by the time the bullets
arrived. He's the quickest bastard I've ever seen."

"Thanks." It was news Mercer didn't need.

In the hallway, Mercer took a second to examine the trail
of blood splattered on the decking. Maybe the fleeing terrorist
wouldn't be so fast anymore. With the pistol held before him,
he followed the blood, keeping himself covered as best he
could. As the trail led him out of the superstructure, he increased his pace, feeling that the terrorist was more interested
in escaping than finishing what he'd started in the pump
room.

Finally coming out into a naturally lighted corridor, the pale sun entering through long rectangular windows, Mercer realized that the terrorist wasn't headed toward the rope ladder. They had come out on the main deck on the opposite side of the tanker and well forward of where it had been left dangling. This close to the main deck, Mercer could feel the radiant heat of the crude oil that covered it. It had been about one hundred twenty degrees when it was pumped from the ground at Prudhoe Bay and had lost little of its warmth since. It actually felt good compared to the sharp October air, but the smell was tremendous, so strong he could see the fumes rising off the slick.

Staring down the expanse of the main deck it was easy to see the footprints left by JoAnn Riggs' last terrorist, their shape distorted as the oil slowly oozed back to cover them but distinguishable nevertheless. In the very far distance, past the manifold towers, a figure ran, favoring one leg as he moved but maintaining a good pace on the slick surface.

Mercer dashed up to the raised metal catwalk that ran down the center of the deck in hopes the dry surface would be quicker going than chasing directly after the terrorist. He was surprised, but thankful, to find an old bicycle propped up against a support stanchion, the tired-looking two-wheeler left there as a convenience to crews who needed to get to the distant bow during routine ship's operations. Every supertanker usually carried them.

In seconds, he was gaining rapidly.

Wolf had been certain he'd heard voices as he and JoAnn Riggs were leaving the pump room. As they'd walked away, he could almost feel eyes on the back of his head, but he hadn't turned to look. It was only after he and Riggs had gotten to the main deck, and he saw the human carnage that had once been his team, that he decided to go back into the ship and dispose of whoever was opposing them. Riggs continued to the boarding ladder and the cabin cruiser. Wolf knew that the pump room would be the logical target for a counterstrike. It was the only place on the ship to prevent her imminent destruction.

As he fled along the deck, running as best he could with

the stinging wound to his thigh where Krutchfield had shot him, he realized that going back had been a critical, maybe fatal, mistake. He had abandoned his training by giving in to emotions. Even if the destruction of the *Petromax Arctica* was averted, he had done his job. Yet he'd returned to the pump room and gotten seriously wounded for his efforts.

Now he raced for the bow, hoping the SEAL who'd shot him would follow. If he was to die on this cursed ship, he wanted the opportunity to take out just one of the Americans.

Wolf looked behind him, hoping to see the SEAL giving chase, and out of the corner of his eye he saw a madman on a bicycle racing toward him on the elevated walkway over his head. He tossed his empty weapon onto the deck, and from the deep pocket of his cargo pants withdrew a wax-coated flare he'd carried with him since the beginning of the scuttling operation. It had been his assignment to ignite the oil lying on the deck just before he and Riggs and the rest of the team fled the vessel.

Mercer heaved the bicycle into a tight skid on the catwalk when he saw the figure below turn and toss away a machine pistol. He let the bike clatter to the deck as he stood to take careful aim with his pistol. Just before he got into a proper stance, the terrorist jerked his right hand, and a red sun burst from his fist, an acrid trail of smoke billowing from the flare he'd been carrying.

"Drop your weapon or this whole ship goes up in flames," Wolf shouted at what he thought was a SEAL on the spidery walkway.

"You don't need to do this. Throw the flare over the side of the ship," Mercer countered. Wolf stood in a pool of oil about two inches deep but covering nearly four acres. Just behind him, the deck bubbled as more crude leached out of an improperly secured hatch cover.

Two hundred thousand tons of highly explosive crude oil. Two hundred kilotons. Facing his own death, Mercer absently wondered if a ton of TNT had more or less explosive force than a ton of oil. He recalled that Hiroshima had been leveled with the equivalent of twenty kilotons. Even if the ratio between TNT and oil wasn't close, he was still standing on a bomb many times more powerful than Little Boy.

He tried to remember what Hauser had said about the gases in the storage tanks. Why did the air in the tanks have to be inert? It was a sign of Mercer's exhaustion that he couldn't remember what it was about oil that made the air in the tanks so important.

"Yes, I do need to do this," Wolf shouted back, the flare waving in his hands like a Fourth of July sparkler, as mesmerizing as a cobra's dance. "If for no other reason than to know you will die with me."

Mercer tightened his grip on the gun, keeping the sights centered on Wolf's chest. Then he remembered. Oil is combustible only in a narrow range of gas ratios; to burn it had to be mixed with precisely 11 percent oxygen. Too much or too little and the mixture was noncombustive unless the oil was preheated first. Hoping that the mix was in his favor and without thinking further, Mercer adjusted his aim and fired off three rapid rounds. The 9mm bullets shredded Wolf's shoulder so that his arm swung uselessly at his side, attached to his trunk by a few scraps of flesh. The flare, its tip burning at several hundred degrees, fell from his deadened fingers, landing with a sluggish splash onto the deck.

Wolf screamed in pain and fell to his knees. He then saw the crimson flare lying beside him, the bright flame shooting from its tip like a tiny rocket motor. He tried to stand, but the wound in his leg and the damage done to his shoulder made his movements so uncoordinated that he pitched forward into the slick. In seconds, he was drowning, unable to turn his face out of the ooze.

As soon as he'd fired and saw that Wolf had dropped the flare, Mercer vaulted over the railing of the catwalk. While the flare had not yet ignited the crude, he didn't want to push his luck. He landed hard, his legs kicking out on the slippery surface so that he fell on his backside, the impact jarring his buttocks and lower back. Agony crashed against the top of his skull. Sliding more than crawling, he reached for the incendiary, scooping it up and holding it high over his head just as the globules of oil that dripped from it burst into yellow flames that landed on his body. He used his free hand to beat out the tiny fires and carefully got to his feet, shuffling to the *Arctica*'s railing. He heaved the flare far out into the Strait, well beyond where the oil had leaked from her holds.

"Mud Skipper, this is Devil Fish. Come in, please."

Mercer stood by the rail watching the flare sputter in the water and didn't want to respond to the submarine lurking below the ship, but slowly he began to hear an alarming noise. He fished the small radio from his pocket. "This is Mud Skipper. Go ahead."

"Sonar is picking up a prop signature, twin screws accelerating away. The signal matches that of the cabin cruiser. Can you confirm you are aboard it?"

He looked down the length of the ship, past where the bridge wing jutted out over the side of the huge vessel. Beyond the stern, he could see the *Happyhour* running from the tanker toward the open Pacific. With Krutchfield and Hauser in the pump room and the rest of the SEALs dead—as well as the *Arctica*'s crew, only terrorists or JoAnn Riggs could be on the fleeing cabin cruiser.

"Negative, Devil Fish. The boat is carrying terrorists. Can you take them out?"

"Affirmative."

The swift passage of the USS *Tallahassee* only thirty or so feet below the surface actually created a disturbance in the water like the movement of some great fish. Mercer couldn't believe the speed of the attack submarine or its incredible agility as it went off in pursuit of the *Happyhour*. Watching intently, he waited for the explosion of a torpedo strike against the vessel's transom, but it never came. The *Happyhour* was just a small speck near the horizon when suddenly a shining black leviathan rose up from the sea directly behind her.

Like a playful dolphin, the nose of the USS *Tallahassee* exploded into the wake of the *Happyhour*, the huge hull coming forty feet out of the water before her incredible weight overcame the inertia of her atomic engines and she smashed back into the Strait, walls of white water blowing out from the impact. Almost as quickly as she appeared, the *Tallahassee* vanished once again. The submarine crash dove as soon as she broached the surface, and as the *Tallahassee* sank under the waves she created a huge vortex behind the cruiser as it tried to escape. Four thousand tons of water rushed back into the void the sub's hull had produced with her brief appearance.

JoAnn Riggs and the pleasure boat *Happyhour* were sucked into the maelstrom, vanishing as if they had never existed. The cruiser was swamped so quickly by the maneuver that a seagull racing above the white-hulled boat was also drawn under and drowned. A few seconds passed and the broiling water calmed. There was no debris to mark where Riggs had died.

Had Mercer not been watching, he wouldn't have believed it. One minute he could clearly see the *Happyhour* racing for the open ocean, and the next it looked as though it had been swallowed by some nightmarish creature, like Jonah being consumed by the whale. Gone. Forever.

"Devil Fish to Mud Skipper, Devil Fish to Mud Skipper. Mission accomplished. Coast Guard reports they will be alongside in two minutes. There are lightering tankers en route to pump off your cargo, and Seattle authorities have been alerted to an oil spill. Response teams are on their way. We are continuing on to our regularly scheduled mission already in progress."

Mercer smiled at the jubilant voice over the radio, not knowing it was the submarine's captain but not surprised later when he found out it was. "Roger, Devil Fish. This is Mud Skipper. Over and out and thank you very much." He began trudging back to the superstructure where a Coast Guard cutter was getting into position to tie up.

With only eight minutes left before detonation, Coast Guard personnel discovered and disarmed the charges placed between the *Arctica*'s double hull. The tide that Riggs and Kerikov had counted on to dump oil all along the shores of Puget Sound was not nearly as high as predicted that day, and the twelve million gallons of crude spilled, though more than the *Exxon Valdez*, did not cause nearly the environmental catastrophe as intended.

A chopper flew Captain Hauser and Lieutenant Krutchfield to a hospital, and both survived. Knowing there was only one more detail to take care of, Mercer was beginning to feel he could finally put an end to the entire affair.

THE UNITED
ARAB EMIRATES

Looking at a globe, it is almost impossible to get any farther away from Seattle than the Persian Gulf. They lie on nearly exact opposite sides of the planet. Yet it was still a little quicker for Mercer to fly first to New York, then, continue east across Europe and on to the Middle East, rather than across the Eurasian landmass. He had no recollection of the transcontinental flight. He slept from the moment he boarded in Seattle until the plane barked its wheels in New York. Because the terrorist attack at London's Heathrow Airport had so disrupted air travel, the only quick flight he could get to Europe was aboard Air France's supersonic Concorde. He would have preferred a slower mode of transportation since he moved through JFK like a zombie and had planned to keep sleeping on the transatlantic leg of his journey. He managed only a two-hour catnap on the slender missilelike aircraft.

In Paris, Charles de Gaulle Airport was absolute chaos as thousands of stranded passengers tried to make their way to the British Isles. Had he been more alert, Mercer would have cared, but as it was, he dozed through the hour layover before his connection to Abu Dhabi.

The brutal glare of the desert sun in Abu Dhabi came as a relief to the cold, damp misery he'd experienced for the past couple of days. It felt as if his bones would need weeks to dissipate the chill of his plunge into the icy water while escaping from Petromax's oil rig. He carried only a small bag of hastily purchased clothing from Kennedy Airport, so he was through customs in minutes, past the enormous duty-free shopping mall in the airport, and out onto the strip of road abutting the international terminal.

Waiting for his contact, a Colonel named Wayne Bigelow, Mercer set his bag at his feet, ignoring the taxi and limousine drivers soliciting fares into Abu Dhabi City, and closed his eyes once again, nodding off as he stood against a lamppost. After he got the chill from his body, his next order of business would be to pay back more of the tremendous sleep debt he'd incurred.

A car horn sounded close by and dragged him back to consciousness. Mercer had formed a pretty good impression of Colonel Bigelow from the telephone call he'd placed back at Sea-Tac Airport and more than half expected to see the old soldier driving a battered Land Rover, one with its top hacked off and a heavy tire bolted to its hood. Instead, Bigelow leaned from the open window of a new Mercedes 600 SEL sedan, its glossy black paint radiant in the sunlight.

"Dr. Mercer, I presume?" Bigelow's accent was strictly Colonial English, like a voice from a bygone era. His silvered mustache was waxed to needle points, and his face was as dark and weathered as tree bark. Even seated in the luxury automobile, he retained a rigid military bearing. Mercer guessed that when Bigelow died, rigor mortis would actually loosen his spine. He liked the older man immediately.

"What's left of him." Mercer pushed himself off the lamppost and, grabbing his bag, walked to the car.

"Sorry I'm late, but I wanted to catch the fireworks this morning. Damn impressive those Hornets your navy uses. Scream like the bloody hounds of hell, they do." Bigelow noted how slowly Mercer walked around the Mercedes and how gingerly he eased himself into the leather passenger seat. "Looks like you and Khalid Khuddari have the same tailor." Mercer's right arm was in a cloth sling to lessen the tension on his more severely torn shoulder tendons.

"It's amazing the sympathy you get with one of these. Hell, even the Air France flight attendants were civil."

"Should have come down on BOAC." Bigelow still used the old name for British Airways. "But I'm sure the flap at Heathrow has mucked them up for a few days."

"So everything went as planned?" Mercer asked. Between the time spent waiting in airports and on planes and the hours he'd lost traveling thirteen time zones east, a full day had passed since he and Captain Hauser had prevented the destruction of the *Petromax Arctica*.

"Like clockwork," Bigelow replied with a grand smile. The Mercedes purred along at about a hundred miles an hour on the ribbon of asphalt bisecting the white desert sand. "I'll let Minister Khuddari fill you in on the details."

"I understand from my conversation with his secretary that he was severely injured in London during an attack at the British Museum and later at Heathrow."

"Siri has a soft spot for him. She made his wounds sound worse than they are. He caught a bunch of shrapnel fragments, nothing even remotely life threatening, and he gave himself a nasty spinal dislocation jumping from an airplane." Bigelow then added fondly, "The pansy fell ten feet and pinched off a nerve for a couple of hours. I've known men who've leaped from five thousand feet without a parachute and walked away with nothing more than a mild limp. I knew he should have gone to Sandhurst rather than Cambridge and the London School of Economics. Lad's too soft by far."

"Known him long?" Mercer smiled at Bigelow's gruff affection.

"Since his father brought him in from the desert when he was a boy. Men like him are the future of the Gulf. They can function in the Western world yet still retain their traditions and their faith, giving each the proper due and maintaining true balance. The fundamentalism so popular now isn't the answer. Whether it's belief in Allah or in modern civilization, the Arabs have to learn not to rush headlong in either direction. Unfortunately, they are so passionate about everything they do that they lose sight of life's subtle compromises."

Mercer chuckled. "I just gave that same speech about environmentalists."

"It applies to everyone," Bigelow replied.

Once in the city, Bigelow parked them in a garage under a modern glass and steel office tower, the space he took having his name on a plaque affixed to the poured concrete wall. "You can leave your bag. In fact, the car is yours while you're here in Abu Dhabi. I hope you enjoy it more than I do. I much prefer my old Rover to these Kraut leather-lined bordellos."

While the building could not have been more than a few years old, Bigelow led Mercer into an area that had the feel of an old Victorian edifice, plaster walls, dark woodwork, and ceilings at least twelve feet high. The effect was disorienting but very welcome in the otherwise sterile city. The doors to Khalid al-Khuddari's office were solid pieces of mahogany, each four feet wide by nine feet tall. Mercer knew they had to be antiques because trees that size were just not found anymore.

The outer office was large, richly decorated, and inviting, the colors hued to those of the outlying desert and the azure of the Gulf to the north. The desk at its far end was as large as a pool table but spotlessly organized, even the cables running from the computer were tightly wrapped to reduce their ugly functionalism. Mercer assumed that the woman coming from behind the desk was Khalid Khuddari's secretary, Siri Patal. He wasn't ready for her exquisitely delicate beauty. He'd expected a heavy, matronly woman like the ones he knew from the Indian restaurants around Washington. Siri Patal could have been a model; her fluid movement and her reed-thin body were exceptional. Thinking a purely chauvinistic thought, Mercer hoped that Khuddari had the sense to have an affair with this woman. He would have, in Khuddari's position.

"Hello, Colonel," Siri said respectfully to Bigelow, who ignored her professional demeanor and gave her cheek a tickle with his mustache.

"Hello, darling. How's my girl?"

"Colonel, please," she blushed and nodded to the corner of the antechamber.

Seated on one of the two leather sofas and leafing through an oil industry magazine, Jim Gibson looked up and smiled

broadly. "Don't you mind me, little lady, you just carry on."
His Stetson and cowboy boots looked appropriate once he
spoke in his booming Texas voice. "Well, jerk my lizard!
They told me you was comin', Mercer, but I said naw,
couldn't be. Mercer is a miner, I said, and the only resource
this country's got other than oil is sand. Since the bottom fell
out of the hourglass market, there's no sense mining that."

Mercer shook Gibson's hand awkwardly with his left, his
whole fist vanishing in the Texan's big paw. "Thanks, Jim,
for everything. I think the world would be a different place
if you hadn't put me in touch with Colonel Bigelow."

"Hell, I haven't talked to you since Nigeria, and the next
thing I know, you're calling me up about government plots
and sabotage. When I heard about the flap at the Alaska Pipeline and knew you hadn't gone round the bend, I did what
any hero woulda done." Gibson laughed. "Taking a lesson
from the Duke, John Wayne, when the Indians are circling,
begging your pardon ma'am, but when they're circling, you
call in the cavalry, right? I'm just glad I was able to help.
And speaking of which, it's time for this hero to get his reward."

Mercer cocked an eyebrow at the brawny petroleum geologist.

"The Crown Prince wants to add to his stables, and knowing me to be a fine judge of horseflesh, he's sending me on
a buying spree through Europe and the States. Told me that
if I happen to find a few fillies that catch my eye, not to be
shy about buyin' them for myself. The check he gave me has
more zeros than a high school chess club." Gibson tipped his
hat. "Miss Siri, Colonel. Mercer, hate to cut this short, but
I've got a plane to catch."

No sooner had Gibson left than the door leading to Minister
Khalid al-Khuddari's chamber opened. The minister wore casual clothing, American-style jeans and an open-necked shirt.
Supported by two canes, his movement into the reception area
was slow but steady, his arms taking much of the strain as
he crabbed forward. Mercer stole a quick glance at Siri Patal
and was envious of the look she gave Khuddari. An image
of Aggie Johnston flashed painfully in his mind. They hadn't

spoken since Alaska. They probably never would.

"Dr. Mercer, it is both a pleasure and a privilege to meet you." Khuddari said, coming close. He looked at Mercer critically, and when he made some sort of personal judgment, smiled. "I'm willing to bet your injuries are a lot worse than they appear."

"Only if I appear dead." Mercer made no move to shake Khuddari's hand because he could only use his left comfortably. He knew that touching an Arab with that hand, which they considered unclean, was a sign of disrespect.

"We've both suffered for this," Khuddari said so quietly that only Mercer could hear. Mercer nodded a silent agreement, recognizing the seriousness of those words and the meaning behind them. Just as quickly as it appeared, Khuddari's serious edge disappeared, and he was again the charming host. "Come into my office. We have a great deal to discuss, a great many war stories to swap. I think even Colonel Bigelow may be impressed by us. What do you think?"

Mercer laughed, "Unless you and I single-handedly defeated Rommel, I don't think much would impress your Colonel."

Khuddari was delighted by the accurate description of his friend and mentor, grinning at Bigelow's scowl.

He led them into his office and took a seat behind his desk, propping his legs on an ottoman and leaning the canes against the wall like dueling sabers. Bigelow and Mercer sat opposite the desk. Because Mercer's internal clock was so messed up by jet lag and exhaustion, he didn't refuse Bigelow's offer of whiskey from the gold-capped flask he pulled from the pocket of his khaki tunic.

"To begin with, my closest friends call me Khalid. I would like to count you among them. May I dispense with your formal title and call you Philip?"

"My friends call me Mercer. Actually, so do my enemies, but that doesn't really matter."

"Then let me say officially, Mercer, the people of the United Arab Emirates and everyone else living in the Gulf owe you a great deal. I'm afraid that without your involvement, what we saw as an internal problem would have mushroomed until it encompassed the entire region. Your timely warning prevented not only a revolution here, but the destablization of the whole Middle East."

Mercer tried to demure, but Khuddari pressed on. "We had known for some time of a revolutionary element here in the UAE, a man by the name of Hasaan bin-Rufti, but we did not know how deep was his involvement with other—how shall we say—less friendly nations. Later, I learned of Rufti's connections with the Iraqis and Iranians when I was in London, but I was too incapacitated to make that knowledge useful here at home.

"Fortunately, as soon as Colonel Bigelow learned that I was delayed in London by a terrorist attack at Heathrow, he rightly deduced that the assault was intended to kill me. On his own initiative, he arrested Hasaan Rufti upon his return from the OPEC meeting. Though we had Rufti, we still didn't know where he had secreted his troops. That's where you came in.

"By linking the attacks in Alaska to Petromax Oil and Southern Coasting and Lightering, you gave us the clue to the location of those troops. In the limbo period during the sale of Petromax's fleet to SC&L, their ship the *Petromax Arabia* had become the *Southern Accent*, a vessel no one had any record of that had sat ignored in our harbor for weeks. We never would have known the tanker's involvement without you. I mean that. The men Rufti had aboard the ship could have stormed ashore and taken over this country faster than Saddam took Kuwait in 1990."

"Am I correct in guessing that the attacks on the Alaska Pipeline and the sinking of the *Petromax Arctica* were the triggers for this Rufti's revolution here in the UAE?"

"As far as we can tell, yes," Khalid said.

"The mastermind behind this whole plot was a former KGB agent named Ivan Kerikov—"

"We know all about Kerikov," Bigelow interrupted. "He was seen in Istanbul last year, meeting with Hasaan Rufti. It was then that they hatched this scheme."

"Not hatched, Colonel, stole," Mercer replied. "We found out from a computer expert Kerikov hired that the program he activated had been in place since the Cold War, planted by a KGB sleeper agent. Years ago, Kerikov came upon the plan and the codes needed to override Alyeska's computers. He'd been waiting for someone like Rufti to come along, someone who would be willing to pay to have the Trans-Alaska Pipeline permanently shut down."

"But why? And why now?"

"By destroying the pipeline and then sinking a tanker carrying North Slope crude, Kerikov and Rufti could guarantee that the United States would abandon its plan to cut off foreign oil suppliers by relying on domestic production and alternative fuels. The President's energy policy, which many Washington insiders and the New York financiers detest, would be scrapped before it was ever implemented."

"So Rufti would use the attacks in America as both a trigger and a diversion while he and his new Iranian and Iraqi allies took over the Middle East." Khalid spoke with a new understanding of how deeply the plot to take over his country truly ran. "By using tactical lessons from the Gulf War and striking when America was occupied by the domestic feuds following the twin oil-related disasters, Rufti could have seized the Emirates in days and the rest of the region in a matter of weeks. Unbelievable! But where did the money come from? It was something the Crown Prince mentioned prior to my going to London. Despite what the rest of the world thinks, not everyone living in an OPEC country is filthy rich. Rufti is a millionaire, certainly, but not nearly wealthy enough to finance an operation as elaborate as this."

"That's where Max Johnston came in, I'm afraid," replied Mercer. "In a way, he paid for the entire thing. At first, it was a simple business decision, but one he later discovered had a much darker side. Because of the President's energy policy, oil companies were scrambling to make as much money as possible in the ten years remaining before the deadline. Johnston was approached by Rufti, and later by Iranians and Iraqis, who promised him that in exchange for some up-front money, Petromax would be given exclusive rights for all future oil explorations in Iran, Iraq, and the UAE. From Johnston's point of view, the 150 million dollars they'd asked for was merely a kickback to the three oil ministers to gain market domination.

"The deal would have stayed in effect even after the U.S. cut off imports, giving Petromax a near monopoly on Middle East crude imported by Europe and Japan. Even if the rest of the world followed our lead on restricting oil consumption, we're still talking about billions of dollars over the next quarter century."

"It's nice that Rufti was negotiating as our Petroleum Minister," Khalid said sarcastically.

"Johnston must have known you were to be assassinated as an obstacle to Rufti's plan, but I don't believe he was aware that Iran, Iraq, and Rufti intended to establish themselves as the dominant power in the Gulf. He believed the deal was with three separate nations, not a triumvirate. Johnston couldn't raise the 150 million without selling some of his assets. Enter Southern Coasting and Lightering. He sold them his fleet of tankers, using the promissory notes of sale and hauling contacts to raise the cash in some sort of financial derivatives fund. I'm not certain how it was all to work out, but in essence he financed his own downfall."

"Excuse me," Bigelow said, "but this doesn't make sense. He sells his tankers to raise money to become sole importer of oil from any new Middle Eastern fields."

"He had just made a deal for drilling rights to half the world's oil supply. I doubt he was concerned with the few million dollars a year he makes on his tankers. But this is where the story gets truly Machiavellian."

"You mean more so," Khalid said mildly.

"I have a friend in Miami who is a leading maritime attorney. He found all the details of what transpired. Up until a year ago, Southern Coasting had been a small outfit in Louisiana, owning a couple of 100,000-ton product tankers that ran between Galveston and Venezuela. Then they were bought, and suddenly Southern Coasting had the money to go buy three VLCCs, a huge step for a company that showed only modest profits last year."

"Who bought the company?"

"Remember the Oil for Food deal the United Nations gave

to the Iraqis a few years ago as a way of maintaining international sanctions yet allowing some humanitarian aid into the country? Part of the proceeds of those oil sales went into Southern Coasting. The company was owned by Iraq and Hasaan bin-Rufti, a fact that Max Johnston was unaware of. He thought he had made the deal of the lifetime. Instead he put his neck in a noose that was about to be pulled."

"You mean Iraq paid for this whole thing? Why bother bringing in Max Johnston if they were going to finance the operation themselves?" Minister Khuddari was quick to point out.

"Two reasons. One, the Iraqis needed to launder the money internationally in a legitimate business deal. During the Oil for Food program, the United Nations was keeping a tight watch on Iraq's money to ensure that they weren't buying weapons. Once my friend Dave Saulman started pulling the thread of SC&L's ownership, the whole tapestry unraveled. What started out as a 150-million-dollar deal for soy and other foodstuffs turned into a tanker fleet with just a few falsified documents and a little bribery. Southern Coasting paid Johnston for his ships, and he turned the money right back over to Iraq, and they now found themselves with a tremendous fortune in their war chest. Some of this money went to Kerikov to set up the destruction of the pipeline and the *Arctica*. For this, he hired commandos and heavily bankrolled PEAL to become his unwitting pawns.

"The second reason was the need to use some of Johnston's equipment, namely his tankers, to carry the huge quantities of liquid nitrogen to Alaska and to act as Rufti's troop base here in the Emirates. Johnston would also be their scapegoat when the operation was over.

"What Max didn't know is that Kerikov and Rufti planned to cancel the deal all along and leave him with the mess following the destruction of the *Petromax Arctica*. Max had already fulfilled his part of the bargain, letting them use his ships and washing their money, so they were going to double-cross him. To ensure he never revealed what he'd done, Kerikov and Rufti's assistant, a man named Abu Alam—"

"Oh, we know Alam," Bigelow said. "The man's a bloody psychotic."

"Right now he's just blood. Maybe a little tissue, but I doubt it. Anyway, Alam and Kerikov kidnaped Johnston's daughter, Aggie. By holding her, Kerikov could threaten Max with her death if their deal were ever made public. Johnston's hands were tied."

"So Max Johnston didn't know that the money he laundered from Rufti would eventually be used to destroy him?" Khalid asked.

"He had no idea. Kerikov and Rufti played off his greed for their own benefit while planning to betray him. It's almost like a Shakespearean tragedy in its scope. It hasn't been reported yet, but the FBI raided Max's home yesterday. I was told by Dick Henna that Johnston had shot himself. I doubt he knew that Kerikov was no longer holding his daughter, so he must have traded the silence of his death for her life."

"And avoided a long stint in gaol," Bigelow said.

"I've known Max for a number of years. He would have gone to prison to make things right. I believe he saw his suicide as a way of rescuing his daughter, not to avoid his responsibilities."

"Did Johnston know that Kerikov was using that oil rig you escaped from?"

"Yes, he did know that. Actually, Kerikov took it over and then told Max about it. But it was too late for him to do anything. He was in too deep."

"And you managed to stop it all before it really even began?"

"Well, it did begin in the United States, but yes, it's over. The twin spills in Alaska and Puget Sound were not nearly as bad as they could have been. Cleanup will still run into the hundreds of millions of dollars, but since this was a terrorist act, the federal government will be picking up a good share of the cost. But here in the Gulf, Kerikov and Rufti's operation never really got off the ground. Colonel Bigelow told me a little about the action this morning. That was where everything finally stopped, Kerikov's plan, Rufti's coup, and the Iran–Iraq pact to dominate the Middle East."

Khalid smiled for the first time since their conversation began. "At dawn this morning, a squadron of American F-18 Hornets from the carrier *Carl Vinson* made a series of subsonic passes over the tanker sitting off the coast, *Petromax Arabia* or *Southern Accent*, whatever you prefer to call it. Your Admiral Morrison phoned me himself to lend U.S. air support to our seaborne counterstrike."

Bigelow continued for Khalid, adding the color that he felt the story needed. "While the fighters were strafing the port side of the tanker with Gatling gunfire and barrages of unguided rockets, UAE special forces boarded the tanker from the starboard, capturing the ship without ever needing to fire a shot. All of Hasaan Rufti's troops were more than happy to surrender after the aerial bombardment."

"Preliminary reports from our intelligence people indicate that they had lists of those to be executed and those who would be loyal to the new regime, as well as timetables for linking up with forces sweeping through Kuwait and Saudi Arabia," Khalid concluded.

"Why didn't your CIA catch on to the troop movements already underway in Iran and Iraq?" Bigelow directed the question to Mercer as if he were responsible for America's lack of hard data.

"You can move troops in school buses and artillery pieces in tractor trailers, and tanks can be deployed like mobile homes. If the effort is coordinated, it's impossible to detect," Mercer lied. He believed it was more plausible that American Intelligence had been caught unaware again, as it had when Saddam Hussein first took Kuwait. Changing the touchy subject, Mercer asked, "So where does this leave us? Is everything settled?"

"Mostly," Khalid said. "The troops we captured this morning, and the division Rufti had poised in Ajman will be tried for treason and executed some time next month. Those who are not Emirate residents—mercenaries and the Iranian and Iraqi instructors—will be deported within the week, probably to face heroes' welcomes, but that's the price we pay for diplomacy."

"What about Rufti?" Mercer asked.

"We have something very special planned for him. Perhaps you would like to watch. It won't be pleasant, but I can assure you it will be satisfying." Khalid checked his watch. "It's time for lunch. Afterward, we'll go see the esteemed Hasaan bin-Rufti."

They dined in a private room at the top floor of Khalid's office building, a sumptuous meal of curried lamb, whose flavor and spice balance kept Mercer eating well past the point when he was full. Though Khalid Khuddari abstained, Wayne Bigelow seemed to have an inexhaustible supply of wines in some private cellar. He found a soul mate in Mercer, bringing out three bottles before the meal was finished and stuffing a bottle of eighty-year-old brandy into his tunic for the ride that followed.

Seated in the back of a limousine racing out into the desert on the Al Ain Road, Bigelow and Mercer, after having shown the aromatic spirit its proper deferential respect, passed it back and forth, drawing from its open neck like soldiers slugging water from a single canteen. The ride, like the meal, was one of celebration. After an hour in the air-conditioned car, the three men transferred to a converted truck, the heavy vehicle reconfigured to make it more usable in the harsh desert environs. Khalid had to be carried from one vehicle to the other. He tried walking, but his canes sank into the soft sand. He withstood the ignominy stoically.

The ride out into the desert was over a tortuous route that was barely a rut in the baked earth, the truck jostling passengers and driver alike as it bucked farther into the empty expanse. The air in the high cab was approaching a hundred degrees, and even the breeze funneling through the open windows was too hot to be a comfort. Abrasive particles of sand swirled though the truck, covering the seats, the dash, the men themselves. If it weren't for the brandy, Mercer would have considered the trip miserable.

Two hours after leaving the main road, the truck ground over the top of an old dry wadi and rumbled to its bottom. The sun was high overhead, blazing at its hottest in the midafternoon. Another truck was parked in the ancient riverbed, a boxy ten-wheeler, its canvas cargo cover faded and torn by years in the desert. Several Bedouins were hunched around a small, smokeless fire a short distance from the truck, their long robes protecting their skin from the brutal solar rays. They stood when they saw Khalid Khuddari shuffling toward them, his canes finding better purchase on the riverbed's hard-pan.

As was the custom of the nomads, Khalid and the Bedouins spoke for a few minutes, gesturing and laughing like old friends reunited after a long absence. Khalid took a cup of strong tea from them, Mercer and Bigelow following suit. After another long exchange that Bigelow seemed to follow with interest, one of the nomads detached himself from the group and went to the back of the truck. Returning a moment later, he placed a large plastic crate on the ground near Khalid.

From within it, a falcon called clearly—as if to welcome her master.

HASAAN bin-Rufti was secured to four metal stakes that had been driven into the ground. He lay naked and spread-eagle under the sun's glare; his body burned raw and blistered by the sun. His hairless body was so rounded and creased by the rolls of fat that he resembled a pillowy Scandinavian sofa covered in bright red vinyl. He'd been drifting in and out of consciousness for hours. The ravaging thirst that burned his throat was matched by the deep rumbling in his empty stomach. He hadn't had a thing for hours now, and the lack of food was drifting his mind and blurring his thinking.

For an instant, he thought he was in a Parisian hotel, trussed to the bedposts by a prostitute he'd hired, his body pinioned while she pleased him in unimaginable ways. He could hear her soft call as her long hair caressed the area between his legs. He moaned at her touch, then suddenly the whore sank her fingernails into his chest and he cried out. The pain was like steel spikes mincing his flesh.

As he came more awake, Rufti found just enough strength to raise his head off the ground and saw a tiny creature standing on him, its noble head looking off into the vacant desert, its wickedly curved beak arrowing down toward his prone form. He knew what was going to happen to him, and the thought sent a new, keener jolt of fear through him.

"She'll go for your eyes first, Hasaan," Khalid Khuddari said as he came into Rufti's view. "As I understand, they are the easiest to get at and one of the more succulent parts of the human body. Once she's plucked them from your skull, she may rest for a while, digesting until she's hungry enough to go after your genitals, another easy target. I suspect Sahara will be able to sever your testicles easily, but she may have to eat your penis while it's still attached."

Khalid whistled, and his saker falcon lifted off Rufti's bloated body and alighted on the glove covering Khuddari's left fist. He stroked the bird's chest, whispering to her softly, reassuring the raptor and praising her beauty. The falcon responded to the gestures happily, preening on his arm and giving him a *kweet kweet* of contentment. Although she wanted to hunt, she would be just as satisfied eating the banquet laid before her.

"I can think of a great many horrible ways to die, Rufti," Khalid continued. "But I believe being eaten alive must be one of the worst. If Sahara has a mind to, she can make this last for a few days. I suspect you'll be dead long before she finishes her repast, but you'll still have plenty of time to think about what you've done and beg for forgiveness from me and the Crown Prince and Allah Himself. I guarantee that we are so far out into the desert that your pleas will never be heard. By all means, you bastard, scream your lungs out. Sahara will enjoy her meal that much more if she knows it's alive.

"Killing you won't bring back the planeload of people you killed in London, or the priest or the little girl in the airport. It won't ever avenge the death of Trevor James-Price. Nor will it forgive you for trying to assassinate me or causing the environmental damage to the United States or attempting to overthrow my country. Your death won't even be a warning to others, because no one will know how you died. Killing you is only to satisfy my desire to feel a little safer at night, to know that there is one less madman in the world. I'll think about your ravaged corpse when I drift off tonight, Rufti, and I'm going to smile."

Khalid waited for a response, but Rufti's spirit had already died. He lay there docilely, not having the strength to even whimper. Khuddari eventually turned away and let Sahara fly from his arm to streak up into the clear sky before swooping to strike at her meal.

Back at the trucks, a hundred yards from where Rufti lay staked to the ground, Khalid addressed Bigelow and Mercer. "This is going to take the rest of the afternoon. He may even live into the night. I want to be here to make sure he's really dead, but you two don't need to wait with me. Why don't you go back to Abu Dhabi and enjoy yourselves? I'll join you for breakfast tomorrow morning."

Mercer was tempted. After all the death he had seen in the past week, Khuddari's version of desert justice was almost too much to bear. However, he demurred, wanting to witness the end of Charon's Landing. The Bedouins built a second fire, erected a sunshade, and brought out a cooking pot for the evening meal. They boiled water for continuous cups of tea. The three men talked desultorily through the afternoon, ignoring the screams from beyond the banks of the wadi.

"So what happens next?" Mercer asked Khalid as the sun dipped below the horizon, turning the sky a rich bloodred before the beginning of twilight.

"I'm taking a few weeks off to recuperate. I'm going to London for a funeral, and then I'll probably go to the south of France or maybe Malaga in Spain with my secretary. I think we both deserve it," Khalid replied with a candor that surprised Colonel Bigelow. "What about you?"

"I was hoping to take your secretary to the south of France or maybe Malaga, but that's out of the question now," Mercer joked to mask his emotions about losing Aggie Johnston. "During my layover in New York, I checked my voice mail and discovered I had a rather intriguing message from the State Department, so I suppose it's back to the mines for me."

Hasaan bin-Rufti stopped screaming just after the desert settled under a blanket of darkness lit only by a sliver of moon and the coldly distant stars. Khalid's falcon rejoined the men a few minutes later, her tight little body speckled with gore, her entire head covered with Rufti's blood.

Mercer, Khalid, and Bigelow spent the night in the Bedouin camp, laughing until well past midnight thanks to the Colonel's wildly exaggerated war stories. Sahara flew off once during the night to continue feeding. None of the men felt she had done enough mutilation of Rufti's corpse. At sunup they returned to the city, leaving Rufti for the jackals and buzzards that had gathered in the night. Khalid left later that day for an extended vacation with a blushing but joyous Siri Patal while Mercer stayed in the country for another few days, resting himself and testing Bigelow's boast that he could drink any man under the table.

Bigelow won all their competitions, but Mercer would have loved to see the Colonel go up against Harry White. The Englishman wouldn't have stood a chance.

ARLINGTON, VIRGINIA

Mercer swung open his front door, reveling in the feeling of being home. He stood motionless for a few minutes, watching the sunlight that played through the three-story atrium. The air was crisp; a sudden and unexpected chill had Washington in its grip, and his furnace was still off. Thinking of such a minute domestic chore as relighting the furnace pleased him more than he thought it would. Everything was finally getting back to normal.

On a table in the little-used living room was a large manila envelope addressed to him. Curious, he opened it and withdrew a single piece of paper and probably the most coveted perk in Washington—a pair of diplomatic license plates. The note read, "A gift from the people of the United Arab Emirates. Park wherever you want to and speed as much as you dare," and was signed by Khalid Khuddari.

Mercer laughed delightedly as he twisted up the spiral staircase. When the telephone rang, he raced up the last few steps, rushed through the bar, and snatched up the handset.

"Thank God you're there." Harry White sounded desperate. "I forgot to buy this morning's paper, so I couldn't check yesterday's crossword answers. Nine down, 'Seduced by Zeus'?"

"Harry, I just got back," Mercer complained, walking behind the bar and noting the four empty liquor bottles in the trash can that hadn't been there when he'd left.

"I know, I know, but you've gotta help me. It's been driving me nuts. Seduced by Zeus? Come on, you know who I'm talking about," Harry wheedled.

"Leda?"

"No, not her, the other one. Zeus came on to Leda disguised as a swan; the one I want was seduced by a golden shower."

Mercer laughed until his chest ached. "Shower of gold, Harry, not a golden shower. There's a big difference, trust me." He pulled a beer from the bar fridge, spying the half-filled wine bottle standing next to the stacks of Heinekens. Harry must have had female company. Further proof was the cigarette butts in the ashtrays. They weren't Harry's brand.

"So, do you know the answer?"

"Try Danaë, I think she was Perseus' mother," Mercer said absently. He thought he'd just heard something from upstairs in his bedroom, a floorboard creak or maybe a piece of furniture being bumped slightly.

"That's it, finally, thank Christ. Hey, Tiny and I and a couple other guys are getting together for some poker tonight. You interested?"

Mercer went tense. There was someone coming down the spiral stairs, soft treads whispering against the antique wood as though stealth was the intention. Mercer whispered directly into the phone. "Harry, someone is in my house. Call the police."

"Of course someone's in your house, Christ, I let her in myself, even gave her my key to use," Harry boomed back.

Aggie Johnston came into the bar from the library wearing

black garter stockings and a matching lace bra and panty set. Over that, she had slipped into one of Mercer's dress shirts, its tails brushing against the smooth skin of her thighs. Her hair was done up beautifully, shimmering like precious metal, and she had artfully applied makeup to accent her best features, which to Mercer were all of them. If seduction had a look, this was it.

"I've got to go now, Harry," he stammered and cut the connection.

"You're early. Dick Henna said you were coming into town later this afternoon. I wanted to be at the airport to meet you." There was a catch in her voice, part desire, part apology.

"I managed an earlier flight," Mercer said, just to say something. He was overwhelmed by her presence. Standing there, she captured his entire vision, as if his brain refused to see anything else. "I didn't think I would ever see you again."

"I didn't think you would either." Aggie moved across the room until Mercer could feel her breath on his skin. Her perfume was intoxicating. "I couldn't stay away. I wanted to, I know that you and I will never last, but I had to be with you. Despite myself, you've charmed me."

"How have you been?" Mercer breathed.

A shadow of annoyance flashed behind Aggie's impossibly green eyes at Mercer for asking when she was trying to seduce him, but she knew he asked out of concern. "I'm all right. It's been a few days so I've had time to adjust."

"So what happens now?"

"Since my father's death, I've been hounded by an army of lawyers. Yesterday I signed my name about a thousand times just to transfer the Johnston Trust into my name. We haven't even begun to go over the Petromax corporate files."

"You're going to take over the company?"

"Ironic that an environmentalist is going to head one of the largest oil companies in the world, isn't it?"

"I can't think of anyone better suited. You'll have an easier time working from within than fighting from the outside."

Aggie smiled, the expression radiating from her mouth to encompass her eyes and her entire character. "That was my thinking as well."

"But what I meant was, what happens between us now?"

She swayed toward him until her body was pressed against his, her small breasts flattened against his chest, one thigh snuggling between his legs. "You take me to bed and make love to me until neither of us can walk," Aggie replied. "The lawyers will eventually track me here, so we've got only a couple of days. After that, Philip? I don't know. You've got your world and I've got mine. Maybe they're the same—only time will tell."

Later that night, much later, in fact, Mercer and Aggie lay on top of the sheets of Mercer's bed in a damp tangle of limbs, their breathing just now returning to a normal rhythm. Seeing the repair work around the skylight over the bed, Aggie asked him who had been responsible for the attack on his home.

"It wasn't your father, if that was what you were thinking," Mercer said. "The FBI found a bunch of receipts from a private investigator in your father's home office. He'd had you followed for a couple of months. Since you moved back to Washington, actually. Henna believes it was nothing more than overzealous parental concern."

"That's how he knew what time I came here that night?"

"Right. And it was the private investigator I heard the night of your father's party leaving the area after the first attempt on my life. He must have followed me home after I dropped you off at your condo in Georgetown."

"He was a sick, greedy man," Aggie said about her father and snuggled deeper into Mercer's arms. "But it's a relief to know he had nothing to do with that."

He explained his theory about Max's suicide, and that seemed to make Aggie feel a little better about her father. There was one detail he would not relate to her, something he didn't even want to believe himself. It was something Dick Henna had told Mercer while he was recuperating in Abu Dhabi with Wayne Bigelow.

The detonating device used to release the liquid nitrogen on the Alaska Pipeline, the one that Jan Voerhoven had triggered, was not the same one used to activate the computer virus in Alyeska's system. That trigger had been activated while Mercer and Aggie were in the Marine Terminal's Op-center, fifteen minutes after the *Hope* explosion. Henna and Mercer had come to the same conclusion.

Ivan Kerikov is still alive.

Get caught reading.

Jake Lloyd reading ENDER'S GAME.

A Message from the
Association of American Publishers